Uncharted Waters

by

Sara DuBose

UNCHARTED WATERS

ISBN # 978-1-907984-55-6

First published in Great Britain in 2012 by Rose & Crown Books
www.roseandcrownbooks.com
(Sunpenny Publishing Group)

MORE BOOKS FROM ROSE & CROWN:

Bridge to Nowhere, by Stephanie Parker McKean
Embracing Change, by Debbie Roome
Blue Freedom, by Sandra Peut
A Flight Delayed, by KC Lemmer

COMING SOON:

Brandy Butter on Christmas Canal, by Shae O'Brien
Redemption on the Red River, by Cheryl R. Cain
30 Days to Take-off, by KC Lemmer
Greater than Gold, by Julianne Alcott
Shadow of a Parasol, by Beth Holland
Changing Landscapes, by Olivia Valentine
Heart of the Hobo, by Shae O'Brien

Dedication and Acknowledgements

Uncharted Waters is dedicated to Steve Searcy, Executive Director of the One Place Family Justice Center in Montgomery, Alabama, and former Commander of the Domestic Violence Bureau of the Montgomery Police Department.

One Place Family Justice Center is one of forty-eight centers throughout the United States whose goal is to meet all the needs of Domestic Violence victims under one roof. For years, Searcy says, DV victims were passed from one agency to another, but OPFJC now provides legal aid, medical assistance, safety planning, transportation and shelter information for victims and their children. Instead of a separate silo approach, Searcy can now walk someone down the hall where a team of professionals is waiting to provide immediate help.

This novel is also dedicated to the forty-eight Family Justice Centers in the U.S., eighty-five throughout the world and another one-hundred and eighteen that are developing. Of this group, there are three FJC in England with nine more on the way. All of these centers work tirelessly to combat domestic violence and stalking.

Special recognition is given to Karen Sellers, Director of Montgomery's Family Sunshine Center, and all of the outstanding people who serve with her. Particular mention should be given to Melanie Beasley, the FSC Outreach Supervisor.

Since 1981 the Family Sunshine Center has served victims and survivors of family violence in Autauga, Butler, Chilton, Crenshaw, Elmore, Lowndes and Montgomery counties. They incorporate services not only to victims with immediate crisis needs, but also those ready to move out of emergency shelters and into self-sufficient lifestyles.

The FSC also provides a non-residential counseling center and a community outreach program for prevention education. Most recently, they have added sexual assault counseling to the services they offer.

I want to also acknowledge District Attorney, Ellen Brooks, who has championed One Place Family Justice Center, the Family Sunshine Center and numerous other projects benefitting Montgomery citizens.

As I began research for this novel, Willie Peak was instrumental in providing an introduction to Bureau Commander, Lieutenant L. P. Gracie with the Montgomery Police Academy. I was soon welcomed by other academy officers: Division Commander, Major J.E. Brown, Assistant Division Commander, Captain B.F. Jurkofsky, Staff Instructors, Sergeant R.D. Culliver, Sergeant S.L. Lavender, now a Lieutenant, Sergeant R.J. Harris, Sergeant R.J. Steelman and Sergeant J.D. Jordin. Sergeant Jordin, who ranked as a Corporal at the time, was of particular help with questions and logistics for this novel.

Although I am old enough to be a mature parent for most of the Police Academy recruits, I soon found acceptance in their classes and even on the parade deck and firing range. It was an honor to attend their graduation several months later.

Other Montgomery police officers interviewed include Sergeant Lance Gambrel, Lieutenant S.L. Campbell, Corporal Steve Smith, Corporal M. Johnson, Lieutenant R.N. Fennie, and Corporal S. Tolliver, who is now a Sergeant. Outdoor firing range information and assistance was provided by Judy Hayes, Range Secretary.

In Tallassee, Alabama I also spoke with Amy Davis, the former Assistant Chief for the Tallassee Police Department and benefitted from a ride-along with Officer D.M. Booth followed by an interview with Lee R. Booth, the Assistant District Attorney of the 19th Judicial Circuit Court.

My friend, Ted Payne, who served as the Executive Director of the Alabama Peace Officers' Association also provided help as well as Corporal Stephen Z. Smith, Crime Scene Technician with the Montgomery County Sheriff's Office.

A special thanks goes to my friend, Debbie Baxter Robison, Director of *Thorn of the Rose*, a Self Defense Class for women and girls. Debbie's help was invaluable as I considered self-defense possibilities for my heroine, Beth Davidson.

Brian Robertson also aided with a technical question and my good friend, Karen Robertson, offered advice, moral support and a listening ear. Other friends who often sustain me include Carolyn, Neville, Emily, Gail, Marjorie, Tutter, Colleen, Doris Jean, Annette, Linda, Anne, Carole, Janet, Dot, Caroline, Daphne, Peggy, Diane, Becky, Sarah, and the Birthday Girls.

I thank my husband, Bill, and daughters DeAnn DuBose and Cherie Preg along with Cherie's husband, Jeffrey. Daniel DuBose and Summer Preg also offered their time and technical support along the way.

Finally, I acknowledge the One who has promised to walk with every believer traveling through uncharted waters and who said,

"So do not fear, for I am with you; do not be dismayed, for I am your God. I will strengthen you and help you; I will uphold you with my righteous right hand." (Isaiah 41: 10 NIV).

STAYING SAFE

Regardless of where you live, you may call:

1. National Alliance of Family Justice Centers toll-free:
   1-888-511-3522
   www.familyjusticecenter.org

2. National Network to End Domestic Violence toll-free:
   1-800-799-7233
   www.nnedv.org

3. Hot Peach Pages/search by country at:
   www.hotpeachpages.net

4. In the UK, help is available through the Women's Aid
   and Refuge, and the freephone 24 hour helpline is:
   0808-2000-247

Since *Uncharted Waters* is set in Alabama, other special
numbers include:

5. One Place Family Justice Center: 334-262-7378
   www.oneplacefjc.org

6. Family Sunshine Center: 334-263-0218
   www.familysunshine.org

Preface

Where do fears come from? Do they arise from the present moment or do they lurk somewhere inside a convoluted corridor of the mind?

At some point in our lives, we all experience fear. Sometimes it may border on terror. Somehow we cope, overcome and carry on. As you escape into this story I trust you will also find helpful information and become more aware, not only of the dangers, but of the precautions we can all take to live a safe and satisfying life. If trouble should ever stalk you, this book will offer the advice and resources to counter your fears. Most of all, it will point you to the author of the abundant life. I make no apologies for the introduction.

Chapter 1

Glancing out the breakfast room window, I noticed an unfamiliar black car in front of my apartment. The male driver appeared to be staring directly at my door. My mind jumped to Donnie but I knew this was wishful thinking. Donnie drives a truck and hardly knows I'm alive.

I took a sip of orange juice, and decided the stranger must be trying to find someone. Our apartment numbers are difficult to read; maybe he's nearsighted like me. I stabbed at the remaining egg on my plate, but it no longer looked appealing. The driver continued to sit.

I stood, picked up the plate, and took a step toward the window. As I stooped for a closer look, the car eased forward and sped away. I made a mental note of the make (a Honda). Easy to do since I work at the Montgomery (USA) Honda dealership. I chastised myself for giving the incident any thought at all.

The cell rang, so I retrieved it from my bathrobe pocket.

"Morning, Beth. How's it going?" Shannon's vivacious voice caught me off-guard.

"Fine." I hoped I sounded normal. The man in the car made me more skittish than I realized.

"Still wanna go shopping and do lunch?"

"Sure." I tried to match her mood. "Let's meet at Eastchase in front of Dillard's around 10."

Shannon was my 3-P gal: popular, pretty and prosperous. Friends since junior high, Shannon's personality pulled me out of my quiet and introspective nature.

I headed for the shower, and allowed myself to linger under the warm water a bit longer than usual. The cell rang once but I ignored it. On the fourth ring, my answering machine cut in, but the caller's words were garbled.

After drying off, I checked the phone and heard a strange voice say, "Hello there, gorgeous. I drove by earlier, hoping to catch a glimpse of you. Well, you're probably in the shower by now." A long pause followed. "Anyway, have a good day. You'll be hearing from me later."

Not recognizing the voice, I listened again. For a second, I thought about Lewis at the office, but this guy didn't sound like Lewis. In fact, I knew all of the employees now and couldn't think of anyone who would leave such a message.

Reaching for the hair dryer, I noticed my left hand was shaking and my mouth felt dry. When I looked at myself in the mirror over the sink, I didn't like the look in my eyes. My mother always said my eyes reminded her of rich chocolate fudge. Now they were more like weak coffee spilled in a saucer.

Twenty minutes later, dressed in jeans and my favorite blue T-shirt, I headed for the door. I rechecked the lock twice, and bolted the second lock. Maybe I was being paranoid. Shannon would think so.

After I got Shannon past the make-up counter in Dillard's, she helped me select some tops that might be appropriate for work. I tried a couple on and she said, "That brown sweater shows off all your curves."

"You think so? I don't won't to attract the wrong sort of attention."

"Is there a wrong sort?" she giggled.

"You know the answer to that one. Look. A man in a Honda was staring at my apartment this morning, and then I got a weird phone call."

"Weird in what way?"

I told her but all I got was a "My advice is to put it out of your mind. Who knows? That guy could have had a wrong number."

"Not likely."

Shannon gave me one of her 'let's move on' looks as she reached for her purse, so I decided to change the subject.

"Say, I like your nails. What's that color called?"

"It's IPC Moonlight Charm," Shannon said.

I glanced down at my un-manicured fingernails and said, "Mine look more like Daylight Alarm."

Shannon laughed, her blue-green eyes dancing as we headed for check-out.

We broke for soup and a sandwich at Panera Bread, and during most of our time, Shannon chatted about her upcoming date with Ryan. I tried to listen. However, since I was secretly mulling over the phone call, I finally asked if she had ever given my cell number to anyone.

"Are you crazy? Chill. You know I wouldn't do such a thing without asking you."

"Sorry," I said. "I'm just trying to solve the puzzle."

"Beth, there is no puzzle. One man is out looking at apartments. Another man happens to call the wrong number."

"I suppose..."

"Come on." Shannon grabbed her check, signaling the end of our conversation.

As we headed back for my car, a black Honda suddenly appeared from around the corner and I jumped.

"What's wrong, Beth?"

"That Honda looks like the one around my apartment this morning."

"You are uptight. Look, it's a family in the car and they're probably coming for lunch. You've got to get your-self together. Tell you what, I'll call tonight – just to be sure you're okay."

As I dropped Shannon off at the parking lot, I assured her I'd be fine but, when a half-pie moon appeared in the sky, I started listening for her call. And later, after I crawled into bed, a worm of worry crept under the covers with me.

Chapter 2

I slept better than I had expected Saturday night, and felt glad to be headed for church Sunday morning. For two years now I'd attended a young adults Sunday school class and, after the eleven o'clock service, some of us met for lunch.

One of the guys, Donnie Crawford, who happens to be a handsome police officer, sat next to me. So, he did acknowledge my existence.

While waiting for the others to arrive we exchanged small talk but, when he asked about my weekend, I blurted the business about the strange Honda and the call. Instead of blowing me off, Donnie looked concerned, and gave my arm a little pat.

"Look," he said, "if you ever get anxious, give me a call."

I nodded. "Thanks. I appreciate it but, hopefully, that's the end of it."

"I know. Probably is … but remember the offer, okay? By the way, are you on any of the social networks?"

"Facebook. Why?" I studied his azure-colored eyes and waited.

"Just be careful about giving too much information, that's all."

As Donnie flashed a reassuring smile our other threesome arrived, so we settled in with a lively conversation – first about an upcoming singles meeting and then the state of the economy. To my surprise, Donnie said he'd like to drop by around four if I didn't have any plans and, frankly, I was glad to have company. Sunday afternoons can be lonely when you're single, especially if you don't have a close family.

Our apartment complex in east Montgomery winds around through a small park with a pond and picnic area, so I suggested we take a walk. Since Donnie seemed to like the idea, I grabbed a quarter of a loaf of old bread to feed the ducks. After closing the door I hid my key in the usual place, a philodendron plant on a wicker porch table.

A light breeze greeted us as we left the sidewalk and headed toward the playground and pond. I noticed how his face seemed to relax when we started out, like I would imagine a young Sean Hannity during a commercial.

"I've always been attracted to this area," Donnie began. "It's kinda tucked away from civilization."

"That's what drew me to it. It's usually quiet, and it's nice to have an apartment so near the park and the Alabama Shakespeare Theatre."

"I bet." Donnie hesitated, trying to match his stride with mine. "It seems to be a safe place to walk. Was yesterday your first scare?"

"Yes. Well, my friend, Shannon, says I'm over-reacting and she's probably right, but–"

"But a woman should be careful or, as they say, be aware of what's going on around her. I don't think you overreacted. Did you get a good look at him?"

"No, not really." I pointed to a duck scurrying in front of us, eager to reach the safe haven of the water. "I think we startled her."

"Yeah. Here, let's see if we can get her attention with your bread."

Donnie took the loaf from my hand and tore a bite size piece for the mallard. She hesitated, but then glided in the bread's direction. Soon others swam in for a hand-out. He passed a slice to me and we enjoyed watching them several minutes before walking on toward a nearby swing. It was one of those with double seats facing each other.

On impulse, I stepped in and took a seat on the side facing the pond. Donnie slid in beside me rather than choosing the seat across. I moved over to make room and crossed my arms over my waist.

"Are you going to be okay?" he asked, as he shifted his body in my direction.

"I think so." A long pause settled in and I cleared my

throat. "Donnie, how long have you been with the police department?"

"Four years."

"You seem to love it. Aren't you a lieutenant now?"

"Right. I was promoted last year. We've got some good guys on the force. It's like a family."

"That must be nice." Feeling self-conscious, I began to fiddle with a loose thread on the button of my new brown top and then looked back out toward the pond.

"Beth, the guys in my unit are having a barbecue next Saturday. Will you be off?"

Startled, I looked at Donnie and realized he was inviting me. "Well, I–"

"You don't have to tell me now. Check your schedule and I'll get back to you."

"Thanks, Donnie. I may have to work, but sometimes Margaret and I swap days. Let me think about it."

"Sure." Donnie rubbed his left hand on the leg of his jean. "How do you like working for Honda?"

"It's fine. I'm at the reception center, you know. All of the incoming phone calls come to my desk."

"So, you determine who the call is for and how to handle it?"

"Yes."

"I guess you have more service calls than anything else."

"That's right. You sound like an employee."

"No, I just try to be observant. Part of my trade."

Donnie popped his knuckles and grinned. I couldn't help but notice his cute dimples, and began to feel my face relax too. However, right after that, he checked his watch, so I knew the visit was coming to an end.

"Well, you may be planning something for tonight, so I'd better go."

He stood up and stepped off the swing, then turned and held one hand out to brace me. Even this little gesture made his muscles tighten, but I tried not to notice. We walked back to my apartment and, as I reached for the key, he pointed to the hanging pot on my small porch.

"What's this called?"

"Portulaca. I got it down at the Farmer's Market."

"It's nice. By the way, I cover Farmer's Market, downtown and the river region."

"Oh … isn't that pretty dangerous?"

"I suppose, but trouble can happen anywhere."

Another pause hung in the air and, for a second, Donnie looked like he wanted to take the comment back.

"Sorry about that," he said.

"It's okay. Look, thanks for checking on me today."

"My pleasure. See you later, okay?" Donnie waited for me to unlock the door and then turned and walked away.

For some reason I felt a sudden burst of energy after Donnie left, and decided I'd head back for the pond to finish off the bread loaf for the ducks. Returning the key to its hiding place, I noticed the wind was whipping up, and a couple of dark clouds hovered overhead, making me wonder if I could finish before the rain started.

Leaves rustled at my feet as I crossed the playground, and the wind picked up even more when I passed the swing where we had sat about ten minutes earlier. My gaze rested on the swing for a moment before hurrying on. A clap of thunder sent its warning as I reached the water and no ducks were in sight. In fact, no one was around now so I brushed the hair from my eyes and just enjoyed watching the effects of the breeze across the water.

After several minutes, I turned to leave. Another thunder boom, then a flash of lightening blazed across the sky and a gust of wind sent a used hamburger wrapper into flight as I rushed back across the park, hoping to make it before the thunderstorm hit.

Only a few cars remained in the parking lot now but, with a full blown rain, I imagined Sunday afternoon adventurers would soon return home. Checking my watch, I almost stumbled, but regained my balance as I reached the porch and leaned over to retrieve the key. It wasn't there. I ran my fingers across the soil of the philodendron again. Nothing.

The rain was pelting now. I scanned the parking lot, looking for any movement or unfamiliar car. Everything appeared the same. My car sat directly in front of the apartment, just as I had left it. My neighbor, Earline, was next to me. Nothing looked unusual.

My eyes traveled down to the porch, and then behind

the legs of the plant stand. Thankfully, the key poked from beneath the back right leg next to the door. I picked it up, wondering if I had dropped it before. No. I distinctly remember seeing it in the plant. In fact, I remember thinking how the large philodendron leaves had concealed it.

Maybe a neighbor's dog had knocked the stand but, if so, dirt would be spilled on the porch. Had someone picked the key up and then dropped it? I had no way of knowing.

I thought about stopping in on Earline, asking to use her phone. But, who, or why, would I call? Turning the key in the lock, my throat felt dry, like someone was rubbing a piece of sandpaper across my vocal cords.

Some people recognize the slightest change in their environment, and I fall into this category. Even as a child, I could tell if a friend moved a stuffed toy on my bed or dresser. Mother used to say I kept close tabs on my stuff and she was right. Maybe it had something to do with being an only child. Regardless of the reason, I always seemed to be aware of change.

Now I moved slowly through the apartment, intent on the process of observation. Donnie would be impressed, I said to myself, as I searched for any new smudges on the carpet, or a change in the angle of a door. My living area and breakfast room face the front of the building so I checked them first and then eased into the kitchen. Nothing appeared disturbed. The oven clock read five-forty five, yet it was almost dark.

The top half of my back door is glass, so I peered out and watched the rain. A frail maple tree was swaying so hard that I wondered if it might become uprooted. Just then, the lights flickered and went out, so I reached inside the cabinet by the door and felt for my flashlight.

Back-tracking into the breakfast room, I flipped the switch, but the flashlight didn't respond. Dead battery, I guess. Now I simply watched the rain, not wanting to take the short hall into the two bedrooms and bath. Just then, the phone rang so I reached for the table to retrieve it.

"Hello. Oh, hi Dad." I let out a sigh, hoping he didn't notice. Dad and I weren't on the best of terms.

"You doing okay?" he asked, but sounding like he didn't care.

"Sure ..." I hesitated.

"What's up?"

"Not much. I did go to church this morning. You?"

"Okay. Just thought I'd call and say hello."

"Thanks." I paused, never knowing what to say to him.

"I plan to take a day off from Alfa next week. Thought I might drive down to see you."

How could Dad take a day off? He was an Alfa agent seven days a week, and in his spare time he ran the world.

"Well, that would be fine." I tried to sound pleasant. "I'm off on Wednesdays and have an occasional Saturday."

"Saturday sounds good."

"Oh," I said, remembering Donnie's invitation, "I may have plans this Saturday. Would Wednesday work?"

Silence. No, there was a hum – the refrigerator and the lights suddenly came back on.

"Dad," I said. "Are you there?"

"I'm here. Saturday is better, but I'll try for Wednesday. Give you a call sometime tomorrow."

"Sure."

"Elisabeth, are you all right?" Dad always called me my full name.

"Yes, I'm fine. We're having some bad weather here, that's all."

"You seem flustered."

"No, I'm okay. The electricity went off as you called."

"Got a flashlight?"

"Yes, Dad." I tried not to appear annoyed. "But it's back on now. Everything's okay. Talk to you tomorrow."

I hung up and moved into the hall before I lost my courage, or the lights went out again. Holding the flashlight like a weapon, I quietly stepped inside the guestroom and looked around. Everything appeared to be in order. The computer had booted itself up again, and the desk chair was positioned just as I had left it.

My bathroom is too small for anyone to hide in, but I did jerk back the shower curtain, thinking about Janet Leigh in *Psycho*. Finally, I crossed the threshold into my bedroom and looked around. Then, even though I know there's not enough space for anyone under the bed, I dropped to my knees and took a look. Boxes ... no body.

Chapter 3

Sometimes I groan on Monday morning, but not this time. It felt good to be back at work, to fix my mind on something productive. The morning whirled. By ten o'clock, I'd taken countless calls and prepared a dozen letters to current customers. At this point, I felt ready for a break so I signed out to the upstairs office to cover for me.

The break room bustled, but several employees looked up to say hello or ask about my weekend. One sales representative, Lewis Bozeman, admired my hairdo, but I hadn't made any changes. For just an instant, I wondered again if Lewis could have placed the Saturday phone call, but I dismissed the thought quickly. No, Lewis was innocent.

By afternoon the in-coming calls subsided, and several salesmen hung around the desk looking lonesome, bored or worried about our lack of customers. More than once during the past month, I'd heard talk of suspected lay-offs. Job security was definitely a concern. Then, almost as if expected, everyone had an e-mail memo requesting a four-forty-five meeting with Ralph Overton, our manager.

Picturing Overton's underside-of-a-mushroom face, I frowned to Margaret who sits across from me at the Welcome Center. She gave me a knowing nod, and we left it at that.

Mr. Overton's office is plush but not overdone. My friend Shannon is an interior decorator, and she says it's well appointed. I find it hard to relate, since almost everything in my apartment looks like Goodwill, and could fit into one small corner of their building.

Most of us arrived on time and took a seat around his

oval table or in a chair against the wall. Overton's tan slacks, lighter tan shirt and pale green tie made my mushroom image mushroom all the more.

Overton was kind, but to the point, and by five o'clock we all could see the hand-writing on the wall. The twelve sales reps would soon be cut to ten, and the six service advisors reduced to four. Two of the thirty men in service might be laid off. Margaret and I would probably have our hours cut. If the situation didn't improve, we could expect part-time within a month or two.

Not welcome news for a Monday, or any day for that matter. Yes, Montgomery, like the rest of the country, was experiencing an economic downturn. I wondered what the rest of the 21st century might hold.

I drove home, pondering what to do with this latest Honda news, and dreading my Dad's phone call. He never seemed to think I measured up.

My mind raced back to an incident when I was a child. Mother had given me a gift for some occasion, and Dad's comment was, "You are spoiling the child rotten. If you keep this up, she will never amount to anything."

Later, when Mother died, Dad retreated into a deep shell of self-pity. I almost felt like he blamed me, so it was akin to losing a dad and a mother. To be truthful, I suppose we both had wallowed in our own pity-party and, in some ways, neither of us had recovered. I was glad Dad had moved to Birmingham two years ago.

While making the last major turn before entering our apartment complex, I even let my mind wander further back to another childhood incident.

Somehow, the details always remained foggy. On this occasion we had attended an Alfa function at the river, and I had announced to Dad that I had just learned to swim. He didn't ask me any details, or even act interested in this news but, late that afternoon, he gave me a push off the pier. It wasn't a hard push like some mean boy, but it was a push.

Since I hadn't really mastered swimming at all, terror gripped my insides as I gulped, gagged, and struggled to pump myself to the surface. Moments later, a pounding headache took over and I remember crying out for God's mercy.

The truly odd part of all this is I can't remember who, or what, saved me, but it wasn't Dad. Somehow it's permanently blanked from my mind.

I asked Mother about it once, but she just said, "Remember, honey, I wasn't there that day. When you came home you didn't tell me about it, and Dad never said a word. Believe me, I do wish I knew."

While I was still immersed in the memory I heard a knock on the glass and realized my neighbor, Earline, was standing in the apartment parking lot, tapping on my window like a woodpecker might tap on a tree.

"Are you all right?" Earline's almost beady eyes heckled me.

Rousing from my reverie, I opened the car door to greet her.

"You had your head down on the steering wheel, so I was concerned about you."

"Thanks, Earline. I'm fine. It's just been a long Monday."

"All right, then." Earline waved me off and pivoted her skinny frame toward her own door.

Frankly, I was not in the mood for more conversation anyway. However, as I pulled my purse from the car, a large reddish-brown lab nudged my knee and looked up with anticipation. I'd never seen this dog before, but he seemed harmless enough. In fact, he appeared intent on getting my attention.

"Okay, boy. How's life treating you?" I held my hand out to let him sniff. "You live around here?"

For a moment I just stood there staring at him, but then sat back down in the driver's seat. Buster considered this a definite invitation, and began to nuzzle my hand and left leg to encourage love.

After a minute, I looked around the car for a possible owner. No one appeared, so I got out and headed for the door. Buster followed. I thought about Shannon's recent advice about getting a dog, but I wasn't ready.

As I opened the door, I remembered the key incident on Saturday, and decided this animal that I had just named Buster must have been the culprit so, saying goodbye, I closed the door in his inquisitive face.

Before I could stick my Lean Cuisine in the microwave,

the phone rang.

"Hello, Elisabeth. It's Dad. Have you finished eating?"

"Haven't started."

"Good. Well, I'm coming down tomorrow night, so we can have the whole day Wednesday. Don't plan anything special for supper. We can eat out if you like."

I immediately thought about my Tuesday exercise class, but didn't mention it.

"Okay ... Dad, I–"

We were cut off. Cell battery, I'm sure. I'd have to charge it and call him back after supper.

Stuffing my Chicken Alfredo in to heat, I began thinking about tomorrow's meal. Frankly, I couldn't come up with anything creative. When you work all day you often take the path of least resistance.

Of course, Dad had offered to take us to a restaurant, but I knew he ate out almost every day, so I headed for the big black box. Checking inside the freezer again, I hoped something would magically appear, but I saw nothing except ice cream and more prepared food. No chicken, beef or meat of any kind, and my father was definitely a meat eater. Nothing to do but go to Publix.

Sighing, I grabbed my make-believe gourmet, gulped it down and made a quick trip to the bedroom. After running a brush through my hair and applying a dab of lip gloss, I started for the car. Forty-five minutes later I was back with a chuck roast, new potatoes, fresh green beans and a container of Marshall's Biscuits.

Suddenly, I remembered I hadn't called Dad, so hurried to grab the cell from my dresser. He answered just before his machine picked up.

"Elisabeth, you forgot me, didn't you?"

"Well, just for a bit. Sorry about that."

"Never mind. Besides, why don't you get a land line, for goodness sake?"

"It's expensive, Dad. The cell works fine."

"Yeah, when you remember to charge it."

"Anyway, what time did you say you're coming?"

"Six-thirty should do it."

"Okay. I'll see you then."

"Sure," Dad said. "I'm looking forward to seeing you."

Closing the cell, I wondered if he were really looking forward to a visit. Reading his mind, or heart, was certainly not easy, but right then I needed to concentrate on getting everything ready. So, after snapping the beans, I put them on to cook, seasoned the meat and potatoes and starting cleaning the apartment. By ten-thirty everything looked presentable and the crock pot was out and ready to turn on on Tuesday morning.

When the alarm went off, my first thought was not Dad, but Margaret. I had forgotten to ask her if she could work for me on Saturday. So, immediately after checking in, I piloted myself toward her desk. She was not her usual smiles, so I asked if she was all right.

"I'm okay. Just didn't sleep well last night." She touched the top of her head as if to smooth one of her many reddish blond curls. Margaret is an all grown up Annie if I've ever seen one.

"Anything bothering you?"

"Just our job situation, but I know it's going to work out somehow. What's up with you?"

"Well," I stopped to scratch my chin. "I should have mentioned it yesterday. Margaret, I need to ask a favor. A friend has invited me to a barbecue Saturday. Could you possibly trade days with me?"

"Is he cute?" Margaret cocked her head to one side and grinned up at me, somehow looking younger than a baby boomer.

"Well, to tell you the truth, yes, but this could be a mercy date."

"Now what does that mean?"

"I don't know. Maybe he feels sorry for me."

"Don't believe it. The man has eyes, you know."

"Thanks, Margaret."

"I'll do it if you promise to give me all the details."

"You've got it."

"Say, did you bring your lunch today?"

"No."

"Me neither. Why don't we grab something at Chick-Fil-A? The gals upstairs have already said they'd cover for me."

"Sounds great. Let's make it at 11:45 before the crowd."

As Margaret and I lingered over our French fries I expected her to ply me some more about Donnie, but we spent most of our time talking about job prospects. She mentioned an upcoming job fair, yet neither of us held out much hope.

Driving back to work, we agreed we'd begin an active search and network with other friends. I didn't tell her what I was really thinking at the moment because bankruptcy definitely didn't fit in my vocabulary.

Chapter 4

I had just peeked through the living room window when I saw Dad sail into the parking lot. He drives a white Camaro which, as any car buff knows, is a head-turner. So is Dad . He's a forty-seven-year-old John Wayne of the silver screen. Sometimes his moods match J.W.'s too.

I checked the clock. Six-thirty sharp. He's always punctual. I stuck the biscuits in the oven before going to the door. They take twenty minutes; ample time to greet him and exchange a few pleasantries before eating. If I remembered correctly, he liked to eat by seven o'clock.

"Hi, Dad," I called. "I see you're right on time."

He slammed the door shut and headed for the trunk to retrieve his bag. "Yeah, I didn't want to keep you waiting." Dad put the duffle bag strap over his shoulder and gave me a little sideways hug. "You're looking good."

"Thanks. You too. How was your trip?"

"Easy, of course. The hour and a half drive from Birmingham is nothing these days."

"No," I agreed, heading toward the sidewalk. "It's not, except for that five o'clock traffic. Anything else we need to take in?"

"That's it. You know I travel light. Why don't I just wash up a little and then I'll take you for dinner."

"No need to. Dinner's ready."

"It is? Why, that's a treat."

When I opened the door, I looked into Dad's river blue eyes and could see he really meant it. "Put your bag there in the guestroom while I check the biscuits."

"Biscuits? I'll be right out."

As he turned for his room my cell phone rang, so I

hurried to my bedroom to retrieve it. Caller ID announced it was Donnie.

"Hi, Beth." His voice sounded warm. "How are you?"

"Fine, Donnie. And you?"

"If you promise me Saturday, I'll be fine."

"Oh, is that so ... Well, I can go."

"Great. Margaret agreed to cover for you?"

"Right. What time should I be ready?"

"I thought I'd pick you up at four if that's okay."

"Saturday at four is great..."

I glimpsed up and saw Dad standing in the short hall. Our eyes met briefly, and I noticed his river blues looked a bit muddy.

"Are you okay, Beth?" Donnie asked. "You sound hesitant."

"I'm okay. It's just that ... well, Dad is here visiting. He just arrived and ..."

"Sorry. You should have told me."

"It's all right. Can we talk later?"

"Of course. How long will he be there?"

"Through tomorrow."

"Fine. I'll call Thursday night. Have a good visit."

"Uh, yes. Talk to you later."

I smiled at Dad when I walked past him toward the kitchen, and could feel his eyes following me. "Got a big date for Saturday, I see. Now I know why this ole man took a back seat."

"No, it's just that I'd already planned something." I stooped to look through the glass oven door, and noticed the biscuits were almost ready. "Why don't you have a seat at the table while I finish up?"

"Need any help?"

"Thanks, but it's about done." I checked the table for napkins then headed for the cabinet to retrieve glasses. "Tea okay with you?"

Dad coughed and said, "Sure, anything is fine."

I could still feel questions in the air while I placed the glasses on the table, so I scurried back to the crock pot, lifted the lid, and reached for my largest serving platter.

Dad said something.

Since I couldn't hear from the kitchen, I continued to arrange the main dish and then poured out the fresh beans. The biscuits were last, but I couldn't find the bread cover, so I just threw a clean dish towel over the top and settled across from Dad.

"Would you like to say a blessing?" I said, wondering how he might answer

"You may."

I bowed my head, thanked God for the food, then asked Him to bless our visit. When I said amen, I heard a sound from Dad's mouth but it didn't sound like amen.

"Well," he said when I passed the roast, "tell me about this Donnie."

"Donnie's a nice guy. I met him at church."

"Oh? What does he do?" Dad took a large serving of roast and potatoes, then handed the platter back to me.

"Donnie's a police officer."

"Police officer?" I watched him raise his eyebrows and pause, as if thinking what to say next. The tree trunk grooves above his nose, intersected with the horizontal lines on his forehead reminded me of a miniature Stone-henge. "Well," he continued, "that doesn't make him a saint, you know. Remember what I told you?"

"Yes, I remember. 'All guys are rascals until proven otherwise.' I've discovered there is some definite truth in that statement, but–"

"You were listening then?" Dad interrupted.

"Yes, I was listening. Here, have some beans."

Dad took the bowl, and then held it until he had my full attention. "How long have you known this ... police officer?" I noticed the sarcastic tone of his last two words.

"About two years. He transferred from another church."

"Well, keep an eye on him, Beth. You never know."

"Yes, Dad. I'm sure you're right. I'll be careful."

We had no sooner finished this theme when he questioned me about work.

"So, how are things going over at Honda? Still like your job?"

"Yes, I do."

"Still find it a challenge?" Dad reached for the biscuits and I passed the jelly.

Again, I thought I detected a condescending edge to his voice, but I ignored it.

18

"Yes, they gave me some new duties a couple of weeks ago and–"

Before I could finish, Dad said, "So I guess they plan to keep you on for awhile?"

"Not necessarily – with this economy in a slump."

"Well, you've got to make yourself indispensable, Elisabeth."

Dad could speak with such authority and assurance! Ever since I was a little girl, I'd had trouble expressing myself or taking a stand, especially with him. Now I pushed the beans around on my plate, wondering what to say.

"Dad, I need to tell you the truth. The manager has already warned us there will be some down-sizing."

He frowned. "And you don't have much seniority."

"That's not the point in my case. They are talking about cutting Margaret and me to part-time."

"Part-time? You can't live on a part-time salary." Dad pushed his plate back from the table, then fiddled with the napkin in his lap.

"I know that, and I'll be looking. We just found out this week."

"Any ideas?"

"Not really, I–"

He cut me off. "Well, like I've said before. I could probably find you something with Alfa. In fact, I bet I could have you placed in Birmingham within a month. How long is your lease?"

I pushed back from the table, planning to re-fill his iced tea. "I've got three more months on this lease, but you know I'd rather live here in Montgomery. Besides, I don't feel led into insurance."

"You don't feel led? What is that supposed to mean?"

"Dad, insurance is a great field. I just don't have a gift in sales."

His voice hardened. "You could develop a gift, you know. I had to. Where are you going?"

"To get you some more tea."

"I don't need tea," he said, his eyes holding me, the tension building.

I stood up, crossed my arms, and surprised myself by saying, "Dad, you are not looking at a twelve year old girl anymore. I'm twenty-two, and I need for you to treat me like it."

"I'm trying to. It's just that you're so all-fired stubborn."

"If so, I got it from you." I tried to smile, still standing with my arms crossed. "Wait here. I'm going to get dessert."

Dad softened a bit. "Dessert? What do you have to offer?"

"Wait and see."

I headed for the kitchen, opened the freezer for the ice cream, and began to cut the brownies, all the time thinking that a minute or two of silence and absence would cool the air. When I returned, Dad looked up and said, "Ah, my favorite." His voice held a definite ring of appeasement.

We ate in relative silence, while the dessert worked its magic. Finally, he spoke.

"Well, it's been a long day. I think I'll turn in early."

"Fine," I said. "When I finish the dishes, I think I'll go to bed, too."

"Good idea." Dad picked up his plate and headed for the kitchen. He also helped me clear the rest of the table but didn't offer to do more. Frankly, I was glad. We'd had enough confrontation for one day.

Before I fell asleep, my mind did a mental re-play of the voice on the answering machine. For just a moment, I thought about a customer who had stood over my desk more than once. The first time, while smiling like the little gecko on the Geico commercial, he had complimented my pleasant phone voice.

I told him that no one had ever said that. He had winked back, calling me the epitome of southern charm. A new look had crossed his face then, and somehow this made me feel awkward.

His name was Harvey ... Harvey Bellinger.

My mind raced on to the next time Harvey had lingered at my desk. What had he said? Yes, it was something like, "I love your name, Beth. It sounds so breathless and sensual."

I remember giving Harvey Bellinger a dismissing nod and quickly turning away. Moments later, he vanished. Then another thought crossed my mind. Bellinger was much older than I – maybe by ten or twelve years.

Chapter 5

The sound of opening and closing cabinets, and maybe the shifting of pots and pans woke me on Wednesday morning. Before I opened my eyes, I saw the picture. Dad was looking for a coffeemaker.

How could I have forgotten to either buy or borrow one before his visit? Last time he came I had promised myself I'd have one before his next trip down. Sighing, I pushed the covers aside, grabbed my robe, and headed for the kitchen.

"Morning, Elisabeth."

"Dad, I'm sorry about the coffee pot. I really meant to buy one this time."

"It's okay. I know you don't like coffee. Tell you what. Why don't you dress and I'll take you for breakfast. You like Waffle House?"

"You know I do, but–"

"No, buts. Now, go get ready."

I knew there was no need to argue. Besides, I love their waffles.

Sometimes conversation goes better in neutral territory, and this morning the Waffle House on Zelda Road seemed to be the perfect place for Dad and me. You see all kinds of people in a place like this and, somehow, at least for awhile, I stopped taking myself so seriously. In fact, I tried to concentrate on Dad.

I asked some questions about his life, and to my surprise, he responded, at least to a degree. He even told me about a recent client he was able to help, so I think this time together eased the tension between us.

After our late breakfast, we took the Union Street exit off the interstate and decided to drive by the Alabama State Capitol. Driving west down Dexter Avenue, I knew Dad would point to the impressive capitol entrance, and mention the star where Jefferson Davis stood when he took the oath of office to become president of the Confederate States of America.

Dad also asked if I remembered him taking me inside the Little White House of the Confederacy just across the street. I acknowledged this childhood history lesson, and we drove on in silence until we reached Court Square.

"You remember what happened here at the Winter Building, don't you?" Dad pointed to his left as we began the slow right turn onto Commerce.

"Yes, Dad. Right up there on the second floor was where the message was sent to fire on Fort Sumter. And, right here at Court Square, wealthy planters once bought and sold slaves."

Dad didn't comment, but as we passed the old Exchange Hotel on our left, he offered more history about dignitaries and presidents who had visited Montgomery. Then he said, "Did you notice Hebe's face is turned north?"

"Who?"

"The fountain back there at Court Square. The statue on top is of Hebe, the Greek goddess of youth. The city fathers turned her to the north, so she could welcome visitors entering the city through the train station and Alabama River boat landing. I used to enjoy hearing my granddad talk about coming down here as a little boy to see the troop trains bringing the Rainbow Division home?"

"Rainbow Division?"

"Yes, the 167th paraded right down Commerce after serving in World War I. The city welcomed them in droves."

We were parked on the north end of Commerce now and, without any discussion, we simply fed the parking meter and headed for Union Station. Dad knew I loved this 1890s Romanesque Revival building sitting on a bluff of the Alabama River.

Although I know little about masonry, I could appreciate the beauty of its stained glassed windows, and the simple elegance of the train shed built on the order of the

Eiffel Tower.

After admiring the architecture of the shed, feeling the breeze from the river, and watching the steamship Harriott pass by, I listened again as Dad told me about his grand-dad who had served as an L&N engineer, and taken his grandson on train trips all over the country, including a ten day jaunt to San Francisco.

"Times were different then, Elisabeth. When I was a kid the world moved at a much slower pace."

For just a moment, I thought about suggesting we take a walk through the nearby tunnel to the river but I could tell Dad was ready to go.

As we turned and headed back to the car I said, "It sounds good. It really does. You know, about those golden years."

"Yes. In a way, I got in on the tail end of them. They say, however, that we need to learn to enjoy the present. Sometimes, I'm not too good at that."

"Nor me. Thanks for reminding me."

When I said that, Dad put his arm around me for a second, then moved it as if he was embarrassed. I wished he had kept it there longer, but it felt good while it lasted.

Driving home, I let my mind wander back to an old childhood dream. In the fairy-tale scenario, I played the role of a sleeping wayfarer. Naturally, a handsome prince, who looked much like my father, would wake me with a kiss on the forehead, turning me into a beautiful princess. But the kiss never came so ... I'd assign myself a part in another fairytale; the role of the ugly duckling.

When we got back to my apartment around five o'clock, I offered to fix us a bite to eat. Dad declined, saying he had an early appointment Thursday morning, and he still needed to finish a proposal. I didn't argue, but did insist he take a few brownies for the road.

Walking to his car he said, "Elisabeth, don't take it too fast with this Donnie guy, okay?"

"I won't. Don't worry. He's a gentleman."

"He'd better be, or he will have to deal with your ole Dad." He opened the car door and asked, "Say, do you plan to keep your Honda?"

"Yes, I think so. It gets good mileage, and I haven't had

many repairs."

Dad ducked his head, sat, and pulled his long legs inside his Camaro. "Well," he said. "They're too small for these limbs, but whatever works for you, Shorty." He looked up smiling. "Take care of yourself, gal. I'll see you soon."

I waved him off, then headed back inside. Somehow, this visit had gone better than I'd expected. Maybe I'd give Shannon a call, see if she had eaten. We could go for a snack supper, and I'd tell her about Donnie and my Dad's visit.

I'd no sooner made a quick trip to the bathroom and dialed her number, when I heard a knock on the door. I closed the phone and hurried to the front. Looking through the peephole, I saw Dad, face forward. Was that impatience on his face?

I didn't have long to conjecture, because he quickly stepped back inside and closed the door.

"Elisabeth, I know this may sound strange. As I was leaving the complex just then, I saw a weird-acting guy pull in. I watched him turn left into your lot, and then sit directly in front of your apartment for a minute or two. After that, he streaked off and whizzed past me again like someone running from a fire. I don't mean to alarm you, but do you have any idea who it might be?"

"No," I answered. "There is a tenant above me. Maybe he was looking for him."

"Well, maybe so. However, you do need to be careful."

"I will. Thanks for telling me."

Dad turned and headed for the parking lot again. I said goodbye, this time with a forced smile. Threatening thoughts were already bouncing off my head wall like a ping-pong ball: the previous drive-by, an anonymous phone call, the key, and now this.

Maybe I could run it all by Shannon again or maybe ... even Donnie ... but I didn't want to wait until Saturday. He had said to call, yet ... I hated to bother him.

Shannon answered her cell on the second ring, and when I asked if she had plans she said, "No, I haven't gone grocery shopping in awhile. How about Taco Bell?"

"Sounds good to me."

24

Shannon has a way of bringing out the best in me but, while eating our tacos and salad, she looked concerned and asked, "What kind of car did your dad see, Beth?"

"I must be a nut," I said. "I forgot to ask."

"No, you've just had a lot going on." Shannon hesitated, stirred her salad and added, "Besides, you didn't want to alarm him."

"Right. He worries about me enough already."

She looked out the window for a long moment and then said, "Say, maybe I should follow you home, just to be sure everything is all right."

"No need. I have on my big girl panties." I patted my thigh and grinned. "I'll be fine."

"All right, but if anything bothers you give me a call, okay?"

"Okay. Thanks."

Shannon and I watched each other walk to our cars, and then she gave me a little toot as I drove away.

Big girl panties or not, I felt a little apprehensive when I pulled into Woodview Apartments. Thankfully, our lots are fairly well lit, and I didn't see any signs of a black Honda near my building. Donnie reminded me to be aware of what's going on around me so, before heading inside, I made sure that I had my key ready and saw no one approaching.

All clear.

I locked the four car doors using the main lock on the driver's side, stepped out, and then hurried to the porch to unlock my door.

Safely inside, I went straight to the cell phone and checked for messages. One. I clicked, and heard a now familiar voice say: "I don't like it. That man is entirely too old for you. This must be stopped. Good night."

The voice. Whom did it belong to? The Harvey guy? If only I'd taken the phone to Taco Bell with me. If only I'd let the voice mail take the message so Shannon could have heard it. Now, I listened again. Who was it? I couldn't be sure. In fact, at that moment, I didn't feel sure of anything.

Chapter 6

Good night? How could I possibly have a good night? I slammed the phone shut and hurried to check the locks on the front and back door. Then I started walking through every room again (it doesn't take long in a twelve hundred square foot apartment), checking the usual places, especially the closets and, yes, under both beds.

You dummy, I said to myself, after looking under my bed. If someone had been in here your thoroughness would have only slowed you down. Well, no one was there, thank God.

Then I rushed to examine the windows, glad for the street light on the corner, yet wishing for more illumination near my bedroom. All windows seemed reasonably secure, all seven of them. And yet, at the moment, it felt like my apartment was nothing but windows, a seven-eyed monster surveying the scene.

Standing in the living room, I reached to turn off the end table lamp when I noticed something I hadn't seen before – the photo album on the coffee table was crooked. Maybe Dad had looked at it while I was fixing supper or getting ready for our outing.

Sighing, I sat down on the sofa and began to absentmindedly turn the pages. Half way through, I found an empty slot right next to shots of Shannon and me posing in our swim suits during summer vacation. The missing picture was one Shannon had taken of me. She had insisted I give her a glamour girl pose. Of course, it wasn't suggestive. Not like some of the shots I had seen on Facebook.

I tried to force my thoughts back to that lazy afternoon at the Perdido Hilton. Was it a dream – that carefree day,

26

with nothing to decide but whether to ride the Orange Beach waves, or bask in the sun by the pool? Lounge and request songs from the good-looking singer in the poolside Tiki hut?

The distraction didn't work. Like a top, my mind started to spin again. Dad wouldn't have removed the picture, or certainly not without asking me. Had someone else been in the apartment while Shannon and I were having dinner? But how, and why?

Suddenly, Harvey or some other nut began operating a leaf blower inside my head.

"You've got to get control of yourself." I said this aloud, but as soon as the words left my lips, the phone rang again. Pulling it from my pants pocket, I sat on the bed and looked. Same number. It was him.

Suddenly, a dry sensation invaded my mouth. I felt partially paralyzed ... like the day I had my tonsils out, and had made the slow climb out of anesthesia.

I couldn't answer the phone because I couldn't speak, and yet, I was just as afraid to hear the message. Four rings. A generic voice requesting a reply, and then ...

"I know you're listening, Beth. Not to worry, sweetheart. We don't have a date tonight. That will come later. Good-night again."

A thought suddenly appeared out of nowhere and buzzed in my head like a persistent fly. About a year ago Dad's sister Beulah had called to check on me. However, she wound up telling me all about her night in the sleep lab. She said a tech had spent forty-five minutes greasing her up. Then he had applied monitors and wires from head to toe, slapped a C-Pap over her face, flipped the lights and said, "Have a good night."

I checked the time on the cell phone. Nine o'clock. Would Donnie be home?

A ring. And again. Three more. Why doesn't he answer? Is his voice mail off?

I closed the phone and put my head in my hands. Where is he? Work? Maybe I could get him at work, but how? He never gave me a number. Reaching for the drawer in my bedside table, I grabbed the phone book and turned to the blue pages.

Under City of Montgomery, the Police Department was listed first. I dialed the number and a woman answered on the first ring.

"Montgomery Police Department. Warren speaking."

"Could you tell me how to reach Lieutenant Crawford please?"

"We have two Crawfords. Did you say Lieutenant?"

"Yes."

"Wait a jiffy."

Wait a jiffy? That didn't sound professional. Maybe she was having a bad day. I waited.

After what seemed like fifty jiffies, she returned saying, "The number is: 251-2607."

This time, I watched my fingers move across the seven buttons, and then I waited for a voice. Three rings later I heard, "Police Department. Murray speaking."

"Murray, is Donnie Crawford in?"

"No. May I say who is calling?"

"Yes, it's Elisabeth Davidson. Can you reach him?"

"Is this an emergency?"

"No. I mean, yes!"

"Your number please."

"It's 319-7752."

"I'll tell Crawford you called."

"Thanks. I–"

The phone went dead, but Murray had my number. How soon he would reach Donnie? I tried to prepare myself. It could be morning. Of course, I could call Shannon but ... for some reason I didn't.

I woke up, still dressed in my Wednesday night clothes. The bedside clock read 3 A.M. Since my mouth had become the Sahara desert, I staggered to the bathroom for a glass of water. After taking several sips, I slowly pushed the half curtain in the bathroom window and explored the night. A crescent-shaped moon hung in the sky like a crooked smile. I didn't smile back.

Everything was still. No unusual cars sat in the parking lot, and no one seemed to have a light on. Before going back to bed, I tested the doors again. They were secure. For a minute, I thought about putting on my sleep shirt but then decided not to bother. In a few hours it would be time for a shower anyway.

I didn't wake again until the alarm went off. Thankfully, I'd set it to music, and the piece was tolerable, not pounding drums or blaring trumpets.

After a shower, I consumed an English muffin and glass of orange juice. By the time I'd dressed and finished hair and make-up, it was seven-thirty and looking cloudy. I grabbed the remote and checked the weather. Don Atwood announced a fifty percent chance of rain, so I decided on my older black shoes and ancient umbrella.

The rain started before I could leave, so I made a dash for the Honda, hearing the cell phone ringing in my purse. It was inevitable that by the time I had unlocked the car and fished inside two compartments the ringing had stopped.

Caller ID identified it as: 410-7705. Donnie. It's about time, I mused to myself. I've got to get to the office. The call would have to wait until the morning break.

Finally, at nine forty-five, I clocked out to upstairs and headed for my car instead of the break room.

"You leaving?" Margaret called.

"No, just have an important phone call. Be right back."

Margaret gave me a suspicious look, but said no more. Secure in the car with the windows rolled up; I pressed 410-7705 and waited. This time Donnie answered and I gave him a quick version of the night before.

"Beth, I'm so sorry. We were out on a long detail and when it was over I hated to call and wake you. Now I wish I had."

"That's okay." Somehow, I felt better just talking to Donnie.

"Beth, the first thing you need to do is get your cell number changed."

"Yes, of course."

"Who's you carrier?"

"Verizon."

"Good. It shouldn't take long. How soon can you go?"

"I think I could do it at noon."

"Tell you what, try for an early lunch. I'll meet you at Verizon and, if you like, I'll pick up your key, run by the apartment, and see about changing your locks."

"That's too much, Donnie. I know you're busy."

"No, I don't report in until two o'clock this afternoon. I've got plenty of time to check a few things and get the new key back to you. If time runs out, I'll leave it with your apartment manager. How does that sound?"

"It sounds perfect. Could you be at Verizon by eleven-twenty?"

"You've got it."

As I put the phone in my purse and headed back to work, I suddenly remembered the mess I'd left in the bathroom. Make-up. A bra hanging from a door hook. Well, I'd have to put modesty aside and be greatful for Donnie's help. Lord knows, I needed it.

When Donnie arrived at Verizon, he had made me a ham sandwich and included a package of chips. While I ate, he initiated the phone number change, so I had little to do but agree to the transaction.

Before he left, he said, "Beth, would you rather we wait on the locks? Maybe it was forward of me to suggest going by without you."

"No," I said. "It's okay. I'll feel safer tonight knowing they've been inspected."

"Sherlock at your disposal, ma'am."

I handed Donnie the key and laughed, not knowing that my friend was about to experience some trouble of his own.

Chapter 7

Donnie later told me how he drove straight to Woodview Apartments and circled the complex once, before parking in the rear near my back door. As suspected, he said I needed better locks, so he headed for Home Depot.

Again, after combing the lot, he parked in the back and began installing the new locks for the front door. Donnie said there was little activity at all that time of day, but he kept his eye out for any suspicious looking character in a black Honda.

By one-o'clock both locks were installed. Donnie was taking a quick look at my windows when he saw someone running past his car at break-neck speed. By the time he reached the back door, the man was out of sight, but experience had taught him to check his car.

Just as Donnie had feared, his left rear tire had been slashed. Donnie's eyes scanned the three look-alike apartments behind mine. All was quiet. Whoever had done it could be safely inside a building.

Was this a coincidence, or had my stalker been on the prowl? If so, did he live in the same complex and, at least on some occasions, drive a black Honda? Donnie didn't know, but he suggested the next move.

"Beth, I want you to pull up all the accounts for anyone who has a Honda, and lives in Woodview. Also, maybe he met you when he came for a service. Do you ever leave your cell phone on your desk?"

"Well, yes. I probably have. Sometimes I walk away from the desk to check on something for a customer. That's careless, I know."

"Yes, it only takes a couple of minutes for a savvy person to record your number. And, like I said before, be careful about giving any personal info on Facebook, and watch for suspicious e-mails."

"I will. Donnie, I'm so sorry I've gotten you into this mess. What about your tire?"

"I'm at Firestone now. It's almost finished. Don't worry; just get started on your task. If this doesn't pull up something we'll keep trying. I'll call you later."

By three-thirty all was quiet at my Honda desk, so I began the job of checking accounts by zip code and then street addresses. I pulled up two in, or near, my neighborhood. One was a 2007 Red Honda Accord for a Mrs. Reynolds, and the other a 2010 Black Honda for a Colonel Wilcox.

The customer card indicated Wilcox had been assigned to another base. No forwarding address given. What next? I thought. Hopefully, Donnie would have some ideas.

I was staring at the screen, mulling over all of this when a piece of good news strolled my way. My boss said I could go home early. Thank God for small blessings! Right then, I decided to scoot by the gym and do my laps. Anything to help relieve some of the stress.

By five o'clock, I felt exhausted from the laps, so decided to skip the exercise class and head home while there was still plenty of sunlight. A late spring breeze caught my hair when I slid into the Honda, so I immediately opened the sun roof.

Road sounds were a welcome relief from the aircon. Taking a deep breath, I tried to forget the last few days. By the time I pulled into the turning lane on the by-pass, I felt better, and began to anticipate the upcoming weekend.

I suppose I was feeling too relaxed, because when I approached the Woodview sign my mind only focused on two things: my Saturday date and the immediate road ahead of me.

When it hit, I instinctively knew it was a bullet – a bullet that completely shattered the window on the driver's side of my Honda.

Two impulses came in rapid succession: to pause and make an assessment for pain and blood, or to make a quick attempt to see the perpetrator.

There was no pain or blood; nothing but broken glass.

Third impulse: to flee. I rounded the corner and reached for the cell phone, dialing 911 as I drove.

"Police Department."

"This is Beth Davidson, calling from my car at the entrance of Woodview Apartments. I think someone has just taken a shot at me. Should I drive to my apartment and wait there for help?"

"Whichever you prefer, ma'am. What is your apartment number?"

"715 Woodview Court."

"I'll send someone right out."

Twenty minutes later a rather young yet weary-looking Sergeant B.R. Lacey arrived to determine the damage and look for a spent cartridge. Lacey's most distinguishing feature was his eyebrows. They resembled two centipedes about to attack each other as they crossed the bridge of his nose.

After several minutes of searching, we didn't find a thing. Lacey said he suspected the culprit had used a pellet gun, but he offered to look for a cartridge back at the Woodview entrance.

"School's out," he offered. "Kids are looking for something to do. They were most likely hiding behind your neighborhood sign, and you were the first target to come along."

"Yeah, you're probably right," I sighed, as I watched Centipede run his middle finger across his brow, as if to prevent a pair of legs from crawling into his eye.

Lacey then helped me remove some of the shattered glass from the window and the parking lot. After signing the accident report, I thanked him and went inside my flat. I quickly checked under windshield repair in the Yellow Pages, and thankfully located a business still open, who promised no over-time charges.

As I drove to Paul's Glass Service, I finally let myself think. Okay. My harasser could be acting out his statement, "This must be stopped." If so, did he intend to kill me or was the shot calculated to simply scare me to death? I didn't know.

On the other hand, Lacey had a point. This might be nothing more than adventure-hunting kids. Right then I'd just wanted to take care of the window and get home. Of course, everything takes time, so when the technician said it would be an hour, I felt thankful for the McDonald's just across the street, even though the entire place reeked with over-cooked French fries.

When I finally got home in one piece, I wanted to call Donnie but didn't. He might think I needed a permanent caretaker. However, when he didn't call on Friday, I felt disappointed. Donnie had sounded so interested in helping me but maybe, I reasoned, he was getting cold feet.

Besides, he had enough to do working over a forty hour week for the police department. Since I was feeling pretty blue Friday night, I asked Margaret if she'd like to have a potluck supper with me, and she readily accepted.

Around six o'clock, Margaret and I pulled out the left-over roast, potatoes and beans. Just as we were finishing our meal with a brownie, Shannon dropped by to check on me. Although she didn't stay long, I was glad she and Margaret could finally meet.

After Shannon left, Margaret and I decided to take a walk by the pond, and then add a more brisk walk through the neighborhood. I almost put the door key in the philodendron again, but changed my mind. I felt safer with it in my pocket.

While we walked, I brought Margaret up to date about the last few days and, when I told her about Thursday's gunshot, she reacted almost like a mother.

Reaching out to pat me on the shoulder, she said, "Please be careful, Beth. Oh, I'm so glad you have that friend on the police force. You are still going to the barbecue, right?"

"Yes. Maybe he'll offer some suggestions. Changing my cell number and locks is certainly a good start. By the way, I want to thank you again for covering for me."

Margaret gave me a big smile as we made the last circle into my drive.

"Glad to. Besides, you're about my daughter's age. Since she lives in Atlanta, I don't get to see her much. Being with you keeps me young."

"Thanks, Margaret. I enjoy your company. Maybe we could take more walks like this in the evening. I certainly need the exercise."

"Me too. Your place is not that far from mine." Margaret suddenly stopped and looked toward my front porch. "Say, it looks like somebody left you a package."

"Package? Where?"

"Right there," Margaret pointed. "Left of your door."

"Oh, I wonder who …?"

"Let's go see."

I reached the porch first, and stooped to pick up a container about the size of a shoe box. It was unwrapped, but had a large purple bow on the top.

"Should I open it?" I asked, looking up at Margaret.

"Well, I guess so. What do you think it might be?"

"I have no idea." I pulled the box tabs apart and stared down on one large wisteria blossom. On top of the flower lay a long, thin piece of paper with a line of type across it.

Standing closer to the porch light, I read it aloud.

"A wisteria may fade, but its perfume still lingers. I will contact you soon to set up our first rendezvous."

"It's him." I looked at Margaret. "He can't call, so now he's resorted to this."

Margaret's face registered trouble, and I'm glad I couldn't see mine.

Taking my arm, she said, "Let's go inside."

I unlocked the door, and Margaret followed me in to the sofa saying, "May I see it?" She shook her head while reading the message again. "This man is an absolute nut!"

"I know, yet what can I do about it?"

"Wait and talk to Donnie," Margaret advised.

"I will, but what about tonight?"

"Why don't you come home and stay with me?"

"That's a nice offer," I said, "but I can't run from this every day."

"Maybe not. However, you don't need to be here alone right now."

"You don't think so?"

"No. Now, go pack a few things. You can sleep in late tomorrow if you like. Of course, give yourself time to get ready for your big date."

"Thanks, Margaret. I think you're right. Spending the night away is probably a good idea. Help yourself to anything in the kitchen while I pack."

Margaret had a nice place in Eastlake. It wasn't plush but the neighborhood is newer than mine, and each townhouse has a unique design. In Woodview all of the apartments look alike.

Margaret made me feel at home right away. We even popped some popcorn; a treat that always seems to calm me for some reason.

At around ten o'clock, I settled down for the night in a yellow and white bedroom. All of the furniture was wicker, so it had a casual and definitely feminine attraction. Frankly, I felt pampered when Margaret watched over me like a mother hen, making me realize again how much I'd missed my own mom over the years.

Everything about Margaret's townhouse seemed perfect until I took a second glimpse at her bedspread. It was decorated with tiny yellow roses and larger lavender-blue wisteria.

Chapter 8

In spite of Margaret's loving care, I had a fitful night's sleep. An elaborate dresser timepiece, decorated with cherubs and more flowers, ticked like a Grandfather clock.

Finally, I took the annoying clock into the adjoining bathroom and, when that didn't work, went back and put a towel over it. A deeper sleep finally settled in around three o'clock, and I then slept in until almost nine. To tell the truth, I wasn't in any particular hurry to go home.

Banana bread and fresh coffee waited in the kitchen, so I decided to give the coffee a try. After I had doctored it up, it tasted good and made the banana bread even better. While eating, I studied the pictures on Margaret's refrigerator.

A shot of Margaret and her daughter caught my eye. They were standing beside a waterfall somewhere, and looked like they were about to enjoy a great day in the sun. I knew it was her daughter because they looked so much alike. Same curly red hair, and almost the same expression on their faces.

I made a mental note to ask her about the waterfall later. Margaret had never mentioned hiking or any hobby for that matter.

Shannon had taught me that you can tell a lot about a person by the accessories in their home. So, after sticking my mug in the dishwasher, I wandered back in the den to see what else I might learn about Margaret.

Even though I'd seen it the night before, her upright Baldwin piano caught my eye first, and immediately brought back memories of early piano lessons before Mom had died.

Mom had been the church pianist, and I could still remember her playing and singing to me as a child. After her death, music had vanished from our home, if you could still call it a home. Sometimes I caught myself humming an old tune, yet it never sounded the same without Mom at the piano.

We'd kept the piano for a year or two, and I'd pull out some sheet music and try to play when Dad was at work. But one day I came in from school and the instrument was gone. No explanation.

I hadn't cried for Mom in two years, but I cried that day and I felt the tears now as I ran my fingers over the keys.

"Why don't you play something?"

I jumped and turned into the face of the young woman in the fridge photo.

"Hi, I'm Annabel, Margaret's daughter."

"Oh, I didn't hear you come in. Sorry. I must have scared you too."

I wiped at my eyes with the back of my hand and tried to smile.

"Is Mom home? Actually, I wanted to surprise her."

"No, she's at work."

"Isn't she off on Saturdays?" Annabel pulled a red curl with her index finger, and then let it spring back in place.

"Well, usually, but she's covering for me. We work together. I'm so sorry. Maybe I could go in after all ..."

"No, Mom didn't expect me. See, Monday is her birthday."

She paused and I filled in the space with, "Yes, I know. I bought her a little gift the other day."

"How nice. Well, since I can't be here Monday, I decided to come today. But ... don't go changing your plans." Annabel picked a piece of lint from her shirt. "I'll just drive over and take her to lunch. During the afternoon I'll shop for her gift. I'm always running behind, it seems. Anyway, Mom and I can do something for dinner. I'm spending the night so we'll have lots of time."

"Are you sure?"

"Yes." Her clear green eyes darted toward me. "By the way, I didn't hear your name. As I said, mine's Annabel. That's one word, not two like most southern names."

She said southern as if it left a bad taste in her mouth.

"Excuse me," I held out my hand. "My name is Beth. Beth Davidson."

"Hello, Beth." She held out a limp hand. "Mom has mentioned you to me several times."

"She has?"

"Yes, she seems to like you. Oh, excuse me. Would you like to go to lunch with us?"

"Thanks, but I need to get home. Your mom had me over because I had a little scare at my apartment last night."

"Oh?" Annabel paused as if she might inquire, but then changed her mind. "Well, no need to rush. Do you need help?"

"No ... I'm fine now. It'll just take a minute to pack. By the way, you have a beautiful room."

"Yes, mother knows I love those colors. Like the bedspread?"

"Well, I ... Yes, it's nice."

Annabel gave me a funny little scowl, then erased it when she spoke. "You sure you don't need anything?"

"No, thank you. I won't be long."

As I stuffed my make-up and other items in my small suitcase, I realized the sheets needed to be changed, so I hurried back to inquire about linens.

"Don't bother," Annabel protested. "It'll give me something to do. You run along. If Mom is covering for you, you must have something important going on."

Annabel waved me off as if she truly doubted her last remark but I said, "Thanks, Annabel. It was great to meet you."

She had already turned, and I heard no reply. I smiled to myself as I remembered how she'd introduced herself the second time: *"As I said, mine's Annabel. That's one word, not two like most southern names."*

I went back for my suitcase and rolled it to the front door, thinking I might call Margaret's daughter A-1. She certainly had a spicy personality. When I called goodbye, Annabel didn't answer, so I decided she must be busy in the kitchen.

Five minutes after arriving home my cell went off, making me jump again. I chastened myself, and answered on the third ring.

"Donnie!" I caught myself, and tried to sound more nonchalant. "How are you?"

"Busy, but fine. You?"

"Okay, thanks." I waited.

"I'm kinda rushed," Donnie said, "Just wanted to see if three-thirty would be all right with you."

"Yes, it's fine. Will jeans be okay?"

"Sure. I've gotta go. See you then."

For the next couple of hours, I tried to stay occupied catching up with laundry, cleaning the apartment and getting my shower. I thought I heard a sound at the front door after my bath, but when I looked through the window, I didn't see anyone.

Then, after dressing, I opened the front door and found a small draw-string sack lying on the rug. When I picked it up, I discovered it was an old tobacco pouch. Closing the door, I felt something hard inside the pouch, so I pulled it open and found another piece of paper rolled around a rock, and held with a rubber band. This was like something from an old "B" rated movie.

My hands started to tremble, as I removed the rubber band and began to read the message. "It's time for our first date. Meet me at the entrance to the tunnel on Commerce Street. Six o'clock. Monday night."

I bit my lip and rubbed my forehead, trying to make the sudden headache disappear. But then, after taking a seat on the sofa, my next thought was sheer gratitude.

Gratitude for this date with Donnie. I pressed my forehead again, trying to iron away the pain, then I stood and walked to the nearest clock which was on the kitchen stove. Three-fifteen.

Like someone in a trance, I headed to the bedroom for my purse and one last look in the mirror. How should I tell him? Poor guy. He had merely asked me for a date. It wasn't fair to bombard him with all of my problems, and yet …

The doorbell rang. Before answering it, I hurried to the medicine cabinet and reached for a bottle of Aleve. I wanted to take ten, but gulped two with a full glass of water. After the medication, I looked at my dazed eyes again and walked to the front. What if it's not Donnie? I asked myself. Get a grip.

Peering through the window, I could only see part of a man. He was tall with dark hair. Looking down, I noticed cowboy boots. I'd never seen Donnie in cowboy boots. Who was it?

"Yes?" I called through the door, forgetting I had a peep hole. "Who's there?"

"It's me. Don."

When I opened the door Donnie took one look at me and said, "Beth, what is it?"

"I don't know." My eyes searched his face, as if to confirm his identity.

Donnie stepped in and led me to the sofa. "Tell me," he said. "What's happening?"

I reached for the pouch but, before handing it to him, I got up and walked to the breakfast table to retrieve the cardboard box.

"Here," I said. "Open the box first."

"Not until you sit down."

I sat and watched Donnie lift the wisteria from the box and then read the message: "*A wisteria may fade but its perfume still lingers. I will contact you soon to set up our first rendezvous.*"

"Okay," Donnie said. "Now let me see what's in your hand."

I gave him the pouch. Trying to read my face as he opened it, Donnie pulled out the rock and the second piece of paper and read, "*It's time for our first date. Meet me at the entrance to the tunnel on Commerce Street. Six o'clock. Monday night.*"

Donnie put the box and the pouch on the coffee table in front of us. Then he turned to me, took both of my hands in his and said, "This guy thinks he has you in the palm of his hand. He doesn't. Now, we are going to the barbecue and we are going to have a good evening. I've been in law enforcement a long time. Trust me. Before the day is over we will have a plan. He is not going to hurt you."

I wanted to believe Donnie but I couldn't. However, a door of belief began to crack just a bit when Donnie added, "*When I am afraid, I will trust in you.*' It's Psalm 56:3. Beth, believe me. I rely on it everyday."

Chapter 9

Shannon often says I need more excitement in my life and, after two hours at the officers' barbecue, I could see what she meant. When we first arrived at Lagoon Park, Donnie announced he was taking me fishing.

"Fishing? Donnie, I've never been fishing in my life."

"Well, now's your chance. Tell me, do you ever get outdoors except for the park at your apartments?"

"Not much."

"I didn't think so. Look, fishing is one of the most relaxing sports in the world. You just sit back, unwind and let it happen."

"Let what happen?"

Donnie parked his truck up near a gum tree and came around to open the door for me. "Let nature work its magic." He held his arm out in a long sweep over the pond, and gave me a moment to look around.

"It's beautiful!"

"Yes, now let me get the gear."

Donnie walked around to his trunk bed and, before I could finish surveying the landscape, he was back with two rods and a tackle box.

"Oh, I need to help you," I offered too late.

"You wanna carry the worms?"

"I suppose so."

Donnie handed me a sticky cardboard carton and said, "Now, follow me."

For the next hour and a half we fished one of the four ponds, and by the time we left I'd caught two bass and four bream. Donnie probably caught twice that many but, since the evening was still before us, we decided not to

42

keep them.

"Another time," Donnie said. "Next time we fish, I'll cook some up for you."

I liked the sound of that. Fishing again. Being with Donnie. It meant that this cute guy in cowboy boots and a semi-western shirt didn't consider me a liability after all.

To my surprise, Donnie had included a bottle of hand sanitizer in his gear. So, after washing up, we were ready for an evening of barbecue and line dancing.

"Line dancing?" I asked, as we entered Pete Peterson Lodge among dozens of other officers and their wives or girlfriends.

"Yep. I guess you've never tried that either."

"No, I haven't," I stammered.

"Well, neither have I." Donnie grinned and led me over to a group of his friends.

"Bo." Donnie held out his hand to a broad shouldered man.

"Bo, I want you to meet my friend, Beth Davidson."

I smiled as Bo turned to greet me. Then, although he wasn't wearing a uniform, I immediately recognized the officer who had written the report for my car window. Sergeant Centipede.

"I know you." Bo offered his hand. "Let's see now. Is it 715 Woodview Court?"

Donnie cut in with, "Say, are you holding out on me?"

"No, she's not," Bo said. "Your friend here just ran into a little fire the other day?"

"What?" Donnie looked bewildered.

"I'm sorry, Donnie. I just didn't get around to telling you."

"Telling me what?" Donnie's wrinkled his forehead in a way I hadn't seen before. Was he mad? I wasn't sure. He certainly did react quickly.

"Donnie, I planned to tell you, but when you picked me up today I thought maybe I'd shared enough. Sometimes a girl has to stand on her own two feet."

"Say folks, I think I need a drink."

Centipede excused himself and headed for a large galvanized tub. I assumed it held soft drinks and maybe some beer.

Donnie led me over to a row of chairs and asked for a full account. When I finished he said, "Beth, like I said before, we need some help with this, and these guys here are some of the best in the business. I'm going to take you over to visit with Bo's girlfriend. You'll like her. Just give me time to talk to some friends. Okay?"

I nodded, wondering if I could adapt to Donnie's *take charge* attitude.

"Look, before I go, will you promise me the first dance?"

I forced a smile, said yes, and followed Donnie over to meet Kathy, a petite brunette who looked only a couple of years older than me. As I suspected from Donnie's remark, Kathy put me at ease right away and introduced me to several wives. After about fifteen minutes of conversation, an officer stood and called everyone to form a line for the barbecue. Donnie quickly headed back in my direction and said he had some good news.

"Tell you what. Let's eat, dance a bit, and then I'll explain some possible plans. Sound good?"

"I suppose so."

I shot a *look grateful* message up to my face as we joined the line, and Donnie introduced me to several more men standing with us. Everyone was so friendly. I wondered if some of them had cooked the barbecue, but Donnie said it was catered by Red's Little School House.

"Have you ever eaten there?" Donnie asked.

"No, but I've heard a lot about it."

"Well, you're in for a treat."

The meal consisted of barbecue, potato salad, slaw, baked beans and several pies for dessert. I've always tried to eat modestly on a date, but this time, I dove in with relish. Somehow, I think my good appetite pleased Donnie, even though he teased me saying, "Yes ma'am. You will need to dance tonight."

Canned country music played in the background during dinner, but after everyone had finished, a live three-man group appeared on a small stage. A fourth guy then walked to the microphone and stated he would be the leader for line dancing.

"Bo says he's good." Donnie grinned and added, "Let's go watch."

We carried our plates to the trash and headed toward the front, along with about six other couples. Bo and Kathy stood beside the dance leader and begin to call some of their other friends forward. Soon one line faced the leader, and within minutes, they simply began to follow the steps of their instructor. Donnie nodded and smiled as we watched from the side.

"That character with the fiddle is terrific," I said, trying to assure Donnie that I was enjoying myself.

"Yes, he reminds me of my Uncle Charlie."

"Does he play the fiddle?"

"No, but he's full of vitality. Maybe you can meet him sometime."

"I'd like to."

"Good. It's a date."

I sighed. Here was another sign of Donnie's good intentions. I hadn't run him off yet.

"All right," Donnie said. "Let's try it."

"Now?"

"Sure. Why not? They are about to start another number."

I nodded, and Donnie took my arm and headed for the dance floor.

"I may have two left feet, but I'm willing to try," Donnie offered.

Standing beside him, we waited for the music to start, and I did my best to copy the instructor's quick foot movements. Donnie and I both messed up the first repetition. However, by the second one, we were able to stay in step, at least to some degree.

I quickly decided that it was best to laugh when you made a mistake, because we were certainly not the only ones who missed a beat or a fast turn.

When the dance finished, Donnie took my arm saying, "Now, I want you to meet Lopez. He's the main guy I spoke to earlier."

He led me through a small maze of dancers and tapped Lopez on the shoulder. Lopez turned and fired a smile, his white teeth standing out against his olive skin. I felt like we were in the presence of an Olympic weight lifter.

"What a lovely young lady." Lopez nodded and reached

for my extended hand.

"Thank you." I felt myself blush.

"Got a minute?" Donnie asked.

"Of course. We move over there by the beer. Yes?"

Donnie nodded and led the way to the beer and beverage tub. After grabbing us a Coke, he followed Lopez outside to the picnic shelters.

We found a seat at the first table, and waited while Lopez took a swig from his Coors. As he raised the can to his lips I noticed the small tat of roses on his right arm and wondered what the police department thought about that.

"So," Lopez began. "Crawford explains to me. You have an admirer."

"Yes." I waited.

"From what Crawford says, he sounds like bully, but we can't assume things. This must be taken ... what is the word? Serious?"

Amused by Lopez's accent, yet knowing I did need to be serious, I took a sip of Coke and said, "Do you two have some ideas?"

"We do," he nodded. "Did Crawford give you plan?"

Donnie cut in and said, "No, not yet. I wanted Beth to unwind some first. Besides, she's teaching me how to dance."

I gave him a slight jab with my elbow as Lopez guzzled his Coors.

"Here's the bottom line, Beth," Donnie continued, "Lopez and I both think you need to take this to our Domestic Violence Unit."

"Domestic Violence? You can't be serious."

"We're dead serious." Donnie held my gaze. "DV has experience with this sort of thing."

"But," I protested. "Isn't domestic violence just for men who abuse their wives?"

"Not all times," Lopez said. "Stalking comes underneath this category. You listen to Don. Lieutenant Wilson is the DV Bureau Commander, and he's had years of experience with these people."

"I don't know. It sounds so complicated." I rubbed my thumb up and down on the Coke bottle and tried to process what they were saying.

"Don't you think it would be worth it to get some relief?" Donnie offered. "Look, I'll go with you if you like."

"Donnie, you've already done enough. That's why I didn't tell you about the car incident. Besides, your friend Bo said he thought it was just some bored kids."

Donnie slapped the table with his hand and said, "That's possible, but be reasonable Beth. Bo didn't know about your stalker."

I studied his face and didn't see any anger; at least no anger directed toward me.

"Maybe I should just show up at the tunnel Monday night. Then I could identify the guy, maybe even reason with him."

Donnie shook his head. "Not a good idea. It's too dangerous."

"Well," I said. "It's still daylight at six o'clock. Just the other day my Dad and I were down in that same location. It's safe. In fact, a police car was parked just a few yards away."

"Beth!"

"All right, Donnie. I hear you." I almost added, *You've said enough,* but instead I said, "I'm just so tired of this havoc."

Lopez fixed his eyes on me and said, "That's why you do it. Go to DV, I mean."

"Okay," I sighed. "I'll think about it. What's involved?"

"Well, you first complete an intake form and offer a synopsis of what has happened so far," Donnie said. "You'll be assigned a case number and–"

"Wait!" I stopped him. "I'm not sure my situation is that complicated."

"You should allow DV be the judge." Lopez looked at me and then back to Donnie. "Well," he said pushing back from the table, "You and Don put your heads to it. I be around if you need Lopez."

Donnie and I both stood and took turns shaking Lopez's hand. To my surprise, Donnie didn't mention the subject again all evening, not even when he walked me to the door and said goodnight. Somehow, although I can't explain it, this made me all the more determined to keep the appointment on Monday night.

Chapter 10

Where in the world have you been, gal? I've been missing you. When you get a chance, give me a call."

It was ten-thirty Saturday night; a little too late to return Shannon's phone call. Besides, the cell needed charging, again. I was always so forgetful.

Besides, I was tired, and wondered how I'd respond if she tried to ply me some more about my mystery caller. Donnie had suggested I not talk about it much until we had made a decision. No, I decided, I needed time to think about what I'd say to Shannon. Tomorrow would be soon enough.

I plugged the phone in the charger and went to bed, thinking about my plan. I'd wear something simple on Monday, some jeans or other comfortable pants. Something I could run in if necessary. The thought made me cringe, yet my mind raced on.

Parking could be a problem but, if possible, I'd take a business slot there on Commerce. Most places closed at five. However, now that downtown Montgomery was being revitalized, locals and tourists were enjoying several new restaurants. Pro and cons, I told myself. Having people around could be a plus, but there wouldn't be many on a Monday.

What are you saying, you crazy nut! The other side of my brain was kicking in and kicking me. *You should listen to Donnie. You shouldn't even be thinking about meeting this guy. You are so all-fired stubborn.*

My Dad's words played ping-pong in my head so I smacked his thoughts off the table, and took up my mental paddle with: *What if I need help and no one is even close to the tunnel? Maybe I should reconsider.*

No. A police car would probably be close by like last time. If not, I'd have my cell phone.

I thought about sitting in the car and waiting to see if I could spot someone watching for me. Then I played a mental scenario of standing beside the tunnel entrance. Neither prospect sounded quite right. A strange mix of confidence and fear bounced in my head. Thankfully, confidence won and I finally fell asleep.

As I showered for church Sunday morning, I wondered if I'd be able to act normal when friends asked the usual, "How are you?" So, while moving on to do my make-up and hair, I practised smiling into the mirror. Of course, I could hide my feelings. After all, isn't that what we all do? We smile and say fine, even if life is falling apart.

I mused about that for a minute. When is it proper to speak up and share, and when is it better to stay quiet? Apparently, now was one of the times to stonewall.

Our singles Sunday school class meets at nine-forty-five, but at ten o'clock, Donnie still wasn't there. I wondered what had happened, because he always had Sunday off. Was he sick or had something come up? When the group mentioned going for lunch after church I didn't feel enthused, but decided it was probably better to stay busy.

Our church service definitely proved a benefit. For one thing, worship helps take your mind off yourself and your immediate problems. I've also noticed how the message often has a direct correlation to my circumstance.

This Sunday Rev. McIntyre's text was Psalm 91. David talks about going to God Most High to hide. He said it's like a secret place where the believer can abide under the shadow of the Almighty. My eyes followed Rev. McIntyre as he read verse 2: *"I will say to the LORD, 'You are my place of safety, my fortress. My God, I trust in you.'"*

Lopez may have a plan all mapped out and Donnie might truly care, I told myself, yet my ultimate hope had better be in Someone bigger than I. Reverend McIntyre began his message and I tried to concentrate. It wasn't easy.

Lunch with friends brought a good diversion but, just as I'd expected, Donnie didn't show up. In fact, I didn't hear anything from him until the drive back to the apartment. The cell rang around two o'clock.

"Beth, its Don."

"Yes, I know."

"How ya doing?"

"Okay, I guess."

"I tried to call you back last night but couldn't get through."

"Sorry. I was charging the cell phone."

"Well, I just wanted to explain why I wasn't at church My folks called and wanted me to come up for services and lunch with them. It's been over three weeks since I've seen them, so I needed to go."

"Your folks live in Prattville, don't they?"

"Yes, you'd think we'd visit more often, but life gets so busy. Maybe you can drive up with me sometime."

"That would be nice."

"Yeah," Donnie sighed. "When we get your situation under control we might all have dinner together."

I liked the sincerity in Donnie's voice. This time he sounded more like he just wanted to help, rather than take charge. I felt myself relax.

"Thanks, Donnie." I paused and then asked, "Is there anything else I need to know about Domestic Violence?"

"Don't think so. Any questions?"

I hesitated. "No, I guess not for now."

"Beth, I don't want to bug you, but I do hope you will think about reporting this to DV."

"I will."

"Are you gonna be okay tonight?"

I wanted to say no, could you come over. Instead, I tried to put a smile into my voice. "Yes, I'll be just fine."

I wasn't. Home by two-thirty, I couldn't think of a thing to do. Call Margaret? No. Besides, I'd see her tomorrow on her birthday. This thought did remind me to wrap her gift. Then, at three o'clock I thought about calling Shannon. After all, she was waiting to hear from me. She didn't answer, so I left a message.

I tried to take a nap, but quickly decided that napping was out of the question. Frankly, I didn't feel tired, just mentally exhausted. By five-thirty, I found myself planning to go back to church. In fact, at the last minute, I asked Earline to go with me and, to my surprise, she accepted.

Earline is one of the shyest people I've ever met, but I decided she was hungry for company too. After church, I asked if she would like to eat a sandwich at my place, and she readily accepted. In fact, she stayed until almost nine. When she left, I decided to read, and finally, before midnight, I put my weary body to bed.

Dreams are strange and sometimes deadly bed fellows. Sunday night I met my stalker in the tunnel, and felt his clammy fingers reach for a button on my blouse. When I resisted, his hands moved to my neck and began to tighten. I twisted my head back and forth, and tried to position an elbow for a stab at his Adam's apple. But, before I could pull my left arm into place, he used a leg to trip me and I fell to the brick floor gasping for air.

As I struggled to stand, he stood over me and sneered, "You could make this easier on yourself, you know. Why don't you come with me peacefully? You'll like what I have to offer."

My attacker held out a hand to help me up, but I leaned the other way and somehow got back on my feet. As I started to run, he laughed and grabbed me around the waist, lifting me off my feet. I screamed and kicked his shin and anything else in the way. One kick must have hit a strategic place, because he groaned and cursed while spinning me around like a dog with snake.

Dreams sometimes include strange props, because in the next scene I watched him grab a blanket and try to smother me. Within seconds my hands and arms were cocooned, and all I could hear was my own muffled moans as the beautiful floral blanket continued to tighten around my face.

The last thing I saw was a faded wisteria blossom as it cut my breath to a thread and then it was over. He wrapped my body in the comforter, carried it to the end of the tunnel, walked to the water's edge and dumped me in the Alabama River.

I woke up thrashing and covered in perspiration, yet relieved to find myself in my bed at 715 Woodview Court. A pale half moon seemed to glower back at me where I had left the blinds cracked, but everything else outside my window remained dark, dictating the body to sleep. If only my mind would listen to the body's call.

Rising slowly, I staggered to the bathroom for a glass of water and almost tripped over my own spread which had fallen to the floor. The water soothed my parched throat as I reflected on the apparent safety of the apartment compared to the river tunnel miles away.

Minutes later, while climbing back in bed, I whispered, "Lord, please let me sleep in your secret place."

Music woke me at six-thirty. No, it couldn't possible be called music. No song. Not even a hint of one. It was more of a beat – an incessant beat. Enough to drive you crazy if you listened long enough. Clicking it off, I realized I felt more rested than expected so I headed for the kitchen for cereal and toast.

Thankfully, sunshine filled the room, lifting my spirits to a level of five as opposed to last night's zero.

After breakfast I chose an aqua top and my comfortable navy blue pants, just in case I was forced into a tunnel run. *Run?* The thought startled me so I erased it immediately, something harder to do when dreaming. While brushing my teeth and applying make-up, I willed myself to dismiss all thoughts of the evening assignment, and to concentrate on Honda's Monday duties.

Arriving at the office, I did a quick desk check and hurried over to see Margaret. My first thought was how fantastic she looked for her forty-six years. Neat. Trim. Radiant eyes. And that saucy curly hair. I told her all of this along with a cheerful sounding, "Happy birthday."

"Thank you, Beth. How was your weekend?"

I knew she wanted, and anticipated, a "great" so I said it. I also thanked her for covering for me.

"My pleasure."

"Say, I enjoyed meeting Annabel at last. Did you two have a good time?"

"We did. It was a nice surprise."

"Well, girl, since today is your real birthday, how about lunch?" I asked.

"That sounds perfect. Where shall it be?"

"You like Olive Garden?"

"Love it, but let's go Dutch."

"No way. It's my treat."

As Margaret and I chatted over lunch, I don't know how I managed to conceal everything about my evening plans, but somehow I did. First, I asked her for more details about her visit with Annabel. Then I told her about the fishing expedition, dinner, and line dancing.

After lunch Margaret opened my gift, and held the sterling silver cuff bracelet up to the light. A grin crept across her face when she read the inscribed message aloud. "Thanks for being my secret sister and friend."

"You're a dear," she said, sliding the bracelet on her arm. "You know I'm old enough to be your mom, yet I like the sound of sister and friend."

"Me, too," I said, as I took my last sip of tea and checked my watch. "Well, I'd like to linger, but our hour is almost up."

"Yes, 'fraid so. It's like the old saying, 'Time flies when you're having fun.'"

As we reached for our purses and slid out of the booth, I mumbled another line to myself, "And time crawls when you waiting for something to happen."

Chapter 11

It was another slow Monday afternoon at Honda. It seems I spent half of my time watching for another dreaded e-mail from our manager, and listening, and hoping, for a call from Donnie. It came after four o'clock.

"How's it going today, Beth?"

"Fine." I heard the catch in my voice and wondered if he noticed.

"I'm at work, but just wanted to check on you."

"Thanks. I'll be getting off here soon."

"Yes, I know. Take it easy."

"I will." Did he know?

"Okay. I'll talk to you later."

I hung up, shaking. Had I wanted Donnie to guess my destination and try to talk me out of it? While I sat there wondering why I was planning to go, I saw Margaret watching me from her desk. I tried to smile but my face muscles were frozen.

After a few minutes, she walked over and touched my shoulder. "Are you all right? You seem pale."

"Yes," I said, looking up at her. "It was Donnie."

"Is he okay?"

"I think so," I heard myself answer. "Yes, Donnie is doing just fine."

As I drove away from the safe haven of the Honda dealership my mind kicked into fast forward. I told myself, *don't rush and don't cut it too close and let it make you nervous.* Nervous? I almost laughed out loud. Nervous was my middle name.

Taking the I-85 interstate, the self talk continued. *Hang*

in there. You're gonna be okay. Try to park in a business slot if you can. This will seem more normal. He may not be watching you park anyway. My guess is he is more intent on getting you into the tunnel.

My heart flopped in my chest. *How reassuring, Beth!*

Soon I took the Union Street exit and passed the Little White House of the Confederacy on my left. Now, there was no time for reminiscing or touring as I had done with Dad. Today I stayed on Union, passing the back of the Alabama State Capitol on my way to Madison Avenue. My mind accelerated. *What ... what if he has a gun?*

Beth, this man wants a date with you. It's not likely he'll have a gun. If by some slim chance he pulls a pistol, remember the cautionary e-mail you received recently: run like mad. Run in a zigzag fashion.

I stared out the windshield, trying to simulate a dash through the tunnel, but my whole body suddenly felt like someone had stuffed me inside a kettle drum during the William Tell Overture. I turned onto Madison and drove west to Commerce. Almost there.

Unlike Shannon, I'm usually on time. I'd be on time today. Now I turned right on Commerce and, after driving a block, I spotted a parking place close to the tunnel. My Honda clock read five-fifty on the nose. The parking meter had fifteen more minutes, but it isn't necessary to feed them after six anyway. I reached for my water bottle and took a long sip, willing away the dryness.

What are you doing here? A tiny voice tried to flood its way into my consciousness. I dammed it up. *After all*, I told myself, *if I could stop this psycho now there'd be no need to spill everything to Domestic Violence.*

Opening the door, I looked from left to right and then down to the end of Commerce. The street seemed strangely quiet. What to do with this permanent arm fixture, my purse? I punched the remote for my car trunk and thought about the recent e-mail warning: "Don't use your remote after exiting your car." Why?

Something about a stranger picking up the signal. I wondered if it were true. Well, too late. I tossed the purse in, covering it with an old blanket. Someone was probably watching. I didn't care.

I checked my watch again. Five-fifty two. I'd enter the tunnel in three minutes, five minutes earlier than planned. *Would he be there? Yes. No. I didn't know.*

Stepping up to the curb, I could feel my heart pounding somewhere in my throat. *One, two three, four.* I counted the beats with each pace and tried to remember how to swallow.

Suddenly, something whisked by. I jumped. The skate board almost scraped my arm but the boy hurried on. *Was he headed for the tunnel? Probably. Would his appearance distract the stalker?* I kept walking and watching the boy as he turned into the tube. I stopped, holding my breath. *What to do next? Had my admirer said to meet him at the entrance or inside?*

I continued to watch the boy, but soon the sound of his footsteps faded. Now I was standing directly in front of the entrance, my eyes traveling down the long cylinder, feeling like a fox in fear of the hound. I saw nothing unusual, and heard no sound except the kettle drum still pounding. Pounding.

I finally took several steps just inside the tunnel and stopped, stifling a cough. Then, I looked behind me. Still nothing. After waiting what seemed like ten minutes, I checked my watch. Six-o-seven. The boy was long out of sight, but did I see someone down at the other end? I blinked.

Trembling now, I moved closer to the tunnel wall, wondering how long it would take me to run back to my car if the man approached. Donnie was right. I shouldn't have come.

Someone sneezed. I looked behind me. Nothing. No, it wasn't a sneeze … it was a train – a six o'clock freight train pulling through the train shed just west of the tunnel. Now came a mournful whistle blow, followed by two more. Ordinarily, I love the sound of a train, but this was distracting. *What should I do?*

I crept several more paces inside the hollow tube, hoping to recognize the person at the other end. The man had definitely moved closer but I couldn't identify him.

"Beth!"

I turned as Donnie touched my arm, and I felt myself

collapse on his shoulder.

"It's okay, Beth." Donnie paused and allowed me a moment of silence. "Are you all right?"

"Yes ... I can't ... I can't believe you came." I hardly recognized my own voice above the roar of the train. "How did you know?"

"Somehow, I knew you were headed here."

"You did?"

"Yes, let's go. It's six-seventeen. I don't believe he's coming."

"What?"

"Our mystery man. He'd be here by now."

"You think so?"

Donnie had his arm around me now, but I couldn't stop shaking.

"Yes, maybe he saw something he didn't like. Maybe he just got cold feet. We'll find out soon enough."

"What do you mean?"

"If he's serious, he won't give up," Donnie said.

"I could only wish."

"Yes!" A familiar voice belonging to a familiar face fast approached. Lopez, dressed in tan work pants and a tattered tan shirt, came toward us. He was pushing a long industrial sized broom.

"So you're the one I saw down at the other end," I sighed.

"Yes. You like Lopez's get-up?" He brushed his side. "Don's idea. Now, you are in no danger this night."

Embarrassed, I thanked Lopez as the three of us turned and walked toward the exit.

Donnie could see I was in no shape to go home alone. Not yet. So, after I had calmed down a bit, he walked me to the car and suggested we meet somewhere for dinner. "Just don't suggest the Renaissance," he grinned. "Pay day is not until Friday."

"What about Martin's?"

"If that's okay with you." He closed the door for me and said, "I'll meet you there in about twenty minutes."

"How did you get off for the night?" I asked through the window.

"One of the occasional perks of being a lieutenant, but

believe me, it doesn't happen often."

I just shook my head and thanked the man who had come to my rescue once again.

Martin's is a down-home style restaurant on Carter Hill Road and, as restaurants go, not too pricy. I ordered the turkey and dressing and Donnie opted for fried chicken. He said Martin's chicken reminded him of the way his mother prepared it.

"My mom's chicken tasted like Martin's too," I said. "I guess it just seems a little much for me tonight." My eyes peddled down to the drops of perspiration perched on my tea glass, reflecting how I still felt on the inside. Struggling with my emotions, I turned toward the café curtains at the window. "My, I still miss Mom so much."

Donnie smiled and was about to say something, when the server brought our food. While we ate, he asked me more about my family, and I realized again how comfortable I felt with him. In time, I decided I might even ask for his take on my near drowning experience, but not now.

When we finished our meal he said, "I hope you saved room for pie."

"After all of this food?"

"Of course. What kind should we get?"

"Donnie, I can't hold a piece of pie."

"Half a piece?"

"Well ..." I could see his determination. "All right, but you make the choice."

"Chocolate!"

He caught the server's eye, and within two minutes, we were staring at a quarter of a pie with four inch meringue. Donnie handed me the knife, so I cut the end off and handed the rest back to him.

"Cheat!"

I laughed, probably for the first time all day, and he quickly took his spoon and smeared a dab of meringue on my nose.

"Copy," I retorted, planting a drop on his chin.

"My, you're a piece of work. Here."

Donnie handed me a napkin and then we both began to assault the pie.

After an hour and a half at the table he said, "Well, you've had a long day, young lady. Maybe I'd better follow you home."

"I'll be all right. You've done enough."

"I want to. Don't turn me down."

I smiled up into one of the most caring faces I'd ever seen, and felt like a cherished lady when he stood and picked up the tab.

Donnie parked beside me at the apartment and came around to open my car door. Walking to the porch he said, "I'd like to come in for a bit if it's all right."

I knew he wanted to see if everything looked safe, so I smiled and handed him the key. Once inside, I noticed that he not only checked the back door, but seemed to pay more attention to each window. When I asked him about it, he just said, "I'm only doing my job."

I let it go at that. Sometime it's best not to ask too many questions. After a few minutes, Donnie headed for the front door and fiddled with the locks again, while I looked down at the floor, searching for the right words.

"Donnie," I began, "you are a true friend ..."

I stopped when he ventured back over the threshold, looked at me and closed the door. His head moved closer to mine, but neither of us said a word. As he leaned in, I lowered my head, thinking he might give me a kiss on the forehead.

"Goodnight, Beth."

When I said goodnight, he lifted my chin and slowly moved his lips closer. I wondered if I should turn away, but I didn't wonder long because an ocean of warmth flooded through me when our lips touched. His almost child-like kiss felt as soft as our chocolate pie and I somehow knew I'd re-live these moments again before the night was over.

Then, just as quickly, Donnie took my hand and simply said, "You are special, Beth, and I will be here for you."

About twenty minutes later, while dressing for bed, my mind did re-play the kiss, but then it wouldn't shut off. It dove back to the earlier events: the drive downtown, parking, walking to the tunnel, a skateboarder, sudden movement from the tunnel exit, a roaring train. *Stop!* I told myself. *You can't keep repeating the terror.*

It was then that I remembered my purse. I considered leaving it in the trunk but I needed the cell phone. Grabbing a cover-up, I slipped on my flip-flops and headed for the door.

The air felt still outside. Quiet. Since I wasn't fully dressed, I didn't turn on the porch light. Besides, there was enough visibility from the street lamp two apartments away. Somewhere in the distance I heard a dog howl, and I thought about the friendly lab that had approached me earlier.

Stepping on the porch, I didn't see a soul so I hurried to the car trunk with my remote in hand. The top popped and I reached inside to lift the blanket. Then, as I started to put the purse strap over my left arm, I heard a voice behind me.

"Don't move!"

A hand quickly slid past my wrist and into the trunk as if to grab whatever he could. I froze. Then, almost without thinking, my hand tightened on the purse. And, calling on a reserve somewhere, I used my other hand to slam the lid on his outstretched arm.

Turning, I caught a glimpse of a black arm. No. It was a black sweatshirt pulled high to conceal a face inside. But it didn't conceal his muffled, yet animal-like, moan. As I dashed for the door, his curse followed. Once inside, I secured the locks and fumbled for the cell phone to call Donnie.

Chapter 12

Could you identify him, Beth?"

"No, his sweatshirt was pulled up over his face. Or maybe it was a mask of some kind."

"Did you see him do anything else around your licence plate?

Puzzled, I said, "No."

"What about his hands? When he reached inside your trunk, was his hand bare?"

"No, I think he wore gloves."

"Then we probably won't have fingerprints. Any idea about his overall size?"

"I'd say five-ten or so," I said.

"Weight?"

"I only got a glimpse. Maybe a hundred and sixty-five or seventy."

"What did he say?"

"Nothing but those two words: 'Don't move.'"

"Was the voice familiar?"

I thought about Harvey Bellinger, the flirtatious guy from a few weeks ago. The one who said he thought my name sounded so breathless and sensual. But, how could I tell with his face partly covered?

"No," I said. "I can't verify the voice."

Donnie and I were sitting on the couch as he wrote everything down on a notepad. When he had finished he turned to me and said, "Are you ready to talk to DV?"

"Yes." My eyes fell to the tiny amethyst ring on my right hand.

"I'd like to go with you if it's okay."

"Thanks. Are you sure?"

Donnie closed the notepad and held me with his eyes. "I think you know the answer to that one."

I nodded, thankful for an ally like him, yet still fearful of what might lie ahead.

After a moment, he tapped his pen on the notepad and said, "You see, once the paper work begins and you're assigned to a case worker, DV can begin a true investigation. In the meantime, you need to collect evidence and start a journal of everything that's happened so far. Log the date, time and place. Write down everything he says and does."

"It may be hard to remember everything, but I'll try."

Putting his arm across the back of the sofa, Donnie said, "That's exactly why you need to start keeping records. You've saved the box and the pouch, haven't you?"

"Yes. What about the phone calls?"

"Your phone records can be subpoenaed if necessary."

"They can?"

"Yes. Listen, Beth. I suggest we get on this right away. Could you take an extra thirty minutes during lunch tomorrow?"

"I think I can arrange it."

"Good, I'll call DV and make us an appointment."

I sighed and looked across at the large living room window. Darkness seemed to be invading us.

"You need some sleep." He reached for my left hand.

"I can't sleep, Donnie."

"Yes, you can. I'm staying with you."

"You can't do that."

"Why not?" He paused. "I understand. Ordinarily, I wouldn't suggest it, but you need protection tonight."

"Donnie, I ..."

"You can trust me, Beth."

"Yes, I know, Donnie. Where ...?"

"I will stay right here." He patted the sofa.

"This sounds like a soap opera."

"Maybe, but we can't help it. Tell me the truth. Won't you feel better with someone here?"

"Yes."

"Then it's done. Now, go to bed, shut your door and I will see you in the morning. By the way, how do you like your eggs?"

"Over-medium," I said as I stood up, grabbed a throw pillow, and bopped him on the head.

Donnie just grinned. But then he rose, leaned down to my level, and planted a firm kiss on my cheek.

Climbing into bed, I did think to take another look at my cell phone. Earlier, in my haste to call Donnie, I had ignored a couple of messages. I pressed play and heard Shannon say, "Well, we are still playing phone tag, Beth. Call me when you can. We have a lot of catching up to do."

Then, pressing again, a familiar voice said, "Beth. Dad here. Look, you said you're not interested in leaving Montgomery, but a gal in my office is doing a lateral move. The spot would be perfect for you. Give me a call."

I noticed the time and then pressed off. No, neither call would be made tonight. Not at eleven o'clock, and not with a man in my apartment – another man who spoke with authority. But ... maybe Donnie's tenacity was not so bad after all.

Donnie was not kidding about breakfast. I woke up to the smell of bacon and biscuits. He'd also sliced some fresh strawberries, and a kiwi.

"I waited on the eggs," he said. "If you will pour the drinks, I'll get started."

"Now, this is service. Orange juice okay?"

"Sure. I couldn't find a coffeemaker."

"Sorry about that." I poured the juice and sat down to watch Donnie at the stove. He seemed to be quite comfortable in my kitchen, and I made a mental picture of how he looked with the red and white dish towel draped over his shoulder. He gave me another peck on the cheek when I left for work and I thought, Is this what it's like for an ole married couple? The idea pleased me as I pulled out of Woodview and turned on the 9.50 radio station. I chuckled to myself for selecting an oldies station but, by the time I reached work, Johnny Mathis was crooning away and I felt better than I had in days. Two stacks of work awaited me at Honda so I plunged in. By ten o'clock I felt ready for a break, and soon found

Margaret. After giving her a brief account of the tunnel and car experience, she patted my hand and said she would definitely be praying. The way she said *definitely* revealed the depth of her concern. Somehow, I didn't think it was time to tell her about my plans to visit Domestic Violence.

Driving to the police station to meet Donnie, I reached for the cell to call Shannon. When she said, "What's going on?" I didn't divulge much, but promised to catch her up later.

"What about you?" I tapped on the steering wheel and waited for the light to change.

"Thought you'd never ask," Shannon teased. "Well, Ryan proposed and I said *yes.* Do you have time to be the maid of honor?"

"Shannon, that's great! You've been keeping quite a secret. Of course, I'll be your maid of honor. Have you set a date?"

"October 25th. How does that sound?"

"Sounds wonderful."

My mind raced ahead, trying to remember if I had anything important going on five months away. No, I said to myself. All I need to do is help apprehend a stalker.

"Listen," she said, "I know you're on lunch break. I'll give you all the details later."

"I'll be waiting!"

Pressing the off button, I thought about how quickly Shannon's love life had evolved. Then, I smiled to myself as I touched my cheek and let my mind drift back to the night before.

After pulling into a parking space at the police station and putting on a fresh application of lip gloss, I remembered I still hadn't called Dad. Well, I'd have to put it on hold. Besides, I needed more time to think of a gentle way to say no to his offer.

Donnie was waiting for me in the lobby, and we took an elevator down to Lieutenant Wilson's office. A mature Indiana Jones look-alike rose from his desk, extended his hand and greeted us. I could tell he and Donnie were on good terms.

Just after Wilson offered us a seat in his small office, his cell phone rang and he asked to be excused a second.

I was glad, frankly, because it gave me time to compose myself and, as I had done with Margaret, to get a feel for Wilson's personality.

In addition to Auburn University football memorabilia, I spotted a picture of Wilson with his wife, and another standing beside his mother when he was promoted to Lieutenant. A family man.

The thought made me feel more comfortable. Then, just as Wilson walked back in, I saw something revealing a sense of humor, a picture of Barney Fife offering some form of instruction to Andy Griffith. I laughed to myself when Wilson began.

"Well, I know your time is limited. Don has already told me you are not exactly sure whom we are dealing with in this stalking case."

"Yes, that's right," I said. "One name does come to mind ..."

Donnie looked at me, wondering I suppose, why I hadn't mentioned anyone before.

"A while back a guy flirted with me, but I didn't give him any encouragement."

"Did this happen only once?" Wilson asked.

"Twice, I think."

"How long ago?"

"The last time was several weeks ago but, like I said, I ignored him."

"This could be the problem."

"I'm sorry?" I asked .

"The fact that you snubbed him. Stalkers have a sense of entitlement. They hate to be rebuffed, especially by someone they admire."

"Wait," I said. "This guy knows almost nothing about me."

"He doesn't have to. He simply sees a beautiful and desirable woman. It's like a hunting instinct."

I turned to Donnie, who nodded in agreement.

"You see," Wilson continued, "stalkers often have a poor self-image. They try to compensate by being cocky. They are primarily interested in their own power and control. Any rejection can set them off. Now then, Don tells me you have two pieces of evidence for us."

Donnie said, "I told him about the box and the pouch."

"Yes, sir. I guess I should have brought them with me."

"That's fine. I want to explain some preliminary paper work first. You can bring the evidence down when you return the forms."

We spent the next ten or fifteen minutes going over the intake papers, and listening as Wilson explained the need for me to fully cooperate with DV. When we got to the part requesting the stalker's name I hesitated, but then wrote: Harvey Bellinger, but was careful to put a question mark after his name.

Satisfied with my explanation, Wilson said, "You will need to notify the security people in your apartment, and your work place. Some might say it takes a village to rear a child, but I say it takes a village to catch a villain. Beth, at this point, you don't need to tell anyone whom you suspect. I'll let you know when, and if, it's necessary."

Donnie must have noticed some change in my expression because he added, "Beth, you could start by reporting this to your friends like Margaret and Shannon. You should also tell your neighbor in the apartment above you."

"Earline?"

"Yes, and like Wilson says, you need to inform your apartment manager and the security people at work."

Lieutenant Wilson must have realized I'd had enough for one day because he stood up and said, "Beth, complete the forms as soon as possible and then give me a call to arrange for a second appointment."

After thanking Wilson, Donnie walked me back to the car. He told me to hang tight and that he'd phone me after exercise Tuesday night.

While I was driving home from exercise class, Dad called.

"Well, what do you say?"

"Hi, Dad."

"Could you come up for an interview sometime later in the week?"

"Thanks, Dad, but I don't think so."

"Elisabeth, you told me your job might be playing out."

"I know. The problem is ..." I pulled into the turning

lane, glad to almost be home.

"Are you thinking about your future?" Dad interrupted.

"Of course, I am. It's just ..."

"It's just that you're missing a real opportunity."

"You may be right. I tell you what. Give me a day or two, okay?"

What was I thinking? Did that come out of me? I hit the steering wheel with my right hand and waited.

"All right, but don't take too long."

"Okay," I whispered in exasperation.

"Elisabeth, are you there?"

"Yes, I've gotta go, Dad."

An hour after arriving home the phone rang. I hesitated to answer, thinking Dad might be calling again. Finally, on the fourth ring, I lifted it from the dresser. Caller ID listed Donnie.

"How are you doing, Beth?"

"Okay. My Dad called."

"Oh?"

"Yeah. He wants me to interview for that Birmingham job with Alfa."

"Are you interested?"

"No, but I need a job."

"Of course." There was a pause and Donnie added, "You are worried about Honda, aren't you?"

"Yes. Like I said, several jobs have already been scrapped and Overton said Margaret and I might be cut to part-time." I swallowed, trying to conceive the unthinkable. "If I move, at least I'd be escaping from the mess here."

"Yes, but ..."

"I know, Donnie."

"Beth, I can't tell you what to do. However, don't make a hasty decision you might regret."

"You're right. I'll think about it, of course."

He said, "Good. I will, too. Keep your chin up. Besides, I might need another kiss."

I smiled into the receiver thinking, yes, I could leave Montgomery, but could I leave a handsome Lieutenant named Donnie Crawford?

Chapter 13

3 days later

The Friday morning Alfa interview went better than I had expected. In fact, late Friday afternoon I received a call offering me a position as a Customer Service Representative.

Now, I really felt the pressure because the annual salary offered was only $2,000 more than my Honda salary, plus I'd have to add moving expenses and the cost of living factor for Birmingham.

Of course, Dad countered. "Elisabeth, you're not comparing apples with apples. You've already told me Honda is expecting more cuts. You could lose out altogether and, best case scenario, you'll be reduced to part-time without benefits. Elisabeth, it's a no-brainer!"

"But, Dad–"

I stopped in mid-sentence because it seemed I'd spent my whole life saying, or thinking, *but Dad*. In fact, life had revolved around what he expected from me.

"Elisabeth," he continued, "Alfa can offer you a promising career with security. You wouldn't turn that down, would you?"

"I just need some time."

Dad exhaled into the receiver. His frustration sounded palpable, making me feel like a four-year-old spilling the orange juice for the umpteenth time.

"There you go again: procrastinating. You've always been a procrastinator. Well, don't wait too long or they might withdraw the offer. Did they give you a deadline?"

"No, not really, but I imagine they will expect to hear

next week."

"Precisely. All I'm asking you to do is think, Elisabeth. You know I've built a twenty-five year career here. If you put your heart in it, you could do the same."

I don't remember what I said after that. However, after our lively phone conversation, my mind settled on one phrase of Dad's rebuttal: *put your heart in it.*

Deep down, I knew I would probably never be able to put my heart into a job with Alfa. Of course, they were an excellent company but I was searching for something else, something I couldn't quite put my finger on.

I can still remember Donnie's call on Friday night. It went something like this:

"Honey, how are you?"

Honey? Donnie hadn't said this before. I could almost taste the word in my mouth.

"I'm okay. Just a little confused."

"Do you want to talk about it?"

"Yes, I guess so. Donnie, it's a good company. Dad's been there twenty-five years. He loves it."

"Would you love it, Beth?"

"I don't know. No, I don't think so. But, maybe I need to keep an open mind."

"Yes, I suppose you do. Do you like Birmingham?"

"It's okay, but I definitely like it better here."

"Why is that?"

"Well ..." I waited. "Montgomery is more my size and ..." I wanted to say, and you are here, but I didn't. Instead, I added, "And the traffic is horrible in Birmingham. It took me over thirty minutes just to get back to the interstate."

"I understand." Donnie stopped. For a moment, I thought we'd been cut off until he said, "I missed you, Beth."

"I missed you, too."

On Monday morning I went to work with my head still spinning with questions and self doubt. Thankfully, Dad hadn't called again. I could thank God for that.

When I checked in at eight, Margaret greeted me with her usual cheer and open-hearted attitude.

"How did it go, Beth?" She reached out to pat my arm and I noticed she was wearing the bracelet I gave her.

"The interview?" I felt distracted and guess it probably showed.

"Yes," she said. "Tell you what. We both have work to do. Maybe we can talk later."

"Lunch?"

"Good, I'd like that. My treat."

"Margaret," I protested.

"No argument. Let's plan on eleven-thirty, before the crowd."

She held her hand up in a high-five so I obliged and then started fumbling through the papers waiting on my desk.

Over lunch Margaret helped me sort through my thoughts and then added, "Well, we haven't heard more regarding Honda job cuts, so maybe our situation isn't totally bleak."

"Maybe not," I agreed. "Do you have any prospects yet?"

"No, but I have enough in savings to last for awhile. Say, what does Donnie think about your options?"

"He's very supportive. On the other hand, I think he'd like for me to stay here."

"So would I."

Donnie came by Honda on his way to work Monday afternoon. I noticed he had a strange expression on his face when he asked if I could take a break. After clocking out with Margaret, he walked me to his truck saying he had some news. We both settled in the front seat and I waited to hear what he had to say.

"Beth, the Police Academy training dates have just been set. Now, I know this might come as a shock, but I think you should apply."

"Me?"

"Absolutely. The process is not complicated. In fact ..." Donnie reached for a folder to his left and handed it to me, "I've taken the liberty of bringing you an application from the Personnel Office." Donnie paused, waiting for me to respond. The look on his face reminded me of a child anticipating a Christmas gift.

"Donnie, is this a joke? I'm not qualified to be a police officer."

"Who says you're not?"

"Well, for one thing, I'm not particularly athletic."

"Come on. You've been going to exercise. You lift weights and do most of the machines. Besides, I can help you train. You can probably do more than you think."

My left hand flew up to my forehead and my fingers begin to rub my eyebrow; a gesture I often follow when surprised or worried.

"Look, I know you've got to get back to work. Just promise me you will think about it." Donnie caught my hand and brought it to his lips. Our eyes locked and a brief kiss followed on the back of my hand.

"When does the training start?"

"I don't know the exact date but you will have enough time for the process. If the department likes what they see in your application, and I know they will, you'll receive a call from a recruiter. After that, you complete a questionnaire, do an interview and the department requests a background check."

"Sounds kinda complicated."

"Not really."

"Is there more after the background check?"

"Well, yes. We can discuss that later. Right now, I just hope you will consider the application. Tell you what. Take it home tonight and look it over. If you have questions give me a call."

I nodded and put my hand on the door handle.

"I know," Donnie said. "You've got to go. Me too."

Always the gentleman, Donnie came around to open the door and walk me back inside. As he turned to go, a sense of anticipation and wonder began to creep up into my head. Could I do it? I didn't know, but the idea held a definite appeal.

Chapter 14

Somehow, my conversation with Donnie gave me a new resolve. Arriving back at my desk, I shot an e-mail to Overton asking for an appointment ASAP, and by five o'clock we were seated across from each other in the conference room.

Overton had called security in, and by five-thirty we had agreed to specific surveillance for my arrival and departure. He also arranged for extra break room and patron waiting room observation for any suspicious characters, and an escort home if I requested it.

When we finished our conference, Overton walked me to the employee parking lot and even opened the door to my little red Honda. I wondered if he noticed the shards of broken glass still visible between the door and the driver's seat. If so, he said nothing. But, after I took a seat, he stood talking to me through the open window.

"Beth, you are showing remarkable restraint, and I admire you for it. It pains me to think of losing you but, like we said before, the economy has us in a bind. I've had a conference with the other officers and we can only give you eight weeks from today. If you find something before then, fine. Is that a deal?"

"Yes," I said. "I understand, and thanks for your concern."

"You're welcome. I wish the situation were different, but we are going to make sure you are safe while you're here."

My mind raced as I backed out and turned into the service road to exit the Honda dealership. Soon my short two years at Honda would be coming to an end, and I had no idea what would come next.

Of course, an Alfa job was still waiting for me in Birmingham and, if Dad had anything to do with it, the position would be stable. I'd be miles away from the stalker but ... far too many miles away from Donnie.

Earline and I arrived home at about the same time, so I decided to spill my story to her too. I was on a roll. Earline listened, and reminded me of one of those cartoon pictures of a timid mouse with ears up and a nose sniffing for the cat.

"Oh, it's scary, Beth." Earline backed away and headed for her apartment. "Yes, I'll be watching out. You know, it's just not safe anywhere these days."

When she reached her door, I watched her look from left to right before hurrying inside, not waiting for my reply.

As I opened my apartment, a deep thirst drew me to the sink for a glass of water. Then I flopped into a breakfast room chair to shed my shoes. At that moment, I heard the muffled ring of my cell and retrieved my purse from the other end of the table.

"Beth, its Margaret."

"My, you got home early."

"Yes," she said. "I wanted to call you right away because I saw Overton walk you to the car. Did you tell him you were taking the job in Birmingham?"

"No, I wanted him to know about the stalker. Margaret, I've just been to the Police Department's Domestic Violence Unit. They suggested I level with Honda so they could keep a look out for the creep."

"Oh, I see ..."

"They also told me to inform the apartment manager, and to tell other friends what's going on."

"That's probably a good idea." Margaret paused and then said, "Beth, I hate to say this, but when Overton walked back inside he came over to talk with me."

"He did? What did he say?"

"Well, that's the part bothering me. He said you'd be leaving in about two months and I could keep my job. Beth, I thanked him, but I didn't promise anything because I wanted to talk to you first."

I hesitated, trying to fit the pieces together. It didn't

take long.

"Don't worry, Margaret." I took a deep breath. "When I told Overton about the stalker, I guess his predicament was solved. He gave me an eight week notice."

"Oh, Beth. It doesn't seem fair. I ..."

Struggling for a reply, I bit the side of my lip and said, "Whoever said life was fair? Both of us can't stay. Tell him yes and get on with your life."

"But what about you?"

"Just pray," I said. "That's what I've got to do. Look, we can discuss it more tomorrow, okay?"

"All right, but I'm not happy with the way this is turning out. Listen, if you want to talk about your visit to Domestic Violence please know I'll be around. Okay?"

"Okay," I groaned.

"I care about you, Beth."

"I know and I care about you, too. Thanks for calling, Margaret."

If I had owned one of those land lines Dad kept insisting I get, I might have slammed it into the cradle. No, I wasn't mad at Margaret; I just needed to release a suitcase of frustration. Instead, I put the cell on the table and reached for the folder Donnie had given me.

The Police Academy application didn't look complicated, yet the reasoning part of my brain asked why should I bother? After all, the Alfa job was practically in my lap, a job that would get me out of Dodge. I'd be foolish not to accept it.

Putting the paper work down, I hurried to change into my jeans and a red T-shirt. Red always makes me feel more in control. Then, after another swig of water, I walked straight to the manager's office to report my stalker.

Gladys Thomas is a beige blond with help. In fact, she's had a little help from there down. Sitting across from her desk, I contemplated her carefully penciled brows. The lids just above her eyes were colored first in an iridescent purple, then violet, then blue. As she greeted me, her mascara lashes blinked several times, reminding me of a peacock.

I say this without disdain because Gladys is an attractive woman, someone who still knows how to color between the lines. Taking a seat across from her, I imagined what Shannon might look like in twenty-five or thirty years.

After a few pleasantries, I told Gladys everything I thought would be applicable regarding the stalker, but I didn't mention the possibility of leaving Montgomery or ask if she might suspend the last few months of my lease. Gladys listened with concern, made a few notes and we were done within ten minutes.

Now, feeling a bit empowered, I headed back to my apartment and was unlocking the door when I spotted it. On the table, sitting on top of the philodendron, perched a large lavender wisteria blossom. A piece of paper was wrapped around the stem. I unwound it and read:

Remember: Flowers are sent for weddings and funerals. I wonder which it will be for you.

Chapter 15

First, I scooted back to my Honda for a quick visual scan. Nothing. No sign of attempted entry and no tire damage. I was about to go inside for my car keys when Earline suddenly opened her door and darted toward me.

"Beth," she gasped. "You won't believe it."

"Won't believe what?"

"A man came by here just a few minutes ago. He got out of his car, looked at yours, and then almost ran to your apartment. I wanted to open my door to get a better look at him, but I was scared. After a minute or two I looked out again just as he sped away."

"What kind of car was he driving?"

"Gosh, I don't know. It was black. Kind of looked like yours, I think."

"A Honda?"

"Yes, I guess so. Did he knock or did you see him?" Earline asked.

"No, I was over at the manager's office. Tell me, do you recall what he looked like?"

"Sort of well built, I guess. About this high."

Earline held her hand up eight or ten inches over our heads.

"Listen, thanks for the lookout, Earline. You've helped a lot."

"I have?"

"Yes, now if you'll excuse me, I need to make a call."

Donnie," I said. "What do you think?"

"Well, he left his calling card. Have you touched it again?"

"No."

"Great. Leave it just like that. Don't guess your friend Earline got the license plate number?"

"No, but I'm beginning to feel like it is Harvey Bellinger."

"You may be right. Listen, I may swing by there tonight to pick up this latest blossom along with your other evidence. Have you filled out the DV forms?"

"Yes, I have."

"Good. Mind if I run it all by DV tomorrow?"

"Of course not. Donnie, how can I thank you?"

"Well …" Donnie's voice took on a playful sound. "I can think of one thing."

Donnie got his kiss, but only a quick one because he was on duty and on his dinner break. When he left, I asked myself the same question I'd asked before. How could I possibly leave Montgomery? Birmingham wasn't that far away but, with busy schedules, just how often could Donnie and I be together?

The prospects didn't look good. I pulled another Lean Cuisine from the freezer, stuck it in the microwave and called Shannon.

For the next fifteen minutes or more, Shannon and I exchanged our stories. Frankly, she's the kind of friend who can listen, and fill in any missing pieces.

"You're in love with this guy, aren't you?"

"Well, I don't know. It's so soon. Let's just say I'm very much in like."

"I gotcha," Shannon laughed. "At any rate, do you want my take on it?"

"Sure."

"Okay. Even with all you're going through, I can hear the happiness in your voice."

"You can? Well, thanks for pointing it out, pal." I paused and then changed the subject. "All right. It's your turn. How can I help with your wedding plans?"

"You can tell me what color to choose for the brides-maids' dresses."

"Me? You're the decorator and color expert. What are you considering?"

"Well, I need your input," she prodded. "As you know, the date is October 25th. If this were you, would you choose fall colors or lavender?"

"Fall colors," I snapped back. "Definitely fall colors." I hesitated and then added, "Well, you asked. By the way, I want to help plan some kind of party or shower for you. Be thinking what you might like."

"Thanks, Beth, but your hands are pretty full."

"Never too full for you. We'll talk about it later."

After my sparse dinner followed by a bowl of ice cream, I sat back down with the Police Academy application and had it finished in less than an hour. Then, when I put the pen down, I started having second thoughts again. Why should I take such a risk when the other job was a given? Was I crazy? Maybe Alfa could wait. Wait until I'd tried and failed to be accepted for training.

Not a chance.

Suddenly, I dreaded talking to Dad. Surely, he'd try to knock some sense into my head. Maybe I needed it and, then again, maybe I didn't.

Chapter 16

Saturday, 12 days later

C ome on," Donnie chided "Let's give it one more lap."
"You've got to be kidding."
"Nope. You wanna be in shape, don't you?"

I was panting as we finished our first lap around Woodview Apartments, but Donnie was unrelenting, determination etched on his face.

"How far have we run?"

"Three quarters of a mile."

"Is that all?"

"Yep. I'll let you drop to a fast walk at one mile, okay?"

"Okay, I'll try. Remember. I'm a walker not a runner."

"You can do it. Breathe like I showed you. That's right. Keep it up."

Donnie had reminded me that the Police Department is no place for wimps, and during those last five minutes of our run, vivid shots from the Academy website rushed to my head. Every officer pictured stood ram-rod straight like Donnie. Tight, firm bodies reflected weekly stints in the Police Academy gym.

Now, as I tried to keep pace with Donnie, it all seemed so hopeless, but I pushed on. Unable to talk, my recent conversation with dear old Dad jumped in to taunt me.

W hy are you doing this?" Dad's words seemed to pound the pavement of my mind. "You're not a guy, Elisabeth. Women shouldn't be in police work."

Maybe he was right. I was nothing but a disappointment to him. I remembered the hurt in his voice when I told him I couldn't accept the Alfa job. Hurt mixed with anger. He acted as if I thought his job wasn't worthy or something.

I had said, "Dad, it's not you or the job. Alfa is a great company. I just feel like I should try the Police Academy."

"Suit yourself, but in two or three weeks you'll be sorry. When it happens, don't call me. The slot will likely be filled anyway."

"I know, but I want to stand on my own feet and not depend on you for everything. Don't you understand?"

"I understand. You are bull headed, Elisabeth. But, good luck. You're going to need it."

Okay, that's it," Donnie called. "Fall back into a fast walk until we get home."

Home? The thought rolled around on my tongue like ice cream. In fact, as soon as the apartment was in sight, I suggested we eat a big fat bowl.

"No way." Donnie shook his head but then relented. "Okay, you can have a small one."

"And you?"

"Same for me."

As we headed through the back door, Donnie tapped me on the shoulder and said, "I have an idea. Why don't I talk to Lamar at the gym? I can tell him about some of the Academy's agility requirements."

"Well, if you think it will help."

"It can't hurt. Of course, the Police Academy has far more equipment than the church, but I believe Lamar will do what he can."

"You think so?" I reached up in the cabinet and handed Donnie two large bowls.

"Beth, I know so. Look ..." Donnie interrupted himself and said, "My, these bowls are big." Then he grinned and continued, "Look, Lamar is a good friend of mine. I can suggest the exercises you need. Is that a deal?"

"Deal."

I pushed the bowls toward Donnie, and watched him wrinkle up his nose as he rummaged through a drawer trying to locate the ice cream scoop. When he found it, he proceeded to dump one scoop of ice cream into each bowl.

Then he carried our servings to the table and waited for me to take a seat. When I was settled he said, "Well, now that I have your attention …"

"What?" I said.

"DV has a rap sheet on your Mr. Harvey Bellinger."

"They do? Tell me."

Donnie sat beside me and said, "Well, for starters, Bellinger is a fairly prominent psychologist in health circles. He's lived here about ten years. In addition to his modest Honda, he owns a Lexus and a home at Lake Martin."

"Wow! You haven't been wasting time, Lieutenant Crawford."

"And neither has he. Bellinger's record shows one citation for carrying a concealed weapon, a criminal trespass and one harassment charge. These are not felonies, mind you, but Bellinger certainly doesn't qualify as a Trinity Church Sunday school teacher."

"I should say not." I slurped my ice cream, trying not to focus on Bellinger's record.

"Speaking of background checks, you know they will run one on you, right?"

"Hadn't thought about it … but I'm squeaky clean."

"No, you're not," Donnie teased. "You should see your face. I can't tell what's dirt and what's ice cream."

"Cut it out, Donnie."

"I will if you'll let me wipe that nose."

At this point I handed him my napkin, leaned in close and waited as he walked over to the faucet, dampened the napkin and gently wiped, and kissed, each smudge away.

Little did I know that in less than forty-eight hours I'd experience more than one surprise.

Chapter 17

Two important pieces of mail arrived on Monday, and I'm not sure which one affected me the more. I stared at the first, a business envelop with no return address. My name stood in bold straight letters but the handwriting was unfamiliar.

Thumbing through the other bills and ads, my eye then fell on a card from the City of Montgomery Police Department.

I turned the card over and read, "You have successfully completed the preliminary investigative process for the Police Department. You must IMMEDIATELY contact the Recruiting Unit to acknowledge receipt of this card and receive further instructions. Failure to do so within five (5) days of the postmarked date will serve as notice that you are no longer interested in this position."

I felt like two people were looking over my shoulder as I read the card again. Donnie stood on one side, nodding and affirming, but Dad hovered on the left, shook his head in disapproval or disgust. I couldn't tell which.

Before I let myself get too excited, I turned back to the business envelope and reached for the letter opener in my desk drawer. When I ripped it open, a familiar parched sensation rose in my throat. One white eight and a half by eleven inch piece of paper folded in thirds held something hidden inside.

I opened it slowly, studied the photo and then read the message, hardly aware I was biting my bottom lip until I tasted blood. After several minutes I placed the envelope on the breakfast room table and reached for the phone.

Donnie suggested we meet for a snack supper at Moe's

on Zelda. He also said to bring the acceptance card and envelope with me. After we placed our orders, he first took my hands in his and said, "Beth, I'm so proud of you. You've passed Phase One so I know you can do the rest. Call the Recruiting Unit tomorrow, schedule your appointment, and they will tell you what to take with you."

I smiled and nodded. Donnie definitely spoke with authority and assurance and I knew he had good intentions.

"Now do you want to show me the letter, or wait until after we've eaten?"

"Let's wait," I said. "This burrito looks too good to waste."

"I agree."

"So," I said, "how has your day gone so far?"

"Routine mostly, but things pick up in the evening."

"I bet." I took a bite of the burrito and tried to imagine what it might be like to work a ten hour shift, especially a night shift. "Donnie?" I spoke with my mouth still half full. "Are new recruits usually assigned to a night shift?"

Donnie wiped his mouth, making me think I probably had sauce on my lips so I instinctively reached for my napkin too.

"Not always, but you should be prepared just in case."

"If so, I hope I'm assigned to the second and not third. I'm not much of a night owl."

"No, you're not. You went to sleep on my shoulder Saturday night, didn't you?" Donnie winked, and I thought about how quickly my disposition improved in Donnie's presence.

"Yes." I smiled back into his tender face.

Then, after a few minutes, his expression changed and I knew he expected me to share the information.

As I handed Donnie the manila folder that Wilson had suggested I use for all communications, Donnie pushed his food aside and studied the new envelope. Then, giving me a nod, he opened it and read, "I wanted to ask you for a picture but you are playing hard to get. Thanks for letting me borrow this bathing beauty shot. The least I can do is reciprocate. I hope you like this picture. Yours truly, Harvey."

I thought Donnie would be upset when he saw that

Harvey had somehow obtained a picture of me but his first words were unexpected. He said, "Bingo. This guy has a weak spot. He's provided exactly what we need." Donnie took his last sip of tea and put the glass down with a thud.

"Well, yes," I nodded. "Wilson said I should try to get a photo of him."

"Exactly. Your stalker has confirmed his identity. I'd say that's quite a break-through. But …" Donnie's face turned serious. "But how did he get this picture of you?"

"That's the scary part. It's the album picture I told you about. Remember?" I dabbed at my mouth again waiting for Donnie's reaction.

"Yeah, you said it didn't just fall out, and you didn't think your Dad took it."

"Right. This happened just before you changed the locks. I told you about leaving the key in the plant when I went for that walk. Thirty minutes later I found it behind the table. Could Harvey have duplicated the key that soon?"

"Absolutely." Donnie pushed his plate back and studied the picture again as he spoke. "I guess what surprises me the most is that he isn't harassing you through the social sites and, best I can tell, he isn't using GPS."

"GPS?"

"Think about it. Remember the night he appeared at your car and you nearly cut his hand off?"

"Of course." I nodded, doing a quick mental cut and paste.

"Well, you said you didn't see him near the car tag and, since then, I've checked your Honda several times."

"For a GPS?"

"Yes." Donnie reached in his pocket and pulled out a tiny flash drive. Holding it to the light, he continued, "Something this small can be easily installed behind a car tag or somewhere inside for that matter. I've been checking, Beth. He's not tracking you with GPS, but he is resourceful. We will have to stay on our toes."

"Okay, so he got the picture the old fashioned way but, thank the Lord, you changed the locks."

"Yes, now remember to never leave your keys unattended, or offer one to anyone."

"I won't." I stuffed the evidence back in the folder and

reached for my purse. "I'll take this stuff down to Wilson tomorrow. Our appointment is over lunch again."

"Good. Do you need me to go?"

"No, I want to start handling some of this on my own."

My first mission on Tuesday morning began at Margaret's desk.

"Well, here he is." I put my hands on my hips and waited.

"Is this the stalker?" Margaret examined Harvey's picture and frowned. Donnie had put everything into a protective covering for safe-keeping.

"That's right. Check out the note."

She turned her chair away from the computer screen and began to read while I studied her face. After a moment she let out a breath and said, "He's acting like a love-sick kid, but at least you have his picture. Can you believe he'd take the risk?"

"No, I can't. It doesn't seem to fit his profile."

"You said he's a psychologist?"

"Yes. Can you believe it?" I shook my head and turned to my desk.

"Live and learn. Well, let me know what Lieutenant Wilson says today. I hope your appointment turns out well."

"It will. I'm finally getting mad enough to take up for myself."

"That a girl!"

"Oh, guess what," I added, facing her again.

"What?"

"I also received a card from Police Department Recruiting. My next step is to call them and set-up an interview."

"Way to go, Beth!"

"Now you're sounding like a kid."

"Got it from hanging around you."

"That could be a scary thought! But don't forget, I'll probably need an hour and a half at lunch. Thanks for covering for me."

"Anytime. You just stay away from the Alabama River."

Chapter 18

O kay," Wilson said. "I'm going to piece this all together and see if we don't have enough to start working on him. In the meantime, go ahead and give your employer and other contacts the name."

"Tell them it's Bellinger?"

"Yes." Wilson picked up the picture and gave my stalker another long look. "We're going to make copies of his photo so you can show it to Honda's security, to employees who know you well, and to the management at your apartment."

"What about other friends?"

"Yes, confide in those closest to you – anyone who might be in a position to spot him. Look, I don't want to overreact, but we've already seen Bellinger move from the 'hearts and flowers' routine to intimidation and threats. When these approaches don't work, some stalkers turn to violence or acting out their frustration. They seem to feel that negative attention beats no attention at all."

Lieutenant Wilson picked up two papers and turned them to face me. "If you should ever need a safe place to stay you may call the Family Sunshine Center. They have a twenty-four hour crisis line and can arrange for shelter." He pointed to the second sheet and said, "This is a map to the center."

I bit my lip again, and thought about the last wisteria incident and Bellinger's message:

Remember: Flowers are sent for weddings and funerals. I wonder which it will be for you?

"On the other hand," Wilson's face softened as he continued, "Bellinger appears to be reverting to 'hearts and flowers' again. He's attempting to court you by wanting to exchange pictures."

I sat up on the edge of my chair and said, "And what should I do?"

Now an almost fatherly expression appeared on his face, a countenance I'd seldom seen in my own Dad.

"There's more than one approach." Wilson paused and then said, "You might send him a letter." He shuffled some more papers on his desk and held a sample letter in front of me.

"A letter?"

"Yes. No two cases are alike, of course, but a stalker needs to know once and for all that his victim has absolutely no interest in a relationship."

I read the form letter as Wilson waited for my response.

TO: _____

DATE: _____

No matter what you may have assumed till now, and no matter for what reason you assumed it, I have no romantic interest in you whatsoever. I am certain I never will. I expect that, knowing this, you will put your attention elsewhere, because that is what I intend to do.

_____

I rubbed my forehead and read it again. No one in his right mind could miss the intent, and yet, would a letter like this cause Harvey to over-react, maybe push him back up to the intimidation or threat level? Wouldn't it be better to ignore rather than antagonize him?

Wilson must have seen my reluctance because he said, "You don't have to decide now, but keep the letter. Apprise the department if, and when, you send it. If you elect to send it, be sure to get a Certified Mail Receipt for evidence. Now then, have you incorporated any of the safety precautions we suggested?"

"Yes, I have. You said stress can impair memory so I'm

keeping a detailed journal of all incidents listing the date, time and place."

"Good. Include what he said, wrote or did. In fact, describe his clothing, his car and include the names of any witnesses."

I shook my head then caught myself, not wanting Wilson to think I couldn't cope or wouldn't cooperate.

I said, "Donnie brought the packages down to you, and I promise to report anything else that Bellinger might mail or leaves at the apartment."

"Perfect," Wilson nodded. "If he deposits anything – devices, boxes, anything at all – don't investigate, but call the police immediately."

"I will. Donnie and I also checked the smoke detector and he brought a fire extinguisher over. Frankly, I don't think Bellinger will resort to anything like this."

"Probably not, but everybody needs this protection anyway." Wilson reached for something behind his desk chair and I waited.

"Beth, since you were last here our department has developed a stalker kit." He fingered the package in his hand. "You and Donnie have already incorporated most of it. However, I'm going to add this air horn, door and window alarms, a disposable camera, hand-held recorder and batteries. We've tried to think of items a victim might need."

As Wilson handed me the large zip lock bag, the word *victim* shot through me like an electric current. Suddenly I felt like a lamp abruptly unplugged. We sat silent for a moment until he said, "Beth, have you thought about an evacuation plan?"

Wilson now seemed to have a direct connection from my eyes to my heart and, although the look was disconcerting, I somehow managed, "Yes, sir. Every day and night ... wherever I am, I check for the closest escape route. If I'm driving somewhere I walk around the car before getting in. Then, while driving, I plan where to turn and what to do if he should follow me."

Looking at my watch, I continued, "Sir, I estimate how much time it will take to the grocery store, the cleaners, church, everything. Like you suggested, I vary my route and park in secure locations."

I caught my breath, thinking of what else to say. Lieutenant Wilson beat me to it.

"Are you able to sleep, Beth?" The fingertips of his hands were touching now, almost in the shape of a steeple.

"It's not the best sleep but ... I've been thinking about something."

"What's that?"

"I realize God's lights are on a timer, too. Sometimes I find myself waiting for the morning."

"I understand."

Did I imagine it, or did Wilson's eyes warm with compassion? I fell into my old habit of wishing I had a Dad like him, wondering how many times during my childhood I had felt the same need.

"If necessary ..." He paused and then continued, "your doctor could prescribe a mild sedative."

"I know, but not yet."

Now Wilson leaned in and said, "What kind of support system do you have, Beth? Are your parents close by?"

"No." I stood up, trying to hold on to what little composure remained. Then I fumbled for my keys, avoiding eye contact. "My mother died when I was a child." Tears began to collect behind my eye balls but I blinked them away. "Dad lives in Birmingham. He asked me to move there, but I don't like to run from trouble, Lieutenant Wilson."

"I can see that and, frankly, I think you will do just fine."

I focused on Wilson's caring face and tried to let his words take root somewhere inside.

Arriving back at Honda, I finally had a chance to phone Recruiting and set up an appointment for Friday week. The receptionist said to bring my birth certificate, social security number, high school and/or college diploma, and any military or marriage certificates.

The phrase "marriage certificate" tripped in my brain for a second but I refocused when she continued with, "Allow two to three hours for an additional questionnaire, an interview, and fingerprinting."

As we hung-up I wondered if, and when, I'd ever finish with this application or if it would *ever* be worth the trouble.

Chapter 19

Thank God, no more scary mail appeared in my box when I got in from exercise class Tuesday night. So, after I had settled inside, I took my shoes off and propped my feet up on the coffee table.

It took no more than a moment for my eyes to fall on the large Bible that lay open in the center of the table with candles, a bowl, and a figurine neatly arranged to the left. I'm not a decorator, but even Shannon had said it made a nice arrangement.

Arrangement indeed. I sighed as I sat there, considering the direct connection between my extreme anxiety, the lack of time for prayer and this book on the table.

After a moment I stood up, walked to the kitchen and poured a glass of iced tea. Then I headed for the bedroom to change clothes. Just after sliding into my favorite jeans and ratty T-shirt, I heard my purse ring and reached inside for the cell.

"Hi, girl. What's happening?"

Shannon's upbeat voice made my lips curl into a smile. "Not much."

"Ah, come on now. I know better than that. What's up with Harvey? Are you handling it all right?"

After hearing about Harvey's note and the picture episode she said, "All the more reason for you to get out of town."

"Get out of town? What do you mean?"

"Look, I have to see a client at Lake Martin this weekend. Here's the deal. I want you and Donnie to come up too. Mom and Dad are there. You and I will stay in the guest room and the guys can bunk in the basement. Ryan and

Donnie need to meet each other, and I know you two can use some rest."

"You can say that again."

"So, what do you think?"

"It sounds wonderful. Let me check with Donnie. What time would you want us to come?"

"Anytime Saturday. The sooner the better. You certainly want time for swimming and a boat ride."

"Shannon, you're just what the doctor ordered. I hope this works out. I'll run it by Donnie and give you a call, okay?"

"Sure. Twist his arm if you must."

"I hear you. He's been a slave driver about this Police Academy application. Maybe I can promise to exercise while we're there."

"Good idea. I'll keep my fingers crossed."

I wanted to say *pray* but, since I hadn't done much of that lately, I just said *bye* and punched 'end' so I could call Donnie. Disappointed to have to leave a voice mail, I headed to the kitchen for a bite to eat.

It was after supper before I got back to the Bible. It's funny (or not so funny) how I could put it off for hours. I started reading where I'd left off days ago – the book of Luke, Chapter 12.

The very first verses convicted me. Jesus was speaking to a huge crowd that was gathered around him. He warned them about being hypocrites; of pretending, and not living the faith. He said something like, *"What you say, or the way you live in the dark, will come to light. No secrets. Truth will out."*

I read on. In the next verse Jesus calls the believer his friend and then says, *"Do not be afraid of those who kill the body and after that can do no more."*

I thought about Harvey, of course. I read on and found help in verses six and beyond. *"Are not five sparrows sold for two pennies? Yet not one of them is forgotten by God. Indeed, the very hairs of your head are all numbered. Don't be afraid; you are worth more than many sparrows."*

As I held the Bible in my lap and exhaled, an old yet new emotion began to work on me: *If God cares about every hair on my head, He certainly hears my sighs now.*

I was chewing on this thought when Donnie called back.

"Hi, beautiful."

I smiled into the phone and began explaining Shannon's invitation. Donnie listened, but seemed reluctant. "Don't you have an appointment with Recruiting Friday?"

"No, that's a week away."

"Oh, good. Well, in that case, I think we should go."

"You do?"

"'Course, if you promise to keep up the exercise?"

"I knew that was coming."

"Somebody has to keep you motivated, right?"

"Right. Actually, I appreciate the persistence. I'd be lazy if you weren't around."

As we hung up I thought, and ... what else would I be if Donnie weren't around?

Chapter 20

Donnie and I arrived at the lake house around eleven-thirty Saturday morning and Shannon met us at the door with her usual enthusiasm.

"Welcome aboard. My, you folks must be hungry. Just look at all this food."

"It's not much," I said. "Donnie baked the beans and picked up chips. All I brought is this potato salad."

"Is this your Mom's recipe?"

"Yes."

"Oh boy. Donnie, look out. It's a recipe to die for."

"Yeah," he replied. "I've been eyeing it, but Beth wouldn't let me give it the taste test."

"How was your drive up?" Shannon put my salad in an already crowded refrigerator and turned to Donnie. "Leave the beans out 'cause we'll be eating soon."

"Beautiful drive" I said. "Donnie's Ford 150, named Truck of the Year at the North America International Auto Show, hugs the road."

Shannon rolled her eyes and asked, "Is it new?"

"No." This came from Donnie, defending himself. "This was just our first real road trip."

"What else did you learn, Miss Truck Expert?" Shannon looked to me for a reply.

"Well, it's the safest full-size pick-up on the road today. It's fuel efficient, boasts great horsepower and displays a remarkable payload capacity."

Donnie shook his head with a playful grin and said, "All right. I had it coming, didn't I?"

I gave him a quick jab in the ribs and replied, "Seriously, it's a super truck. I wouldn't mind having one myself."

"Okay," Shannon offered. "Should we eat now or go for a swim? To tell you the truth, I'm famished."

I got so tickled at Shannon. She was already pulling the potato salad back out of the fridge and then motioned for me to put the silverware and plates on the table. Just then, Ryan walked in with a large bag of ice in one hand and a gallon of tea in the other. We introduced the guys and, after directions from Shannon, they immediately began filling the plastic cups for lunch.

"Are your parents eating with us?" I asked.

"No, they're meeting friends at Kawliga but should be here by mid-afternoon. Ryan, please put this ham on the table. Donnie, would you pour the chips in that green bowl?"

Shannon stopped to take inventory and then said, "Mom's looking forward to seeing you, Beth."

"I'm anxious to see her, too. It's been a while."

We exchanged a few more pleasantries and took our seats at the small table on the screened porch. Shannon asked Ryan to say grace, and then we began passing food as we watched a pontoon boat slowly cruise by.

"Now that's my Mom and Dad's speed." Shannon motioned to the boat. "In fact, they don't take Cuddy out much anymore."

"What's Cuddy?" I asked.

"The speed boat. You know. It's the same one we've always had. In fact, Ryan will take us out whenever you say."

I glanced at Donnie, wondering if he'd had much experience with boats. He looked up and caught my smile so I just said, "That sounds nice. It's a perfect day for it."

"Oh, me!" Shannon jumped up from the table. "I forgot the chicken. It's a wonder I can remember my name after that appointment this morning."

"So," I said. "You've already seen your client?"

"Yes, I met them both at nine o'clock and you wouldn't believe their place."

"Where do they live?"

"Over in the Ridge."

I passed the chicken to Donnie and asked, "Is that the new development you told me about?"

"Well, it's not so new anymore, but it's certainly one of the pricier ones."

Donnie looked up and said, "Beth tells me you're a decorator."

"Well I try, but today I needed you guys over there to help me."

"How's that?" Donnie spoke with true interest.

Shannon must have realized she'd been dominating the conversation, so she turned to Ryan and said, "Tell them what I told you about the Stallworth place."

Ryan rolled his eyes and said, "Well, I haven't seen it, of course, but Shannon says it's a hunter's paradise. Stallworth travels all over the world on safaris and big game hunts. Apparently, he wants his lake house to look like something from *Out of Africa*. By the way, who brought the beans? They're delicious."

Donnie held up one hand and then Ryan continued.

"Anyway, they wanted Shannon to give her opinion about the alligator."

"Alligator?" I almost bit my finger instead of the drumstick.

"It's a crocodile," Shannon corrected.

Ryan shrugged, "Whatever."

"Anyway," Shannon continued, "Mrs. Stallworth thought the croc should go outside, but her husband said he'd paid the taxidermist far too much to relegate him to the outdoors. Excuse me. Isn't that their natural habitat? Anyway, we're still debating that one. By the time I left, Mr. Stallworth was saying that he wanted it perched on a rock in the den."

Donnie laughed and I just shook my head, trying to imagine the Stallworth Zoo.

After lunch, Ryan helped Donnie move our overnight bags inside and later, while Shannon and I cleaned up, we heard the two of them in the basement playing pool. Soon we were deep in girl talk.

"How are you coming with the wedding plans?" I asked this while rinsing our plates for the dishwasher.

"I've ordered the bride's cake and it's gorgeous."

"Might have known," I teased. "What about the groom's?"

"Ryan's working on it. After hearing about the Stallworth place, he may want it decorated in a wild animal motif."

"Probably. Do you have a caterer?"

"Yes. By the way, when it's your turn remember to select the caterer right away." Shannon covered the left-over chicken and licked her fingers. "They book months in advance."

"They do?"

"Yes, and you may need one sooner than you think."

"Oh come on, Shannon."

"I'm serious. Can't you see how Donnie looks at you?"

"What?"

"Stop being so humble. Donnie looks like he could eat you up."

"You think so? Well, there may be days when he wishes he had. I've kept him so busy lately." I reached for a paper towel to wipe my wet hands and handed one to her. She took it and looked me in the eye.

"A man needs to be needed, girl. Don't you forget that."

Before I could reply, Ryan and Donnie appeared back at the top of the stairs in their swim trunks. I wondered if they had heard any of our conversation. Thankfully, their faces didn't reflect it.

"You girls ready for a dip?" Ryan shot his fiancé a thumb's up.

"I am. How about you, Beth?" Shannon headed for our room and I followed.

Minutes later, standing in front of Shannon's mirror, I felt a little conspicuous in my two-piece bathing suit, but then decided it looked more modest than Shannon's one-piece. I hesitated at the door and then turned back for a T-shirt cover-up.

Shannon had already arrived on the screen porch with the guys. Through the window I could see that Ryan was rubbing Shannon down with suntan lotion. As I walked out to join them, Donnie looked up, a pleased expression on his face. Maybe he'd already been over-exposed to the female figure.

"Y'all ready for a boat ride?" Ryan eyed some keys on a table by the back door.

"No, we'll swim first," Shannon said. "I'd rather ride in late afternoon."

Ryan shrugged his shoulder and held the screen open

for Donnie and me. Once on the dock, Shannon spread her beach towel out saying she couldn't wait to catch some rays. Donnie's face etched a question mark. I guess I read his mind.

"You'd rather swim, right?" I asked.

"Sure," Donnie said. "I've been looking forward to this."

"Me, too."

"There are some floats and stuff in that cabinet over there," Shannon called over her shoulder.

Donnie lingered. "You want one?"

"Later," I said, as I eased down the wooden ladder into the lake.

He dove in, and I must admit I enjoyed watching him when he popped up, swam several yards and then looked up to spot me. Giving him a quick wave, I slid in and began to dog paddle while my body adjusted to the cool temperature.

After a bit, I swam out to him and we both treaded water and commented about the landscape and other homes ringing the lake.

"Did Shannon's folks build this place?" Donnie wanted to know.

"I don't think so. We've been coming up here since we were teenagers, and I think she said they bought it from another family."

"It's nice," Donnie offered as he made a quick turn to look back toward the pier.

"Yes, some of their friends have even finer places, but I like this one."

"Me too. You ready for a float?"

"I think so."

After several smooth strokes, he was back at the pier and I heard Shannon ask him if we wanted a drink. I shook my head, so Donnie reached in the cabinet and tossed a float out to me, and then grabbed an old inner tube.

It didn't take long for the early afternoon sun to work on us, so Donnie suggested we move to the east where some hardwoods and willows provided shade. Soon I began to feel more relaxed than I had in weeks, and his face told a similar story.

"You're an excellent swimmer, Donnie Crawford."

I contemplated this good-looking police officer floating beside me, and wondered why he would want to give me the time of day.

"Well, you're not bad yourself."

"I don't know about that. Swimming doesn't come easy for me."

"No? Why not?"

For just a moment I wondered if telling him would be like a child picking at a scab. However, after studying his inquisitive and caring face, I decided it was time.

"Well …" I pushed my arms through the water, moving closer to him. "Donnie, I had a scary experience when I was about six years old." I paused, willing myself to continue.

"You want to tell me about it?"

"Yes … It happened during an Alfa picnic at the river. Mom couldn't go for some reason, so I was looking forward to a day out with my Dad." I stopped again, the memory taking me by the throat. "I guess I wanted Dad to be proud of me so I told him I'd just learned to swim."

"Had you?"

"No, it was a lie, or at least a broad stretch of the truth. I'd probably flapped my arms up and down in the shallow end of a pool and called it swimming."

"I see." Donnie nodded, waiting.

"Anyway, that afternoon while talking to a friend, my Dad just pushed me off the end of the pier. I guess the water was no more than eight or ten feet deep, but when you're six years old and can't swim, anything over four feet can scare the willies out of you."

"Of course," Donnie confirmed. "What happened next?"

"What you would expect, I guess. I felt frantic, yet somehow kept telling myself he'd jump in and rescue me."

"Did he?"

"No, I …"

"It's still painful, isn't it?" Donnie looked into my eyes like he might want to pick up the little girl from long ago, but he just said, "Do you want to keep going?"

"Yes. Somebody dove in or else I wouldn't be here now. I have no idea who saved my life that day. I guess that's been blocked out of my head somehow."

"Did your Dad ever talk about it?"

"No, not once."

"Have you questioned him?"

"I can't."

Donnie's eyes drifted up to study a cloud for a moment, but then he turned back and said, "Why? Are you afraid of the answer?"

"I guess so." I bit my lip, trying to imagine what kind of father would abandon his child.

Then I heard Donnie say, "Beth, it's been sixteen years. I think you need to ask."

We were out for a late afternoon boat ride with Shannon and Ryan when Donnie suddenly turned to me and whispered, "Beth, I'm sorry."

"Sorry for what?"

"For trying to give you advice earlier today."

I pushed some hair out of my eyes and concentrated on the feel of his arm around my shoulder. "It's all right. I probably needed it."

"Well, I've been thinking about something I read not long ago." He removed his arm then took my right hand in his.

I wondered what was coming and asked, "What's that?"

"Whoever wrote it said, 'The very best we can give each other is our respect not our advice, and certainly not our judgment.'"

He squeezed my hand and nodded. Ryan started to say something, then stopped and turned back to concentrate on his destination. Still in a whisper, Donnie said, "What I really want to say is, I love you, Beth."

During those few moments everything on the horizon seemed to serve as a frame for his face, and his words became the artist's signature. I tried to speak, but Donnie held his finger over my lips.

"Don't. Not right now. I just wanted you to know."

I smiled and nodded.

Ryan slowly turned the boat around to who knows where. It didn't matter; Maybe we were going to Shannon's parents' home. And maybe, just maybe, I was finally beginning to find mine.

.

Chapter 21

Back at work on Monday, I went from Margaret telling me I looked radiant and my explaining why, to Monday afternoon when another piece of unwanted mail arrived in my box, bringing back the old sense of dread and foreboding.

"It's been a week and I haven't heard a peep from you," I read his familiar scrawl. "Now that's almost a rhyme. Anyway, I thought you might be more considerate. So, who knows? I may have to take matters into my own hands, or maybe I'll give you a rest."

There it was. Intimidation. Well, I told myself, I could move through stages too. I threw the mail on the coffee table, popped my knuckles and then stared out the window and chastised myself.

For weeks my apartment had felt like a prison, and somehow, I'd become my own jailor. In fact, while at home, I rarely let myself outside for the obligatory fifteen minutes of sunshine and exercise. Well I'd had enough, and this time I wouldn't let fear take over. Anger maybe, but not fear!

Grabbing the keys beside the mail, I decided to go for a walk. After all, why should Bellinger keep me from a normal life? After locking the door, I put the key in my pocket and headed straight for the pond. Then I circled back through the park almost daring him to appear.

However, another part of my brain chastened itself for not asking Earline or someone to accompany me. Somewhere and somehow I needed balance. I was sick of Bellinger buzzing around in my head like a mosquito, especially when I had almost no repellant.

After the walk, I made a quick snack supper and surfed

the channels on TV. Nothing looked interesting, not even *Cops*. Then, when Donnie called around seven o'clock, I found myself venting my frustration to him.

This time he said, "I won't tell you what to do, Beth. But don't forget, the rejection letter might be a possibility. Have you heard anymore from Wilson?"

"Not yet," I said. "Should I give him a call?"

"Maybe. Let's see what tomorrow brings."

Tomorrow brought nothing, but I did remind my boss, Ralph Overton, about the Friday appointment with Recruiting. Two more days passed and still nothing. I read Bellinger's note again and noticed the last phrase: "... or maybe I'll give you a rest."

When Donnie and I met for dinner on Thursday night I just said, "Let's assume he's giving me a rest."

"I hope you're right, Beth. Don't assume too much though. In other words, don't let your guard down completely. Okay?"

I agreed, but an idea began to form in my mind while Donnie paid our check at Ming's Garden. Then, on the short drive home, I rehearsed it. When he walked me to the door after this work-night date, I was the one who initiated the kiss. Then, as he grinned down at me, these words came out of my mouth, "I'm letting my guard down when I say this, Donnie Crawford. I love you."

I met Tabesha Griffin soon after arriving at the Police Academy Recruiting Office on Friday morning. She held out a small brown hand and smiled. I decided that we both wanted to exude confidence, but our handshake wasn't convincing. In fact, she reminded me a little bit of a rag doll with two brown buttons for eyes.

"Did you bring all of the stuff they wanted?" she asked.

"Yeah, I think so. I've got the certificates and diploma."

"Me too. Are you scared?" Now her button eyes came to life and rolled from side to side.

"Yes," I admitted. "You?"

I didn't tell her that I felt like I was exploring a house under construction, and at any minute I'd fall through some insulation on the second floor.

"Scared to death," she said. "You think the test will be hard?"

"Well, I have a friend on the force and he says it's not too bad." My voice sounded funny. Like I was catching a cold.

"Sure 'nuff?"

Before we could say anymore, a Lieutenant Bishop appeared in the foyer. He looked haggard and pasty, like someone who spent too much time giving tests. As he turned to hand Tabesha her papers, I studied him from the side. His profile reminded me of that baker man on the US map: the one with an Iowa head, a Missouri stomach, Arkansas legs and Louisiana feet.

After handing me the same *Montgomery Police Department Pre-Employment Questionnaire*, Bishop suggested we take a seat against the wall to fill it out.

When he walked away, Tabesha said, "Gosh, he's scary looking, and this thing is twice the length of that first application and the In-word Survey."

I thought for a second and realized she meant the IS5-R Inwald Survey. Why it was called that I had no idea. After we took a chair, I quickly turned to the last page of the questionnaire and agreed with Tabesha. "Yeah, this thing is twenty-two pages. But look, we've made it this far."

She puffed some air and said, "You've got that right."

As we settled in, trying to manage the papers on the small desks, Tabesha said, "Wonder why there are only two of us here today?"

"Well, I think we're going to have an interview, too. Maybe they can only handle a couple of us in one morning."

"Yeah," Tabesha bit her pencil. "I guess so."

Now, shuffling through the pages again, I wondered how many recruits had received a different notification card, one reading, "You do not qualify because ..." I also considered if I might be the next one struck.

Staring at the first paragraph, I read, "*Throughout the remainder of this packet* (it was definitely a packet) *you will be asked to make statements about your life. Based upon these statements, the polygraph examiner will ask you a series of questions, including relevant and irrelevant questions to determine if you have been completely truthful. In*

*order for you to avoid problems on your polygraph examina-
tion, please **DO NOT** falsify, misrepresent, lie about facts,
leave out, neglect to mention or purposely withhold any
information about your background."*

Leave out. Neglect. Withhold. My mind jumped to the
long-ago near-drowning experience. Ridiculous. Surely I
wouldn't need to go there. I read on.

"You must be sure that you are completely frank, truthful, and honest in answering the questions."

Continuing, I lifted a quick *"Lord, help me".*

The first few pages involved previous employment
history, with information regarding any reason for being
fired and I wondered if this question might eliminate more
of us. Well, Honda hadn't exactly fired me. The current
parley was down-sizing. I turned to page four.

*Before going to the next section, be sure that you have
not failed to list any jobs that you have been fired or forced
to resign from. The polygraph examiner is authorized by the
Montgomery Police Department to ask you if you have been
truthful in listing all jobs from which you have been fired or
forced to resign.*

Criminal activity questions were addressed next – questions regarding personal or property theft, breaking into
a vehicle or home, any illicit sexual activity, kidnapping,
assault, forgery, false reporting, resisting arrest, pornogra-
phy, organized crime, family violence, court appearances
and so forth.

Even though I hadn't involved myself in any of these
activities (unless I counted the time I stole a pencil sharp-
ener from my second-grade classmate), just pursuing the
list made me tired. How would it feel to be asked some of
these questions on a polygraph?

Another section of the questionnaire involved the illegal
possession, sale or use of drugs. No problem here, except
for some prescribed steroids during a sinus infection. In
the Traffic Violations section I had to guess at two dates:
one for accidentally running through a stop sign and
another for a speeding ticket. I hoped those two citations
wouldn't cause any trouble.

When I looked at my watch it was already ten-fifteen,
and I still had seven pages remaining. As I read questions

about my ambition, reason for wanting the job, friends, and family, I remember feeling almost thankful I didn't have to list siblings and indicate their addresses, vocations, history and so forth.

But then, before I could feel too smug, I came to a disturbing question. It read, "What is the most important thing you have ever lied about in your life?"

There it blazed again – a neon sign in my head. The pier incident. My mouth went dry. I couldn't go there? Concentrate on something else, I told myself. Anything. What about the time you told your parents the lie about the math test? Wouldn't that do?

I looked at my watch again and decided to leave the slot blank for a second, but whoever wrote this questionnaire was clever. The next question read, "Are you nervous? If yes, explain."

My eyes bounced over to Tabesha. She looked intent, and I wondered if she might be on the same page. I couldn't tell. Then a uniform walked by and I looked up. It was Bishop. He hesitated, nodded, and then smiled as if to say, "I know it's tough. Keep going."

My eyes fell on the nervous questions again and I checked yes. I wrote, "Yes, I'm afraid I can't remember the most important thing I've lied about. The one that jumps in my mind is the time I ..." I wrote frantically, hoping to finish before Lieutenant Bishop appeared again.

At eleven o'clock he stood in the doorway, looking even more like the baker man. Tabesha continued to write, but when he approached her chair, she looked up, her eyes vaulting to his face in panic mode.

"Miss Davidson." He nodded in my direction. "You may follow me. Miss Griffin, Corporal Pruitt will interview you when you're finished."

The Recruiting officer led me down the hall to a small office, and gestured to the one chair in front of his desk. After taking his seat across from me, Bishop picked up a stack of papers, and I realized he was holding my original application, the Inwald Survey and the questionnaire I'd just completed.

When he donned some clear-framed glasses and riveted his eyes on me, I decided that he now resembled a picture I once saw of a Smokey Mountain bear gazing inside a tourist's car. Suddenly, my red Honda became that car, and I was the grizzly's next meal.

Lieutenant Bishop took his time turning the pages, and I began to feel like I might never eat again, at least not until I'd removed the cotton-like substance I felt in my mouth. I wondered if he could tell.

Finally, he looked up and said, "On question # 36 of the survey you indicate you feel more upset than other people when you think someone is angry with you. Could you explain?"

I swallowed, but it didn't help the dryness. Bishop lowered his glasses and let the silence rest between us. I was about to speak when he said, "Don't be nervous. There is no right or wrong answer."

"Well," I began. "I don't like to upset anyone."

"Are you a people pleaser?" I thought I detected a condescending tone to his voice.

"If I feel someone is in the wrong, no."

Bishop sniffed, waited and then said, "But you aren't comfortable when someone is angry with you?"

"Sir," I said, "although I don't like confrontation, I try to handle it the best way I can."

"I see ..." He paused, then apparently felt satisfied and moved on. "You wrote false for question #98, yet you added a question mark beside it. Tell me why? The question reads, 'I have had to get a restraining order to protect me from someone I feared would harm me.'"

Lieutenant Bishop sat up straighter and leaned over, as if he thought I might not speak loud enough.

Suddenly, I almost regretted I'd added the question mark yet I'd wanted to be truthful. So, taking a cue from him, I held my shoulders up and briefly explained my experience with the stalker, saying I had not yet requested a restraining order.

Bishop listened, nodded and then finally replied, "So, do you think being a police officer is a way for you to get even, or prove yourself?"

"No, but maybe being an officer will help empower me to take up for myself and to contribute something to others being abused."

Again Bishop nodded; his faced revealed nothing. He turned the page and then said, "You indicate you sometimes care a little too much about getting approval from other people. Elaborate."

"Yes, sir," I began. "I sometimes feel I don't always please my Dad, and this bothers me."

"Are you an only child?"

"Yes."

"Do you live with your parents?" Bishop gave me another *bear in the glass* expression. Was it a look of disapproval, or was I over-reacting again?

"No." I tried not to let him intimidate me. "My mother died when I was twelve and Dad lives in Birmingham."

"How does your father feel about a law enforcement career for you?"

I moistened my bottom lip, trying to remain calm. "Well, to tell you the truth, he doesn't approve."

"And ..." Bishop scratched his chin with his right claw. "How are you responding to this?"

"Well," I sighed. "I would naturally prefer his approval but–" I faltered and then added, "Dad doesn't relish women in police work. He may think I'm too weak for the role."

"What do you think, Miss Davidson?"

"I think I'm stronger than I appear ..." I paused to put my thoughts together, "And, to tell you the truth, I believe this is what God wants me to do."

Lieutenant Bishop gave me a strong nod and responded. "I like a woman who can speak her mind. Okay. Now let's move on to today's questionnaire."

As he slowly turned through the twenty-two pages, I sent up a silent prayer, hoping he'd not find anything to press me about. When he reached what I determined to be the half way point in the survey, he stopped and looked up again.

"Miss Davidson, I see you've only listed a steroid for a sinus infection. Never used a tranquilizer?"

"No, sir," I said. "I've never used a tranquilizer."

Our eyes met, but he didn't press me. Bishop turned a page or two and then said, "You've cited a couple of traffic tickets but nothing more serious, and you indicate no outstanding debts. Is this correct?"

"Yes, sir."

"Good." He moved on and then said, "Hobbies. I see you've listed reading and writing short stories. Had anything published?"

"No, sir, but I hope to one day."

My answer surprised myself. This was the first time I'd ever admitted this desire.

Lieutenant Bishop's face seemed satisfied, but I knew we were close to the question that had bothered me the most. Only one line was offered for a response, so I had kept my answer brief.

The question read, *"What is the worst thing that ever happened to you?"* I had simply written: "A childhood swimming incident."

I waited, hoping he would pay it no attention. After what seemed like a child's long wait for punishment he read, "What is the best thing that ever happened to you?"

Startled, yet relieved, I heard him say, "Is this really the best thing? You wrote, "When I became a Christian."

"Yes, sir. It is definitely the best thing."

Once again, our eyes locked but I couldn't read his thoughts. I watched him quickly turn the pages, and then my breath caught again when he cleared his throat and paraphrased the question and answer about lying.

"You once lied and said you could swim when you couldn't. Not good." He paused. "Is this the only lie you've ever told?"

"No, I'm sure it's not, sir."

"So, are you saying a Christian can still lie?"

"Yes, sir, but ... there's a difference. When we tell a lie it grieves us more."

As I tried to study Bishop's face again, he seemed intent on something else. Finally, he spoke. "Lieutenant Donnie Crawford. I see you found out about the job from Crawford. How do you know him?"

"Crawford and I are friends from church." I tried not to smile too broadly, but I wondered if Bishop could hear the music in my voice.

"He's a good man. Well, that about does it." Bishop shuffled through the last few pages, stood up, and announced, "Take a five minute break and then see me in the next room for fingerprinting."

Getting up and moving about can certainly help with stress, so I felt more relaxed when Lieutenant Bishop and I met for fingerprinting. After filling in my name, address and the date on the small blue and white finger-printing card, he instructed me to wash my hands, and then to evenly distribute black printer's ink on my fingers.

Bishop demonstrated how to carefully roll my finger from nail to nail and then place each one on the front side of the card.

When the fingerprinting was done and the ink washed away, Bishop revealed a *time for hibernation* look and said, "We are finished for the day. You will be getting a notice concerning if, or when, to schedule a polygraph. If it's in the affirmative, allow at least an hour and a half."

I guess I had hoped for a more positive closing statement, but in one sense, I felt thankful to simply be dismissed.

Chapter 22

Hi darling. How are you?"

Donnie's voice sounded sweeter than I could ever recall as I took a deep breath and sighed, "Fine, I think."

"You know the definition for fine, don't you?"

"No, what?"

"It's frustrated, insecure, neurotic, and exhausted," Donnie laughed. "Seriously," he added, "was it rough?"

"Yes, but I know you're not surprised."

"Not really. Where are you?"

"Just pulling out of Recruiting. You timed it well."

"Look," Donnie continued, "my mom called earlier today to invite us for lunch Sunday. Are you up for it?"

I hesitated, and supposed he could read my mind.

"Look, if you're too tired, they'll understand."

"No," I said, as I turned onto Highway 80. "I want to meet them. I guess she wants us after church, right?"

"Right. Tell you what. You're off for the rest of the day. Why don't you go home and take a long nap? If you don't feel like a date tonight I understand."

"You're not getting off that easy," I teased. "Besides, I need your take on the interview and stuff."

"Good deal. I'll see you at seven. Why don't I pick up a couple of Chick-Fil-As on the way?"

"Sounds wonderful. Whoops!"

Changing lanes, I dropped the phone in my lap and when I retrieved it he said, "Maybe I'd better buy you some ear buds. Anyway, take that nap, girl. I know you're exhausted."

Bless his heart; Donnie listened to every word of my explanation of the day's events as we settled in at my breakfast table with the Chick-Fil-As. In fact, I'd never dated a guy with better listening skills.

At one point he said, "I tried to tell you to expect some personal questions, didn't I?"

"Yes, you just didn't tell me how personal."

"'Fraid I'd scare you off. Anyway, it should be smooth sailing now." He rested his chin in his hand and smiled at me.

"You think so?"

"Yeah. The worst part it over."

"What about the agility test?"

"We're working on it. Say, why don't we walk around the complex before I leave?"

I stood and took our trash to the kitchen. "Are you kidding?" Then, seeing he wasn't, I said, "Fine. Stand at attention while I get my sneakers."

After Donnie and I said good night, I had a phone call from Dad. Somehow, he remembered the testing and interview date, and wanted to hear the outcome.

"It was long. Tiring."

"Well, *police work* will always be tiring."

I should have anticipated his negative response and caustic tone, but I hadn't ."Is it over?" he pressed.

"No, I still have the Polygraph."

"That should be interesting."

"Yes, well, I'm ready to get it behind me."

"Do you know how long before you'll hear something after that?"

"No, not exactly."

"How much longer do you have at Honda?"

"About five weeks."

"Well," he said. "If money gets tight, let me know. Maybe I could help out a little."

I felt my muscles tighten in my back, but knowing he was sincere, I simply said, "Thanks, Dad. Hopefully, that won't be necessary. I should be fine."

After we hung up, I thought about Donnie's *fine* definition: frustrated, insecure, neurotic and exhausted.

On Saturday morning, I finally got caught up with apartment pick-up and cleaning, and then settled in for some long-delayed ironing. Around noon, Margaret called to ask about Friday's happenings, and said she wanted to treat me to a meal at Mimi's.

When I protested she said, "Look, once you become a police officer we may not have many dinner dates. Besides, we need to celebrate."

As I clicked the cell shut, I thanked God for my sweet friendship with Margaret, and then finished up so I could buy a few groceries and take a leisurely bath before our six o'clock date.

After placing our order at Mimi's, Margaret wanted to know all about my experience with Recruiting and, like Donnie, she listened intently while I replayed each event. She seemed to know when to comment and when to just nod with approval.

After she had heard me out I asked her about A-1, but I called her Annabel, of course.

"Annabel is doing okay physically, but I think she's dealing with some stress right now."

"Is it her job?"

"No ..." Margaret hesitated. "It's something else. Beth, I've never shared this with you. Annabel is adopted."

"Adopted?" I shook my head, thinking I'd not heard her correctly.

"Yes, I'm sorry I didn't tell you before."

"But, she looks so much like you," I stammered. "The red hair, the curls."

"I know. Everyone says that. In fact, even the social worker used to marvel over our resemblance. Maybe I still enjoy this thought so much that I find it hard to discuss."

"Yes," I said. "I'd probably feel the same way."

Margaret diverted her eyes to another couple passing by our table and then said, "Yes, George and I were so happy with our little girl. I'd never dreamed I'd have to rear her by myself."

"You told me your husband died when Annabel was only four."

"A heart attack. She barely knew him."

Margaret looked away again, and I wondered how painful our conversation was for her. After a pause, she continued. "It's hard for a girl to grow up with only one parent. You know all about that."

"Well," I said. "I did have my mom during the formative years. In fact, in may be even harder for a girl to lose her Dad."

"Maybe. It seemed especially difficult for Annabel during her teen years, and I sometimes wonder if she'll ever marry."

"Oh, I suppose she will," I said. "Maybe she just hasn't found the right man."

"Maybe not. Anyway, right now she seems intent on finding her birth parents."

The server placed our water and salad on the table, and seeing we were deep in conversation, eased away.

"Really? Has she had any success?"

"Well, it was a closed adoption. We didn't even meet the mother. Annabel plans to search some of the internet sites. They tell me it shouldn't be too hard these days."

"And how do you feel about this?"

"Mixed emotions, I guess." Margaret took a bite of her salad, but I wondered if she even tasted it. "I've always had Annabel to myself. Selfishly, I'd like to keep it that way. But more than anything, I want what's best for her."

I pushed chopped veggies around on my plate, trying to think of what to say.

"You know," she continued, "parents always want to protect their children."

"They do?" I stopped, wondering what she would think of my Dad's behavior and then I said, "Yes, good parents do."

Margaret took a breath and said, "Nobody knows, of course. Finding her birth parents could be fulfilling, or she could be opening a Pandora's Box. I just hope she's not in for more disappointment and heartache."

"Me too." I reached for a roll and then added, "This must be so hard for you."

Margaret paused again and then said, "And for her. Say ... I just had a thought. Why don't you come up to Callaway Gardens with us over the Fourth of July? Annabel and I have just cooked it up, and I know she'd love to have you along."

"You think so?" My mind continued to churn over the adoption issue, but I could tell that Margaret wanted to move on. Going to Callaway sounded like fun, but I certainly didn't have money to blow on a trip.

Margaret must have picked up on this because she quickly added, "My brother has a cabin he lets me use. The cost would be minimal."

Our meal arrived, so we pushed the salads aside and admired our entrée, tilapia for me and barbecue for her. The server placed more rolls in front of us and re-filled our water.

"Okay," Margaret asked. "Will you consider it?"

I grinned and said, "It sounds wonderful. Could I let you know later?"

"Of course. Now listen, if Donnie wants you to do something with him, I understand. How is he, by the way?"

"Great, I think. I'm going up to meet his parents tomorrow."

"Sounds pretty serious to me." Margaret passed me a roll and we both dove into our meals. In fact, we even finished by splitting a piece of key lime pie.

D o you remember me telling you about my Uncle Charlie?" Donnie asked as we pulled away from church on Sunday.

"Yes, you mentioned him when we went to the officers' barbecue in Lagoon Park."

"That's right. Well anyway, my folks have invited Uncle Charlie and Aunt Gertrude for lunch, too."

"Do they live in Prattville?"

"Yes. In fact, their house is only a few blocks away. Dad and Uncle Charlie have always been close, and the two of them are enough to provide entertainment for any party."

"Sounds like fun."

Donnie pulled onto I65 and said, "Did you enjoy your dinner with Margaret last night?"

"Yes, of course. She's almost like a mother to me." I thought about our adoption discussion, but didn't think I should share it without asking Margaret first. So I said, "In fact, she's meeting Annabel in Callaway Gardens over the fourth, and has invited me to go with them."

I studied Donnie's face for a reaction.

Donnie nodded and said, "Are you going?"

"I don't know for sure. What do you think?"

"Sounds like a great girls' outing to me. Besides, you may not have time for another trip any time soon."

"I guess you're right. Margaret says we'd stay in her brother's place, but I still hate to spend the money."

"I know, but you should consider it, Beth. Everybody needs a break."

We drove on to the Prattville exit, and before I knew it, Donnie was turning into his parent's place, a ranch style house from the 60s.

But just as we were getting out of the car, his mother came running out of the carport door saying that Aunt Gertrude appeared to be having a heart attack.

Chapter 23

The next hour and a half felt like a dream in slow motion. Donnie knew exactly what to do for his Aunt Gertrude; minutes after our arrival, he assessed the situation. While his Uncle Charlie called the hospital, Donnie had Aunt Gertrude chew two aspirin. Then he and I followed their car to the ER.

Donald and Cindy, (Donnie's mother and Dad) agreed to stay behind and put the food away.

Once in the ER, Donnie and Uncle Charlie explained the situation to the attending physician while I waited in the hall. Later, the physician told us that Donnie's quick action had probably saved his aunt's life.

After Aunt Gertrude was given some blood-clotting drugs, she was transported by ambulance to Montgomery's Baptist Hospital, and surgery followed in less than three hours.

One beautiful thing I observed through all of this was Uncle Charlie's devotion to his wife. During surgery, he leaned toward us and said, "I've always told my beautiful bride that she's a heart-stopping woman. However, this is not what I meant. I may look like old Snuffy Smith but, if God spares her, I'll quit acting like him."

"Listen here," Donnie chided. "You've never treated Aunt Gertrude like that. In fact, you and Dad are my mentors."

Uncle Charlie winked at me and said, "I'm glad he didn't dispute my good looks. At any rate, Donnie knows how to pick a good-looking woman. I'm so glad you were here today. You've really been a comfort."

"Thank you, Mr. Crawford," I blushed, not used to receiving compliments.

He quickly corrected me by saying, "Please just call me Uncle Charlie."

Sometime during all of the evening turmoil, Donald and Cindy Crawford had run the lunch food down to Donnie's apartment. Around nine o'clock that night, we gathered in Donnie's small dining room for a meal.

I guess I will always remember Uncle Charlie's blessing that night, because I've never heard anyone speak with such honesty and dependence. It went something like this:

"Our Father, here we stand with our dirty hands and hearts. In fact, sometimes we must look like little kids in soiled diapers. But, in spite of this, you love us, and provide for our every need including this food. Thanks for saving my Gertrude today, and if it's your will, give us some more years together. Praying in Christ's name, Amen."

As our chairs shuffled under the table, Donnie looked at me and said, "Do you see what I mean about Uncle Charlie?"

I nodded, happy to feel so comfortable and loved in the Crawford clan, especially by Donnie.

Back at the office on Monday a cute smiley face card peeked out from under my mouse. My mind murmured: *Bellinger.* How did he get past security? Then, as I looked up, I saw my sweet friend Margaret, and tried to relax.

"Good morning," she called across the aisle.

Smiling back, I reached for the card and read, "This is your official invitation to Callaway Gardens. I talked to Annabel this weekend and she's delighted with the prospect. Pine Mountain, Georgia awaits the Three Musketeers."

"Thanks Margaret." I waved the card toward her desk and said, "I'll be with you in a minute."

After checking my desk for e-mails or any notes from Overton, I strolled over to Margaret and leaned against her desk.

"So, what do you say?" She cocked her head to one side and waited.

"You are so thoughtful, and I really want to go."

"So is it a deal?" she pressed.

"It looks doubtful."

Her face fell, so I added, "It's finances. You understand."

"Of course. But don't say no yet. You can let us know at the last moment."

"Thanks Margaret. I'll remember that."

Staring at my checkbook Monday night, I saw no reasonable way to make the trip with Margaret and Annabel. I had my meager savings account, but knew I needed to keep a cushion for an emergency.

I was busy paying a few bills when Donnie called from his Aunt Gertrude's hospital room with good news. Her Montgomery cardiologist had declared her stable, and reported minimal heart damage. In fact, he gave her an excellent prognosis.

Right after taking my shower Monday night, the phone rang again. Earline sounded alarmed.

"Beth, that Harvey fellow drove by here again just before dark. Did you see him?"

"No," I said. "Are you sure it was Bellinger?"

"Yes. It was the same car. He sat in front of your apartment for about ten minutes. I guess you weren't in from work yet."

"No," I said. "I had to pick up some stuff from the grocery. Did he do anything strange?"

"Nothing except scratching off like a teenager. Well, anyway, I just wanted to make sure you're all right."

"I'm fine Earline, and I appreciate your call. Keep your eyes open."

"I will. By the way, how do you put up with this creep?"

"Not very well, I'm afraid. Just when I think life is getting better he strikes again."

Chapter 24

After work on Tuesday, I went straight to the gym so I could practice with two new machines that Lamar said were identical to some machines at the Police Academy. In fact, Lamar had promised Donnie that he would help me become proficient in their use. I felt that I needed to honor their efforts.

When I finally arrived home, a note in the mailbox immediately aroused my curiosity. In the note, Gladys Thomas, my apartment manager said she'd like to see me early on Wednesday morning. My first thought concerned my rent, of course. But rent was not due until Wednesday. Could she have some new info regarding Bellinger?

Maybe. But even though she lived in the building, she apparently didn't want me to bother her right then.

As I headed inside my apartment, another piece of mail stuck out from a circular. I hadn't noticed it at first. The return address was The Montgomery Police Department/ Recruiting Division. This time I took a seat at the breakfast table and read,

This is to inform you of your scheduling for the Police Department Polygraph. Please report for your Polygraph at one of these times:
Ten o'clock: Wednesday, July 1 or
Ten o'clock Friday, July 3.

So, I had passed the interview. I read the notice again.

Wednesday, July 1? That was tomorrow, I reasoned. But better to report on Wednesday, my off date, than request another absence from Honda.

Relief and dread bounced around in my head while I continued to study the paper. Last Friday's interview had left significant doubts about my ability, but I'd arrived at this final fifth phase. Now, if I could only pass it.

As I took my shower and dressed for bed, my mind tried to push me into several corners. Maybe I hadn't passed Phase Four at all. Maybe the interviewer had offered trick questions to the Polygraph Administrator. Maybe he'd be ready to ... The cell interrupted my negative harangue.

"Good evening."

"Donnie!"

"Surprised to hear from me?"

"Yes. I mean no."

"How are you, sweetheart?"

"Better now that you've called. Are you at work?"

"Yes, I'm taking a late snack. What's happening?"

"I heard from Recruiting," I said.

"And ..."

"The Polygraph is tomorrow."

"Great. That means you aced the first four phases. What time?"

"Ten o'clock."

"All right! Get a good night's sleep, okay?"

"I'll try, but ..."

"But what?"

"Never mind."

"Go ahead. Tell me."

"Well, I also had a note in my box from Gladys Thomas. She wants to see me about something in the morning."

"So?"

"Oh, I don't know, Donnie. I just wonder if it has something to do with Bellinger."

"Beth ... You can't worry about every little thing. It's a waste of energy."

Donnie sounded impatient. Maybe he was just tired.

"I'm sorry," I said. "You're right. Guess I'm too paranoid. Are you okay tonight?"

"I am now. This afternoon was another story. We had a domestic violence call, and some gun fire."

"What ...? Donnie, are you all right?"

"Well, we had to arrest two guys. One of them was so

doped up he shot at Mike and me, but he only hit the black and white."

"When did this happen?" I felt myself shaking and sat down in the hall, still holding the phone.

"About five o'clock. Listen, a call's coming in. I gotta go."

"Donnie, I ... Listen, take care of yourself."

"I will, darling. You, too. Goodnight."

How could I possibly go to sleep? Not with my mind trying to comprehend Donnie's scary experience. I didn't even ask how, or where, it had happened. Now my doubts about the note and the Polygraph seemed minor.

I could have lost him.

Looking at the clock, I thought about calling Shannon. No, not a good idea, but I needed someone to talk to. What about Margaret? With the phone still in my hand, I stood up and headed for the sofa.

Half way through punching Margaret's phone number I stopped. Why upset her this time of night? She had enough to worry about.

"Lord," I stammered. "What's wrong with me? I've got to learn to depend on You."

I picked up the Bible and turned to Donnie's favorite verse, Psalm 56:3. *"When I am afraid, I will trust in you."* After all, Donnie said he relied on it everyday.

When I finally turned out the lights at ten o'clock, I realized that I still had a lot to learn. A lot to learn about Donnie and police work, and certainly a lot to learn about my own doubts and fears.

Chapter 25

W
ell, good morning, Beth."

Gladys Thomas stretched her hand across the desk, and asked me to take a seat in her small living area set up like an office.

"I hope my message didn't worry you," she said as she reached inside a drawer and lifted a ledger. Her eyelids were a blend of peaches and strawberries today. In fact, a little juice seemed to be running down the side but I tried not to notice.

"Late last night I thought maybe I should have told you more, especially since the news is good."

"Oh? Well, I could use some good news. Tell me."

"Yesterday I received a check on your behalf." She nodded and blinked with satisfaction.

"You did?"

"Yes." Gladys turned the ledger around for me to take a look. "See. It's a check for your entire rent for July. I haven't made the deposit because I wanted to run it by you first."

She had clipped the check to the ledger, and I immediately recognized Dad's handwriting.

"You look surprised." Gladys paused, waiting my response.

"I am. No, flabbergasted is more like it."

"Well, if you don't have a problem with this, should I go ahead and make the deposit?"

"Let me think about it. May I call you later today, or tomorrow, if I can't reach Dad?"

"Of course. You always take care of your business in a timely manner. Just call when it's convenient. By the way, have you had any more trouble from that Bellinger guy?"

"Not exactly." I stood and headed for the door. "Earline said she saw him sitting out in front of the apartment the other day. That's about it."

"Good. I'll keep my eyes open too."

"I'm sure you will. Thanks, Gladys."

"All I have to say is this: You have a generous Dad."

"Yes, this is a generous gift. I just need to decide if I should accept it."

As I drove to the 10 o'clock appointment with Recruiting, I wondered if I should call Dad or wait until after the polygraph. I certainly wanted to express my gratitude, but what if he was negative again, or said something to upset me? I was still thinking about all of this when the cell rang.

"Beth, it's me. Can you talk?"

"Of course, Donnie. Are you okay?"

"I am. Just wanted you to know I'm thinking about you this morning."

"Donnie Crawford, you're the one who needs attention. Last night sounded awful. Did you sleep?"

"Like a baby. In fact, I just got up. Honey, I shouldn't have told you all that stuff."

"Yes, you should, and I want every detail when I see you tonight. I've been so worried."

"I know. It's okay now. Look, try to relax during the polygraph. Don't let him shake you up. You're gonna do just fine. Say, it's nine-forty-five. Are you almost there?"

"Yes, I'm about to turn in."

"Call me when you're done, okay?"

"Okay. I will."

"Love you."

"You too. Bye."

Pulling into the parking lot, I grabbed my purse and headed for the restroom to freshen up. My watch indicated ten until ten so I decided to wait on the phone call to Dad. Besides, one hour couldn't make that much difference.

An anxious face glared back at me from the mirror, but I tried to ignore her and applied a little blush. A lieutenant stood at attention just outside the restroom door. Had he been waiting for me? I tried to smile when he asked, "Are you Miss Davidson?"

"Yes."

"It's time to begin our exam. Follow me please."

I watched Mr. Erect Lieutenant trek past the open door where I'd been interviewed on Friday, and I tried to amuse myself with this name I'd just given him. After all, he hadn't introduced himself.

Then, as if he could read my mind, he turned and said, "I'm Lieutenant Hamel and I'll be administering the polygraph in this room. Have a seat."

Hamel motioned to a chair, then settled his rock-like body behind a desk. There was a typical laptop, but it was connected to numerous wires, tubes and various other contraptions.

"Is this your first polygraph?"

Hamel seemed to be staring at his nose when I nodded and replied, "It is, sir."

"Well, you may be nervous, and that is perfectly normal."

I studied Lieutenant Hamel's fossil eyes and massive forehead, looking for a sign of compassion. He merely turned away, fingering his badge and then began straightening some papers beside all of the paraphernalia. Surely he was somebody's uncle, brother or son, yet he didn't look like he belonged to anyone but the police department.

"Try to be comfortable," Hamil continued. "I will explain everything as we proceed. Nothing is designed to harm you. We only want to determine if you are being honest and truthful. Remember, ninety-nine percent of the truth is still a lie. Do you understand?"

"I do, sir."

"First, I will explain each diagnostic instrument. The sensors record the fluctuations or physiological changes taking place in your central nervous system when I ask questions."

He fingered a blood pressure cuff and I nodded.

"Doctors check your specific blood pressure numbers. We need to see if those numbers go up, down, or stay the same when you answer questions. Therefore, your pressure will be taken continuously throughout the exam. As we go through six or seven charts, you will feel the cuff squeeze your arm. Your skin may turn a bit red, and your arm may tingle but nothing dangerous is involved."

The tone of Hamel's voice sounded like someone explaining an electric chair, but I nodded and waited for him to continue.

"Now, you may not be familiar with pheumographs." He looked at me like I was a first grader. "Pheumographs (he fingered two rubber tubes) are placed around your chest and abdomen. When your chest or abdominal muscles expand, they employ transducers to convert the energy of the displaced air into electronic signals. In other words, they calculate your respiratory rate."

I pondered the tubes, thinking they looked like the cords on my Dad's land line phone.

"Now then," he continued. "The third set of sensors will be placed on two of your fingers. This measures your electro-dermal activity, or changes in your sweat glands."

I examined my morning application of fingernail polish. Lieutenant Hamel must have noticed because he said, "Your polish will not interfere with the test. And, finally, this last sensor goes on your thumb. It will gauge relative blood flow changes."

I felt a slight dizziness. Had the blood already gone somewhere? But I nodded again, eager to get this whole thing behind me.

"Now please go to the polygraph chair, and notice the special cushion. This is a motion-sensor cushion, so while you are taking the examination you must remain perfectly still."

Shifting to the chair I thought, *He doesn't know me. I'm never perfectly still.*

"Do not move your hands, feet, arms, legs or any other part of your body."

"But what if I need to sneeze or have an itch?"

Lieutenant Hamel's eyes flashed like yellow caution lights. Then he said, "Miss Davidson, officers don't itch or sneeze. Surely you can be still the six or seven minutes while the chart is recording. Applicants are expected to cooperate." He leaned across his desk and continued to hold me with his blinking eyes. "Do you think you can cooperate?"

"Yes, I think so," I said, and then I wondered if his comments were all part of the test.

There is no need to go through the long process of the polygraph. Suffice it to say, he finally hooked me up to all the monitors. Then he explained how I should respond to inquires regarding lying, or concealing information about serious crimes, illegal drugs, theft and so forth.

Sometimes he repeated questions, or even instructed me to lie some of the time. I know it sounds contradictory, but I suppose there's a point to it all. Frankly, the hardest part was being still for the six or seven minutes during each phase.

Finally, when he felt ready to dismiss me, Lieutenant Hamel rose from his desk like a gorilla rising on two feet after a good meal. He did shake my hand, however, and I remembered to thank him for his time.

My eyes had to adjust to the bright sunlight when I stepped back out on the asphalt. It felt like leaving the theatre after an early afternoon matinee. Then, suddenly, I felt sleepy and hungry at the same, so I decided to head for Taco Bell rather than stir up something at home.

Seated with two soft tacos, I reached for the cell to call Donnie. As expected, he insisted I tell him everything and he gave a hearty laugh when I described Hamel, the gorilla.

"Well, my darling," Donnie offered, "It's over. Can you celebrate tonight?"

"I can if you're up for it?"

"Of course, I am. I need to see you, Beth."

He emphasized the term *need* so I wondered what that might mean.

"Donnie, are you okay?"

"Yes, I'm fine."

"What about Aunt Gertrude? How is she?"

"Still improving. In fact, Uncle Charlie is back in high gear."

"That's good. Look, there's something else I want to mention when you have time."

"Why not right now?"

"Okay. Well, I had a surprise this morning."

"You did? What?"

"It's about my Dad."

"Is he all right?"

"Oh yes. I think so. This morning I went by to see Gladys Thomas, and she informed me that Dad has paid my rent for this month."

"Really?"

"Really. Not long ago he mentioned helping out with finances, but I guess he knew I wouldn't ask. Do you think I should accept it?"

There was silence for a moment, then Donnie said, "Yes, I think you should. I know you and your father have had some ups and downs, but he might be offended if you don't accept."

"Thanks. I needed a man's take on it."

"You're welcome. So, since my time is limited with this work schedule, can you just meet me at Ming's tonight?"

"I'd love to. See you then, sweetheart."

"May I hear that word again?"

"Sweetheart?"

"Ah," Donnie sighed. "Hold that thought until tonight."

"I will."

"Love you, babe."

"You, too."

Still on a high from hearing Donnie's voice and from the nourishment of one taco, I punched in Dad's office number. He must have been sitting at his desk, because he answered on the first ring.

"Hi Dad. It's Beth."

When he responded with his "Good morning, Elisabeth," I wondered why I always said, "Hi Dad. It's Beth." After all, I was his only chick, and he could certainly recognize my voice.

"Dad," I started again. "I don't know how to thank you for your great gift."

"Oh? You know about it already?"

"Yes. Ms. Thomas showed it to me this morning."

"Right. Well, I feared you might not accept it from me, and I wanted to help."

"This is a *lot* of help. Certainly more than I could have

expected, and it came at a perfect time."

"Glad to do it." He cleared his throat. "Say, how are things going with the Police Academy?"

To my surprise, his voice sounded more upbeat, almost encouraging.

"It's moving along. I had the polygraph this morning."

"You did? I bet that was grueling."

"Yes, but I'm glad it's over." A thought suddenly jumped in my head, so I pounced on it. "Say, Dad, I've been thinking about something and need your advice."

"You do?"

"Yes. An older friend at work has invited me to go to Callaway Gardens for the fourth. Her brother owns a cabin there, so the trip wouldn't be costly. Do you think I'd be foolish to go?"

Silence. Did he hear my question?

"Dad," I said. "Are you there?"

"Yes, I'm here, Beth."

Had he actually called me Beth?

"No." Again I could almost hear him thinking. "No," he started again. "I don't think the trip is foolish. You probably need a little vacation."

"Do you mean it?"

"Of course. Well, I have a client waiting to see me. Guess I'd better go."

"I understand, and thanks again for everything."

"You're welcome. I'll talk to you later."

I closed the cell phone and reached for my second taco. It was cold, but it tasted delicious.

Chapter 26

After calling Gladys and telling her to deposit the check, I changed into shorts and went for a walk around the complex. I needed to jog of course, but it was much too hot. Then, following a shower and a quick devotion, I picked up the cell to call Margaret at work.

"How's everything at Honda today?" I asked. "Are you able to run the place without me?"

"Barely," she laughed. "What about you? How was the polygraph?"

"Scary, but I survived. Look, is the invitation still open?"

"Of course. Are you coming with us?"

"I'd love to. Decided I need a break."

"That a girl. Say, I've been thinking. You and I will drive up Friday night after work. How would you like to invite Donnie for the day on Saturday?"

"Oh, Margaret, you're sweet to ask, but I don't know."

"Come on. He probably needs a change too. It's not that far. If he gets an early start, we could have the whole day together. Believe me, there's a lot to do at Callaway."

"Well, it sounds wonderful." I scratched the itchy spot on my nose, the spot I'd felt ever since the polygraph. "I guess I could check with him tonight. Oh, what about A– … Annabel? Have you mentioned this to her?

"No, Annabel won't care. It's not like he's spending the whole weekend."

"Your thoughtfulness is showing again, Margaret. Tell you what. Donnie's working tonight, but we are planning a quick supper. Why don't I give you a call after that, say around eight?"

"Perfect. Well, I see a customer coming this way. Talk to you later."

I arrived at Ming's a little early so I could put the order in to save time. Donnie had told me that he wanted sweet and sour chicken, and I selected the chicken fried rice. The host gave me a nice booth by the window, so I watched for Donnie's black and white and thought about how little he had shared about the domestic violence incident. Would he drive up in his usual police car, or had the damage been too extensive?

Less than five minutes after I placed our order, the server brought some chips and red dip. Since I managed to get my fingers sticky on the first bite, I headed to the ladies room to wash up. When I got back, Donnie was already seated, but jumped up when he spotted me.

As I walked past, our server offered me that polite smile and nod so characteristic of Orientals.

"You don't look exhausted from your exam this morning," Donnie offered while giving me a quick peck on the cheek.

"Well you're the one who should be exhausted."

"Why?"

"The domestic violence case, naturally." I slid in the booth and Donnie took a seat across from me and grabbed a chip. "I want you to tell me everything."

He smiled. "Are you sure?"

"Yes. Everything."

"Well, Mike and I were cruising our usual area when we got a call about a disturbance on Clay Street. Say, we're supposed to be celebrating the completion of your exams."

"We are," I said. "Keep going."

I gave Donnie my most determined look, so he wiped his mouth and continued.

"Okay. Dispatch said a resident on Clay Street reported a lot of noise and possible gun fire next door. Since this was the second summons to this same address, we knew it could mean trouble."

"Second in one day?" I reached for a chip, but handled the messy dip more carefully.

"No, the first call came about a week ago. Anyway, by the time we arrived everything appeared to be quiet, at least from the street. That's not too unusual when the occupants spot a police car outside. So we documented our arrival time. Then, I walked around to the side of the house and Mike headed for the front door. Mike said that a frail twenty-something year old woman slowly cracked the door about six inches and called, 'What do you want?'"

I leaned in so Donnie wouldn't have to talk so loudly.

"Well, we could both hear conversation inside now. Guess they were planning their strategy. So, when Mike told her we had received a disturbance call, someone must have pushed her aside, because a sumo-wrestler-sized guy opened the door wider and stood with one hand on his hip. I made a quick call for back-up just as the guy reached into his pocket and pulled out a small snub-nose revolver. Then I drew my Glock and said, 'Drop the weapon. Hands in the air'"

"Did he?" I gasped.

"No. I might as well have been a fly, because he aimed and then shot at Mike who had jumped, or stumbled, behind a tall holly bush. I fired then, hitting the guy's arm. His weapon fell to the pavement. Then after I yelled, 'Shots fired. Officer down,' into my shoulder mike, Mike subdued him with his taser." Donnie held the salt cellar in midair to demonstrate. "The guy was stunned," Donnie continued, "but he still stooped to retrieve his revolver. Mike kicked it aside and I held my Glock on the wrestler. By this time, back-up units began to arrive and we were able to hand-cuff the guy and evaluate the woman's injuries."

Even in the dim light of Ming's, I think Donnie must have seen color drain from my face, because he shook his head and said, "I should have waited and told you this later."

"No," I said. "If I'm gonna be a cop, I need to know. What happened next?"

"Not much. We checked the house for any children or other occupants, and then completed our arrest. Mike and I didn't see the car damage until we hit the street. It's not bad. Repairs should be finished by tomorrow. You probably noticed I'm in a different car tonight."

"No," I confessed. "Guess I was too glad to see you."

Donnie grinned, and then put his finger to his lips when the server appeared with our order. After he walked away, he said, "Now, that's enough of this for tonight. Let's enjoy our meal."

I wanted to ask more questions. Maybe I needed to assuage my fears, but since Donnie's face was firm, I picked up my fork to begin.

"Still not good with chop sticks, aye?"

I shook my head and diverted my eyes to the outside window. An older couple had just stepped up to the sidewalk, holding hands. Suddenly, I wanted to grow old with Donnie, but I just said, "Let's eat."

After a few bites of chicken fried rice and several sips of tea, I decided that a change of subject might be in order.

"How long since you've had a break, Donnie?"

"I don't know. Awhile, I guess. Why?"

"Could you give up a whole day for me on Saturday?"

"Well I guess so. Wait. I thought you were going to Callaway Gardens."

"I am. Margaret has invited you to spend Saturday with us."

"What ... Come now, let's reason together. With all of you women, that might be scarier than the D.V. episode."

"Donnie!"

"Okay, let me check my date book."

"Little black book?" I quizzed.

"Something like that." Donnie reached in his pocket and pulled out a thin notepad. He pretended to study over a page and then said, "Why, that redhead is not until Sunday. I suppose I could reserve Saturday for Beth Davidson."

Once again, I smiled at the handsome police officer sitting across from me. But as we stood to leave Ming's, another face with emerald green eyes planted itself in my mind; a face topped with curly red hair. A face belonging to Annabel.

Chapter 27

After transferring my stuff to Margaret's Ford Expedition on Friday afternoon all we had to do was swing by her townhouse for a cooler and a few staples for the cabin pantry. The drive to Callaway takes about an hour and a half but, when we neared the I 85 exit for Pine Mountain, Margaret called my attention to a magnificent sunset forming behind us.

I had no sooner turned to see it when the cell rang.

"I miss you, Beth." The phrase seemed to tumble out of Donnie's mouth.

"You too." I smiled into the phone.

"Where are you?"

"About twenty minutes from our destination I think."

"What's the sunset like?"

"It's gorgeous."

"Yeah. Wish I was already there. Hold tomorrow night for me, okay?"

"You've got it."

"Look,. I plan to be there around eight-thirty or nine in the morning. Will you be up by then?"

"For you, yes." My eyes flipped to Margaret as she took the exit, and a ripple of contentment washed over me when I read the look of approval written on her face. After allowing the scenery to work on us for a while, she broke the silence.

"Do you want to stop for a light supper at the inn? It's on me."

"Margaret, I ...."

"Come on. You need to try their muscadine ice cream."

"Their what?"

"That's right. It's probably the only place in the world that serves it."

Accustomed to her generosity, I sighed and simply said, "How could I resist? But, what about Annabel?"

"She likes to take an afternoon hike and then get a shower. I'll call from the restaurant and check, though."

By the time we pulled into the parking lot at the inn, a magenta sky seemed to explode in all directions, and I sent up a plea for a similar one for Saturday. Reds, purples and pinks hovered and hugged the massive wood and stone inn, and a blanket of warmth beckoned us into the lobby.

Margaret stopped to phone her daughter, while I headed down the hall for the restroom. When I returned, a hostess escorted me to a table where Margaret was already seated. Annabel, it seems, would just meet us at the cabin.

I can't explain it, but somehow I felt relieved all through the meal and down to the dessert of muscadine ice cream. Margaret had definitely become a mother figure, and I relished time alone with her more than I could explain.

A-1 was playing solitaire when we arrived at the chalet-style cabin, but she stood up to greet us, and even helped unload the Expedition. When we finally settled in and I had unpacked my gear in a cozy bedroom loft, the three of us played a couple of games of Hearts.

Before ten o'clock, Annabel stood, yawned, and then said something about needing her beauty sleep. Quite frankly, I felt tired too, and wanted to be fresh for Donnie in the morning.

Donnie arrived at eight-thirty sharp, and we all sat down to breakfast on the cabin porch. Margaret had made some delicious cinnamon rolls to go with my contribution of bacon and eggs, and Annabel's offering of cheese grits.

I made a mental note to pick up some of the special mill grits from the Pine Mountain store, since Donnie complimented A-1's tasty casserole.

I also remembered a long ago remark from my mother: *The way to a man's heart is through his stomach.*

Nestled in a mature forest of pines, oaks and hickories, the Camp Callaway chalet provided an excellent retreat for enjoying nature. In fact, at one point, Donnie commented on a chorus of squawking birds.

"What are they?" I asked.

"Don't you know a blue jay?" Annabel answered almost too quickly.

"Oh," I said.

Donnie answered with, "Yes, they're quite a chorus. We could call them *Jays in Blue*."

Annabel's approving laugh followed, so I just nodded and asked if anyone needed more coffee or juice.

"Let me get it," Donnie insisted. "I haven't done anything to help."

"What about those steaks you brought for tonight?" A-1 demurred.

"Well ..." Donnie jumped up to get the coffee. "I hope I can grill them to your liking."

Annabel kept a smirk on her face as she admired Donnie, so I decided to follow him to the kitchen, just in case he decided to offer refills on both beverages.

"It's about time I got you alone for a moment," Donnie said. He kissed me on the cheek. "This is one fine place, isn't it?"

"Yes," I said. "In fact, we had a rain shower at bedtime and it sounded great on the tin roof."

"I bet. Say, you take the orange juice. I have the coffee."

"Okay. Donnie ..." I stammered.

"What?"

"Oh, never mind."

"Is everything all right?"

"Yes, of course. Let's go."

Would you like more coffee?" Donnie asked Annabel. "Yes, thank you." She held her mug up and gave him a little wink. "Mom and I were just discussing what we should do first. Are you two up for a hike?"

Donnie looked at me and I said, "That sounds fine. Where would you like to go?"

"Several trails are available. One of our favorites is Laurel Springs."

"Beth and Donnie might want to go on their own," Margaret offered.

I could have hugged her on the spot, but bit my lip instead.

Donnie eyed me again, but then replied, "Whatever you all want to do is fine with me."

"Well, let's all do Laurel Springs." A-1's eyes flitted to their faces and then stabbed me. Her look was framed with red cheeks to match her hair, yet it was anything but winsome. I watched her mouth twitch and her eyes narrow as if in deliberation. "Then," she continued, "if the two lovebirds want to be alone they can take another trail later. Is that okay with you, Beth?"

What could I say but, of course, so I nodded and said, "Of course."

Nobody told me that the Laurel Springs Trail is five miles long, but fortunately we moved along at a rather fast clip. Margaret and Annabel walked ahead of us most of the time, and the younger redhead seemed to delight in giving us a history of the Appalachians.

She also pointed out a mountain laurel thicket and pieces of Hollis Quartzite in the path. Donnie seemed especially impressed with the quartzite, so Annabel told him that much of the original architecture in Callaway showcased it.

"If we have time, we can go see the Ida Cason Memorial Chapel. The chapel is built with the quartzite, and is absolutely beautiful."

"It sounds nice," Donnie said. He took my hand.

I felt relieved, but wondered why my palm was sweaty. We walked on without much conversation until A-1 slipped on a rock and stumbled in our direction. Donnie instinctively reached out to brace her fall, and as she lingered a bit on his shoulder, I thought to myself: that's the oldest trick in the book. Maybe this girl does need to find a man.

Thankfully, we were coming to the end of the trail at this point, so Donnie took my hand again and made what I thought was a bold pronouncement.

"Last night I got on the computer and enjoyed reading about the Day Butterfly Center. If you two will excuse us, I think Beth and I will go exploring over there."

"Good idea," Margaret said. "Annabel and I have seen it a couple of times. You two kids have fun. Beth, you have my cell and the cabin number. Call us later if you like. If not, we will just see you back at the cabin."

I shot a look at A-1. She was watching Donnie with a cool, steady stare; something calculating and probing in that unblinking look. Was she dreaming, or planning something? I couldn't be sure.

Chapter 28

Did you know the Cecil B. Day Butterfly Center is the largest glass-enclosed tropical conservatory in North America?"

We were standing in the foyer of the center when Donnie looked up from the brochure in his hand and said, "Now, it may take awhile to see the film and do the tour. What do you think?"

"Let's do both if there's time."

"Sure. Do you want to browse the gift shop first?"

"No, let's tour the conservatory."

"Sounds like a plan."

From the moment we stepped inside, Donnie and I were surrounded by flying colors.

"How many species do you think are here?" I asked.

"I have no idea." As he spoke, a rose and black creature flew past his waist and then another landed on his arm. I held a finger out to the butterfly, and in a moment, a tiny feeler foot moved to me.

"They taste with their feet," Donnie said.

"How do you know that?"

"Read it online. Now watch that one over there on the flower."

"The hibiscus?" I said.

"Yeah. See how he takes the nectar? He drinks with that straw-like tube. It's called a proboscis."

"Oh," I told him. "You're sounding like Annabel now."

"Sorry," Donnie laughed. "But ... I do think it's interesting."

"Me, too."

We wandered on past a fountain filled with lily pads

and exotic water lilies, while tiny winged creatures of every imaginable hue flew overhead. It made me feel like we were on the screen of an old fashioned Disney film; maybe *Snow White.*

"Look up higher," he said.

"What?" I lifted my chin. "Oh, talk about color."

A parrot perched on a willow limb just over our heads, then his mate called from a higher branch. After having a one-sided conversation with the parrot, my eyes were drawn back to the water below. Striped fish swirled in patterns just inches from our feet, and more butterflies landed on the low-lying branches of lush plants, all perfectly suited for the surroundings.

"Ready to go?" he asked.

"No, but it's time. People are waiting behind us. Besides, there is still more to see."

Donnie opened the exit door saying, "May I make the call?"

"You bet. What next, sir?"

"Well, I saw a sign back up near the entrance."

"A sign for what?"

"Hang on. You'll see."

"Come on," I chided.

"All right, sweetheart. If it's all right with you, let's skip the film this time. I want to get us a snack lunch and then ..."

"Then what?"

"I'd like to take you to the chapel."

We stopped for take-out pizza at the Vineyard Green, and then followed the signs to Ida Cason Callaway Memorial Chapel. Pulling into the visitor parking lot, we were surprised to hear deep-throated music reverberating through the trees.

"What's that?" Donnie looked at me.

"I don't know. Is there an organ in the chapel?"

"Maybe. Guess I should have picked up cordon bleu instead of pizza."

"Get out of here," I popped back. "We finished breakfast five hours ago, and my stomach is doing the pizza dance."

"Mine too," he grinned.

Donnie came around to open my door and I handed him the drinks. "I'll carry the pizza," I said. "Did you bring napkins?"

"Yes, I got a double supply for my little girl."

Following the music and a winding trail, we soon spotted the stone chapel nestled beside a pristine lake. A family of three walked just ahead of us, and we could hear someone coming up from behind, yet still at a distance.

"That's Mozart, isn't it?" I asked.

"I think so. Do you recognize the song?"

"Not really, but it's beautiful."

The family stopped at the chapel entrance, and then found a pew just inside to the left. Donnie looked at me and said, "Why don't we sit here by the lake first?"

"Good idea."

As we found a seat on a large rock, the person behind us suddenly turned back toward the parking lot. Maybe the pizza smell made him hungry.

"Do you think we're far enough away not to disturb anyone," I whispered.

"Yes. Let me help you get the tops off the tea."

"What could be better than a concert in the forest, and freshly baked pizza?" I asked, when he handed me a drink and the larger slice.

"Well, I can think of something better."

"You can? What?"

"Oh, let's wait and see. Here, take this napkin."

Donnie spread the paper napkin in my lap, and then I watched his eyes graze the landscape around us.

"I'm so glad Margaret included me, Beth."

"Me too. It wouldn't be the same without you."

"You don't think so?"

"I know so. Besides, you bought me some pizza." I took another bite and followed it with a sip of tea. Then, turning toward the chapel, I saw the young family get up to leave. "People seem restless sometimes, don't you think?"

"Definitely," Donnie agreed. "I think we're over-exposed to entertainment. Not many folks can just sit quietly and enjoy the world around them anymore."

"You're right."

"Listen." He put his pizza slice down for a moment.

"What?"

"Do you hear the tapping?"

"Tapping?"

"Yes. Oh, there he is?" Pointing up to a sycamore tree, he said, "It's a pileated woodpecker."

I squinted and turned, following the sound to the tree. "Oh, yes. I see him."

"The red head is a give-away. Maybe he's trying to keep time with the music."

We laughed, and then Donnie's eyes turned serious. After a moment he said, "When you are finished I need to tell you something."

"Okay."

I wiped my mouth again and reached for the tea while he waited. Donnie seemed to be searching through some hidden compartment in his mind. Then, a wooden receptacle close by the bench caught his eye, and he quietly gathered our trash.

I watched him walk away and wondered if he needed to discuss a problem. Maybe he wanted to tell me more about the recent domestic violence case. When he turned to come back to me, his face looked flushed, so I stood and walked toward him.

"Honey," I said. "Is anything wrong?"

"No, but would you come with me?"

Donnie took my hand and then turned to face the other side of the lake. "Let's take this trail."

"Okay, but we'll be farther away from the music."

"We can still hear it over there." Now he squeezed my hand and began to lead us around the edge of the water to the other side.

"Watch your step," he said as the trail dipped. I thought about A-1's obvious slip, and almost laughed.

"Watcha thinking?" he asked.

"Don't you know?"

"Annabel?"

"Yes. Shame on me. At any rate, Annabel knows a good looking guy when she sees one."

As I said this, he stopped and touched my chin, turning it to face him. Now I can't remember if the organ was still playing, if any people were around, or even if any woodpeckers or other birds were making sounds.

All I saw was Donnie's face, and all I heard were the words, "There's an old song that says, 'I only have eyes for you.' It's true for me, Beth. I love only you."

"You do? Well, I ..."

I couldn't talk, because Donnie's lips got in the way. A tender kiss followed, and then a hesitation to see if anyone was around. I didn't see the bench, but he did. Taking me by the arm, he led me to it and motioned for us to sit down.

"Beth, I'm nervous."

"Why?" I said. "You've kissed me before, and no one is watching."

"God is, so I want to do this right."

"Do what?"

"Tell you something important."

"What?" I asked.

"Let me try to explain it with a little story. When I was about five years old we lived next door to a man I admired a great deal. In fact, I guess he was the first police officer I'd ever met."

I smiled, and nodded for Donnie to continue.

"Boyce probably served on the first shift in those days, because he came home in the late afternoon. I'm sure he was tired, but if he found me outside, he always took time to talk or inquire about my day. Sometimes he'd invite me to sit on the porch with him and he'd tell me about catching a bad guy. Well, as you can imagine, his behavior left a lasting impression on me."

"I can see that," I said. "Is this why you decided to become a policeman?"

"Yes, but there's more." Donnie looked at me as if he were about to share a long-kept secret.

"My bedroom faced the Boyce's house, so sometimes after supper I'd go to my room and peer through my window into their kitchen."

"And what did you see?" I leaned in closer to Donnie and ran my fingers down his cheek.

"It's a sight still locked in my memory. I'd watch Boyce walk up behind his wife while she stood at the sink. He'd put his arms around her waist, and then into a sink full of dirty dishes."

"Oh my, I like this guy."

"I don't suppose he ever saw me watching, or on some occasions, listening while he snuggled close to her. I'll always remember that sight. Beth, we've only dated for about three months, but we've been friends for almost two years so..."

I waited, still not knowing for sure what he wanted to say. However, as I watched the mid-afternoon sunshine reflect specks of gold in his eyes, I began to suspect before the words were formed.

"Beth, if you are willing, I want to repeat that kitchen scene with you ... and ...

Donnie slid from the bench and turned his knees in toward me. This can't be happening, I thought. It's got to be a dream. However, when Donnie reached for my hand, our eyes locked and he continued.

"I had a little speech all worked out, but my thoughts are running together." He rubbed the top of my hand and said, "Sweetheart, you and I have chosen a profession that plays a small role in keeping our society in check. Our job is also to set an example in our community."

He's not going to propose after all, I chided myself. This is a pep talk.

"Well," he continued, "I believe God wants the Christian home to be a little picture of the perfect union between Christ and His bride, the church. Beth ..." Donnie paused. "Like Christ, I want to serve you the rest of my life. I'm not an ideal police officer, and won't be a flawless husband, but I'd like for us to wash dishes together. Have a family. Submit to each other and just let God direct everything we do."

My mind jumped back to the morning a couple of months ago when Donnie fixed our breakfast. Sweet as that was, it couldn't compare to what he was saying now. As I began to nod my head, I felt something like a dam breaking behind my eyelids but it didn't matter.

"Beth, will you marry me?"

"But," I stammered. "What about the Police Academy?" I wiped a tear from my eye.

"I know," he said. "We can wait until you graduate in about five or six months. If for some reason you decide you don't want to finish, that's all right, too. Besides, you do want a family someday, don't you?"

"Yes, of course."

"Well," he said. "Did I hear a yes, or not?"

Taking both of Donnie's hands, I began to stand and he rose beside me. Then, turning with my back to him, I placed his arms around my waist and said, "Hmmm. I think your hands can reach into the sink just fine. Yes, lieutenant. I'd love to be Mrs. Donnie Crawford."

When I said this Donnie nuzzled the back of my neck. Then he turned me around in another embrace and whispered, "The best day of my life is fast approaching, yet I suppose this one is the next best. Now, hold on for just a minute."

Donnie reached in his pocket and pulled out what looked like a tiny white coin purse. My mouth went dry when he unsnapped it, and slid out a gold ring with a small, but beautiful diamond in the center. Placing it on my finger he said, "This ring is my promise to love you for the rest of our lives."

I gazed at the ring, and then into Donnie's face and replied. "I never imagined such happiness but ..."

Before I could finish, he said, "I know. Life is full of surprises."

Little did we know.

Chapter 29

Donnie heard the noise first, and instinctively turned to his right.

"What is it?" I said.

"Be quiet."

Crossing my arms, I turned back to the bench and sat down. After a moment, we heard another rustle, and then a sound like someone running in the brush. I moved in the direction of the sound, but saw nothing.

Donnie had his hand on his right pocket now, and I wondered if he might be reaching for his Glock or another weapon.

We waited. Then, after maybe a minute with no more sound he said, "Maybe I'm paranoid, but I think someone was watching us."

"Me too. Do you want to head back to the truck?"

"Yeah. We'll keep our eyes open. It could just be some nosey teenager."

"Probably," I said. "Did you see anything?"

"Not really, but I didn't like the sound of it."

We quickly turned toward a trail that would take us back to the truck, and just before we reached the second row of cars, I saw the profile of a man that looked strangely familiar.

"Donnie," I said. "Is that him?"

"Who?"

"Bellinger."

I had no sooner spoken the dreaded name, when the guy jumped inside a black Lexus and spun out of the parking lot.

"I can't believe this, Donnie." I said this as I ran behind

my fiancé, hoping we weren't in for a chase.

"Hurry," he called. "I want to see that tag number."

We ran to the truck, not taking time to buckle up. But by the time we reached the parking lot exit, the Lexus had already maneuvered the next major turn and was on its way into the maze of holiday traffic.

Donnie hit the base of the steering wheel with the inside of his right hand, and I could see the frustration seizing his face.

"This guy just won't leave you alone." We sat at the intersection of the parking lot and a major turn inside the gardens. "Listen," he continued, "how long has it been since you contacted Wilson?"

"A couple of weeks," I said. "Remember? The last time Wilson and I talked he suggested I write Bellinger that firm letter stating my lack of interest. I understand this rationale, but I'm afraid of setting him off even more."

"More than what you're experiencing now?" Donnie chided.

I looked down at my trembling hands, and noticed how the engagement ring had turned almost completely around on my finger. Donnie saw me looking at it and said, "I'm sorry, honey, but this man won't give up. I don't want him ruining your life. We've got to do something."

"Okay," I said. "You're right. What do you want to do now? Go back to the cabin?"

"I don't know. Why don't you call Margaret and see what they're doing?"

A-1 answered the land line, and said that something had come up and she was packing to head back to Atlanta. I hoped she didn't hear the smile in my voice.

"Mom is resting a bit, but says she's looking forward to that steak tonight."

"Can you stay until after dinner?" I asked this as politely as possible.

"No I can't. Maybe Donnie will eat a second one. He looks like he can handle it."

I smiled to myself, knowing that Annabel was probably right.

"Okay," I said. "Have a safe trip home. Tell Margaret

we'll be back before long. If I can talk Donnie into it, we may swing by the gift shop to browse, and to buy some of those delicious grits you fixed for us."

"Good. Oh, by the way, some guy called saying he wanted to see you, Beth. He sounded like an old friend, so I told him you were headed for the Butterfly Center, and that I had also suggested you visit the chapel."

As I shut the cell phone, I felt as if my whole body was suddenly being filled with butterflies, and if I took a deep breath they would all die.

Chapter 30

Someone at Honda must have heard you and Margaret talking about your trip to Callaway." Donnie placed the steaks on the grill, and put the platter down to face me.

"Yeah, but how did Bellinger find out?"

"Who knows? Some employee tipped him off, I guess. At any rate, you've got to be more careful."

"I know, but ..." I stopped to look back toward Margaret's kitchen. She was still standing by the window making our salad. "Donnie," I started again. "I'm so sorry about getting you into this mess."

"Well, at least I'm a cop, right? Look on the bright side." He wiped his hands on a paper towel and winked at me.

Margaret raved over Donnie's filets, and when we showed her my ring she said, "How in the world did you keep your secret for over an hour? I guess this just shows I'm not as observant as a police officer. Congratulations! Have you set a date?"

Donnie said, "As soon as she'll have me, but we do plan to wait until after graduation."

"I'm thrilled for you both," Margaret exclaimed, still holding my hand. "We'll have to plan a shower for you, Beth. Say, do you think you could spare a Saturday in the early fall?"

"That sounds great to me," I said as I loved her with my eyes, and then helped her clear the table.

"I tell you what," Margaret offered as Donnie and I began to do the dishes. "Since Donnie has to get back tonight, why don't you two go watch the fireworks together? You now have something to celebrate besides the Fourth of July."

I've always been like a little kid when it comes to fireworks, and this night was no different, only better. We arrived at the lake just as the sun was setting, and Donnie found us a seat close to the action.

He even bought two double ice cream cones, and didn't even mention trying to exercise it off. Later, during the extravagant light and sound display, I thought about Shannon, and decided to give her a call.

"Guess what!" I shouted into the phone.

"Beth, you sound like you're having a party. What's going on?"

"I'm engaged!"

"You are? Wow, that's wonderful. Congratulations. Where are you? It's so noisy I can barely hear you."

"We're celebrating at Callaway Gardens, and that noise is the fireworks display."

"All for you? No, just kidding. So ... Don is giving up his independence on Independence Day. Now that is something."

"Yes, it is."

"Way to go," Shannon gushed. "But listen, I can hardly hear a thing. Maybe we can get together to celebrate one day next week."

"Yeah, that sounds great. Besides, I want us to talk about plans for you and Ryan. Don and I are thinking about a couples party, okay?"

"Super. We need to do something special for you too. Okay, I'll see you soon."

It was hard telling Donnie goodbye at the cabin doorstep that night, but when I passed Margaret's room, she was still up, and waiting to hear all of the details of Donnie's proposal. She also tried to ease my fears about the Bellinger appearance, and urged me to plan another appointment with Lieutenant Wilson.

Before heading back to Montgomery on Sunday morning, Margaret mentioned the possibility of going to a special Callaway Chapel service. However, the moment she said it, she stopped, looked me in the eye and recanted. "No, maybe it would be best for you to attend your Sunday evening service."

As Margaret pulled out of the drive, I nodded and looked down at my shiny new engagement ring. My next thought was: *Well, I've shared the news with my substitute Mom. When should I tell Dad?*

Chapter 31

It hit me during the Sunday night service. Here I sat beside the finest man I had ever known, and yet my fiancé and I had not included my Dad in this marriage equation.

Donnie seemed to always be able to read my moods and thoughts so, after the benediction, he asked me what was wrong and I told him. We were seated in the car before he spoke again.

"You're right. What do you think we should do?"

"I'm not sure, honey."

"Do you have your cell phone?"

I nodded and Donnie continued.

"We could drive up and see him tonight."

"It's six o'clock already," I said. "We'd be so late getting home."

"If it will give you peace of mind it's worth it. Besides, I should have considered this before. Forgive me, Beth."

"There's nothing to forgive." I ran my fingers down the pleat on my pants leg and said, "I suppose I've lived my early adulthood almost as if he didn't exist, but he is my father."

"If he's home, let's go. Do you want me to talk to him?"

"No. Since you two haven't even met I should do it. Are you sure you're up for this tonight?"

"I am. If we put it off he may be more hurt."

Donnie cranked the truck and pulled out of our church parking lot as I punched in the numbers. Dad answered on the second ring, and my voice quivered as I spoke.

"Good evening, Dad," I began. "How are you?"

"Doing well. Are you all right?"

"Yes, I'm feeling great. It's just ... Well, I know this is the spur of the moment, but may I come up?"

"To Birmingham? Tonight?"

"Why, yes. I have something important to tell you."

"It must be very important." He paused and then said, "Well, okay ... but drive safely."

"We will, Dad."

We. Why had I said we? Would he ask who? He didn't. Should I say more? I didn't.

"Fine." Dad's voice seemed hesitant and quizzical when he added, "I guess I'll see you around seven-fifteen or so."

"Right, Dad."

I gave Donnie a nod, and he responded with a quick salute as we pulled out on the interstate. I didn't say much on the way up. I suppose Donnie and I were too deep in thought, wondering what to say, and what kind of reaction we might encounter.

Donnie did mention that he thought Dad's gift of the July rent was something of an olive branch, and I agreed.

As we pulled into Inverness Woods (a perfect name for the hilly neighborhood of moss-covered oaks and hickories), I was attacked by an overwhelming thirst, and by the time we parked in Dad's drive, I could barely speak.

Donnie sensed my dilemma so we prayed before going to the door. Donnie asked for God to give us peace and wisdom.

As we took the walk to the door, I peeked through the glass insets in the garage because Dad had left the garage lights on.

"Wow! That is some car." Donnie exclaimed.

"Yes," I said. "Dad is proud of his Camaro. I got to ride in it when he was down for that visit."

At this point, the front lights came on and Dad opened the door. We both turned to face him and I said, "Dad, this is my friend Donnie Crawford."

Realizing *friend* didn't exactly capture our new relationship, I looked at Donnie, but he seemed content with the introduction and held out his arm to shake hands. Dad took his hand, yet I thought I detected some reluctance.

"Well," Dad said. "Do come in."

Dad was using his formal voice as we followed him

through the foyer and into the den. The room had a strange smell I had never detected before, maybe a cross between peppermint and mothballs. I glanced around.

Everything looked neat, arranged for efficiency, and sterile. As I've said, I'm not a decorator, but a few throw pillows and accent pieces would add some color and warmth.

"Would you have a seat?" Dad offered. "What about something to drink?"

"I'd like a glass of water. How about you, Donnie?"

"Yes," Donnie said. "Water will be fine."

I immediately thought about Donnie's definition of fine, and wondered if he felt frustrated, insecure, neurotic and exhausted. No, I reminded myself as we took a seat on the sofa. We prayed and God would supply. Wouldn't he?

Dad handed me a glass and then turned to Donnie and said, "So, what brings you two out this time of night?"

I took a deep breath and said, "Dad, you know Donnie and I have been dating awhile and ..."

Dad took a seat in his recliner, but I think he was too tense to recline. He said, "About three months. Is that right?"

"Yes, sir," I said as I watched the ice bob up and down in my glass. "Actually, we've been friends for almost two years."

"I see." Dad turned to Donnie and said, "You are a police officer, I believe."

"I am, sir."

"You are also responsible for my daughter's application, are you not?" Now Dad shifted his position in the chair and winced.

"No sir. I did share the opportunities with Beth, but she made her own decision."

Taking up for Donnie I said, "Dad, we've talked about this and I told you I think God is directing me."

Dad's eyes seem to scrutinize me as if he either didn't grasp, or want to believe, my answer.

"Well," he said. "I don't intend to argue with God or with you. On the other hand, it's hard not to be concerned."

"It's normal for you to be concerned," Donnie offered. "You love your daughter and want the very best for her, but I'm here tonight to tell you I love her, too."

A look of disbelief with a touch of anger seemed to cross Dad's face for a moment. Then he wiped his fingers across his mouth as if to camouflage it.

At this point, I jumped in with, "Dad, Donnie proposed to me last night and we've come here to share our joy with you, and to ask for your blessing."

Dad stood and walked over to the fireplace, staring at an imaginary fire left over from some February night. All we could see was his back, and if this back had been carrying a billboard I think it would have stated, *Closed for the Season.*

I looked at Donnie, but couldn't read his expression. Maybe he was trying to reconcile an older man's dream with a younger man's desire. I didn't know.

Finally, Dad turned to me and said, "Beth, you've always liked to hit me with a surprise. However this time, you've gone overboard. Think about it. Your mother and I dated almost three years before we married and ..." Dad rubbed his forehead as if lost for language. Then he started again. "Frankly, I think you and Donnie are being too hasty."

"Yes sir," Donnie took up for me. "I'm sure it seems sudden to you, but Beth and I plan to wait about five or six months." Donnie took a sip of water and placed his glass on the end table. "Beth can still back out if she feels I'm not right for her."

I gave my head an annoyed little shake, and then turned back to Dad. He was silent, so I filled in with, "We plan to wait until after I graduate from the Academy."

Donnie's face softened. I guess my newly discovered confidence boosted his because he said, "If the class starts as expected, she should finish in early December. If so, we could get married over the Christmas holidays."

A Christmas wedding. I liked the sound of it. But, as I studied Dad's face, my enthusiasm fell.

Standing ramrod straight, he rubbed his palms together and replied, "Well, I've expressed my concern, but you both seem determined to go your own way."

Dad began walking toward the foyer, so we followed. After opening the door, he stepped aside. He then put one arm around me and held the other arm out to Donnie for a final handshake. I felt as if I was watching his heart shut down like the electronically controlled garage door housing his Camero.

"Well ..." Dad stopped and gave me a staccato peck on the cheek. "I guess there's nothing left to say. Have a good-night."

Chapter 32

Donnie tried to console me as we headed home but sadness is contagious. Actually, I think we both felt a bit numb.

"Do you want to grab something to eat?" he offered.

"I'm not hungry."

Just as I spoke, the cell rang. I fumbled through my purse, and then realized I'd left it under the passenger seat. When I finally said hello, the ringing had stopped but, within a minute, it began again.

"Beth?"

It was Dad.

"Beth ..." Dad paused as if he might be struggling. "A few minutes ago I accused you of being hasty, yet I'm the one who made a hasty judgment. Look, if you haven't passed Applebee's could you meet me there for a snack?"

Holding my hand over the receiver, I asked Donnie what he thought, and within twenty minutes, we were all seated in an Applebee's booth. Now, my Dad is not an overly demonstrative person but, on that July 5th Sunday night, we did obtain his blessing.

The rest of the week was hectic. On Monday I received a notice to report to Police Headquarters for a staff interview with three police majors, all from a different division. Thankfully, I was able to set this up for the next day.

Then, when the interview was over on Tuesday, I was issued a conditional offer of employment, followed by a handful of additional paper work. With forms complete, the staff sent me to the police physician for a physical.

I was about to decide that there was no way I could see

Lieutenant Wilson, but right after scheduling a psychological exam for Thursday, I took the elevator to Wilson's office and brought him up to date about the latest episodes with Bellinger.

We had a productive chat, and I agreed to send Bellinger the rejection letter.

As it turned out, the Thursday psychological exam was not as grueling as I had expected. Maybe I was getting used to being interrogated. At any rate, after the exam they set up a payroll and clothing requisition for Friday.

When Donnie called Thursday night I was exhausted, but he cheered me when he said, "Honey, you're on your way."

"I thought you said that last time."

"Yeah, I guess you're right. However, when the Academy starts to invest money and time, you can really begin to get excited. Are they sending you to Azars for your uniform?"

"Yes."

"All right. Pick out something sassy."

"Sure," I countered. "I get one color choice, right?"

"You'll look ravishing to me. Oh, sorry, I'm getting a call. Talk to you later and don't forget to save Saturday for me."

"Who else? I only have eyes for you, remember? See ya."

I finally mailed the Bellinger letter on Friday morning, and called Wilson's office to let him know.

I then enjoyed a lunch date with Shannon, and gave her a play by play of the July 4th proposal. When she mentioned giving me a shower, I suggested that she and Margaret co-host an event, and Shannon promised to give her a call. We also picked some tentative dates for a couple's barbecue for her and Ryan.

On Friday, July 17th the final Police Academy letter arrived without flourish or fanfare. No congratulations. No "We are pleased to inform you." I was simply asked to report for Orientation on Monday, July 26th.

When Donnie called that afternoon I shared the letter with him and was surprised by his reaction.

"Beth, expect congratulations from me and from your friends. Don't expect it from the Police Academy at this point. Their job is to toughen you up, to make you into a strong cop. I hate to say it, but this is just the beginning.

Right now we need to count your blessings."

I knew Donnie was right. God was working. After all, even though the Academy appointments had caused me to miss the equivalent of two more days, Honda had kept me through July 15th so there were no serious financial concerns; especially after Dad's generosity with the rent.

To my relief, even though I could still sense some reluctance on his part, Dad was trying to accept my future husband.

"Look," Donnie said, interrupting my thoughts. "We can enjoy our own celebration. I'll see you around six-thirty."

Donnie called it a mystery date, but I hadn't expected a white tablecloth candlelight dinner at his place.

"I picked the flowers up at Publix's," he said. "Are they okay?"

"They're more than okay. I ... I shouldn't have said so much about the Academy letter."

My eyes grazed the room, paying it more attention than I had when his Aunt Gertrude was so sick. Poor Donnie. He and Dad must have used the same decorator.

"Look, we need to celebrate. This is your big night. We can also call it our engagement dinner."

Donnie held out my chair, gave me a kiss on the cheek and disappeared into the kitchen for our salads. My eyes drifted around the room while he was gone. Like me, he obviously had made the most of hand-me-downs, but I decided that between the two of us, we'd have more than enough.

Later while we ate, I suspect Donnie read my mind, because he suggested that I start thinking about our wedding date.

"Your birthday is December 22nd," he said. "I don't guess you want two big celebrations on the same day?"

"Why not? Don't you think a husband is a good birthday gift?"

A sunburst smile erupted on Donnie's face. Then he declared, "Well, you might think so this first year, but will I be your energizing bunny who keeps on giving?"

"Maybe, if you continue to beat your drum." I laughed and wiped my lips with his cloth napkin. "Say, did you borrow these napkins from your mother?"

"I did."

"Donnie, everything is perfect."

"Not quite. In fact, Lopez calls my place Flintstone's Flat. Anyway, I wanted this to be a special night."

"It couldn't be better, but why should I act like some kind of princess. Let me help you."

"Not tonight, baby. Sit tight. I'll just be a minute."

Donnie reached for our salad plates and disappeared. After a brief appointment with his kitchen, he returned with two filet mignons, some twice-baked potatoes and a side vegetable dish.

"Mom supplied the veggies," he confessed.

"Your mother is a special lady." I paused, trying to express my feelings as I watched him place our dinner plates on the table.

"Donnie, I'd like for your mother and I to be close."

"You will. In fact, I can already tell she's fond of you."

I took a sip of water and said, "Really? What makes you think so?"

Donnie waited as I released the glass, and then he took my hand and said, "When I told my folks about our engagement, Mom said you will be the daughter she always wanted. Dad agreed." I looked into Donnie's eyes and let his words wash over me. Then I repeated them to my heart. For a moment, it felt almost like the time Mother hugged me after the swimming episode.

I guess Donnie could tell I was far away somewhere, so he gave me some time before he said, "Well, let's see if you like the steak. I certainly hope you do, because it's about the only thing I can cook."

As we picked up our forks Donnie said, "You're a beautiful woman, Beth. I can't believe you've agreed to marry a guy like me."

"Candlelight is deceiving," I chided. "But ..."

He jumped up and said, "I forgot the wine. You will let me serve you a glass of wine for our engagement dinner, won't you?"

When he returned and poured a small glass of Lambrusco, I followed his lead by lifting the glass as he said, "Here's to us, and many happy years ahead."

As our glasses clicked, I felt as though I'd known this man all my life.

At around eleven o'clock Donnie kissed me one last time at my apartment, and I said, "Donnie, I feel like I'm on cloud ten instead of the proverbial cloud nine."

"Me too. But to get you in shape for those agility tests, I need to be back around seven-thirty in the morning. Can you make it?"

"It's a deal."

After Donnie left, I picked up the Academy letter again, this time with a smile. I'd had my celebration after all. A big one. Now with eight to ten days off, I'd have time for exercise and some needed rest.

However, I forgot to factor in a person who would rear his ugly head again the very next day.

Bellinger.

Chapter 33

Donnie and I put in a good hour and a half of warm-ups, sit-ups and other exercises, followed by a jog. Afterwards, we fixed ourselves an old-fashioned breakfast. When he left around ten, I headed for the shower and then planned to pick up some groceries and swing by Shannon's apartment to show her my ring.

The mail truck caught my eye as I pulled out of the parking space, so I waited, hoping my last Honda check might have arrived. Bellinger's bold print darted to my eyes the moment I opened the mail slot.

I decided to use the pocket knife in my purse to open the envelope, and face whatever happened to appear on the page. This time, the stationery was tombstone gray, and Bellinger had selected a blood red ink.

"When will you ever wake up?" he wrote. "Can't you see that punk is not good for you? You wasted your Fourth of July when you could have spent it with me. Well, I'm giving you one more chance. I'll pick the time and place – so just sit tight! H.B."

A month or so ago this message would have sent me into orbit, but now I began to think of how I could fight back, or at least not let him terrorize me. Like I had feared, my rejection letter had failed.

I knew it had reached him, because I had the Certified Mail Receipt. Was he just ignoring it? Well, I'd show this new material to Donnie and Lieutenant Wilson, and then decide the next move.

Putting all the mail aside, I drove on to Shannon's apartment, careful to watch just in case he might be following me. Shannon had pizza and a fruit salad waiting when I arrived, so we enjoyed a special girl time.

In fact, she made such a big deal over all the plans she and Margaret were making for my shower that I didn't even mention Bellinger. When we finished eating, I was glad I hadn't spoiled our visit when Shannon told me to follow her down the hall to her second bedroom.

"Close your eyes," she cooed. "All right. Now you can open."

A sparkling champagne wedding dress hung from a hook on the closet door, and a bridal veil lay neatly on the guest bed.

"I bought it in Atlanta last week," Shannon said. "Like it?"

As I nodded my head like a chicken, I thought about my sticky pizza fingers, and turned to her half bath to wash up.

"That's right, my messy friend. Pizza sauce and wedding garments don't mix." She watched me dry my hands and then said, "So take it down and have a look."

Shannon's dress was exquisite in every detail, and I knew in an instant that it must be expensive.

"So," she said. "When I'm done you can borrow it if you like. Do you have time for us to try it on?"

"You model it," I said. "Tell you what. I need to make a phone call. Knock on the door when you're ready."

Shannon grinned, and I left her to fuss with the special underwear and tiny zippers. Ten minutes later, I stood beside my friend and pronounced her the most beautiful bride I'd ever seen.

She just smiled and said, "It could be perfect for you, too. Here. Try it on."

"Ah," she said as we both stood before her bedroom door mirror. "You look incredible. So here's the deal. You may want to shop for your own dress, but if not, this one will be waiting. Or ... ," She seemed to be grabbing ideas out of the air. "You could just use the veil to complete the 'something borrowed' line of the wedding chant." I hugged my long-time friend and thanked her profusely for her offer. Then I checked the time on my cell, and knew I'd better leave for groceries. As I headed for the Honda she called, "Remember, the shower date is September Second. Be sure to put it on your calendar."

Sunday was spent with Donnie's parents and Uncle Charlie and Aunt Gertrude. In fact, Aunt Gertrude helped prepare lunch, and while the women did the dishes, she announced she'd like to plan a small party for Donnie and me.

Before I could say anything, Donnie and Uncle Charlie walked in.

Uncle Charlie put his arm around my waist saying, "I vote for one of those towels and tools parties. Right, Donnie?"

Donnie winked at me and replied, "I knew I could count on you, Uncle Charlie."

On the drive back to my apartment, Donnie offered to deliver Bellinger's last note to Lieutenant Wilson's office, and said he'd also tell him about our Callaway Gardens experience.

As we said goodnight, he told me, "Beth, this guy may be nothing more than a big bluff, but I plan to keep my eyes open. I hope you know you're the most important person in my world, and I'm longing for the day when I can introduce you as my wife."

Eight days later

All the talk about bridal parties and wedding dresses flew out the window on the first day of Police Academy Orientation. Donnie, of course, had tried to warn me, but I wasn't prepared for Day One.

When I arrived, I spotted Tabesha on the second row, and hurried to sit beside her. We barely had time to speak before a hush settled over the room, and twenty-six pairs of eyes darted to the front.

Orientation began with an introduction of the Academy Staff, and since I'd had zero exposure in Chain of Command I wondered if I could remember the difference between Major, Captain, Lieutenant, Sergeant, and Corporal, and who was who.

What did all of the stripes, stars, colors and clusters mean? One thing was certain. I'd better learn fast.

Frankly, I couldn't help but admire the freshly pressed uniforms, polished insignia, and shoes as clear and shiny as mirrors as the staff formed a line before us. Each officer stood tall and erect, even female Corporal Dorsey who was no taller than me.

Yes, I could almost see assurance, determination and no-nonsense wrapped around them like a wall, and wondered if any of us would ever be able to scale it. No wonder Donnie wore the uniform with pride.

"Davidson, are you on vacation already?"

Surprised, I uttered the appropriate reply, "Sir, no sir!"

"Well, get with the program. Look alert!"

"Sir, yes sir!"

Caught within the first ten minutes, I threw my shoulders back and made eye contact with ... I strained to read his name tag. Was it Lieutenant Conway (the Bureau Commander) or Sergeant Hamilton (a Staff Instructor)? I vowed to have their names memorized by the next day.

Later, when the introductions were complete, only two staff members remained. One of them, Sergeant Hamilton, reminded me of a picture I'd once seen of Goliath, the Philistine giant who had taunted David.

Yes, Hamilton was the one who had intimidated me. Now he paced up and down in front of our desks, and then stopped to stare at us – one at a time.

I counted the seconds in my head, and when I reached thirty he bellowed, "Are you a bunch of idiots? One of you left your keys in your car!"

Ignoring the bulge, my left hand flew to my pocket as if to confirm the obvious, and from the corner of my eyes, I noticed a similar response from others recruits sitting around me.

"Who will have the guts to come and tell me?"

From the back of the room, I heard a desk squeak and a sound like feet hitting the floor. Afraid to turn, I watched a top heavy guy heave his way to the front, and then try not to react as the officer waved the keys back and forth in front of his face.

"If you want to last through this day you better wake up, Humphrey. Who ever heard of a police officer leaving keys in his car on the first day of training?"

"Sir. No one, sir."

"Return to your seat before you do something else stupid."

"Sir, yes sir."

After this bit of ridicule, the other instructor, Corporal Boltwell, distributed more paper work and began offering instructions. "Put the date in the top right hand corner. What is the date, Kendrick?"

Boltwell eyed the recruit on my right side.

Kendrick started, hesitated, and said, July 25th, sir."

"Wrong date. Big mistake, Kendrick. How will you prepare reports when you don't know the date?"

"Sir, I can't, sir."

"Can't is not in an officer's vocabulary. Erase the can't or you will be erased. Understand?"

"Sir, I understand, sir."

As we finished the assignment, Corporal Boltwell issued further instructions.

"Now, put your first initial, middle initial and last name on your papers and pass to the left. Recruit Jeeter, stand and gather the papers from the back to the front."

I heard someone in the back of the room rise and then Boltwell cut in with, "Move it. You guys have to move with a sense of urgency. Collect the papers, Jeeter."

"Sir, yes sir."

"All right." Corporal Boltwell reminded me of an eagle perched on a treetop. "Take a five minute break, and meet me on the practice field. In the meantime answer me in unison. What do you do when you pass an officer in the hall?"

"Sir, Move to the wall. Stand at attention, sir."

"What should you be prepared to do when addressed, Davidson?"

Trembling, I answered, "Sir, Be prepared to defend my direction, mission and maybe even my existence, sir."

"Correct. You are all dismissed."

I hurried to the bathroom, wondering if my breakfast was about to reappear. Then, when I looked in the mirror, something else caught my eye: pink lip gloss and a hint of blush. Make-up was definitely forbidden in this place but habits die hard. I grabbed a tissue and removed every hint of color before hurrying to exit.

As I stepped back into the hallway, a navy blue uniform appeared so I hit the wall and stood at attention.

"Where are you headed, Davidson?" Sergeant Hamilton bared his teeth as he grunted at me. I wondered if he used ten penny nails for toothpicks.

"Sir, Practice field, sir."

"Very well. Carry on."

I knew what was coming next. Agility tests. As I stood at attention in the second line of four rows, Donnie's warning echoed in my head.

"The Agility tests will be your biggest hurdle."

Chapter 34

Y ou will be tested for endurance, agility and ability. If you should fail, you can be re-tested only once, and the re-test must occur within forty-eight hours. Any questions?"

Sergeant Hamilton sneered and then sneezed. So ... officers did sneeze!

No one dared laugh or ask a question as we stood there. I suppose fright had frozen our tongues. Hamilton's steel gray eyes moved from one recruit to another, and then he patted his right leg as if he were eager to begin.

"You are expected to complete five events, and you are allotted ninety seconds per event. There are twenty-six of you here today. Tomorrow you may only number nineteen. Stand tall Dorset. This is not a playground. Humphrey, your shoe is untied. Fix it now."

"Sir, yes sir."

I held my shoulders up, looking straight ahead, afraid any eye movement would arouse his attention.

"Corporal Boltwell will now introduce you to the five events in the agility portion of your tests. Listen up. Your future depends on today's performance."

Corporal Boltwell, whose proboscis looked like an eagle's beak, was perched on an incline just west of us. Then he flapped his wing-like arms and glided within five feet of me. Once again, I avoided his penetrating probe and tried to concentrate on chocolate. It didn't work.

"Davidson, what is that bulge in your pocket."

I patted my right hip and said, "Sir, it's just some change, sir."

Flickers of annoyance shot from his eyes. Then he

called, "How do you expect to perform with money jingling in your pocket?"

"Sir, I cannot perform with change in my pocket, sir."

"Remove it and get back in line immediately."

"Sir, yes sir." I ran to the flag pole stand and dumped the money in a heap. When I returned to my station he continued to frown at me. I suppose he wanted to extend my torture with this non-verbal jab. Finally satisfied with my humility, he shrugged his shoulders and began.

"About face."

Fifty-two feet fumbled into an about face position, and Recruit Jeeter, who was standing next to me, started giggling. Boltwell took flight around all twenty-six of us and stood facing him.

"Jeeter, do you think you are applying for kindergarten?"

"Sir, no sir."

"You're a joke, Jeeter."

I smiled, but then quickly pulled my lips in as if blotting fresh lip gloss. Thankfully, Boltwell didn't notice as he pointed to the car some forty feet away.

"The car is in neutral. You are to push it for fifteen feet. Your stopping point is clearly marked. Any questions?"

I'm not sure who, but someone murmured, "That's not hard."

Eagle ears Boltwell heard him however, and taunted us with, "It will be with me sitting in it."

Thankfully, I was in row two position five, so I could observe several peers first. I watched as some chose to push with their arms, and others turned away from the rear end of the Crown Victoria and pushed with their shoulders.

Donnie had suggested I use my shoulders, so I waited and worried through nine of ninety second episodes.

I also thought about my ten-year-old birthday party, when my parents had invited six of my friends to go bowling. Since I'd never bowled in my life, I had stood there waiting for my turn, yet fearing the thought of winding up in the gulley.

"Davidson!" Boltwell flew toward me and cawed, "Davidson, pretend this vehicle is stalled in the middle of Eastchase Boulevard, and you're the only officer around. Move this baby out of the traffic before the light changes."

He then perched in the driver's seat and gave me the signal.

Answering with all of the force I could muster. "Sir, yes sir," I took my position in the middle of the rear bumper and began to push. She moved. Slowly, but she moved.

I heaved myself at the Crown Victoria as if I was saving a grandmother from the flames, and I began to count the seconds in my head. Thankfully, my count was off and I somehow made it.

Boltwell's eyes flickered back toward me. Was it a look of surprise, affirmation or "I'll get her next time?" I couldn't tell, but for just a moment, I felt like a foster eaglet on her first flight.

It was a good thing that we could rest between events, because the next assignment looked impossible. We had to scale a six foot wood or chain link fence.

Since I'm not very agile, I studied each candidate before me, and then tried to visualize exactly where to position my hands and feet. I noticed that every recruit chose the chain link fence, and I remembered my childhood dog. By taking a running leap and using his claws for support, Fluffy could sail over our chain link almost in a moment's notice.

Well there was a weight difference of about ninety pounds between Fluffy and me, but I decided that I could at least match him with my zeal.

When Boltwell called my name, I made the run with ease, but my right foot hung half way up. I managed to regain balance and probably lost no more than three seconds in the effort.

Boltwell declared, "Ninety seconds on the nose," and I could feel myself exhale for almost as long.

Everyone's perspective is different, I suppose, but I didn't think the next event looked quite as difficult. Maybe I say this because I once crammed myself into my mom's clothes dryer. And on several occasions I had enjoyed pretending to be a circus acrobat by walking the top of our retainer wall.

Boltwell woke me from the reverie by pointing out the

obvious. "You have ninety seconds to run and then step through the simulated window. After that, you will attempt to scale the one by six foot balance beam. Now don't look smug. This could be a burning house, or you could be chasing a crazed killer."

It was as if he could read my mind. I snapped to attention when my name was called, and by the time I was half way through the event, I had developed more respect for the challenge.

The next event, I decided, would be my Waterloo. This time we were given ninety seconds to run twenty-five yards, and then drag a one hundred and sixty pound dummy for fifteen feet.

Somewhere deep inside my psyche I heard myself say, Donnie Crawford, you knew about this one. Why didn't you offer to serve as my guinea pig?

While waiting my turn, I did some stretches and almost wished we could practice on each other.

My mind wandered as I remembered a story I had once heard. *Years ago, a southern farm hand was promised a free watermelon if he could eat the entire melon by himself. The guy accepted the challenge, but asked to be excused for a half hour. When he returned he promptly devoured the melon, to the surprise of a gathering crowd.*

"How did you do it?" The challenger asked.

"Easy," the farm hand replied. "I had a melon about that size at home, so I had a chance to test myself."

"Davidson, you're next."

My stomach tightened.

Boltwell shouted, "Go!"

I ran, wondering what one hundred and sixty pounds might do to my back, but once I had a grip around what appeared to be shoulders, it didn't seem so bad. Well, not until the last five feet. I say this because my left heel hit a rough spot in the dirt. As I tried to swing the dead weight away from the spot, the torso slumped into the cavity and I lost my balance. I figured my time must be up, but I heard Tabesha on the sidelines.

"Hurry. Go. You can do it."

"Eighty-nine seconds," Boltwell announced.

Tabesha shot me a Crest Whitestrips smile as I nodded

my thanks. We had both passed the Agility test.

Now, as he dripped with perspiration, Boltwell declared a twenty minute break. He ended with, "Next up is the Ability test. You will either make it or exceed it. Dismissed."

With fingers interlocked behind our necks, Tabesha and I took the last five minutes of our break to practice sit-ups. I could only do twenty-four in the sixty second allotment, so Tabesha suggested I rest.

"You gotta do one more," she said. "But if you're too tired, you sho' can't do it. Time me. Okay?"

I watched how Tabesha arched her back and raised her body. She was accurate, graceful and deliberate. No wasted movement. No rag doll now.

Just then, Boltwell sailed into the gym and everyone lined up and stood at attention.

"You are well rested," he announced, almost in a mocking tone. "Now for the Ability test." He paced between the rows. "As you know, this test is in three segments. You will complete timed push-ups, sit-ups and a one point five mile run. We will begin with push-ups."

Nervous, but not panicked, I watched as Boltwell suddenly executed a right face and looked at me. "Are you prepared for push-ups, Miss Davidson?"

"Sir, yes sir," I said.

"Well, so we will see. My timer is ready. Begin."

Boltwell dropped to one knee and counted. I could almost feel his breath in my ear. What he didn't know was that Lamar had trained me on this one, so I managed all twenty-two push ups in sixty seconds.

"Not bad Davidson. I must confess, you surprised me."

"Sir, thank you, sir."

"Next." He rose and moved to Kendrick, and then on down the line. Tabesha was the last in our row. She passed with ease.

Sit-ups were next, and I wished I could have one more practice. No, this was it. My face flew to Tabesha, who gave me a thumbs up and a nod. This time Boltwell remained standing, but as he hovered over me, the tension rose.

"What about it, Davidson? Can you do twenty-five sit ups in sixty seconds?"

"Sir, yes sir," I said with all the determination I could muster.

"Very well. Begin."

For the next sixty seconds, I pictured Tabesha's slim body, and then imagined myself clicking off those sit ups like an athlete in the Olympics. It worked. Twenty-five sit ups in sixty seconds. I'll probably never do it again.

We ran the one point five miles as a group, and all but one of us made it. However, three other recruits failed some segment of the Agility test, and all were told to take one re-test within forty-eight hours.

Boltwell didn't make a public spectacle of the four recruits, but I did notice a dejected look on Jeeter's face when he collected his belongings and left the gym at lunch.

Back at the academy by one o'clock, our Friday afternoon was mainly consumed with administrative paper work, seating, locker assignments and placements in class counselor groups.

I felt relieved to hear we could take our questions and problems to an assigned counselor. Relieved that is, until I discovered my counselor was none other than Corporal Boltwell.

At five o'clock I finally headed for my red Honda. I sighed. One day down. Eight hours out of six hundred and forty. One day out of eighteen weeks. I had no way of knowing what tomorrow would bring.

Chapter 35

Yesterday was the easy part," Sergeant Hamilton roared as he marched back and forth across the parade deck inspecting our formation. "The Police Academy is not a cakewalk. Look at it this way. If you perceived yourself sitting on a café stool gorging donuts, erase it from your mind."

My eyes fell on Hamilton's amble girth, and decided that food references must come to him with ease. However I had to admit, the tummy extension looked solid; more like a permanent fortification than a temporary inner tube. He also had wide shoulders, and constantly pulled them back as if posing for a family photograph. Goliath in all his glory.

"Speaking of that," he continued, "we are here to train your body and your mind. The mind part may be hard for some of you. Right, Jeeter?"

"Sir, yes sir." Jeeter whimpered.

"All right. Let's test your minds. You're first, Massey. Give me the quote of the week."

"Sir, yes sir," Massey called. "The quote of the week is: 'Do not follow where the path may lead.'" He paused and then said, "Leave a trail instead."

"Wrong," Hamilton bellowed. "Let's hear from you Baxter."

"Sir, yes sir," Baxter yelled from the rear. "The quote of the week is: 'Do not follow where the path may lead. Go instead where there is no path and leave a trail.'"

"Right. Now, you recite it to ole Massey until he gets it."

"Sir, yes sir."

Hamilton continued pacing up and down our formation, evaluating our stance, clothing and over-all attitude. More than once he ordered a recruit to do ten or more push-ups, or take a jog around the block. Finally, we were given a break and told to report to the gym.

Brute strength is not enough in this profession. As you build strength it's imperative that you learn how to use it to restrain and subdue." Pacing again, Goliath continued, "It takes muscle to subdue a suspect or shoot a target, but a good officer must know when and how to do so. Or when and how to enforce the law."

He stopped, and his shoes clicked the gym floor as he did a right face turn.

Then, no more than six inches from a pale face, Hamilton shouted: "Are your shoes tied today, Humphrey?"

"They are ... I mean, Sir, yes sir."

"What about car keys? Did you remember not to leave them in your ignition today?" Before he could answer, Hamilton replied for him. "So, we've got one recruit beginning to use his mind. Who knows about the rest of you numbskulls? Well, time will tell."

Hamilton took a deep breath, and when he blew his whistle, my hands instinctively flew to my ears. He peered at me but then moved on.

"We are about to begin an uphill fitness challenge of exercise, running and weight training. Give your attention to Corporal Boltwell as he begins roll call."

For some reason, Boltwell instructed us to answer roll call saying, "One thousand and one, one thousand and two, one thousand and three." As the voices rumbled and echoed across the gym, I wondered how I could feel tired at nine o'clock in the morning. Tired before exercises had even begun.

Stretching was next, so I willed my mind to be alert, and willed my ears to hear above the bellow of Boltwell's voice, and the scraping of tennis shoes across the gym floor.

When Boltwell decided we'd had enough warm-ups, he led us in about twenty minutes of floor exercises, then gave us a fifteen minute break before our mile and a half run.

Most everyone darted outside or to the locker room. I just flopped against the gym wall and tried to inhale and exhale slowly. Anything to calm myself down.

Sitting there with my head bowed, I didn't see him coming, but I sensed something, or someone, moving deliberately in my direction. Tabesha, who was sitting to my right, tapped my arm and said, "Beth, somebody's looking at you."

When I looked up, I could feel tension draining from my body.

"Hi, Beth."

As he held out his hand, I scrambled to my feet, dusting off invisible wads of lint from my shirt.

"How's my girl?" Donnie's tender face searched my eyes and found his answer.

I was about to introduce him to Tabesha, but she had already headed for the locker room.

"Can you go outside with me for a minute?"

"Yeah." I tried to smile. "Fresh air might help."

As Donnie pushed the heavy gym door, I wondered if he could sense my frustration.

When we were out of ear shot I said, "Tell me, what am I doing here? I must be crazy!"

"No, you're not crazy." Donnie looked at me almost like a parent reasoning with his child, and yet his eyes were tender. "You are in pursuit of a worthy mission. Let's go to the truck. I have something to show you."

Ordinarily the July heat would already be oppressive by mid-morning, but thankfully, we felt a breeze as Donnie opened his truck cab, and picked up a small red foil gift bag that reminded me of Christmas.

"You may think I'm the crazy one Beth, but I couldn't resist buying this for you last week."

"What is it?" I asked as he handed me the package.

"Well, I was just browsing the internet and happened to Google *Christmas in July*."

I lifted a small see-through box from the bag, and found a beautiful silver bell with some sort of inscription engraved on the front.

Before I could open it, Donnie said, "It's for our first tree. Look, I know it's early. I just couldn't resist."

I turned the ornament toward the sunlight and read, *Beth & Donnie, Our 1st Christmas Together.*

"Donnie, I ..."

"Now don't go all sentimental on me."

"Looks like you're the sentimental cop in this equation, but I love it," I said. "How is it you do these things when I can't kiss you."

"Rain check? Say, if you don't have too much homework, how about a supper date? Besides, even recruits need a little fun."

"Homework is gonna take two hours at least, but a girl's got to eat. What time?"

"Let's aim for seven, but I'll call you later. Look, to save you a trip to the locker room, I'll bring the gift with me tonight."

I handed the beautiful ornament back to Donnie, and waved as he pulled out of the parking lot. Somehow, taking a July jog didn't seem so bad after all.

Our first assignment after lunch was to listen to a lecture from Corporal Stedman. Now if Hamilton looked like Goliath, and Boltwell resembled an eagle, then Stedman could be compared to young Greek philosopher, maybe a Socrates or an Aristotle. His reasoning went something like this:

"Some of you may be better suited to flipping hamburgers, selling cars, developing software or serving as a price checker for Dollar Tree. I don't know. However, no career offers me more satisfaction than law enforcement."

I watched Stedman point to his badge, and then using a yard stick, point to a recruit.

'What did you do before coming to the Academy?"

"Sir, I worked for Guardian Credit Union, sir."

"Fine. Do you think you can now be a guardian of lives, property and of the public trust?"

"Sir," Massey answered, "I think so, sir."

"You've got to know so, Massey."

Stedman pointed again. "What about you, Jeeter? What did you do?"

Jeeter hesitated and then said, "I cut grass, sir."

"Cut grass. All right. What kind of goal or standard did you set for yourself when cutting grass?"

"Well," Jeeter said. "I tried to do my best and make their

yard look nice."

Someone snickered to Stedman's disgust.

"Jeeter had a worthy goal, but I suspect he could finish several lawn jobs and call it a day. Right, Jeeter?"

"Sir, you're right, sir."

"Right. Most jobs can be completed. Not police work. This job is not like counting twenty dollar bills at Guardian Credit Union, or taking a break from cutting grass. A police officer may go off duty, but in a sense, he or she is never off duty."

Stedman whirled around and pointed his yard stick toward me. "Davidson, what did you do before coming to the Academy?"

"Sir, I was a customer service representative for Honda, sir."

"Was the customer always right, Davidson?"

"Sir, no sir, but I was to treat each one as if he were."

"Not a bad answer. In fact, remember this in your new profession. You are to treat everyone with respect. Don't be too heavy handed or it may backfire."

Stedman paused and then said, "Before you finish this Academy you will be able to recite the four paragraphs of the Police Officer's Code of Ethics, and you will be expected to live it everyday. Do you understand?"

"Sir, yes sir!" Our voices rang in unison.

"Does anyone not have their homework completed?"

Silence.

"All right. Put the date, your first initial, middle initial and last name next. Follow this with your new student ID number and pass to the left. Take the papers up from the rear forward."

When we had finished, Stedman tapped his yard stick on the floor, and spoke in a fast staccato. "Take out a piece of paper for today's notes."

The sound of twenty-something clicking notebooks and the shuffle of feet followed, but I watched Stedman, knowing more comments or instruction were forthcoming. I'd have to learn to hear above the noise.

"You must learn to transition your mind in a moment's notice. For instance, suppose you get a SID call. It's agony."

What's a SID call? Oh, yes, I know, I told myself.

"You try to console the family, and then you get a Code Six or a shooting."

A shooting? All of this in the same day?

"Yes, a shooting." Stedman repeated himself. "This could all happen in one day. Are you prepared?"

I checked the time. Three o'clock. No, I wasn't prepared for one more hour. How could I ever be prepared for a SID, a Code Six (whatever that meant), or a shooting, especially if all three came within eight to ten hours?

Chapter 36

While enjoying an Arby's sandwich that night, I mentioned the afternoon lecture to Donnie. His response was immediate.

"Beth," he said. "I know you've only had two days of training but let me ask you something."

I nodded, waiting.

"Has the Academy staff tried to teach you everything you need to know in these two days?"

"Of course not," I said, dabbing my sandwich in the Arby's sauce, and trying to grasp his point.

"Okay. Your training is stretched out over eighteen weeks. Think about what you've already learned." Donnie sipped his tea and continued, "When December rolls around you'll be far more prepared than you are right now, right?"

"Right," I nodded. "Look, I'm sorry. It's just been a little overwhelming."

"I know. What did you find the hardest today?"

"Well," I said, "we had a test on the first chapter. The questions weren't so difficult, but Stedman kept blaring out the time. He'd hit his yardstick on the floor and call, 'Five more minutes!' then 'Two more minutes!' then 'Thirty seconds!' and finally, 'Pass 'em up!' It's unnerving."

"Yes. It's also a strength builder. You're learning to think under pressure. In time, the staff will loosen up. Let me ask you something else." Donnie had finished his sandwich and was now giving me his most intense look. "Did you hear or sense any form of compassion today?"

Meeting his gaze, my mind charged back to Stedman's lecture. "Yes, there was something. Stedman was tough, yet when Humphrey asked him how he handled the recent SID case he said, 'When the shift was over I took the couple some flowers.'"

"You see?"

I nodded and silence fell between us for a minute. I could tell he wanted to say more, but he didn't.

"What is it, Donnie?" I pressed.

"Beth, before you get even busier, I'd like to show you a few self-defense moves. Maybe even purchase some mace. Do you have any objections?"

"No, not really. With a guy like Bellinger around I need all the help I can get."

"I agree." Donnie hugged me with his eyes and we let the subject drop. After a moment he said, "I'm glad you like the bell."

"It's perfect. Just think. In six months we can hang it on our first tree."

"What kind of tree do you like, Beth?"

"A tall one," I said, reaching my hand way above our heads.

"Me too. Let's buy a real one, okay?"

"Let's do. We always had a real one when Mom was alive."

"And after that?"

"Artificial"

"I thought so." Donnie reached for my hand and said, "There's nothing artificial about you, sweetheart."

I didn't respond because I knew Donnie was about to say more. For just a moment he turned toward the window, and then he looked back at me.

"Beth, I don't know how I'd live without you."

I smiled and then paused before saying, "I hope you won't ever have to."

Saturday afternoon

I didn't expect Donnie to bring a self-defense video to my apartment, but frankly, it seemed easier to watch another woman encounter an attacker than to engage in mock combat with Donnie.

The video was short, so once or twice Donnie replayed certain segments and offered comments and suggestions. Then, before helping me review the next two chapters in the Blue Book, he gave me a lesson regarding the proper use of mace. Naturally, he couldn't provide the mace used by police officers, but when used properly, he assured me, the one he selected could be effective.

When Donnie left that night I wondered if I'd need the mace or the self-defense instruction before I finished the Academy. At least they were confidence boosters, and confidence was a valued commodity with Harvey Bellinger around.

Chapter 37

Monday

Y**ou live in a glass house and are being watched."
If he only knew, I said to myself, as we watched
Corporal Stedman pace back and forth in front of
our classroom.

"Your badge, if you ever obtain one, is a public trust. Your duties are well articulated in the Police Officer's Code of Ethics, and you will memorize every line of this code. More importantly, you will live it. Do you hear me?"

"Sir, yes sir," we called, still standing at attention.

"At ease. Take a seat."

After a shuffle of feet, books and papers, Stedman said, "Baxter, give me a one word definition of ethics."

"Sir, *conduct* sir."

"Massey." He pointed to the back row.

"Sir, *responsibility* sir."

"Davidison."

"Sir, *honor* sir." I shouted a little louder than necessary for someone in the second row.

Corporal Stedman continued to call names and hear our answers and then he said, "Where does this statement originate: '*As a law enforcement officer, my fundamental duty is to serve mankind.*' Let's hear it, all of you."

"The Code of Ethics, sir. First paragraph, sir."

"What does all mankind mean?" Not waiting for an answer, Stedman said, "It means everyone, in spite of age, health, color or creed. You are not to demean or use force unless it's absolutely necessary. You will remain calm, even in the face of ridicule. Even if someone spits on you."

Then turning to the last man on the first row he said, "Can you do that, Jeeter?"

"Sir, yes sir."

"I see some of you using hand sanitizer. That's fine," Stedman pronounced. "But, listen up. You can't afford enough Purell, or latex gloves for this job. You like to bathe? Well, some folks don't. Have you ever seen gangrene? You will!"

Stedman continued his lecture by reciting the Code of Ethics and offering examples, line by line. When the clock indicated our time was up, he concluded with: "That which does not kill you will make you strong!"

Kill you. Kill you. Those words didn't affect me much until Monday evening when Dad called.

"Beth," he began. "How are you?"

"I'm okay, Dad. What's up?"

"Well, I need to let you know about an incident just brought to my attention."

"All right," I said.

"Beth, do you know a man named Harvey Bellinger?"

"Harvey Bellinger?" My voice sounded like air coming out a balloon.

"Yes," Dad repeated. "Harvey Bellinger."

"Why do you ask?" I managed to say.

"I have a friend in Montgomery who just faxed me an incomplete Alfa life insurance form. This guy, Harvey Bellinger, attempted to take out a policy on your life."

"He did?" My heart suddenly began to jump rope in my throat, making it so parched I could barely speak.

"Yes. Do you remember Joe Nichols?"

"No, I don't."

"Well, fortunately, he remembered you. Nichols met you at an Alfa function years ago. When he saw the name on the form, it rang a bell and he was kind enough to call me for verification."

Dad went on, but my mind was in a haze. He said something about Nichols rejecting the application since Bellinger couldn't produce any insurable interest information. Then Dad said, "Nichols also figured you didn't owe this guy any money."

"No, of course not," I managed to say.

"Beth, I think you should report this to your friend."

"Donnie?"

"Yes, he can probably advise you about how to handle it. Let me know if he needs a copy of the application."

"Thanks. I will, Dad."

There was a long pause and then he said, "I don't want to frighten you Beth, but we shouldn't ignore this."

"I know, we shouldn't," was all I could say.

"Beth," Dad added, "are you going to be all right?"

"Yes," I said as we hung up. Then, as I put the cell back on the table, I sighed aloud. "Yes, one way or another, I'm going to be all right."

Chapter 38

Donnie called five minutes after Dad and I hung up, but since he was in the middle of something big, I didn't tell him about the life insurance. Besides, I wanted some time to think about the implications. To start (if I may say so) thinking like a police officer.

Well, one thing was certain. Bellinger had not accomplished his mission with Alfa insurance. If he were planning to kill me what could he gain? On the other hand, could there be some unscrupulous insurance companies out there; companies that might issue him a policy? Well, I decided not to go there. Not think about it.

But then again, if some company did offer him a policy, how could he know they would honor it if I died? Would they be reliable? Was Bellinger smart enough to think this through? After all, he was a psychologist. Wasn't he supposed to know all about human behavior?

On the other hand, did Dr. Bellinger think, and act, like a reasonably intelligent person? I didn't think so.

When I finally went to bed I put the mace close by – just in case.

Wednesday

A lot of things in your life are about to change."
I looked up into Sergeant Hamilton's face and wondered if he knew something I didn't. No, he was obviously talking about what any recruit might expect now, during training, and afterwards on the street.

"You are going to become attached to each other, and

believe it or not, to some of us. You've heard of *Band of Brothers*. Well, this is what you, or we, are becoming. I remember when I lost a friend of mine. It was hell. I wanted to quit, and to be honest ... well, it was my mom who helped me the most."

I thought: *Goliath has a mom? Well, he may even have a heart.*

"My mom said, 'Son, give yourself some time and you will get your focus back.' I did, and I did." He looked away, scratching a spot on his chin.

So ... officers did itch.

"Now that's enough sentiment. Today, we will finish discussing the objectives and duties of police patrol – the backbone of the Police Department. Remember this men and women. Your role, like a diamond, has many facets but it can probably be summed up with these two words: *Protection* and *Service*. Now for today ..."

Hamilton droned on with his lecture, but when he came to the part about the who, when, what, where, why, and how of report writing, I gave him my undivided attention. Finally, he asked if anyone would like to summarize what he had just said, and before I could stop myself, my hand flew up.

"All right. Give it to me in one sentence, Davidson."

"Writing a report is like painting a picture," I said. "You need to remember all of the details."

"That's two sentences, Davidson. Who else wants to try?"

I should have known. Oglethorpe, the tall, bookworm guy in the back, stood up and said, "Like Michelangelo, a police officer should observe everything around him before he crafts or paints his report."

"Excellent," Hamilton beamed.

I watched Oglethorpe smile with satisfaction, but then the smile slid from his face when Hamilton added, "Of course, you stole your idea from Davidson, so at least for that answer, I can only give you both a grade of fifty."

Several guys in our loose *Band of Brothers* snickered, but Hamilton sneered at them and continued his talk. When I thought that I could endure no more punishment, he said, "Okay. You have your handouts. Study the material regarding precincts and shifts for tomorrow. Begin to learn the Codes. Now, I'm sure you've read the chapter for today. Take out a clean piece of paper for a test."

Forty-five minutes later the papers were turned in and Hamilton said, "Tomorrow, we will have a guest speaker with thirty-five years of experience in law enforcement. He gives lectures all over the country. You are in for a treat. His name is Lieutenant Wilson, and his subject is Domestic Violence."

I didn't know whether to applaud or cry.

Chapter 39

Donnie had been out of town on Tuesday, but when he phoned Wednesday night I spilled the beans about the life insurance.

He said, "Beth, you've got to tell Wilson."

"He's gonna be busy with his lecture and all. I ..."

"Beth."

"All right, I will. But what can Wilson do about Bellinger trying to take out an insurance policy?"

"He can investigate. You know that, Beth."

"Yeah, I know. I just don't want anything to interfere with my training."

"It won't. In fact, the Academy should be aware of your situation."

"I don't expect any special privileges," I said as I twirled my index finger through a strand of hair.

"Say, haven't you been there long enough to know they don't play favorites?"

"Yes, I guess so but ..."

"Stop worrying. This could be the break you need."

"I don't know. Maybe."

Some of you may have already experienced domestic violence," Lieutenant Wilson began. "Some of you carry scars and baggage. You know what it's like to be hurt and abused."

At one point, Wilson's eyes rested on me, but then he quickly scanned the room and moved on.

"We live in an *I* generation. IPods, I Phones and I could go on ... Police officers need to develop a *we*, or *you*, attitude. Selfish, me-centered, individuals do not belong in this field."

I studied Wilson's face, and decided that my first impression of him had not changed. He carried himself with an Indiana Jones-type assurance, and yet he was a gentle man; unselfish and caring.

"Remember this," Wilson continued: "All of us belong to the same gene pool. We hurt and bleed. Your job will be to offer understanding, compassion and hope to the victims of domestic violence, and to help build a sound and complete case against the perpetrators."

I noticed nods from several of my classmates as Wilson began to walk in front of us, maintaining eye contact.

"What I'm about to say may surprise you. Sixty percent of all 911 calls are for domestic violence, and when you're called, be prepared. Victims can't shop for a cop. When you wear the uniform, you are responsible. You are the calming influence or damage control. Once you walk in the door you *are* involved.

"Later today I will talk to you about the whys and hows of DV report writing, but for now I'll just say, don't take short-cuts. Handle each case wisely. You could be involved in a lawsuit, and may be required to rolodex your mind for facts. Remember litigation can happen, and with a lawsuit, the bullseye is on our backs."

Lieutenant Wilson gestured by patting his back and continued. "Are there any questions so far?"

Massey raised his hand and said, "What are some of the causes of domestic violence?"

"Good question. Well, let's hear from some of you. What do you think?"

"Drugs," Humphrey offered.

"Right. What else?"

"Alcohol." This came from someone in the rear.

"Good," Wilson said. "Alcohol offers temporary liquid courage. "Anything else?"

"Some folks are just mean," Jeeter added.

Wilson nodded and said, "Absolutely. Left to our own devices we'd all be totally self absorbed, wouldn't we? When we look at a domestic violence case, the perpetrator usually exhibits a specific course of conduct, with an attempt to exercise power and control over another person."

My mind jumped to my first contact with Lieutenant

Wilson, when he had explained the typical stalker's power and control mindset.

"How many of you can remember what it's like to ride on a see-saw?"

Hands flew up across the room.

"Okay," Wilson explained. "If someone uses his weight to hold you up in the air too long what is he saying? Isn't the person in essence shouting, 'I've got you where I want you – it's my call?' What about this: suppose he jumps off? Do you see how power and control is in the see-saw?

"When you receive a DV call and go into a home, you can see, hear and almost taste the tension. Don't make it worse. As I said before, you are damage control."

Tabesha raised her hand and asked, "But what if everything seems calm when you arrive?"

"My next point," Wilson acknowledged. "There are three stages, or cycles, of violence. It's like the face of a clock."

Wilson turned around and drew a clock face on the chalkboard, and spaced the stages on the clock face: calm, tension-building and acute.

"Let's say you get a call from a dispatcher who reports an acute situation, but when you arrive everything appears calm. What happened? It could be nothing more than a face-saving device. Or, the victim may believe the spouse is only experiencing a temporary lapse of sanity, and all will be well tomorrow." Wilson paused and shook his head.

"Again, the victim might be afraid of future retaliation. Whatever the reason, everything may appear to be calm when you arrive. However, once you are gone, the cycle will likely repeat itself the next day or in a week or two. Like I said, the stages are calm, tension-building and acute."

I wrote as fast as I could, wondering if this is what I was experiencing with Bellinger.

"Now, here is something else hard to swallow. You may wonder why some women stay in an abusive situation. Well, that's another subject for the afternoon session. For now I'll just say, leaving is a process, and in extremely serious situations police may be dispatched five times before the violence turns into a homicide."

Homicide. Those three syllables stomped in my head as Wilson turned back to his clock and drew an X to the right of the acute line. I wondered what it meant, but he quickly supplied an answer.

"This X represents a flash point in the cycle I described. Imagine a couple in a relatively calm stage. It's six o'clock and they are tired from a long day's work." Wilson hesitated and then said, "By the way, ladies–" he eyed Tabesha and me – "when is the best time of day to communicate with a husband?"

"After supper," Tabesha offered.

"You are absolutely right. But what usually happens? Well, maybe I should ask, what often happens?" Not waiting for an answer, he continued, "The wife wants to share and talk about her day, while the husband wants to hunker down and be quiet. Men you see, protect their freedom, while women want an emotional connection. They want to secure, feather and embellish their nest. Sometimes a wife or husband brings up a subject at the wrong time, and this could become a flash point."

Some of what Wilson was saying was new information for me. In fact, I almost felt like this was a marriage seminar as I made mental notes and thought about Donnie. Did we spend too much time discussing serious issues over a meal? Well, I'd work on that now so I'd be a better wife later. Thanks, Wilson.

"As I said ..." My mind jumped back to Wilson's speech. "In the afternoon we will discuss your DV investigation and what to include in your reports, but now I want to conclude with this brief outline of the traits of a DV offender.

Again, Wilson turned to the chalkboard and wrote,

Characteristics of an offender.
1. Low self-esteem
2. Abuses alcohol and drugs
3. Accepts violence as proper behavior
4. Does not accept the negative consequences of
   abusive behavior
5. Blames others
6. Pathologically jealous
7. Believes he/she is superior

Wilson concluded his morning presentation without

saying anything about a stalker, but when I reviewed his list, Harvey Bellinger seemed to match at least six out of the seven characteristics.

My classmates scurried out almost immediately. I suppose they were hungry. At any rate, I lingered, wondering if I should approach Wilson. I didn't have to wait long because, after rearranging some papers on his lectern, he walked over to my desk.

"Good morning, Beth – or is it afternoon?" Wilson checked his watch and waited for a reply.

"Eleven fifty-six," I said, "but your talk was so informative I didn't notice the time."

"Thanks. How are you, Beth?"

"I'm all right, but do need to tell you that Bellinger tried to take out a life insurance policy on me."

The expression in Wilson's eyes changed, and I watched him take a deep breath as he sat down in the desk beside me.

"Tell me more."

As I told Wilson about my Dad's call, he gave me an understanding nod and then said, "Beth, this guy is continuing to leave a paper trail. Ask your Dad to fax that application to me ASAP. Once I see it, we'll decide what to do. In the meantime, be cautious, especially during times of transition. Now, if need be, where did I tell you to go if things should take a negative turn?"

"The shelter?"

"Right. The Family Sunshine Center has a record of your file, so no explanations are necessary."

"Right." I bit my lip, holding emotions in check.

Since Wilson is a heart-reader, his eyes ricocheted away and then he said, "I promise you, our department will be riding herd on this guy, and will also be in closer touch with you."

I searched Wilson's eyes again, finding what I needed. Maybe everyone did belong to the same gene pool. Well, maybe everyone except Harvey Bellinger.

Chapter 40

The next week seemed like a blur as our class covered criminal and civil cases, and issues involving federal and state procedures of law enforcement. Naturally, we spent time covering burglary, robbery and auto theft and then moved on to death investigation.

With everything going on in my personal life, I didn't find this last subject comforting.

Sometimes our class would divide into squad groups to study and quiz each other. I also found it interesting to comb the newspaper for actual cases, and speculate about possible outcomes. Other times I'd just make up my own bizarre scenarios and attempt to reason through the crime. Somehow, this helped to take my mind off of my crazy world.

One Saturday night when Donnie and I were together, he helped me lighten up by sharing a cop joke. It seems a certain guy was driving erratically on a busy highway. When the police stopped him the suspect lowered his window. After taking one whiff, the officer's suspicions were confirmed, so he handed him an alcohol breath analyzer saying,

"Here. Blow in this thing."

"I can't do that."

"Why can't you do it?" the cop queried.

"'Cause I'm an azz … thmatic and it could trigger a su-vere attack. You'd haf to call the paramedics."

"All right," the officer replied. "We will go to the station for a blood test."

"Can't do that, sir."

"Why can't you?"

"'Cause I'm a borderline hemo ... pheliac and you'd have to call the paramedics."

"Okay. Then get out of the car and let me see you walk this white line."

"Can't do that one either," the man slurred.

Exasperated, the officer said, "Why can't you?"

"'Cause I'm drunk!"

My laugh prompted another story, and soon the worries of the week began to slide from my shoulders. I even decided to share an incident with Donnie.

I said, "Did you see the newspaper article about the man who held up a service station wearing his personalized athletic shirt?" Not waiting for an answer, I continued. "Shouldn't he think about being caught on tape by the store camera? I believe the writer said it took the cops less than two hours to find Burdelli, number thirteen."

"It does happen," Donnie chuckled. "Wait and see."

"Wanna hear another one?" I said, enjoying the attention. "I made this one up."

"Okay, let's have it."

"Well, one night a woman prepares a meal for her husband, but is disappointed when he eats small portions."

Donnie raised his eyebrows – wondering, I suppose, where this was going.

"After waiting and coaxing him to eat more meatloaf," I said, "the wife slips from the room and calls 911. When the cops arrive some thirty minutes later she explains. 'I called because my husband won't eat his dinner.'"

"Won't eat his dinner?" one cop repeats. "You called 911 for such a trivial matter?"

"It's not trivial," she says. "You see he's always giving me excuses for not eating, so I wanted to cure him from lying once and for all. Yes, he's gonna need you."

"All right. Why?"

"I put Lysol in his meatloaf."

Even though I thought my joke was a little corny, Donnie's grin broke into a hearty laugh as I stood and headed to the kitchen for dessert. When I returned, I offered him one of his favorites: a chocolate brownie – and just for fun, I let him watch me squirt a dab of Cool Whip on the top.

After dessert and a short stroll to walk off a few of the calories, Donnie helped me study for the dreaded legal issue exam slated for Tuesday. In fact, he drilled me for so long I felt like I'd half memorized the Criminal Laws of Alabama and the Alabama Law Enforcement Handbook.

However, in spite of all of this, Donnie said the exam could be tricky. The multiple choice questions were phrased in such a way that you might sometimes need to concentrate on the most appropriate answer.

Our Monday classes and preliminary drills confirmed Donnie's assessment, so I found myself burning the midnight oil again Monday night, and wondering if I might be too tired to think at all. Part of the problem for all of us, I suppose, was the effort to maintain our daily physical conditioning and homework assignments. I especially remember how I felt on Monday night when Donnie called me from work. About all I could say was "Pray for me."

Instead of just agreeing to do it, Donnie said, "Let's pray before we hang up," but before he could say *amen,* I almost fell asleep.

The Tuesday legal issues exam took almost two hours to complete, but I felt like I had passed. When the grades came back the next day, I was more than a little surprised with a score of ninety-four.

I could almost see Donnie's smile as I shared the news by cell Wednesday afternoon.

"I'm proud of my girl," Donnie said.

"Thanks to you," I sighed.

"The credit is all yours. I'm just your coach. Now, let your mind rest a little."

"What about firearms?" I protested.

"You can handle it. In fact, aren't you doing okay with the lecture part?"

"Yes, but ..."

"What did I tell you, Beth?"

"You said to take a day at a time."

"That's right. Should we get a snack tonight?"

"Sure. Want me to meet you somewhere?"

"If my time is tight, maybe so. I'll give you a call later.

"Sounds good to me. See ya tonight."

Donnie called back around five-thirty and asked if I could meet him at Applebee's around six-fifteen. Even though the drive takes less than twenty minutes, I pulled out of the parking lot around five-fifty, hoping to get a booth to save time. As I left the complex, I spotted a small dog tied to a post near the apartment sign. He didn't appear to be wearing a collar, and he looked agitated.

I decided to circle the median for a better look. Seeing no sign of a leash or an owner, I pulled over into a parking spot and got out. The dog whimpered and pulled on the rope.

"Hi there," I called as I walked closer to the victim. He thumped his tail once, but gave me no other acknowledgement.

"Hi boy," I tried again.

"Hi girl."

The voice startled me, and it took no more than a second to realize who it belonged to. Bellinger was standing about twenty feet away, and my instincts shouted, *you can make it to the car before he reaches you.*

First I backed up a step or two, and then I turned and ran. Thankfully, I hadn't locked the door, so this saved me three or four seconds. As I slammed the driver's door shut, hit the lock button, and put the key in the ignition, his hand touched the door. It was no more than a touch, because my Honda had fired to life as I pushed the gas and sped away.

Checking the side and rearview mirror, I saw him standing in the parking lot. Then I watched as he raised his hand in a fist-like motion, and then turned toward the dog.

I pulled out on Carmichael Road and looked again from the passenger window. Bellinger appeared to be untying the animal. How could he have known I was about to leave the complex? He wasn't aware of my phone conversation with Donnie. Had he just happened by, expecting to use the dog in some other capacity?

As I headed toward Applebee's, I tried to call Donnie. A car suddenly pulled out in front of me, and I chastised myself for trying to call again while driving. Certainly, I didn't need to have a wreck now. How would I explain reckless driving to Recruiting?

I checked the rearview mirror again, hoping Bellinger wasn't tailing me. On the other hand, maybe he'd follow, pull up into Applebee's and then ... Donnie would nab him.

As I continued down the by-pass, I thought about the little dog again. What kind was he? Looked like a mixed breed; not the kind of pet for Bellinger. He'd have a boxer or a Rottweiler. At that moment, I felt like a Rottweiler might be lunging for my throat.

As I pulled into Applebee's, I still saw no one in pursuit. Why had I been so careless when leaving the apartment? Usually, I'd check for unusual cars.

Now, I peered at the Honda clock. Six-twelve. Donnie would pull up any minute. Should I wait or go inside? After all, the welcoming sign read, Applebee's: Your Friendly Neighbor Grill.

Then, just as I opened the door, I heard him.

Chapter 41

Hi, gorgeous!"

Looking at the clock again, I opened the door, stood, and then leaned into Donnie's shoulder as we headed toward the restaurant.

"What's up?" Donnie asked. "You look kinda beat."

"I am." So much for waiting until after dinner to talk about serious subjects, I thought.

Donnie stopped and turned my chin to face him.

"Bellinger," I said. "Let's go inside."

The Applebee's crowd was so sparse that the greeter was standing at the entrance, all smiles.

"Welcome to Applebee's. Table or booth?"

"Booth," Donnie said, as she turned and led us to a secluded spot.

"Is this okay?" She placed a large menu in front of each of us and then said, "My name is Melissa. I'll be your server tonight, but will give you a few minutes to decide."

"Thanks Melissa," I smiled back, wondering if she had read my mood at some level of women's intuition.

"Okay," Donnie said as she strolled away. "What's this with Bellinger?"

"He was in the parking lot when I left a few minutes ago."

"Doing what?" Donnie's eyebrows corrugated with concern.

"Imagine this. He had a dog tied to the Woodview entrance sign."

"A dog?"

"Yes, and sucker that I am, I got out of the car to check. Bellinger was waiting. He was no farther away than the

197

saxophone on the wall over there."

Donnie turned to the decorative sax and said, "Then what?"

"I made a break for it, and barely peeled off in time."

"Do you think he tried to follow you?"

"No, I didn't see anything."

Melissa was back now, staring down at us with her pen in hand. I ignored her.

"Should I call Gladys Thomas or anyone?"

"Probably too late now."

"What can I get for you?" Melissa wanted to know.

We took a minute to order, and when Melissa walked away, Donnie reached for his phone. Within seconds, he had Wilson on the phone and briefly related what had happened.

"All right . Oh? I see . Good. Okay ... I'll tell her," Donnie said. "Yes, she knows that. Anything else?" There was a pause then, "Good idea. Thanks."

"What?" I held Donnie with my eyes.

"DV interviewed Bellinger, and his classification is ORI-Stalker."

"Meaning?" I said.

"ORI is Obsessive Relational Intrusion. It's simply the repeated and unwanted invasion of your sense of privacy by someone who desires and/or presumes an intimate relationship. However, considering the previous phone calls, the notes and now the attempt to purchase life insurance, Bellinger has definitely moved into the threat category. The label: ORI-Stalker."

"So ..." I said, feeling somewhat annoyed.

"So, he'll be under more strict surveillance. Wilson will notify Recruiting. So ... you'll have about twelve more officers on his tail."

I sighed and said, "I guess I should be thankful."

Donnie nodded knowing, I suppose, that I wasn't done.

"But," I continued, "these guys can't follow me home, check my apartment every night and watch as I leave every morning."

"No, they can't. However, you can give me a call when you get home, and phone me or DV if anything looks suspicious when you leave for work."

I propped my hands on the table, plopped a cheek in each hand and countered with, "I'm just so tired of all this, Donnie. When is it ever going to end?"

Just as I said this, Melissa appeared, so I moved my elbows from the table and tried to look alert. Donnie held his reply in check, waited for Melissa to leave, and then said, "I don't know, Beth. I do know this: I love you and will do all I can to protect you."

"Yes." I tried to appear reassured. "I guess I just want to feel safe."

Donnie nodded, waited,and then said, "Safe, yes. But ... Beth, life is never totally safe."

"What?"

"Think about it. Do you or I ever know what is going to happen – even in the next minute?"

"No," I stammered. "We don't."

"We do what we reasonably can to protect ourselves and others, but our ultimate security can only rest in ..."

"I know. You're right, Donnie. I'm sorry."

"No need to be."

"Donnie ..." I brushed a strand of hair from my eyes and picked up my fork. "What did Wilson mean when you said, 'Good idea. Thanks'?"

"What I've just told you."

"Oh ..."

Somehow, eating a meal with someone you love helps your disposition, and this was no less true that Wednesday night. Then, just as a precaution, Donnie followed me home and surreptitiously checked the locks, before giving me a long and loving goodnight kiss.

When I finally finished the homework assignment, prepared for bed and then read my Bible a bit, I felt better. Then around eleven o'clock I climbed into bed.

Everything was quiet until I heard an unfamiliar noise. I sat up, listened more closely, and then realized it was just the hissing of the mosquito truck as it made its second round for the summer.

Too bad there was no repellant for a certain human pest!

Chapter 42

One week later

Give me the quote of the week, Jeeter."

"Sir, the quote of the week is, 'The block of granite which was a blockage in the ... the ... '"

"Wrong, Jeeter. Humphrey, give me the quote of the week."

"Sir, the quote of the week is, 'The block of granite that was a problem in ....'"

"Wrong! Give me the quote of the week, Griffin."

Tabesha arched her back and said, "Sir, the quote of the week is, 'The block of granite which was an obstacle in the pathway of the weak, became a stepping stone in the pathway of the strong.' Thomas Carlyle, sir."

"Correct, but that's last weeks quote. Davidson, do you know this week's quote?"

"Sir, yes sir. The quote of the week is, 'It requires less character to discover the faults of others, than to tolerate them.' J. Petit Senn, Sir."

Jeeter mumbled under his breath and Boltwell turned on him saying, "Exercise something besides your tongue, Jeeter." Then, without looking at anyone in particular, he said, "Griffin and Davidson, work with Jeeter and Humphrey until they learn both quotes."

"Sir, yes sir," we called in unison.

Corporal Dorsey, the only female officer in Recruiting, appeared on the parade field then. "All right. Hit the deck. I want to see twenty push-ups."

"In this rain?" Oglethorpe sighed, and then caught

himself.

"Who said that?" Dorsey demanded.

"Sir, me sir"

"What?"

"Ma'am, me ma'am," Oglethorpe corrected.

"Make it twenty-five for you, Oglethorpe."

"Yes, ma'am. I mean, Ma'am, yes, ma'am."

We hit the dirt and started counting as Dorsey walked between our rows, smiling and stretching like a cat in the sunshine. I heard Jeeter jabber something again, but I made the *Ssh* sound, not wanting anything to add minutes to our torture.

Mud squished between my fingers as I took a breath and counted eighteen, nineteen, twen – before falling into a mud rut and then scrambling back to position.

"Are you finished, Davidson?"

"Ma'am, no ma'am. I have one more."

"Let's see it then."

I did the final push-up and stood, just as Jeeter sneezed, almost in my face.

"Cover your mouth before sneezing, Jeeter."

This came from Stedman as he strode up beside Dorsey and said, "All right. Take a ten minute break and meet me in your classroom. I hope you're ready for your afternoon mock trial."

I wasn't. After all, this particular mock trial was listed as *The City of Montgomery versus Beth Davidson*. I was accused of robbing a local service station, and I knew that a couple of the mock witnesses had plans to do me in.

Thankfully, all of this trial business was merely aimed to prepare us for the many authentic trials we would one day face. Somehow, I survived the afternoon, and to tell the truth, I did feel better informed and competent by four o'clock that afternoon.

On top of that, the defense stated my guilt had not been proved beyond a reasonable doubt, and the jury declared me *not guilty*.

When I checked my cell after class, I had a message from Wilson instructing me to call him. Phone tag came next, but he did get back to me around seven saying

Bellinger was still being watched, and that there was no further evidence of any other life insurance applications.

Naturally, I shared this news with Donnie when he called that night, but we didn't dwell on it. In fact, Donnie tried to lighten me up with a question.

"Tell me something." Donnie spoke in his most serious voice. "Did someone post bail for you at the trial today?"

"No, but I'm free as a bird."

"Not guilty then?"

"Not guilty."

"Were you nervous?"

"A little bit, but it was a good learning experience."

"Thats a' girl! Say, what's on docket for tomorrow?"

"Firearms." I said this with more confidence than I felt.

"All right," Donnie said. "Be sure to listen up."

"You bet I will. Any advice?"

"Just one piece. Be sure to tell the instructor that you're left-handed."

Still feeling a little cocky for surviving another day, I decided to give Margaret a call before plunging into the homework. However, as soon as she said hello I knew something was wrong.

"Margaret," I said. "It's Beth. Are you okay?"

"Beth! I was about to call you."

"Really?"

"Yes. Frankly, I don't quite know what to say, but we need to talk."

"Okay."

"Well first, are you all right?"

"Yes, classes and homework keep me busy but I'm well. Sorry I haven't called you before now."

"That's okay. I understand."

"So tell me. What's on your mind?"

"Well Beth, I talked to Annabel this morning and she has some news about her birth parents." Margaret hesitated, waiting I suppose, for my reaction.

"Good," I said. "I'm listening."

"Annabel has found her birth mother who is a former hair stylist, and once owned her own beauty shop. However, she hasn't located her Dad. Several years after her mother gave Annabel up for adoption she married a much older man. They live ... Beth, are you sitting down?"

"Yes." I could hear the impatience in my voice. "I'm sitting down."

"Beth, they live at Lake Martin with an adult son from his previous marriage.

"Okay," I said, still not comprehending the significance of all this.

"Beth, the parents are Harold and Martha Bellinger, and their son's name is Harvey."

I don't remember if, or how, I responded to Margaret. I just remember her saying, "Beth ... Beth ... and within twenty minutes, she was standing at my front door.

Chapter 43

Would you have ever dreamed this was possible?" I asked Margaret as I handed her a cup of green tea.

"No, not in my wildest imagination."

I took a seat in the chair across from her and said, "Life can certainly be convoluted. Who knows? Maybe my stalker has experienced some trauma too."

"Are you trying to take up for him?" Margaret gave me an incredulous look.

"No. I'm just trying to understand. Have you shared this with Annabel?"

"Not yet. I was too shocked to say much of anything. Actually, I didn't want to tell her until I'd spoken with you." Margaret took another sip, put her cup down on the coffee table and waited.

"Thanks Margaret. Tell me, did Annabel tell you what she planned to do with the information she does have?"

"No, but I think she definitely wants to meet them sometime in the future."

"How do you feel about that?"

"It makes me nervous for you and for her. I think she should know the truth. On the other hand, what if she thinks I'm exaggerating just to keep her away from her birth mother? Beth, am I making any sense?"

I let some thoughts roll around in my head like marbles and then said, "Yes, of course you're making sense. Do you want me to talk to her?"

Margaret looked away and then answered. "You're already up to you neck in responsibility. I couldn't ask you to do that."

"You didn't ask. I offered. Tell you what. Why don't you think about it and then let me know if I can help?"

"That's a good idea. Look, I'm keeping you from those books." Margaret nodded toward the mound of material on my breakfast table then stood, picked up her tea, and handed it to me. "Don't quibble with this any more tonight. Just take care of your studies and try to get some rest."

As we walked to the door she turned back and said, "Beth, have you handled any guns yet?" The words had left her mouth, but she seemed to regret them.

"No. No pistols or shotguns yet. We start with the Glock tomorrow."

"Glock?" she asked, as she stepped out into the night.

I put my left hand on my hip as if drawing a gun. Margaret just shook her head and walked away.

D on't be like that female recruit who complained to her instructor saying, 'Officer, this gun makes too much noise and it smokes.'"

Stedman had our undivided attention and finished his little joke with, "'Okay. Nelson, go in and get this little lady a pistol that doesn't make noise and doesn't smoke.'"

I could feel a grin spread across my face as Stedman followed his story with a question. "So, are you ready to be serious and learn how to properly handle a firearm?"

"Sir, yes sir."

Our voices sounded too loud and probably too confident for Stedman, so he came back with, "Remember, the weapon is not what's between the hands, it's what between the ears."

Seeing that we were properly chastised, he then continued with a DEA video, followed by a lecture on firearms safety and shooting fundamentals. I paid particular attention to his instruction on stance: feet a little more than shoulder width apart. Knees bent. Shoulders forward of the hips.

I watched and tried to run this through my mind, but found it more helpful when he said, "Emulate the way a fighter stands."

"Every movement is important." Using a dummy weapon in his holster, Stedman demonstrated. "First, look at your threat and bring your Glock straight up. Then pull in your other hand, your off hand, to support it. Keep your thumb and index finger high on the tang. You will be using the first pad of your finger to press the trigger, using continuously increasing pressure. Don't squeeze. Allow the gun to fire. Push the bullet out. Relax. Become one with your weapon."

"Allow the gun to fire," he repeated. "As it settles back on center from recoil, you will reset the trigger while still looking where the front sight was. This is your follow-through."

The words and phrases began to circle in my mind, and then they sped to my stomach where they lined up like cars at the Talladega racetrack.

Stedman went on about grip, sight picture, trigger control, breathing, and recoil, warning us by saying, "Ninety-five percent of shooter error is recoil." He also stressed the importance of scanning the target, and yet keeping a three hundred and sixty degree view of the world around you. Frankly, it all sounded next to impossible for the neophyte.

"You looked pre-occupied, Davidson."

"Sir, no sir." I said. "I'm just trying to retain everything."

"Not to worry. It'll come together when you're on the range."

Some of it did. Some of it didn't. But once we appeared at the firing range just off Highway 80, I sensed that there was no turning back. For the next several days we practiced our ball and dummy drills, shot from the five, seven, fifteen and twenty-five yard lines, and had our four instructors drill us almost beyond endurance.

Finally, by the end of the week it began to take shape – even the special lessons on loading and unloading our weapons, night firing and four hours on shotgun fundamentals.

Overall, I decided the hardest qualification was learning to shoot with the less dominant hand, but Tabesha said she was more afraid of shooting from a down-and-disabled position. I tried not to even think about this one.

In spite of our first five days with firearms, it turned out to be an almost perfect weekend; all except for one phone call. Annabel called me around nine o'clock Sunday night, and our conversation went something like this:

"Hi Beth. It's Annabel." Then, after my brief greeting she launched in with, "My, you must think the entire male population is after you."

"I'm sorry," I said. "What do you mean?"

"Well, if Donnie Crawford wasn't enough, you've aligned yourself with the whole Montgomery police force, and also manufactured this elaborate case about being stalked. Women like you will stoop to almost anything for attention."

"Annabel, I ..."

She didn't let me finish, and all I heard on her end was an exasperated sigh and a click.

Chapter 44

My first inclination was to call Donnie. Surely he would sympathize, advise or just listen while I released my frustration about A-1. But I waited. After all, that's what my mom always advised me to do. "Think before you speak, or act," she would say, and usually, I was glad I'd taken her advice. I was still rehashing Annabel's lashing when the cell rang again.

"Am I calling too late?" Margaret asked. Her voice was unsettled.

"No," I said. "Of course not. It's only nine-thirty."

"Has she called you?"

"Who?"

"Annabel."

"Yes," I admitted. "We just hung up."

"What did she say?"

"Annabel thinks I fabricated the stalking story for attention."

"Yes I know. When she called me yesterday I decided to share the truth about Harvey, but I guess she's wants to meet her biological family so much she can't believe Harvey could do such a thing."

"I think you're right."

"It's easier to just block out anything negative," she continued. "Beth, I had a feeling she might call you, but I didn't expect her to accuse you of lying."

"That's okay, Margaret."

"No, it's not okay. I'm so ashamed of the way she's behaving." Margaret faltered and then said, "Beth, I hate to say it. Annabel is jealous of you. I saw how she acted around Donnie. Naturally, I realize she wants someone to care about her, but she tries too hard and probably runs guys away."

I didn't know what to say, so all I could manage was an, "I see."

"Look Beth, I've said enough, but please try not to let this worry you. Just pray for her, okay?"

"Yes. I'll remember both of you. Tell me, are you all right otherwise?"

"I am." Her voice was tentative, and then she abruptly changed the subject and said, "Oh, how did the gun thing go this week?"

"It was intense, but I've learned a lot."

"I'm proud of you, Beth."

"Thanks, Margaret. You know, I really do miss you."

"You too. I'm looking forward to our shower on the second."

"So am I, but I hope all of this is not too much for you."

"Are you kidding? It gives me something to look forward to."

Some of you are vertically challenged." Hamilton gave me a nod and smiled. I think this was a first.

"Others … Well, other folks are endowed with height and weight, yet don't know how to use it. Today we will show you how to build on your strengths. First, let's talk about degrees of resistance, and degrees of compliance enforcement."

Jeeter raised his hand, but Hamilton ignored him, and continued by saying, "In other words, think of it this way. The greater the threat, the greater the force you will use. Understand, Jeeter?"

"Sir, yes sir," Jeeter called, and even though he was standing one row away from me in the gym, I could see his shoulders relax.

"Now then," Hamilton continued, "what I'm about to say may surprise you. Remember your first two weapons of defense: your body posture and your voice."

Standing as rigid as the picture of Stonewall Jackson in my high school history book, he walked the first row, eyeing a different recruit as he spoke.

"A slow, deliberate inflection in your voice implies you

are in control." Hamilton suddenly turned and walked the other way saying, "If you maintain a confident demeanor, voice commands may be all that's necessary." Then, apparently not satisfied, Hamilton walked the second row, my row, with this decree: "It's almost like the parent-child relationship or a punishment-reward concept." He stopped in front of me and said, "Davidson, did your Dad ever just give you that look?"

"Sir, yes sir," I said, seeing my Dad's face reflected in Hamilton's scan.

"All right," Hamilton barked as he spun around and returned to his lecture position. "I have Davidson's attention, I have your attention, and you will have your suspect's attention. However, there is one exception to posture and voice control, and that is when the subject is under the influence of alcohol or drugs."

I saw several nods from the group, and then heard Massey say, "What if another person has dared the subject to behave a certain way?"

"Important point. Peer pressure does play a role, but an officer's demeanor still works to his or her advantage." Hamilton paused and I could almost see a thought bubble above his head when he said, "Here are a couple of signs of potential resistance. If your subject is scanning the environment, or is verbally evasive, watch out. These are two clues for trouble."

Trouble. The word began to jump rope in my head, but I made it stop. I had to hear and retain what came next. My life might depend on it.

Chapter 45

We took a break, then returned to the gym for hands-on defense tactics, with Hamilton and Boltwell as our primary instructors.

"Pain compliance using pressure points and joint locks will be our subject this afternoon," Boltwell smirked. "You will practice on each other, and before it's over, Hamilton and I may even join in the fray."

Well, hearing something described, and actually doing it are two different stories, so I suppose a confession is in order. After long descriptions and several demonstrations, I was paired with Oglethorpe. My instructions were to encircle Oglethorpe's neck from the rear and then, using my fingertips, apply upward pressure to the sides of his neck.

It worked. Oglethorpe scowled, and before I could count to three, he gave the "stop it" signal by a quick clap of his hands.

Empowerment. Piece of cake. Self assurance. Not for long.

Boltwell swooped down on me from behind, and within seconds I was on the ground pleading for mercy.

I was not looking forward to the next session: strategic kicks and baton strikes. However, when Hamilton offered special protective shields for these maneuvers, I did feel a measure of relief.

My turn for a baton strike didn't come until mid afternoon. Standing as tall and confident as possible, I tried to imagine myself at bat. I backspaced to a time in seventh grade when, mad at being the last one chosen for the team, I struck the ball with all the force I could muster.

Of course, it will probably never happen again, but on that beautiful spring day, I hit a home run and my teammates applauded. This time I drew the baton back, swung, and only heard a muffled thud.

"A good lick, Davidson." I looked up into Hamilton's face and realized he knew I needed some encouragement.

Defensive tactics continued for the rest of the week, and with practice, we all seemed to develop more confidence. In fact, when Donnie called on Friday afternoon I said "Honey, I got Oglethorpe between the mastoid and the mandible, and exerted pressure to the hypoglossal, glossopharyngeal and vagus nerves."

Donnie chuckled and then said, "Tell me. How long did you work on those pronunciations?"

"More than a minute," I shot back. "Maybe I'm just trying to cover my lack of finesse with handcuffing."

"Oh?"

"Yeah." I sighed into the cell. "I don't understand the strong and weak side approach, or how to effect the kneeling and prone position."

"You'll get it," Donnie said .

"Are you sure?"

"Yes, sweetheart. You will grasp it in time."

Time. Somehow, as we hung up, the word seemed to flood my mind, and one part of me wanted to erect a dam to hold time back. I needed more hours for study, tests, and wedding plans.

However, another part of me wanted to skip all of this fuss and just be married and settled into my home with Donnie. Everything would be perfect then. Well, maybe not perfect, but with fewer problems and questions. Or would it?

I checked the time, caught myself, and thought. *I'm a prisoner of time, with only one and an half hours before Donnie arrives with our snack supper.*

But somehow, I made good use of the opportunity, and after we ate Donnie reviewed those handcuff positions with me. Before leaving, he even suggested we start reading the Bible together. When I agreed, he turned to Matthew 6: 25-34.

Although we both knew those verses well, they provided a fresh heart application, especially verse 34 when Jesus said, *"Therefore do not worry about tomorrow, for tomorrow will worry about itself. Each day has enough trouble of its own."*

Little did I know.

Chapter 46

Saturday morning's sunshine held party promises; promises until I spied Ballinger's tightly-folded note protruding from the philodendron. In fact, I probably wouldn't have seen it had I not gone outside to water the plant.

The note read, "You think you're smart, don't you? Your fancy friend in the police department tells me I should stop seeing you. Well, I won't be leaving more notes at your apartment. I have other options. Harvey."

My eyes combed the parking lot again, but I knew it was far too late. After all, Donnie had left around eleven Friday night, and it was now ten in the morning. Bellinger probably dropped the note off sometime after midnight. Of course, friends at the apartment had promised to look out for him, but who is up from one until six in the morning watching for a stalker?

Well, at least I had one more piece of evidence to share with DV. I dropped the note beside my stalking journal, and headed to the kitchen for coffee.

Yes, coffee. Somehow, my weird hours and constant study had driven me to caffeine. Dad would be happy. I had no sooner flipped the switch on the coffeemaker when the cell rang.

"Good morning, Beth."

"Hi Shannon. I hear you're busy planning a party."

"That's right. You coming?"

"You bet. What time should I be there?"

"Come about one-thirty so we can take some pictures before your guests start arriving."

"Okay," I said, "And thanks for doing all of this, friend."

"Margaret's done a lot too, you know. It's been fun working with her. Remember, tell Donnie he can appear around four and help take the loot home."

I can't believe it," Donnie said later. "We actually need this truck. I didn't know you had so many friends."

"Well," I explained. "There are twelve gals in our Sunday school class, and then I have those friends from Honda and some from high school. Tabesha came too."

"We're both blessed," Donnie sighed, as he balanced several boxes and headed for Shannon's door. I could tell he wanted me to count our blessings rather than focus on our mutual enemy.

"Be careful now," Shannon cautioned. "You have one or two breakables in that load."

I stayed behind to help Margaret and Shannon pick up, while Cindy and Aunt Gertrude pitched in with the dishes. By five o'clock Shannon's apartment was almost back to normal, and our hostesses even packed a container of leftovers for our supper.

Donald and Uncle Charlie were waiting back at Donnie's apartment, so they helped us unload. After our meal, Cindy Crawford surprised me my saying that she and Donald wanted to offer help for our wedding.

"I'm not a caterer of course, but maybe I could assist with whatever refreshments you might like for the reception."

"Are you serious?"

"Of course. You and Donnie are both so busy, we'd love to help in any way we can."

I thought about this sweet mother-in-law to be. She had said nothing about my not having a mother, but was just stepping into a much needed role.

"What about the bride's cake?" Donnie teased. "I think Beth might go for that."

"Tell you what," Mr. Crawford joined in, putting one arm around my shoulder. "You pick and I'll pay. Isn't that what a good Dad is supposed to do?"

Mr. Crawford looked at me with such acceptance that I just smiled and said, "How could I possibly turn down an offer like that?"

Later, while saying our goodbyes, Cindy pulled me aside and confided, "These men have no idea about what goes into even a small wedding reception, but we two girls can pull if off, don't you think?"

As I gave Cindy a hug, I hoped she could feel my gratitude and love.

Jumping back into a police officer mindset wasn't easy. The next week was consumed with more patrol techniques, officer/violator contact, traffic control, offense and accident reports and more exams.

On top of that, we continued with physical training, officer survival and even a much needed session on stress management. By the weekend, I found myself thinking like my former co-workers at Honda: "Thank God It's Friday."

Okay. We're all set," Donnie said when he phoned Friday afternoon. "Red's Little School House will deliver the barbecue and stuff at six o'clock tomorrow night. All we need to do is bring our gift and show up."

"Perfect! But Donnie, I still feel guilty."

"For what?"

"For making you plan all the arrangements." I plopped on the sofa, resting my chin in my hand.

"No. Like I said, it only took a phone call. You bought our gift, and I think Ryan is gonna love that Foreman's grill."

"Shannon too. A gal welcomes any kitchen help she can get."

"Is that a hint?"

"Absolutely," I tossed back. "Look, I'd better decorate the clubhouse tonight if Gladys says it's okay."

"I understand," Donnie said. "Wish I could help you. Are you still planning a cowboy theme?"

"Yeah. Party City had some colorful bandanas and other western motif. I'll also add some fall decorations to match the color scheme."

"Good for you. Shannon will be impressed."

"Well," I said. "Maybe a little of her skill is rubbing off on me."

"I should say so," Donnie encouraged, "but call me if you need anything."

As far as I could tell, our barbecue bridal shower for Shannon and Ryan was a success. Naturally, I knew most of Shannon's friends, but we both enjoyed meeting Ryan's buddies, and some of the guys and gals who would be in the wedding party.

"All of this wedding talk is making me anxious for my bride," Donnie said as he helped me clean up Saturday night.

"Yeah, it's getting close," I agreed. "Do you think you'll get cold feet at Shannon and Ryan's wedding next week?" Before he could answer I added, "You still have time to back out, you know."

As Donnie lifted the last trash can, he turned and winked at me saying, "Not on your life, sweetheart. I'd never let you get away."

I wanted to offer some help to Shannon during those few days before her wedding, maybe even create some more memories.

Wishful thinking.

I should have known our Academy training wouldn't leave a spare minute. In fact, I had to take my Tuesday lunch break just to rush by Penolia's for a final fitting of my muted rust color bridesmaid dress.

I admired the dress again on Friday, as I scooted in for our afternoon session: a talk from Corporal Tatum entitled *Preserving the Crime Scene.*

So instead of thinking about a romantic late-October wedding, I was forced to concentrate on surveying and securing all evidence in a murder, or potential murder scenario.

I eyeballed Corporal Tatum, an attractive and deeply-tanned woman who stood no more than five feet four, but whose pixie-cut dark hair and dark eyes seemed to say she could handle anything thrown her way. In fact, in spite of her beauty, she looked like she rarely had time for anything except blood and ... well, you get the picture.

"You will need to think fast as you call for assistance and back-up," Corporal Tatum admonished. "Here is a list of what to do. Jot it down."

I poised my pen on the notebook, and scribbled as she spoke.

217

1. *Assess victim's needs and call for back-up.*
2. *Administer emergency aid and notify medical person-nel.*
3. *Survey and secure the scene, and be aware of any escalating situations.*
4. *Note all persons present, and apply communication and any necessary defensive skills.*
5. *Document all statements of victims and suspects.*

On and on it went, as Tatum described how to map the crime scene into the hot, warm and cold areas. How to observe the evidence, check for weapons, chemicals or hazardous material, create a crime scene log, ask the right questions, maintain safety, take appropriate photos.

It occurred to me to check her left hand. Yes, she wore a wide gold band on her ring finger.

How could anyone learn to do all of this? I asked myself. *Better yet, how could a woman manage this intense life-style and still maintain any home life?*

"Note the time, weather conditions, any odd circum-stances or possible changes to the scene," Tatum contin-ued. "In other words, take extensive notes, because you will need to transfer all of this information to the investiga-tive officers, including your departure time."

Departure time. I wondered if our departure time was near. No, Corporal Tatum had a CD to share. The CD included an actual area crime scene, complete with pictures of an ax-handle beating and a slit throat.

I felt nausea rising in mine, but pretended all was well as I rubbed my fingers together. When Boltwell turned and asked me what was wrong, I frowned and said, "Writer's cramp."

I wondered if he could see inside my brain.

Chapter 47

I'd rather be judged by twelve than carried by six,"
Stedman stated. "Who said that?"

Several of us shook our heads as we waited. I didn't
know the author, but it didn't take a genius to understand.
It's far better to be tried by a jury than to be transported
by pallbearers.

With a satisfied sneer on his face, Stedman continued.
"We all say it. Amen? Here's another one. 'I lace my boots
in the morning and plan to unlace them at night.'"

"Sir," Oglethorpe interjected. "Better you than the
coroner, right?"

"Right. Now listen up. You may get chill bumps when
you push an old lady's car from a busy intersection, but
you'll experience more than chill bumps when you apprehend a felon with a dangerous weapon. Okay, Oglethorpe,
you want to share your brilliance. What are the typical
sensations we feel in an emergency?"

"Audio exclusion, sir."

"Yes, diminished hearing. I should have guessed you'd
choose that one. What else?"

Stedman's eyes scanned the room, so I raised my hand.
When he nodded to me I said, "Dry mouth and accelerated
breathing, sir."

"Good. What else?"

Massey caught his attention and called, "Sweating, sir.
Also tunnel vision and loss of fine motor skills."

"Excellent, but there's two more. Let's hear it from you,
Jeeter."

Jeeter looked lost in thought, but then offered, "Blood
pressure and ..." He stopped and looked at Tabesha who

219

held two fingers to her wrist. Then he said, "Pulse rate, sir."

"Well, I had to drag it out of you. When a person is stressed, all these sensations will hit, and hit hard." Stedman stopped, turned to the wall and then back to us. "Everything you experience here in the Academy is for a purpose. For example, why do you think we put a wrist band on your arm when you first arrived? Which arm is it on?"

"Our strong arm," Humphrey called.

"Good. You're catching on, Humphrey. I thought you'd never make it. While I have your attention, give me the quote of the week, Humphrey."

"The quote is, 'In order to be walked on, you have to be lying down.' Brian Weir, sir."

"Are you lying down, Humphrey?"

"Not any more, sir."

"All right. Enough of the pep talk. Now, who wants to be tasered first?"

No one moved. I didn't even hear a cough.

I tried to imagine myself in another place: Shannon's wedding. Yes, I was walking down the aisle of Eastlake Baptist Church. And, although we hadn't had rehearsal yet, a certain groomsman stood at the front watching me.

"Oglethorpe, come to the front."

Oglethorpe glowered as he swaggered toward Stedman, trying to appear nonchalant. I watched his eyes flash to the ceiling and then the floor. Was his armor slipping?

"What kind of inward fermentation should I experience?" Oglethorpe asked.

Stedman hurled back, "What?"

"How is this taser going to feel?"

"Like hell, man. Are you ready?"

Stedman pulled and pointed the taser, and before I could take a breath, Oglethorpe's knees buckled and he crumbled to the ground.

"Wow!" Jeeter ejected.

"Thanks for volunteering to be next, Jeeter."

Everyone waited a moment as Oglethorpe came to. His face was colorless, and when he struggled to his feet, we didn't hear any fifty dollar words; just an appreciative acknowledgement for the gift of life.

"What did it feel like, man?" Jeeter wanted to know.

"Well," Oglethorpe said. "Have you ever stuck your finger in a 220 socket?"

Shannon didn't have to find a substitute bridesmaid for Saturday. I survived the taser, and as I journeyed down the aisle to Donnie, I counted off the days to our wedding.

Two weeks later ...

Hi, Beth," Dad said when he phoned from work Friday afternoon. "Have you and Donnie made any plans for Thanksgiving?" Before I could answer he continued with, "If not, I'd like to come down and take you out for lunch."

"That sounds great, Dad."

"In fact," Dad continued, "I have an appointment with someone on Wednesday afternoon and could stay overnight if you're not busy."

I turned to the academy schedule to confirm what I already knew. We were off from mid-afternoon Wednesday through the weekend.

"Dad, I'd like that."

"Good," he said. "Besides, I want to hear more about your wedding plans – see if I might still help."

"Thanks, Dad. I ..."

"Fine. I'll call from Nichol's office so you'll know when to expect me. Bye."

As we hung up, my mind remained fixated on Nichols. Wasn't he the guy who notified Dad about the life insurance attempt? Well, this appointment was probably totally unrelated, or was it?

I poured my coffee, but even after adding the sugar and cream, it tasted bitter; maybe like brewed pencil shavings.

On Monday morning Boltwell's first words were, "Give me the quote of the week, Jeeter."

"Sir, the quote of the week is 'Success is the ability to go from one failure to another with no loss of enthusiasm.' Sir Winston Churchill, sir."

Boltwell beamed.

"Well, we are about to deal with those jokers who know little but defeat; men and women involved with drugs, meth, and prostitution. We will also be amplifying what you've already learned regarding day and night building searches. It should be a good week."

Good week? I chewed on that thought for a moment, and then remembered this was a three day work week before Thanksgiving. Maybe I could make it after all.

My Tuesday mail included a yellow envelop with no return address. Opening it, I immediately spotted the name and felt relief. Margaret's Thanksgiving card included a note. It read: "Blessings to you, friend. Call me. I have some news."

It's always good to hear Margaret's voice, but old friends are good at reading moods, and I seemed to pick up on Margaret's immediately. After a brief chat she said, "Annabel called last night." She paused. "Beth, she plans to spend Thanksgiving with the Bellingers. Well, I just thought you should know."

Chapter 48

After exercise on Tuesday night, I felt a sudden urge to call Mrs. Ryan Jamison. When Shannon heard my voice she exclaimed, "Beth, I've meant to call you for two days."

"That's okay," I said. "How was your Caribbean cruise?"

"Wonderful! The websites don't do it justice. We just got back Sunday. Are you okay?"

"Yes," I said. "Just busy. Graduation is a week away."

"What? I can't believe it. May we come?"

"If you want to. No ... I take that back. You'd better be there."

"Wouldn't miss it for the world. Say, your other big day is coming up too. We checked the dress, and unless you're worried about it, I don't think it needs a cleaning. I only wore it those two hours."

"It'll be fine, Shannon. Are you sure you want me to wear it?"

"Look, I don't have a sister except you. Ryan and I will get it to you soon."

I planned to work on our wedding invitations over the Thanksgiving holidays, but one event changed everything.

It happened late Wednesday afternoon during a heavy thunderstorm. I had just put a pecan pie in the oven, when a local radio station announced hazardous weather conditions, with ten inches of rain in the past five hours.

Dad called around two-fifteen to say he was on his way. I almost offered a word of caution, but then decided he wouldn't appreciate daughter intrusion. After all, Dad was

the Alfa agent. He dealt with weather and accident investi-
gations all the time.

Looking back, I wonder if speaking up might have
made a difference. Only God knows. However, as the rain
increased and the clock hand moved past three, I began
to worry. The drive from Alfa to my apartment should only
take fifteen minutes.

Thinking about Dad's old cliché, misery loves company,
I clicked the TV remote. Don Atwood, Channel 12's local
weatherman, was making wide gestures with his hands,
and spoke with an almost breathless anticipation of a
second Noah's flood.

Reporters from throughout the city shared live and
blotchy scenes of flooded streets, and drainage ditches
unable to handle the deluge. Drivers were cautioned to
avoid low-lying areas, since a mere two feet of water could
lift and move a car. Six to ten inches of rushing water
might knock a man off his feet.

Putting the remote down, I walked to the window. No
sign of Dad. Just as I started to pray, the phone rang.
It was Margaret. She wanted to know if I was all right,
and then rehashed Annabel's plans for visiting her birth
parents over Thanksgiving.

I wondered if Harvey would be there but didn't ask. I
had no sooner closed the cell when it rang again, and I
answered on the first ring.

"Beth, I'm here with your Dad." Donnie was trying to
sound confident, but I heard an edge in his voice.

"Where are you?" I demanded.

"We're about five minutes from your place. Beth, everything's okay."

"What? What do you mean?"

"Your Dad got trapped in a flooded area east of here
and ..."

"But ... Where were you? You cover the River Region."

"Right, but on my way to work I got the Double Zero and
headed over."

"Double Zero? Oh, no. What happened to Dad?"

"Here," Donnie said. "I'll let you talk to him."

Dad came on, and except for his usual cliché he sounded
like a stranger.

"Beth, I have some good news and some bad news."

Not caring to play games, I said, "Let's hear it, Dad."

"The good news is your ole Dad is alive."

"Yes, I hear you. Thank God."

"But ... the bad news is I lost the Camaro."

"Lost the Camaro? What happened?"

Silence ... and then, "I'll tell you when we get there. In fact, we're turning on Carmichael now."

Beth!" Dad sputtered my name as he came through the door. His face was ashen, and his navy blue suit soaked. Donnie stood behind him, concern stamped on his face, his clothes also dripping.

"Dad," I said. "Are you all right?"

I motioned to the nearest chair, but he shook his head and just stared at me.

"Yes ... Yes, I am."

"What happened?"

"I tried to make it. The water looked less than a foot high, but I was wrong."

"I see," I said, feeling a minor role reversal. "I'm just thankful you're okay."

"Me too." Dad turned to Donnie and said, "You need to get back to work."

"I'll go in a minute."

Donnie glanced at me, so I agreed. "Dad's right. We'll be fine now."

"Are you sure?" I could almost see a debate going on in Donnie's head as he concurred, and headed for the door saying, "Okay. I'll call you later."

I wondered how Donnie would handle his wet clothes, but didn't mention it. Surely he had a plan. As for Dad, I soon learned he had put his small carry-on and brief-case in the passenger seat of the Camaro, and was able, with Donnie's help, to retrieve them just before the current sweep the car away.

Thankfully, his personal items like credit cards were in his suit pocket, but car registration papers and other documents were gone.

Tackling the immediate need first, I found Dad my old brown bathrobe, and while most of his clothes ran through the dryer, he shared the rest of the story.

"Well, when I left Nichol's office and reached that next intersection on McGhee, a police officer was about to set up a road block," Dad said. "As you know, that area is quite low, so I did slow down. However, when the water didn't appear high, I decided to chance it."

I shook my head as I pictured the spot, but waited for Dad to continue.

"Big mistake, because there's a significant dip near that service station, and the drainage ditch couldn't handle it. Before I knew it, the Camaro was afloat like a leaf."

"What happened then?"

"Well I felt helpless. First, I tried to open the door. That didn't work, of course. Then I looked up and saw the officer wading toward me. It was like watching a movie in slow motion. By this time, the current was pushing me toward the mall parking lot. I don't know how many minutes passed, but the next thing I knew, I was hung up on some sort of telephone relay station, and the cop motioned for me to shield my head as he hit the top of the sun roof with his baton."

When Dad said this my hands flew to my head as I tried to picture the scene.

"Then, almost at that moment," Dad continued, "I saw Don on the other side. As the sun roof shattered, he reached in and I somehow handed him the briefcase and carry-on. It's all kind of hazy now."

"Yes ... I'm sure it is, Dad."

Just then, the dryer sounded a familiar ding, so I stood and headed for the laundry room. As I walked away from Dad, a scene from sixteen years ago began to buoy its way into my head.

Chapter 49

Later in the afternoon, Dad made some calls regarding his Camaro, and arranged for a rental car until he could decide what to do. Then during supper, Donnie phoned to suggest we join his family for Thanksgiving lunch.

With everything going on, Dad agreed, and as the two of us lingered over dessert Wednesday night, I noticed the tight lines just above his nose began to relax.

"Your pie is delicious," Dad sighed. "Tastes just like your Mom's, in fact."

"Really?" I let the words sink in. Dad rarely mentioned Mom anymore. I watched as he took another bite. His eyes explored the darkness through the breakfast room window. After a long pause he spoke again.

"Yes, you remind me so much of your mom, Beth."

"I do? Well, I will take that as a compliment."

Silence sat between us again. In fact, I could even hear the ticking of the clock in the next room. I wondered if I should ask the question tumbling in my mind, but then Dad spoke.

"Beth, your Mom and I had an idyllic marriage."

"Yes," I said. "I know."

"It's been so hard to talk about her and ..."

I smoothed the ragged edges of the placemats; mats Mother had made years before.

"Your Mom was the sort who never knew a stranger but I find it hard to meet new people and to relate. Frankly, I have to push myself."

"You've done well with Alfa, Dad."

"Maybe so, but the credit goes to your mom, and a few

strong company mentors like Nichols. By the way, Nichols asked about you, and I told him you were working with the police department concerning that Bellinger guy. I believe you said there is no new evidence regarding any life insurance."

I nodded and then said, "Dad, something else is on my mind. Something that happened years ago."

He looked startled, so I added, "It's not about Mom."

"Well ... okay. What is it?"

I took a deep breath and said, "Dad, when I was about six years old you took me on a company picnic and–"

"Beth," Dad stopped me. He shook his head and dropped his napkin beside his plate. It lay there, looking like the dead Eurasian dove Donnie and I once spotted during a jog. "Look, I've wanted to talk to you about this for a long time, but it's painful."

"Painful? Why? I'm the one who–"

"Yes ... well, after what happened today, maybe I'm beginning to grasp how horrible that experience was for you. You probably thought I forgot you or didn't care."

"Right on both counts," I affirmed, pushing my chair back a bit.

Dad shook his head and replied, "I have no excuse."

I glared at him, still trying to comprehend a father's neglect.

"Believe me," he said. "The event has plagued me for years."

"How so?" I crossed my arms as if to shield myself from more rejection.

"Your mom and I had just settled into this new role with Alfa, so I had almost zero experience and even less confidence. When you announced you could swim, I believed you."

"Those two statements don't compute!" I could feel my blood pressure rising. My mouth was dry.

"I know, but I did it because I believed you could swim, and at that moment, my boss, Joe Nichols, asked me a critical question. Beth, there is no excuse. I was temporarily distracted."

Dad's eyes drifted toward the window as if probing the darkness again, then he turned back to face me.

"Beth, by the time I'd answered his inquiry, I turned and realized you were in trouble. I suppose Nichols felt partly to blame, because he jumped in before I could, and that's the story."

"But couldn't you have talked to me afterwards? Said something?"

"Yes ... But I rationalized by telling myself you were okay. I was wrong."

Dad's face looked more contorted than it had hours earlier, when he had stood in my doorway soaking wet.

There was something about his features and present predicament that began to soften me so, hardly thinking about it, I reached for his hand. For a moment, he just inspected our hands, but then he took his thumb and began to slowly rub it back and forth across my index finger. A sudden tenderness invaded his eyes, and I began to feel a bond with Dad for the first time.

Our Thanksgiving lunch with Donnie's family seemed to strengthen the bond. In fact, after the meal the five of us discussed wedding plans almost as enthusiastically as men discuss football.

At least, that's what Donald Crawford said. When Cindy reiterated her offer to make party sandwiches, Dad agreed, but said all other pick-up foods were on him, and he also wanted to pay the photographer and any other expenses.

Suddenly, Mr. Crawford looked at me and winked. Then, he said, "Beth, you may not be planning a groom's cake, but if you are, may I have the honor?"

"Of course," I said. "As long as it's chocolate. Right, Donnie?"

"Right. With a crocodile on top."

"What's this?" Cindy asked.

Donnie grinned at me, so I just said, "It's a joke. He'll explain later."

On Friday, Dad arranged to keep the rental car and later return it to a Birmingham office. Part of me wanted him to stay, but I knew the paper work following the accident would keep him involved for the remainder of the weekend.

Dad left around ten-thirty that morning, but his first real bear hug lingered for hours.

After changing the sheets in the guestroom and straightening up the apartment, I started on the wedding invitations. When I had about two dozen behind me, I decided to give Margaret a call.

"Hi there," I began. "It's Beth."

"I know your voice girl," Margaret teased. "Did you have a nice Thanksgiving?"

"We did," I said, wondering how I could ever explain what had happened, yet knew we'd get to it soon enough. "What about you? I know you missed Annabel."

"Yes, but she's on her way home this afternoon."

"Really? I thought she planned to stay several days."

"Well, she changed her mind." Margaret paused and then said, "Annabel and I only talked for a minute, but just from the tone of her voice, I could tell she had some concerns about Harvey.

"Oh?"

"Yes ... Well, she didn't say much. I'm reading between the lines. Guess I'd better let her tell me what she wants and not ask too many questions. Beth ... I have a feeling this family situation is going to take time, and it could get complicated."

"Yes," I said. "It could become very complicated."

Chapter 50

Saturday morning seemed bright with promise, especially after Dad called to say all looked well with his insurance coverage. When I asked if he planned to purchase another Camaro he said, "No, I don't think so. After all, I'm not exactly a young man anymore."

"You look great to me," I said. "But whatever you choose, be sure you have wheels before the wedding. You are going to give me away, aren't you?"

"I could never give you away," Dad countered. "Let's just say I'll agree to this marriage to Donnie. He's a great guy, Beth."

"Thanks Dad. That's all I need to hear."

"Beth, there is one more thing I want to say."

"What's that?"

"Well, I'm going to try to communicate with you more."

"Really?"

"Yes, I used to adhere to the slogan *silence is golden.* Now I know it's not."

"That's right." I struggled with my thoughts but then heard myself say, "When I was little, I remember you giving me that line when I traipsed through the house making noise."

I could have said more. I could have said *his* years of silence had nearly killed me, yet what would that accomplish?

The next words out of my mouth were, "I love you, Dad."

"I love you too, Beth."

I spent the rest of the morning writing more wedding invitations and thank-you notes. By early afternoon, the

231

temperature was sixty-five degrees so I decided to take a drive.

When I first stepped outside, the stray lab I had named Buster was sniffing the sidewalk, so I stopped to speak and scratch him behind the ear. Recognizing my scent, he rolled over in submission, so I kneeled to admire his gorgeous red coat and offer more serious attention.

Of course, by this time I needed to wash my hands, so I hurried back inside before heading for the Honda.

It's seldom that I hit the road without deciding where to go, but today was different. For one thing, Donnie was filling in for another officer, so we hadn't made plans for Saturday night.

I'd already read the Academy homework material, so this felt like a free day; maybe my last one before graduation and the wedding.

I pulled out on Carmichael and then turned north on the by-pass. For a moment, I thought about going up toward Wetumpka and Redland Road, but all at once, I felt an urge to revisit Lagoon Park, and see Pete Peterson Lodge where Donnie and I had our first date.

After putting my blinker on and making a quick lane change, I turned into Lagoon Park, passing the ballpark on my right, and then a golf course. Several cars sat in both parking lots, and I remembered how these family settings had put me at ease that day with Donnie.

Continuing down to a dead-end, I made a right turn on Gunter Park, and began to enjoy the meandering drive to the entrance. Soon I spotted the sign for the lodge, and hung a sharp right. I noticed again how the turn was so sharp that you could look to your right and trace your path, so I let my eyes comb the road. No one appeared to be following me.

Moments later, I approached the sign: *No Fishing Except for Approved Special Events* and I smiled, remembering Donnie's thoughtfulness when he planned our special fishing event months before.

The road dipped then as I spied the ponds and picnic areas to my left. Taking the circular drive into the lodge area, I parked in almost the same spot Donnie had chosen; between the lodge and the first picnic station.

For a moment, I just sat, letting my mind drift back to that late spring day. Then I reasoned that I had come this far, why not get out and re-trace our walk, Donnie's fishing instructions, and his attempts to put me at ease?

Stepping out of the Honda, I locked the doors, put the cell in my pocket, and headed for the water. After no more than three or four steps I detected movement above me, and looked up just in time to spot an eagle soaring only about twenty feet overhead.

His magnificent head and wing span amazed me, as I considered how few eagles were seen in our state. Then, to my surprise, a second one followed close behind, and I remembered that eagles often hunt or fish in pairs.

Just like Donnie and me, I mused. Maybe I'd call state Wildlife Management later. Let them know about my sightings.

Strolling on, I passed the first picnic area and spotted the table where Donnie, Lopez and I had sat to discuss my stalker. I also thought about how the two of them later appeared at the river tunnel to protect me.

Now, deep in thought, I ambled to the left and headed up the slope to the pond where Donnie and I had fished. When I reached the top, I focused on the wooded area and began to look for an eagles' eyrie hidden somewhere within the dense branches. I didn't see any tight arrangement of sticks in the trees, but I suddenly felt tightness in my chest, a gut instinct that something or someone was watching me.

Just as I turned back toward the pond and the parking area, I saw another car pulling in beside mine. A black Honda. I waited, my feet frozen to the ground. The driver's door opened and he stood, his right hand shielding his eyes, as he peered in my direction.

My hand flew to the bulge in my pocket, and I gave the 911 dispatcher my name, location, and a one sentence description of the scene.

Now less than a Frisbee throw away, Bellinger was moving toward me. He was wearing a faded red Polo shirt and kakis. His straw-colored hair was slightly parted, and combed forward to cover a bald spot. As he drew closer, I spied a fake Rolex watch on his left wrist. At least, I called it a fake to match the rest of him.

I could run, but knew I couldn't make it to my Honda, and no matter which direction I took, he would catch up. I could scream, but the nearest neighborhood was a half mile away. No one could hear me.

I could wave at passing cars in the distance, but the highway stretched out a good mile east of me. All speeding cars, intent on their own mission.

Think, Beth. Ignore the dry mouth. Control your breathing. Prepare to use what you've learned. Pray. Think.

Bellinger had passed the pond now, and was moving up the incline. The woods were behind me. I would not let him take me there. No way. I took a step forward, and planted my feet in the earth, waiting.

"Good afternoon."

As he spoke, Harvey Bellinger made a gesture almost like someone tipping a hat. His voice, however, was tense, coiled like a snake ready to strike. He stood no more than ten feet away.

"Good afternoon." My voice sounded foreign, but firm.

"You are out enjoying this weather, I see." His eyes darted about, probing the setting.

"Yes." I cleared my throat. "It's beautiful."

"Not as beautiful as you."

I forced a fake smile and said, "Thank you."

"Well, at least you're talking to me. I suppose that's some progress."

I put my hands on my hips and said, "What do you want?"

Bellinger shook his head. "I only want the chance to get to know you better. That's all." He held his palms up, as if to show me he was harmless, and then took a step forward.

"Look," I said. "I'm flattered, but I have a boyfriend. In fact, we're engaged."

This was not the information he wanted, yet it was too late to take it back. Bellinger lunged forward, grabbed my wrist and pulled me toward him. As I strained, he stopped for a moment then jerked again.

I stumbled down the incline, but once I had secure footing, I remembered to turn my arm like a page in a book. As expected, this quick movement threw him off balance long enough for me to run a few steps back toward the car.

At this point however, time and space were in his favor. I'd covered no more than a yard or two when his arms quickly encircled my waist. Was this it? No. I wouldn't give up this easily. Raising both arms in the air, I reached behind me, grabbed his ears and dropped my weight all in one swift movement. He tumbled to the ground to my left, and my knee rocked forward into his jaw.

Surprise, and maybe some mild pain registered on Bellinger's face after the fall. Ugly red veins threaded the whites of his eyes, and as he shifted his legs, I tightened the knee hold. When he tried to roll, I tightened again.

How long could this last? On the self-defense video, the actors quickly moved from one tactic to another.

Now, Bellinger's face twitched and his upper teeth bit into his bottom lip. Afraid he might try something; I made a "V" with my index and middle finger, and shoved the bottom of the V on either side his nose, pushing upward, my fingers curled like claws over his two eyes.

He didn't resist. I waited. Waited, that is, until he took a sudden breath and spat on my hand. Instinctively, I raised my palm and heard him say, "You think you're something, don't you? But I feel you shaking."

"You're right." I said. "There's no shame in shaking. The shame is seeing someone throw away a career."

"Big talk from a girl fighting for survival."

"Maybe ... But now that I have you on the ground, I'm the counselor, and I suggest you stop looking back on your past and gazing around for someone to exploit. It's time you took a new direction."

Bellinger flinched but I went on. "Listen. In your last note you said something about options. Well, believe me, if this behavior doesn't stop, my only option will be to pursue criminal charges."

When I finished my speech (a speech I didn't know I had in me) Bellinger's eyebrows were corrugated, but his eyes remained closed. His mouth too. In fact, he was still silent when the black and white rolled down the hill and into the Pete Peterson parking lot.

I kept my grip on Bellinger, but did raise my right hand as if to signal our location. There was no need. Two officers practically flew in our direction, one with his Glock in the air.

While waiting, I took several quick breaths. Breaths to convince myself that I was still alive. Moments later, as I continued to help hold him during the arrest, I tried to keep the mental and physical exhaustion at bay. After all, this was my first real handcuffing, and I needed to know I could do it.

While the officers informed Bellinger of his upcoming trip to the station, and escorted him to the police car, my stalker still had no more words for me. Only a look of surprise, mixed with something else I still can't define.

I'm sure my face registered relief and extreme fatigue. At least, that's what my rearview mirror told me about five minutes later when I flopped in the Honda.

The park's beauty was lost to me now because late-afternoon clouds were floating in, concealing the sun. As the engine roared to life, and I began to complete the circle out of the parking lot, I gazed up over the pond again, hoping to see the eagles.

They were nowhere in sight. And, although I took my time pulling away, I had no delusions of locating their secret home.

As I climbed the hill leaving the lodge, I watched as a familiar vehicle made its way down the hill, and sped towards me as if on a mission. Just before we met, almost head-on, the driver stopped, opened the door and raced toward me.

It didn't take me long to open my door and fall into Donnie's arms. He held me in the tightest embrace I can ever recall, and then I pulled back to study his face.

Donnie said, "Kathy's handling dispatch today. Remember? You met her here at the Lagoon Park barbecue."

"Yes, I remember."

"Anyway, after declaring a 10-33, she phoned me. Beth, I came as quickly as I could, but see you already have everything under control."

"I do?"

"You do." Donnie smiled, and at that moment, I realized that Beth Davidson was beginning to learn how to manage a few things on her own.

Somewhere I've read that human emotions are fickle, and Sunday afternoon was a perfect example. After enjoying another lunch with Donnie's family, he took me home, sat me down on the sofa and said, "Beth, I'm going to be honest with you. The more I think about something, the more alarm I feel. Look. Maybe we're making a mistake."

"What?" I rubbed Donnie's engagement ring with the thumb of my right hand. I also tried to brace myself. He looked toward the door, and I wondered if he wanted to bolt, to escape the apartment and escape from me. I waited.

"Beth," he started again. "You've become the most important person in the world to me, and I don't want to lose you."

"I see," I said. Relief flooded somewhere inside me, and I wondered if Donnie noticed.

"Beth, I'm being blunt. You could have been killed yesterday."

"I realize that, Donnie."

"Well, don't you see? Here we are, trying to start life together and ..." A thin line etched its way across Donnie's forehead.

"Donnie, are you afraid?"

"Yes," he flared. "Look, for a couple of years now, I haven't worried so much about my own life, but the more I think about yesterday the more ..." Donnie's voice trailed off.

"Donnie," I said. "What did you tell me less than three month ago?"

He shook his head so I continued. "You reminded me how our lives are never totally safe. You said we don't even know what is going to happen within the next minute."

"Yes ..." Donnie hesitated, "But this is different."

"How?" I persisted. "How is it different?"

"Well, when I first told you about the Police Academy, we weren't in love like we are now."

"What does that have to do with it? Listen, do you believe God brought us together?"

"Yes, I do, but ..."

"And don't we both believe He has called us into this profession?"

"Yes, I think so."

"Well, if we're gonna trust Him with our love, we've got to trust Him with our lives. Right?" I moistened my parched lips, not sure I was handling this well.

Donnie nodded, and then took my hand. He said, "Beth, I've always known I wanted to settle down, get married and have a family someday. Do you really think we can have a normal family with both of us in law enforcement?"

"Normal? What's normal?" I fired back, and as I said this, I watched a grin creep up to his face.

"Listen. It's my turn to remind you of something you read to me a while back." I took a deep breath and continued, "It comes straight from headquarters. Therefore do not worry about tomorrow, for tomorrow will worry about itself. Each day has enough trouble of its own.'"

Donnie shrugged but added, "But what if I can't handle your staying in this field?"

"Then I'll leave, and concentrate on our having a little Donnie."

"You will?"

"Yes!" I nodded with all the resolve in me, and then I threw both arms around my fiancé. I held him, until he finally pulled back long enough to replace the hug with a one-of-a kind Donnie kiss.

Chapter 51

Shannon called me around eight o'clock Sunday night to say that she wanted to run the wedding dress over. Naturally, I didn't protest. After all, we both knew I might need to make some minor adjustments, decide on jewelry, or plan accessories.

After a round of female chit-chat, I told Shannon about the Lagoon Park incident, with as little fanfare as possible. I didn't want to portray myself as some kind of hero.

When Shannon asked me about the maneuver I used on Bellinger, I suggested she take a self-defense course, or borrow Donnie's video. Frankly though, I could see she was far more interested in collecting recipes and decorating their new apartment.

In addition to the wedding dress, Shannon brought me a recipe for baked Alaska. I didn't have the heart to say it might be months, or years, before I'd have time to try it.

Then, as we hugged each other goodbye that Sunday night, I could tell we were turning a corner in our relationship. Shannon would always be my friend, but our lives were taking on a new dimension, and neither of us would ever be quite the same.

These thoughts began to take root during my final week at the Police Academy. In fact, I still wonder how the staff pulled everything together, as we reviewed the Code of Ethics, studied the various divisions and shifts and even had a demo from the K-9 force.

Somehow, I had always wanted a dog so I felt a special kinship with the K-9 troop, and later, when I discussed it with Donnie, we speculated about the fine four-legged friend we would enjoy one day. Then, as the final week drew to a close, I also began to look forward to another pre-wedding celebration.

The Friday night towel and tool party was a roaring success. At least these were the words Uncle Charlie used, as he and Donnie admired the hammer, screw drivers and other paraphernalia a man can't live without.

Uncle Charlie even laughed and said, "You know, I 'spec Gertrude and I even recouped our expenses." He put his arm around me when he said that, and I watched my Dad and Donald smile from across the room.

Donnie and I invited a number of our police buddies to the party of course, and I particularly recall a comment Corporal Stedman made just before leaving. Smiling, he shook Donnie's hand and said, "Socrates once declared: 'By all means, marry. If you get a good wife, (and you and I have both picked a good one) you'll become happy; if you get a bad one, you'll become a philosopher.'"

Other towel and tool officers also had good wishes for us, and I was reminded again of what Sergeant Hamilton had said, "We had become a *Band of Brothers.*"

Dad didn't stay overnight at my apartment, because he still had some loose ends to take care of before coming back for graduation on Monday, December 7th.

When I look back on the graduation ceremony that day, I can still see Dad beaming and taking pictures with his new digital camera. Thanks to him, we have several group shots of our class and the instructors.

He also took a number of cut-ups with Jeeter, Humphrey and even Oglethorpe. In one shot, Oglethorpe has a huge grimace on his face because I am attacking him between the mastoid and mandible. Tabesha is looking on with a satisfied giggle.

Here's another interesting tidbit about my Dad at the graduation reception. I couldn't help but notice how he took some time away from the camera to talk to my friend, Margaret.

Three weeks later, Dad came back for the big day. When our pastor, Rev. McIntyre, asked "Who gives ... I mean, who presents this woman to this man?" Dad's kiss on my cheek was captured by the wedding photographer, and even today, this picture is one of my favorites.

To be honest, I guess my favorite photo is one of Donnie and me kneeling, just before being pronounced man and wife. I say this because you can only see our backs. We are holding hands facing the chancel, and I've labeled the picture with a promise Donnie and I claim; a verse printed in our wedding program.

Some guests may wonder why we selected this verse, but there are at least three of us who understand. "When you pass through the waters, I will be with you; and when you pass through the rivers, they will not sweep over you" (Isaiah 43:2).

The silver bell with the inscription: "Beth & Donnie, Our 1st Christmas Together" has hung on a real Christmas tree for four years now, and in a few months our little Donnie will arrive.

So far, we've passed through only one quagmire of troubled water, yet I'm sure there are more to come. When they do, I trust we will remember the verse, Isaiah 43:1: "Fear not, for I have redeemed you; I have called you by name; you are mine."

I'm also happy to report that my handsome officer still puts his arms around me at the sink, and slides his hands into a sink full of dirty dishes.

THE END

The Author

From riding shotgun in a police cruiser to firearms training and other Police Academy strategies for staying alive, Sara DuBose turns a corner for her latest novel, *Uncharted Waters*. This time her "in the flesh" research offers romance, suspense and moments of sheer terror.

Author and speaker Sara DuBose is a first place winner in *Putting Your Passion into Print* and a first place fiction winner with the Southeastern Writers Association. She is also the author of four previous novels: *Where Hearts Live, Where Love Grows* and *Where Memories Linger* form a trilogy, and *A Promise for Tomorrow* is a stand-alone.

One reviewer wrote, "Sara DuBose is as good a southern writer as one would expect to find. Her unique and heart-warming book is a gem."

Sara's articles and stories appear in eight anthologies with Multnomah, Barbour and David C. Cook. Titles include *Stories for a Woman's Heart, Stories for a Faithful Heart, God Allows U-Turns* and *God Makes Lemonade*. She has written over 200 articles for magazines and authored one non-fiction book assignment called *Conquering Anxiety*.

Sara's novels are promoted through some of her original contacts as well as via radio and TV interviews and blogs. She has served as a featured author and speaker for the Alabama Book Festival and for the Emerald Coast Writers Conference. Sara regularly offers inspirational and motivational presentations for conferences, retreats, universities, churches and libraries, and serves on the board for the Alabama Storytellers Association.

During her leisure Sara enjoys reading, family time, travel and sitting in a tree stand with her husband Bill, a deer hunter. To learn more or to arrange a speaking engagement Sara may be reached at: www.saradubose.com.

Rose & Crown

BRIDGE
to
NOWHERE

STEPHANIE
PARKER
McKEAN

SAMPLE CHAPTER

Bridge To Nowhere

A Miz Mike Novel

by

Stephanie Parker McKean

ISBN# 978-1-907984-42-6

Best-selling crime author Mike Rice – or Miz Mike to her friends – is by nature inquisitive. (Or meddling, to her friends.) She also has a heart of compassion that gets her into trouble time and again, and her inability to really hear what God is saying to her doesn't help! So when a beautiful young stranger begs her to investigate the death of her sister, Mike is soon not-too-reluctantly embroiled in a mystery that involves the whole town of Three Prongs. She finds herself rapidly immersed in the illicit subculture in Texas Hill County – from dog fights to kidnappings, jealousy and murder – and her life is thrown into chaos as she takes in two troubled young-sters, to boot. And that's without the animals thrown in!

Mike's crazy crush on the town heart-throb, retired film star and rodeo champion Marty Richards, fuels her impossible fantasies about the two of them hooking up. But when he does finally ask her out, her need to track down culprits and bring them to justice gets in the way every time. Will they finally settle on a date and keep it? And more importantly, will Mike's M&M fantasies ever grow roots in a real relation-ship?

BRIDGE TO NOWHERE is the first book in the Miz Mike series.

Chapter 1

Perhaps I *was* careless, because my mind was chained to my failing Pastor Garth Seymour detective series, but still, it seemed to me the teen driver of the red car was to blame.

I had just left my Three Prongs office when he careened around the corner and barreled down the street towards me, seemingly blind or indifferent to the fact that I was crossing the street in the path of his sports car. I partly leapt, partly tumbled, and totally fell, out of the vehicle's path. As a career, writing is unfortunately a static occupation. One does not get enough exercise – or at least, I don't. At forty-something, I am hearty. Fast movement, like fleeing from a monster car, reduces me to breathlessness. Gracefulness has never been one of my faults at any age or weight, though. I landed in a disheveled heap in front of my long-time heartthrob, Marty Richards.

In my defense, I must add that Marty would be pretty much *any* woman's heartthrob. Even nearing fifty, he was Texas-tall and slim. His wide shoulders and narrow hips shot a breath of life into the Western-cut clothes he wore, from the tooled leather boots and leather belt with his name engraved on the back, and a wide silver buckle bumping up against a flat hard belly, to the pale Stetson that held his cinnamon-brown hair in near-submission. He sometimes complained that his hair was etched with grey, but as he bent down over me to check for injuries all I could see was the red, catching glints of light from the sun and tossing them back playfully; and the fabulous blue eyes, dark as day flowers around the edges and pulsing with yellow around the pupils.

I wasn't sure whether my difficulty in breathing was from Marty's closeness, or my forced rapid movement. My hazel eyes (which I determinedly refer to as *green*) are too big for my face; thus I am sometimes unfairly accused of staring at people. But if someone had accused me of staring at Marty now, it would not have been mendaciously. I drank in the close details of his person like a water-starved plant.

My own light brown-red hair (which I determinedly refer to as *red*) fought its way out of the bun I had stuffed it into earlier with less than expert skill. It fell around my face and blew across my lips as I devoured details of Marty that I was seldom close enough to see. I was thankful that it – my wind-blown hair – did not block my view of the ex-rodeo-television-movie star. His full lips smiled easily, and the lines around his eyes and mouth hinted at a sense of humor and kindness, but of course I had already memorized those qualities from my dreams.

To his credit, Marty managed not to laugh. Instead he solemnly helped me to my feet, even though his cheeks puffed in and out suspiciously and his full lips quivered under the ends of his cinnamon-sprinkled mustache.

"Good morning, Miz Mike," he boomed in his rich movie star voice that rose and fell with the gusto of a friendly spring breeze. "Are you okay?"

My real name is Michal Rice, but 'Mike' serves to admirably hide my identity as a female writer for the Pastor Garth Seymour series. Critics of the series lament the fact that Seymour lacks the salient grey cells of Agatha Christie's Hercule Poirot. Since I lack the fine brain cells of Christie, I'd have to agree with them. My books win accolade from fans, however, thanks to Seymour's unfailing integrity, unshakable faith in God, and predilection for solving crimes through his *aperçu* in recognizing things nefarious in drag.

Now, with my pantyhose torn, my knee bleeding, and my clothes of dubious labels bundled up around my aching body – there was Marty, asking me if I was okay. I wasn't, of course, but I could hardly admit that to him. His magnetism threatened to pull the truth right out of me: I had been the one who had sent him flowers and candy for Valentine's Day two years prior. At the time, he had jumped to the conclusion that his secret admirer was the girl at the drugstore, and had started dating her.

Remembering that my pedestrian qualities had not improved from a rollicking tumble over the curb and across the sidewalk, I managed to bite my cheeks – hard, on the inside – and stop the ebullient confession from spilling out into the warm Texas air. Instead, I nodded.

That simple gesture sent a blast of pain racing up through my neck to explode inside my head.

My legs tried to shake me loose, although I couldn't tell

whether that was a reaction to pain or to the overwhelming effect of Marty Richards himself standing next to me, holding my arm and smiling into my eyes.

Over the years I had linked Marty's name and mine together in my dream life – secretly, of course, as the names could never be connected in *real* life. Since I love chocolate, the voice in my head referred to us affectionately as the 'M&Ms'. Sometimes, while trying to round out a plot or to extricate poor Pastor Garth from some huggermugger of a mess I'd penned him into, I would find myself doodling lines of M&Ms across empty paper.

And then there was my secret M&M game. Even though dark brown might be perceived as a masculine color, my love for chocolate wrote the game rules: brown was for me, and yellow was for Marty. Marty's love, whether real or imagined (and yes, at my age, and with my knocked-about-old-car-looks, it was imagined) spun sunlight into my life. Thus I sorted out the M&Ms, keeping the browns and yellows hidden in a container inside my desk drawer. The other colors were poured out in a dish that sparked my desk with its brightness and invited visitors to my office – and me – to munch and crunch on chocolate rainbows.

Marty insisted on walking me back to my office. By then the utopia of close contact with him had erased from my memory the fact that I had just been *leaving* my office. He need utter no blandishments to win my heart; with his strong arms supporting me, I was in danger of liquefying and falling into a helpless heap on the sidewalk ... again! It took heroic effort to bite back all the extemporaneous conversation that bucked through my mind like a calf at a rodeo: *If I follow you home, can I keep you? ... Marry me, and I'll be a better horse trainer than the Horse Whisperer ...*

The promise of turning myself into a horse trainer would have been particularly spurious, considering that I am rather frightened of the huge, unpredictable animals. Marty, however, had trained horses for Westerns and television commercials. He owned his own small entertainment business and traveled around to schools, birthday parties, and other large gatherings to give pony rides and display the tricks of his own horse, Cactus, to an appreciative audience.

Marty was a hero of mine for several reasons, not the least of which was his proactive determination to keep our small hometown of Three Prongs Western. Everything he did – including the name he chose for his horse – defined Marty's Western ilk. In a town that boasted of its cowboy heritage, my heart boasted of only one: Marty.

Forgetting the diet soda I had been walking to the corner convenience store to purchase before the rude red car attempted to eat me, I allowed Marty to settle me into my padded desk chair in front of my computer. Ignoring my objections, Marty fetched a wet paper towel from the bathroom and bent down in front of me to mop the blood off my torn knee. I held on to the arms of the chair, lest I be tempted to throw my arms around his broad shoulders.

With his fabulous purple-blue eyes throwing gold sparks at me, Marty pushed his Stetson back from his forehead and chuckled. "You do get yourself into some real pickles, Miz Mike."

I bristled. "I *had* to choose that spirited horse when we went riding! It was what Pastor Garth would have done!"

He laughed. "Yep – some real pickles."

"And you should have told me that horse was afraid of thunder."

Marty shook his head. "Not thunder, Mike – lightning. He's close to being deaf at his age, you know. Thunder doesn't bother him a bit."

I *hadn't* known. Nor had I known that Marty would be the one to rescue me downstream where the horse and I had parted company after a faster, wilder ride than I had intended.

Anger against Marty was impossible to nurse at such close quarters, though, and I found myself smiling mindlessly back at him and forgetting to breathe when he pushed a strand of loose hair gently out of my face. "You take care of yourself now, Mike. I wasn't planning any more rescues today."

Sadly, Marty's coming to my rescue seemed to be part of a repeating pattern that I was helpless to control – like with my vehicle, Old Blue. Deer are a real threat on late-night drives in Texas Hill Country, but I am usually a careful driver. Thinking that Marty was ahead of me and had already arrived at the children's benefit that he was scheduled to sing for, I had driven perhaps a bit recklessly that night. I hadn't wanted to miss a note of his compelling songs – many of which he had written himself.

I missed the deer. In fact, I missed the entire herd, but poor Old Blue plunged into a series of neck-wrenching spins that would scare the parts out of even a new car. One tire peeled right off the rim.

Marty stopped to pick me up and take me to the benefit with him, since the car was far enough off the road not to be a traffic hazard and there was no time to change the tire.

What a joy it was to spend the evening with Marty and

know he would be my escort home! But by the time the concert ended and he took me back, my neck was screaming in such pain that I made a less than alluring hostess. Moreover, whereas Blue quickly recovered from the incident after brief treatment consisting of a new tire, I wore a neck brace for several weeks. The brace tilted my chin up into the air, forcing me to strike a constant and unintended pose of disdain. At least for the duration no one had noticed my huge greenish eyes and accused me of staring at them!

Now, my insides were quivering like a parcel of startled daddy long-legs spiders as Marty brushed hair out of my face and smiled at me. Fortunately, Marty was not one for light dalliances. If he had kissed me, I would have fainted.

He had to repeat the question twice before I heard it. "Will you be there?" he asked again. "At eleven?"

Because Three Prongs is a small town, I was able to leap to the meaning of the question. Of course, I wished I could believe that I had made the leap because Marty's soul and mine had somehow knit together. Friday was shrimp day at *The Spanish Tile* restaurant, so named both because it had risen up out of immense limestone blocks along the Old Spanish Trail, and because the roof was the only one in Three Prongs that had been constructed with red rounded brick tile.

Filling plates from the seafood buffet on Fridays was a Three Prongs tradition, due in part to the fact that the town offered limited choices for dining, but also because the food was excellent. It seemed as if the entire town showed up for Friday's seafood buffet. The secret to getting a table was to get to *The Spanish Tile* early. Only on rare occasions had I managed to finagle a place at Marty's table.

So: Marty was inviting me to have lunch with him.

I returned his smile and nodded. "That would be great," I managed in a voice not quite my own. "Marty ..." I wanted to keep him with me as long as possible. "Did you see what happened? Who was driving the car that nearly hit me?"

He stood up, and I immediately missed the close contact we'd shared a moment before. He laughed. "That, Mike, was Three Prongs' newest joke." Then he sobered. "Of course, it's not really funny considering that it's a downright sin."

"Yes," I said, following my own line of reasoning. "If not a sin entirely, at the very least, it is very rude to try to run over innocent people."

He was shaking his head. "No. I mean about the 'long, lean cheating machine'."

"What! Are we talking about the same thing – the car – or

did I miss something else?" My face colored at the admission that I had missed his earlier question about lunch.

"I know you're like me, Mike. We stay out of bars and away from the night life and drinking and the like ..."

What a thrill it was to have Marty say we were alike! M&Ms! I knew it! Before long, we would be marching down the church aisle, and then I could finally give up my silly schoolgirl game of holding mock weddings with brightly colored M&Ms lined up as guests, as Brown and Yellow – Mike and Marty – walked the aisle between them.

"But you must know Zolly Gilmore, that feller who owns Borderbound Watering Hole, the bar? You must have heard about some of his antics."

I nodded. "I've heard that he held a bronc-busting contest with live horses in his bar one night and never repeated it because of broken furniture. I think a few people even got hurt."

"Yup. That was just one of many. The taxi is his newest one."

"Taxi? He started a taxi service in Three Prongs?"

"Yep. That was his car, and if you hadn't been so intent on scrambling to safety–"

"Which was the wise thing to do, surely!"

He nodded in agreement. "If you hadn't, you would have noticed the 'taxi' signs on the sides – magnetic, peels off. He can put them on and remove them at will."

"Why go to all the trouble and expense to start a taxi service and then take the signs off the taxi? Doesn't make any sense, if you ask me."

"You don't understand, Miss Michal Rice, because you have an inner beauty and keep your thoughts on pure things like the Bible tells us to. The taxi isn't a taxi at all, although his wife thinks it is. The whole thing is a ruse. He slaps the taxi signs on that car and runs around with Candy."

"Candy? I thought his wife's name was Carmen."

"Exactly. Candy is that big ... uh, that blonde barmaid of his with the almost-white hair. No one seems to know her last name or anything else about her. She just showed up in town one day and went to work for him, and he keeps her in that trailer behind the bar – the place he lets his band practice in. Well, they don't get to go into the back. That whole half belongs to Candy ... and Zolly, when he spends the night, which he does almost every night."

"No! And his wife?"

"Poor thing hasn't got a clue. She's even taken the taxi around town on a lark, thinking it's legit."

"How awful!"

"Well, I don't believe I've ever heard anyone accuse Zolly of being a nice feller. Anyway, that wasn't Zolly driving just now. It was that kid from the children's home down south of here, Jared Silvers."

"He ought to lose his license," I said darkly.

"Can't lose what he doesn't have. He's too young for a license. Give him a break. He needs one."

"What do you mean? Who is he? Is he in some kind of trouble, or is it just his driving record that's a debacle?"

"Now don't get mixed up in this, Mike. I know how you like to try to find out about everything and help."

How could Marty know that? He must have talked to Ron. My son had the mistaken belief that one of my bad habits was sticking my nose in other people's business.

"Jared's had it about as rough as a kid can, growing up with no parents," Marty continued. "If church folks would have taken him in, I reckon he wouldn't be hanging out with the likes of Zolly now."

Marty had a point. I nodded in agreement, and for a moment, I even felt guilty. My son Ron was an adult, a married man. His wife, Faith, was a nice creature, although plain. She had long, wavy, light brown hair and eyes that were a true clear green; they made mine look hazel by comparison. Her face was oval, and her nose was long and thin, reminding me of a greyhound. Ron thought she was beautiful.

My son was unaware – thankfully – of the secret antagonism I held against Faith. Before Ron married Faith, he had briefly been engaged to my best friend's daughter, Irene. Donna Johnson and I had been inseparable, partly, perhaps, because we had both lost our husbands at nearly the same time … well, we hadn't lost them really, since they were in Heaven and we knew where to find them. Anyway, Three Prongs residents often said of us, "Mike and Don, huh? Hmm. Let's make one of them the chair on this committee. They know how to get things done."

Donna's daughter and I were nearly as close. I liked to think that Irene and I had matching red hair and that after she and Ron married, people would see us together and mistake her for my daughter. Actually, her hair was a rich, dark red, unlike my pretends-to-be-red locks.

Irene had a young, innocent beauty that maintained its breathless quality into womanhood. When Ron met Faith and dropped Irene like a scorpion crawling up into the palm of his hand, I suffered as much heartbreak from their breakup as anyone. I felt I had been robbed of the daughter I'd always wanted and never been able to have.

Donna suffered, too, but she assured me that parents don't make matches for their children in the United States and that Ron was free to choose. She insisted that Ron's marriage to Faith would not ruin our friendship, but she was wrong about that. Shortly after Ron and Faith married, Donna took Irene and moved back to Georgia to be closer to her parents. For a while we stayed connected through phone calls, e-mails, and occasional letters and cards. Then Irene married the high school agricultural teacher in their town and started having children, so Donna became the quintessential grandmother. She and I lost the treasured connection of friendship that we had attempted to maintain.

By this time Ron and Faith had started a family of their own. While I nearly always mind my own business, some grandmothers (like Donna) tend to get carried away and become too involved in the lives of their children and their children's children. Donna put grandmothering Irene's children in front of our long-distance friendship. It was natural, I suppose, since blood is thicker than water and all of that hullabaloo, but I still felt that Donna held a grudge about Ron's cool treatment of Irene. I know *I* held a grudge against my son for a while. Then I discovered that it was easier to forgive Ron and shift that resentment to Faith.

Ron was beautiful for a man. He had blond hair, blue eyes, and chiseled face with a deep cleft in his chin and dimples when he smiled. I would have chosen a matching wife for him – like Irene, with her young, haunting beauty and red hair – but Ron did his own choosing and was stuck with Faith. At least the grandsons – four-year-old Alex and two-year-old Ryan – turned out to be beautiful children who resembled their daddy.

Anyway, as I thought about my grown son and my empty nest I wondered what had kept me from offering a home to a kid like Jared. My husband, Alfred, had died several years earlier, and the big house on the small ranch was ... empty.

"You know," Marty added, rescuing me from the unstable well of memories that my mind had plunged into briefly, "I've been able to get Jared to come to church with me a few times. He likes the kids his age, but he's kind of shy. If you see him around town, you might invite him too."

I bit my lip and nodded. Marty was my hero, and I could never reach the peerless heights he held in my estimation, but I could try to copy his example when possible. "I'll do that," I said resolutely, ignoring the pain zipping through my knee and the slight ache in my neck and back – souvenirs from

Jared's driving.

"Great! I'll see you at eleven." Marty doffed his hat, a natural gesture for him, and left.

The room swam large and empty in the wake of his exodus. I sat in the chair, quieting my breathing and urging my mind to people the office again with Marty. My heart skittered around in my chest like a frightened mouse. I felt younger than I had as a schoolgirl, when I'd endured many a hopeless crush.

I looked down at my rumpled clothing that covered the too-much-of-me that existed and decided that I best leave the whole M&M thing to the dream world, where it belonged. In real life, movie heroes like Marty Richards do not fall in love with old frumps like me, and it would be to my advantage to remember that my past had been blessed with a reasonably good marriage, a wonderful son, an okay daughter-in-law (even if she didn't have red hair and wasn't fish-jumping pretty), and two priceless grandsons. That was already more blessing than I deserved in this lifetime. Best leave Marty for someone drop-dead gorgeous who can match his golden qualities. I only hoped it would not be someone like our town's left-over hippie, Hyacinth Walker.

Hyacinth had an aggravating habit of yawning for no reason. She taught yoga and ran an art colony, adopting New Age ideas as her own. She had openly ogled Marty for a long time.

Hopefully it also would not be Three Prongs *Sidelines* newspaper editor Bea Hernandez, whose misanthropic edge tended to shred friendships.

Both women were frankly a bit foolish when it came to Marty. Unlike me, they fawned over him in public. I was one of Bea's rare friends and had, in fact, worked with her for nearly ten years. Hyacinth, on the other hand, I avoided. She attempted to force-feed everyone she met with unpalatable doses of New Age and Eastern religions, fluffed up and scrambled together so their idiosyncrasies were hidden.

No doubt Bea and Hyacinth would both arrive at *The Spanish Tile* at eleven. Bea put the paper to bed on Thursdays and was fairly free on Fridays. Hyacinth, unlike her name, was a virulent burr, trundling her noxious self around town several times a day.

Realizing that my half-date with Marty might fall prey to Bea or Hyacinth made me glance uneasily at the clock. With a sigh of relief, I realized I had time to attempt to make friends with my computer and get some work done. I was writing the seventh in the Garth Seymour series, and even though the number seven is God's number of perfection in the Bible, it wasn't boding well for me. The Pastor Garth series had slowed in sales. As the royalty checks slimmed, my waist continued to expand. I realized that if I intended to continue eating and purchasing necessities like new clothes to house my ever-increasing size, I'd best get the new book finished quickly – and finished well. Searching for new inspiration, I had rented the Three Prongs office and moved into it; therefore it was even more imperative to finish the book and sell it, because rent was coming due.

Of course, if I found myself unable to pay the rent, I could always move my office back to the ranch outside town. However, there were too many distractions for me at home. The dogs enjoyed romping, long walks. Keeping the ranch the unique, picturesque land that God had formed, with live oak trees extending olive green foliage over fields of romping blue-bonnets, mandated hard manual labor, sometimes having to spend entire days in temperatures closing in on 100 degrees as I cut down the non-native mountain juniper trees. Cedar was a greedy water-user, not content to go dormant like the native foliage did during droughts. Streams and water levels in wells dropped as cedar marched across the land. The limbs, with their needle-like leaves, shut out sunlight and trapped whatever rain did fall, starving grass and other plants beneath.

An equally noxious non-native resident was the fire ant, so named because its bite stings like fire. The critters are aggres-sive and will attack savagely if their mounds are disturbed. Besides inflicting pain and discomfort on humans, they prey on native wildlife. Gone were the horned toads that had once called the Texas Hill Country home. Snakes were scarce, and every year kindhearted people rescued fawns that had been partially eaten alive after birth by the venomous ants; fire ants can smell the wetness of baby deer and attack in droves, entering through the baby's nose and killing the fawns unfor-tunate enough not to find rescue. I waged a harsh war against the marauders, treating fire ant mounds with chemicals that promised to kill them. Unfortunately, those so-called "silver bullets" only caused a mass exodus, and the fiery little beasts simply took up residence in a new area.

I also found myself chasing armadillos in an attempt to get close enough to photograph them, crawling through dry creek beds looking along the banks for animal burrows and taking pictures of wildflowers rioting along the banks. I was occasionally rewarded for my efforts by getting close enough to take a picture of a shy ringtail or even a grey fox.

At home, it was too easy to forget that I was a writer, not an artist. It was too easy to plant myself on the screened-in porch with an easel and take up paints and one of Ron's borrowed sign-painting brushes and begin painting vividly colored monstrosities that would never sell at any art show. Besides, in Three Prongs, I was close to the post office, convenient for mailing manuscripts back and forth to my agent. It was possible to watch a parade of interesting possible book characters flow past my large plate glass windows, each new and unique person an inspiration for the written canvas expanding under the labor of my fingertips on the computer keyboard.

It was as difficult to close my mind to the memory of Marty moving around the office as it would have been to turn down a chocolate chip cookie with extra chocolate chunks. I placed my fingers on the keyboard and willed myself to remember the book hero I had created instead of the real-life hero who had just left the office.

The door, which already stood open to invite the warm spring day inside, filled with shadow, and I blinked in surprise. My disheveled appearance after the car incident strummed regret through my mind in rude, sour notes as I feasted my eyes on the vision of loveliness before me.

She was a couple of inches shorter than my five-nine, and she was slim where she should have been and full where fullness was no crime. Her gold hair swept over her shoulders like a sunlight-spangled cloud. As she moved closer to me in her tight Western-cut jeans that looked better on her than they would have looked on a sales rack, I could see that her eyes were a light, friendly blue. She brushed her long blonde hair impatiently back over the shoulder of her checkered Western shirt; she was slim enough where she should have been slim that she was able to thrust her hands into the pockets of her jeans as she read the name plate on my desk. "You're Mike?" she asked in disbelief. "You're the Mike Rice who writes about Pastor Garth?"

I managed a nod. I had been mentally comparing the lovely stranger to Faith and thinking that my daughter-in-law would not stack up favorably next to her. If I could have chosen Ron's wife for him after he'd parted with Irene, this young woman was the epitome of who my choice would have been.

"Mike?" she asked again. "A ... a woman writes those books?"

On second thought, perhaps Ron would deserve better. "Gender is not the big kahuna in writing," I said icily. "A woman is–"

She waved my words away impatiently. "I know all that. I'm

a woman, after all. I just didn't know that 'Mike' was a woman. Anyway, I need your help, Miss Rice. I'm so ... I'm desperate!"

I gawked at her like a trout-eating bear, then realized that wasn't helping either of us. How could such a lovely girl be desperate about anything? Surely with those looks, the world is hers to command?

"What's wrong, dear?" I asked, hoping I was not about to be asked to stick my nose in someone's business.

I brightened. If she were pregnant and unwed, I could invite her to come live with me until after the baby was born. My overactive imagination instantly conjured up images of helping her raise a beautiful baby who would look like Ron.

"My sister has been murdered, and I ... I need you to find out who did it."

I gasped at first, but then relief drifted over me like pollen from a live oak tree in bloom, smacked by a blast of north wind. This was going to be so easy. I was not dealing with a pregnant, unwed mother, a drug addict, or a person wanting to commit suicide. I had tried to help all those in the past with varying degrees of success, even amidst my son's derisive comments about his mother's inability to mind her own business. But this I could dismiss easily.

I was already shaking my head. "You need to go to the sheriff's department, dear. I don't investigate things. I make up crime stories – make-believe – and let my character solve them in the story. It's fiction, not real. I'm not a detective. I'm only a mystery writer, not a solver."

"I know that," she said patiently, "but I've already been to the sheriff's office, and they don't believe me! They say ... they just dismiss me because they think Julia's death was an accident. I know better."

"Julia, you say?" I mused out loud, trying to remember. "Was that –

"Yes," she said, with tears growing up around the lower rim of her eyes like crystal gardens. "My name is Lynette Clarissa Greene. I'm undercover right now as Clara Greene. I came here from Alabama last week to do my own investigating, since the police are just blowing it off. Julia was planning to divorce Thor. I'm sure you know him – Thornton Dean? He used to be county commissioner, and he sells real estate now."

I nodded. I had known Thor for a long time and had, in fact, a standing invitation to visit his ranch. Even though I always minded my own business, I had just been too busy to make the trek to the southern end of the county where Thor's ranch was located. He had drawn me a map to the ranch a long time ago, but I had lost it. When I had worked for Bea at the paper, I had reported on county commissioner court meetings. Until Thor met Julia, Bea and Thor had dated. That threw the three of us together at community events.

I looked at Lynette and mused, "As I remember, it was a gas leak that caused your sister's death. She walked into her mobile home, switched on a light, and an electrical spark ignited the propane in the house. The whole place exploded. Sheriff Cruz–"

"Doesn't believe she was murdered."

"I've known Brent for years, dear. He's an honest man and seems to be a good sheriff. He's been re-elected three times."

"Her murder was carefully concealed. Money can do that."

In spite of my resolve not to become involved, I was instantly alert. "Whose money? Do you think Thor killed his wife because she was going to divorce him?"

"That was what I thought at first. Julia had written me, you know."

Why do people assume I know things that are none of my business? I rarely mixed myself up in other people's business.

"She told me she was going to leave him, and Thor knew she was planning to. He was the one who helped her rent the mobile home that blew up." Fresh new tears sprouted up in the crystal garden and shed clear liquid petals down her face. "But I got a job with Thor as his secretary. He doesn't know I'm Julia's sister."

I gasped. "Lynette ... or Clara or–"

"You can call me Lynette or Lynn even. Clarissa is my real middle name. Everyone I've met in Three Prongs knows me as Clara, so just don't call me Lynette around anyone else."

"You are playing a very dangerous game!"

She smiled and brushed the garden of tears out of her eyes. "No. Thor's not dangerous. Now that I'm working for him, I know he didn't do it. He's really torn up over her death and feels like it was his fault because it wouldn't have happened if she hadn't been in the process of leaving him."

"Why did she want to leave?" I asked, forgetting to mind my own business.

Lynette apparently did not hear the question. "Anyway, Thor owns this big ranch. His house and office are up near the front gate. He has several houses scattered around the back roads. He lets his help live in them since they're so far out of town. I'm staying in one of those."

Lynnette pulled a list out of the back pocket of her jeans. I was amazed there was room for it there, as nicely as she filled up her denim.

"Thor was my first suspect," she said, flipping open a slim notebook, "but now I've crossed him off the list." She looked up at me quickly. "I only did that because of the facts. Remember when it happened?"

A fresh batch of tears welled up in her eyes. She was waiting for me to reply, and my mind cavorted like a feeding white bass as I tried to remember details. When I was silent, she answered softly, "Two months ago, at the annual Three Prongs Founder's Day Rodeo and Parade. Thor rode in the parade and then participated in the rodeo until ... news came ... about Julia." Fiercely, she rid her eyes of the new tears. "Julia stayed home that day because some people knew about the separation, and she didn't want to be bothered with too many questions from people. But Thor's son from his first marriage, Nat, is still on the list. Nat is a druggie."

I gasped in dismay.

"He lives in San Antonio but comes up to visit. His dad decided to try a tough love approach to get Nat off drugs and threatened to write him out of his will. If that had happened, Julia would have inherited everything, because there are no other children. Thor's first wife remarried and moved to Australia."

I interrupted her. "Lynette, it seems to me that you need to take your list to Sheriff Cruz and explain all this to him."

"He can't do what you can."

"What do you mean, Lynn? As I told you, all I do is write. The sheriff can actually investigate. He has the training and the manpower."

"But you can pray!"

I blinked at her in surprise.

"You can spread this list out and pray over it like Pastor Seymour would. Ask God who killed my sister."

"I need a Diet Coke," I muttered to myself.

"What?"

I shook my head. "Sorry. Bad habit – talking to myself. Also the Diet Cokes. But the caffeine helps me think, and I don't drink coffee."

"Do you want me to run down to the store and get one for you?" she asked. "I'd be glad to."

She was a real find, this young girl whom I would have selected for my son to marry – since he had dropped Irene for Faith. Faith! What kind of a name is that for a person anyway? Faith belongs in the Bible and in a believer's life, but why name a child with an idea-name?

I smiled at Lynette and shook my head. "No, but thanks."

She continued down the list. "My number one suspect is Hollis Newbark."

I thought of Hollis. His white hair was not unlike Candy's – no one knew if hers was natural or contrived – and his crawly caterpillar-like eyebrows tended to rise up over pale eyes in a seemingly constant state of surprise. I couldn't really think of anyone in Three Prongs whom I disliked, but I distrusted Hollis Newbark. I had no objection to his name on Lynn's list of suspects. Besides, he and Thor were former business partners, and now the two seemed to despise each other for, some undisclosed reason.

"Then, of course," she continued, "there's Buddy Turner –"

"Buddy?" I interrupted. "Why would Thor's maintenance man want to kill your sister? What motive would he possibly have? Granted, he is an alcoholic and undependable but–"

"I have to put down every name connected with her," Lynette answered, "just like you do in your books. I have Neil Peters down, too, because he rented her the house. I even have that barmaid – Candy someone – because Thor said she threatened Julia once."

"Why would she–"

She shook her head, spilling waves of blonde hair around her face. "I don't know! I don't know why anyone would want to hurt Julia. But you can spread this list out and pray over it and let God show you who did it."

"It doesn't work that way, Lynette, honey."

"You mean God doesn't care about my sister or who killed her?"

"Of course He cares! The problem isn't God – it's me! I'm not always good at hearing what He's trying to tell me."

"Can you ... just try?" Fresh tears replaced the old pools in her eyes, and she tried unsuccessfully to blink them away. Her courage and quiet dignity moved me. She squared her shoulders and bit her lip.

I took the list and tried to tell myself that I was not really accepting involvement by accepting the paper.

Lynette saw me studying the name on the list that she had crossed out, Thornton Dean. She smiled wanly. "Thor bought my entire family plane tickets for the wedding eight years ago. I didn't get to go because I had chicken pox, so Thor sent me a box of chocolates. Julia sent me a picture of them at the wedding. I thought Thor was the most handsome man I'd ever seen, and I was happy for my sister."

"Doesn't Thor recognise your name?"

"No. Julia and I were actually half-sisters with different last names, and Thor just sent everything to the family and included my first name, 'Lynette,' on the box, which is why he hasn't connected me with Clara."

"I still think you're playing a dangerous game, Lynn. I think you should leave this investigation to someone else."

"Oh good! You will help! I knew you would understand."

I started to protest, but she threw her arms around me in such an ebullient hug that I would have felt guilty to refuse. She would have, after all, been a quintessential daughter-in-law. As a Christian, I knew God hates divorce, which meant I hated it too, but if Ron ever did divorce Faith ...

I looked at Lynette Clarissa Greene and was reminded of sunlight beams bouncing over floorboards in the summer, drawing patterns of bright hope on every object they touched. This girl with a halo of bright gold hair and eyes that sprouted tears like crystal flowers was a keeper.

"I will do what I can, with God's help," I agreed. "Nothing is too hard for God, and nothing is impossible for Him, but I am only a clay vessel." I noted her look of confusion and smiled. "The Bible says God took dust and breathed life into it and created the first man. That makes us all ... well, never mind. You can read that on your own in the Good Book. I was just trying to explain that sometimes the part of me that is not spirit gets in the way of what God is trying to accomplish through His Spirit."

Lynette was watching me with the kind of nervous trepidation reserved for fireworks when they're about to explode at close range.

I halted my flow of words. "We'll talk more about all this later."

She nodded but still looked uncertain. A quick flash of intuition warned me that perhaps Lynette would not make as good a wife for Ron as Faith did, because Lynn didn't seem to be a Christian; however, that flash was so swift and sudden that I couldn't glom on to it while under the spell of the stranger's sunny smile.

"How does your family feel about your involvement in all this, Lynette?"

"They don't know. They think I just came here for the funeral and stayed because I liked the town and found a job. I had been working with my dad in the family business at home, and they're glad I'm getting a chance to get away from home and get more experience in the job market. They didn't come themselves. They don't care."

"What a thing to say! Why?" I asked, finally getting tangled up in business that was not my own.

"Well, Julia was Miss Alabama, and–"

"Goodness! She must have looked at lot like you. I know her by name, but I don't believe I ever met her. I've known Thor for years, but I haven't seen him much since he married Julia. I don't believe I ever saw her at all, come to think of it. From what I understand, she busied herself taking care of animals and loved ranch life."

"You compliment me falsely by comparing me to Julia," my dream daughter-in-law said humbly. She pulled a picture out of the checkered pocket of her Western shirt, and I suddenly realised that she must not carry a purse. Crumpled money tumbled out onto my desk as she showed me the picture of her deceased sister. To me, the resemblance was there, even if only a slight one. Julia's hair was the bright red I had always hankered for, and her amber eyes and the slight sprinkling of light freckles across the bridge of her nose gave her face a sparkle of friendliness and good humor.

"They didn't have children," Lynette said softly. "That was one reason for the split. Thor wanted to start another family before he was too old. He's almost fifty, you know."

"Fifty isn't old!" I protested.

She didn't argue but cast a quick glance of surprise in my direction that told me she considered anyone who didn't think fifty was old about as sound as a water bed. "Julia wanted to straighten Nat out before they had their own children. Besides, she wasn't sure if she could get pregnant. That's why my parents didn't go to the funeral."

"Because she couldn't have children!?"

"Because as Miss Alabama, she won all these scholarships and travel opportunities and had the chance to really make something of herself. My dad's business is small and slows down in the summer months."

"What does your father do, dear?"

"Anyway, Julia ran with a wild crowd and had a baby and wasn't even sure who the daddy was. She gave it up for adoption, and our folks had a fit. They only had two daughters and would have given anything for a son to help dad with the business – although he'd be getting pretty old by the time the baby grew up."

"Around fifty?" I suggested derisively.

Ignoring my sarcasm, Lynette nodded. "They did come here for the wedding because they were hoping Julia had changed, but they didn't come for the funeral because someone had written them that Julia was running around on Thor ... drinking and stuff."

I searched my mind. Three Prongs was small, and rumors ran rampant. I had never heard such rumors about Julia. "Do you think it was true?"

She shook her head vehemently. "No! I don't believe that about Julia nor Thor." She blushed. "He's too old for me, of course."

"Yes, I know. Nearing fifty." With a sudden spate of knowledge, I wondered if Lynette's real objective in coming to Three Prongs had been to chase Thor. While it was true that a great number of years separated them in age, Thor was a wealthy man and would be a good catch for the young girl. She would probably outlive him, and Texas community property laws would render Lynn a wealthy widow after Thor's death. Also, she had eliminated his name from her list of suspects rather briskly.

"Thor is all torn up over Julia's death," Lynette repeated, "and he's never said anything bad about Julia, even though she was in the process of leaving him. The sad thing is, Julia let my parents down so often over the years that they believed the lies someone told them about her. Anyway, about Thor ... he got enough from Julia's life insurance to pay for the funeral but very little else. I was able to check that out when I first started working for him. Buddy Turner and Neil Peters insist the mobile home and the gas lines were all in good repair. Surely they wouldn't lie."

And this was where Lynette's deductions were flawed. Neil Peters was a slumlord at best, under investigation by the district attorney's office. An elderly woman in one of his mobile home units had handed her Social Security checks over to him for years with the understanding that he would purchase groceries for her and pay her utility bills. She starved – or froze – to death and wasn't found for several weeks. The electricity had been off for months, the propane tank was empty, and the only groceries consisted of several unopened cans of chili – food she couldn't tolerate because of her aged and frail digestive system. I almost hoped Peters *was* involved with Julia's death because I wanted him put away for life; homicide involvement would seal the district attorney's case against the monster.

Buddy was an alcoholic with an uncertain work record, but violence had never been one of his trademarks.

Lynette was tapping her long, slender fingers against the list. "I don't know Hollis, although I know Thor is upset with him for some reason. I can probably ask some questions and find out more."

"Do be careful, dear."

She nodded absently. "I've seen Nat a couple of times but never got to talk to him. No loss there, I would say."

I summoned up a memory of the unhealthy-looking young man with the long brown ponytail and tattooed body. Anarchy had redrawn the features on his young face – bar fights and drunken car wrecks were chronicled with scars, a drooping eye, and slashed eyebrow.

"So we agree about leaving all these names on the list?" she asked eagerly. "If Hollis wanted to get back at Thor for something, he picked something devastating that hurt a lot of other people too. And I haven't found any truth about Candy whatever-her-name-is and Thor, but I know it was only a rumor that they were having an affair."

How could Ron possibly say I need to mind my own business? I wondered. Here's yet another rumor I've never even heard.

"I've got to go now," Lynn said, "but I'll leave you with this list. I kept a copy at home." She tore the pages out of the notebook and handed them to me. "I included directions to Thor's house, since Buddy and Neil have places on the ranch. Even though I know Thor's not involved, I figured you would want to talk to him yourself. Besides, you might be able to ferret out information about what happened with Hollis – you know, as a writer. Maybe you can ask questions about their real estate business or their relationship while he was county commissioner."

I nodded.

She hesitated, then gave me a quick hug that warmed my heart before she left.

The room seemed dark and empty without her coruscating presence, and I felt suddenly old and foolish. What could I possibly do to help that beautiful, sweet young girl? I greatly feared that I was destined to disappoint her.

I fell on my knees and poured out my heart to God. Then, forgetting to check the clock and count down the hours until I could meet Marty for lunch, I set out in search of a murderer.

END OF SAMPLE CHAPTER

BRIDGE TO NOWHERE *is available from all good online stores, or better still, support your local brick-and-mortar bookshop by ordering through them!*

Rose&Crown
Inspirational Romance
www.roseandcrownbooks.com

(an imprint of the SUNPENNY PUBLISHING GROUP)

MORE BOOKS FROM ROSE & CROWN

Bridge to Nowhere, by Stephanie Parker McKean
Embracing Change, by Debbie Roome
Blue Freedom, by Sandra Peut
A Flight Delayed, by KC Lemmer

COMING SOON:

Brandy Butter on Christmas Canal, by Shae O'Brien
Redemption on the Red River, by Cheryl R. Cain
30 Days to Take-off, by KC Lemmer
Greater than Gold, by Julianne Alcott
Shadow of a Parasol, by Beth Holland
Changing Landscapes, by Olivia Valentine
Heart of the Hobo, by Shae O'Brien

MORE BOOKS FROM the SUNPENNY GROUP
www.sunpenny.com

Lightning Source UK Ltd.
Milton Keynes UK
UKOW051631091012

200301UK00015B/15/P

And, departing, leave behind us
Footprints on the sands of time.

Resignation
Henry Wadsworth Longfellow

From the earliest humans to the present day, there has always been a compulsion to 'leave one's mark': early cave art includes thousands of hand outlines, while many churches in Britain have foot outlines inscribed in lead and stone. These two extremes span almost 30,000 years during which time all kinds of persons, real and legendary, have left visible traces of themselves. But 30,000 years ago seems almost recent, when compared with the finding of some (admittedly controversial) fossilized human footprints in rocks apparently contemporary with dinosaur footprints that are tens of millions of years old.

Most of the footprints – and hand-prints, knee-prints, and impressions of other body parts – are clearly not real, having allegedly been impressed into rocks around the world by such high-profile figures as the Buddha, Vishnu, Jesus Christ, and the Virgin Mary, as well as a vast panoply of saints, whose footprint traces and associated stories occupy two chapters. Their horses also left hoof-prints, and other animals are represented too. Not surprisingly, the ubiquitous Devil has a whole chapter to himself – but giants, villains and heroes, such as King Arthur, also feature strongly. Witches, fairies, ghosts and assorted spirits have made their mark: there are many modern instances of phantom hand- and foot-prints, the latter often bloodstained and indelible. Modern mysterious footprints are rarely graven in stone, but are rather more ephemeral, being left on the earth by monsters such as Bigfoot, or aliens who have briefly stepped out of their spacecraft. All these tales, old and new, may have some deeper meaning, and there is a chapter on the significance of footprints, as revealed in customs and folklore.

Hundreds of imprints are described in this book, which concludes with location details for more than 100 imprint sites all around the world, and also includes 138 illustrations.

Janet Bord lives in North Wales, where she runs the Fortean Picture Library with her husband Colin.   They have written more than 20 books since their first successful joint venture, *Mysterious Britain* (1972).

FOOTPRINTS IN STONE

The significance of foot- and hand-prints and
other imprints left by early men, giants,
heroes, devils, saints, animals, ghosts,
witches, fairies and monsters

Janet Bord

By the same author

Mazes and Labyrinths of the World

Fairies: Real Encounters with Little People

The Traveller's Guide to Fairy Sites

With Colin Bord

Mysterious Britain

The Secret Country

A Guide to Ancient Sites in Britain

Earth Rites

Sacred Waters

Ancient Mysteries of Britain

Atlas of Magical Britain

The Enchanted Land

Dictionary of Earth Mysteries

Alien Animals

Bigfoot Casebook

The Evidence for Bigfoot and Other Man-Beasts

Modern Mysteries of Britain

Modern Mysteries of the World

Life Beyond Planet Earth?

The World of the Unexplained

FOOTPRINTS IN STONE

The significance of foot- and hand-prints and other imprints left by early men, giants, heroes, devils, saints, animals, ghosts, witches, fairies and monsters

Janet Bord

Heart of Albion

FOOTPRINTS IN STONE
The significance of foot- and hand-prints and other imprints left by early men, giants, heroes, devils, saints, animals, ghosts, witches, fairies and monsters

Janet Bord

Front cover *Background:* King Arthur's Footprint at Tintagel, Cornwall; photo by Paul Broadhurst. *Top right:* Hands at Belvoir Castle, Rutland; photo by Charles Walker. *Centre right:* Shoe outline at Barrowden Church, Rutland; photo by Bob Trubshaw. *Bottom right:* Hand petroglyph at Gorham, Illinois; photo by Frank Joseph. *Top left:* Footprints at Pirra Martera, Switzerland; photo by Andreas Trottmann. *Centre left:* The Devil's Footprint in the Frauenkirche, Munich, Germany; photo by Dr Elmar R. Gruber. *Bottom left:* Bronze Age foot at Gladsax, Sweden; photo by Klaus Aarsleff.

Back cover Footprint at Dunadd fort, used for inauguration of the kings of the Scotish kingdom of Dalriada; photo by Janet Bord.

ISBN 1 872883 73 7

Heart of Albion Press
2 Cross Hill Close, Wymeswold
Loughborough, LE12 6UJ

albion@indigogroup.co.uk

Visit our Web site: www.hoap.co.uk

Printed in the UK by Booksprint

Contents

Acknowledgements

My thanks are due to the many friends and colleagues around the world who have contributed footprint information, including Klaus Aarsleff, W. Ritchie Benedict, John Billingsley, Dr Elmar R. Gruber, Scott Lloyd, Ulrich Magin, Andreas Trottmann, Jennifer Westwood, Dwight Whalen – but most especially to my long-time comrade in the exploration of the byways of Britain, whose enthusiasm for footprints triggered mine: Tristan Gray Hulse. I am also indebted to Ruth Bidgood for granting permission to reprint her poem 'Hoofprints'.

Most of the pictures were supplied by the Fortean Picture Library: especial thanks are due to Klaus Aarsleff, John Billingsley, Paul Broadhurst, John Robert Colombo, Dr Elmar R. Gruber, John L. Hall, Jane and Ian Hemming, Frank Joseph, Dr Thomas J. Larson, Kristan Lawson, Gerd Schmidt, Sennis Stacy, Lars Thomas, Andreas Trottmann and Charles Walker for allowing their photographs to be used.

Janet Bord
North Wales, January 2004

Hoofprints

The legend was always here,
at first invisible, poised above the hill,
stiller than any kestrel. Idle hands
carved hoofprints on a rock
by the hill path. The legend, venturing nearer,
breathed warm as blessing. At last
men recognised it. A magic horse
had leapt from hill to hill, they said,
the day the valley began. Could they not see
his prints, that had waited in the rock
till guided hands revealed them?
From the unseeable, legends leap.
In the rock of our days
is hidden the print of miracle.

Ruth Bidgood
Selected Poems (Seren Poetry Wales Press, 1992)

Chapter One

The meaning of hands and feet

And, departing, leave behind us
Footprints on the sands of time.

Resignation
Henry Wadsworth Longfellow

Footprints on a sandy beach show where we – and other mere mortals, and their dogs – have recently passed by; footprints in stone are a visible record of the eternal presence of a super-being – God, the Virgin Mary, a giant, a ghost, a fairy, the Devil, a saint, King Arthur... they are all represented in the folklore of footprints, and also in this book. 'Footprints' also includes the imprints of other body parts, for in addition handprints are often left, also finger-prints, sometimes knee-prints, while more rarely found are ribs, buttocks, the heart, or even a whole-body imprint. Animal tracks also feature – mainly horses' hoof-prints – and sometimes even the imprints of inanimate objects like a dagger or chariot wheels.

The explanations for the existence of these imprints are almost as many and varied as the imprints themselves, and an insight into their significance might be gained by taking a look at the symbolism of hand- and foot-prints around the world: they are certainly of significance worldwide. The foot was believed to have magical powers which could be used for good or evil; the hand too was highly symbolic and demonstrative. It was used as a charm to ward off evil, and amulets were often in the shape of a hand, such as the Hand of Fatima, a brass and silver hand with thumb and fingers extended. Fatima was the daughter of the prophet Mohammed, and the hand amulet encapsulated much Islamic symbolism.[1]

In some parts of the world, for example southern India, a palm dipped in red paint and pressed, fingers outspread, on the house wall is used to avert the evil eye. At a Madigas marriage ceremony, the hand would be dipped in the blood of a sacrificed sheep or goat and then pressed on the wall near the door of the room where the pots were kept.[2] Similar customs were widespread throughout India: in Gujarat, the bride and groom would dip their hands in vermilion and mark the doorposts.[3] In North Africa also, handprints were used to avert the evil eye, paintings of red hands being applied by the Moors, and the Arabs in Kairwan, above the doors and on the columns of their houses. It was reported from Persia (now Iran) in the late 19th century that 'a rough representation of a hand, or generally the imprint of a right

1

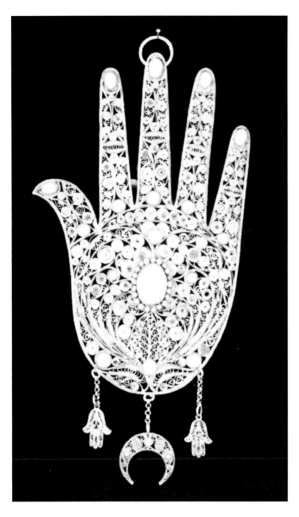

*Hand of Fatima: a 19th-century
Turkish amulet designed to
keep away the evil eye.*

hand, in red, may be seen on the wall or over the door of a house whilst in building, or on the wall of a mosque, booth, or other public building.' The Persians said it was the hand of Albas, a brother of the prophet Mohammed's grandson, one of the victims at the massacre of Kerbela in 680 who had his right hand cut off.[4]

Red handprints were also made by some American Indians: they were sun symbols, and were also used as charms to keep evil at bay.[5] In Yucatan (Mexico), red hand imprints have been found on the walls of the ancient temples, and they too were probably placed there to keep away evil, rather than being, as was once thought, simply masons' marks.[6] A similar practice was widespread thousands of years ago, and many hand impressions have also been discovered at sites of prehistoric cave art (see Chapter 2). Other recorded hands with magical significance come from Bronze Age Sweden, Ancient Egypt, Greek vase painting of the 5th-century B.C., an Assyrian votive, Red Indian chiefs' robes, the stern of Caligula's galley, and 10th-century Saxon robes, among many others.[7] Opinions vary as to the significance of the most ancient hand imprints, but it seems undeniable that here is an example of a practice

*Hand impressions on a house
wall in southern India.*

that has survived over thousands of years, and even to the present day in many parts of the world.

In wishing to avert the evil eye, the people who used powerful symbols for that purpose were also hopeful of attracting good fortune towards themselves and their families, and so to some degree hand imprints can be regarded as good luck symbols. Footprints were also regarded in this way in some circumstances, though they did have their negative aspects too. Positively, they were sometimes used in rituals intended to promote healing or fertility, for animals as well as humans. Around Gilwern in South Wales, 'wise men' used spells and charms to cure animal and human ailments. For 'foul in the foot', the wise man would dig up a turf bearing the affected animal's hoof-print, mumble some words over it, and then place it high in a blackthorn bush. As it rotted, so the disease was supposed to depart.[8] In India a cure for human paralysis was to rub the victim with earth taken from the footprints of a running dog, the intention being to transfer the animal's power of locomotion to the sufferer.[9]

These practices both used 'real' footprints, but the stone variety were sometimes actively used as well. Childless women would visit the shrine of St Remaclus at the Groesbeeck well at Spa in Belgium for nine days, there drinking a glass of the holy water and placing a foot in the saint's footprint by the well in hopes of stimulating their fertility and becoming pregnant.[10] In Ireland the water from bullauns (rock basins) was sometimes used for healing purposes, as at the old ruined church of

*Hand outlines carved on a wall
in Belvoir Castle, Rutland.*

Killalta. There the bullauns (which were said to be the saint's knee-prints) contained water all year round, which was used to remove warts.[11] In France too the same practices were commonplace – and still occur in some locations. For example, at Ménéac in Morbihan (Brittany) children who were late in walking were taken to a rock where the Virgin Mary and Baby Jesus had supposedly left their imprints. The mother would put her own foot and knee on those made by the Virgin, and her child's feet would be placed in the Baby Jesus's prints. The water from certain imprints was also drunk to partake of its health-giving properties.[12] The belief that the footprints left by superior beings, be they real or mythical, were able to promote fertility is shown by the saying that wherever the Virgin Mary walked, the most lovely flowers on earth would spring up. A streak of lush green grass on the Tyrolean heights of Austria would cause people to say that 'Alber, the Spirit of the Alp, has walked this way', while in Swabia (south-west Germany) it was believed that the places where elves and fairies walked stayed greener for longer than other areas of grass. In the French village of Solférino a bronze plaque was set up bearing an image of Emperor Napoleon III's footprint, and the message that he set foot on the soil of the Landes in August 1857 'in order to make it fruitful'.[13]

Just as 'real' footprints could be used for good, so too could they be used for evil purposes. In some parts of the world, it was considered dangerous to leave one's footprint exposed: your enemies might put a piece of glass or a sharp stone into it and thus injure you, a belief held by some Australian aborigines. The Maoris would walk along stream beds when in hostile territory, to ensure they left no footprints that could be used against them. In Burma and northern India, a sore foot was sometimes seen as proof that an enemy was trying to cause harm. Dust from an intended victim's footprint was often used to create a link with the intended victim: it would be burnt or buried in a graveyard, in order to kill the victim. Or the dust might be used as a love charm, as was the case among the negroes of the southern United States, who would carry it with them in a bag, to make their chosen one follow them.[14] In Herefordshire in England, it was believed that a witch could be identified by hammering a tenpenny nail (whether only a tenpenny nail could be used is unclear!) into the alleged witch's footprint, and if she returned and pulled out the nail, she was believed to be guilty.[15] A tale from Lindfield in West Sussex tells of a

Hand outline carved on a pillar in Thriplow church, Cambridgeshire, possibly by Mathies Prime in 1691, whose name was also carved.

witch who lived near the Witch Inn, and it would seem she had some financial stake in the inn, since it was her custom to stick pins in the footprints of people who had been there, so that they would return and have another drink![16] From all these tales we can deduce that there was generally believed to be some subtle link between a person and their footprints.

Even today, in Western society, footprints can sometimes be used for harmful purposes, or for good, depending on which side you are on. Criminals (admittedly very careless ones) sometimes reveal their whereabouts by leaving their footprints in snow, leading from the scene of the crime to their hiding place. Criminals can also be convicted by the evidence of footprints found in the soil at the crime scene, because the unique impression of the shoe sole matches shoes later found in their possession. Fingerprints have been a valuable aid to solving crimes for over 100 years, the first conviction by fingerprint evidence occurring in 1892 in Argentina. Two children found murdered in their beds were thought to have been killed by a man who had been rejected by their mother, but a bloody thumbprint found at the scene matched the mother's prints, and when confronted she confessed to the crime.[17] Even in the more distant past, footprints have identified the guilty party. A miraculous icon in a monastery near Drama in Macedonia was often attacked by the

Mexican Aztec mythology, with the god Yacatecuhtli, the patron of merchants, top left, carrying a cross-road marked with divine footprints.

Bulgarians. The footprint of a Bulgarian officer who tried to damage it was permanently impressed into the floor, and his identity thereby established.[18]

The belief in past centuries that a person could be magically harmed through his or her footprint was widespread, and the methods used varied according to the local custom.[19] It is clear that people intuitively understood that the footprint was not ephemeral, but somehow a part of the person that made it, with a continuing connection to them. It naturally follows that if a person's footprint were to be perpetually visible, a perpetual link to the creator of the print would also exist. Hence the importance that was placed on the many footprints of saints and other holy people. Not only did a footprint in stone 'prove' that the saint had stood on that spot, but it also provided the pilgrim with a personal link to the saint, in the same way that he or she could partake of the saint's holiness by touching a relic such as a

6

bone or something that had belonged to or been held by the saint: the 'contagion of holiness'. By standing in the saint's footprint, the pilgrim believed he or she could benefit from the saint's virtues. A similar belief may have been held in past centuries in Celtic Britain, when the new king or tribal ruler was required to stand in a stone footprint during his inauguration ceremony, possibly so that he would benefit from the superior qualities of his predecessors. (Some examples of inauguration stones will be found in Chapter 2.)

In the surviving Graeco-Roman remains around the Mediterranean and in Egypt and North Africa, footprints have often been found: bare and sandalled, sometimes as part of mosaic designs, sometimes cut into rock slabs. They were often found in sanctuaries, where they may have symbolised the presence of the god or goddess. It is also possible that pilgrims or worshippers may have stood in the footprints during their visit to the sanctuary, as a way of linking with the divine presence. Footprints were also found at thresholds, and as with other symbols that may be found at doorways, these probably represent the desire for safe passage for those entering or leaving, as well as being a symbol to keep evil away (like the handprints on walls by doorways, mentioned earlier).[20] The doorway of course represents the movement from one form of existence to another, and therefore is potentially dangerous, so footprints by doorways may also be a warning to take care. Christ's footprints on the Mount of Olives represent where he stepped from the physical realm of existence into eternity. (See Chapter 3 and 'Footprints to Visit') In Mexican Aztec iconography, footprints symbolized the invisible presence of the god. Divine footprints can be found in codices (manuscripts of ancient texts) where they appear on the bodies of certain figures to show the god's presence. In rituals performed to celebrate the arrival of the gods on earth, ground maize flour was placed on a rush mat and when a small footprint appeared in the flour, those present knew that the gods had arrived: The priest said, 'His Majesty has come.' [21] In parts of Scotland and Ireland it was once the custom to look for St Brigid's footprints in the ashes in the hearth on St Brigid's Eve, their direction indicating good or evil fortune (See Chapter 4).

The belief that a deity or divine personage could leave some of their power behind in their footprints is shown by the practice in some parts of the world of not allowing such people any contact with the earth. They always had to be carried, because if their feet touched the ground, their life-force would drain away into the earth. Montezuma, the Mexican Aztec Emperor, was always carried on the shoulders of noblemen; the king of Persia, while indoors, walked on carpets that no one else was allowed to walk on, while outdoors he rode in a chariot or on horseback. Joseph Campbell calls this 'the insulating horse, to keep the hero out of immediate touch with the earth and yet permit him to promenade among the peoples of the world'.[22] There are many instances in folklore of famous personages' or saints' horses leaving hoof-prints in rocks: maybe those animals performed the same function, standing in for the saint or whoever it might be, so that they did not dissipate their energy, but instead harboured it so that when they did themselves leave a footprint on the rock, it was especially powerful.

Imprint symbolism is wide-ranging, extending from birth at one end of the spectrum to death at the other. Womb-like caves were thought to be birth-places: Zeus'

*The headman of a mountain community in north Togo showing where the
first man came down from Heaven (Essoda). Photo: Dr Thomas J. Larson.*

birthplace is marked by a cave shrine on Mount Ida in Crete, while in southern
Africa, all humans and animals were believed by the Anyanja tribal group to have
originated in a hole in the ground east of Lake Nyasa, where they left their footprints
on a rock as they emerged.[23] Similarly in southern Botswana, where at Metsing there
is a flat outcrop of rock in which is a deep hole with a spring at the bottom. The local
tribe believed that this was the site of Creation, and that from out of the hole came
all the animals, then a one-legged giant called Metsing, then the Bushmen, then the
first Bantu and other tribesmen, all leaving their footprints in the wet soil. The giant's
footprint is a natural depression in the rock, but all the others are rock engravings,
comprising crude human feet (the largest of these having six toes), and many animal
tracks including lion, baboon, rhino, hippo, and others.[24] Also in Africa, the Kabiye
people of Togo held sacred a line of tracks on the mountains at Yade, believing them
to mark the place where the first man and woman came down from Essoda or
heaven. Their son and daughter founded the first settlement of Kabiye people.[25]

These visitors were welcomed, but at the end of the life-cycle, visits from the dead
were rarely a cause for celebration, and efforts would be made to stop the dead from
revisiting the places where they once lived. The Finno-Ugrics of Scandinavia would
cover the footprints of a funeral procession with ashes, to stop the corpse from
finding its way back home.[26] Perhaps the purpose behind footprints inscribed on the
slabs of prehistoric burial chambers was similar. In Brittany footprints have been

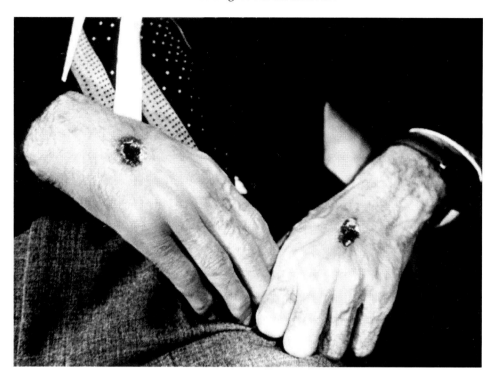

Stigmata in the hands of Antonio Ruffini, an Italian stigmatic who built a chapel south of Rome at the place where he saw a vision of the Virgin Mary.
Photo: Dr Elmar R. Gruber.

found that are surrounded by meandering lines: were these intended to control and encompass the footprints of the dead who were buried there, to stop them returning to haunt the living?[27] Alternatively, the meander might represent a maze, with the whole emblem being an invitation to follow the dead and communicate with them through sacred or ritual dance, perhaps in a trance state. Footprints have also been found on a Roman period cremation urn from Jutland, and on Christian gravestones.[28] Perhaps these were also intended to pin down the ghosts and stop them walking... or perhaps they were there in their good-luck role and symbolised the hope of resurrection. If the dead did manage to sneak back, you could also use ashes to locate and identify them, since it was widely believed that the returned dead, as well as guardian animals and spirits, and troublesome demons, could be located by means of the footprints they left in ashes strewn on the ground. In England it was once believed that if ashes were scattered on the hearth on St Mark's Eve, and a footprint was found in them next morning, that person would die in the coming year.[29] Some of the ghosts recorded in Chapter 9 also left footprints in dust.

The footprints recorded in folklore usually commemorate the visit of some superhuman being, the event being described in the story that often survives to explain the imprints. Where a saint or other holy person is involved, the site is imbued with sanctity and has a powerful significance for the pilgrims who visit it. It is open to all, and anyone can visit and partake of the power, real or imagined, of the

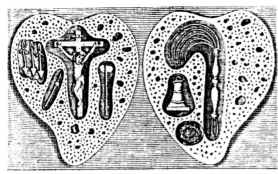

Cum Clara pectus explicat.
Fulget Crucis myſterium.

The emblems of the Passion embossed on the heart of St Clare of Montefalco, as revealed after autopsy. (From the Acta Sanctorum *vol.III, August, 673)*

place. At many of these special places, the pilgrims have developed rituals, usually involving a certain procedure that must be followed, in order to 'activate' the benefits to be obtained there. Sometimes pilgrims leave offerings: at certain French imprints such small items as money or pins or little wooden crosses or flowers would be left in the imprint, in hopes of receiving healing.[30] In South Dakota (U.S.A.), the Sioux Indians would leave offerings of tobacco and beads on a rock bearing human footprints.[31]

On a much more personal level, however, some people claim their own private sacred imprints, which take the form of stigmata. Probably the earliest case of a person receiving stigmata, in the form of wounds in the palms and feet where the nails pierced Christ's body at the Crucifixion, and in the side where he was speared, dates back to St Francis of Assisi in the thirteenth century, and there have been many cases in the almost 800 years since then.[32] In St Francis' case, it was even reported that the heads of the nails could be seen in the palms of his hands and in his feet, outside the flesh, and that the points of the nails came out through the backs of his hands and feet. Some stigmatics also bore the marks of the crown of thorns around their heads, others had stripes on their body from the scourging. Even more remarkable was the case of St Clare of Montefalco in Italy, who had the emblems of the Passion embossed on her heart during a vision. She died in 1308 and her body remained incorrupt. It can be seen in her shrine at Montefalco, along with the heart on which were found a thumb-sized crucifix, a scourge, a crown of thorns, and other symbols after her death. Unfortunately they are no longer clearly visible.[33] St Veronica Giuliani (c.1640–1727) also received the imprint of the emblems of the passion on her heart, reportedly seen when her body was opened up 30 hours after her death, and so too did St Clara of the Cross. Similar miracles clearly also happen in other religious settings, for a traveller in western Nepal, visiting the monastery named Ku-tsap-ter-nga in the district of T'hak, saw numerous interesting relics including a lama's skull which had 'the Tibetan letter A embossed as it were on the bone, for he had meditated so long on this basic vowel-sound, which lies at the root of all existence, that it had produced its written symbol miraculously inside his skull'.[34]

*Pilgrims' graffiti at
St Winefride's Well,
Holywell, Flintshire.*

The average person cannot claim such a personal link to the sacred as is shown by stigmatics and lamas, but nevertheless the urge to make a lasting personal connection is a deep one, as evidenced by the quantity of pilgrims' graffiti (usually names and drawings) at holy sites, such as St Winefride's Well at Holywell (Flintshire) or saints' shrines in cathedrals. Sometimes pilgrims leave their foot-marks, for example at Capel Ffynnon Fair (the chapel of St Mary's Well) at Cefn Meiriadog (Denbighshire), where foot outlines, and some hand outlines, can be seen scratched into the stones around the well.[35] This same urge to leave one's mark can also manifest itself in a non-religious setting. Think of the Chinese Theatre in Hollywood, California, with its forecourt full of the footprints, handprints and signatures of the stars (See 'Footprints to Visit'); or even Bolsover Castle in Derbyshire, where visitors since the 1820s have signed their names inside the outline of shoes on the lead roof.[36] In North Yorkshire, the 19th-century squire of Ebberston Hall would lure his girlfriends up onto the roof and trace the outlines of their hands and feet.[37]

Practices similar to this (though usually without the hint of fetishism!) may not be as rare as one might at first imagine. Folklorist John Billingsley described how he found 19th-century markings on lead sheeting on the roof of St Peter's church in Sowerby (West Yorkshire), including signatures and hands and feet. The feet are shoe-prints, and they have a spoked wheel design on the heel, a feature which also appears on the wrist of some of the handprints.[38] Could this be intended for self-protection, or simply a good-luck symbol? It is interesting that the same spoked-wheel design is also among the repertoire of symbols found on the footprints-of-the-Buddha icons in Asia, where the design represents the Wheel of the Law. Archaeologists recording details of graffiti discovered on the tower roof of Cookley church in Suffolk counted no less than 163 shoe impressions with dates from the 17th to 19th centuries, and some names were also found, as well as a few tracings of hand outlines.[39] The lead in the tower of the church at Ilketshall St Lawrence, also in Suffolk, carries foot outlines that have inside them designs including a crown, a swastika, and a hanged man.[40] All these designs must have had a meaning within folk magic, now forgotten, but probably to do with promoting good luck, or keeping evil fortune at bay. Another church where footprints were found on the roof is Edmondthorpe in Leicestershire, where hundreds of shoe outlines bear dates from the early 1700s to the mid-1980s.[41]

Kitten footprints on a brick placed on the exterior chimney wall of a Norfolk cottage.

Possibly the practice of inscribing shoe outlines on church roofs is somehow linked with the equally widespread custom of concealing old shoes within the fabric of domestic dwellings, often inside the chimney, and likely done with the intention of keeping away evil spirits, which might enter through the chimney. The same intention may have also manifested itself in another form: the impressing of animal tracks on bricks in the process of manufacture. In the former exterior wall (now inside the conservatory) of her cottage in Norfolk, folklorist Jennifer Westwood pointed out to me a brick bearing the clear impression of what appeared to be a kitten's footprints, obviously impressed there at the time of the brick's manufacture. The brick had been placed on the exterior of the chimney, suggesting that even if the kitten had accidentally walked on the wet brick, it had later been used as a good-luck charm and sited so as to protect the cottage and especially its chimney. In the same vein, human and animal (cat, pig, ox) footprints were found on over 300 bricks at the Roman bath-house at Vindolanda close to Hadrian's Wall during an archaeological excavation in 2000, though there is no evidence that these marked bricks were recognised as having any special powers.[42]

While staying in Cornwall and visiting old churches during 2001, I chanced upon an old sheet of lead in the nave of St Cleer church which had been brought down from the roof. I was intrigued to find that it bore several shoe outlines, with 18th-century dates scribed inside them. Later on the same holiday I found another shoe outline, engraved into the lead still in place in a church tower. After so many examples have come to light in the course of my research, I am now confident that the roof lead of many other English churches will also be found to carry foot-outlines. A few examples that can be visited will be found in the entries for England: Gloucestershire and Rutland, and Wales: Powys in 'Footprints to Visit'. There is clearly a deep-seated impulse to leave one's mark at any significant place one has visited, an impulse which also takes the form of lighted candles, flowers, coins and other offerings left at sacred places, carved name-graffiti, and it may be a similar impulse which inspires us to take photographs, especially ones showing ourselves at the places in question. In the 1960s, Elise Baumgartel, who was excavating on Monte Gargano in Italy, asked her workmen why they were adding their own hands and feet to the hundreds

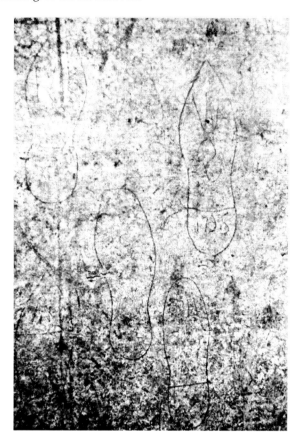

*Shoe outlines on lead from the
roof of St Cleer church,
Cornwall.*

of such impressions already to be seen in the sanctuary of the church of Monte San Angelo, and they told her they did it so that something of themselves would be ever-present in the holy place.[43] This impulse links us incontrovertibly with the people of thousands of years ago who have left more than 100 million rock art motifs around the world, including among them, of course, many hand and feet impressions.

Footprints and other marks in the landscape usually immortalise the presence of a saintly or supernatural being, acting as proof of his or her presence at that place, but there are some legends where the visible proof takes the form of a bare patch on the ground rather than the definite shape of a body-part. In mid-Wales in 1821 John Davies was executed for highway robbery, and his last words allegedly declared that as a sign of his innocence, God would not allow the grass to grow on his grave for at least a generation. The so-called Robber's Grave in Montgomery churchyard (Powys) remained bare at least until the beginning of the 20th century, though more recently grass has grown there, leaving only a small patch bare.[44] The 'proof of innocence' theme reappears in Halifax (West Yorkshire) where a hand-mark on a wall at Piece Hall is said to have been made by a fugitive from justice, who declared his innocence before God as he was dragged away by police, leaving his handprint behind him. Similarly in Pennsylvania, there is a mysterious handprint in cell no.17 of the old Carbon County Jail in Jim Thorpe, said to have been made by Alexander Campbell in 1877 as he was being taken from his cell to be executed as an accessory

The Robber's Grave in Montgomery churchyard, photographed around 1897–8
when the cross-shaped bare patch could still be clearly seen.

to murder. He swore he was innocent, and said the print would remain there for ever as proof of the truth of his statement. It has been painted over more than once, but has always reappeared. Even demolishing the wall failed to get rid of it: in 1930 when the sheriff wanted to end the legend he had the wall replaced, but was shocked to find that the handprint reappeared.[45]

Another bare-grave story concerns a man who was famed for his swearing, and it was said while he was still alive that because of his blasphemy grass would never grow on his grave. He was eventually buried at Luskentyre on Harris (Western Isles) and sure enough, according to Alasdair Alpin MacGregor, writing in 1937, despite the site being sown with grass seed, 'not a blade will spring upon it'. He also told of another grass-free site, on the island of Pabbay in the Sound of Harris, where there was a battle between the MacDonalds and the MacLeods several hundred years ago: the islanders used to say that grass would never grow on the spot.[46] It was also said that for some while afterwards, no grass would grow on the hill at Ashingdon (Essex) where King Canute fought and won a battle.[47] The most famous bare-topped hill must however be Dragon Hill below the Uffington White Horse in Oxfordshire. The chalky-white patch on its summit was said to be the place where St George killed the dragon, and no grass would grow where the dragon's blood fell.

14

The hand-mark on the north gate at Piece Hall, Halifax. Photo: John Billingsley.

There are said to be barren patches the size of footprints at two sites of duels in England: at the site in Tavistock Square, London, there was also once a barren patch which marked where one of the duellists fell and died. According to 19th-century records, there were over twenty footprints, maybe even as many as forty, and when folklorist Jennifer Westwood visited the Square twenty years ago she was able to find bare patches 'which could be taken for footprints'.[48] At Skipsea Brough in East Yorkshire, four footprints marked the site of a duel fought by two brothers. They were two or three inches deep, and clearly right and left feet, placed the correct distance apart for a duel. In another version, there were only two footprints, left by two men who fought over a woman and killed each other. The belief was that if the prints were filled in, the men would return to haunt the spot, and so it was customary to make sure that they were kept clear of grass.[49] In the same area, at Hutton Cranswick, two bare footprints on a hill mark the place where Tommy Escritt used to stand and pray for the conversion of the village.[50]

The inventiveness of people the world over is shown by the wide variety of ingenious stories 'explaining' how the so-called foot-prints, hand-prints, finger-prints, knee-prints and so on came to be. Here are a couple of tales that don't fit into any of the following chapters but are worth recording nevertheless. Giraldus Cambrensis (Gerald of Wales) wrote of a boy's finger-marks in the church dedicated to St David

15

The bare patch on top of Dragon Hill, to the left in the distance, can be clearly seen. In the foreground is part of the head of the Uffington White Horse.

at Llanfaes near Brecon (Powys) which had impressed themselves on to a stone at the church. The boy leaned on the stone when trying to remove young pigeons from their nest, and perhaps as a punishment by St David for his act, his hand stuck fast to the stone and it was three days before it was released 'by the same divine power which had so miraculously fastened it'. Gerald actually met the person, by then an old man, who claimed to be the boy to whom it had happened. The stone bearing the finger-marks was preserved inside the church 'among the relics', it clearly being considered as some form of relic of St David.[51] Far away in the Caucasus (Abkhazia) a foot was imprinted at the time of the building of the Pitsunda church in the 10th–11th centuries. It was said that the architect had a wager with the man building the town's water supply: whoever finished his task last would commit suicide. The church architect was the loser, and he left his footprint in the wet mortar on the dome as he threw himself to his death.[52]

An amusing interlude before we enter the strange world of footprint-lore is provided by a few instances of animals allegedly bearing finger-marks, such as the squirrel, the dark lines on whose back are the marks made by Krishna's fingers when he stroked it.[53] The large black spot on each side of a haddock behind the gills is caused by St Peter's finger and thumb, and was made when he took the tribute money from the mouth of a fish on the orders of Christ.[54] Alternatively, the spots were made by Christ himself, since according to Scottish fishermen the fish provided to feed the five thousand was the haddock, and the marks were made at the time of that miracle.[55] In yet another explanation, the black marks were caused by the Devil's sooty fingers as he grabbed a fish by accident when trying to find his hammer in the sea. He was building Filey Brig (East Yorkshire) at the time.[56] Apparently the pig has six dark pea-sized rings on the inside of each foreleg, these said to have been caused by the pressure of the Devil's fingers, when he entered a herd of swine which ran into the Sea of Galilee and were drowned (the so-called Gadarene swine).[57] It used to be said of someone whose face was pockmarked that 'The Devil has thrashed peas upon him.'[58]

The Devil will make many more appearances in this catalogue of imprints, since he was said to have been responsible for the creation of so many of them. However he is probably outnumbered by the saints and other holy figures, and it is clear from this that a majority of the footprints and other impressions of body parts, both human and animal, were more than simply visual records of a supernatural presence, but played a more serious part in people's inner lives. The holy footprints helped bring an otherworldly dimension to the landscape which they knew so well, imbuing it with sanctity and reminding people of the spiritual aspects of life. In the following chapters I hope to convey something of the magic of footprints, be they ancient ones in cave art, the visible traces of saints or sinners, or evidence for modern mysteries that are still enthralling us today.

Chapter Two

Imprints from prehistory: fossil footprints, cave and rock art, and inauguration stones

> We admit we don't know exactly what made the prints, but we do know one agency that didn't, and that is man in the Carboniferous.
>
> A.G. Ingalls demonstrating how scientists discourage objective debate, in 'The Carboniferous Mystery', *Scientific American*, 162 (January 1940), 14.

Footprints have been found which appear to be genuine human footprints, dating back several million years – these are scientifically acceptable and have taken their place in the record books. However, alleged fossilised human footprints have also been found which are rather more controversial, since they apparently date back to a time *before* the known emergence of man. Even worse, they have also been found in the company of dinosaur footprints – and dinosaurs are believed to have become extinct over 64 million years ago, whereas the earliest acceptable traces of man date back only 4–5 million years. Does this mean that the proponents of theories about the existence of now-lost civilisations on earth were right all along? Could human populations have existed which have left no traces other than their footprints in stone (and a few anomalous artefacts)? There are several hurdles to jump before the answer can comfortably be 'Yes' to those questions. The rock layers where the footprint was found could have been wrongly dated; the so-called footprint might be nothing more than a footprint-shaped depression in the rock, or a distorted animal footprint; a hoaxer may have carved it and/or placed it into the wrong archaeological context. All these possibilities must be borne in mind when looking at the evidence for impossibly early man.

First let's look at the safe footprints, those the scientists have validated. Perhaps the most famous set of tracks, probably of an adult and a child walking side by side, was discovered in 1977 at Laetoli in north-west Tanzania. More than 50 prints were discovered, extending for around 80 feet, and they were preserved because they were made in volcanic ash which was then covered by further falls of ash that hardened. They are believed to date back around 3.75 million years, and they prove that hominids were walking upright at that time.[1] In addition, the feet are judged by many experts to be indistinguishable from 21st-century human feet, rather than having the expected ape-like characteristics, suggesting that humans very similar to ourselves had developed earlier than the fossil evidence has yet revealed.[2]

Other early footprint finds are relatively recent, being 'only' a few hundred thousand years old. Three sets of human footprints on the Roccamonfina volcano in southern Italy are fossilized in volcanic ash dated to between 325,000 and 385,000 years ago. Known locally as 'devils' trails', the tracks were made by people only 1.35 metres tall, possibly children, and some handprints show that one walker put down a hand occasionally to steady him- or herself in the descent of the volcano.[3] The footprint found in a former sand dune at Terra Amata in southern France, where evidence of hominid campsites at least 300,000 years ago was also found, was human in form,[4] and similarly 'modern' were the footprints found preserved in hardened volcanic ash during the construction of a dam near Demirkopru in Turkey in 1970. They were dated to 250,000 years ago, and a vivid picture was painted of a man desperately running to escape a volcanic eruption.[5] Anatomically modern feet are also said to have left the footprints found in 1997 on the shore of the Langebaan Lagoon north of Cape Town in South Africa. They were judged to be around 117,000 years old.[6]

By comparison with all the prints listed so far, those discovered in caves such as the Tuc d'Audoubert in Ariège, France, date back a mere 15,000 years, and are contemporary with the cave art that features a little later in this chapter. The marks of fingers and heels found around the clay bison at Tuc d'Audoubert may have been made by children playing while an adult made the bison. However the imprints could have been more significant than mere childish doodles, and could have been created in order to count game animals, or the numbers in the tribe, or record some period of time. Foot-, knee- and hand-prints found in other French caves were also probably made by children, either accompanying adults or exploring. Researchers have noted the preponderance of children's footprints in caves, always unshod – suggesting they may have left their footwear at the cave entrances. In the Chauvet Cave in southern France, 80 footprints apparently left by a boy around 8–12 years old have been found, covering 150 feet and leading to the so-called 'room of skulls' where bear skulls were found. The boy's footprints are accompanied by a dog track: 'the first pet in history'?[7] In the Niaux cave complex (France) where many footprints have been found in the several kilometres of caves, one set of about two dozen is placed in a 'rectilinear' pattern as if with the conscious intention of creating an artistic design.[8]

The closer we come to the present, the more common, relatively speaking, do prehistoric footprints become. Four adults left their prints about 8–9,000 years ago in the Mesolithic period on the foreshore at present-day Uskmouth (near Newport, South Wales), one of them being a relative giant with size 12 (UK) feet,[9] while fossilized footprints found on the shore at Formby (Merseyside) date back around 5,000 years to the Neolithic period. The tracks of animals such as wolf, wild boar, goat, sheep, deer, unshod horses and aurochs have also been identified at Formby. It has been possible to distinguish the tracks of males and females and children, and to interpret them as men moving faster, possibly tracking or herding red deer, with the women and children moving more slowly – perhaps gathering seafood. The feet also

Fossil footprints found by convicts during blasting in a sandstone quarry at the Nevada State Prison in 1882.

reveal abnormalities such as missing toes, arthritis, etc. All these tracks are however elusive, being regularly covered by the tide and by sediment.[10]

These scientifically acceptable reports are very different from the mixed bag of so-called fossilized human footprints that I have managed to glean from numerous sources of varying reliability. It's not always possible to separate the good from the bad, and the possible explanations listed earlier should always be borne in mind: primarily hoax and misidentification. The third possibility – that some of these footprints constitute proof that humans were living on earth millions of years ago – entails a great leap of faith, but even so it should not be discarded out of hand. Orthodox science doesn't know everything, and sometimes dons blinkers when faced with anomalies.

These footprints (only a selection from the examples on record[11]) were all discovered during the late 19th to late 20th centuries, and they are presented here in chronological order of their discovery. The first example demonstrates the need for caution in dating footprints, and also how modern scientific techniques can solve earlier puzzles. In 1878 footprints were discovered in a Nicaraguan quarry and examined by Dr Earl Flint who was in Central America collecting antiquities. They were at a depth of 16–24 feet, preserved in a mudstone layer, and he believed they dated back at least 50,000 years, and possibly even 200,000 years. However when

Dinosaur tracks interspersed with apparent human tracks, at Dinosaur Valley State Park, Texas. Photo: Dennis Stacy.

geologist Dr Howell Williams re-examined the site in 1941, he was able to ascertain that in fact they were no more than 5,000 years old, a finding confirmed in 1969 when radio-carbon dating was carried out on the soil layer below the mudflow. The conclusion was a date of c. 3000 BC, when early agriculture was underway in the area.[12] The humanoid footprints found during rock-blasting at the Nevada State Prison near Carson City in 1882 were genuinely ancient: their location in the rock strata dated them to around 2 million years ago. However, there was immediate doubt as to their origins, since they were 18-20 inches long and 8 inches wide, with a 3-foot stride, and so unlikely to be human! It was decided that the most likely source for the tracks was the ground sloth (Mylodon), the remains of which were also found in the same deposits.[13]

An 1890 newspaper report described how blasting in a Texas quarry had revealed seven gigantic human footprints on a rock shelf. The prints were almost 2 feet long and 4 feet apart, and 'deeper indentations' at the ends of the toes showed that the being had long curved nails. In addition, a heavy object appeared to have been dragged over the rocks, 'probably a club', according to the press account. Alarm bells ring at this point: not only was the being an apparent giant, if he had feet that were 2 feet long, but he was behaving according to the current stereotype and wielding a club.[14]

An age of 7 million years was given by W. Freudenberg to the fragmentary human footprints found in a clay pit at Hol in Belgium early in the 20th century. He analysed the prints and noted clear dermal ridges. The pattern of the lines matched modern human feet rather than those of apes. The little toe was short, rather than long like an ape's, and his analysis suggested that modern rather than primitive humans were responsible for the footprints.[15] Seven million years is pretty unbelievable, but the ancient footprints which have received the most publicity must be those discovered in 1910 in Dinosaur Valley State Park, along the Paluxy River in Texas. In 1909 three-toed dinosaur tracks were found: the following year two boys fishing in a tributary of the river found human footprints 15–18 inches long, accompanying dinosaur tracks. Humans living with dinosaurs over 64 million years ago? The waters were muddied in the 1930s by the carving of fake human footprints, and over the following decades controversy raged as to whether the footprints were genuinely human, or simply misinterpreted dinosaur tracks. In 1984 Glen J. Kuban made a discovery that appears to have settled the argument: the toes of dinosaur prints had been filled by a sediment that had later hardened to rock, leaving a track with a human-like appearance.[16] (A museum displaying the footprints from the Paluxy River, and others, has been opened at Glen Rose in Texas: more information on the Creation Evidence Museum can be found in 'Footprints to Visit'.) If the idea of humans living alongside dinosaurs seems unlikely, the next example is positively beyond comprehension. A fossilized partial shoe-print was found in Nevada in 1922 by John T. Reid, a mining engineer and geologist, while he was searching for fossils, and those who examined it agreed that details of the threads that sewed the shoe could be clearly seen, especially in photographs magnifying the marks 20 times. The only problem was, the rock the print came from dated back over 200 million years! If this is not a hoax, and there is nothing to suggest it is, then either humans wearing shoes were around millions of years ago, or the print was, as one learned doctor tried to explain it away, a 'freak of nature'.[17]

In 1932 more apparent footprints made by a giant were found, on gypsum rock on the western side of White Sands in New Mexico. Ellis Wright who discovered them was a government trapper, and his finding was confirmed by a party of men he took out to the site. They saw thirteen human footprints 22 inches long by 8–10 inches wide, clearly imprinted into the rock.[18] Although the footprints found in Rockcastle County, Kentucky, in 1938 were more acceptably human in size, there was nothing acceptable about their apparent dating: they were found in a rock outcrop dating back around 300 million years! They were reported in a sober manner by Professor W.G. Burroughs, head of geology at Berea College. He said: 'There are three pairs of tracks showing left and right footprints... Each footprint has five toes and a distinct arch. The toes are spread apart like those of a human being who has never worn shoes.' They were about 9 inches long and 4 inches wide, or 6 inches across the spread toes. Other scientists studied them, and so too did a sculptor, who concluded that the footprints were not carved. In this case there seem to be only two possibilities: Either the footprints were of impossibly early humans, or they were made by an unknown amphibian with human-like feet.[19]

A tantalisingly brief report in *The Field* magazine, some time around 1948, mentioned that the imprint of what appeared to be a shoe had been found near Lake

The fossilised shoe-print found near Antelope Springs.

Windermere in Cumbria. Fair enough so far, but the information that it was in what was believed to be Ordovician limestone, dating back around 450 million years, places the report in either the realm of the fanciful, or the ground-breaking. Without further information, the puzzle remains.[20] Genuine prehistoric footprints were discovered at a depth of 4–5 feet when a farm track was being constructed in El Salvador in 1955, but the investigators judged them to be a 'mere' 1,200–1,800 years old.[21] A 'fossil footprint with ribbed sole' discovered in the Gobi Desert (China or Mongolia) in 1959, with the alleged age of at least 2 million years, was identified as being nothing more exciting than 'fossilised wind or water ripples in sandstone'.[22] Equally unlikely to be genuine is the 'footprint' measuring 44 by 21 inches found in sandstone, depth not mentioned, at Baxter Spring, Kansas, in 1963. It was of a right foot with perfect toes and an indentation caused by the ball of the foot. Proof that giants once roamed the American continent... or a hoax? [23]

An apparent shoe imprint discovered in Utah in 1968 has not yet been successfully explained away, despite its seeming impossibility. It was discovered by William J.

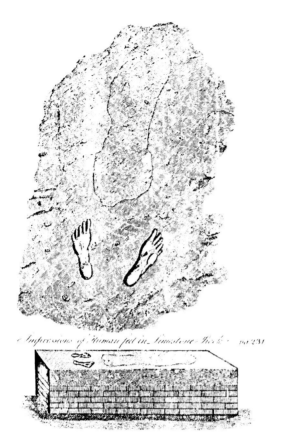

An 1822 depiction of the Mississippi Valley footprints which were later taken to New Harmony.

Meister who was fossil-hunting in the Wheeler Shale near Antelope Springs. He described how he found it: 'I broke off a large, approximately two-inch thick slab of rock. Upon hitting it on the edge with my hammer, it fell open like a book. To my great astonishment I saw on one side the footprint of a human with trilobites right in the footprint itself. The other half of the rock slab showed an almost perfect mold of the footprint and fossils. Amazingly the human was wearing a sandal… The footprint was clearly that of the right foot because the sandal was well worn on the right side of the heel in characteristic fashion.' The big problem is, the rock was dated to 505–590 million years ago.

Although the validity of the footprint was accepted by a professor of metallurgy, it was also rejected by a professor of geology. But its supporters also included Evan Hansen, who was a shoe repairer for many years. He interviewed Meister, and after careful examination of the find he concluded, 'Both sole and heel are some hard material like leather, or plastic, so this was a shoe with a hard sole, it was not a moccasin or any other simple foot covering or soft material.' Simulacrum or fossil footprint? As Ulrich Magin commented: 'What is certainly needed is a scientific and unbiased study of the print by geologists and palaeontologists.' [24]

Also discovered in the late 1960s were some controversial human-like tracks near Tuba City, Arizona. E. Cummings was forced to land his small plane on a dirt road, and it was then he noticed the tracks beside the road. If genuine, they date back 200 million years and could be further evidence for the coexistence of humans with dinosaurs. However, despite considerable scientific research over many years, their validity is still unproven, and sceptics may be disturbed to learn that the major support for these tracks comes from creationists, as was also the case with the Wheeler Shale footprint and of course the Paluxy tracks. The involvement of creationists doesn't necessarily mean that the tracks are not genuine, of course, but non-creationist scientists are likely to be more circumspect in their pronouncements.[25] In 1983 another human–dinosaur juxtaposition was reported, this time from Turkmenistan in Central Asia. Professor Amanniyazov of the Turkmen Academy of Sciences agreed that the footprint, found next to a giant three-toed dinosaur print in rock 150 million years old, looked human, but that didn't mean to say it was human.[26] Prints found in Southwest Virginia in 1991 also looked human, but were soon identified as those of a giant sloth, like those found at Carson City in 1882.[27]

There have been other discoveries of anomalous footprints which might also have originated millions of years ago (if any of them did...), but in the cases which follow there is also the possibility that they may have been artificially created, and relatively recently, as they were found on exposed rock outcrops rather than hidden in underground strata. In that respect they are in some respects similar to the footprints which fill the following chapters, many of which are also located on rock outcrops. It is often impossible to tell whether any given footprint is a natural depression that just happens to resemble a footprint, or has been carved by human hands in the recent or distant past, or is a genuine fossilised footprint thousands or even millions of years old.

In 1822 Henry R. Schoolcraft described how he had discovered a slab of limestone rock bearing two human footprints, at Harmony in the Mississippi Valley. The rock was located in a quarry, and the footprints had been seen in earlier years by the French and during the development of St Louis, but it is not clear whether the slab was cut out of the rock in quarrying or whether it had always been simply lying around. So it is impossible to judge the age of the footprints, and whether they were natural or manmade. However the interesting fact gleaned from Schoolcraft's report is that the slab was removed by Father Rapp and taken to his Rappite community's village of New Harmony (Indiana) where his followers were said to regard the footprints as 'the sacred impress of the feet of our Saviour' (as quoted by Schoolcraft, but it was actually the Archangel Gabriel whose footprints they were believed to be). There is more information on these footprints in Chapter 3, where their acceptance as the footprints of the Archangel is described: folklore of this kind in the making is rarely recorded.[28] Towards the end of the 19th century, Herbert P. Hubbell found a footprint stone which had already been absorbed into the local folklore. It was near the mouth of the Little Cheyenne River ('in Dakota Territory', so presumably South Dakota), on a rocky hillside, and three moccasined feet were clearly marked in line about 4–5 feet apart – left, right, left – as if made by a person running. A local Indian told Mr Hubbell that the Indians considered it to be a 'medicine' rock and worshipped it. Beads and trinkets had been found there, probably left as offerings.[29]

Some reports give few details of the footprints that have been discovered. An 1890 press report described a rock outcrop in a stream near Lincolnton (Georgia) where 'a perfectly defined imprint of a man's bare foot' had been found.[30] The *American Anthropologist* reported in 1896 the finding of a human footprint 14 inches long in a large stone 4 miles north of Parkersburg (West Virginia),[31] while in 1910 a man digging a well near Gravelbourg (Saskatchewan, Canada) found a rock with a 10-inch footprint on it. It is not clear whether the stone was actually found in the hole, or just happened to be lying around. Apparently the footprint was not noticed until the light struck it at a certain angle, and so it could have already been above ground but never noticed before.[32]

Footprints of apparently moccasin-clad feet on rocks in McIntosh County, Oklahoma, were first noticed in 1956 by the farmer riding across his land. Researcher Stan Morrison, working at the site in 1986, counted almost a dozen footprints, two of them bare feet, and he also found what appeared to be a runic inscription (the letters BM) and petroglyphs which, he believed, gave the site an ancient astronomical function. He suggested that the pair of bare footprints were 'the positioning marks for the chief priest or shaman...and directly in front of them is a bathtub-sized basin'.[33] This brings to mind the Graeco-Roman sanctuaries with carved footprints which possibly symbolized the presence of the god or goddess, where pilgrims would stand to make contact with the divine presence; and also the use of footprints at inauguration sites, to be discussed later in this chapter. In the 1960s more footprints were discovered in Oklahoma, a few miles east of Tulsa. Troy Johnson removed earth and roots from a sandstone outcrop and discovered human and animal footprints, which he felt were genuine fossilised tracks never before exposed to daylight.[34]

There have been many more discoveries of this kind, but it is time to move on to other matters. But first, let us make a quick trip to Atlantis, to see the footprints recently discovered there... One of the claimed locations for Atlantis is the tiny Bimini Islands in the Bahamas 55 miles east of Florida. Expedition Project Alta-III, led by William Donato, went to Bimini in autumn 1997, and while they were looking for signs of a human presence there in prehistoric times, project member Donnie Fields saw a human footprint close to the sea. A search revealed two dozen prints, leading from the beach and into the water towards East Bimini. A geologist dated them as 7,000 years old, from a time when the two islands were a single land-mass.[35]

Most of these discoveries have been of genuine footprints, ancient and fossilised, their survival being totally fortuitous, but sometimes presenting a major headache to science, especially when they appear to date from the time of the dinosaurs. More scientifically acceptable are the footprints and handprints which form part of the art of prehistoric man, discovered in caves and on rock outcrops around the world. There are many recorded examples of hands and feet in cave art, dating back as far as the Upper Palaeolithic (last part of the Old Stone Age) which covers the period from 40,000 to 10,000 years ago. Hands can appear as prints (often red) or stencils --

Stencilled hands and wild horses in the Pech-Merle Cave (Lot, France).

there are hundreds of stencilled hands in the cave of Gargas in the French Pyrenees, dating back around 27,000 years. Some of them seem to be mutilated or deformed, and it is not known whether they genuinely had fingers damaged or missing, perhaps from frostbite, or whether the fingers were bent in some form of sign language. However it seems more likely that they simply show the manual dexterity that is to be expected from artistic humans, rather than being evidence of 'a macabre self-mutilating cult'.[36] Not all researchers would agree with that assessment, and the possibility of ritual amputation has recently been revived, following the discovery of a ritual deposit in a Polish cave which included human finger bones, dated to around 30,000 years ago. The suggestion is that fingers may have been amputated in a ceremony, as a form of atonement or sacrifice.[37]

Among many other examples worldwide, hundreds of stencilled hands also decorate Argentinian rock shelters such as the Cueva de las Manos, thought to date back to c.7000 BC (see 'Footprints to Visit'), and Australian caves, such as Art Gallery in Carnarvon Gorge, Queensland (see 'Footprints to Visit').[38] They are still being discovered: in 1995 a hiker accidentally found a cave in Wollemi National Park near Sydney where there are scores of Aboriginal rock paintings up to 4,000 years old; the designs including humans, god-like figures and animals, as well as outspread hands.[39]

There is nothing to be gained from listing all the caves where hands appear, but it might be useful to see what interpretations have been placed upon them by different

This stone with a carved hand design was found in the Neolithic cult-house at Hornsherred, Zealand, Denmark. Photo: Klaus Aarsleff.

scholars, and also what links we can find with more modern expressions of hands and feet. A survey of 343 examples of Palaeolithic 'negative hands' on cave walls, 10,000-30,000 years old, made in 2003 by Dr Charlotte Faurie and Michel Raymond of the Université Montpellier II, found that when compared with 179 French students the proportion of left-handers was the same, a fact the researchers found surprising. 'The frequency of left-handers is highly variable from place to place in the present world (ranging from three percent among Inuit people to 27 percent of the Eipo people of New Guinea), and handedness is subject to natural selection, so the theoretical chances that the frequency remains the same for 10,000 years is very low,' said Dr Faurie. She also suggested a meaning for the negative hands: 'the rock is the border between the real world and the imaginary/spiritual world, and... they put their hand on this border to enter the spiritual world.' [40] Other possible explanations include: 'a signature, a property mark, a memorial, a wish to leave a mark in some sacred place, a record of growth, "I was here"...' [41] 'The visitors, probably for the same reason as modern Australian aborigines do on their sacred rocks, impressed their hand prints as testimony to each individual's right to enter, not simply because it "identified" him like a fingerprint, but probably because... the hand is to primitive people directly linked with a human's personal spirit.' [42]

The urge to leave one's signature at a place with which one has interacted still persists. Folklorist Jacqueline Simpson reported how in the 1970s, when stripping old

A cast of the feet carvings on a stone at the Petit-Mont passage-grave.

wallpaper, she found marks left by earlier decorators, one from before the First World War, and one probably from the late 1930s. Both men had outlined one of his hands, and added his name and the date; they had also outlined their implements.[43] I have also found the signatures of decorators in similar circumstances – and added my own. Was this decorators' custom of marking walls also originally intended to convey good luck, or protection? In Chapter 1 I referred to an Indian custom of placing handprints on walls in order to avert the evil eye, and the same thing happened in the Assam area of India at the time of the Wangala (rice-gathering ceremony): 'it is the custom to mix flour with water, and for the assembled people to dip their hands into the mixture and make white hand-marks on the posts and walls of the house and on the backs of the guests.' [44] Presumably this was also intended as a form of protection or good luck.

Hands and feet are sometimes found on prehistoric megalithic burial chambers and as part of other outdoor rock art, both from prehistoric times and also much more recently. The hands with outstretched fingers, found occasionally on rocks at Neolithic burial sites, have been interpreted as sun symbols, for example by Johannes Maringer, German historian of religion, who described how, 'In the north, just as in the west, [of Europe] the megalithic cult of the dead seems to have merged with sky, or solar, worship. The surface of the slab covering a grave at Bunsch, in Ditmarschen, [Germany] reveals not only a number of cup-like hollows, but also incised drawings of a four-spoked wheel, several pairs of hands, and a foot – in other words, symbols of the sky, or solar, cult.'[45] Maybe this sun symbolism can also explain the use of a hand in more recent times as a protection against the evil eye: the sun with its light rays is more powerful than the forces of darkness.

Numerous carvings of feet have been found on burial chambers in Britain and Brittany. The two feet engraved on a slab at the Petit-Mont passage-grave (Arzon, Brittany) are, according to G.R. Levy, at the centre of a maze, which is here formed by meandering lines, and may represent 'the primeval maze of entry to the divine world', the maze also being 'indicative of the soul's wanderings'.[46] The symbolism may indicate that the dead person's soul has passed into other realms, and may even express some fear of the unwanted return of the dead, the meandering lines acting as a kind of barrier to prevent the dead coming back to haunt the living. (See 'Footprints to Visit') The most famous British prehistoric footprint stones are among the Calderstones (Merseyside) which probably once formed a passage grave. Several carved feet are accompanied by symbols among which were spirals, again perhaps symbolising the maze.[47] (See 'Footprints to Visit') Feet, six in total, were also found carved on a slab covering a burial inside a round barrow at Pool Farm, West Harptree (North-East Somerset), first excavated in 1930. The feet were accompanied by cup-marks, a common feature of prehistoric rock art whose meaning is still unknown.[48] (See 'Footprints to Visit') The only other known example of Early Bronze Age foot-carvings in Britain was found on the southern wall-slab of a stone-lined grave in a round barrow at Harbottle Peels near Alwinton in Northumberland.[49] In addition to the death symbolism, it is also possible that where carved feet appear at prehistoric burial chambers, they were left there by people visiting the tombs of their ancestors, as a form of votive offering, in the same way that foot outlines have been left at sacred sites such as churches in recent times.

The foot also makes an appearance at the most famous British prehistoric site, Stonehenge, though not in the same context as the carvings just described. The 17th-century antiquary John Aubrey was the first to describe a large depression shaped like a friar's heel on one of the stones, but not the one now commonly known as the Heel Stone, though confusingly that also bears a mark resembling a heel. Aubrey's heel-stone is no.14 in the outer circle, and in his *Monumenta Britannica* he explained how it came to be there: 'when Merlin conveyed these Stones from Ireland by Art Magick, the Devill hitt him in the heele with that stone, and so left the print there'. Another version of the story is that the Devil was secretly building Stonehenge and realised he was being watched by a friar, so he threw one of the huge stones at him, catching him on the heel, and leaving a permanent heel-shaped mark on the stone.[50] It is strange that the genuine examples of prehistoric footprints carved on megaliths and rock outcrops do not seem to have inspired similar folklore.

Carvings on burial chambers may not have been intended to be seen, or only perhaps on special occasions. Carvings on rock outcrops, however, presumably were meant to be on permanent display, conveying a symbolic message to all who came there. These open-air 'notice-boards' have been in use since prehistoric times, and right up to the present day, though the message left by the earliest carvers is often now unclear and can only be guessed at. Often the carvings are also impossible to date. Both hands and feet feature in the displays, though rarely together. However, cup-marks sometimes occur with footprints, and though the significance is not understood, at least the presence of cup-marks indicates that the carvings are prehistoric, and probably Neolithic, or 4,500–6,000 years old. The highest cup-marked rock in Europe, at c.9,000 feet in the French Alps, La Pierre aux Pieds has 82 feet and 80 cup-marks carved on it.[51] Bronze Age rock engravings in Scandinavia, dating back c.1,500 years, sometimes show footprints and shoe-prints in association with boats. Again the meaning is not known: perhaps the footprints were worshipped as representations of a god – 'virtually the equivalent of a cult image'[52] – or as a concrete expression of the presence of the divine being. Richard Bradley suspects they are connected with death, and may mark the path from the grave to the next world, the shoe-prints being 'the *hel-shoes* [footwear used by the dead in Icelandic mythology] of the recently deceased.'[53] (See 'Footprints to Visit: Sweden')

The meaning of carved hands seems somewhat clearer and, as mentioned earlier, they seem to symbolise the sun, with the outstretched fingers representing the rays of light. There are numerous examples in European rock-art, especially in Scandinavia and at the famous site of Val Camonica in northern Italy (see 'Footprints to Visit'). Sun-symbolism, not just by means of hands, is very widespread in prehistoric rock-art, and it is not difficult to understand how important sun-worship must have been, considering the fact that the presence of the sun is vital to mankind, and without it we all would die.[54]

Outdoor carvings of hands and feet have been discovered in many other parts of the world. There are around 200 'podomorphs' (pairs of feet) carved on Mt Tindaya on Fuerteventura in the Canary Islands: the mountain was a holy shrine of the Guanches, the indigenous people who disappeared soon after the Spanish arrived on the island.[55] In Australia, a rock in the bed of the Laura river (Queensland) has carvings of hands and feet with fingers and toes spread; its date is unknown. When carvings of human footprints were first noticed by European settlers, they were attributed to whichever religious or folklore figure may have been part of their culture. The Aborigines believed that footprints of humans and animals were made by the creator when the rock was softer, and some of the giant animal tracks were thought to have been made by dinosaurs, though this explanation probably does not extend to the larger human footprints that have been discovered.[56] Human footprints, or mundoes as they are known, feature frequently in Aborigine rock art. As in Europe, the meaning is often unclear, but they probably encapsulate folk beliefs and ritual practices, and a long line of footprints may be an invitation to follow a ritual trail.[57] (See 'Footprints to Visit')

In Pakistan above the Indus river runs the Karakoram Highway, and when this was being constructed, rocks carved with prehistoric carvings of symbols and inscriptions were discovered (and probably some were destroyed). One, in the barren rocky landscape between Thak-Gah and Buto-Gah, shows a hunting scene, a footprint and a palm-print with four spread fingers.[58] Engraved footprints and painted handprints feature regularly in the rock-art of Southern Africa; the best rock paintings are found in the mountainous regions and are often accompanied by red or white handprints.

These vary in size, with small ones close to the floor showing that children also made handprints, as in the much earlier cave art described earlier in this chapter. One of the finds was of a cave with one rock wall covered by hundreds of later stylized handprints: earlier handprints were made by covering the hand with paint and pressing it on the wall.[59] Dating the South African rock art is difficult, but some could be as old as 12,000 years, while other paintings are likely to be much more recent.[60]

American Indian rock art is voluminous and ubiquitous, from Canada down through the United States (see 'Footprints to Visit'), Mexico and Central America, and throughout South America (see 'Footprints to Visit: Argentina'). As might be expected by now, footprints and handprints feature widely in the rock art of the Americas – and as we have already seen elsewhere, dating is often imprecise. Usually, but not invariably, the footprints are engraved on rock, while the handprints are painted, by impression or stencilling. This variation may suggest that feet have different symbolic or ritual functions from hands. Hand motifs are particularly common in the Americas, often the 'blown-stencil' technique having been employed, where the hand is placed on the rock face and pigment blown from the mouth around the edge of the hand. One smoke-blackened cave wall in the Santa Lucia Mountains of California has 246 white handprints on it, these having been made by coating the hand with paint, pressing it on the wall, and then scraping the dried print to make it look skeletal. This possibly suggests that at least some hands indicated a ritual identification with the dead. Another hint of the significance of some handprints appears at a southern Californian location where the smaller handprints of young people are found with diamond and zigzag designs which are associated with puberty rites. Those prints may have been made as part of the ceremony of initiation, to cement the youngsters' membership of the tribe.[61]

Although some of the petroglyphs and paintings were likely to have been merely doodles, it is probable that most of them had a definite purpose. However, the world of the rock artists is so far removed from our own, that we cannot easily translate their meanings. Hints and suggestions, links with similar designs in other parts of the world and at long-distant times, all provide tantalising glimpses into the lives of the artists and their kin. Footprints and handprints are shorthand messages which to some degree have been passed down through the generations, though their meanings may be somewhat obscured by the time they have reached the 21st century. Researcher Paul Devereux found he was using his intuition to interpret some intriguing footprints he discovered in Pony Hills, a remote location in the New Mexico desert. A life-sized human footprint beside a rock carving of a figure holding 'a tall upright stick with an umbrella-shaped top' he saw as part of shamanic rituals, the shaman figure holding a ceremonial staff in the shape of an hallucinogenic mushroom. In the same area Devereux discovered a trail of tiny footprints across rock ledges and flat rocks towards a large rock pool, which he instinctively felt were the footprints of the Water Baby, a spirit helper of the shamans.[62]

Ancient petroglyphs may need to be interpreted using unorthodox methods, because of the lack of written documentation as to their purpose. By contrast, the use of inauguration stones in Celtic lands is relatively well documented, since these footprints were still in use only a few hundred years ago. There are still a few of them surviving in Scotland and Ireland, though probably there were once very many more. The ease with which they were discarded, despite being known to be 'special', is shown by a note from John S.A. Cunningham in *Notes and Queries* (published in 1866) in which he recalls a letter he received in 1862 'from a gentleman in the county Sligo, stating he had in his possession "a red sandstone flag in a rough state, engraved with a human foot-print in the centre", and "until lately it had been used as a door flag in one of the peasant's cottages on his estate"; mentioning it was held in high estimation by the country-people in the neighbourhood, and asking me could I throw any light on its probable history or uses.'[63]

Stones such as this one, with one or two life-size footprints carved into them, were used when a king or chieftain or overlord was inaugurated into his role, and he would have stood in the footprints to take his vows. The footprints may have symbolised his predecessor, so that the new incumbent would be expected to 'follow in his footsteps' in upholding the tribal customs and generally being a good ruler. Having been used by so many generations of rulers, the stone would have become imbued with power, and the act of standing in the footprints would help bring home to the new ruler the importance of his task in upholding the standards of his predecessors. The use of stone may also have symbolized a direct link with the Earth, and the king's role in maintaining within his kingdom the health and fertility of the Earth and his subjects and livestock. There were many provincial kings and territorial chiefs in Ireland in the early Christian years, and one of the conditions of the ceremonial was 'That the inauguration should be celebrated at a remarkable place in the territory appointed of old for the purpose, where there was a stone with the impression of two feet, believed to be the size of the feet of their first captain, chieftain, or acquirer of the territory'.[64] There used to be a Proclamation Stone, with two foot impressions on it, on Cnoc na Dála or Carnfree Inauguration Mound in County Roscommon.[65] One surviving example is St Columba's Stone, near Londonderry, which has two foot-sized depressions. The chiefs of the O'Dohertys used this stone at their inaugurations.[66]

Stone inauguration seats would sometimes have been used in Celtic areas instead of stone footprints, a custom which was also widespread in other parts of the world. But it is feasible that the use of stone footprints in inauguration ceremonies was also practised widely, and some of the engraved stone footprints that have survived, but without traditions or folklore attached to them, may well have once been used in inauguration ceremonies. Stone seats were certainly used worldwide, and the practice has not died out: it was traditional for the British monarch to be crowned on a throne beneath which was placed the ancient Stone of Scone, Stone of Destiny, or Coronation Stone, a rock whose origins are lost in the mists of time.[67]

In Scotland there are several surviving footprint stones, all of which were probably inauguration stones though there is no actual documentation to support this. However the best-known and documented Scottish inauguration ritual site is now lacking its footprint stone. This was located near Loch Finlaggan on the island of Islay in the Inner Hebrides (Argyll and Bute), and was known as the Stone of the Footmarks. It was a rock about 7 feet square with footprints cut in it where the chief of Clan Donald (the MacDonalds) would stand, sword in hand, to take the oath. The

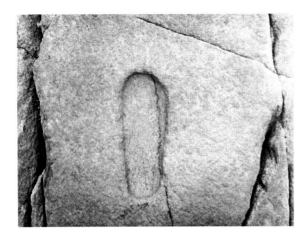

*The foot imprinted on a
rock at Dunadd fort.*

stone was destroyed in the early 17th century. One such installation of Donald as Lord of the Isles took place in Kildonan church on Eigg instead of on Islay, possibly around the mid-15th century, and was described by Hugh Macdonald who, it is believed, presided at the event. 'There was a square stone seven or eight feet long and the track of a man's foot cut thereon, upon which he stood, denoting that he should walk in the footsteps and uprightness of his predecessors and that he was installed by right in his possessions.'[68]

There is also said to be a footprint stone on the island of Berneray in the Outer Hebrides (Western Isles), known as Beinn a' Chlaidh Stone, which was an inauguration place of the Lord of the Isles.[69] At Clickhimin near Lerwick in the Shetland Isles, an important prehistoric site with substantial stone remains, there is a flagstone (now part of the causeway) on which two carved footprints can be seen, and these demonstrate the earlier importance of Clickhimin as a royal centre.[70] (See 'Footprints to Visit') Scotland's best-known footprint stone can be seen at Dunadd fort (Argyll and Bute), where it is prominently displayed on top of the hill, alongside a carved boar, an Ogham inscription and a stone basin. This was traditionally the inauguration site of the Kings of Dalriada.[71] (See 'Footprints to Visit') Two other possible inauguration stones recorded in Scotland were the Clach na Luirg (Stone of the Footmark) at Halkirk in Caithness, and the Ladykirk Stone on South Ronaldsay (Orkney), whose legend will be told in Chapter 4.[72]

This far-reaching historical round-up of feet and hands has extended over millions of years from the age of the dinosaurs until almost the present day, and the wide spread of cultures and locations conveys a sense of the power that imprints have had down through the centuries and millennia. Their influence has survived to the present day, in the form of a wide variety of legends and traditions that purport to explain them, and the following chapters will clearly demonstrate the power that footprints and handprints have had, and definitely still have, in many cultures.

Chapter Three

Sacred stones: the footprints of Buddha, Jesus, and other holy beings

> ‘ He had a well-shaped foot, small and delicate.’
>
> Pilgrim from Piacenza, c.570, describing Christ's footprints in the pavement of Pilate's judgement hall in Jerusalem.[1]

Most footprints in stone have been identified or 'explained' at some time in the past, and these explanations have been passed down through the generations in folklore. Many of the explanations have a religious theme, with Christianity naturally being predominant in the West; but this lore is not exclusively Western, the Eastern religions having their fair share of imprints. It is only the personnel of the stories who are different. The Christian footprint folklore is strongly weighted in favour of the saints, about whose imprints a whole book could easily be written: in this one I have devoted the following two chapters to them, while this chapter concentrates on other holy figures.

In the two previous chapters, mention has been made of Creation stories involving imprints, in Southern Africa and in Togo, and the appearance of gods is also recorded elsewhere. A missionary in Kiribati (the Gilbert Islands) in the South Pacific during the mid-20th century noted giant footprints carved in the rocks. These were locally believed to be the footprints of giants who came from the sky, and their existence was researched by Erich von Däniken when he visited the islands in 1980. He was able to find some of the footprints: some were 4 feet long, others were of normal size, but many had six toes (see also Chapter 8).[2] The gods and ancestral beings take many forms, according to folklore. In Australian Aborigine lore, Djanggawul and his two sisters were mythical beings who moved through the land during the Dreaming, and their sexual organs were so long they dragged on the ground and left traces which can still be seen.[3] The 'Bon Dieu' or 'Almighty God' who left his mark in France was in fact the Lord, or Jesus, rather than God. At Lognes (Yonne), a depression on a standing stone is known as 'Le Pas Dieu' ('God's footprint'), while at Arleuf (Nièvre) there are two cavities on two large rocks identified as the shoes of 'Bon Dieu', again meaning Jesus rather than God.[4] Further east, God's toe-print featured in the *Shih Jing*, which told the story of Kiang Yuan, mother of a king, who was childless until she happened to tread in a toe-print made by God, whereupon she became pregnant.[5] The footprints of God also feature on a modern item of jewellery, the so-called 'Footprints Cross'. Based on the poem 'Footprints', it 'is adorned with sculpted waves framing a single trail of footprints on a sandy beach.' On the reverse is the inscription: 'Footprints. When you saw only one set of footprints it was then that I carried you.'[6] God's footprints visible on the landscape, or God's footprints in a personal, portable form: the expression may be different but the impulse which created it is the same.

Of the few traces left by Biblical Old Testament figures, the most famous must be the almost 6-foot long Adam's Footprint on Adam's Peak, a mountain in south-west Sri Lanka (see 'Footprints to Visit'). But is it Adam's Footprint? It all depends on your religion. In Muslim legend, this is the place where Adam landed when he left Paradise and began his life on earth, but to Buddhists the footprint belongs to the Buddha and marks the place of his last contact with the world. For Chinese Taoists it was made by their first ancestor, Hindus visit the footprint of the god Siva, while Christians identify it as the footprint of St Thomas.

This extract from an account of a pilgrimage to Adam's Footprint dates from 1801: 'A considerable number of devotees... lately applied to our government in India for permission to visit the mark of Adam's foot, in Ceylon.... There is a tradition that the first man was created on the top of a high mountain in Ceylon, hence called Adam's Pike; and there is the shape of a man's foot cut out of the rock, about six feet in length, which they pretend to be the print of his foot. Near this mountain there is a reef of rocks extending to the continent, called Adam's Bridge; for they say it was made by angels, to carry him over to the main land.'[7] One version of the story of the making of Adam's Footprint tells how in Paradise the peacock was at the entrance on the lookout for approaching danger and ready to warn Adam; the role of the snake was to assist in repelling any danger. But Iblis (the Islamic name for the Devil) charmed the animals and was able to enter Paradise. When Adam was expelled from the Garden of Eden, he descended on to the peak which later took his name, Eve alighted at Jeddah on the Red Sea, the snake at Isfahan, the peacock in Hindustan, and Iblis in Khorasan. Adam stayed in Sri Lanka for 100 years, and then went to India across the islets and reefs known as Adam's Bridge.[8]

Abraham was the first of the patriarchs of Israel, and he rebuilt the Ka'bah, the sacred shrine of Islam at Mecca in Saudi Arabia that was first built by Adam. It is today a major pilgrimage site, the Hajj or pilgrimage to Mecca being one of the Five Pillars of Islam. To make the pilgrimage to the place where Abraham left his footprints is obligatory for every Muslim, at least once in his or her life, if the circumstances of their lives permit. The place where the concluding prayers are said is the pavilion which today houses the *maqam ibrahim,* the stone where Abraham stood to set the cornerstone of the Ka'bah and where he left his footprints.[9] To the north-west is the Sinai peninsula, in the southern part of which is Jebel Musa (the mountain of Moses), believed to be Mount Sinai. Moses lived in a cave on the mountain, and he is said to have stood in a certain hollow when the glory of the Lord passed by. This is near the chapel at the top of the mountain, and the impression of Moses' head and shoulders is said to be still visible on the stone.[10]

Also near the Red Sea is the site of Moses' Hot Baths, visited by the famous traveller Sir Richard Francis Burton who was one of the first Englishmen to visit Mecca, in disguise, in the mid 19th century. Moses left behind the marks of his fingers and

Carving on a bench-end in Launcells church, Cornwall, depicting Christ ascending into Heaven and leaving his footprints on the Mount of Olives.

nails: 'On one side... is the hole opened for the spring by Moses' rod... and near it are the marks of Moses' nails – deep indentations in the stone, which were probably left there by some extinct saurian. Our Cicerone informed us that formerly the finger-marks existed, and that they were long enough for a man to lie in... ' Sir Richard also described seeing the Prophet Mohammed's tooth-mark at the Kubbat al-Sanaya (the Dome of the Front Teeth): Mohammed lost a tooth when attacked by infidels, and it touched a stone in the wall as it fell, leaving a permanent mark there.[11] Mohammed also left his footprints in numerous places, such as at the Dome of the Rock in Jerusalem, in Damascus, and in mosques in West Bengal, Bangladesh, and Gudjarat.[12] At Masjid al-Badawi in Egypt, where a large mosque was built over the tomb of Ahmad al-Badawi, founder of a large Sufi brotherhood, it is customary for pilgrims to perform certain rituals, the main one being to rub a stone which bears the footprints of the Prophet.[13] In Iran can also be found saintly footprints, those of a 9th-century religious leader, Imam Reza, being located in the shrine of Qadamgah at the

*The footprint of Jesus Christ on the Mount of Olives, as reproduced in a pilgrims'
token from Jerusalem made of linen c.1600, and cut to the exact shape
and size of the footprint (length 260mm), and touched to the original.*

village of Mahmudabad.[14] Still in the Middle East, though stepping back a few
centuries, one of Moses' most famous exploits was leading the Israelites across the
Red Sea as they escaped from Egypt, and according to the 6th-century bishop
Gregory of Tours, 'They say that the ruts which the chariot-wheels made remain to
this day and that, as far as the eye can reach, they can be seen at the bottom of the
sea. When the motion of the sea begins to cover them up, they are miraculously
renewed and made just as they were before, as soon as the water becomes calm
again.' [15]

The footprints of Jesus Christ, the central figure in the Christian religion, have not
surprisingly been widely recorded, most famously on the Mount of Olives east of
Jerusalem, the place where Jesus spent his last days, and from where he is believed
to have ascended into Heaven. Early in the 4th century St Helena built a church over
the traditional site of the Ascension, but it was later recorded that no one had been
able to roof over the actual place of the Ascension, and it had to be left open to the
sky.[16] (See 'Footprints to Visit')

Jesus also left his knee-prints at Jerusalem, in the Valley of Jehosaphat, where,
according to Bede, the 7th–8th century historian, there is 'a stone inserted in the
wall, on which Christ knelt when he prayed on the night in which He was betrayed,
and the marks of His knees are still to be seen in the stone, as if it had been as soft as
wax.' [17] In Jerusalem, the stone where Jesus was tied during the scourging (Mark
15:15), still bearing the marks made by his body, can be seen. (See 'Footprints to
Visit') A pilgrim to the Holy Land in the 6th century wrote of seeing, in the church of

Jesus being scourged as a punishment before crucifixion.

Holy Sion in Jerusalem, 'the column at which the Lord was scourged, and it has on it a miraculous mark. When he clasped it, his chest clove to the stone, and you can see the marks of both his hands, his fingers, and his palms'. The same pilgrim visited the church of the Holy Wisdom, Sancta Sophia, also in Jerusalem, and saw the seat where Pontius Pilate sat to hear Jesus's case. Jesus had to stand on an oblong stone during the proceedings, and 'his footprints are still on it. He had a well-shaped foot, small and delicate. From this stone where he stood came many blessings. People take "measures" from the footprints, and wear them for their various diseases, and they are cured. The stone itself is decorated with gold and silver.' [18]

After the death of Christ, St Peter the Apostle was in Rome, and while walking along the Appian Way he had a vision of Christ who was walking towards Rome carrying a cross. 'Domine, quo vadis?' (Lord, where are you going?) Peter asked him. Christ replied that he was going to be crucified again, and vanished – leaving his footprints behind. After this vision, Peter returned to the city for his own execution by crucifixion, and he continued to spread the word after he was imprisoned there. In the 9th century a church was built at the place where Peter had his vision, and named the Church of Domine Quo Vadis? A copy of Christ's footprints in stone is at the entrance to this church; the original footprint stone can be seen in the Chapel of the Relics in the Basilica of San Sebastiano. (See 'Footprints to Visit') This church was originally the Basilica Apostolorum ad Catacumbas, and the bodies of Saints Peter and Paul were taken there in AD 258, later being returned to their original burial places elsewhere.[19]

The marks inside St Govan's Chapel, said to be the imprint of Christ's ribs.

French folklore identifies many footprint-shaped markings on rocks as being the places where holy figures once trod, among them being Jesus. At several locations he appears as a baby with his mother the Virgin Mary, for example on the path to Notre-Dame du Haut, near Moncontour (Côtes-d'Armor), where a small footprint is identified as that of the Baby Jesus, rested there for a moment by his mother when they were fleeing Herod's wrath. (See also Chapter 5 for further examples.) The Baby Jesus' footprint was also imprinted on one of the stones of the Well of Bon Dieu at La Grande Verrière (Saône-et-Loire), after he quenched his thirst at the well. At Saint-Symphorien-de-Marmagne (Yonne) a shallow basin is said to be the footprint of our Lord; the mark of his walking-stick is nearby.[20] In Arles (Bouches-du-Rhône) Jesus left his knee- and foot-prints after appearing there among a gathering of bishops. They had assembled for the consecration of the first Christian cemetery, created by St Trophimus who had been sent to Arles in the year AD 46 to convert the Gauls. While present at the consecration, Jesus is said to have blessed the cemetery himself, and knelt there, leaving his knee- and foot-prints as proof of his presence. The stone with the imprints became the altar in the Chapel des Paysans between Arles and Pont-de-crau. Another chapel, called 'la Genouillade' (Place of the Knee-caps), was built at the actual site of the appearance, and rebuilt in the 16th century.[21] Jesus' footprint was also preserved at Poitiers (Viene), where a chapel called Pas de Dieu (the Lord's Footprint) was built where St Radegund had her cell. An hour before her death, this pious nun had a visit from a beautiful young man, the Saviour, who came to tell her of her imminent death, and he also left his footprints. There is said to be a stone in the cathedral at Reims (Marne), preserved behind the main altar, which bears the

The original footprints of Jesus found at the Tomb of Jesus in Kashmir. The marks on the feet are different from those of the holy men of Hinduism and Buddhism, and supposedly represent the scars from crucifixion wounds.
Photo: Dr Elmar R. Gruber.

imprint of Christ's buttocks: he sat on it to rest while engaged in the construction of the main doorway.[22]

In south-west England there is a legend that St Joseph visited the area, and brought Jesus with him. Places in Cornwall linked to this legend are the Jesus Well at Minver, and a holy well at St Just where there was a stone on which Christ had stepped and left his footprint.[23] Tradition also took him further north, into South Wales, where at Penylan Well (Cardiff) marks on a stone were said to have been left by Christ when he visited the well.[24] Further west in Pembrokeshire, Christ also features in one version of the legend of St Govan's Chapel, a tiny stone cell dwarfed by the surrounding cliffs. In the east wall inside the chapel is a crevice barely large enough to admit an adult, and the tradition was that Christ had hidden himself in this crevice which had opened up to receive him when he was being pursued by his enemies. (In other versions, it was St Govan, or the Gawain of the King Arthur story, who hid in the crevice.) Marks faintly visible on the rock were said to be the imprint of Christ's ribs.[25] (See 'Footprints to Visit')

The footprint of the infant Jesus can be seen on a rock in the church of the Virgin Mary at Sakha in Egypt, supposedly dating from the time when the Holy Family lived

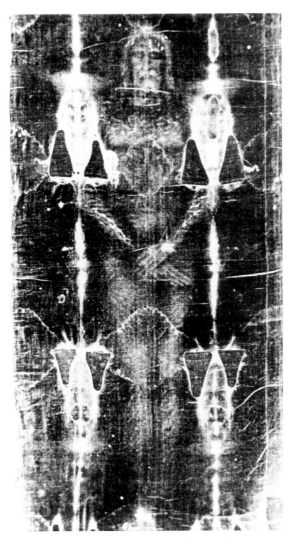

*The image, said to be that of
Christ, on the Turin Shroud.*

in Egypt. (See 'Footprints to Visit') During that same period, Jesus also left his handprint on a rock which he prevented from falling from a mountain and on to the boat carrying the Holy Family, after the mountain had 'bowed in admiration before him'. Almeric, King of Jerusalem, cut out the piece of rock with the imprint and took it to Syria in 1168, but in the 13th century it was reportedly being kept at the Church of the Holy Virgin north of Minya in Egypt.[26] Christ's footprints are (or were) also to be found in the pilgrimage-church at Einsiedel (Saxony, eastern Germany) and in a hermitage on the Rosenstein in Swabia (south-west Germany). The latter were known as the Herrgottstritte, or Lord God's Footsteps, and were much visited by pilgrims – until 14 June 1740, when the reigning Duke, who disapproved of the reverence paid to the footprints, ordered that the stone be blown up.[27] A large rock footprint identified as that of Jesus is in a mountain stream in the Philippines – somewhere on a sacred mountain near Tayabas south-east of Manila.[28] Rather more easy to locate are the footprints of Christ on his alleged tomb at Srinagar (Kashmir), India. One modern version of his life tells how Jesus spent his 'lost years' between the ages of 13

42

The face of Christ from St Veronica's Veil held in St Peter's Basilica, Rome.

and 29 travelling and studying in Asia, and after his 'death' on the cross he actually returned to Kashmir and was known as Yuz Asaf. The prophet of this name was a holy man from a foreign land who performed many miracles before dying of old age in AD 109. He became a saint of one small sect of Muslims, and many believed him to have been the same as the Christian Jesus. A crucifix and a rosary accompanied the footprints carved on his tomb, and the scars of the crucifixion wounds were also included.[29] (See 'Footprints to Visit') Christ's footprint continues to be found: at the end of 2000, two lumberjacks in Bosupu in Equatorial Guinea found a 3-foot-long human footprint in a tree, which was interpreted as heralding Christ's imminent Second Coming.[30]

Also appearing in 2000, though not given any prophetic significance, was the face of Christ apparently visible on an aerial view of the Crystal Palace football pitch at Selhurst Park in South London.[31] It resembled the famous face of Christ on the Turin Shroud, a holy relic which retains its mystery despite numerous scientific attempts to determine once and for all whether the clear image of a male body is that of Jesus Christ. According to tradition, the image was mysteriously formed when he was wrapped in a linen shroud after his crucifixion, and the sceptics have not yet shown that the tradition is false. Today the shroud is preserved in the cathedral at Turin in Italy.[32] (See 'Footprints to Visit') Other images of Christ on cloths, which were believed to have been created miraculously by direct contact with his face, include the Mandylion of Edessa and the Veil of Veronica. These are generically known as acheiropitoi – 'not-made-by-hands' images. The Mandylion was the most famous

*The Angel's Footprint in the
church at Fécamp.
Photo: Andreas Trottmann.*

miraculous image of Christ during the 6th to early 13th centuries. It was said to have
been created when Abgar, King of Edessa, heard that Christ was a healer and invited
him to Edessa to cure him. On receipt of Abgar's letter, Jesus told the messenger that
he could not go to Edessa, but he promised a cure for the king. He washed his face
in water and when he wiped himself on a towel, his image was somehow imprinted
on the cloth. On receiving this, and a letter from Jesus, Abgar was cured and
converted. There is a Mandylion on public display in a church in Genoa; see
'Footprints to Visit'. St Veronica's Veil was a *sudarium* or cloth for wiping sweat,
and came into existence when St Veronica offered Christ a cloth with which to wipe
his face as he carried the cross to Calvary. When he handed it back, she found his
features miraculously imprinted on the cloth. In the following centuries it was
displayed in Rome and visited by countless pilgrims: a cloth claimed to be the
original relic is still preserved at the Basilica of St Peter in Rome.[33] In 1981 a modern
equivalent of the Turin Shroud came to light in Liverpool, following the death of a
West Indian man from cancer of the pancreas. A nurse was scrubbing the mattress he
had lain on, and found that the bleach she was using was not removing the marks left
on the mattress. When it was examined, there was found to be an outline of the
man's body in his death position. The buttocks, upper legs, back, shoulders, left arm
and the face had all been somehow permanently imprinted on the mattress, through
the man's pyjamas and a sheet. Attempts were made to explain this phenomenon:
perhaps, some suggested, it was caused by alkaline body fluids which had somehow

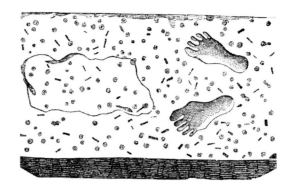

*Gabriel's footprints on the
stone at New Harmony.*

leaked out and through the action of enzymes created an image of the man's body. If such an explanation were true, shouldn't there be many more examples on record of this happening? [34]

Angels are also represented in footprint folklore, and a great many of the reports that I have collected feature specifically the Archangel Gabriel (one exception is the 'Pas de l'Ange' – Angel's Footprint – inside Holy Trinity church at Fécamp in Normandy, France – see 'Footprints to Visit'). In Rome, an altar dedicated to Isis in the Capitoline Museum bears the imprint of two feet, and these were once believed to have been made by the Archangel Gabriel.[35] In Jerusalem, the mosque standing on the site of Solomon's Temple contains a piece of rock called Hadjr-el-Sakhara (the locked-up stone) which was believed to have been brought from Heaven by the Archangel Gabriel, whose fingermarks are visible upon it, along with the footprints of Mohammed and his horse.[36] Gabriel also made an unexpected visit to Mount Athos in Greece in the year 980. A junior disciple was reading the office alone in one of the churches of Karyes when a stranger (Gabriel) arrived, who told him to preface the Ninth Ode with the words 'Worthy it is to magnify thee, Mother of God'. He also wrote the words with his finger on a stone which became as soft as wax. This stone was later forwarded to Constantinople.[37] Also removed from its original location was a piece of limestone discovered early in the 19th century at the edge of the Mississippi River at St Louis (Missouri) which had human footprints on it. The stone found its way to New Harmony in Indiana, the home of the community of Rappites presided over by Father Rapp, where it was believed that the footprints were those of the Archangel Gabriel. The story was that some time between 1815 and 1824 Gabriel had appeared to Fr Rapp. He (Gabriel) appeared as a tall, well-built hermaphrodite – with a masculine body and female breasts. The angel foretold the swift-approaching and violent End of the World when only the Rappites would be saved: they had only to be celibate, and to obey the commandments of God. Then he disappeared, leaving his footprints on the stone he had stood on.[38]

In Ireland, it was the Angel Victoricus whose apparition appeared to St Patrick when he was held in slavery, to comfort him and tell him when he would escape. Also, as the time of his death drew near, the same angel told Patrick that he was not to return to Armagh to die, and gave him instructions for his burial. Victoricus became known simply as Victor, and pilgrims to the ruined Skerry church (Magheramully, Co. Antrim) visit the spot where the angel appeared to St Patrick, and see the rock with the hollow which is said to be the Angel Victor's footprint. He left it there when he ascended into Heaven before St Patrick's eyes.[39] (See 'Footprints to Visit') Angels' chariot wheels left their mark near St German's Well (the Well of Tears) in Cornwall, after the angels' intervention to rescue St German when he was suffering persecution at the hands of his enemies. One day they were so rebellious in church that he had to leave hurriedly, and he made his way to the cliffs at Rame Head. There he wept in agony at his failure, and the Well of Tears symbolises his sorrow. Seeing his enemies advancing, St German called to God for help, and then saw a flaming chariot rushing towards him. Two angels lifted him inside and they rose into the air. After cursing his enemies, St German was taken to other lands where he lived a holy life. By the well, the chariot wheels had burned permanent marks into the rocks.[40]

Assorted non-angelic religious personages have also left permanent marks, like St Gaudentius, the first bishop of Novara, who found the gates of Ivrea (Italy) closed one night, so went to sleep on a rock and left the imprint of his body on it.[41] In France, a Capuchin friar locked in the tower of Ham (Somme) was so used to privations that the stone which served as his pillow had yielded to the weight of his head and was permanently marked with his face and his ear.[42] Near the old church at Aghadoe (Co. Kerry) in southern Ireland was a circular stone with two hollows that were said to have been made by the knees of a friar who knelt there for nearly 200 years, engaged in prayer and meditation.[43] As already mentioned in Chapter 2, the mark of a friar's heel can be seen on one of the great stones of Stonehenge, made when the Devil threw the stone at a friar who was secretly watching him at work. Further north in Derbyshire, the Devil in the form of a dragon was driven off by a monk who stood on a rock with his arms outstretched in the shape of a cross. He was concentrating so hard on his task of exorcism that his feet sank into the rock, leaving two holes on the face of Winlatter Rock.[44] Near Beit Jala not far from Jerusalem (Israel) is a shrine dedicated to El Khudr, the mysterious 'Evergreen One' who was said to have discovered the Fountain of Youth. When a Greek priest was administering Holy Communion in the church of El Khudr, he spilled the bread and wine on to his foot. They made a hole right through which never healed and eventually caused his death, and also made a lasting mark on the flagstone beneath. At a later time, a sick man visiting the church unintentionally knelt to pray on the same flagstone and was healed on the spot. Further cures were also reported.[45]

The symbol of the foot may have been used sometimes to signify the act of pilgrimage, or to indicate that someone was a pilgrim. On Inishcealtra in County Clare, one of the cross-slabs in St Caimin's church has the inscription 'Cosgrach Laighnech', a large cross, and two footprints. Peter Harbison interprets this as meaning that a person called Cosgrach came on pilgrimage from Leinster.[46] A stone in the church at Llanelltyd in Gwynedd also bears a faint footprint, and an inscription stating that a person named Kenvric placed it there before setting out on a pilgrimage.[47] Further south in Wales, at Nevern in Pembrokeshire, the course of a pilgrim path is still visible, and in the rock at one point there are steps in the shape of footprints, which have been worn smooth from the passage of thousands of pilgrims. The path led from Holywell in the north-east of Wales to St Davids in the

The pilgrim route at Nevern, with foot-shaped steps cut into the rock.

south-west. There are crosses incised in the footprints, and the footprints themselves may have been carved, for it is unlikely that the rock could have been worn away so deeply by passing feet, even despite the great number that must have trodden here down the centuries.[48]

Religious fervour was often the accepted reason for the appearance of footprints, as was the case with the so-called prints of John Wesley, the well-known Methodist preacher, which were locally believed to be visible on the stone slab which covered his father's grave at Epworth (North Lincoln). Wesley was active in the 18th century, and it was said that he preached barefoot while standing on the slab. Walter White wrote of the prints in the late 19th century: 'The tradition has not yet died out that John Wesley once stood barefoot to preach on his father's tomb, and grew into such a fervour that his toes burnt hollows in the very substance of the stone.'[49] Religious fervour may also be thought responsible for the footprints of another Methodist, Tommy Escritt, which were to be found on a hill overlooking the village of Cranswick (East Riding of Yorkshire). On his walk to work every day he would stop and look out over the village for a few moments, praying for its conversion. 'There to this day [1890] are the marks of his feet, for no grass grows on this place, so sacred to his memory; a place to which visits and pilgrimages are made, as to some dear spot or holy place.'[50]

Finlay Munro's footprints, which always return if destroyed.
Photo: Andreas Trottmann.

The next three footprints were made as a proof or reminder of something. A footprint-shaped dent in a flagstone in Smithills Hall near Bolton (Greater Manchester) was often referred to as a blood-stained footprint, and believed to produce fresh blood at a certain time each year. It was said to have been made by George Marsh, a Lancashire Protestant martyr who was questioned at Smithills Hall by the magistrate who lived there, and accused of 'preaching false doctrine'. He stamped on the floor and called for a permanent memorial of the injustice of his treatment, before being taken off to be burned at the stake in 1555. It was also said that early in the 19th century the young men of the hall lifted the stone and threw it out, but they had to fetch it back after alarming noises were heard indoors. (See 'Footprints to Visit') Brindle church (Lancashire) has a footprint with a story: in the wall above a stone coffin beneath the eastern gable of the chancel is an indentation that resembles a foot, and the story that attached to it told how it was made by the 'high-heeled shoe of a Popish disputant' who averred that if the doctrine he supported was untrue, then let his foot sink into the stone. Unfortunately for him, 'the reforming stone instantly softened and buried the papistical foot'.[51] Travelling preacher Finlay Munro also called for a miraculous proof of his words, when he was preaching close to a cairn near Dundreggan in Glen Moriston (Highland) in 1827, and was being heckled by some young men who called him a liar. He said: 'As a proof that I am telling the truth, my footprints will forever bear witness on this very ground I stand on.' And so they did, for over 150 years, with people visiting the footprints and standing in them as part of the custom. However, since the early 1990s they are no longer to be found, having apparently been deliberately destroyed.[52] (However... see also 'Footprints to Visit'.)

The footprints of Vishnu beside the Ganges at Hardwar. Photo: Dr Elmar R. Gruber.

Just as in the West, where Christianity is the predominant religion, the footprints of Christ and the saints and other religious figures are described, so too in the East, where Buddhism is widespread, do we encounter tales of the Buddha's footprints, and in addition imprints of various kinds left by lamas and gurus and other disciples of Buddhism. In India, where Hinduism is a prominent religion, figures from their pantheon have also left their imprints. Vishnu, an important creator god, left his footprints at the bathing-ghat called Hari ka Pairi on the River Ganges at Hardwar, where the great festival of Kumbha Mela is held every twelfth year. The stone bearing the footprints is inside its own little temple, where it is revered by pilgrims. (See 'Footprints to Visit') Vishnu also left his footprint on a boulder at the city of Gaya, which became a sacred place, symbolising the intersection of the two realms, the mundane and the spiritual. The Vishnu Pada Temple was built over the footprint, and in the centre of the temple a silver-plated octagonal basin surrounds the footprint, which is about 16 inches long. Pilgrims throw offerings of rice and water into the basin. 'It is by performing the shraddhas here on Vishnu's footprint that the devout pilgrim gets the great and maximum merit that the place is capable of giving.'[53] (See 'Footprints to Visit') Rama was an incarnation of Vishnu, and while on an expedition to the south of India he left his footprints on a stone in the Deccan, and in a cave where he slept.[54] Parvati, who became the wife of the god Siva, left her footprint on the tiny rock island of Sri Pada just off the southernmost tip of India. Hindu worshippers built a temple round it, and pilgrims came from afar to venerate it.[55]

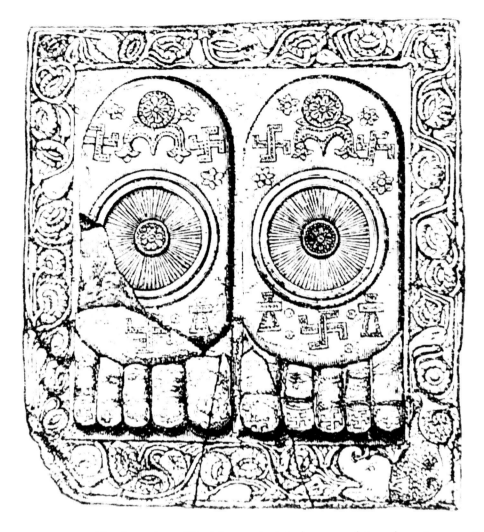

The footprints of Buddha as depicted on a sculpture from Amaravati.
From Schliemann's Ilios *(1880).*

Mention has already been made of the famous footprint on Adam's Peak in Sri Lanka, and of the various identifications. As Buddha's footprint it is an important focus for Buddhists and other pilgrims, and has been for centuries. Notable visitors include the 5th-century traveller Fa-hsien, who recounted how Buddha had placed two footprints on the island, as he wished to convert the wicked dragons that originally roamed the land. Marco Polo wrote about the island and the footprint in the 13th century, and then in 1344 Muslim traveller Ibn Batuta made a special visit to the island so that he could visit the footprint – however both of them regarded it as Adam's Footprint rather than Buddha's.[56] There are other Buddha footprints on the island, a 380-foot high stupa having been built over one by King Gajabahu in the 2nd century. A pair of footprints on a stone plaque was seen by traveller Thor Heyerdahl in the early 1980s in the entrance hall of Sri Lanka's National Museum.

They had been found near Jaffna on the north of the island, but Heyerdahl believed them to have strong links with the Maldive Islands to the south-west. He saw strange symbols on the plaque, similar to those he had found in the Maldives, including a conch, a fish, a sun-wheel, and swastikas. He had also found other carvings of footprints accompanied by symbols, during his excavations in the Maldives.[57] The symbols which he puzzled over were probably the 'Seven Appearances', symbols which were often placed on carved replicas of the Buddha's footprint. They are the swastika, fish, diamond mace, conch shell, flower vase, Wheel of the Law, and the Crown of Brahma, and they symbolize the enlightenment of the Buddha.[58] Representations of Vishnu's footprint also often carry incised symbols.[59] The wheel symbol often appears in Indian Buddhist sculpture: for example, there is one behind the empty Buddha's throne in one of the sculptures from the Great Stupa at Amaravati, dating from the 1st century BC. Although the throne is empty, the Buddha's presence is symbolised by the footprints in the place where his feet would have been had he been there.[60] (These footprints have been transferred from the India Museum to the British Museum.)

The strongly Buddhist countries to the north of India – Tibet, Nepal, Sikkim, and Bhutan – are rich sources of footprints and other imprints, made by the Buddha himself and also by priests and followers. Several examples are mentioned in the account of Fa-hsien's travels during the years 399–414: 'Tradition says that when Buddha came to Northern India he visited [Udyâna] and left behind him a foot-print. The foot-print appears to be long or short according to the faith in each particular person, and such remains the case up to the present day... ' Footprints we can take in our stride... but Buddha's shadow? 'Half a yôjana [between 2 and 5 miles] to the south of the capital of Nagarahâra there is a cave. It is on the south-west face of the Po mountain. Buddha left his shadow on the rock inside. Looking at it from a distance of ten paces or so, it is like Buddha's actual self, with his golden complexion, his thirty-two greater and eighty lesser characteristic marks, all brightly visible. The nearer one goes, the more indistinct it becomes, appearing as if it were really He.' As if a shadow were not ephemeral enough, in another place in the north of India Fa-hsien wrote about the imprints of drops of water, to be found at a monastery called Fire Domain, where Buddha converted an evil spirit. A shrine was built at the place, and 'when the shrine was being dedicated, a saint took water to wash his hands, and some drops fell upon the ground. These drops are still here; and however much they may be brushed away, they always remain visible and cannot be removed.' Another footprint was left at Pâtaliputra in Magadha: 'When Asôka destroyed the seven pagodas, with a view to building eighty-four thousand others, the very first large pagoda he built was at a distance of over three li to the south of the city. In front of this there is a foot-print of Buddha's, over which a shrine has been raised, with its entrance facing north.' [61]

During the 16th century, Karmapa Mikyo Dorje was travelling through Tibet, and at one point he carved a statue of himself out of stone. He asked the statue, 'Are you a good likeness of me?' to which the statue replied, 'Yes, I am.' Karmapa squeezed a lump of stone that was left over, as if it were butter, and left his palm-print and finger-prints on it. The statue and the imprinted stone were removed to the residence of the present Karmapa at Rumtek monastery in Sikkim. Karmapa Mikyo Dorje left his footprints and the hoof-prints of his horse in the rock at Gangri Thokar, the retreat of Longchenpa, a great saint.[62] Guru Padmasambhava was another holy man who left his footprints on rocks in Tibet, also his handprints, and body-marks; and he also left huge handprints which were always visible on four specific lakes.[63] The sixteenth Karmapa, Rangjung Rigpe Dorge, left his footprints on the water of a small lake in the area of Drong Tup while on a journey in 1937, and those footprints are said to be still visible, even when the lake is frozen.[64] Shetak in Tibet is one of the power-places of the Nyingma School, and in Guru Padmasambhava's Crystal Cave can be found, in the rock of the roof, a small footprint said to be that of Yeshe Tsogyel, the Guru's consort. The footprint of the Guru himself can be seen by the altar in the Moon Cave where he lived at Dawa Puk.[65] The sacred Mount Kailasa in Tibet is the site of very many footprints, including those of Buddha, Milarepa, and many other holy men.[66] These few examples are a random selection from the many, probably hundreds, of footprints and other imprints recorded for the Himalayan region. They are far too numerous to list more of them here, but their ubiquity and variety make them worthy of a study in their own right.

Buddhism in China has also produced similar traditions, including another shadow imprint. Ta-Mo, the first Chinese patriarch, lived in the monastery of Shao-lin-ssu during the 6th century AD. The monastery was at the foot of a sacred mountain near the holy city of Têng Fêng, and it was said that Ta-Mo sat in silent meditation for nine years, gazing at a stone, and then died. His shadow had impressed itself upon the stone, which was kept for the faithful to view.[67] The footprint of Sakyamuni Buddha is said to lie under a stupa in the grounds of the White Pagoda Temple at Damenglong, which was built in 1204 to honour his visit to the area. Hua Shan is one of China's sacred mountains, a religious centre for millennia. According to legend, the demi-god Yu the Great was called upon to deal with major flooding, and one of his tasks was to split Hua Shan in two, because it was blocking the water's outlet to the sea. He was assisted by a giant, and his handprint is said to be visible high on a cliff on East Peak.[68] In Japan a Buddhist monk left his footprint on a rock on Cape Ashizuri (which means 'foot stamping') on the island of Shikoku. The story of what happened was told in the early 14th century by a wandering Buddhist nun, Lady Nijo. She described how a monk and his disciple had lived there, until one day the disciple left in a boat with a companion. When the old monk cried, 'Where are you going without me?' the young man replied, 'We're going to the realm of Kannon' (a bodhisattva – one who worked for the salvation of all – who had a wide following) and both men in the boat turned into bodhisattvas. The old monk was so distraught he wept and stamped his foot on the rock, leaving his footprint there. That was how the cape got its name.[69]

Further south in Thailand, it was once the custom for a child's hair from his top-knot to be saved after cutting, and the long hairs taken with the child on a pilgrimage to the holy footprint of Buddha on the sacred hill at Prabat. There the hair would be presented to the priests, and the custom was that it would be made into brushes with which to sweep the footprint. However the priests were being offered so much hair every year that they could not make use of it all, and so they would quietly burn the surplus.[70] There are several Buddha's footprints to be seen in Thailand: traditionally they were left so as to guide people to enlightenment. Three examples, in Lamphun,

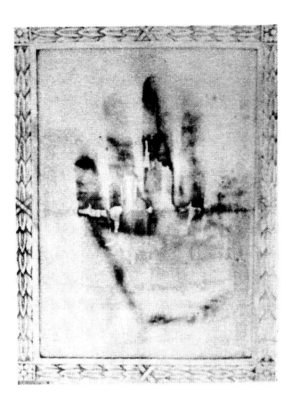

The cloth from Jasna Gora, with the imprint of a hand burned upon it.

Saraburi and Samui, are described in 'Footprints to Visit'. In 2002 the events that followed the discovery of a puddle in the shape of Buddha's footprint demonstrated the crazier side of human nature. Thousands of people flocked to the top of Had Sai waterfall in Pungna province in Thailand to see the puddle, which was believed to somehow be able to relieve pain and bring good fortune. The latter did not extend to an unfortunate frog living by the puddle, which was viewed as the site's guardian. So many people rubbed talcum powder on to its skin in the hope of seeing the winning lottery numbers that it became weak and close to death.[71]

This chapter closes with some miraculous hand- and finger-prints in a religious setting. St Cunegund was an 11th-century empress, the wife of Emperor Henry II who founded a monastery and cathedral at Bamberg (Germany). She founded a convent at Kaufungen and appointed her niece Judith or Jutta as superior, but the young abbess was found to be not attending properly to her duties. St Cunegund reprimanded her with a blow across her cheek, and the finger-marks could be seen until her dying day. The imprint had the effect of impressing both the abbess and the community, and was a permanent reminder to them of the need to devote themselves to their task.[72] In Chapter 9 there is a ghost story in which mystery finger-marks were seen on the victim's face. There are many examples on record of hand- and finger-prints burned into cloth or paper. A collection of relics held in Rome in the Church of the Sacred Heart (see 'Footprints to Visit') includes part of a chemise that had belonged to an abbess, on which a dead abbot had left the imprint of his burning hand; a shirt from Belgium upon which the owner's dead mother had left the

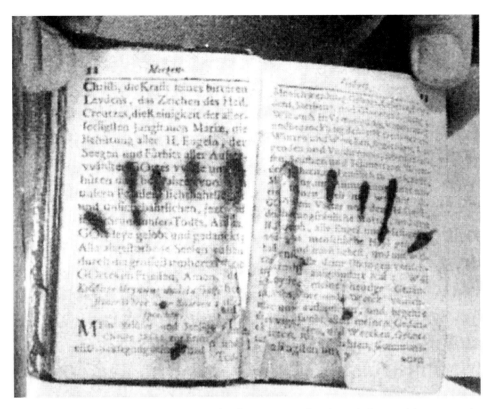

The Hackenberg prayer-book with burned finger-marks.

burnt mark of her hand; the nightcap of a Lord Warden with his wife's burnt finger-marks on it, left by her in 1875 to show their daughter that she needed masses saying for her; and a nun's pillow marked in 1894 by the finger of a companion who had died the previous day, indicating that she required twenty days of prayers.[73] Such postmortem burn marks were taken to be evidence of survival, or messages from souls in purgatory who were undergoing torments by fire, and often they needed to complete some unfinished business back on earth, as described in the following examples.

A consecrated cloth bearing the burned impression of a hand was held at Jasna Gora, a Polish shrine in Czestochowa, and was described around 100 years ago by a priest named Alfred Reichel: 'I was participating, along with two colleagues, in the pilgrimage to Czestochowa. A monk in charge of the sacristy led us around to show us the sights. He took us into a vaulted side-passage, and with great solicitude showed us, among other things, a small metal chest – he did this very rarely, he told us. Then he lifted the lid and we saw a corporal [cloth used in the Eucharist] bearing the imprint of a man's hand, a hand which must have been red-hot. The upper layers of the folded fabric were completely charred, while the burns diminished on the lower layers. In the spaces between the fingers the linen threads were intact, while in the places where the muscles in the hand stand out, we could clearly see a more serious degree of burning in the fabric; at the outer edges it became less serious. The origin of the imprint was given with this story: Many years ago, two monks of the Order of St Paul had promised each other that the one who died first would supply the other with a sign from the next world. At the time of the story, the one monk had already been dead a long time and had not given the least sign. The other monk was thinking of this as he was just finishing the celebration of the mass, folding the corporal nine times, as always. A pernicious doubt stole over him – perhaps there is, then, no life after death. At this moment a hand appeared, rested upon the corporal and disappeared immediately. The burned imprint which it left on the linen cloth, folded nine times, will always prove how hot that hand was.'

In addition to cloths bearing burned hand-imprints, there are also examples of such burns on prayer-books, like the one which originated with the Hackenberg family in Czechoslovakia. It was examined in 1922 by a Dr Stampfl, the director of a seminary, who described what he found. 'On page 18 we find the burned imprint of a little hand. The charred marks go through 10 pages and reach the inside cover. We can clearly distinguish the five fingers, the palm of the hand, and a part of the wrist... The imprints of the thumb, the index finger and the little finger are more heavily imprinted... The fingers give the impression of being composed only of bones.' The explanation for the imprint was that a member of the family undertook a pilgrimage to fulfil a pledge made to his dead father, and during his journey home he saw a vision of his father while he was sleeping, who thanked him for the pilgrimage and said he would leave a sign of his deliverance, in the form of a burned handprint in his prayer book, which the pilgrim duly found on awakening.[74]

There are other examples of burned hand imprints left on book pages, one such being a collection of Biblical stories called the *Kada Codex* which was created in Hungary in the 17th century. Stephen Kada was a Hungarian bishop who died in 1695, and it was said to be the deceased Kada who left his hand imprint burned into the book pages one dramatic night in April 1696, after there had been several nights of strange happenings in the monastery at Privigye. He was said to have appeared to Father Franciscus Hanacius and requested that a mass be held at his grave and that prayers be said for the release of his soul from Purgatory 'where it has been burning for 100 days'. Father Hanacius requested proof of identity, which is when the book-burning took place, and 'the mark of a man's right hand appeared on the cover and on the first 100 pages of the book'. It was said that page 101 – immediately opposite the last burned page – was not even yellowed. Unfortunately no one can check this, because the book was (allegedly) destroyed by a fire in 1952 at the ancient convent of Cintra in Portugal where it was kept. I cannot help feeling that caution is needed when considering such stories as this – especially when the date on which the strange events began at Privigye is given as 1 April. Dr Joe Nickell also expressed caution over burned handprint phenomena, and with regard to the Hackenberg case he noted that the print was of a child-sized hand although allegedly produced by an adult: but it had to be small to fit on to a small prayer-book. As Nickell noted, 'The scaling of the size of the hand to fit the page is a detail that points to an amateurish forger; so is the crudeness of the anatomy… since both the thumb and little finger appear proportionately too long.' Nickell went on to demonstrate how a burned hand imprint could be faked by making a cast-metal 'hand' and heating it before placing it on to the pages of a book.[75]

A handprint was once used as a signature on documents, and so the burned imprints of the hands of the dead could be interpreted as their signature, proving their survival of death. That is… if they are genuine. As with the stone footprints, all are a mixture of fabrication and folklore, and they live on because they fulfil people's need to believe in the supernatural (that which transcends the natural world).

Chapter Four

A saintly presence I
St Antony to St Martin of Tours

> Mostly natural cavities in the Stones, though probably improved
> by the Chisels of ye Monks
>
> Richard Fenton, *Tours in Wales*, 323 – Williams' MS (1814) in
> appendix III.

Saints, being special people credited with supernatural powers, were believed to be capable of amazing feats, and one of these was the ability to leave their footprints and other imprints impressed in solid rock. Being permanent rather than ephemeral, the footprint would be there for ever, representing the saint and empowered on the saint's behalf to perform healing and other miracles. In addition, it could be touched and venerated, just as pilgrims have always done at those locations where saints' relics are preserved. Relics usually comprise parts of the saint's body – a fingerbone, or a skull, for example – or pieces of their clothing: anything which has been in direct contact with the saint, even if simply touched by him or her. The footprint in stone follows in this tradition, since according to the legend which often accompanies it, it marks the place where the saint once stood. Of course this is usually not true, and very often the saint specified never went anywhere near the site of the footprint. But even so, knowing this does not make the footprint any less potent, and it can still claim a spiritual link, however tenuous, with the person said to have made it, and its power for the pilgrim is thus undiminished.

Although footprints are the imprints most often preserved in the landscape, imprints of other body parts such as hands and fingers are recorded, sometimes heads, and even on occasion the imprint of a saintly bottom can be viewed. There are also numerous tales of saints' beds and chairs, these descriptions being given to rocks which are the right kind of shape for sitting or lying on, but unless there is also said to be the impression in solid rock of the saint's buttocks or whole body on the chair or bed, they have been omitted from this collection.

As with all the footprints and other imprints in this book, the question arises as to how they originally got there. Laying to one side any discussion of the likelihood that the stories of the imprints' formation are literally true, it seems probable that sometimes a naturally footprint-shaped depression caught someone's eye, and then it only needed one story-teller to see it for an instant tradition to arise. If a stone carver were also handy, the footprint could be 'helped' a little. Maybe some of them

*St Anthony of Padua. From
Acta Sanctorum (1867).*

were carved 'from scratch' in order to create a focus for a religious story, in which the footprint would feature as a kind of sacred relic. People cannot resist a good story, and if it incorporates magic and mystery, so much the better. In Ireland, for example, it was often the case that hollows in stone slabs, known as bullauns, were interpreted as the marks left by saints' knees, caused by their spending so much time praying. Saints' imprints have proved to be a useful way to bring the saint and his influence to remote rural communities. Saints' imprints are to be found wherever saints are venerated, most especially in countries with a large Catholic population, though by no means exclusively. In India it was customary for models of the holy footprints of Hindu saints to be carried in palanquins to the temple of Pandharpur on festive occasions. Here the footprint clearly 'stood in' for the saint.[1]

Some Christian saints have proved especially popular in the footprint stakes, such as St Martin of Tours in France and St Patrick in Ireland, and the choice of the saint to whom a footprint is attributed obviously depends on which one is best-known in the location, rather than him or her ever having visited the place. I am presenting the saints' footprints and imprints of other body parts in alphabetical order of the saints, with the realisation that very many have been omitted: a whole book could easily be devoted to saints' imprints.

St Antony of Padua (1195–1231) was a Franciscan preacher who was born in Portugal, went as a missionary to Morocco, and spent the last years of his relatively short life preaching in France and Italy. A stone step in our Lady's church in Portugal (possibly in Lisbon) is marked with a cross which was said to have been made by the finger of St Antony of Padua when the Devil appeared to him.[2]

St Augustine depicted on a banner painted (oil on canvas) in 1895 by Baron Corvo for St Winifride's Well, Holywell (Flintshire, Wales). It was carried in pilgrimage processions and is now in the Well Museum at Holywell.

St Arnulf (also Arnoux; a courtier who was later bishop of Metz, and eventually became a hermit at Remiremont; died 640) left the mark of his skull on the rock he used as a pillow in a cave at Tourette-les-Venues (Provence, France).[3]

St Athanasius the Athonite was an abbot from Trebizond who became a hermit on Mount Athos in Greece and died there c.1003, killed by masonry falling from his church. He built the first monastery on Mount Athos, and according to legend, he battled with demons at the spot now marked by a hilltop shrine. After one such battle, in which he broke his ankle before driving them off, his footprint was impressed in the basin of a fountain, the spot now marked by a cross.[4]

St Augustine of Canterbury was the leader of a group of forty monks sent to England by Pope St Gregory the Great in 596 to preach to the heathen. They arrived on the Kent coast in 597 and were welcomed by King Ethelbert. The landing place was probably Richborough, where 'our father Augustine, as he stepped out of the ship, happened to stand upon a certain stone and the stone took the impression of his foot as if it had been clay'. The footprint stone was venerated during the Middle Ages at a chapel to which it had been taken, pilgrims visiting on the anniversary of St Augustine's burial in hopes of healing.[5]

St Baglan (*fl.* 600) left his knee-prints on a stone near Llanfaglan church (near Caernarfon in Gwynedd, North Wales), which as its name suggests was founded by

A modern stained-glass window depicting St Winefride and her uncle St Beuno, at St Winefride's Well, Holywell, Flintshire. He put her head back on when she was decapitated by an angry suitor, and the well sprang up where her head had fallen.

this Celtic saint. (Confusingly, the Llanfaglan in Glamorgan, South Wales, was founded by an entirely different St Baglan!) [6]

St Besse, so the story goes, escaped from the massacre of the Theban Legion, in which he was a soldier in the 3rd century, and sought refuge in the mountains of the Soana valley in northern Italy. In another story, St Besse was a holy man and a shepherd in the mountains, envied by other shepherds for the quality of his sheep. Two of them threw him from the mountaintop, but his body was not discovered for several months. It had been covered by the snow, and its location was marked by a beautiful flower. During the fall, St Besse's body had imprinted itself permanently on to the rock: a chapel was built at the site at Cogne, and pilgrims still visit to venerate him. Fragments of the imprinted rock are taken away as relics.[7]

St Beuno lived in the 6th–7th centuries, a Celtic saint most associated today with Clynnog Fawr in Gwynedd (North Wales), where his well is still located, and formerly also his tomb. Beuno left several imprints, including his knee-prints in a rock in the middle of the river at Llanaelhaiarn (Gwynedd) where he used to kneel to pray. He also left his footprints at Trefdraeth on Anglesey, and a stone named Maen Beuno in the church at Clynnog Fawr bears an incised cross, said to have been made by St Beuno with his thumb.[8]

St Boec was also known as St Vouga, St Vio, and numerous other similar names. Like other Irish saints, he used a floating stone as a boat. He sailed across to Brittany

The remains of St Boec's stone boat at Treguennec in Brittany – a rock with a hollow imprinted by the saint's head.

(France) from Co. Wexford and landed near Penmarc'h (Finistère). The stone returned to Ireland and can still be seen near St Boec's church at Carnsore Point, but a chunk of it remained in Brittany and is just outside the graveyard by the saint's chapel at Treguennec. It carries the imprint of St Boec's head, and pilgrims visited it to obtain a cure from fever by resting their heads in the depression.[9]

St Bozon, patron saint of Bousenot (Vosges, France), threw a rock from the church belfry and it landed 3 km away. His efforts in lifting and throwing the rock caused the imprints of his fingers to be left on it.[10]

St Brieuc (also Brioc, but not Briac who is someone different!) was a Welsh-born saint who flourished c.500 and, according to tradition, used to meet his chum St Illtud at a megalithic monument (destroyed in 19th century, except for three stones) at Coadout (Côtes-d'Armor, Brittany, France) and together they would kneel to pray, as a result of which their knee-prints could be seen on the rock.[11]

St Brigid (also Bridget, Brigit, Brigitte, Bride, Ffraid): As the variety of spellings shows, St Brigid was (and still is) venerated widely throughout Northern Europe, especially in Ireland, Wales, Scandinavia, Alsace, Flanders, Portugal. She may have been more than one person, but the most important Brigid came from Kildare in Ireland, where she was abbess and died c.525. Her birthplace was believed to be at Faughart (Co.

St Brigid's Well in Kildare,
Ireland. Photo: Kristan Lawson.

Louth), where there is now a shrine to her, and she left her knee-prints on a rock in the stream. She knelt on the rock to pray for guidance when her father wished her to marry against her will. She also plucked out one of her eyes so that she would no longer be attractive to her enforced suitor, placing the eye on another stone close by. Her suitor reacted with anger on seeing her, leaving the mark of his whip on the eye stone, and the imprint of his horse's hoof on a third stone.[12] (See 'Footprints to Visit') In Kildare her footprint was said to be on a stone beside her well in the old graveyard at Ticknevin. The well water was believed to cure warts if the correct procedure was followed, which included three visits, and leaving pins by the well. Brigid's knee-prints were on a stone by her well at Riverstown, also in Co. Kildare, and at Kilree south of Kells in Co. Kilkenny, on a stone between St Brigid's Well and the ancient church. The stone is called Gloonbride (Glún Bhrighde – St Brigid's Knee).[13]

The Scottish Hebrides islands take their name from Brigid, Hebrides meaning Isles of Bride, and on St Brigid's Eve (31 January) 'the ashes should be raked smooth on the hearth so that her footprints would show in the morning and all know whether or not she had visited and blessed the house. By the direction of her footprints the good or evil fortune in the coming year was known, for if her steps pointed inward towards the smoored [covered] fire she brought good fortune but if they were going away

*St Cado giving the Devil a cat
in exchange for building
the bridge.*

from the hearth it was an omen of ill fortune or even death.' [14] The same procedure was followed in parts of Ireland on St Brigid's Eve.

St Brigitte is remembered in Brittany (France), traditionally passing through on her return from the Holy Land, although in reality she probably never went there. She left her footprints on a large rock in the river near her chapel in Plounévez, her handprints on a rock near St Brigitte's Well in Finistère, when she fell on to the stony ground, and her knee-prints on a rock near Dinan. In the last instance, she was being followed by a nobleman who had designs on her virtue, so she leapt from the top of a hill while making the sign of the cross and, protected by her guardian angel, with one bound she leapt the valley at the bottom of which is the pool of Kergournadeac'h. In the course of her descent, two holes were made in a rock which perfectly resemble knee-prints, and these can be seen close by the little chapel dedicated to her. [15]

St Brochan left his head-print on a stone east of the old ruined church in Clonsast parish in Co. Offaly (Ireland), and people with headaches would place their heads in the depression in hopes of a cure. [16]

St Buduan (*fl.* late 6th century) was another Irish saint who used a floating stone as a boat. St Columcille and St Buduan sailed across to Scotland, but their missionary work was not appreciated and they had to make a hasty retreat, in the course of

63

which St Buduan was left standing on a rock on the shore. It broke away and Buduan sailed home on it; it now lies at the mouth of the Culdaff River in Co. Donegal, and the saint's five finger-marks can be seen.[17] It is also known as St Bodan's Boat.

St Cadoc (also Cado), a 6th-century Welsh saint, is commemorated in Brittany (France) on the Ile de Saint-Cado near Belz (Morbihan). The islet is connected to the mainland by a causeway, which was traditionally built by the Devil, he expecting to get the soul of the first person to cross in payment. However, St Cadoc sent over a cat instead, which angered the Devil and he made as if to destroy his work. St Cadoc made the sign of the cross and rushed to stop him, but he slipped and left on the rock a mark known as the Glissade de St Cado (St Cadoc's Slide).[18] (See 'Footprints to Visit')

The north Breton version of Cadoc is Cast, and St Cast gave his name to the village of Saint-Cast-le-Guildo (Côtes-d'Armor, Brittany). He was one of many saints who traditionally performed the miracle of making an imprint in solid rock in order to prove something, or to convince people of the truth of their promises. St Cast stamped hard on a rock and imprinted his foot on it, in order to confound a nobleman who was demanding a miracle, and by his action showed that he was truly a representative of God.[19]

St Christopher was a martyr, now the patron saint of travellers, with his cult being traced along medieval pilgrim routes in Europe. He left his footprint in the church of St Trinita della Cava near Sorrento (Italy).[20]

St Clodoaldus (also Cloud) was a 6th-century prince who gave up his claim to the Frankish throne and became a monk and then priest. Saint-Cloud to the west of Paris (France) was where he died, and pilgrims used to visit a paving stone larger than the others on the corner of a little street leading to La Place de l'Hôtel-de-Ville, on which is a depression said to be the saint's footprint, and known as the Pas de Saint Cloud.[21]

St Coemgen (anglicised as Kevin), 6th–7th-century Irish abbot, founded the famous monastery at Glendalough in Co.Wicklow, where he died in 618. In the years before the monastery came into being, Kevin lived as a hermit by the Upper Lake, where St Kevin's Bed (a cave) and St Kevin's Cell can still be visited. St Kevin's Seat was a rock on which were shown the marks of his leg and his fingers. A few miles south of Hollywood (Co. Wicklow), in Kilbaylet Upper, the King's Stone has a foot-shaped hollow, made by St Kevin when, as a giant, he stepped on to it from Slieve Gad, and thence to the next ridge.[22]

St Columcille (also Colmcille/Columbkill/Colm/Columba) was born in Ireland where he founded several monasteries, then moved to Scotland in 565 and stayed there, mostly on Iona, and so traces of him are found both in Ireland and Scotland. He left his knee-prints on a circular flat stone in the centre of the churchyard at Clonmany (Co. Donegal), where there is also a well named after the saint, the water from which runs into the sea, and it was once customary for the cattle to be driven down to the beach on the saint's day, 9 June, and made to swim in that part of the sea where the well water mingled with the sea water.[23] The bullauns on a boulder known as Colm's

St Columba in a stained-glass window in the Chapel of St Margaret at Edinburgh Castle. Photo: Andreas Trottmann.

Stone (Cloch Cholaim) at Kilcolumb (Co. Kilkenny) were interpreted as the imprints of his head and knees, and people would go there to cure headaches.[24] (See 'Footprints to Visit') He also left his knee-prints on a stone near his well in Kilconickery parish (Co. Galway);[25] and his thumb- and finger-marks (six altogether) on a limestone boulder by the lane to his church in Glen Columbcille (Co. Clare).[26] The imprints of his fingers were left on a stone slab known as Colmcille's Pillow, close to a round tower on Tory Island (Co. Donegal): water from the finger depressions was used by women giving birth, to help ease their pain.[27] His footprints were imprinted on a rock near Gartan Lake in Co. Donegal, when he jumped on to it from the top of the hill of Cnoc a' Toighe when being chased by enemies.[28] The marks of his ribs are on the shore below Killeanny on Inishmore in the Aran Islands (Co. Galway), at the place where Colmcille had a dispute with St Enda.[29]

St Columba's landing point in Scotland is traditionally said to have been near Southend village at Keil Point on Kintyre (Argyll and Bute), and near the ruined chapel and St Columba's Well can be seen 'a flat rock bearing on its top the impress of two feet, made, it seems, by those of the saint whilst he stood marking out and hallowing the spot on which his chapel should rest.'[30] (See 'Footprints to Visit')

St Cornély, as he appears on the exterior of his church at Carnac.

St Columbanus was also a 6th–7th-century Irish saint, but he travelled south to France and Italy, founding the monastery of Bobbio in the Apennines. On the summit of La Spanna mountain, near the cave where St Columbanus was wont to pray and meditate, is a rock bearing the impression of the saint's left hand. Local peasants would place their hand on it in order to be healed of their afflictions.[31]

St Cornelius (supposedly, he was the martyr and Pope St Cornelius who died in AD 253) was known as St Cornély in Brittany, the patron saint of horned animals (*corne* = horn), with an atmospheric church in the town of Carnac. He was a sensitive man, according to the folk-tale which explains how his footprint came to be imprinted on a rock at Moustoir near Carnac. As he arrived there, he heard a woman swear and a boy insult his mother, and he was so saddened he jumped back, landing hard on the large stone which now bears his footprint.[32] It is also said that when he was being chased by pagans he and his people fled in a chariot. As they approached the sea, he stopped and turned to face his pursuers. He cursed them and turned them all to stone where they stood: they are still to be seen in Brittany today – the hundreds of standing stones at Carnac. The course of St Cornély's chariot wheels appears as lines in the cornfields where the plants grow faster and appear greener.[33]

St Cybi (also Cuby in Cornwall) was a 6th-century saint who founded a monastery at Holyhead on Anglesey (Wales), leaving the print of his foot there on a rock at the east end of his church in the town.[34]

St Cynllo, Celtic saint associated with Llangoedmor (Ceredigion, Wales), left his knee-prints, 'Ôl Gliniau Cynllo', there, in the rock where he knelt to pray.[35]

St Cynwyl, 6th-century Celtic saint of Cynwyl Gaio (Carmarthen, Wales), also left his knee-prints in a rock where he knelt to pray, which stood in the river. In previous centuries the farmers would scoop the water from the hollows in the rock and pour it over the backs of their cattle to prevent them catching any diseases. At his holy well, Ffynnon Gynwil, were said to be the prints of his knees, elbows, and boots.[36]

St Damhnat of Tedavnet (her principal church) was an Irish nun in the 6th century and she was the focus of a midsummer-day pilgrimage to her well in Lavey parish (Co. Cavan), close to which was a flagstone with a hollow, said to have been worn by the saint's knees. The hollow was large enough to hold two or three quarts of water, and this was used by the pilgrims to heal their sore knees.[37]

St Deiniolen *(fl. 600)* was a Celtic saint, a disciple of Beuno, who gave his name to Llanddeiniolen near Caernarfon (Gwynedd, Wales) and left his footprint on a stone near the church.[38]

St Edern, son of Beli, a king of Gwynedd in 6th-century Wales, was patron of Llanedern on the Lleyn peninsula and of Bodedern on Anglesey, and at the latter place he left hand-marks on a stone which he threw a quarter of a mile into a field. The stone was later blown up and pieces used to build a house.[39] In Brittany he was the local saint of Lannédern, and his stone bed was located nearby. He used to sleep there under the moon and stars, and left the imprints of his neck and back on the granite bed.[40]

St Eligius (also Eloi, Loy) was originally a goldsmith in 7th-century France who became a bishop, preaching and founding monasteries in various parts of France. On the edge of the valley of Brézou (Limousin) is St Eloi's Rock, where he rested while watching work going on at the Abbey of Solignac, and he left his knee-prints on the rock.[41]

St Evette (also known by other names, e.g. Avoye or Avée) is said to have sailed from Britain to Brittany on a stone boat, part of which is still preserved in Pluneret church (Morbihan), and sickly children were once placed in it to give them strength. She left her knee-prints on a rock, along with the marks made by her rosary hanging at her waist, and the print of her right hand on which she leaned when she was tired, at Esquibien (Finistère, Brittany).[42]

St Ferreolus (Ferréol) gave his name to a stone with five hollows, resembling a giant hand, at Lorgues (Var, France), which was known as St Ferreolus' Quoit. A folk-tale had Our Lady of the Angels, St Joseph of Cotignac, and St Ferreolus playing a game of *bouchon*. St Ferreolus collided with a tree while preparing to throw his quoit, stumbled, and dropped it. He had been gripping it so tightly that his fingers left their imprint.[43]

St Fiacre (also Fiachra) was a 7th-century Irish hermit who moved to Meaux east of Paris (France): his name came to be used for taxi-cabs, which used to be hired from the hotel Saint-Fiacre in Paris. He left behind him in Ireland, at Ullard in Co. Kilkenny, his knee-prints on a stone by St Fiachra's Well, and water from the hollows was used to treat sores.[44] In France St Fiacre created a hermitage at Breuil near Meaux, but when he was measuring out a piece of ground for an extension, the ease with which he created a trench caused him to be denounced as a sorcerer using magic. Devastated by the accusations, he sank on to a rock to await the arrival of the bishop, whereupon the rock melted in sympathy with the saint's plight, forming a chair taking his body imprint. The rounded, indented stone was placed in the village church, by the saint's tomb, while in the forest, earthworks marked the trench he had miraculously created.[45]

St Finbar (also Finbarr, Barr, Barre, or Barry: 6th–early 7th century) gave his name to Kilbarry in Co. Roscommon (Ireland); in the churchyard is a boat-shaped stone 8 feet long with a modern statue of St Barry on top of it. The stone was said to float, and it was known as St Barry's stone boat, he having used it to cross the River Shannon: his knee-prints on the stone 'prove' the truth of the story. The local people continued to use the stone boat after St Barry was dead, but when they lost their innocence, the boat sank.[46]

St Florina, a virgin saint living in Gaul, was persecuted for her chastity and she used to hide from her persecutors in a rocky valley that has been named after her. One day she leapt across a 50-foot chasm to escape her enemies and left her right footprint where she landed, and her left footprint on the rock she jumped from.[47]

St Gertrude was commemorated at Neustadt in Germany and her footprints were said to be visible on the road between Neustadt and Carlstadt. They were not imprinted on to rock, but showed up as green patches when the grassy path was brown and as brown patches when the path was green.[48]

St Govan, the 6th-century Welsh hermit, has an improbably-sited chapel dedicated to him, in a cleft between high cliffs at St Govan's Head in Pembrokeshire. Inside this tiny building, according to legend, St Govan hid in a narrow crevice when pirates raided the area, and the rock closed around him, the marks of his ribs being permanently imprinted on the rock. In case this story sounds familiar, the ribs are also claimed as Christ's, and the story therefore appears among the accounts of Christ's imprints in the previous chapter.[49] (See 'Footprints to Visit')

St Gredfyw (also Rhedyw) was a 6th-century saint who came from Brittany and left several rock imprints around Llanllyfni (Gwynedd, Wales): in addition to his bed and seat, his knee-prints, his thumb-mark and his horse's hoof-print are all recorded in the local folklore.[50]

St Gwyn, together with St Gwyno, St Gwynoro, St Ceitho, St Celynin (probably 6th century): These are the five saints from whom the village of Pumpsaint (*pump* = five in Welsh) in Carmarthenshire took its name. They were said to be a set of quins who, during a thunderstorm which overtook them on their pilgrimage to St Davids, took refuge in the system of caves and tunnels which can still be seen at the Dolaucothi Roman gold mines, all resting their heads on the same block of stone as they fell asleep. Over time, their heads made hollows on the stone, and it was eventually thrown out: it now stands erect at the site. The Five Sleepers took another stone for a pillow, and this also has hollows to hold their heads. They will not awake until King Arthur reappears, or 'a genuine and faithful apostolic bishop occupies the throne of St David'.[51] (See 'Footprints to Visit')

St Gwyndaf Hên was a missionary saint who travelled from Brittany to Wales. A chapel dedicated to him once stood on the bank of the River Ceri at Troedyraur (Ceredigion), while in the river was a flat rock with holes said to have been made by the saint's knees after he prayed there. Local people would bathe their feet in the water in the holes to cure wounds and sores.[52]

St Helen was a Scandinavian saint of the 12th century, whose tomb and well are at Tiisvilde on the island of Zealand (Denmark), and pilgrims would visit the place and perform rituals in hopes of being cured of their afflictions. One legend told how her body floated on a stone to Zealand after she was killed in Sweden. Her body was carried to Tiisvilde and buried where she was first laid down, after it became too heavy to be moved further. The stone which acted as her boat remained close to the shore, and the marks of her hair, her hands and feet remained visible on it.[53]

St Herveus (Harvey; Hervé) was a Breton saint, a 6th-century abbot born in Brittany but the son of a British bard, and he was blind from birth, according to his *Life*. He was a wandering monk and minstrel, but he eventually settled with a community at Lanhouarneau (Finistère) where he died. His footprints are on a rock at the village of Guémenez nearby.[54]

St Illtud was an important 5th–6th-century Welsh saint. He was said to be a cousin of King Arthur, and one of his knights. His knee-prints at Coadout in Brittany have already been mentioned, under St Brieuc, with whom he was accustomed to pray.[55]

St Jean caused his footprint to appear on a stone to prove his honesty, according to a French legend. The saint (probably St John the Evangelist on a mythical visit to France) was passing through Saint-Clément-de-la-Place (Maine-et-Loire) and stayed there briefly, but when he left, his host suspected that he had not paid for his stay and so pursued him. In order to defend his honesty, St Jean said: 'It is true that I have paid, just as it is true that my foot will be engraved on that stone.' And sure enough, this was seen to have occurred – and when the landlord went back, he found the saint's money.[56]

St Justina of Padua was an early female martyr, her legend (most likely untrue) telling how she was condemned as a Christian by Emperor Maximian and pierced through the breast with a sword. At Venice in Italy, a stone was preserved that bore her knee-prints, after she prayed when fleeing the governor who pursued her for her wealth and beauty.[57]

St Landrada was Abbess of Münster-Bilsen in Belgium in the 7th century, and while she was praying one day, the heavens opened and a finely worked cross came down on to a hard stone beside her. She heard a voice telling her it was a gift. She worked to clear the land for a new church, and erected the altar herself. The stone was impressed with the cross she had received from heaven, as if it was made of wax, and was visible for a long time afterwards.[58]

St Lawrence was a 3rd-century Roman deacon and martyr, traditionally killed by being tied to an iron grid and roasted alive. The Basilica of San Lorenzo fuori le Mura was built in Rome in 330 beside St Lawrence's burial place, and the crypt contains the imprint of his body.[59]

St Leocadia died in prison in Toledo in Spain c.303. She was patron of Toledo, and also of St Ghislain (in Belgium). It was said that she made the sign of the cross with her finger on the prison wall, and as if it was wax, the cross was impressed into the stone.[60]

St Madeleine (probably St Marie Madeleine – or Mary Magdalen – who according to medieval French legend came to France from Palestine and lived there as a hermit). She left her mark near two rivers in south-west France. Her footprints are on a rock carried by the saint, which found its way to an island in the Charente; and a rock 500 metres from the left bank of the Vienne bears the imprints of her slipper.[61]

St Magnus was the son of a Viking ruler of the Orkney Islands (Scotland) who lived in the 11th–12th centuries. He was a pirate before converting to Christianity, and he eventually died a violent death at the hands of his cousin, becoming a Christian saint and martyr. He was another saint who traditionally used a stone for a boat, in St Magnus' case when he wished to cross the Pentland Firth to Caithness on the Scottish mainland. He afterwards carried the stone, now known as St Magnus's Boat, or the Ladykirk Stone, to Ladykirk (St Mary's church) at Burwick on the Orkney island of South Ronaldsay, where it can still be seen. It carries the imprint of two human feet, traditionally the saint's, and it is said that at one time delinquents were punished by being made to stand barefoot in the footprints for a set period of time.[62] (See 'Footprints to Visit')

St Manawla left her mark in her home territory of Co. Clare, Ireland. Two hollows on a rock between Dysert O'Dea and Rath Blamaic are her knee-prints, made when she carried off the round tower of Rath. She coveted one of the round towers built by St Blawfugh of Rath, so at night she uprooted it and carried it in her veil, intending to take it to her monastery. St Blawfugh chased after her, and she flung the tower away. It landed and stuck upright beside Dysert church, but the effort caused St Manawla to overbalance and she fell on her knees, leaving their impression in the rock. This must be one of the few saint's knee-prints that were not made during the act of praying![63]

St Martin of Tours.

St Martin of Tours (c.316–397) was a popular saint in the Middle Ages, and there are many examples of his imprints, especially in central France, with 4,000 churches dedicated to him in that country alone. He was born in Hungary, became a monk, and eventually Bishop of Tours, though still living like a monk, and he founded numerous monasteries. His cult spread quickly after his death, and he was famed as a miracle-worker. His imprints often carried a reputation for being able to achieve pilgrims' desires, such as the footprint at Cinais near Chinon (Touraine): a young person wishing to marry within the year had only to place his or her foot in St Martin's footprint for this to happen. Fever patients went to St Martin's footprint at Iffendic (Ille-et-Vilaine) and left coins and small wooden crosses in the print.

The traces of his presence are widespread, and not only his footprints are represented. At Sobre-le-Château (Nord), the Pierres-Martines have a hollow which was formed by St Martin's back when he lay down there. Sometimes St Martin was able to work miracles that benefited no one but himself. At Viabon (Eure-et-Loire), a rock has two holes representing his foot- and knee-prints: he knelt there to pray because he could not decide which was the way to the village. When he lifted his head again, he could see the cross on the steeple at Viabon. On occasions St Martin had to outwit the Devil, as in Provence when the Devil proposed that they play the game of three leaps to decide the ownership of the land between Toulon and Saint-Nazaire. The saint, having successfully leapt the valleys, sprang so strongly for his third leap that his foot imprinted itself in the rock above the Kakoye and left a depression 60 cm long and 15 cm deep.[64]

More saints, and more weird and wonderful folk-tales describing their powers and exploits, will follow in the next chapter.

Chapter Five

A saintly presence II
St Mary, the Blessed Virgin, to St Wolfgang

> 'For those who believe in divine apparitions, the sand on which
> Mary left her footprints, the leaves of a hawthorn or live oak on
> which she appeared, and the stone on which she sat bore her
> signature and were meant by her to be kept and used in memory
> of her visit.'
>
> William A. Christian Jr., *Apparitions in Late Medieval and
> Renaissance Spain*, p.212

Many saints, both male and female, left permanent reminders of their presence in the form of rock imprints; indeed many of the most popular saints were female and accordingly they were often named as the creators of miraculous footprints, none more so than the Virgin Mary whose influence was and still is ubiquitous and powerful. It is true that some of the footprints described here, those belonging to perhaps lesser-known saints, cannot now be easily found, though they probably still exist if only one knew where to look. Others retain their power and are still visited and venerated by pilgrims – 'Footprints to Visit' lists some of the most accessible.

St Mary, the Blessed Virgin, was the mother of Jesus Christ and accordingly is the most important saint in the Christian canon. However very little is known about her origins, her life, or even where she died (the two main claimants are Jerusalem and Ephesus, her tomb still being shown at the former). She has now been venerated for two millennia, and her cult remains especially powerful today. She figures strongly in Christian folklore, and has traditionally left more footprints than probably any other saint.

Her footprints are particularly widespread in France. At Font-Sainte, Apchon, Riom-ès-Montagnes (Cantal), are ancient sacred springs where an apparition of the Virgin Mary appeared to shepherdess Marie Galvin, asking her to restore a sanctuary, in the 17th century. The Virgin left her footprints on the threshold stone of Font-Sainte, and a triple spring began to flow where she touched a rock with three fingers.[1] She left the mark of her thigh on a rock where she fell from fatigue, while fleeing the wrath of Herod – near Moncontour (Côtes-d'Armor)[2] – whereas in Deux-Sèvres she was being followed by the Devil and so she flew to Heaven, leaving her footprint in the rock, which began to soften beneath the Devil's feet, and he was held prisoner. He also left his claw-marks on the same rock. The footprint was located near Saint-Laurent Chapel, and was venerated by pilgrims.[3]

A 19th-century vision of the Virgin Mary, when she appeared to children at La Salette in France. A healing spring appeared at the site.

The Blessed Virgin Mary left her footprint on a rock on the summit of a hill at Pontarlier (Doubs); it acted as a memorial to the time she extinguished a terrible fire at Pontarlier by dousing the place with torrential rain.[4] At Agde church (Hérault) her knee-print on a stone commemorates the occasion when she halted a tidal wave.[5] She left two knee-prints in the base of a cross when she knelt to pray while on her way to Mass at Saint-Mars d'Egrène near Passais (Orne).[6] She had another encounter with the Devil in a wood at Commequiers (Vendée) where there are two dolmens (prehistoric stone burial chambers): one has a right footprint said to be Satan's, the other has a left footprint said to be that of the Blessed Virgin Mary.[7] The footprint on a rock at the well of Saint-Gré at Avrillé (Vendée), said to be that of the Virgin Mary, is also a left foot.[8]

Three interesting tales concerning the presence of the Blessed Virgin Mary in Brittany show a varied reaction to her, the first being particularly surprising. She was said to have appeared at a rock called 'Roc'h ar Verhès' (Rock of the Virgin) at Saint-Coulitz (Finistère), but was not well received by the people of the village, who threw stones at her. She fled to the other side of the ravine, and a sanctuary was built there for her. There are several holes on the Rock: the two biggest are her footprints, while the small ones were made by the stones thrown at her.[9] At Ménéac (Morbihan) there are on an exposed rock the traces of three footprints of the Blessed Virgin Mary, though some people see a footprint and a knee-print, with two child's footprints between them. She was passing this way while travelling between Nazareth and Egypt during the flight from Herod (but her map-reading seems not to have been very reliable),

VIVA

MARIA SANTISIMA

MADRE DE DIOS.

**Esta es verdadera medi-
da de la sandalia de la
Virgen Santisima, que
se conserva con gran
veneracion en un Mo-
nasterio de España.**

El Papa Juan XXII concedió
trescientos años de indulgen-
cias á todos, besando tres veces esta medida, y rezando
tres Ave Marias.
Dicha indulgencia confirmó
Clemente VIII en el año 1603,
y se puede ganar cuantas veces
se quiera por las benditas almas
del Purgatorio, y para mayor glo-
ria de la Reina de los Angeles.

*Se permite sacar de esta medida
otras, y todas tendrán las mismas in-
dulgencias.*

MARIA

MATER GRATIÆ,

ORA PRO NOBIS.

*The Virgin Mary's footprint:
a holy picture which is the
Measure of Our Lady's
sandal (actual length 188mm);
Madrid 1881.*

and some people say that she knelt on the rock with the baby Jesus while a procession went past. It was once customary for mothers to take their children, if they were late in starting to walk, to the Virgin Mary's footprints, in the hope that help would be given. The mother would place her foot and knee in the Virgin's two imprints, and the child's feet would be placed into the prints of the baby Jesus. Families with children still visit the site, and there is an annual *Pardon* with a procession whose route includes the footprint stone.[10]

At Ergué-Gabéric (Finistère), the Virgin Mary's footprint on a rock is accompanied by the imprint made by the plague when it tried to enter the village. The plague took the form of an aged wild woman, who touched people with a white stick and thus gave

74

them the plague. The villagers of Elliant across the River Ster Wenn were afflicted by the plague, and so they decided to make a pilgrimage to the shrine of Our Lady of Kerdévot in Ergué-Gabéric, to call for her help. The wild woman followed behind the procession, no doubt hoping to spread the plague across the river. As the people crossed the water by means of stepping stones, they saw a vision of Our Lady standing on one of the stones, and she cured each pilgrim as they passed her. But she prevented the old woman from proceeding further, and thus stopped the plague spreading to the parish of Ergué-Gabéric. The stone on which she stood retained the imprint of her foot, and also that of the old woman, or the plague, in the shape of a horseshoe: the two prints 'confront' each other. The stone was later moved to the foot of the calvary outside the chapel at Kerdévot, which is still a major place of pilgrimage for the *Pardon* on 8 September.[11]

The Blessed Virgin Mary also left her footprints elsewhere in Europe, and a few more examples follow. Doubtless there are many more that I have not yet heard about. The Virgin's footprints are in the Käppele pilgrimage church near Würzburg in Germany.[12] In north-west Spain, at Mugía north of Cape Finisterre (Galicia), in the sanctuary of the basilica of our Lady there is a large flat stone, said to be the keel of a stone boat in which she sailed to Spain to encourage St James the Greater (who is buried at Compostela) in his preaching. She left the imprint of her feet on the stone and, according to the local fishermen, the stone keel sways slightly.[13] Over the centuries the Virgin Mary has appeared in visions to numerous people in Spain, sometimes leaving her footprints behind.

For example, at Cubas in Central Castile, 12-year-old peasant girl Inés Martínez saw the Virgin Mary six times in March 1449, in fields close to the village. When questioned about her visions, one of the things she remembered was that the Virgin Mary had left small footprints on a stretch of sand. She said they were like the footprints of an 8-year-old girl, and other witnesses also saw the footprints and agreed they were tiny. (Seeing our Lady as a child seems to have been something of a Spanish speciality – even the great Teresa of Avila saw Her as a child – which remains to be explained.) The place where the footprints were left was regarded as sacred, and the sand was taken for use in cures. People would walk round the site or go down on their knees as if visiting a saint's relic. In 1592 Isabel Besora had a vision of our Lady while watching her sheep at Vallbona in Catalonia: she was touched on the cheek, and a mark like a red rose was left there.[14]

In Italy, Mary had earlier left her footprints at another vision site, at Caravaggio in Lombardy, in 1432. In 1428 she had touched an elderly visionary and left a mark on her shoulder at Monte Berico, a mountainous site near Vicenza where a spring appeared as foretold by the Virgin. The *Capo della Madonna* (the Madonna's Head) was impressed on a rock on Canneto in the mountains between Rome and Naples. The ascent to Canneto is made from Sette Frati near Atina, and when visiting the village in 1894 Dom Bede Camm was told the legend of Our Lady of Canneto. A shepherd boy saw a vision of the Virgin Mary who requested that a church be built in the mountain-pass at the spot where she appeared. The shepherd was loath to leave his sheep to die of thirst in the barren mountains while he went at once to tell the priest, as our Lady had asked him, so she placed two fingers on the rock and a

The Virgin Mary's footprint on a rock above Llanfair (Gwynedd).

river (the Melfa) gushed forth. The boy went to the village but no one believed his story. Returning with him to the mountain, they followed the miraculous river to its source where, instead of a vision, they found a wooden statue of our Lady standing on a little hill (where the church now stands). Soon the whole population of the village was assembled, and they decided to carry the statue away, but as they did so, it became heavier. (This feature is commonly found in the foundation legends of shrines.) They placed it against the rock, and when they lifted it up again, having received a sign from the Virgin Mary, it was again lighter – and had left a mark on the rock where the head had rested. Later a chapel was built over the place where the *Capo della Madonna* had lain.[15] In southern Ukraine a monastery grew up at the mountaintop site where our Lady left her footprint on a rock during a vision. A spring began to flow at the rock whose water was believed to have healing powers, and pilgrims came to visit. The rock and its footprint are now protected in a silver shrine in a church at Pochaev monastery, which is one of the most important shrines of Russian Orthodoxy.[16] (See 'Footprints to Visit')

On Jersey in the Channel Islands, there is at St Helier a chapel dedicated to Notre Dame des Pas, which may mean Our Lady of the Footprints, referring to the Virgin Mary's appearance at the spot where afterwards there was to be seen a rock bearing footprints. The location of the rock was just off Green Street, but its present whereabouts are not known to me.[17] Our Lady also left her footprint, and her knee-print, in Scotland. The footprint was formerly to be found on a large stone at Our Lady's Well south of Stow church (Scottish Borders), where there were also relics of the True Cross, and these, in addition to the healing powers of the well, attracted many pilgrims. The footprint stone seems to have disappeared 200 years ago.[18] Our Lady's knee-print was on a stone where she was said to have knelt in prayer, in Kirkmaiden parish by the Mull of Galloway (Dumfries and Galloway) where, as the name indicates, a church was dedicated to the Virgin Mary.[19]

Wales has some unusual and interesting traditions concerning the legendary presence of the Blessed Virgin Mary. There are several footprints and other imprints said to have been made by her just inland from the Welsh coastline between Barmouth and Harlech (Gwynedd), the tradition being that she landed at Llanfair ('Mary's church enclosure') where the church is still dedicated to her. Accompanied by her maidens, she climbed the hill behind the church. Feeling thirsty, they knelt and prayed, and a well, Ffynnon Fair (Mary's Well), sprang up. Mary left the imprint of her knees on a rock beside the well, and older inhabitants of Llanfair remember that she was also supposed to have left the imprint of her breast. The group then walked into a field on the hilltop, where Mary's sandal came loose. As she fastened it, she left her footprint and her thumb-print on a rock. She and her maidens walked on to the lake known as Hafod-y-Llyn and bathed there, and for ever afterwards yellow water lilies always grew there in remembrance.[20] A little further south, by the side of an old road from Dyffryn Ardudwy inland to Cwm Nantcol, by a ruined farm known as Llam Maria (Mary's Leap), was another stone with a clear footprint, unhappily smashed in the early 20th century when the road was being metalled. The name Mary's Leap refers to the legend of a powerful lady, or giantess, leaping from the top of the hill called Moelfre on to this stone. Just as has happened elsewhere, a saint has become transposed into a giant in local folklore. Further south again, tradition reports that Mary leapt to the outskirts of Llanaber, leaving her footprint on a stone on top of the hill called Wenallt.[21] It seems likely that in the past the three imprint sites were linked, perhaps in a story of Mary leaping from one to the other: they are more or less in a straight line north – south: Llanfair – Llanbedr – Llanaber.

Still in Wales, at Uwch Mynydd, on the Lleyn Peninsula (Gwynedd) overlooking Ynys Enlli (Bardsey Island) and close to a pilgrim track, is a holy well known as Ffynnon Fair (St Mary's Well), close to which is said to be a rock bearing the imprint of Mary's hand, and also that of her horse's hoof.[22] There are many other St Mary's Wells in Wales, around eighty in fact, but not many of them can also claim our Lady's footprint.

In conclusion, and as a change from her footprints, there was recorded a belief that the dent on the back of a date stone was, according to a Coptic legend, caused by the Virgin Mary's tooth, the date being the first food she ate during the Flight into Egypt.[23]

St Médard (died c.558) was a French bishop of Noyon and Tournai whose cult dates from the 6th century, and one of the folk beliefs was that St Médard could control the wind for 40 days following his feast day, similar to the British belief in the weather being foretold by that occurring on St Swithin's Day. This belief is evident in one of

*St Michael protecting a soul from demons during the Last Judgement;
a detail from statuary on the façade of Bourges Cathedral.*

the tales concerning St Médard's footprints, which is set around the Margeride mountains in southern France. Suffering from the effects of a strong north-easterly wind, St Médard chased it with his stick as far as the Cave of Oule at the highest point of the Margeride. There he imprinted his foot on the rock and, sinking his stick beside the print, he cried: 'Wind, blow as much as you like, you will not blow any more from this direction.' And ever since, the wind, which blows in summer every morning from sunrise until 10, stops at the south-eastern slope of the Margeride.[24] St Médard also used his footprint to help settle a boundary dispute, after the farmers of Picardy appealed to him for assistance. Having made his decision, he had a large stone brought to mark the boundary and set his footprint on it as if it were wax not stone, this act giving greater authority to his judgement.[25]

St Mewan (also Mevennus, Méen, Meven, Maine) was born in South Wales in the 6th century and went with his relative, St Samson of Dol, first to Cornwall and then to Brittany where on his arrival in that country he left his footprints on a large stone at Cancale. A few beads fell from the rosary he carried at his waist, and left their own small holes in the stone. (This is not actually possible, since strings of beads as prayer-counters did not appear in Europe until some time around the 12th century.) His principal foundation was at St-Méen, which area was the home of a fearsome dragon. St Mewan placed his stole around the monster's neck, led it to the river, pushed it in and drowned it.[26]

St Michael must be one of the best-known of the European saints, and in Britain he is linked with high places, numerous hilltop churches being dedicated to him.

A scene from Revelation depicting war in Heaven, with St Michael casting down the dragon Satan and his angels to the earth.

Biblically Michael was an archangel who battled with the Devil, and he is often depicted slaying a dragon (who represents the Devil – referring to Revelation 12), or weighing souls. His cult began in the East, first of all in Asia Minor, then moving into the Byzantine world, and thence to the West, where there was a famous apparition of St Michael seen on Monte Gargano in Italy in the late 5th century. The vision site in a cave on Monte Gargano was chosen by St Michael for his shrine, and when some local people went there to give thanks for their victory in a war, they found the archangel's footprints in the rock floor: St Michael had consecrated the cave. The cave was walled up and became a church, and a replica of the shrine was set up on Mont Saint-Michel in Manche (northern France) by the 9th century. Indeed, a piece of marble from the Gargano, on which St Michael had stood, was taken to Mont Saint-Michel to validate the French shrine. Pilgrims visiting the shrine on Monte Gargano still today outline their own hands or feet and add their initials, to commemorate St Michael's footprint.[27] The pilgrims also take away chips of stone from the cave as relics.

St Michael also left his footprint (actually his boot-print) on a rock by the road leading to the chapel of Sainte-Barbe at Le Faouët (Morbihan); and on the hill of Mont-Dol (Ille-et-Vilaine) where he leapt from Mont Saint-Michel in order to rid the hill of the Devil (more information on this event can be found in Chapter 7 and in

*St Non depicted in a window
in the Chapel of Our Lady and
St Non, close to her holy well
at St Davids in Pembrokeshire.*

'Footprints to Visit').[28] In 1455 St Michael appeared in a vision to a shepherd near Navalagamella in Castile (Spain). He was in a holm-oak, and after giving the shepherd a message, he left his handprint in the tree trunk. The shepherd dared not at first tell his story, but after he woke up crippled he revealed what had happened and he was carried to the tree, where the hand-mark was seen by everyone. He recovered his health at a mass said for him, and became the keeper of the saint's shrine at the place of the vision. The shrine still survives today, but not the tree.[29] St Michael also left his fingerprints on a pointed stone, part of a prehistoric burial chamber, near Llanfihangel Lledrod (*Llanfihangel* translates as 'Michael's religious enclosure') in Ceredigion (Wales), the stone being known in the early 19th century as Llech Mihangel (Michael's slab), but later becoming known as Carreg Samson

The stone with St Non's knee-prints, at St Non's Well, Dirinon.

(Samson's Stone), showing that 'ownership' had shifted from St Michael to a giant, or that the saint himself had transmuted into a giant in the minds of the local people.[30]

St Mildred, 7th-century daughter of a King of Mercia, returned to England following her education near Paris, and found a great square stone miraculously prepared for her to step on as she came ashore at Ebbsfleet. It retained the marks of her feet and was taken to the religious house (the abbey of Menstrey) at Minster-in-Thanet (Kent) where Mildred had become a nun. Her tomb became a place of pilgrimage following her death, and diseases were cured using water containing a little dust from the footprint stone. It was said that the stone always returned if removed, and eventually an oratory was built to house it.[31]

St Non (also Nonn, Nonne) was a 5th-century Welsh saint about whom not much is known, except that she was the mother of St David, the patron saint of Wales. She may have been a nun in Pembrokeshire, seduced by Prince Sant; or else she was the daughter of a chieftain and married to Sant. She also lived in Cornwall, where her church and well can be found at Altarnon, and she may have died there, or at St Davids. Most of the information about St Non comes from the Life of St David written in the late 11th century by the Welsh scholar Rhigyfarch. Concerning the birth of St David, he wrote: 'The mother, in her travail, had near her a certain stone, on which she leaned with her hands when hard pressed by her pains; whereby the

*The author kneeling in
St Noyale's knee-prints
on her prie-dieu at
Les Trois Fontaines.*

marks of her hands, as though impressed on wax, have identified that stone for those who have gazed upon it: it broke in half in sympathy with the mother in her agony. On that spot a church has been built, in the foundations of which this stone lies concealed.'[32] The church referred to now survives only as a slight ruin (Capel Non), and the whereabouts of the handprint stone are no longer known, but the site at St Davids in Pembrokeshire is most evocative, above the cliffs and close to St Non's holy well.

Dirinon in Brittany (France) was the place where St Non died and was buried, her tomb being located in a chapel close to the church. Dirinon has also been claimed as the place where she gave birth to St David (there known as St Divy or Divi), but this appears to be a late addition to the traditional legend of her knee-prints. Not far from Dirinon is the saint's well, and a rock bearing the imprint of her knees, where she was wont to kneel to pray. So went the legend in the 18th century. By the early 20th century the rock was said to be the place where she gave birth to St Divy: above her knee marks is the hollow where she placed the newborn baby, for the rock softened like wax to serve as a cradle. It was believed locally that a visit to the stone could heal babies born with a certain blue vein between the eyebrows, known as the illness of St Divy. St Non ensures they do not suffer the premature death the ailment heralds.[33] (See 'Footprints to Visit')

St Noyale (also Noyala, Nolwen, and the same as Newlyna, of Cornwall) came from Britain, sailing to Brittany with her nurse on a leaf, or on a branch, depending on which source you consult. She died at the hands of a chieftain when she rejected his advances. He decapitated her at Bézo, but she picked up her head and carried it for some distance ('30 leagues') before dying of exhaustion at Ste-Noyale, where her chapel and well can be found. Not far away, at Les Trois Fontaines near Noyal-Pontivy (Morbihan), can be found her stone bed and her prieu-dieu (praying stool) – a rock with her knee-prints. The three springs at Les Trois Fontaines are said to have sprung up from three drops of blood which fell when St Noyale rested here while carrying her severed head.[34] (See 'Footprints to Visit')

St Odilia was the 7th–8th-century abbess at Hohenburg in the Vosges mountains of France where pilgrims still visit her shrine, especially seeking cures for blindness and eye ailments: she was allegedly born blind but later gained her sight. Near the well on the mountain of Sainte-Odile (Vosges) are three deep grooves in a rock into which you can put your hand. They are the marks of St Odilia's fingers, made when she was escaping the control of Duke Alaric (or Adalric) her father, who wanted to marry her off, whereas she wanted to consecrate her virginity to Christ.[35] At Hohenburg is the Zähren-capelle, the chapel of tears, with a stone containing two hollows which are the marks of St Odilia's knees, impressed on the stone when she knelt there.[36]

St Ólann was the confessor of St Finbar of Cork (6th–7th century) and his well is near the ruined church of Aghabulloge which he founded in Coolineagh, Co. Cork, Ireland. Also close by is St Ólann's Stone, a boulder which bears the impression of his feet. On the saint's day (5 September), as well as at other times, pilgrims circumambulate the well, stone, and the Caipin, a phallic healing stone.[37] (See 'Footprints to Visit')

St Osith founded a nunnery at Chich (which is now St Osyth in Essex) and retired there in 673. According to the saint's legend, Danish pirates attacked the nunnery and when Osith resisted capture, the pirate chief beheaded her. A holy well sprang forth where her head fell. She picked up her head and carried it to the church, where she placed her bloody hands on the door, leaving indelible marks.[38]

St Padrig (Patrick), not the Irish Saint Patrick but another living later, probably in the 7th century. He is said to have founded the church at Llanbadrig on Anglesey (Wales): his boat was shipwrecked off Ynys Badrig on the Anglesey coast and he scrambled ashore, leaving the marks of his feet on the rocks of the cliff-path and near his holy well. He later founded a church there at Llanbadrig to commemorate his survival.[39]

St Palladius, 5th-century bishop, was St Patrick's predecessor in Ireland, sent there by Pope Celestine. After failing in Ireland he moved to Scotland which was where he died, and in Glen Lyon, at Camusvrachan (Perth and Kinross), is the Chraig Fhianaidh, or Stone of the Footprint, said to be marked with the footprint of St Palladius.[40]

St Patrick is now mainly associated with Ireland, but he was not Irish: he was born somewhere in western Britain around 390 and taken to Ireland by pirates while still young. He came from a Christian family, and after his years of slavery he went to be

The young St Patrick tending his master's animals during his enslavement; he also became a devout Christian at this time.

trained as a priest, traditionally in France. He was appointed to work in Ireland as a missionary, to where he returned c.435, becoming a bishop, and he is now the country's patron saint, and also Ireland's most popular saint, which accounts for the number of places where his imprints are to be found.

There are rocks with St Patrick's footprints on them at Sheestown (Ossory), at the well of Toberpatrick at Dungiven (Derry, Northern Ireland), and on a stone on Knockpatrick Hill, Graney, near the site of St Patrick's Well (Co. Kildare),[41] while an ancient stone cross at Cooley, Inishowen (Co. Donegal) has a mark on its base which is traditionally identified as St Patrick's footprint.[42] One of the major pilgrimages is to Lough Derg, also in Donegal, where on an island in the lough was the place (its exact location now unknown) called St Patrick's Purgatory, a cave which was thought to be an entrance to the Underworld, and where St Patrick had a vision of Purgatory. One of the places visited by the Lough Derg pilgrims was called 'Lackevanny', a stone covered with water and bearing St Patrick's footprints. They

St Patrick's Purgatory, as depicted in a 14th-century manuscript.

would place their feet on the stone under the water, and the experience was said to be healing and refreshing.[43]

St Patrick's footprints are also found outside Ireland. There is said to be one of his prints on a rock on the mountain Cronk ny Arrey Laa (also known as Slieau-Ynud-ny-Cassyn, the Mountain of Footprints) in the south-west of the Isle of Man, made when he landed there from Ireland.[44] In south-west Scotland, at Portpatrick (Dumfries and Galloway), there was a rock beside St Patrick's Well, known as St Patrick's Vat, which carried his hand and knee imprints, now lost because of quarrying.[45] St Patrick's knee-prints were once almost commonplace in Ireland. Lady Wilde, in her *Ancient Legends of Ireland*, described an occasion when, working as a missionary, St Patrick created his knee-prints as a demonstration of the power of God. (The location is not given.) 'When St Patrick was one time amongst the Pagan Irish they grew very fierce and seemed eager to kill him. Then his life being in great danger, he kneeled down before them and prayed to God for help and for the conversion of their souls. And the fervour of his prayer was so great that as the saint rose up the mark of his knees was left deep in the stone, and when the people saw the miracle they believed.' The people at the next village also demanded a miracle, and so he drew a circle and caused a well to flow there, where he had placed his prayer-book.[46]

The pilgrimage to Croagh Patrick (Co. Mayo) included a rock known as St Patrick's Knee, bearing a hollow in which the pilgrims knelt to say seven paters, seven aves, and a creed, before continuing on their bare knees over a rocky route.[47] Also in County Mayo, three stones each containing a bullaun (rock hollows which probably once had a ritual use) are located at different sites near Killeaden, and it was believed that St Patrick knelt on each stone to pray, leaving his knee-print behind. The three stones marked the points of a triangle, and anyone inside the triangle was thought to be safe from war.[48] A stone with three bullauns, said to be the imprints of St Patrick's head and knees, is to be found near the round tower at Roscam near Oranmore (Co. Galway). The head-print is larger than the knee-prints, being 8 inches deep, and it was believed that a person suffering from a headache could gain relief by placing his or her head in the hollow.[49] Patrick Logan, who wrote a book on Ireland's holy wells, saw the imprint stones as 'the saint's visiting cards'. Once, when visiting the holy well in Carna townland at Mullaghhorse, Co. Cavan, he asked a local man how he could be sure that St Patrick had visited this place, to which he got the reply: 'Of course I am sure he came here. How else could he have left the track of his knees in that stone?'[50] He left his foot- and knee-prints at many other Irish locations, including Ballysadare (Co. Sligo), Bridgetown (Co. Wexford), Cahir (Co. Tipperary), Moycullen (Co. Galway), Plumb Bridge (Co. Tyrone), Skerries (Co. Dublin)(See 'Footprints to Visit'), Tempo (Co. Fermanagh), Tuam (Co. Galway).[51]

Footprint stones were often included in the rituals which pilgrims followed at the Irish holy wells, as at St Patrick's Well, Oran, Ballydooley (Co. Roscommon). A visit made by C.F. Tebbutt in 1961 was described in detail by him in a folklore journal. The stone with the saint's knee-print stood about 10 yards from the well, and was actually labelled 'Knee Stone'. He summarised the ritual which pilgrims were supposed to follow, and this included a visit to the knee stone where St Patrick is supposed to have knelt.[52] (See 'Footprints to Visit') At the Hawk's Well at Tullaghan (Co. Sligo) were stones said to bear the marks of St Patrick's hand and back, where he fell from his horse, and also the mark of his horse's hoof. At the time, St Patrick was pursuing a demon known as the Fire-Spitter, who was poisoning all the wells as she fled ahead of him, knowing that eventually he would need to stop for a drink. Sure enough he became more and more thirsty and prayed for a drink. Suddenly his horse stumbled, he fell off, and where he landed, in addition to leaving imprints on the stones, a well sprang up. He refreshed himself and resumed his pursuit of the Fire-Spitter.[53] Four indentations left by St Patrick's fingers are to be seen on a stone at Tobernalt Well (Co. Sligo), and placing your own fingers in them is said to cause a transfer of some of the saint's power to you.[54] (See 'Footprints to Visit') Finally, in Killaha parish, Co. Mayo, a stone at the old church of Cross Patrick was said to have imprinted on it the outline of the saint's bottom.[55]

St Peter the Apostle had strong associations with Rome, being bishop of Rome and the first pope. He left the marks of his knees on a paving stone now in the church of Santa Francesca Romana, alongside the imprints of the knees of St Paul. (See 'Footprints to Visit') The two men knelt together, praying that Simon Magus, a magician from Jerusalem, would be dropped by the demons that held him in the air after he jumped from a high tower. He was trying to prove that his magic powers were stronger than those of the Christians. The prayers of the two saints were answered, and Simon Magus fell to his death. Afterwards, water that gathered in the knee-print hollows was believed to have the power to cure the sick, who would come to collect it whenever it rained. St Peter also left the impression of his head in the Mamertine Prison, when he returned to the city and was imprisoned there. He caused a spring to arise miraculously in the prison, when two other inmates asked him to baptise them.[56]

St Philip Neri went to Rome (Italy) in the 16th century after the city was sacked, and persuaded the aristocracy to do voluntary church work, founding the Oratorian Order for this purpose, and introducing the oratorio into worship. Items from his life, and paintings of him, are held in the church of St Filippo Neri, including a chalice with the marks of his teeth, which he is said to have bitten in the passion of his devotion to the Precious Blood.[57]

St Pierre Morin: This French monk was carrying stones to build a church at Guignen (Ille-et-Vilaine) when he heard a heavenly voice telling him that the church was finished. He seized a stone and threw it into a field, his hand sinking into the rock as if into a lump of clay, and leaving his handprint permanently upon it.[58]

St Procula (Procule), shepherdess of the Aveyron, was being chased by Count Gérard, so she took refuge in the midst of a mass of rocks, where she collapsed with exhaustion. The pressure of her hand, her arms and her body caused the rock to soften, and depressions were left where her body touched the rock.[59]

St Quirinus (Quirin) gave his name to the French town of St Quirin (Moselle), and when he was returning there from his pilgrimage to Palestine, and nearly home, he sat exhausted on a chair-shaped rock, leaving there the imprint of his sacred bottom.[60]

St Radegund was a 6th-century queen of the Franks, married unhappily to King Clothar I, whom she left after several years, becoming a nun and devoting the rest of her life to the Church. Miraculous cures were reported at her tomb soon after her death, and she is said to have left her knee-prints at Péronne (Somme) on a stone on a calvary where she knelt when she was insulted by pagans. In another version, she was travelling on foot with her child and rested on the stone, but she slipped and in falling her knee-prints were marked on the stone.[61]

St Remaclus (or Rémacle) was an Aquitaine nobleman in the 7th century who became a monk and later an abbot and a bishop. He left his footprint on a rock on the edge of the Amblève near Spa (Belgium): it happened as God's punishment when the saint fell asleep while saying his prayers. God let one of his feet sink into the rock – presumably he did not go so far as to trap it there. Women wishing for children would place their foot into St Remaclus's Footprint.[62]

St Rivalain was a reclusive Breton hermit in the 6th century, and a disciple of St Gildas, who left his handprint on a granite rock in the middle of a river at St Rivalain in the parish of Melrand (Morbihan). It was formed when he was being followed by a nobleman, and leapt across the river, landing on the rock with such force that his hand was imprinted on to it.[63]

St Ronan was a 6th-century Irish monk and hermit who fled to Brittany to escape his fame, and not any other saint with the same name. He sailed to France from Ireland on a stone, and this stone later became a stone horse and followed him around. When he died his body was brought back to Locronan (Finistère), the place where he had originally landed, in a cart drawn by two wild oxen, and the cart's wheels left permanent tracks in two rocks at Locronan. At the end of the 18th century childless women would rub themselves on the stone horse, and it was said that the mother of the duke of Coigny was born after such a ritual was performed, twenty years after her father married her mother. St Ronan's tomb is inside the Pénity chapel adjoining St Ronan's church at Locronan.[64]

A strange story was told about St Ronan's funeral procession. It was said that he had an opponent in Locronan, a woman by the name of Kébèn, who carried on doing her washing rather than watching the passing of the corpse with due respect. ('The traces of her knees' were said to be still visible on the stone where she used to kneel to do the washing.) She then attacked the cortege and hit the saint's body with her washing bat. The body turned to stone, and became the effigy which now lies in the Pénity. Every seven years, at the time of the *Troménie* or great pilgrimage, the mark of the bat reappears on the left cheek of the granite figure. After the procession around all the sites associated with the saint's legend, the pilgrims venerate the saint's relic in the Pénity, walking round the tomb and kissing his face.[65]

St Selevan was probably a Welsh or Cornish saint of the 6th century, who gave his name to the Cornish village of St Levan, where he was said to enjoy fishing from the cliffs at a place afterwards known as Old St Levan's Rocks. The path he was accustomed to take across the fields was said to be still visible, his footprints marked by finer grain from the corn that grows there, or greener grass when the land is under pasture.[66]

St Senan (Seanán; Senanus) was a 6th-century abbot-bishop born at Kilrush who founded several monasteries and finally settled on Scattery Island (Co. Clare, Ireland). In that area there are several stones with his imprints, including knee-prints on Scattery Island, and on a stone on the seashore at Kilrush, to which countrymen passing by would bow, take their hats off, and mutter prayers. At Dunas, near where the saint lived, a flat rock on the edge of the well bore the impressions of his hands and knees. People would try to kneel in the marks as they drank from the well, and touching the marks would help in curing illness.[67]

St Stapin has a chapel consecrated to him on top of a mountain near Dourgues (Aude, France), the site of a pilgrimage on 6 August, the saint's day. The lame, the paralysed and anyone who was sick would go to the chapel and encircle it nine times, then proceed to a platform where there were rocks bearing the saint's imprints. Each pilgrim seeking a cure had to place the affected limb into the hole or mark which was believed to cure that body part, and he would then be cured.[68]

St Teilo was a 6th-century monk and bishop, born in South Wales, who as Theleau was also venerated in Brittany. St Theleau's House was a megalithic tomb near Landeleau, which collapsed during a hunt for treasure there. A huge stone formed the capstone, or roof, and on the underside could be seen the impression of two large hands, said to be St Theleau's. He was in the habit of lifting off the roof of his house in order either to enjoy the sun, or so that he could pray in the open air.[69]

St Thomas was one of Jesus's apostles, who is believed to have travelled to India to undertake missionary work, and to have died and been buried there. The Portuguese identified the footprint on top of Adam's Peak in Sri Lanka as that of St Thomas. (See also Chapter 3.) Interestingly, footprints found on the other side of the world, in Central and South America, have also been identified as those of St Thomas. Seventeenth-century Spanish missionaries believed that there had been a Christian missionary in the Americas many hundreds of years before, who they said was St Thomas, and his footprints have been reported in Brazil, Peru, Colombia, and Paraguay, allegedly tracing the route of his travels.[70]

St Twrog (*fl.* 600) was, according to late tradition, a disciple of and secretary to St Beuno. He gave his name to the village of Maentwrog (Gwynedd, Wales), which literally means Twrog's Stone. The boulder in question can still be seen beside the church, and according to legend it was thrown there from the top of the nearby hill Moelwyn by the saint, or in another version, by a giant named Twrog, who was angry with some villagers and intended the rock to kill them. The imprint of his fingers was left on the rock. (See 'Footprints to Visit') This is not the only instance in which saint and giant overlap in the folklore: possibly the saint is believed to have superhuman powers, and by extension he physically becomes a giant in people's minds. Also, after the people were exposed to Protestantism the

A stained-glass window inside Maentwrog church shows St Twrog standing with his hand on top of the stone where he left his finger-marks.

St Tydecho's Well bearing the marks of his fingers at the bottom of the hollow.

cults and legends of the saints would after a time have become less prominent in their memories, allowing other traditions to take over.[71]

St Tydecho, in addition to being a 6th-century Celtic saint, was said to be related to King Arthur. His main centre was Llanymawddwy (Gwynedd, Wales), where he was eventually buried, and in the hills above the village the landscape is rich in Tydecho folklore. The stream is called Llaethnant (the Milk Stream) from a story that the saint's milkmaid one day accidentally spilt the contents of her milk-pail into the water, turning it white. Indeed the stream does run white, the water foaming as it rushes over innumerable boulders and little waterfalls. Gwely Tydecho, the saint's bed, is a rock shelf on the hillside, and close by is his well, Ffynnon Dydecho. This is a hollow in a rock slab, and St Tydecho left his fingermarks at the bottom. To complete the saint's landscape, a rock formation can be viewed as the saint's head; while not far away is his chair, a hollow in a rock.[72]

St Valay was a Breton saint, who left his footprints near Dinan (Côtes-d'Armor). One day he was fleeing from some women who wished to stone him, and they all arrived together on the edge of the Réhories valley. St Valay called on God for help, and leapt across the valley on to a rock, where he left his footprints. The women continued to chase him, so he leapt again and crossed the Rance, landing at Lanvallay, where he left another imprint.[73]

St Vincent, with his sisters St Sabina and St Christeta, was killed in Spain early in the 4th century for refusing to renounce the Christian religion. When he was told that he would be put to death, he put his foot on a stone which retained his footprint as if he had stepped into wax. The soldiers who were leading him were struck by this miracle and obtained a few days' more life for him from Dacian, the prefect of Gaul, but despite fleeing he and his sisters were all caught and murdered at Avila, of which they are now the patrons.[74]

St Wolfgang was a 10th-century bishop of Ratisbon (now Regensburg) in Germany who died in Austria in 994. He was buried in the crypt of the church of St Emmeram in Ratisbon, and miracles occurred at his grave. He was canonized in 1052. The Austrian town of St Wolfgang grew up at the place where the saint built his cell. He had chosen a solitary place where he prayed before throwing his axe into a thicket. Where it fell he took to be the place where God intended he should build his cell, and the axe is still on display in the town. In the church is a rock with marks that are said to be the saint's body, foot and hand imprints, though a colleague reports that 'the imprints are not convincing and certainly of natural origin'.[75]

This concludes my selection of Christian saints' imprints – of necessity only a small sample from the vast quantity of such tales recorded in the folklore of the Christian world.

Chapter Six

The hoof-prints of horses and other animals

The holes said to have been made by the horse's feet are
supposed to be nothing more than the boundaries of four parishes.

White's Directory of Lincolnshire (1856)

Saints' imprints were the subject of the previous two chapters: this time it's the turn
of their horses. Although various other animal species will also appear in this
chapter, horses are by far the most prominent, and many of them were ridden by
saints. The ubiquity of horses' hoof-prints shows how dependent people once were
on horses for their transport, something we have mostly forgotten in our age of
soulless travel by motor car and aeroplane. Travel by foot or on horseback meant
that the traveller was more aware of the landscape through which he was passing
than is usually the case today. Whizzing along straight stretches of tarmac encased
in a glass bowl is not conducive to any sort of affinity with the landscape: views are
seen as they flash past, but there can be no appreciation of detail, and certainly no
sense of oneness with the land. All generations before the invention of the infernal
combustion engine had a totally different relationship with their immediate
environment from that of today. So many people at the start of the 21st century have
travelled to far-distant lands, and yet so few of them have any real familiarity with
their home surroundings. Even 100 years ago, people rarely travelled very far from
home: it was difficult, expensive, and anyway largely unnecessary. A rare visit to the
nearest large town was an adventure – but the country people knew the local fields
and tracks, woods and streams, in minute detail. Their world was more
circumscribed, but no less rich, than ours – each rural parish, in any part of the
world, carries its hidden history, and to the person in the know, each stone has its
story.

A rounded hollow in a stone may resemble a horse's hoof-print – but to make such
a print, the horse must have had magical powers, or was ridden by someone
endowed with supernatural abilities. That someone was of course a local holy man
or hero – or the Devil himself. Welsh saints seem to have been frequent travellers,
judging by the number of horse's hoof-prints that were associated with them. North
Wales folklore tells how St Asaph traversed the countryside on horseback in a series
of jumps, one of which was from Onnen Asa (St Asaph's Ash-tree) at Tremeirchion
two miles into the present town of St Asaph. Halfway up the hill between the parish
church and the cathedral, there used to be a black stone in the pavement with a
mark which was identified as St Asaph's horse's hoof-print, but the stone is no longer
there.[1] St Beuno's horse also left its footprint in North Wales, on a stone called

Carreg March, the stone with St Engan's horse's hoof-print.

Beuno's Stone somewhere near the village of Gwyddelwern.[2] Further south, at Llangoedmor (Ceredigion) a stone bears the name Ôl Troed March Cynllo, meaning literally the Footprint of Cynllo's Horse.[3] St Tegan's horse left multiple hoof-prints on the cliffs in Llanwnda parish near Fishguard (Pembrokeshire) when the saint emerged from the sea after riding to Wales from Ireland on horseback.[4] More seaside hoof-prints were left by St Elaeth's horse at Amlwch on Anglesey (North Wales): the saint rode into the sea in Llanallgo parish and came ashore at Amlwch, where his horse's hoof-prints were afterwards visible on a flat rock.[5]

Although often today only sketchy details survive, at one time all imprint stones would have had their own mini-sagas, bits of which have been gradually forgotten as the years pass until perhaps only the name of the stone remains, to alert us to the fact that it was once a significant feature in the landscape. If the details are recorded by some interested person before the last keeper of the tale dies, they can be saved for posterity, and luckily this has often happened. Sometimes however the details change completely, and a site acquires a new modern relevance. An example of this is the stone known as Ôl Troed March Engan (Footprint of Engan's Horse – also called Carreg March, Horse's Stone) at Castell Cilan near Llanengan on the Lleyn peninsula in Gwynedd. St Engan was the same person as Einion, a king of Lleyn in the 6th century, whose brothers Seiriol and Meirion were also saints. It was once believed that the rain-water which collected in the hoof-print had healing properties, being especially useful for curing warts. In more recent times, the connection with the saint has largely been forgotten, and a new legend is current, concerning a local doctor practising in the area at the end of the 19th century. It was said that Dr Williams was very fond of his drink, and one stormy night while in a drunken state he was called out to Cilan. Off he went on horseback, but in his befuddled state he was galloping towards the clifftop. His horse suddenly stopped, just before the precipice above the sea was reached, and saved the doctor's life. The horse's hoof-print was left in the stone at the very spot, and it was known as Ôl Traed y March (the horse's hoof-print).[6]

One of the places where St George was said to have fought the dragon was in North Wales, at the place now called St George, not far from St Asaph (Denbighshire), and his horse's hoof-prints were imprinted on the coping stones of the churchyard wall. It is impossible for any Welsh church to have been dedicated to St George in the pre-Norman period (c.1150 at the earliest), which suggests that the custom of healing horses at the well at St George, and probably also the tradition of the saint's horse's hoof-prints, have been adopted from the tradition of an earlier native saint. The original name of the parish was Cilcadoc, meaning the Cell, or Retreat, of Cadog, so perhaps he was the first saint. However there may also be a link with St Asaph, since the town of that name is not far away, with its tradition of the saint's horseback leap. There is other horse-related folklore in the area, and the sites can be linked almost along a straight line which follows the line of the old Roman road between Chester and Caerhun. All this fragmentary folklore hints at a rich history now sadly lost.[7]

Just over the Welsh border into England, a strange story is associated with Ledbury in Herefordshire. Catherine Audley (Katharine de Audele), who lived there in the late 14th century, was described as a recluse; she was a holy woman who was called a saint, and her raised status is evident from the story that survives, describing how her mare and colt were stolen. St Catherine prayed that the mare's hoof-prints would lead to the thief, but she (a maid) led the animals along the course of the brook in an attempt to hide their tracks. However the hoof-prints of both animals, and the imprints of the pattens of the maid, were permanently graved into the stones of the stream bed, and the saint was able to follow them and recover her animals. Afterwards, the marked stones were collected by local people and used as charms against robbery. In another version of the story, the theft took place at Tedstone Delamere in Herefordshire, the animals being led away along the Sapey brook after being stolen from a local farmer. The trail was easy to follow, as horseshoe-shaped marks had been left on the rocks of the stream bed.[8]

French folklore has many tales of saints' imprints, as already shown in the two previous chapters, and not unexpectedly there are also numerous tales of saints' horses' hoof-prints. The saint most frequently mentioned in the French tales is St Martin, and a selection of the most interesting ones follows. There are many footprints attributed to St Martin himself at Druyes, but one said to be his horse's hoof-print marks the place where the animal struck the rock and caused a spring to

94

*St Gildas's horse's hoof-print
close by St Gildas's Well in
Brittany.*

gush forth. At Lavault de Frétoy, his horse left its hoof-prints when it slipped on an uneven rock. The place where it slid is marked by an area that is shiny and smooth – it has been used to sharpen axes. When St Martin visited the church of Sainte-Colombe (Doubs), he rode through a wood and past a rock at which a witches' sabbat had taken place. The horse was startled and fell, leaving its knee-prints on a rock.

St Martin's Stone at Assevilliers (Somme) has two large hollows, three deep grooves, and a natural basin, forming the imprint of the saint's horse's backside. When St Martin was engaged in a terrible struggle with the Devil, his horse reared and fell against the rock.[9] In another encounter with the Devil, at Saint-Martin du Puy, they were disputing who could jump the furthest on horseback. St Martin jumped to Montigny-sur-Canne and left the imprint of his horse's hoof at Saint-Martin du Puy and his horse's knee-print at Montigny. At Mont Foran, a beggar (the Devil in disguise) offered to guide St Martin through the forest. But suddenly he quickened his pace and threw the saint and his horse on to a rock with the intention of launching them into the void. The animal, terrified by the sight of the abyss, took off under the lash of its master's whip and leapt with one bound across the valley as far as Mont Foran where it landed. The place where its hooves first touched solid ground is marked on the rocks, and the grooves are the marks of the whip.[10] Another footprint of St Martin's horse, made while they were climbing a steep and slippery rock, is

95

near Vorey, and close by is St Martin's Well (a rock cavity) where offerings are left. At Vertolaye (Puy-de-Dôme), mothers used to rock their sick children in the footprint of St Martin's horse. Elsewhere in France, other of St Martin's and his horse's footprints were used for healing purposes, sometimes involving the rainwater that was gathered from them.[11]

The saints seem to have been keen to show off their horses' jumping prowess. St Gildas de Rhuys, despite his French name, probably came from Wales: he was educated in South Wales by St Illtyd in the 6th century; he also lived as a hermit on Flatholm Island before moving to Brittany at the age of thirty and settling at Rhuys where he eventually died. His tomb can be seen in the abbey church at St Gildas-de-Rhuys, and on the coast not far away, by the saint's well and cave and statue, is a hollow in a rock which is said to be the imprint of St Gildas' horse's hoof, made when it leapt from the Île de Houat nearly 10 miles to this spot.[12] One version of the story tells how St Gildas was on the island when he heard the Rhuys bell tolling for vespers. Realising he was late, he jumped on his horse to the mainland, and that is when the hoof-print was formed. (Another version of the tale is given in 'Footprints to Visit'.) The horse of St William of Gellone (a Benedictine monk who lived from 755 to 812 and known in France as Guilhem) also made a gigantic leap – at Lou Pahon, L'Herault. St William was on his black horse, taking a relic of the True Cross to Gellone (later known as St-Guilhem-du-Desert), where he had founded a monastery, when he heard shouting and then saw a troop of Saracens rushing after him. He ordered his horse to jump the river in one leap. The effort used in doing this was so intense that the horse's head and right hoof left their imprints on the left bank, and its tail left its mark on the opposite bank.[13]

Other saints whose horses were reported to have performed prodigious jumping feats in France, in addition to SS Martin, Gildas and William, were Julien, Maurice, Capraz, and George.[14] French folklore also records many instances of local heroes whose horses left their hoof-prints permanently imprinted as proof of their presence at that place, and of their superhuman qualities, Roland being the most ubiquitous.[15] He was the greatest of the paladins who attended Charlemagne, dying in battle at Roncesvalles in 778. Charlemagne was king of the Franks and Holy Roman Emperor, and his famous horse Bayard left its hoof-prints in Belgium after leaping across the valley of the Ourthe river while in pursuit of the 'Four Sons of Aymon', who were characters in a medieval romance. Bayard also made his mark in the Forest of Soignes and at Dinant, where he opened up the rock that took his name with one blow of his powerful hoof.[16]

Bayard originally meant a bay-coloured horse, and the fame of Charlemagne's horse meant that the name was widely used in later times. It features in a tale of horse's hoof-prints from Lincolnshire, known as Bayard's (or Byard's) Leap. The location is Ancaster Heath west of Sleaford, and one version of the story was that a shepherd had been given the task of getting rid of a local witch, and he had to do this by persuading her to climb up behind him on his horse as it drank at a pond outside her dwelling, where he would then stab her and she would fall into the pond and be drowned. Why she should obey his strange request is not stated, but she did, and was stabbed, and in agony she dug her long, sharp claws into the horse Bayard's

*King Arthur's horse's hoof-print
on a rock close to Llyn Barfog.*

back, whereupon he leapt a distance of 60 feet. The witch had already fallen off and drowned, as planned. In another version, a knight was riding past when the witch jumped up behind him and in his fright Bayard made three great leaps. The events, whatever they may have been, left holes in the ground said to have been caused by the horse's hooves, and these were later marked by the placing of large horseshoes at the site.[17] (See also 'Footprints to Visit')

Numerous other larger-than-life heroes made death-defying leaps on their magnificent steeds. Wild Humphrey Kynaston was a Shropshire outlaw in the time of Henry VII who 'robbed the rich to give to the poor, and sold himself to the devil'. His horse was believed by some to be the Devil himself, and was shod backwards so that he could never be tracked down. When being chased one day, he leapt from the top of Nesscliff Hill to Ellesmere, at least 9 miles (or the jump might have been from Nesscliff to Loton Park and thence to the Breidden), leaving his hoof-marks somewhere – exactly where was in dispute. Another version was that the amazing leap was one of 40 feet across the River Severn, with the hoof-print being left on a rock on the riverbank at a place once known as Kynaston's Leap.[18] Huw Daniel was also escaping from his enemies on horseback when he leapt to his death rather than be captured. This legendary event took place near the village of Llanfachreth in Gwynedd, being commemorated in the name Rhiw Daniel (Daniel's Hill). Daniel leapt from high rocks to his death, and a certain stone has a hole right through its

King Arthur's horse's hoof-print at Loggerheads.

middle, said to be where the horse trod. Daniel's remains are said to lie behind a wall, covered by a large slab of rock.[19] Owain Glyndwr, a 15th-century Welsh nobleman (also known by the English version of his name, Owen Glendower), led the last major rebellion of the Welsh against the English and became a Welsh national hero. Much of the folklore relating to him centres on Corwen in Denbighshire, and close to the town there is said to be a stone bearing the imprint of his horse's hooves. At Craig y March (Rock of the Horse) in the Pumlumon area (Powys), hoof-prints on the rock show where his horse Llwyd y Bacsie walked up the rock face.[20]

All these heroes are, however, eclipsed by the great King Arthur. He will reappear in Chapter 8 in his own right, but meanwhile his horse(s) also left their marks in various English, Welsh and French locations. In western Cornwall on Goss Moor near St Columb, a large stone has four deep marks which look rather like horse's hoof-marks, and are said to have been made by King Arthur's horse when he lived at Castle Denis and hunted on the moors. The stone may be the capstone of a now-lost dolmen, the Devil's Coit.[21] In west Wales, not far from Llyn Barfog which is a fairy-haunted lake above Aberdyfi (Gwynedd), there is a rock named Carn March Arthur (Arthur's Horse's Hoof), bearing Arthur's horse's hoof-print, left when Arthur came to the area to kill a monster that lived in the lake, his horse leaping across the Dyfi estuary to reach the lake (or, in another version, it was made when the horse leapt across the water to escape from the king's enemies).[22] (See 'Footprints to Visit') Another of King Arthur's horse's hoof-prints is to be seen on the similarly named Carreg Carn March Arthur (Stone of Arthur's Horse's Hoof), located in north-east

Wales at Loggerheads (Flintshire/Denbighshire border). (See 'Footprints to Visit') This is a roadside boundary stone, on to which King Arthur's magical horse Llamrei landed after he leapt, with King Arthur in the saddle, from the nearby hill Moel Fammau. The neighbouring hilltop in the Clwydian range is Moel Arthur, which still carries the banks and ditches of an Iron Age hillfort, these probably giving rise to the belief that King Arthur's palace was located here. He was in residence when it was reported that a Saxon army was on its way from Chester, and he and his knights were ready when the enemy made their way up the hill. A mighty battle ensued, with Arthur being chased from Moel Arthur to Moel Fammau, and that was when he leapt off the hill, to avoid being killed.[23]

King Arthur was a human being (if he really lived, a controversy I do not propose to enter here) who became cloaked in an aura of mystery, and was credited with larger-than-life abilities, something which is also apparent in tales about other less-well-known personages. In Germany's Black Forest, in the Wutach valley beyond Stühlingen, there was and maybe still is a castle on a steep hill, the castle of Hohenlupfen. At a tournament there, the daughter of the lord answered the love-making of a knight by daring him to prove his love for her, and the dare she named was for him to ride upstairs and leap through the window out on to the rock below. When he made preparations to do what she had requested, she told him it was only a joke, but he went ahead all the same, and leapt out, luckily harming neither himself nor his horse. He refused to see the lady again, however, and married someone else. The event was permanently marked by the horse's hoof-print which was left on a stone at the castle.[24] Another tale of love gone wrong comes from Alspach (Vosges, France), where there was once a young knight who harboured passionate (and sacrilegious) feelings for a nun. While trying to meet her, he was thrown from a steep rock overlooking her convent, and his horse's hoof-prints were left in the rock. An evil lord in Brittany also suffered his downfall as a result of wrongdoing. The village of Tremec (Finistère) was once a town, until he burned and destroyed it. Afterwards he sat on his horse surveying his handiwork from a local vantage point. The horse was shocked to see what his master had done, and tipped him into the bog. The horse's hoof-prints are clear to see on the rock where they were standing.[25]

Horses belonging to both evil and saintly people worldwide, real and legendary, have left their hoof-prints for posterity. In India, holes in the rock at a temple on the Brahmaputra river at Gauhati are said to have been made by the hooves of the horses of Krishna, when he visited with his consort Rukmini.[26] In Scotland, a rock with natural cup-marks near Kilmichael Glassary (Argyll and Bute) is said to carry the hoof-prints of the horse of 'Scota, daughter of Pharaoh'.[27] In South Wales the district of Blaenau Gwent was said to be the site of a battle between the Welsh and the Normans. At Rhyd y Milwr (Warriors' Ford), Trefil, holes in the stream bed were said to be the hoof-prints of the black army's horses.[28] In France at a place called Sainte Baume, horses' hoof-prints on the edge of a precipice were said to commemorate a miracle when the lives of two merchants travelling at night were saved when their horses were held back by St Mary Magdalen as they were about to fall to their deaths.[29] In Haute-Savoie, the plain between Reignier, l'Arve, the mountain range of Bornes, and the mountain of Saint-Sixt, is strewn with rocks each of which has a

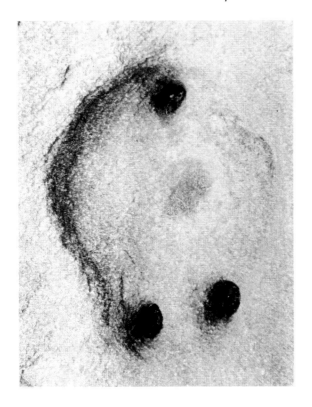

*Hoof-print left by the
horse of the giant Bodo
on the Rosstrappe.
Photo: Gerd Schmidt.*

name, such as the Death Stone, the Fairies' Stone, the Devil's Stone – and one called the Horse's Hoof-print. The explanation for this harks right back to the time of the Flood, when a horse that was not among those allowed on to the Ark, seeing the water rising all round, climbed on to the rock of Arbusigny. People came and tried to climb on its back, but it reared and kicked out with its hooves. The deep hollows still to be seen on the rock were caused by these antics.[30]

In Germany, a magical horse belonging to the princess Emma (or Brunhilde, depending on which version you read) left its hoof-print on the Rosstrappe, a large rock outcrop near Thale in the foothills of the Harz mountains. Bodo was one of many giants who once lived in the Harz, according to folklore – or a knight, in another version of the story. He was in love with Emma, the king's daughter, and pursued her through forests and mountains and valleys on horseback. When she reached the Hexentanzplatz (place where witches dance) her horse halted and she gazed fearfully at the 1,000-foot drop to the river below, wondering whether she dare chance the leap across the chasm to the cliff on the other side of the valley. As Bodo came ever closer, she spurred her horse on and they jumped, reaching the safety of the cliff and leaving a 4-foot-deep hole in the rock where her horse's hoof had landed. Bodo was not so lucky and fell into the abyss, where he is said to live on in the form of a black dog, guarding the princess's gold crown which fell from her head as she leapt to safety.[31] (See 'Footprints to Visit') In the U.S.A., several impressions in the ground measuring about two feet in diameter are described as the tracks of a giant horse, and they commemorate a war between the Dakota groups in

1853. They are located near the Mandan Dakota village of Fishhook on the Fort Berthold Indian Reservation in North Dakota.[32]

Chapter 7 will reveal many instances of the Devil leaving his indelible mark as a result of numerous escapades, but since he often travelled on horseback as he went about his evil trade, the marks of his horse's hooves have also been recorded. In South Wales, a white horse carried a bag of money on its back and left its hoof-prints on a rock at a farm in Cwmtillery, and it was there that work on the building of a church began, the money being used for this purpose, and the horse being used to carry stones. When the men began to argue over who owned the white horse, it kicked up its heels and disappeared in a flash of flame – which made people wonder if it came from the Devil. The church site was therefore abandoned, and eventually the new church was built at Blaina (Blaenau Gwent).[33] Another Welsh tale concerning the Devil and a horse which left its hoof-print comes from near Bala (Gwynedd), though the horse involved did not actually belong to the Devil. An attempt was made to consign the Devil, who was causing trouble in the locality, to the depths of a pool in the River Dee, known as Llyn-y-Geulan Goch. His Satanic Majesty was captured in Llanfor church and, in the form of a cock, was carried on horseback to the river pool: the journey across two fields was made in two leaps. On reaching the water, the Devil was not keen on being thrown into the pool, but agreed to jump in if his captors lay face down. They heard a splash and assumed he had jumped in – and the tradition is that the foaming of the water proves he is still there. The horse that carried him is said to have left its hoof-print on a stone at the riverside, but no one knows exactly which one.[34]

Another tale of the Devil being involved in building a new church was recorded at Batcombe in Dorset. The architect made a pact with the Devil, but after the Devil had helped in the construction, the architect refused to pay him, and so the Devil damaged the building irreparably. His horse knocked down a pinnacle, which could not then be replaced, and horse and Devil disappeared in a snowstorm, leaving behind the horse's hoof-prints in the ground behind the church. In another version, the architect's name was John Minterne, and it was his horse that knocked off the pinnacle, after he jumped from Batcombe Down over the church with the aid of the Devil.[35] Still in England, the Devil's Doorway was said to be an entrance to the Underworld: it was a fault in the slate rocks behind Polperro, Cornwall. The Devil's horse left its hoof-print there as it carried its master through.[36] In northern England, according to a medieval account in the *Chronicon de Melrose*, the Devil on a black horse charged through the sky to the sea during a storm in August 1065. 'The tracks of this horse were seen, of enormous size, imprinted on a mountain at the city of Scandeburch [Scarborough]. Here, on top of several ditches, men found, stamped in the earth, prints made by the monster, where he had violently stamped with his feet.'[37]

Two tales from Scotland include hoof-prints left by horses following events in which the Devil or his demons were involved. The medieval magician Michael Scot was tired of constantly hearing his demons crying 'Work! Give us work!' and he fled from them on horseback, crossing Caithness and Sutherland and arriving at the Cromarty Suitors, famous headlands in north-east Scotland. He leapt from the North Suitor to the Southern Suitor, leaving his horse's hoof-prints on both of them. But the demons still caught up with him and began clamouring for work, so he ordered them to make 'a rope of sand long enough and strong enough both to girdle the earth and to bind the moon to the earth as well'. They work constantly at this task, and you can sometimes see lengths of the rope on sandy beaches, before it is washed away yet again by the tide.[38] Another magician with northern Scottish connections was Donald, the Wizard of Reay, who had been taught by the Devil in Italy. One day they met in Smoo Cave in Sutherland and had a violent quarrel. Donald fled on horseback, and his horse's hoof-marks were left by the entrance to the cave.[39]

The Devil on horseback was also involved in this tale from the U.S.A., located at the small town of Bath in North Carolina, although it was not his horse that left its hoof-marks. The alleged events took place in 1850, when a Mr Elliott entered his stallion for a race to be held on the common. During a trial run, which took place when Mr Elliott was rather drunk, he saw a stallion which was almost as fine as his own, and he hurried to overtake horse and rider. The mounted stranger said that he too was planning to enter the race, and that he was sure to win. The drunken Elliott took exception to this, and challenged the stranger to a race there and then, to determine which horse was the faster. He vowed to win the race, or else to drive his horse to hell, and they set off at full gallop. Suddenly Elliott's horse whinnied as if terrified, turned off the road, leapt into the air and threw Elliott off its back. He hit a tree and was killed; the horse died of a broken neck. The stranger was never seen again, but his horse's tracks were followed as far as the place where Elliott had met his death: they stopped abruptly and no continuation could be found. The puzzled townspeople could, however, smell burning pitch. The final four hoof-prints made by Elliott's stallion remained permanently visible, dug into the ground near a large pine tree, and despite being covered up from time to time, they were always revealed again. In 1925 author Charles Harry Whedbee camped overnight by the tracks, carefully covering them with dirt before sitting against a tree with the intention of watching them throughout the night. He believed that he had fallen asleep only briefly, but when he examined the tracks at dawn, they were 'sharp and clear and deep again, just as though they had never been covered.'[40] (See 'Footprints to Visit')

It was not only horses that were used for transport: mules, asses and donkeys were also once widely used to carry people from place to place, and there are therefore accounts of their hoof-prints being left on rocks. Continuing with the Devil's involvement in such tales, his mule was said to have left its hoof-print in the base of Mathon cross not far from the old castle of Marsais in Poitou, France. This happened after a confrontation between a nobleman from the castle and the Devil. The nobleman attacked him with a sword which he drew from a scabbard filled with holy water, whereupon the Devil retreated and left behind his mule in acknowledgement of his defeat. But the mule would neither eat nor drink, and would only kick out when offered oats. The Devil reappeared and mounted the mule, which tried to knock the cross over as it passed, but only succeeded in leaving its hoof-print on the base.[41] The Devil also features in a tale from Aquitaine, though it was not his mule that left its hoof-print behind. St Jouin used to sleep under an elm tree near the village of Mavaux and the Devil seized his opportunity and stole the saint's money. The bishop St Hilary came on his mule to deal with the matter, and the mule stepped back in alarm on seeing the Devil, leaving its hoof-print on a rock. The same bishop's mule also left its hoof-print on a stone at Ligugé (Aquitaine), when the bishop went to see St Martin in his cell. The mule bowed down before the saint, and left its hoof-mark, the place thereafter being known as The Mule's Footprint.[42]

St Leonard's mule features in a story from the Forest of Pauvain in Limousin, where this popular saint is believed to assist women in childbirth, as well as those unable to conceive. While living in the forest as a hermit in the 6th century, he is said to have assisted Queen Deuthéric who was hunting in the forest when she was overcome by labour pains. He accepted a gift of that section of the forest which he could ride around in one night on his mule, and it is said that marks on the rocks were left by his mule's hooves. There are also numerous hoof-marks in France left by St Martin's donkey, for example near St Martin's bed, at Suc de la Violette, where three hoof-prints were left, and at Beauvray where a foot-mark was left when the donkey jumped the valley of Malvaux in one bound, to escape the pagans who were chasing the saint. St Martin's donkey also left its knee-prints when it fell down on to one of the stones covering St Martin's Well at Thil-sur-Arroux.[43]

Two stories of mule-prints from France involve the Blessed Virgin Mary. She and the baby Jesus were being carried by a mule on their flight into Egypt, and stopped by a well at Changy (Saône-et-Loire) to quench their thirst. The donkey left four hoof-prints on a rock by the well. The other tale concerns the countess of Foix (Gironde) who was visiting her domain on the back of a mule, which suddenly stopped and would go neither forward nor back, and stamped its foot into a rock, imprinting its hoof-print. The Countess was surprised by the mule's behaviour, and lifted the stone to examine it more closely. Underneath she found a miraculous image of the Virgin Mary.[44] The mule whose shoe was imprinted on a stone pavement in Avila in Spain had been used to settle a controversy. The 12th-century Saint Peter del Barco had lived alone for many years in a rocky hollow on the bank of the River Tormes. He knew his end was near when a miracle occurred: the water from the spring he used daily turned into wine. After his death, there was an argument over whether his body should go to Barco or Avila and the bishop decided to settle the dispute in an apparently unusual way, but it is a theme which recurs often in the folklore of saints. The saint's remains were placed on the back of a blindfolded mule. It went straight to the church of St Vincent in Avila and there dropped down dead. So that was where St Peter was buried, and the mule's shoe-print in the church proves the truth of the story.[45]

In Ireland, St Patrick's ass left its knee-prints on a stone near Cross Patrick in Killaha parish (Co. Mayo);[46] while near the summit of Carrick Hill, north of Edenderry (Co. Offaly), is the Mule's Leap, where eight holes are said to be the footprints of a mule which ran off with a saint from Carrickoris church.[47] Lest it seem that mule and donkey footprints are confined to the West, that is not the case, and similar tales are known from the Eastern world. In China, Heng Shan mountain in Shanxi bears the hoof-print of the donkey of Zhang Guo Lao, one of the Eight Immortals, who rode his donkey backwards. There were different reasons given for this, one being that the donkey was a piece of paper which Zhang would blow on to turn it into a donkey,

St Manchán's cow can be seen at the top of the window in Boher church, Co. Offaly, above the image of the saint.

and the first time he did this, the donkey rushed off at speed and just happened to change direction as Zhang flung himself upon its back, so he ended up facing backwards. Alternatively, Zhang was said to be unable to leave beautiful places and so would ride away backwards so that he could gaze at the scene for as long as possible. The hoof-print was left to commemorate the donkey's surprise at being ridden backwards.[48]

Most of the accounts of cows leaving their hoof-marks come from Ireland, probably because there are numerous magical cows (*glas*) in Irish folklore. In Co. Armagh, the area west of Slieve Gullion is known as the Glen of the Heifer, in reference to the story of a cow which gave milk to everyone – until someone milked it into a sieve. It stamped its foot in anger and left the valley, never to return, though its hoof-print can still be seen on a stone beside the Kilnasaggart pillar stone.[49] On the eastern Burren in Co. Clare, the hoof-marks of legendary cows like the Glasgeivnagh and Glas gamhnach can be seen in the form of hollows on the rocks, while on Glasgeivnagh Hill the marks on the rocks were made by the grey cow of Lon mac Leefa (Lionmhtha).[50] In Co. Cork, St Gobnait, a patron saint of beekeepers, is linked to the story which gave its name to the townland of Lackavihoonig – the flagstone of the thief. The saint caught a thief who had stolen a cow and calf, and she fastened them to the flagstone where she had caught them, so for ever afterwards their tracks were visible on the stone.[51] At the Early Christian monastic site of Clonmacnois (Co. Offaly), close to the Pilgrim's Way, is a stone sunk into the ground which has two deep hollows in it, said to have been made by St Ciarán's cow when it stumbled. In the same county, at Lemanaghan, a trackway which was probably also a pilgrim's route has stone flags with depressions said to have been made by the hooves and tail of St Manchán's cow when it was being led away by thieves. By following these tracks, the saint was able to retrieve his cow. It had already been slaughtered, but not eaten, and so he restored it to life and took it home again. It was another magical cow which yielded an endless supply of milk, and until quite recently it was customary only to give milk away at Lemanaghan, never to sell it. The saint and his cow can be seen depicted in stained glass in Boher church nearby, where is also displayed the wonderful shrine of St Manchán.[52]

Stolen magical cows also feature in some Welsh saints' legends, such as that of St Winifred of Holywell (Flintshire). When thieves stole a cow from church lands, they led it along a stony path thinking that its tracks would not be visible, but it drove its hooves deep into the ground, so that their imprint was visible on the stones as well as on the dry ground, and its owners were able to follow the route the thieves had taken and recover their cow.[53] In South Wales, St Tatheus' cow was stolen from the monastery at Caerwent (Monmouthshire) by the king's servants. They killed it and tried to boil it, but it could not be cooked. St Tatheus found the cow's hoof-print near the monastery, 'marked in a wondrous manner in a stone', and was able to follow its tracks to the palace, where he miraculously brought the cow back to life and took it home.[54]

The only reference to a bull's tracks I have found comes from remote Scottish islands: the Monach Isles to the west of North Uist. On the island of Ceann Ear is the Loch of the Virtues, said to be the home of a water-horse. This monster was so troublesome to the island people that they even resolved to move away from Monach, but a woman named NicLeoid said she had a powerful bull which she had been feeding up in the hope that one day it would be strong enough to kill the water-horse. When she thought it was ready, she led it to the loch-side and let it graze there, watching for the water-horse to appear. The bull began to roar, and was digging into the ground with its hooves and horns. Soon the water-horse emerged and a tussle began on the loch-side. The water-horse was out of its element and it looked as though the bull would win: but it made the mistake of following the water-horse into the loch when it retreated, and in turn was out of its element. The water was being churned up so much that the onlookers could not see who was winning the fight, until eventually the water calmed, and neither bull nor horse was ever seen again. All that was left to commemorate the event were the marks made by the bull with its hooves and horns before the epic battle began, and those marks became permanent.[55]

A few oxen have left their imprints, one example in Norfolk having given its name to the farm where it is now located. The Oxfoot Stone is at South Lopham (on private property), and folklore tells how the hoof-print was made by another of those

The claw marks of the black dog which ran through Blythburgh church.

magical cows which gave endless milk freely to the poor during times of famine, but when things improved it struck its foot against the stone and disappeared.[56] In Wales, St Elian came from Rome with his family and oxen, according to a 15th-century version of his life, landing at Porth Ychen (Port of the Oxen) on the north coast of Anglesey near the present settlement of Llaneilian, where he built his church. The hoof-marks of Elian's oxen were said to be visible on the rocks where the party landed.[57] Also in Wales, at Cerrigydrudion (Conwy) the Devil was being a nuisance at the local church, and had to be captured and dragged across Denbigh Moors by two huge oxen. As they remorselessly dragged him closer to a lake on the moors he struggled hard, and their efforts caused the oxen to leave the marks of their hooves in the rocks, before they succeeded in dragging him into the water, and despatching him. However they had to enter the water too, and so they perished along with him.[58] At Saint-Vran in Brittany, there is a rock imprinted with the hoof-prints of four oxen which drew a cart carrying St Lin. The saint hadn't told the driver of the ox-cart where he wished to go to, but when he arrived at Saint-Vran, at the place where there is now a chapel dedicated to him, the oxen refused to go any further, despite being beaten, and as a result their hoof-prints became imprinted in the rock.[59] At Ronzières (Puy-de-Dôme) there is a rock with an ox-hoof imprinted on it, and the custom was for girls who wished for a husband to put their foot in the hoof-print and leave offerings of daisies.[60]

An assortment of other creatures, real and imaginary, have left their imprints on rocks around the world. The Lamb Stone was a small stone at the base of a standing stone on Milfraen Mountain (Blaenau Gwent) in South Wales which was a way-marker for travellers from Abergavenny, so named because it was said to bear the miraculous imprint of a young lamb's foot.[61] In the Auvergne region of France, on the Rocher de la Chèvre (Goat's Crag) at L'Allier were said to be visible the imprints of a goat and a wolf, as well as two people. They illustrate a drama which occurred when a wolf seized a goat, and the young girl tending the goats on the hill ran to save it. The wolf seized her too and held her under its paw while it tore its prey to pieces with its teeth. A nearby monk heard her cries for help and rushed to her rescue. He called upon the wolf, in the name of God, to drop its prey, and the wolf lay down docilely at the monk's feet before leaving quietly. Since that time, the foot-, paw- and hoof-prints of each animal and person involved can still be seen on the rock.[62] In County Clare in Ireland, a rock known as the Navel of Ireland that was taken to Quin from Birr, carries not only the finger-marks of the famous Irish hero Finn MacCumhail but also V-shaped marks that are said to be the footprints of the cockerel that crowed when St Peter denied Christ.[63]

Dogs' paw-prints are occasionally seen: in Scotland and in France, prehistoric cup-marks are sometimes interpreted as dogs' footprints, for example St Martin's dog in the Ardèche and Velay. At Champagnac (Creuse), there is a standing stone which looks like a woman, and is called Lady Stone. The marks of a dog's paws can be seen, and these were made by a fierce mastiff which the pages set on to St Valeria who, in a desperate attempt to avoid the dog, turned herself into a standing stone.[64] In County Kildare (Ireland), the so-called grave of King Cormac of Munster in the ancient cemetery of Killeen Cormac at Colbinstown is marked by a pair of pillar-stones, one of them having the imprint of a dog's paw. There was a dispute about the place of the king's burial, and when the cart bearing the corpse drew near, a dog leapt on to a stone in the cemetery, leaving its pawprint on the stone to show where the king was to be buried.[65] (See 'Footprints to Visit') In Eastern England, the phantom black dog which rushed through Blythburgh church (Suffolk), terrifying the congregation, left its claw marks permanently burned into a wooden door at the back of the church as it quitted the building.[66] (See 'Footprints to Visit') King Arthur's dog Cabal left its footprint in Wales, an event described by Nennius in the early 9th century. The location was a cairn known as Carn Cabal or Cafall, on the hill Corngafallt not far from Builth Wells (Powys). The cairn was built by King Arthur who was hunting the boar Troynt (the same as the great boar Twrch Trwyth described in the legend of Culhwch and Olwen in the *Mabinogion*) on the hill: he placed the stone with the paw-print on top of the cairn. Since that day, even though the stone may be taken a long distance away, it always magically returns to the cairn.[67]

The dogs whose paw-prints were left on stones were clearly supernatural animals, and so too were the fairy dogs which left their tracks on the sands of Scottish islands. The footprints of the fairy dogs were also found in snow and mud, and were said to be very large. A man who saw a fairy dog on Tiree, next day visited the sand dune where he had seen it, and found the imprints of a dog's paws, 'as large as the spread of his palm'. Also on Tiree, it was said that a family spending the summer in a shieling (a rough shelter used by shepherds at summer pastures) heard noises on the turf roof at night, and next morning found deep indentations which they believed had been left by the paws of fairy dogs.[68] Fairy dogs were believed to frequent the sandy shore of Luskentyre on Harris, but no one ever saw them, only their large paw marks – and if anyone walked in their tracks he became mad.[69] Death was the fate of anyone stepping in the paw-marks of the fairy dogs on Iona's white sands, though it was actually considered lucky to see the imprints.[70]

The ephemeral traces of magical creatures bring to a close this catalogue of supernatural animals which left their footprints behind, often permanently in rock, sometimes fleetingly in sand.

Chapter Seven

The Devil stamps his foot (or hoof, or claw)

> I call'd the devil, and he came,
> And a thrill of astonishment through me ran.
> He is not ugly, he is not lame,
> But a perfectly charming agreeable man.
>
> Heinrich Heine, *Buch der Lieder*, 1827; trans. John E. Wallis, 1856

Perhaps Heine overstates his case, but the Devil certainly knows how to appear agreeable; he is a complex character, a creature of many parts, and a master of disguises. He has appeared in human form; he has appeared in demonic form: he is a being of extremes, unpredictable, capable of anything, and totally unreliable. Artists' depictions show him as a man, as an animal, as a part-human being, sometimes with horns, with hooves, with bird's claws, with bat's wings, as a monster totally lacking in human attributes; but he is frequently depicted as a goat, whose cloven hoof is his identifying feature. He is ubiquitous in folklore, and has left his hoof-mark on rocks worldwide in proof of his existence. The tales often refer specifically to the 'cloven hoof', as for example at Aragon, a village in L'Aude (France), where Satan came to tempt St Lupus of Troyes, and finding himself powerless struck angrily at the rock and left the mark of his cloven hoof.[1] On the island of Jersey, the coastal granite outcrop known as Rocqueberg in St Clement parish is said to carry a cloven hoof-print made by the Devil.[2] In Perthshire (Scotland), a cloven hoof-mark close to a well on a farm near Abernethy caused the well to be known as The Devil's Well;[3] while the Devil's Stane in Belmuire Wood on the north side of the River Ychan (Aberdeenshire) was said to bear marks looking like cloven hoofs, which must therefore be the 'impress of the devil's feet'.[4] Also in Aberdeenshire, the Cothiemuir stone circle at Keig has a recumbent stone with hollows that are called the Devil's Hoof-Marks.[5] Elsewhere, hoof-marks and hoof-prints are also referred to, as in the Loire gorge in France, where two crevices on the rock face of the so-called Saracens' Castle commemorate a jump made by the Devil. He jumped on horseback off the rock and into the river, leaving his horse's hoof-print and also one of his own: Le Fer du Diable – the Devil's Horseshoe.[6]

The Devil was often involved in trouble of some kind, usually connected with his antipathy towards the Christian religion. At Mayfield in East Sussex, St Dunstan was building a wooden church: each morning he would find the building leaning, having

a

b

c

The Devil's feet are depicted in a variety of ways:
a. The Devil who appeared to Dr John Faustus, in an 18th-century chapbook
illustration, had cloven hoofs.
b. The feet of this Devil, dragging away a child he has bought, appear to have toes
with claws. After a woodcut from the Rider of the Tower *series (Augsburg, 1489).*
c. The Devil presenting a demonic pact to Theophilus has apparently normal
human feet. This early 13th-century illumination is from the Psalter of
Queen Ingeborg of Denmark.

d

e

f

d. The Devil dancing with witches at the Sabbat has cloven hooves.
From Collin de Plancy, Dictionnaire Infernal *(1863 edition).*
e. Christ and the Devil, whose feet are birdlike with long, sharp claws.
From Omvaarherris dod oc Pine *(1531).*
f. The Devil flying off with Over church, Cheshire, appears to
have cloven feet with long pointed toes.

111

The basin on Great Rock was said to have been made by the Devil when he stepped across from Stoodley Pike. Photo: John Billingsley.

been pushed over during the night by the Devil. He would straighten it up again, and so the battle continued. The Devil had to bide his time until after St Dunstan's death, when a stone church was being built. At night he would undo all the previous day's work, and he also went to the stone quarry to annoy the workmen, leaving his hoof-marks on the rocks there.[7] In West Yorkshire he left his hoof-print on Great Rock, Stansfield, Hebden Bridge, when he stepped across from Stoodley Pike during a wager with God that he could win the souls of the folk of Upper Calderdale. When his hoof slipped from the top of the rock, it skittered down the face of the outcrop and cracked it from top to bottom.[8] He was also working to halt the spread of Christianity in North Yorkshire, according to another folktale, this one centred on Hood Hill where a large block of stone has a foot-mark on the top, known as the Devil's Footstep. The rock was originally on Roulston Crag, another hill close by, where the first missionaries were preaching: the Devil flew in and landed on the rock, in an attempt to dispute their words. Failing, he flew across the valley, afterwards known as the Devil's Leap, with the rock still attached to his foot because the top of it had melted on contact, and the rock fell on to Hood Hill with the Devil's footprint impressed into it.[9] In West Yorkshire he left a giant hoof-print on the Cloven Stone at Baildon Bank, Shipley, while the hoof-print on the Cloven Stones at Rivock on Rombald's Moor was said to have been scorched on to the rocks. These latter stones are now covered by forestry plantations.[10]

Some folktales refer generally to the Devil's foot-marks or footprints, not specifying hooves, cloven or otherwise, and there are several other examples in England, in addition to those already given. The Devil's Stone at Birtley (Northumberland) has a

The Devil's Stone at Birtley, the surface of which bears the Devil's footprints.

flat surface in which are holes said to have been made by the Devil when he leapt across the river to Lee Hall, a distance of about half a mile. However he didn't make it, and fell into that part of the North Tyne river afterwards known as Leap-Crag Pool, and allegedly drowned.[11] (See 'Footprints to Visit') On the witch-haunted Pendle Hill in Lancashire, a stone in Ratten Clough above Sabden bears two distinctive footprints said to have been left there by the Devil when he jumped from Hameldon Hill, upset at the building of Clitheroe Castle on his territory. (See 'Footprints to Visit') The footprints are of slightly differing sizes, and one is misshapen, said to be because the Devil has a club-foot. This may be one reason why he is sometimes depicted wearing shoes with long pointed toes: in order to hide his deformity.[12]

Further south, in Chester, there was once said to be a Devil's Footprint actually inside the Cathedral. Its existence was recalled by Edward Thomas in 1906: 'When I became a chorister in Chester Cathedral, in the year 1828, I, as was the custom with all new boys, was shown by the older choristers a flag at the north-east corner of the Cloisters on which was a mark, said to be the Devil's Footprint, and was told that if the flag was removed and replaced by a new one, on the following morning, the footprint would again be there.' Folklorist Richard Holland found what may be the footprint when he searched for it in 1998, but my own search a few years later was thwarted because that part of the cloisters was out-of-bounds due to building work.[13] Even further south, in Kent, the Devil left a 15-inch footprint on a stone near the church gate at Newington. Unable to tolerate the sound of the church bells ringing, he stole them one night, put them in a sack and jumped down, overbalancing as he

The Devil's Footprints beside St Davids Cathedral.

landed and impressing his foot into the stone. The bells fell out of the sack into a stream and were never seen again.[14] The reason the Devil didn't like the sound of the church bells was because their ringing was believed to be able to dissipate diabolic power, an attribute they acquired after being formally consecrated. Church bells were also believed to be able to prevent destruction by lightning and storms. An act of theft perpetrated by the Devil in Cornwall is precisely dated to the year 1592, when he stole the fishing nets of the fishermen of Mousehole and Newlyn, in order to use them himself. As he made his escape, the deed was discovered, and he was pursued by the choir of Paul church, who chanted prayers and other parts of the church service at him as they ran. Trying to escape by jumping across the valley, his foot sank into a stone on the Tolcarn, a pile of rocks above St Peter's church, Newlyn, and he overbalanced, dropping the nets on the carn where they turned to stone. Apparently the petrified nets and the footprint can still be seen today, but they are very difficult to find and the perilous ascent is not recommended.[15]

There are also a few Devil's footprints dotted around Wales. At Llanblethian (Vale of Glamorgan) St Quintin is said to have lamed the Devil (exactly how he did this is not recorded), and he was in pain for three days as a result. Marks on the hillside are known as the Devil's Right Kneecap and Left Foot.[16] The Devil fought with St David on the roof of St Davids Cathedral (Pembrokeshire), but he was pushed off by the saint and landed on a flat graveslab in the churchyard, where his footprints can still be seen.[17] As the graveslab is relatively recent, this story cannot be much more than 100 years old. (See 'Footprints to Visit') Further up the Pembrokeshire coast, at Dinas Head, there are said to be some steps in the rock that are known as the Devil's Footprints; and another lot on a rock between Llanwenog and Llanarth (Ceredigion).[18] (This is a popular area for Devil impressions, since his hand- and knee-prints are also shown at Llanarth, as will be revealed shortly.) Further north in Wales, on the side of the mountain Cader Idris (Gwynedd) is a rock called The Rock of the Evil One, named after an occasion when the Devil joined the local people for cards and dancing on the mountain, and in dancing with them he left the marks of his feet on the rock.[19] On Llanymynech Hill (Powys/Shropshire border) there is a hollow known as the Devil's Footstep at the mouth of the Ogo Hole, a cave on the hill, but no folklore has survived to explain the name.[20]

In Scotland the Devil left his footprints in mud at Dingwall (Highland), and the story of what happened also explains why horseshoes placed above the door of a building will keep the Devil out! The Devil apparently wished to be shod with iron horseshoes, but during the operation the pain was so great he asked the blacksmith to stop. To make the blacksmith stop, he promised that neither he nor any of his devils would ever enter a building where there was a horseshoe placed above it. With the shoes removed, the Devil rushed to cool his burnt feet in a creek near the castle, and the heat caused his footprints to bake hard in the mud and still be visible today. Anyone able to walk in them was said to have good fortune, but the stride is too long for it to be possible.[21]

The Devil's Footprints can of course be found in other parts of the world, and a few examples follow. In France, the war between the Devil and St Michael, as described in Revelation 12, was popularly located in the Breton/Normandy landscape, and after Satan was vanquished by St Michael, he made a massive leap from the Grand-Mont to the Petit-Mont (Normandy), where he wanted to build himself a palace. But he misjudged the jump and fell on to an enormous rock where his footprint, and the marks of his horns, can still be seen. In Brittany a natural hollow in the Roche du Diable at Ercé-en-Lamée (Ille-et-Vilaine) is the Devil's Heel. He came here to rest and contemplate his estates, and each time he visited, he tried to jump over to the Pierres Grises (grey stones) which were guarded by the good fairies. But his efforts were always in vain, as he was held back on his rock by an invisible force more powerful than his own. In his annoyance he jabbed his heel into the rock and jumped into the river. He also left his heel-mark at Hénon (Côtes-d'Armor) at the place called le Cas Margot, when he struck vigorously with his foot in preparing to leap over the valley.[22] In Germany the Devil left his footprints on the Devil's Pulpit at Baden-Württemberg,[23] in the Kreuzkirche at Dresden,[24] and in the 15th-century Frauenkirche in Munich (see 'Footprints to Visit'); while in Italy he left a footprint near Caprie in the Val di Susa (Piedmont) [25] and another at Castel San Niccolò in Casentino. In Turkey, there is said to be a Devil's Footprint on the Devil's Table (Seytan Sofrasi), a mountain south of Ayvalik, and in Lithuania, the Devil's Footprint can be found on a large boulder on Sacred Grove Hill at Sarnele.[26] (See 'Footprints to Visit') Three examples of the Devil's footprint in the United States of America are in

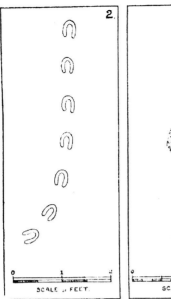
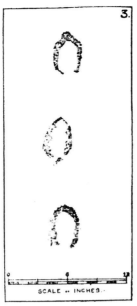

The Devil's Hoof-Marks, which were seen in the snow in Devon during February 1855.

California, Connecticut and Massachusetts. The first is on a rock on the bluffs overlooking Point Vicente near Long Beach;[27] the second is on a granite boulder near an Indian church in Montville, it being made when the Devil was leaving the area.[28] The example in Massachusetts is at Ipswich, where the print of his cloven hoof can be seen on a rock on Meetinghouse Green. It was made following a confrontation with the Rev Mr Whitefield, after which the Devil was thrown from the top of the church steeple.[29] (See 'Footprints to Visit') The Devil appears to have been wearing moccasins when he stepped on a rock about a mile west of the courthouse in Brockville, Ontario (Canada): early settlers said that since the rock was millions of years old, only the Devil could have left a footprint in it, and therefore it was known as the Devil's Rock.[30]

Although the foregoing accounts describe impressions that resemble footprints in shape and size, which have often formed the basis for a folktale invoking the Devil as the footprint's creator, common-sense tells us that these events are not real. However what are we to make of modern-day reports of strange tracks in the snow? Although more of these will feature in Chapter 10, with a variety of interpretations, it seems appropriate to include at this point those modern tracks which have been ascribed to the Devil. The most famous of them must be the so-called Devil's Hoof-Marks which appeared overnight in the snow which blanketed Devon on 8–9 February 1855. The tracks were about 4 inches long by 3 inches broad and resembled a donkey's tracks, sometimes apparently cloven and sometimes not, though they were in single file and with a stride of between 8 and 16 inches. They covered many miles (some accounts said as many as 100) in one night, and were seen in gardens, crossing roofs, passing through small holes in hedges and over tall walls, in fields and on roads – wherever there was snow to capture them. A vast number of tracks were reported in the South Devon area around Dawlish, Exmouth, Newton Abbot, Topsham, and it was easy to see that no one creature could have

The rock on Mont-Dol which has the Devil's claw-marks on top of it.
Photo: Andreas Trottmann.

been responsible for them all, unless it possessed supernatural powers, or was even the Devil himself. It seems feasible to suggest that many animals contributed to the tracks: cats, donkeys and ponies, hares, polecats, rabbits, badgers, otters, rats and mice, birds – in fact anything that might have been abroad that night and left its footmarks or, in the case of the smaller creatures, body impressions as they moved through the newly fallen snow – these have all been suggested, as well as other more farfetched explanations: gypsies, hoaxers, UFOs, lasers, sea monsters, for example. But the name 'Devil's Hoof-Marks' has stuck, and the last word on this mystery has yet to be written.[31]

This is not the only instance of mysterious tracks being found in the snow in relatively modern times, and attributed to the Devil.[32] Two strange reports from the 20th century come from Scotland, the first being located probably in the early years of the century, and near to Cromdale in Lower Speyside (Highland). James Alan Rennie saw footprints 19 inches long and 14 inches wide, with a stride of 7 feet, running in a straight line across snow-covered moorland. He followed them for half a mile, until they ended at the foot of a pine tree – but then he picked them up again and saw that they went across a field, down a hill to the river's edge, and disappeared opposite the village churchyard. A local ghillie said they had been made by the Bodach, a Highland giant or bogeyman.[33] Perhaps this has some link with another weird Scottish experience, reported by another reliable source, which occurred between Cluanie and Glengarry (Highland) some time before 1960. Author Otta Swire and her husband were driving through a frozen, snow-covered landscape, wondering if they would be able to complete their journey, even though they had chains on their tyres, as a recent snowfall had removed all traces of other vehicles from the road. They noticed a small loch close to the road, and on it were the 'marks as of cart wheels, clear and unmistakable in the new-fallen snow which covered the ice.' They stopped the car and got out to investigate: they could see no house or person or footprint in the snowy landscape, and especially there was nothing to see at the point where the wheel marks began and ended. Later they were told that they must have seen the tracks of the Devil's coach wheels, as he drives across the moors in winter and his wheel marks are often seen on lonely frozen lochs.[34]

I have wandered away from the track I was following, which was the marks allegedly made by the Devil himself, so without further ado let us return to the Devil's feet. He was sometimes visualised with claws or talons rather than cloven hoofs or normal human feet, and some of the tales of his escapades reflect this. Several of these took place in France, like the time he had an epic struggle with St Michael on Mont Dol (Ille-et-Vilaine). (See 'Footprints to Visit') The Devil was thrown down so heavily that he scratched the rock with his claw. St Michael made a hole in the mountain with his sword and threw the Devil into it, but he naturally extricated himself and lived to fight more battles with the Christian religion and its representatives.[35] One of these was St Enimie, who was following the Devil as he ran into the River Tarn (in the Toulouse area of south-west France). She prayed fervently, and in answer an enormous rock fell on to the Devil's back. But he was still able to escape through a crevice in the river bed which led to Hell. As proof of the story, there can be seen the mark of his claw on one of the rocks that the saint caused to fall on him.[36]

He also left his claw-mark at Aubune, when he was again routed, this time by the Virgin Mary. The occasion was the building of a chapel in memory of 8th-century leader Charles Martel's victory near Avignon, and the Devil said it would not be finished, grabbing a huge rock in order to smash the structure. But our Lady, who was at the altar, pointed her distaff at the rock and the Devil fled in despair, leaving his claw-mark on it.[37] At the abbey of St Victor at Marseilles, a granite column beside a well was said to bear the mark of the Devil's claw, made when he visited the monastery with the intention of corrupting the saintly inhabitants. He was disturbed and scratched the column with his claw as he made his getaway (though in fact the 'claw-mark' was a worn carving of an acanthus leaf).[38] The Devil also left his claw-print in the Devil's Cave on Monte Tezino in Umbria (Italy);[39] while in Sicily there was said to be a letter held in the safe of the cathedral at Agrigento which had been marked by the 'fiery claw' of the Devil.[40]

His claw-marks can also be seen in various parts of Great Britain, for example at Llandogo in Monmouthshire, left on a stone there after he had been worsted by the monks of Tintern Abbey nearby. The Devil was in the habit of preaching to the monks from the Devil's Pulpit on a rocky outcrop high above the River Wye, but he really wanted to get closer, and offered to preach a sermon from within the abbey building. The monks agreed, but once he was inside they threw holy water over him, which burned him and caused him to flee to Llandogo, where he left the mark of his claw on a stone before leaping the River Wye back into England.[41] Perhaps he fled all the way to the Isle of Skye, where many of the black rocks on the shore are scarred by the marks he made when sharpening his claws. The marks are apparently like the scratches a cat makes on a chair or table leg, except that they are larger and deeper.

Otta Swire remarked that when the Devil revealed himself in human form in Skye, he had horns and claws but no tail. Her mother had been told by an old man in Skye that 'the reason the Devil had no tail was because God took it to make women out of it. Adam's rib made the good women and the Devil's tail the fascinating ones.'[42]

When he ventured south again, the Devil spent some time at Kirkby Lonsdale (Cumbria), where he built the bridge which became known as the Devil's Bridge. The story was that he built the bridge for an old woman whose cow had strayed across the River Lune, on the understanding that he should have the soul of the first creature to cross it. He was expecting that to be the old woman herself, as she went to fetch her cow, but she realised what he was up to, and threw a bun for her dog to fetch, and so the Devil was thwarted yet again. One of the coping stones on the bridge has several parallel scratch marks, supposedly made by the Devil's claws.[43] Further south in Shrewsbury (Shropshire), the Devil is said to have left his claw marks on one of the bells in the steeple of St Alkmond's church: he appeared during a storm in 1533 when mass was being held, and shot up the steeple where he damaged the clock and a bell and knocked off one of the pinnacles.[44] This dramatic event is recorded in the Taylor MS Chronicle of Shrewsbury, where it specifically refers to the 'dyvyll' appearing 'when the preest was at highe masse, with great tempeste and darkenesse' and that he 'put the prynt of hys clawes upon the 4th bell', the result of his visit being that for a time he 'stayed all the bells in the churches within the sayde towne so that they could neyther toll nor rynge'.[45]

This tale has echoes of the account of the black dog which tore through Blythburgh and Bungay churches in Suffolk during a storm in 1577, also causing damage and leaving its claw marks on one of the church doors, as already described in the previous chapter. The Devil's claw-marks are also to be seen on the Devil's Beam, one of the timbers in Barnhall, a house at Tolleshunt Knights (Essex). The Devil killed the man who was keeping watch over the partly built house, in revenge for its being built in the Devil's Wood where he had presided over satanic orgies. After killing the watchman he destroyed the house and threw its timbers about, crying 'Where this beam shall fall, there shall ye build Barnhall.'[46] The 'claw-marks' are in reality mortise peg holes. Also at Tolleshunt Knights, the Devil's claw-marks can be seen inside All Saints church, on a tomb half in the wall. It was said he scratched at the tomb to try and get at the body of the knight buried there. The Devil's claw-mark can also be seen in another Essex church, that dedicated to our Lady at Runwell, where the mark of a hand with claws appears to be burned into the wood of the 15th-century south door.[47] In Canterbury (Kent) one of the earliest churches was that dedicated to St Pancras, dating probably from the early 7th century but now ruinous. Tradition tells how there was a heathen temple on the site, used by King Ethelbert before he was converted to Christianity, and it was the destruction of the temple and its replacement by a Christian church which so angered the Devil that he attacked the building and left the marks of his claws in the walls of the south porch. Yet another natural disaster may again be behind the story of the Devil attacking the church, since in 1361 a hurricane destroyed the new roof and killed a chaplain.[48]

There are also numerous accounts of the Devil leaving his finger-marks and during these events he must have appeared in his most human guise. The marks he left on

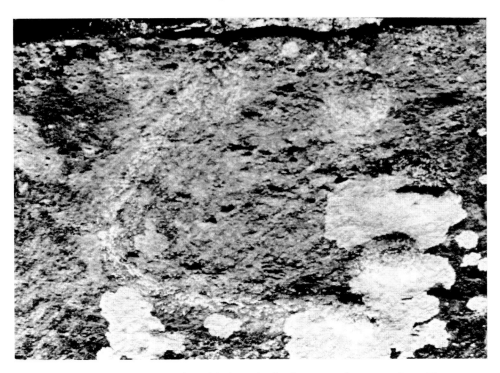

The Devil's handprint in the old chapel of Kilneuair. Photo: Andreas Trottmann.

the parapet of an exterior stair at a ruined church on Sanday in the Orkneys are known as the Devil's Finger-Prints, and are said to date from the time he was unsuccessful in persuading the worshippers to forsake Christianity.[49] Further south on the Scottish mainland, at Saddell Castle in Kintyre (Argyll and Bute), the Devil left his finger-marks after a terrifying night-time encounter with a tailor. The man was challenged to spend a night alone in the graveyard of the abbey of Saddell, and he took with him what he needed to make a pair of trousers. He was sitting cross-legged on a tombstone when the Devil appeared from beneath a grave slab, asking the tailor as he emerged: 'Do you see this great head of mine?' and so on through the various parts of his body. The tailor answered that he did see him, but 'I'm too busy making my breeks.' When he had finished, he took to his heels with the Devil in hot pursuit. He just managed to get through the castle gate before the Devil caught him, and slammed the gate shut. In his anger, the Devil grabbed one of the stone gateposts, and the imprints of his fingers and thumb are still visible.[50] This appears to be a peripatetic tale, since in another version the location was the church at Fincharn or the old chapel of Kilneuair (see 'Footprints to Visit') at the southern end of Loch Awe (Argyll and Bute), and in this instance the tailor's 'companion' in the graveyard was a mouldering corpse rising from its grave. In the version told of Dornoch cathedral (Highland), a human skull rolled towards the tailor who was sitting cross-legged in front of the altar. It grew to be a full-size skeleton, which left the imprint of its finger-bones on the door-post as it chased the tailor. In the Beauly Abbey version (Highland), the skeleton blew out the tailor's candle.[51]

120

In Wales the Devil's finger-marks were said to be visible on a 'huge stone pillar' a few miles from Llanon (Ceredigion) which he had been intending to use in the building of Devil's Bridge, but abandoned in alarm when the cock crew and he realised he had nearly been caught out in the daylight.[52] Deep indentations on a stone thrown at Beguildy church (Powys) by the Devil are said to be his finger-marks: he threw it from Craig-y-don rocks near Knighton but it fell short and landed on farmland. When the farmer tried to move it, a thunderstorm erupted and so he left it alone.[53] The Devil was involved in a battle with a giant when he threw a stone at Battlegore, near Williton in Somerset, leaving his handprint on it. The stone may be part of a prehistoric chambered tomb.[54] The Devil was battling with another giant in North Yorkshire and they were hurling rocks at each other across the valley where Semerwater lies: one stone on the water's edge is said to have the Devil's finger-marks on it.[55] Also in North Yorkshire, a rock bearing the Devil's finger-marks lies somewhere on Gatherley Moor, after he threw it at the people of Hartforth from Gilling, shouting 'Have 'at thee, black Hartforth, but have a care o' bonny Gilling.'[56] I mentioned earlier the footprints he left on Pendle Hill (Lancashire): in the same area lies a scatter of stones known as the Devil's Apronful, which he had intended to throw at Clitheroe Castle in order to destroy it. Failing to hit his target, he threw the stones down, and two of them are today large rocks near Whymondhouses, both with the Devil's thumb and finger marks on them.[57] In Bedfordshire a house on the site of Odell Castle was haunted by the ghost of Sir Rowland Alston, and the haunting was so bad that an exorcism was carried out. The ghost was put in a pond where he stayed for 100 years, but then he emerged again with the intention of resuming his ghostly antics. The Devil was waiting for him and followed him to the church, presumably hoping to take control, but Sir Rowland squeezed in through the keyhole, leaving the Devil thwarted outside. In his rage he shook the church, leaving five giant finger-marks on the porch's stone pillar.[58]

There are as usual numerous stones in Brittany and elsewhere in France that carry the Devil's finger-marks, like the 16 foot tall Christianised standing stone called the Lande-Ros Stone at Noyal-sous-Bazouges (Ille-et-Vilaine), left there after the Devil had been fighting with St Michael.[59] Also in Ille-et-Vilaine, at Plerguer there is a natural rock known as the Devil's Castle which has on it hollows that look like an open hand and a fist. They illustrate the effort Satan put into carrying the rock in order to construct the hill. A stone beside the road from Saint-Pol-de-Léon to Plougoulm (Finistère) has ten small holes on its surface, as if made by hooked fingers pressing into the stone. The Devil had come to Cléder to see the work being done by St Ké and he was enraged to see the fine spire of the Kreizkêr church in St-Pol-de-Léon. He seized a rock to throw at it, but the Virgin Mary stopped the rock halfway and it fell harmlessly on to the heathland where it buried itself in the ground.[60] Further afield, the marks left by the Devil's claws can be clearly seen on a stone at Roskilde in Denmark called, not surprisingly, the Devil's Stone. It is deeply scored with grooves, said to have been gouged out by his claws as he tried to stop himself being thrown out of town.[61] (See 'Footprints to Visit') The Devil also left the marks of his fingers on a stone to be seen in the basilica of Santa Sabina in Rome (Italy). It was thrown at St Dominic by the Devil, angered at seeing him praying inside the church. The heat from his hands blackened the stone, and his burning fingers made three

Footprints in Stone

holes in it.[62] In Latin America, the red hands found in caves and on rock faces, already described in Chapter 2, were often attributed to the Devil.[63]

Other parts of the Devil's anatomy have also been known to leave their mark. In Wales his knees and elbows (or hands and knees, depending on which version you read) made four impressions on a cross-inscribed stone in Llanarth churchyard (Ceredigion). On a stormy night a noise was heard coming from the belfry, and the vicar went up to investigate, carrying bell, book and candle up the narrow winding staircase. He discovered the Devil in the act of stealing a bell (presumably to stop it being rung, since it was usually believed that the Devil could be kept at bay by the ringing of bells and other loud noises) and began reading an exorcism ritual, which caused the Devil to depart speedily up the staircase and on to the roof of the tower. He had nowhere else to go when he saw the vicar coming up after him, and so he jumped off the parapet, landing on the cross-stone.[64] The Devil was usually recorded as carrying stones rather than bells and, as we have seen, leaving his finger-marks on them. Sometimes the effort involved caused the marks of other parts of his body to be permanently imprinted on the stones. Near Uchon in France, his claws and his back were marked on a rock resting on another, called Devil's Rock, on which moss is said never to grow. He had been carrying it to use as a keystone for a bridge, and a young girl had been promised as his reward for building the bridge, but her fiancé made the cock crow early, thus deceiving the Devil into thinking that dawn had broken, and he beat a hasty retreat, dropping the rock as he fled from the light. His back also made a hollow in a standing stone at Bazouges-sous-Hédé (Ille-et-Vilaine) and on the opposite face a groove was made by his belt: these show how hard he worked in carrying stones to construct Mont St-Michel. His head made an impression on a stone at Plerguer (Ille-et-Vilaine), again when he was carrying stones to build Mont St-Michel. In the east of France, in the Morvan (Nièvre), the Devil wagered that he could carry an enormous rock to Saint-Léger de Fourcheret between Mass and Vespers. He loaded it onto his shoulder and marched at speed, but hearing the bell for Vespers before he arrived he abandoned the rock, leaving an imprint, presumably of his shoulder, on it.[65]

There are even a few accounts of rocks with the marks of the satanic buttocks on them. One such is Satan's Stone near Rushton Spencer church on the Staffordshire/Cheshire border. It was one of many he had carried to the marsh when the church was being built, in his attempt to thwart the building altogether. Marks on the stone were said to show where he had sat to rest.[66] At Aron in France, the Devil's Chair was a circular hollow in a granite block, formed under the weight of the Devil who rested there one day when, having made a bridge for the local people, they gave him in payment a cat instead of a person.[67] (This probably refers to the familiar legend of him claiming the soul of the first person to cross the new bridge, his desire then being thwarted by the ingenuity of the people, who were perfectly well aware of what he was up to, and easily outwitted him. This happened so many times, one would have thought he would have grown wise to it. Perhaps His Satanic Majesty was endowed with more brawn than brain. Tales like this one, with a positive outcome, show that folk-religion in the middle ages was not all doom and gloom and eternal damnation, but that optimism was also a feature: the Devil could be vanquished.) He also sat on the edge of a rock-pool in a burn that flows past the

122

village of Newmill near Keith (Moray), leaving hollows in the shape of a seat.[68] In the Jura mountains of Switzerland near the chapel of Vorbourg there is a rock with a hollow that resembles a human body resting on its left side. Pope St Leo IX chased the Devil from the chapel when blessing it in 1049, but, wishing to go back into the chapel after the pope had left, the Devil hid behind the tower of Saint-Anne and slept on a stone which softened under the weight of his body. An alternative explanation for the shape of the stone is that the impression was in fact made by the pope himself, who was suspicious of the Devil's intentions and, fearing his return, lay in wait for him on this rock, which softened in his honour so that his shape was permanently impressed on it.[69]

This listing of impressions caused by the Devil's body concludes with a few instances of inanimate objects linked to the Devil leaving their impression. Both the Devil and giants were often said to carry huge rocks in their aprons, which explains why the Devil sometimes left the mark of his apron-strings on a rock. Satan's Stone at Rushton Spencer, recently mentioned as having the impression of the Devil's backside, also has grooves said to have been burnt into the rock by his apron-strings.[70] The Devil once had the intention of building a bridge to link the Isle of Man to the mainland, starting from a promontory near Seascale in Cumbria, but as he was carrying the foundation stone his apron-strings broke and the stone, afterwards known as Carl Crag, fell to earth. Two white lines could be seen on it, the marks of his apron-strings, or so it was said, but later the rock was covered by blown sand.[71] Off the west coast of France, on the Île d'Yeu (Vendée), small holes on the upper face of the capstone of the dolmen La Roche aux Fadets were said to have been made by the burning tripod on which the Devil sat every Saturday accompanied by his acolytes. Finally, just to remind ourselves that he was not the benevolent old gentleman he might have liked to appear, on the edge of a well by the church of Lanlef (Côtes-d'Armor) is the imprint of a piece of gold Satan placed there to pay for a child which its mother had sold to him.[72]

Chapter Eight

Giants, villains and heroes, including King Arthur

> The crofter undoubtedly believed that these prints [on two hillside boulders on South Uist] had been made by a striding giant, for had not several of his sheep been killed by lightning when standing near one of them!
>
> T.C. Lethbridge, *Gogmagog: The Buried Gods* [1]

Mythological giants and human villains and heroes tend to overlap, since in folklore heroes like King Arthur take on mythic status and develop a stature to match their status, in other words they are seen as giants, with the capability to do the same sorts of things that giants do: lifting and carrying and throwing huge rocks, for instance, or leaping across valleys. I will start by recounting instances of King Arthur himself leaving his imprints, then assorted other heroes usually of lesser fame than the great King Arthur, though they are often well-known within their own territory, such as Owain Glyndwr in Wales or Roland in France, with a few villains mixed in. Finally, a clutch of 'real' giants and some accounts of their bizarre antics.

Since King Arthur was said to have been born at Tintagel Castle in Cornwall, it is fitting that his footprint should have been permanently imprinted on a rock at that impressive cliff-top site.[2] (See 'Footprints to Visit') His finger-prints were said to be on a stone at Dyffryn Ardudwy (Gwynedd) which he threw from Moelfre Hill a couple of miles away.[3] Arthur's finger-marks and knee-prints were also imprinted on a stone up in the hills near Dorstone (Herefordshire), close to the prehistoric burial chamber known as Arthur's Stone. One version of the story says that this stone was originally part of a larger construction than survives now, and that the marks were made on it when King Arthur lifted it up on his back to place on top of upright stones.[4] Other tales say that Arthur killed a giant here, and the hollows were made by the giant's elbows. Or they were made by Arthur's knees as he knelt to pray; or it was a quoit he used when playing the game of quoits, and the marks were made by his fingers and thumbs. Yet another version claims the hollows as the imprints of Jesus's knees when he knelt on the stone to pray.[5]

King Arthur's horse's hoof-prints have already been listed in Chapter 6: he was after all a great warrior and would have travelled around the countryside on horseback, so his horse probably left its mark as often as the great man himself. In his role as warrior, Arthur naturally would have carried a sword, and on the stones called Maen y Cleddau (Sword Stones) on the moors above Barmouth (Gwynedd) are marks resembling a sword blade, said to have been made when Arthur threw his sword

King Arthur and his Knights at the Round Table.

against the rocks.[6] (On the Denbigh Moors in North Wales there is also a Stone of the Sword (Maen-y-Cleddau), this one being fractured after being struck by a giant's sword.[7]) King Arthur seems to have been fond of throwing things, which fits in with his giant status. In Northumberland near Sewingshields are two rocky outcrops half a mile apart, known as King's Crags and Queen's Crags, with a rock called Arthur's Chair. While sitting there, he was quarrelling with his wife Guinevere, who was sitting on Queen's Crags. He threw a rock at her, which bounced off her comb and landed between the two crags, where it still lies today, and the toothmarks of the comb are permanently imprinted on it.[8]

Almost equally as famous in Britain as King Arthur is Robin Hood, the outlaw who with his band of merry men became for ever associated with Sherwood Forest in Nottinghamshire. However his sphere of activities extended further than that, and in addition landmarks in areas where he never operated were named after him and his supposed exploits. He left his finger-marks on a stone which he threw from Werneth Low (Greater Manchester) towards the Cheshire Plain: it landed in the River Tame, near Arden Mill.[9] Further south in Herefordshire, almost on the Welsh border, Black Vaughan was a larger-than-life villain from Hergest near Kington. He was said to be Sir Thomas Vaughan who died in 1469 in the Battle of Banbury, and whose effigy can be seen in Kington church. His spirit was said to have been captured in a snuff-

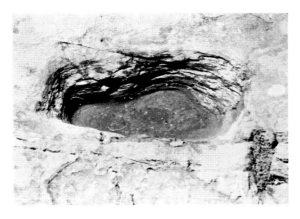

King Arthur's Footprint
at Tintagel.
Photo: John Billingsley.

box and laid for a thousand years at the bottom of Hergest Pool. (This story is clearly not contemporary with the alleged events, since snuff was not available in England until at least 200 years after Sir Thomas's death!) There used to be two foot-marks visible in the grass under an oak tree near Hergest, at the place where Black Vaughan used to stand to watch the deer, and it was said that the grass never grew there because of his wickedness. However by the time folklorist Ella Mary Leather spoke around 100 years ago to someone who claimed to have seen the footprints when he was a boy, they had disappeared.[10] A Cornishman who found his way into folklore was John Tregagle (sometimes Tregeagle), who lived in the 17th century, a harsh steward involved in a lawsuit who gained notoriety and thus became celebrated in Cornish folklore as a villain. He was a giant who involved himself with the Devil; he also threw a boulder which fell at Clapper, his finger-marks still visible on it.[11]

The origins of Jack of Kent, a figure from Monmouthshire folklore, are not so clear. He may have been one of several people, including Father John of Kentchurch, or Dr John Kent of Caerleon, or Siôn Cent, a 14th-century rector of Kentchurch, or an amalgam of all of them. In folklore he was a giant who was famed for outwitting the Devil. He also leapt from one famous Monmouthshire hill to another – from the Sugarloaf to the Skirrid (Ysgyryd Fawr) – leaving his heel-mark when he landed. The so-called heel-mark is an ancient landslip, said to have been caused by an earthquake at the time of Christ's Crucifixion.[12] It has been suggested that Siôn Cent and the Welsh hero Owain Glyndwr may have been one and the same, the latter living in hiding under a pseudonym. Glyndwr certainly left his mark in Welsh tradition, as well as his imprints on the landscape. He is particularly associated with Corwen in Denbighshire, that part of the Dee valley being one of his home areas. He is said to have been born in the mid-14th century; he fought in the Scottish wars of 1385 and 1387. In 1400 he was declared Prince of Wales and thereafter led several attacks on English forces; in 1404 he formed a parliament in Machynlleth, and began to establish Wales as an independent state. He achieved many military successes against the English, but the tide eventually began to turn, and nothing is known of him after 1415.

Many Welsh landscape features are associated with him in folklore, several of those in the Corwen area being imprints. On the hill Pen-y-Pigyn above Corwen, a viewpoint overlooking the town is known as Glyndwr's Seat: close by is his footprint

*Owain Glyndwr's Footprint
on a rock above Corwen.*

in a slab of rock. His knee-prints are on another stone just outside Corwen; and his dagger left its mark above the south chancel door of Corwen church, after he threw it down there from Pen-y-Pigyn.[13] (See Footprints to Visit') Further west in Wales, at Llanymawddwy (Gwynedd), 6th-century North Welsh king Maelgwyn Gwynedd, who was wont to quarrel with the local saints, left the marks of his buttocks permanently visible on a rock above Pumrhyd, overlooking the village, where he sat to rest while hunting. St Tydecho was the local saint, and the rock just happened to be his seat. He and Maelgwyn were not on good terms, and so when he had to use magical powers to release Maelgwyn who had became stuck to his rock seat, the latter was forced to stop persecuting St Tydecho and make amends.[14]

In Scotland, a 20-foot standing stone called Ulrach Fhinn (Fingal's Armful) overlooking Loch Caravat on the island of North Uist was, as the name suggests, lifted by Fingal, who left the mark of his thumb upon it.[15] Fingal is the same person as Finn MacCool, which is the anglicized name of the 3rd-century (if he really did exist, which is doubtful) Irish hero Fionn mac Cumhaill, who was also the giant who built the Giant's Causeway. There are numerous other variants of his name.[16] He also left his mark in Ireland, for example in County Clare where a giant rock called Cloughmornia or Cloughlea, near Ballysheen, has long gashes in it where Fionn mac Cumhaill and his warrior band tried to sharpen their swords on it. Fionn's finger-marks were imprinted on a rock that was moved from Birr to Cullaun House near Quin. The rock was known as the Navel of Ireland, and it is the same rock that was said to be imprinted with the footprints of the cock that crowed when St Peter denied

The Metlakatla Man: The Man Who Fell to Earth.
Photo: John Magor/John Robert Colombo.

Christ, already mentioned in Chapter 6.[17] Fionn's finger-marks and thumb-mark were also said to be on a boulder known as Finn's Seat, which was located near Parsonstown on the road to Dublin, but has now been removed.[18] In County Monaghan, the townland of Lurganearly supposedly got its name from a stone on Mullynash Mountain which bore the footprint of an earl, *Lorg an Iarla*.[19] King Cormac Mac Art, legendary Irish high king, left the mark of his head on a stone, thereafter known as the king's stone, when he was born at Cormac's Well near Kesh in Co. Sligo.[20]

In France, the ubiquitous hero Roland, whose horse we met in Chapter 6, also left imprints in various locations. His knees, foot and cudgel are supposedly on a rock at Nérignan (Gironde); his footprint is on a rock at Roquecor (Tarn-et-Garonne); another footprint is at Saint-Aman, and a few kilometres away in the valley of Roncevaux (Roncesvalles, just over the border in Spain), a rock bears his boot-mark. When Roland and Charlemagne arrived at the town of Tardets, where the Pyrenees begin, Roland wanted to frighten his enemies with a show of strength. He climbed to the summit of the Madeleine and picked up a huge rock, intending to throw it over the mountains into the Spanish villages. But while he was raising his arm, his foot slid on the wet ground and the force of his throw was weakened. The rock fell on the French side of the mountains and is now an isolated rock 20 metres tall near Lacarry: it still bears Roland's finger-marks. Charlemagne himself left a footprint, in a granite block near a waterfall some distance from Gérardmer (Vosges).[21]

Footprints and other imprints are ascribed to all kinds of famous people, not necessarily in the long-distant past. Marie Stuart (the 16th-century Queen of Scotland known as Mary Queen of Scots, who married the French dauphin in 1558 and became Queen of France in 1559) left her footprint on a rock near Morlaix in Brittany.[22] Somewhat earlier, in the second century AD, Lucius of Britain was said to be a king and church founder, including Westminster Abbey among his foundations. However, he was probably not a real person. Nevertheless, he did manage to leave his finger-marks on a rock pulpit above the town of Chur in Grisons (Switzerland) from where he preached to people in the valley below, in a voice so strong that it could be heard 12 miles away. Legend tells how he abandoned his British throne and emigrated to Chur, where he became a bishop and was martyred, his relics being held in the cathedral there.[23] In Hungary, an adventurer prince left his footprint after a jumping match with a giant. They were trying to jump across the valley of the Ipoly (Eipel), and the prince's footprint was left on a stone slab: it appeared to be the impression of a bocskor, which is a kind of shoe and legging made by wrapping cotton round the foot and leg.[24]

Historical and legendary figures in other continents than Europe have also left their imprints. In Africa, the famous explorer David Livingstone reported in 1857 having seen footprints on rocks at Pungo A Ndongo in Angola, which were said to have been made by Queen Ginga, or Jinga. She ruled Angola from 1624 to 1663, leading a long fight against the Portuguese, though Pungo A Ndongo fell to them in 1671. She was mainly remembered, however, for her hunger for men, and for killing each lover after the first night. She was so powerful that she could press her foot into a stone and leave a footprint. Jalmar Rudner visited Queen Jinga's footprint in 1966 while travelling in Angola; some children took him to a rock floor where, between two giant boulders, he saw 'a perfect footprint, about 22.5 cm long and at least 13mm deep in the coarse rock… a beautifully hammered and polished engraving'.[25] In Asia, the 'Chinese Columbus', early 15th-century explorer Admiral Cheng Ho (Zheng He), left one footprint in Penang, now in the Temple Batu Maung, and he left the other on the island of Langkawi, 96 km to the north.[26] Across the world in Canada, a rather unusual imprint can be found in British Columbia. The Metlakatla Man is a full-size full-body imprint on a horizontal rock on Robertson Point, an area rich in Native Indian archaeological sites. The Coast Tsimshian Indians told the story of the man who fell from Heaven: he was a great chief and shaman who went into a trance and levitated, disappearing into the clouds. Several days later he was seen falling from the sky, landing unharmed on the rock slab and leaving his outline permanently impressed. He would have stayed longer in the sky, but there was no food up there. The intaglio figure was probably of spiritual significance to the Indians, who have occupied the area for around 5,000 years.[27] (See 'Footprints to Visit')

As remarked earlier, heroes and villains, who are often based on people who once lived, rather than being totally imaginary, have tended to take on a mythical status, and in so doing have also grown in size, often becoming thought of as giants. Folklore also has many giants who were never anything else: they were often given names, and had an important place in the legendary history of their territory. They got involved in many escapades, often involving shows of strength, and in so doing

The Tibblestone, thrown by a giant who left his fingermarks on it.

they often left their finger-marks or footprints. Cornwall's giants included Bolster, whose size is shown by the fact that he could stand with one foot on St Agnes' Beacon and the other on Carn Brea, these two landmarks being 6 miles apart. One day, when striding between them, Bolster stooped to drink out of the well at Chapel Porth, and rested on a stone, leaving his finger-marks on it.[28] Giants were often said to throw rocks about, and the stones known as cromlechs or quoits, believed to be the remnants of prehistoric burial chambers, were ideal for giants' playthings. There are several impressive structures of this type in West Cornwall, and it was said that depressions on the stones were made by the giants' fingers.[29] They also left footprints at prehistoric sites, one good example being on a horizontal rock on the outcrop called Creeg Tol which overlooks the famous Boscawen-Un stone circle.[30] (See 'Footprints to Visit')

The giant who lived at the Roman town of Silchester in Hampshire went by the strange name of Onion. He is said to have thrown the Imp Stone about a mile from Silchester to a site by the Hampshire/Berkshire boundary, the giant finger-marks on it proving that he was the culprit.[31] A giant in Gloucestershire threw a stone from

Tom Hickathrift meets another giant and kills him; from an 18th-century chapbook.

Dixton Hill where he lived, slipping in the process and leaving a scar on the hillside. The projectile went astray and landed at the road junction known as Teddington Hands. Known as the Tibblestone, it may once have been a boundary marker during its long life: holes on its surface are said to have been made by the giant's fingers when he threw it.[32] (See 'Footprints to Visit') In north-west Bristol, on Blaise Castle Hill south of Henbury, there is a 'giant's footprint' on a small area of limestone pavement. It was said to have been made by Goram (or Gorm) a slow, lazy giant who was in conflict with the more lively giant Vincent; Goram's rock chair can also be seen.[33]

The legendary giant of the Norfolk Marshland and the Wisbech area of Cambridgeshire was Tom Hickathrift, and there are still numerous relics from his legends. These include the remnants of three old crosses, known as Tom Hickathrift's Candlesticks, and one of them, still surviving in the churchyard at Tilney All Saints, has indentations on top which are said to be the marks of his finger and thumb.[34] (See 'Footprints to Visit') There is a small carved figure on the exterior of Walpole St Peter church (Norfolk) (specifically at the exterior corner intersection between the north wall of the chancel and the east wall of the north transept – for anyone wishing to look for it), said to represent Tom Hickathrift, and to its left an indentation in the wall was made when Tom threw a stone (or a cannonball) at the Devil.[35] Also in eastern England, but further south between Dedham and Ardleigh in Essex, there is a building known as Cole's Oak House which has a stream flowing beside it, and in the stream bed is said to be a huge footprint made by the giant King Cole as he strode from his castle at Colchester to Ipswich.[36]

*Tom Hickathrift's Candlestick
in the churchyard at
Tilney All Saints.*

On the prominent Shropshire landmark known as The Wrekin, certain bare earth patches, where grass never grows, are said to be the marks of the feet of the giants who created the hill from the earth they dug out of the bed of the River Severn.[37] In West Yorkshire, the Pennine giant Rombald left his footprint on the Cow and Calf Rocks above Ilkley (see 'Footprints to Visit');[38] while the giant of the North York Moors in North Yorkshire was called Wade. His wife was Bell, and they were very fond of throwing rocks about. The Roman road which in its original unmetalled state can still be followed across the moors, is known as Wade's Causeway and was made by them. They also had a child who inherited their penchant for throwing rocks about: one day he became impatient for food and threw a huge rock at his mother who was milking her cow. She was not hurt, but her body left an impression on the stone which remained visible until the stone was broken up for road-mending.[39] On the Isle of Man, whose lore includes several giants and their doings, a huge granite block was lifted from the castle rock at Peel Castle by one of them and hurled half a mile against the opposite hill, the giant's handprint being afterwards visible.[40] The standing stone at Ballakilpheric, known as the Giant's Quoiting Stone, has the marks of the giant's huge hands on top of it. Along with four other stones which together made a stone circle, all marked with the giant's handprints, it was said to have been thrown by the giant from a mountain 2 miles away to the north, Cronk ny Irree Laa.[41] A few miles further north, at Lerghydhoo to the north-east of Peel, there is a circle of white quartz standing stones known as the Giant's Fingers, on which the marks of a giant's fingers can still be seen. A Scottish and an Irish giant were quarrelling, and the Irish giant picked up a rock to throw at his enemy, but it split in three, making the standing stones.[42]

Giants were also very active in Wales, especially throwing rocks around, and one giant who threw a huge rock called Carreg Samson from Uwch Mynydd on the Lleyn Peninsula (Gwynedd) left the impression of his fingers upon it.[43] The giant was often named as Samson – though one mark on a rock near Dinas Mawddwy (Gwynedd) was called Sawdl Efa (Eve's Heel), and was left by Samson's sister![44] Another North Wales giantess left the marks of her feet half a mile apart, one on the north side and the other on the south side of Llyn Peris in Snowdonia (Gwynedd).[45] Near Beddgelert (Gwynedd) there is a place called Llam Trwsgwl (literally 'clumsy leap'; or maybe the name should be Llam Trosgol, an abbreviation of Llam tros Golwyn, 'the leap across the Colwyn') where two giants held a jumping contest by the River Colwyn. One of them jumped right across the river, a distance of 75 feet, and left a huge footprint on a rock above the river. Also near Beddgelert, two giants were having a stone-throwing contest near Dinas Emrys, the hillfort where one of them lived. They also fought with steel balls, according to one version of the story, and wrestled with each other until they both died. Holes once to be seen in the area were said to mark the places where the steel balls landed.[46] At Maentwrog, also in Gwynedd, St Twrog's Stone stands close to the church door, and according to one tale it was thrown there by the giant/saint Twrog from a hill 3 miles away. There was no church on the site at the time, and he was aiming to destroy a site of worship used by pagan Celts in the 6th century – unlikely behaviour for a giant, but possibly something of which a saint would have been capable! The giant's thumb- and finger-marks were said to have been left on the stone. This is one story where giant and saint are one and the same person: see also Chapter 5.[47] (See 'Footprints to Visit') In Conwy (formerly part of Denbighshire), two hollows in fields at Llannefydd go by the name Naid y Cawr a'r Gawres (The Leap of the Giant and Giantess) and show where the giant and his wife landed when they jumped from the top of Mynydd y Gaer, an Iron Age hillfort.[48]

Scottish giants too were an energetic lot. A footprint on the Giant's Stone at Scurdargue (Aberdeenshire) resulted from a fight between two giants;[49] while no less than three huge stones were thrown from the hillfort of Knockfarrel near Strathpeffer (Highland) over to the old church of Fodderty. A giant challenged Fionn (Finn MacCool), who lived with his Fenian band on the hillfort, to a stone-throwing competition, and Fionn put forward a dwarf to take the challenge. The giant and the dwarf stood together on the hill, and the giant went first, throwing the Eagle Stone, which three men could not lift, across to Fodderty. The dwarf went over to the stone gateposts of the old fort, which seven men could not lift, and threw first one and then the other the same distance, so that all three stones afterwards stood upright together. One of them is said to have the marks of an enormous finger and thumb as proof of the tale.[50] On the Isle of Lewis (Western Isles) the giant Ciuthach fought with Fionn at Dun Ciuthach (his fort, also known as Dun Borranish) and on a rock nearby there are said to be the marks of the giant's shoulders and buttocks.[51] On South Uist, also in the Western Isles, a crofter showed archaeologist T.C. Lethbridge two giant's footprints some time in the first half of the 20th century. One was on a boulder on a hill-slope, the other was on a stone some yards away, on a causeway in a loch. Lethbridge said that the first footprint was 18 inches long and 'perfectly clear' and had probably been 'improved by human agency'; the second was less clear. The crofter believed the footprints to have been made by a striding giant, their supernatural nature being proved by the fact that some of his sheep had been struck by lightning when they were standing near one of the prints.[52]

The name of the most famous giant in the Orkneys is Cubbie Roo (also Kubby Roo or Cubbierow). On Rousay a huge stone slab called the Finger Steen, on the cliff edge at the Leean, was thrown there by Cubbie Roo from the Fitty Hill on Westray, the next island 8 miles away. Cubbie Roo's finger-marks can still be seen on the stone, and fishermen were in the habit of placing pebbles into the marks, in order to ensure a good catch and a safe return home. Throughout Orkney, bare patches of grass on the hillsides, where no heather would grow, were known as Cubbie Roo's footprints.[53]

The Shetland islands were also a rich stamping ground for giants, indeed they were believed to have been instrumental in shaping the islands. One of them, Atli by name, was accustomed to throw stones, and he raised the Ve Skerries, a group of rocky islands out to the west. He overbalanced while trying to throw an extra-large rock, which fell short and landed in the Muldra Burn in Aithsting. When he fell, his knee caused a dent in the hill which goes by the name of Atla Scord.[54] One Shetland giant who lived in the hills known as the Kaems fell over while carrying a huge creel of trows (mischievous trolls) he had captured. He landed on one knee and that place is now a gap in the hills called K'neefell. His other foot made a gash which filled with water and became a loch. At Pettawater it is said that the marks made by all his toes can still be seen.[55]

In Ireland, traces were also left by the many giants that once inhabited that island. In the north-west, in County Donegal, a standing stone in the townland of Bellanascaddan had two cupmarks which were said to be the finger-marks of a giant who lived in a nearby fort.[56] In County Monaghan, the Long Stone on Mullyash Hill (also Carn Hill) has on it the marks of a giant's foot, hand and knee, having been thrown here from Slieve Gullion.[57] Inishkeen round tower, also in Monaghan, was said to have been built in one night by a woman (presumably a giantess) who brought three apronsful of stones for the purpose. A large footprint said to be hers can be seen in the bed of the Fane River.[58] In Connemara, County Galway, the Stone of Curreel (Clogh-na-Curreel), between Coreogemore and Slieve Moidaun, is a huge block the size of a castle. The giants Curreel and Moidaun were good friends, until Moidaun ran off with Curreel's wife. Curreel was asleep at the time, but when he awoke he saw them making off across the plain, so he seized his stone pillow and threw it after them. The marks of his five fingers and thumb can still be seen on a corner of the stone. Folklorist G.H. Kinahan commented, on telling this story: 'It may here be observed that in the co. Donegal the giants are all said to have had five fingers besides the thumb; but on the three "giants' stones" that I have seen in that county there are seven impressions instead of six.'[59]

A giant who lived at Leam, also in Connemara, was challenged to a battle of strength by the Devil. After several feats they were still equal, and the giant suggested they jump across a chasm with a 'pillow' (a 6-foot stone) on their backs, but the giant tripped the Devil and he fell into the chasm. The place was called Leam (a leap) after the event, and on the stone, which was stuck in a bog, could be seen the marks of the giant's hands and the Devil's paws, impressed there while they were each holding it on their backs.[60] In County Clare, Hughey's Rock commemorates a giant of that name. It is at the northern end of the Edenvale ridge, near Ennis, and was thrown there from Mount Callan at another giant, but it missed its target and broke in two. Hughey's finger-marks were permanently impressed into the stone.[61]

Gargantua is the giant most often referred to in French lore, his fame having grown following his appearance in the high literature of France, in Rabelais' book *Gargantua*. He was famed for his enormous appetite: he once swallowed five pilgrims in a salad. Because of his popularity, marks said to have been made by giants on stones in France are almost always attributed to Gargantua. A dolmen near l'Ile-Bouchard (Indre-et-Loire) has the imprint of his thumb, and his handprint is on other stones. Cup-marks or basins on the Rocher aux Ecuelles (Bowl Rock) at Getigné (Vendée) are his knee and elbow impressions. His footprint is on a rock at Saint-Jacut du Mené (Côtes-d'Armor), made when he launched himself on to another rock 3 km away where there is a second footprint. The giant footprint made by a sabot (clog) at Saint-Priest-la-Plaine (Creuse) is known as Gargantua's Footprint; while the Pierre de Samson, an erratic boulder at l'Ain (Rhône) has two holes which are said to be the footmarks of Samson, made when he was sporting with Gargantua. In Normandy, the (unnamed) giants who erected the Menhir de Gouffern left the marks of their heads and shoulders on the standing stone.[62] Giants are also to be found in the folklore of other European countries, such as Hungary. In the parish of Ipolyságt, there is a stone seat where the Giant of Drégely was wont to sit, though the two footprints in front of it, and said to be his, are only of human size. Another footprint, that of the Giant Palást, is 26 inches long, which sounds more like it. Even more gigantic is the giant's heel imprinted into a rock called the Giant's Stone, near Szotyor in Háromszék, for it is 5 feet in diameter.[63] Somewhere near Orkney in South Africa there is on a rock outcrop an upright footprint which appears to be nearly 6 feet tall. Appropriately it is known as Goliath's Footprint.[64] The most remote giant's footprints in the world must be those on the Gilbert Islands (part of the Republic of Kiribati) in the Pacific Ocean. There are several sets of footprints carved on the coral rocks of Tarawa, an atoll where there was a battle in the Second World War. One of the footprints is said to be that of the giant Tabuariki: it is 3 feet 9 inches across its twelve toes, and 4 feet 6 inches long. He was able to pick coconuts without climbing the trees and his other footprint is on another island 20 miles away.[65]

Just as imprints of feet and other body parts provided visible proof that the saints have passed this way, so too did a wide variety of imprints serve to demonstrate to the country folk the 'truth' of folk-tales, myths and legends.

Chapter Nine

Supernatural beings:
ghosts, witches, fairies and spirits

> He found a strange pain on his arm, and… found the exact mark
> of her hand and fingers as black as cole
>
> A witch tale from London dated 1704

You might think that ghosts would have no place in a book about footprints, since their otherworldly quality means they don't leave any. Indeed, a figure seen by someone which has been found to leave no footprints in a location where it should have, is almost certain to be a ghost. But of course there are always exceptions, and sometimes ghosts do appear to have left footprints or, more often, handprints. Just how something that is non-physical can leave physical traces, no one has yet been able to fathom, and indeed such cases are mostly ignored since they present awkward questions concerning the nature of reality.

One classic example of an apparently solid person who didn't leave footprints, and must therefore have been a ghost, was reported from remote Sandwood Bay at Cape Wrath in north-west Scotland. In 1949 a fishing party on the beach saw a man who looked like an old sailor, walking along a sandy knoll and disappearing behind a hillock. Thinking he must be a poacher, the ghillie went to speak to him, but soon came back with the news that not only could he not find him, but he had left no footprints in the sand. Numerous other visitors to Sandwood Cottage and the nearby bay have reported either seeing a similar figure or experiencing the sound of footsteps and other noises at the cottage.[1] The lack of footprints in snow rather than sand was the notable feature of a post-Second World War sighting in Derby. A young woman was walking home after a late shift on a cold, dark night. Snow was falling and there was snow on the ground. She noticed a figure walking ahead of her: it appeared to be a nun. The witness was intrigued because the nun was wearing men's boots with trailing laces and, wishing to get a closer look at this strange figure, she attempted to catch up with her. She was unable to do so, and watched in amazement as the nun reached the bridge over the Markeaton Brook, walked through a wall and disappeared. When she turned to look back the way she had come, she could see only one set of footprints in the snow – her own. She later learned that the bridge was known as the Nun's Bridge and the street was Nun's Street, and that there used to be a convent where the ghost disappeared.[2] Ghost-hunter Elliott O'Donnell once rented a house in St Ives, Cornwall, and often heard footsteps outside his bedroom door. So he sprinkled flour and sand on the floor and fixed cotton across the passage. That night he heard the footsteps again – but there were no footprints and the cotton was unbroken.[3]

A large number of ghosts leave audible rather than visible 'footprints': reports of ghosts often describe how the frightened occupant of an apparently haunted house hears the clear sound of someone walking around upstairs, or along a corridor, or down the stairs, but when they investigate there is never anyone there – not anyone visible, at any rate. One representative example from the many that could be cited took place at an old vicarage near Carmarthen in West Wales in the first half of the last century. The family of the new vicar often heard footsteps in the house, when they were sitting down to their evening meal. The sounds were in the passage outside the dining room and on the stairs, and were heard nearly every evening for two years or so. The schoolmaster son of the vicar also reported that on a few occasions, when descending the staircase, he felt he had been passed by an invisible entity making its way upstairs: he heard its footsteps coming up the stairs, and then behind him as they passed.[4]

There are rare reports of inexplicable footprints appearing in houses that are believed to be haunted, for example Adlestrop Park in Gloucestershire. It was reported that a pair of bare footprints was found in front of a desk, which could not be removed by cleaning (presumably they were on a wood floor). They stayed for about a month, until one day someone working in the room felt a cold breeze pass by, and found that the footprints had gone.[5] Some time during the last century, a couple living in a house in Old Windsor (Berkshire) experienced poltergeist effects, among which was a smell of burning in the bedroom after they had had new lino laid. They found that a line of footprints had been burnt into the lino from the bed right across to the door, and they were never able to remove them (or to explain them).[6] In December 1965, parapsychologist Tony Cornell was called in to investigate a haunted shoe shop in Wisbech in Cambridgeshire. Among all the strange happenings (some of which Cornell felt had human rather than paranormal causes), one of the most difficult to explain was the discovery in a bare storeroom on the top floor of a line of footprints in the dust. There were six or seven, leading from the window to the fireplace – but they were all right feet, and there were no other footprints of any kind to be seen.[7] In the 1970s, a house in Haslingden (Lancashire) was affected by strange occurrences, such as objects disappearing and reappearing, footsteps, a child heard sobbing, a noise like coal being tipped into the cellar, a black-suited man seen on the stairs, and, especially interesting, a child's footprint was found in coal dust in the cellar. The print did not match that of the child living in the house, but on one occasion the ghost of a boy was seen to rush up the cellar steps and disappear.[8] Again in a cellar, a line of footprints was found in a newly laid concrete floor in a house in London Road, Devizes (Wiltshire), even though the door had been kept shut so that the concrete could dry.[9]

During a poltergeist outbreak in a cottage in the village of Dodleston near Chester in 1984, a line of barefoot footprints was found running up a newly plastered and painted wall from the bottom to a height of about 7 feet. They were a different size from the feet of anyone present, and anyway each footprint had six toes! They

137

appeared to be made from dust from the floor. Next day, as the occupants had found a can of the emulsion paint that had been used on the wall, one of the party repainted it. Next morning, the first person downstairs found that the footprints were back. There had been three people in the cottage overnight, and it would have been difficult for anyone to have crept downstairs unheard in the night, because of creaking doors and creaking stairs. The prints were again six-toed, but were not in exactly the same positions as before. They were again made from dust from the floor. Again the wall was repainted, and this time the footprints did not come back.[10] A ghostly big cat, possibly a pet lion kept by a bishop who once lived there, was said to haunt Spynie Palace at Elgin (Moray), home of the bishops of Moray for 500 years. A lady visiting the house in 1995 saw a huge paw print on the floor in the ruined kitchen range, which naturally made her apprehensive.[11] In past centuries in rural England it was believed that any footprint found in the ashes in the hearth on St Mark's Day would be that of a person who would die within the next year. Also, strewn ashes were in many cultures believed to reveal the footprints of the dead and of troublesome spirits and supernatural beings, as already described in Chapter 1.[12]

Mysterious footprints have also been found out of doors, usually in the snow. In the mid-18th century a man called John Turner died in a heavy snowstorm near Rainow in East Cheshire. The mystery arose from the discovery of a single woman's shoe-print in the snow by his side, which no one has ever been able to explain.[13] (See 'Footprints to Visit') In 1855 at Ipplepen in Devon, a trail of footprints, apparently a woman's shoe with heel- and sole-prints clearly visible, was seen in the thick snow on the thatched roof of Penrae, a former farmhouse. The occupant Mrs Hall did not go around the house to see if the prints continued there, because it was snowing heavily, but her dogs behaved as if frightened by something for a couple of hours, after which time they were suddenly normal again.[14] Some time during the 20th century, friends of writer Jessica Lofthouse saw mysterious footprints in the mountains of the Lake District when they were walking there one wintry April day. They had climbed from Wrynose Bottoms by Gaitkins, following new footprints in the snow. They were exceedingly puzzled to see that the footprints clearly led to the centre of Red Tarn, which was frozen and snow-covered. In the centre the footprints ended, but there was no hole in the ice.[15]

In the 1950s, the father of writer Doug Pickford had an unnerving experience in a snowstorm when driving a shop van in Staffordshire. He offered a lift to an old lady in Quarnford, and she walked round the back of the van. Mr Pickford waited for her to climb into the passenger seat beside him, but she never appeared. Thinking she may have fallen in the heavy snow, he got out to rescue her – but found no one, only her footprints which stopped by the cab door.[16] Folklorist Katy Jordan, a most reliable witness whom I know personally, said she had seen a strange footprint in the snow when she was a child in Wiltshire in the mid-1960s. She was walking with friends near Oare in the Vale of Pewsey when they found a naked footprint in the snow by the hedge, with no other prints nearby. It looked oddly twisted, and it clearly spooked the children, as they quickly made their way back to the safety of home.[17] Inexplicable footprints were seen by security men working in the Kingfisher shopping centre in Redditch (Worcestershire) in the early 1980s, and the guards also experienced other strange occurrences. The footprints would appear on the wet floor of a car park underpass in the early hours of the morning when it was raining, and would accompany the footprints of the security guard, sometimes leading one way, sometimes another.[18]

Ghostly handprints are usually found indoors, and a few examples follow. At the White Hart Inn at Caldmore Green, Walsall (West Midlands), strange happenings were reported from the attic, where a mummified child's arm was found in 1870. During the last century, footsteps were heard up in the attic, and the print of a very small hand was seen in the dust on a table in the attic, although no one could have been up there. The attic was locked and the landlord had the key.[19] At Hawksworth Hall (West Yorkshire), a ghostly negro page-boy was said to leave dirty handprints on the pillows.[20] In a recent poltergeist case somewhere in Britain, the precise location details of which are not available, the focus of attention was a 12-year-old boy, and among the phenomena experienced were handprints appearing on his bedroom wall. Although they were a child's prints, the hands were smaller than the boy witness's.[21] Similarly, a young woman who moved into a new flat in Tillicoultry (Clackmannan) in the 1990s experienced poltergeist-like phenomena, including the sound of running footsteps, and one day two sticky handprints were found on her living-room mirror. She commented: 'The prints seemed perfectly formed. I placed my own hand over the top of them to gauge their size and they were about half the size of mine and obviously belonged to a child. Nobody smaller than myself had been in the flat.'[22]

For no apparent reason that I can think of, all these handprints have been children's, and that same pattern continues. In March 1991, a newly married couple arrived at the Bell Hotel in Thetford, Norfolk, for their honeymoon stay. However during their first night, they experienced strange happenings including the appearance of the ghost of a teenage girl, and next day learned that the room was known to be haunted, but they decided to stay in it, as what they heard intrigued them. They noticed that the glass cover over a 15th-century wall painting had what appeared to be finger-marks on it in a place where no human hand could reach; and on the third day of their stay a small handprint, but without any fingerprints, appeared. A couple of months later, psychical researcher Tony Cornell visited the Bell Hotel and examined the glass cover. He could see two handprints, as would be made by a hand pressing on the glass, but he could think of various reasons why there was no straightforward explanation (unless the glass had been removed for cleaning, a long time before) – and the prints were again those of a child.[23]

At another hostelry, Royal Stag Inn in Datchet (Berkshire), a ghostly handprint appears on the window facing the churchyard. The story is that during the 1800s, a labourer visiting the pub on a cold winter's evening left his young son in the churchyard to entertain himself while he drank inside. Feeling cold, the child tried to attract his father's attention, and failing to do so, he pressed his hand on the window before sinking into the snow and dying of exposure. When the handprint puts in an appearance, which it does from time to time, sometimes it lasts only a few hours, at other times it is visible for months. When it appeared in 1979, the glass was removed and scientifically examined, but nothing unusual was found that could explain the phenomenon.[24]

La Mano Morta, or
Dead Hand: the hand imprint
burned into the convent
door at Foligno.

Another mysterious handprint on glass was said to have been made by a mother who killed her baby. It was on a bedroom window of a house on Dunkirk Hill, Devizes (Wiltshire) and appeared to be stained into the glass. It could not be removed by cleaning, and even if the window pane was replaced, the handprint would reappear on the new piece of glass. This happened many times, and the records of the reglazing were to be seen in the accounts books of Wiltshire's glaziers in the town.[25]

An intriguing report from the early 20th century may have some bearing on this and other cases. A man by the name of Viel from Bucharest reported in the French scientific journal *La Nature* that when he was a boy, he had melted the hoar frost from a glass window pane one cold winter's day by placing his warm hand against the frost. Afterwards, when all the frost had melted off the pane, the boy's hand could be seen apparently etched into the glass, and despite frequent washing, the handprint could not be removed and was still faintly visible after 30 years. It showed up as slightly iridescent when the sun struck it at a certain angle, and the report suggested that it was caused by the fact that glass can absorb tiny amounts of compounds of potassium or sodium from human perspiration, which then makes the glass slightly iridescent.[26]

During the last twenty years a house in Manchester Road, Burnley (Lancashire), has been haunted by a little girl, who was seen by the occupants. They also found mysterious handprints, but not small ones, as would be expected. When the owner was decorating his hall ceiling, he felt the step-ladder being shaken, and saw that higher up the stairway, a large handprint, twice the size of his own hand, had appeared on the wall. It was like a watermark, and slowly dried out and disappeared. A much smaller handprint was seen on a back bedroom window three storeys up, in a location too inaccessible for it to have been made by burglars.[27]

'Margery' with materialised hand.

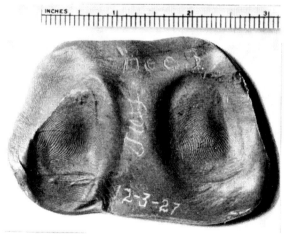

Psychic thumbprint in wax, made by control 'Walter' on 3 December 1927.

Ghostly handprints made by children have figured largely in this chapter, but there are post-mortem handprints made by adults on record, and indeed some examples have already been given in Chapter 3 where several with a religious setting are summarised. Another such account comes from Italy in the year 1859, where at Foligno a community of nuns were grief-stricken following the death of Sister Teresa Marguerite. Twelve days later, her ghost was seen by her close friend, and they even held a conversation. The ghost struck a door panel with her open hand, saying (in

Italian) 'Here is a token of God's mercy' before vanishing. The impression of a human hand was left burned into the wood, and literally burned, since the smell of burning, and black smoke, were also experienced. The nuns believed it truly to be the handprint of Sister Teresa, because it was small, and she had had a small hand. A few weeks later, in the presence of a magistrate and clergy of Foligno, the dead nun's hand was placed on to the burned imprint, and fitted it exactly.[28]

The Spiritualist era of the second half of the 19th century and the early 20th century produced some truly weird, and scarcely believable, phenomena, among which was the production of 'spirit' hands and other body parts in paraffin wax. The most famous medium with this ability was the Polish man working under the pseudonym of Franek Kluski in the first part of the 20th century, who was investigated by parapsychologists in France. A receptacle containing melted paraffin floating on warm water would be placed near the medium, and the materialised entity would be asked to put its hand, foot, or face into the paraffin. After setting, plaster of Paris could be poured into the mold or glove, and a model of the body part could be obtained. The hands would show lines which did not match those on Kluski's hands. In the late 1920s, the American medium 'Margery' tried similar experiments, using dental wax to obtain the impressions of the thumbs, fingers and whole hands, as well as fingerprints, of her control, 'Walter'. Bizarre photographs show 'Margery' seated at a table, both hands held by controls, and with a large hand materialising from between her legs and pressing on to a piece of wax. 'Margery' would always be closely controlled during her seances, for example in a 1931 sitting with one person, she was tied to her chair with surgeon's tape so that she could move neither her hands nor her feet. A detailed investigation by experienced researchers from the American Society for Psychical Research, undertaken at the time, concluded that, 'There is no evidence of fraud… These "Walter" phenomena are definitely proved by the evidence to be supernormal.' They also believed that the impressions were not 'identical with that of any known person or persons.'[29]

Some unfortunate witnesses actually carried the impression of a ghostly hand or fingers on their person after being hit by an invisible assailant. In a tale from 17th-century Bratislava (Slovakia), the ghost of respectable citizen Clemens Janos was haunting a young girl about a year after his death in 1640. He wanted her to visit his mother and get money to give to people in need; he also wanted his widow to put a statue of St Mary in the cathedral so that he could escape from Hell. His widow refused, but the ghost continued to haunt young Regina, and one night she was slapped by an invisible hand which left finger-marks on her face. The ghost asked her to visit his widow again, but Regina wanted proof that he really was a ghost. He put his hand on a cloth-covered box and left the imprint of his finger on the box. His friends later confirmed that it was Clemens' finger, as he had had a knuckle amputated when alive, and this deformity could be seen on the imprint. A cross, as if made by a hot iron, also appeared on the box, and there were other signs which convinced everyone of the ghost's identity, so that eventually the statue he wanted was placed in the cathedral and his money given to the poor.[30] Another phantom slap was administered early in the 20th century to a man in Suffolk, who was spending a night in the haunted Hall at West Stow. A girl was said to have been murdered by her lover in the room where he was sleeping – until suddenly woken by a sharp slap on his face. The next day he saw in the mirror that there was a red mark, the size of the palm of a hand, on his cheek, which took several weeks to fade.[31] In Kendal (Cumbria), the proprietor of a haunted café was pushed down the stairs in 1981, and she claimed to be able to feel the imprint of a hand on her back for a couple of hours afterwards. The report does not say whether she got anyone to check if her skin had been marked by the blow.[32] During poltergeist activity in a house in North Belfast (Northern Ireland) in 1989, a child was slapped around the face, leaving the imprint of fingers clearly visible.[33] The same thing happened in a house in the Woodrow area of Redditch (Worcestershire) in 1978. A little girl was experiencing poltergeist-type phenomena, and one night was slapped across the face: her parents came into her room on hearing her screaming, and saw a handprint on her face.[34] At Blackpool's Lobster Pot restaurant in Lancashire, the waitresses would be grabbed by a ghost which left red finger-marks on their arms and legs.[35] In 1991, a poltergeist was making its presence felt in a house in Martley (Worcestershire) and someone staying there overnight saw a dark figure and felt a smack on his leg: next morning, finger-mark bruises were visible.[36] In a strange late 1960s report from America, ghostly forces were active in a house where the witness's father had recently died: there were sightings of a man inside the bedroom, and the figure of a large man was seen moving across the windows from outside. On one occasion the witness and his fiancee were going up the front steps when they heard a loud slapping noise. She screamed: and there was a large, bloody handprint on her arm – but there was no one else around.[37]

The last report introduces the theme of bloody imprints. A large proportion of the ghostly handprints, and some footprints, that I have come across, are in the form of bloodstains that cannot be removed, usually permanently staining the floorboards of an old house. Sometimes the bloodstains are simply that, and do not represent a body part, but nevertheless they still act as a perpetual reminder of some event in the past, real or mythical, just as do most of the impressions and imprints recorded in this book. In County Clare (Ireland) a haunted house near the Fergus is said to have just such a memorial, in the shape of a small patch of blood on the wall which 'comes out' as a dark spot every year at about the time an old nurse was found dead in the room with a deep cut in the back of her head in the mid 18th century.[38] It is usually murder which the bloodstain commemorates, as at Clopton House in Warwickshire, haunted by a priest who was murdered there. A thin dark stain on the floor is said to be a bloodstain, left when his body was dragged along.[39] A perpetually damp stain on the floorboards of the Chapel Room at Husbands Bosworth Hall in Leicestershire was said to be either wine or blood, left when a priest tried to escape Cromwell's men. He either spilled the consecrated wine, or cut his hand.[40] Market Bosworth Hall, again in Leicestershire, also has a bloodstain, this time on a ceiling, and shaped like a girl's hand. It is a permanent reminder of the death of Ann, daughter of Sir Wolstan Dixie who lived there in the 18th century. She was allegedly caught in a man-trap that her father had set to catch her lover. Taken back to the hall bleeding profusely, she bled on to the floor, the blood seeping through to the ceiling below.[41]

Glamis Castle (Angus) was said to have once had a bloodstain that couldn't be removed: it was in King Malcolm's room where Malcolm II was murdered in the 11th-century. The floor had to be replaced to get rid of it.[42] Holyrood Palace in

Edinburgh had a permanent bloodstain outside the Queen's Apartment, where Rizzio, Mary Stuart's servant, was murdered in 1566.[43] In Shropshire there are two old houses with bloodstains, the first following a murder, the second rather different from the norm. The murder took place in Condover Hall when it was owned by Lord Knevett in the 15th or 16th century, according to the local tradition, which also tells how he was murdered there, stabbed by his son when lying in bed. He leapt from his bed and ran through the chapel, but collapsed and died from blood loss. Somewhere along the way he left a bloodstain on the floorboards which cannot be removed. The other tale relates to Plaish Hall near Cardington, where a group of clergymen was playing cards one Sunday night. The door suddenly burst open, was locked again, burst open again – and on the third occasion the Devil appeared among them. All fled except for the host, who was never seen alive again. Nor was his body found – only a bloodstain in the shape of a human body, which was on the floor, and could never be removed.[44]

All these bloodstain memorials have been indoors, but there are also a few located outdoors. Near Llansannan (Conwy), there is an old stone stile where dark red stains appear in damp weather, and they are said to be the blood of a maiden who was 'foully murdered' there by a jealous lover one dark and stormy night.[45] Another variant of the 'bloodstain as memorial' theme comes from Leicestershire, where in Hinckley churchyard there is a tombstone which is said to sweat blood on the anniversary of the murder of Richard Smith in 1727, killed by a soldier who lost his temper, and never paid for the offence.[46] Bloodstained stones that commemorate violent death also feature in saint-lore. There is a stone in a church in Pozzuoli, near Naples (Italy), where St Januarius is said to have been beheaded, and it bears the marks of his blood. On his feast-days the stains become moist, at the same moment when St Januarius' blood, preserved in two phials, usually in a dried form, liquefies in Naples.[47] St Nectan was another saint whose head was cut off. According to his legend, after the beheading he carried his head to a well between Stoke and Hartland (Devon) where he stopped and set it down on a stone. Blood ran from the head on to the stone, and became a permanent memorial to the saint.[48]

The everlasting bloodstain in Machermore Castle near Newton Stewart (Dumfries and Galloway) took the definite shape of a handprint, but there seems to be no story associated with it. It was said to have reappeared even when that part of the floor was replaced with new boards, in an attempt to eradicate it for good. The imprint was in the so-called Duncan's Room, which was said to be haunted, though by the time the writer J. Maxwell Wood came to sleep in the room, some time around the late19th or early 20th century, no one took any notice of the old belief. However, he afterwards wrote that, as he heard a clock strike midnight, he heard footsteps coming near to the door of his room, and even to enter. The room was moonlit, and he saw no one, but he heard the sound as of a drawer being opened and closed, in the corner of the room where the bloody handprint was. He sat up in bed and called out, but no one answered. He heard a noise like the rustling of silk, passing through the still-closed door, and the footsteps receded into the distance.[49]

The reason for the bloody impression of a thumb and fingers on a wall in the old manor-house in Darlington in north-east England is said to be the murder in that

The footprint on the flagstone at Smithills Hall. Photo: Smithills Hall.

room of Lady Jarratt during the Civil War, killed by soldiers for her ring. They cut off her arm to get it, and afterwards her ghost, minus one arm, was seen sitting on the churchyard wall. Also in north-east England, the Old Hall in West Holborn, South Shields (Tyne and Wear), was said to have the marks of two bloody fingers and a thumb on one of its mantelpieces, which no amount of scrubbing would remove, and they even showed through new coats of paint. Ghosts of a lady in white and a soldier were seen in the house, but their possible link to the bloody imprints is not known.[50] In one version of the story, the bloody prints were a reminder of the murder in the 1770s of a merchant by a ship's captain.[51] In Buckinghamshire, it was said that the bloody handprint of a murdered woman appeared on the shield in the De Crispin family coat of arms whenever a member of the family was about to die. This was the result of a murder in Norman times, when the wife of a De Crispin of Hitcham Manor near Taplow was discovered by her husband in his brother's arms and slain. The murderer never repented, and was cursed so that the family would never die in peace.[52]

There are probably enough stories of indelible bloodstains in Britain alone to fill a whole book, and I will conclude with possibly the most well-known, the bloody footprint of the martyr George Marsh. It is at Smithills Hall near Bolton (Greater Manchester), where Marsh, a Protestant preacher born locally in the early 16th century, was made to attend for examination by a Justice of the Peace when he refused to embrace Catholicism. At one time it had been a crime to be a Roman Catholic, but when Queen Mary came to the throne she re-established Catholicism and so Protestantism was outlawed. Marsh steadfastly refused to revoke his religion,

The face at St Andrews, said to depict the martyred Patrick Hamilton.

and after his examination by Roger Barton and others at Smithills he is said to have angrily stamped his foot on the flagstone floor, and 'appealed to God for the justness of his cause; and prayed that there might remain in that place a constant memorial of the wickedness and injustice of his enemies', as the story goes. He was burned at the stake in Chester in 1555. But his footprint remained at Smithills, a vaguely foot-shaped cavity in a flagstone, which is said to become wet and red once a year, an everlasting reminder of his martyrdom. It is said that Marsh's ghost has been seen at the hall; and when some young men living there removed the flagstone early in the 18th century and threw it into a field, there was so much noise and disturbance that it had to be quickly replaced.[53] (See 'Footprints to Visit')

Witches feature in just a handful of tales relevant to this collection of imprints. They were more likely to have been involved in interfering with other people's footprints than leaving their own: they knew what evil purposes could be pursued by means of a person's footprint. The strangest witch imprint must be the witch's heart on a wall at King's Lynn (Norfolk). A diamond shape above a window in Tuesday Market Square has a heart within it, said to be the heart of a witch who was hanged in the square below. She was Mary Smith, who was executed for being a witch on 12 January 1616 after having allegedly made a contract with the Devil, cursed various people, and confessed to other things which were together taken as proof of her witchcraft. As she was taken to the gallows, she is said to have predicted that her heart would burst from her body and fly to the magistrate's window.[54] (See 'Footprints to Visit') A Dunstable (Bedfordshire) witch was said to have been burned at the stake, but after death she haunted the priory of St Peter where the priory

*The Pierre aux Fées with
'fairy' footprints.
Photo: Andreas Trottmann.*

church now stands, and when she touched the prayer books, her fingers left singe-marks on the covers. It was said that she was exorcised by enticing her into a bottle and burying it. However the location of the burial in the churchyard was unknown, so no further human burials could be made at the priory in case the bottle containing the witch's spirit was accidentally broken, thus releasing her again.[55] There is another impression formed at the time of a burning, though this time it was not a witch who died, but a Protestant martyr. Patrick Hamilton was killed in the early 16th century at St Andrews (Fife), and a tortured face appeared in the stonework of a tower at the site.[56] (See 'Footprints to Visit')

A tale from London, as late as 1704, tells how a woman was suspected of being a witch and was tested by being thrown into the river to see if she floated, showing she was a witch, or sank, showing she was innocent. She 'swam like a cork', and her tormentors kept her in the water for some time. When she did get out, she hit one of the young men on his arm and told him he would pay for what he had done. 'Immediately he found a strange pain on his arm, and looking at it found the exact mark of her hand and fingers as black as cole'. He was afraid, went home, and died in pain.[57] Did he die of fear caused by auto-suggestion, like the Australian natives who were victims of the pointing-bone? In Ireland, the Witches' Stone near the round tower at Antrim was a bullaun, a rock with hollows carved into it, but the holes were said to have been made by the elbow and knee of the witch who built the round

147

tower: the easiest way for her to get down from the top was to jump![58] Another witch left a memorial to her innocence on a tombstone in Bucksport, Maine (U.S.A.), according to folklore. The tombstone belongs to Colonel Jonathan Buck, who is said to have ordered the execution of a witch in the 17th century when the anti-witch mania was at its height. As she died, she cried that her foot would be seen on his tombstone after his death as proof of her innocence, and indeed there is a vague foot-like shape on the white marble. It is also said that the mark reappeared even after the original stone was replaced.[59]

A rock with a series of tiny depressions on its surface can sometimes look, to the eyes of the romantic soul, as though it is marked with the footprints of fairies, which probably explains why stones can acquire names like the Pierre aux Fées or Fairies' Stone. The Pierre aux Fées at Col du Pillon in Switzerland looks as though marks caused by natural erosion suggested fairy footprints to people who saw them, and thus stimulated the carving of further footprints to enhance the effect. (See 'Footprints to Visit') In fact, considering how many stories of fairies and other Little People there are in folklore and mythology, they have left very few footprints behind. There are accounts of tiny shoes having been found in Ireland, showing signs of wear and presumed to have belonged to Little People, but no actual footprints. Perhaps they are so tiny that they are easily missed! There was a strange case in North Carolina, U.S.A., in 1976 when an 8-year-old boy claimed to have seen a little man not much bigger than a Coke bottle: he doesn't seem to have been called a fairy, but he was certainly one of the Little People. Tonnlie Barefoot was playing in a field of dried cornstalks at Dunn when he saw the little man, dressed in black boots, blue trousers, and a blue shiny top, with a black 'German-type hat' with a pretty white tie. He seemed to be reaching for something in his back pocket, then froze, squeaked like a mouse, and ran off fast through the cornstalks. He left footprints 2.25 inches long and 1 inch wide, and the marks of boots could be made out. A fortnight later, a 20-year-old woman saw a little man as she went home from a party in the early morning. He shone a tiny yellow light across her eyes, and ran away when she screamed, leaving footprints on the hard ground.[60]

Most of the folklore descriptions of fairy footprints that I have found have come from France: for example, in central Côtes-du-Nord (Brittany), fairy footprints and marks made by the nails of their sabots can be seen on rocks in the hills where they were believed to live.[61] The marks of fairy fingers are said to be visible on two of the stones that make up the Coat-Menez-Guen prehistoric passage-grave at Melgven (Finistère),[62] and another prehistoric monument, a standing stone which is part of the so-called Witches' Cemetery at Bouloire (Sarthe), has a fairy's footprint on it.[63] Continuing the link with prehistoric sites, some dolmens (burial chambers built of huge stones with a capstone across the top) in Anjou bear fairy imprints. One at Soucelles has a deep claw mark, made when a fairy leapt from it and across the River Loire. The Fairies' House at Miré, another Anjou dolmen, has three hollows under its capstone. Two of them were made by the hands of the fairy who carried it there, and the third was made by his head. There is also said to be the imprint of a fairy's saucepan on the dolmen![64]

According to Alasdair Alpin MacGregor, 'the Isle of Lewis is teeming with Little Folk' and at one of their strongholds at Ness, near the Butt of Lewis, there is a stone with a fairy footprint on it.[65] In Scottish folklore there is a kind of fairy creature known as the Urisk who is half-human, half-goat, with long hair, long teeth and long claws. Like the Brownie, he would do work around the house and on the farm. Urisks lived on their own, but craved friendship and sometimes followed travellers at night, as well as haunting lonely pools. There is said to be an Urisk footprint on a rock in Glen Lyon (Perth and Kinross);[66] while on the Isle of Luing, one of the Slate Isles in the Inner Hebrides (Argyll and Bute), there lived in Glen Dubh the *ghlaisrig*, the spirit or demon of the glen. On the hillside is said to be a large stone with the imprint of a giant clawed hand, said to be the demon's.[67] The mystery creature which left its imprints in snow in Kintail (Highland) also had long claws. It featured in a folk-tale about the murder of Murdoch MacRae, whose body was found at the bottom of a precipice. Strange sounds were heard at the spot, and in winter the snow was marked as if by round feet with long claws, although the snow all around was untrodden. The location was thenceforth believed to be haunted by an evil spirit.[68] The Isle of Man had a mountain hag or Cailleach who fell into a crevice while 'mountain-hopping': she was stepping from the top of Barrule to the top of Cronk ny Irree Lhaa, and left the mark of her heel on a rock.[69] On the remote islet of Rona, in the Atlantic Ocean north of the north-westerly tip of Scotland and north of the northern tip of the Isle of Lewis, there are rocks deeply scored as if by the claws of giant beasts. These marks are said to have been caused when St Ronan visited the rocky islet and found it covered by terrible beasts, all with bears' claws, which he subdued by walking towards them, while they dug their claws into the rocks in an effort to keep a foothold, although they were all the time being pushed back by an invisible force until they disappeared into the sea, and the saint was alone.[70]

The mythology of other races and religions also features fearsome creatures which leave their permanent imprints as proof of their existence, and sometimes they are semi-human, like the garuda, which is half-man, half-bird. In one tale from Tibet, a disciple of the guru Jigten Sumgön (1143–1217), while meditating alone in a cave, heard a noise and saw a giant snake encircling the monastery three times and looking in through the window of Jigten Sumgön's palace. This was the naga, a semi-divine serpent, and the disciple thought it was about to harm the guru, so he changed into a garuda and chased the naga away. The naga left the mark of its body at Rölpa Trang, and the garuda left its claw-mark on the rock where it landed at Dermo Mik. Both creatures left imprints near the river of Khyung-Ngar Gel.[71] More weird monsters will feature in the next chapter, but this time they will be real, or almost – just not quite accepted by Science, yet...

Chapter Ten

Footprint evidence for modern mysteries: monsters and aliens

'It's a two-legged cow with wings.'

Mrs Ed Shindle, on finding hoofprints left by the Jersey Devil, January 1909

During the second half of the 20th century popular culture spawned a rich harvest of publications dealing with mysteries of all kinds. Many of the mysteries concerned living creatures – or more often, allegedly living creatures, since hard evidence for the reality of their existence was and has usually remained scarce. The search for these elusive creatures has become known as cryptozoology, and it embraces the search for certain extinct creatures which are believed by some people to still survive in remote areas, as well as the search for new species which have not yet been officially recognised but which have been claimed to have been seen by many people.

Planet Earth's secrets are by no means exhausted, and there still exist pockets of habitat which are largely unexplored by humans, and where even quite large unknown creatures may live. New species are regularly discovered, admittedly not usually large ones, but there have been some recent surprises, such as the discovery in the early 1990s of the Vu Quang ox (*Pseudoryx nghetinhensis*) on the Vietnam–Laos border. Standing around 3 feet tall at the shoulder, over 4 feet long and weighing around 176 pounds, it cannot be called a small and insignificant find. Numerous other mammals, as well as birds, fishes, reptiles, amphibians and invertebrates, have been discovered and rediscovered [1] – but the really big catches, the mammoths and man-beasts, remain in concealment… at least for the time being. They continue to tantalise the searchers, as do other unofficial but suspected creatures, by leaving evidence which is encouraging but not conclusive – such as footprints. Another modern mystery which is equally elusive, but which also sometimes leaves footprints and other imprints, is the UFO and its crew. Despite more than 50 years of intense interest, however, no alien has been captured and no unearthly spacecraft is yet available for study by officialdom (despite sensational reports to the contrary).

This survey of the footprints of mystery creatures begins with the mammoth (*Mammuthus primigenius*), a creature which definitely once existed, but which does

Thylacine.

not exist now – or does it? Its extinction would seem to be incontrovertible: it was a massive creature, closely related to the elephant but standing almost 11 feet high, and surely such a monster could not survive unseen anywhere on earth in the early 21st century. Maybe not, but a claim that he had seen living mammoths was made less than 100 years ago by a Russian hunter. He was describing what happened in 1918 when he was in the Siberian taiga (swampy coniferous forest) and found and followed large footprints in the mud. The tracks were about 70 cm by 50 cm and belonged to a four-footed creature. He also found a huge pile of dung, and noted that the tree branches 10 feet up had been broken. He followed the footprints for days, and eventually found the creatures that had made them. They were living in the forest, and he didn't name them as mammoths, but said they looked like elephants with long dark chestnut hair and big white tusks. It was generally believed that mammoths lived on the barren treeless plains known as the tundra, rather than in the forests, but it was many years after the hunter told his story that scientists concluded that the mammoths had lived in the taiga rather than on the tundra.[2] There have been other reports of living mammoths and mastodons, but I have no other good reports of footprints seen.

Much more recently proclaimed extinct is the thylacine (*Thylacinus cynocephalus*), also known as the Tasmanian wolf or Tasmanian tiger, which probably still survives in small numbers in Tasmania, and perhaps also on the Australian mainland. There is a persistent trickle of convincing sighting reports of this carnivorous dog-headed marsupial, despite it being officially extinct since 1936, and some reports mention footprint sightings. One such report was made in 1986 by Turk Porteus, an old

151

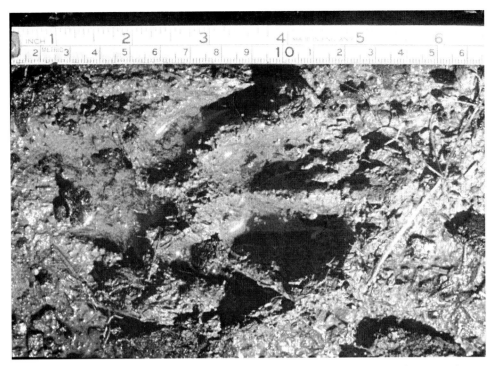

The mystery footprint at the Llangurig farm.

bushman who was familiar with the thylacine before it became officially extinct, and recognised their tracks. He could therefore certainly be trusted when he claimed to have seen a female thylacine, and followed its familiar tracks, in 1986 near the Frankland River. He also found the tracks of two cubs, which indicates that the species is increasing in number. He commented: 'You can't mistake a tiger's footprints because they walk right up on their toes.'[3]

Both the mammoth and the thylacine are known to have lived – it is only their present-day survival status which is open to question. Big cats of various kinds are also real animals, but their presence in certain places is disputed, if those places are ones where the animal reportedly seen is not native. These are known in cryptozoology as OOP (out-of-place) animals. Australia has its fair share of them, including many ABCs (alien big cats) which have left their paw-prints as well as being seen and even photographed. The cats are often but not always black, the prints are usually large: for example, in 1975 ten people followed a trail of cat-like, four-toed footprints measuring 13 by 14 cm for 1.5 km after a girl and a neighbour both saw a metre-tall black panther in the Southern Highlands of New South Wales. Sightings have continued for years in that state and in Victoria, and there is virtually no doubt that big cats are living and thriving in Australia – where there are no native big cats.[4]

Most people in the United Kingdom are by now aware of the big cat sightings that are reported periodically in certain parts of the country, especially the south-west and other parts of England, but also in Wales and Scotland – indeed the so-called

Surrey puma was being reported as long ago as the early 1960s, when there was an avalanche of sighting reports. However, most people are also aware that the big cat is not native to the British Isles, and so the identification of the animals seen (often only briefly glimpsed, it must be said, and usually from a distance) is sometimes disputed. However, physical evidence including footprints has also been obtained on numerous occasions: I even saw and photographed a 5-inch-long footprint myself when investigating big cat reports in Wales in 1980. A farmer living on a remote sheep farm near Llangurig (Powys) believed he had a strange animal lurking in his barn among the straw bales. He had heard unusual snoring noises and found large footprints in the mud. In addition, several sheep had been found killed in a way not typical of dogs or foxes. When the police came and explored the barn, their quarry had gone, but they did find wet bales as if they had been urinated on, a strong smell, and strange droppings 3–4 inches long. A month later, a farmer only a few miles away saw a cat-like animal running across some fields, 'in leaps and bounds like a cheetah'. It left tracks 'the size of a small palm with claws about the size of a finger'.[5] This is just one incident plucked from literally hundreds, many of them also having footprint evidence to prove the reality of the sighting.

Similar reports are also frequent in other parts of Europe, and in North America too: pumas are native to certain parts of the United States and Canada, but melanistic (black) ones are not supposed to be. However, many of the witnesses report big black cats, and so too do witnesses report big cats of whatever colour in parts of North America where they are no longer supposed to be living. Even more unexpected, however, are reports of maned mystery cats emanating from North America: pumas may be, but lions are certainly not a native species! One 8-foot-long creature with a mane and long tail, seen near Roscoe, Illinois, in May 1970, left tracks measuring 5 by 4.75 inches.[6] Seeing big cats that shouldn't be there isn't a modern phenomenon, as a provocative headline in the *Edmonton Bulletin* (Alberta, Canada) for 26 August 1929 demonstrates: 'Here's a New Scare for Timid Souls in Edmonton'. It goes on to describe a 'strange beast with huge footprints… twice the size of those of a St. Bernard dog', seen by some boys who used to gather in a cave under a bridge on Mill Creek. They found that the creature had been using their meeting-place for sleeping quarters, and had left footprints inside the cave and in the soft earth along the creek bank. Those boys who saw it thought that it was a lion.

The reports cited so far in this chapter are only a drop in the ocean of data relating to 'extinct' and out-of-place creatures, and anyone whose interest in that topic has been aroused should obtain a series of books by Dr Karl Shuker, a zoologist and prolific writer who has as wide a knowledge of mystery animals worldwide as anyone.[7] We must move on to some even stranger footprint reports, since they may belong to animals whose existence, past or present, is not (yet) accepted by mainstream science. It is probably safe to refer to them as monsters, since monsters are large, unnatural and may be imaginary.

The first group of monsters is from watery habitats, be it swamps, lakes or the sea. Because of the nature of their normal environment, their footprints are only left when they venture out on to dry (usually muddy) land, and therefore reports of footprints are rather scarce when compared with the number of sightings of the creatures

An old postcard depicting the Loch Ness Monster as she might look when out of the water, on one of the few occasions when she has left any physical traces.

themselves, which are usually made when bits of them protrude from the water. The most famous water monster is of course Nessie, or the Loch Ness Monster. There have been a great number of (usually fleeting) sightings of her during the last century, but very few of those have been on land, only about 25, and strangely most of them were in the 1930s or earlier. The witnesses' terrestrial encounters with Nessie were usually short-lived and distant, so there was no opportunity to notice if the creature left any tracks or footprints. However, in the 1930s it was reported that a carpenter by the name of Alec Muir saw the monster cross the road near Dores. He stopped his car and went back and found 'a depressed area of moss' where he thought it had lain, and 'a visible trail to the loch', but no further details are known.

The only real footprint report of which I am aware dates from December 1933, when big-game hunter Marmaduke Wetherall found strange footprints on the loch shore near Dores. He is quoted as saying, 'It is a four fingered beast and it has feet or pads about eight inches across. I should judge it to be a very powerful soft-footed animal about 20 feet long. The spoor I have found clearly shows the undulations of the pads and the outlines of the claws and nails... I am convinced it can breathe like a hippopotamus or crocodile with just one nostril out of the water. The spoor I found is only a few hours old, clearly demonstrating that the animal is in the neighbourhood where I expected to find it.' Unfortunately what the hunter failed to notice was that all the footprints were made by the right hind foot of a hippopotamus! It was of course a hoax: someone had taken a mounted hippo foot to the lochside and carefully imprinted it on the soft ground.[8] Perhaps the Nessie-hunter should consider himself lucky: according to a tale from further north in Scotland, from Lake Barrachan in Sutherland, the clothes of two missing fishermen were found on the shore, surrounded by large hoof-prints.[9]

Canada's most famous lake monster is Ogopogo, who allegedly inhabits Lake Okanagan in British Columbia. There are several reports of footprints being found: in 1949 a trail of 'cup-shaped imprints' was found, 6 inches wide and with eight toe-marks, which came out of the water and re-entered it a short distance away. 'Elephantine footprints' 6 inches deep in firm sand were seen in 1960; and only a few years ago a woman saw an Ogopogo partly out of the water and found tracks in the sand.[10] The monster of Lake Pohénégamook (Quebec) was also said to leave circular imprints on the sandy lake-shore or in shallow water; while the creature which left its prints on the sandy shore of Lake Memphrémagog (Quebec) was said to be alligator-like. The witness was Dr Curtis Classen, a military surgeon, who in October 1935 saw it crawl out of the water and said it looked to be about 10 feet long. Further prints were found two years later by John Webster on the same beach.[11]

The slimy three-toed monster of the Nith River at New Hamburg in Ontario was also said to resemble an alligator: it had a large green body perhaps 8 feet long, and its trail was like that of a bicycle tyre, with three-clawed feet, according to people who saw it in 1953. The question was: could an alligator, possibly brought back when small from Florida, survive a Canadian winter?[12] Much further south, in Arkansas, the White River Monster, seen by witnesses in 1971 all along the river system, appeared to be leaving footprints measuring 14 by 8 inches, again with three clawmarks.[13] In South Carolina, the Scape Ore Swamp lizardman, who was being seen near Bishopville in the summer of 1988, also left three-toed clawed footprints.[14] Some reports of Bigfoot, to be described later in this chapter, also mentioned three-toed footprints.

In Australia the traditional lake monster in Aboriginal folklore is known as the bunyip, among other names. One report from the Lachlan River near Oxley in New South Wales in 1847 describes how a farm worker out searching for the milking cows in a reed bed came across a strange animal grazing there. It had a thick mane of hair, large pricked ears, a long pointed head, and tusks, and a large tail, and it shambled off when it saw the boy, who next day took two men to the place where they found its tracks, which they described as broad and square, rather like the impression a man's hand would make when spread on muddy ground.[15] There have been numerous other sightings of bunyips, but few footprints reported: often the creatures were in the water when seen.

One of the most often written-about water monsters of recent years is also probably the most inaccessible. Mokele-mbembe may be a living dinosaur, but getting to his habitat to study him is not an easy trip for his haunt is the Likouala swamps of the northern Congo in Africa. There have been a few sightings in recent years, and the native peoples have offered many first-hand reports of the creature, which is said to be the size of an elephant with a long tail and a long neck. Similar creatures with different names have also been reported from remote areas of Zambia and Zaire, such as the Chipekwe of Zambia's Lake Bangweulu, where the monster was actually seen in 1954 by a non-native, Alan Brignall, who was sure it was not a lizard or a crocodile or a turtle, but something thought to be extinct. Lake Tanganyika's monster left three-clawed footprints bigger than an elephant's, as reported in 1934, and Mokele-mbembe also leaves three-clawed footprints – unlike any other known

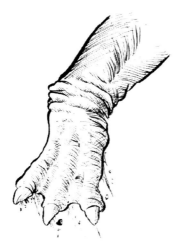

Mokele-mbembe and its foot,
depicted by Richard Svensson.

animal's.[16] There are several descriptions of sightings of Mokele-mbembe's footprints in a book about the search for the monster: *A Living Dinosaur?* by biologist Roy P. Mackal, who has also searched for the Loch Ness Monster. The people of Dzeke village used to see the monster come from the jungle and go into a pool in the swamp over several months in 1979. It left footprints in the sand the size of elephant's tracks and with claw marks. Mackal himself was shown a track through the jungle and possible footprints, when he was near Dzeke in 1980.[17] Although no one has been able to leave the Likouala area with conclusive proof of Mokele-mbembe's existence, it seems clear that there is a real mystery awaiting solution.

For obvious reasons, the footprints of sea monsters are even more rarely seen than those of lake monsters. There are, however, a few intriguing sightings on record, such as that which occurred on the west coast of Tasmania in 1913: not only were the footprints seen, but also the creature that made them. Two men who were prospecting in the area between Macquarie and Port Davie on the west coast were walking along the shore just before sunset when they saw a strange creature in the dunes. It was 15 feet long, with a barrel-shaped body, small head, thick arched neck, no tail or fins, shining chestnut fur and four legs. When it saw them, it reared up and was standing about 4 feet tall. It then bounded down to the sea and disappeared under the water. It left circular footprints 9 inches in diameter with 7-inch clawmarks, and both men, being familiar with seals and sea-leopards, and being shown pictures of sea-lions, said it was none of them.[18]

A representation of the Barmouth monster, based on the girls' descriptions.

In Scotland in 1962, a man walking his dog near midnight on the beach at Helensburgh on the River Clyde (Argyll and Bute) saw a luminous monster 30–40 feet long. Jack Hay was alerted by the whimpering of his dog, and then 'I saw the thing – about 40 yards away. I made out a massive bulk with a sort of luminous glow from the street-lamps… It did not move for about a minute, then seemed to bound and slithered into the water. I saw the thing swim out. It had a long body and neck, and a head about 3 feet long…. There was a strong pungent smell in the air.' He walked to where it had lain and found 'a giant footprint. It looked like three huge pads, with a spur at the back. The thing was not a seal. I have been a sailor – but it was not like anything I have ever seen.'[19] In 1950 a man visiting a beach in west Devon had found footprints on the sand after the tide had gone out: they were hoof-like but not cloven, 6 feet apart, deeper than a man's tracks, and led in a straight line from under a steep cliff directly into the sea.[20] In the 1970s, footprints were found at the water's edge in various west Wales locations: in 1971 at Llanaber they were 12-18 inches in diameter; in 1975 at Penmaenpool they were 'a little larger than a good-sized dinner plate and… webbed'; and earlier that same year, at Barmouth, six girls saw the creature that left its prints on the sand, as it made its way into the sea. It was about 10 feet long, with a long tail, long neck and huge green eyes. Its 'feet were like huge saucers with three long pointed protruding nails… Its skin was black, patchy and baggy.'[21] Footprints have even been reported from the bottom of the Atlantic Ocean, 3 miles down! In 1957 Dr A.A. Laughton of the National Institute of Oceanography reported how he had photographed strange footprints on the seabed when he lowered a camera with attached electronic flashlamp over the side of a ship.[22]

If the witnesses are to be believed, and if they are not simply misrepresenting or failing to recognise conventional species, their reports, and all the reports from people who have seen strange creatures in the water rather than on land, provide intriguing evidence for the existence of species so far unrecorded. There are similar

In a drawing of the Mylodon from the 1920s, some children come face to face with this allegedly extinct monster.

tantalizing hints that unknown land animals are living unseen in some of the still-remote corners of the world. These creatures present tiny pieces of themselves in the form, for example, of footprints, or brief sightings, evidence which intrigues but proves nothing. One of these mystery creatures is known as the Nandi bear, named from the Nandi district of western Kenya in east Africa – it also has numerous local names, such as *chemosit* or *chimiset*. Some reports may result from failure to identify known creatures seen only briefly, but there are still enough strange sightings to tantalize the monster-hunter, and numerous reports of large footprints. The Nandi bear may be a giant unknown species of hyena, or it may indeed be some kind of bear: some witnesses said it stood on its hind legs and left tracks like a bear's. Other reports were different: 'huge footprints, four times as big as a man's, showing the imprint of three huge clawed toes'; or 'enormous pug marks, the size of dinner-plates… spade-shaped and turned inward… a hyena enormous enough to leave footprints as big as those would have himself been a fabulous beast'; or 'round, saucer-like spoor, with two-inch toenail marks… does not fit the paw of any known wild beast that raids stock'. It has been suggested that the Nandi bear might even be a chalicothere – an extinct mammal rather like a horse, but with long forelimbs and large cat-like claws instead of hoofs![23]

Left: *This drawing of the Jersey Devil was printed in the* Philadelphia Evening Bulletin *in January 1909, and shows the creature seen by Mr and Mrs Nelson Evans at Gloucester City, New Jersey.* Right: *These footprints were said to have been made by the Jersey Devil; the photograph appeared in* The Sun *newspaper in St John, New Brunswick, in 1909.*

Equally intriguing is the *mapinguary* of Brazil, which may be a modern version of the Mylodon or ground sloth, a shaggy quadruped able to stand on its hind legs to browse on tree foliage. Officially they lived millions of years ago and are long extinct... but reports from Amazonia suggest that a 6-foot species weighing around 500 pounds may still survive. Its footprints are strange: they are said to be shaped like the bottom of a bottle, and to point backwards. Ground sloths apparently walked with their long claws curved inwards, leaving tracks which looked as though they were pointing backwards; and the rounded track may be made by the tip of its long, heavy tail. To add to this creature's bizarre reputation, it is said that its weapon is bad breath! Three *mapinguaries* are said to have been captured at various times, but the hunters had to release them because of the smell they gave off. This may arise from a special gland which gives off a foul-smelling gas: a highly effective defence mechanism.[24]

Unidentified monsters are not confined to remote unexplored jungle regions, however. One of the strangest creatures, the bat-winged 'Jersey Devil', made its appearance in the North American state of New Jersey in 1909, more precisely in the Pine Barrens, a desolate sandy forested area yet close to dense population. The creature's origins were folkloric and pre-twentieth century, but when it re-emerged in January 1909, thousands of people claimed to have seen it or its footprints as it came out of its den in the Pine Barrens and showed itself in more than thirty towns. The way the mass hysteria spread reminds us of other monsters that briefly hit the headlines but were never caught: Spring-Heel Jack in the 19th century, the Mad Gasser of Mattoon, Illinois, in 1944, and the Monkey Man in India in 2000, to mention just three.

The Jersey Devil or 'kangaroo-horse' had big wings and hooves, and left lots of tracks in the snow as it wandered around. Some were large hoof-prints 3 inches across, some smaller, and the tracks tended to end suddenly, as if the creature had taken off again. The sheer quantity of footprints left during the week the Jersey Devil was in town is reminiscent of the sudden overnight appearance of the so-called Devil's Hoof-Prints in Devon in 1855, as already described in Chapter 7. In the hundred years since the Jersey Devil was the talk of New Jersey, he has occasionally reappeared, and the rumours of his death appear to be greatly exaggerated. He has been the inspiration for numerous hoaxes: the police were called in when strange tracks were discovered in the Pine Barrens in 1952, but they were found to have been made with a bear's foot on a pole. In more recent times there have been reports of giant birds seen over the United States, especially in Texas in the 1970s, but none has been killed or even photographed. In New Jersey anything untoward that happens, such as howling noises heard, footprints found, banging on sheds, unexplained animal deaths, tends to be blamed on the Jersey Devil.[25]

From time to time truly outlandish events are reported that involve monsters with apparently supernormal characteristics, and it is unclear whether the witnesses are in a state of heightened tension and therefore misinterpreting normal creatures, or whether inexplicable paranormal forces are really at work, as they imagine. One such case from recent times took place in the late 1990s in Utah, when Terry Sherman and his family bought an uninhabited ranch. They weren't worried by the fact that the local Ute tribe wouldn't go on to the land and called it 'The Path of the Skinwalkers', a name referring to tales of shape-shifting witches. However the Shermans got their first taste of the ranch's weirdness even as they moved their belongings in, when a huge wolf appeared, apparently tame and allowing itself to be stroked, before grabbing a calf in the paddock. Though shot at many times, with heavy-calibre guns that would have killed an elk, it trotted off apparently uninjured. They followed its footprints into the thicket – until they suddenly stopped as if the creature had vanished into thin air. On another occasion, when Mr Sherman and a team of paranormal researchers saw a strange creature in a tree and another standing at the base, and fired on them, they vanished, leaving behind only a three-toed footprint with claws, which 'closely resembled the print of the dinosaur velociraptor'. These events are the tiny tip of the iceberg in this most weird case, and have been chosen because of the footprints that were seen.[26]

A much older case that centred on a paranormal creature that could leave footprints, yet whose identification remained problematic, was the so-called 'Haunting of Cashen's Gap' which took place on the Isle of Man in the early 1930s. A remote farmstead was apparently haunted by a usually unseen mongoose known as Gef that knew – and spoke aloud – several languages. It proved particularly elusive whenever attempts were made to photograph it, but footprints and teethmarks were obtained

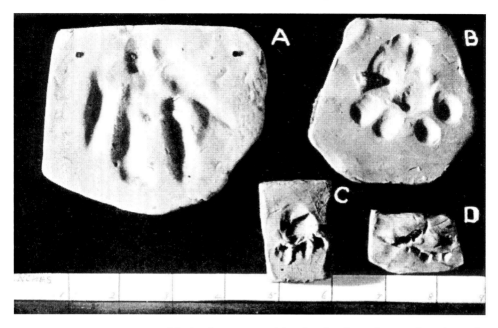

Marks that were said to be the footprints and teeth marks of Gef the phantom mongoose.

by researchers and sent to the Natural History Museum in London for the opinion of a zoologist. R.I. Pocock gave his opinion of the prints in a letter dated 5 October 1935. What was said to be the 'right fore paw with "fingers" extended', he stated 'does not represent the foot print of any mammal known to me, except possibly a raccoon, an American animal.' The alleged 'right fore paw with "fingers" in normal position' Pocock stated had no connection with the first print, though they were both said to be the right forepaw. He added, 'Conceivably it was made by a dog. There is no other British mammal that could have done it.' The third print, very small and said to be Gef's hind paw print, was dismissed by Pocock who said it had no connection with the previous print: 'There is no mammal in which there is such a disparity in the size of the fore and hind foot.' He was equally dismissive of the so-called tooth marks which Gef claimed to have made with his top jaw. When asked how he avoided also impressing his lower jaw if he bit on plasticine, Gef said: 'I did not put it in my mouth like a piece of bread; I put my teeth down on it.' However Mr Pocock's comment was, 'This does not appear to me to represent tooth marks.' In this case a hoax by lonely teenager Voirrey Irving, who was always closest to Gef, has to be a distinct possibility.[27]

The mention of a hoax reminds us to always be aware of this possibility, however impossible the task of hoaxing might seem at first glance. One set of footprints that was accepted as genuine for many years turned up on the coast at Clearwater, Florida, in 1948. They appeared to come out of the sea and meander along the shore for more than 2 miles before disappearing back into the water. They were large: 14 inches long and 11 inches wide – and three-toed. What could have made them? More tracks were found 40 miles away up the Suwannee River, and there were people who claimed to have seen a strange creature that might be responsible. Cryptozoologist Ivan T. Sanderson went to Clearwater to investigate, and made plaster casts of sample footprints. He concocted the theory that the monster was a giant penguin blown off course by bad weather: he did not think that the tracks were hoaxed, for they were too deeply imprinted to have been made by a man, and extended for too long a distance. Not until 1988 was the truth revealed, by which time Sanderson was dead, and never knew how wrong he had been. Tony Signorini admitted to having had a pair of three-toed boots cast in iron, which he then put on and used to make the 1000+ tracks – and he still had the boots, to prove he was telling the truth.[28]

The Devil's Hoof-Marks and other strange tracks in the snow have already been mentioned (see Chapter 7), but there are also other instances of similar mysterious tracks, apparently animal in nature. The so-called Wild Beast of Barrisdale, said to have been responsible for tracks found in the snow by the shores of Loch Hourn (Scotland: Highland), is clearly more folkloric than factual, but nevertheless the tales may originally have been based on genuine mystery tracks. They were described as being circular ('not unlike the bottom of a bottle') or alternatively cloven, and were often seen in the snow in the hills of Knoydart as well as on the sand edging Barrisdale Bay. A crofter who claimed to have seen the Beast in the late 19th century described it as three-legged, and with gigantic wings. Except for the three legs, it does sound reminiscent of the Jersey Devil.[29] More recently a woman living in Hull (East Riding of Yorkshire) in 1957 when she was a child found footprints in the newly fallen snow in her garden. They were 4 inches across, shaped like a cloven hoof, and were 12 inches apart in a straight line. They came to a stop in the middle of the garden. At the bottom of each print was not compressed snow, as one would expect, but dry concrete could be seen (presumably a concrete path).[30]

A feature of many of the mystery footprint reports is that no one saw the creature that made them (if indeed they were made by creatures and not simply a natural phenomenon of some kind: James Alan Rennie actually saw 'footprints' being made across a snow-covered lake in Northern Canada in 1924, created by blobs of water which formed when warm air met the low temperature and condensed on to the snow[31]). Giant human-like footprints have been found all around the world, and they coincide with reports of man-beasts, the most familiar of which are the Yeti of the Himalayas and the Bigfoot or Sasquatch of North America and Canada. The general assumption is that the man-monsters made the giant footprints, and at first sight the multitude of prints do appear to provide striking evidence for the genuine existence of these beings. The problem is to correctly categorize the prints: some may be misidentifications of tracks left by other creatures, especially if they are not clearly defined; some may be hoaxed (not impossible, even over long distances: remember the giant penguin tracks); some may indeed be the footprints of unknown hominids. With that in mind, here is a quick run-through of just a small sample of the literally thousands of humanoid footprints on record.

In Australia, the giant man-beast is usually known as the Yowie, though a variety of Aboriginal names occur in different states. Although there are records going back hundreds of years, only in the 1970s did this monster receive any widespread

*Man-beast hunter Igor Bourtsev holds a cast of a footprint
found in the Gissar range in August 1979.*

publicity. A report from early in the 20th century describes handprints as well as footprints being found. The witness was poet and bushman Sydney Wheeler Jephcott, who was in the bush in October 1912 when he saw scratches on a gum tree which he thought had been made by a large hand with strong nails. He soon heard that a neighbour, George Summerell, had come across a hair-covered hominid about 7 feet tall, drinking from a creek. Jephcott went to the place, a creek between Bombala and Bemboka in New South Wales, and found many footprints in the mud which resembled a long human foot but had only four toes. The handprints were also human-like, but the little fingers appeared to be set like the thumbs. A couple bush-walking in the Blue Mountains of New South Wales in April 1979 found a dead kangaroo with some of its flesh torn away, and then found a massive four-toed footprint in the sand. They felt they were being watched, and saw something tall and shaggy among the trees. Other descriptions of Yowie footprints describe five toes, and some only three, while others don't appear human at all. Such discrepancies also surface in the records of Bigfoot footprints.[32]

Persistent man-beast reports have come out of China, especially Hubei province where there are thick forests and snow-covered mountains. Scientists working in the mountains in 1979 came across a hundred manlike footprints in the snow, from 8 to 17 inches long. South of China, 'monkey men' have been reported from the area where Burma, Thailand and Laos meet. An American soldier stationed in Vietnam saw giant footprints from the air, and when he examined them he found them to be 18 inches long and 8 inches wide, pressed deep into the ground, and with a 4-foot stride. Malaysia has reports of man-beasts, and so too does Sumatra, where it is known as the Orang Pendek or Sedapa. Many reports have come from the remoter regions of the former USSR and Mongolia where the creatures are known as Almas. In the Gissar Mountains of Tadzhikistan, an expedition was camping out in 1979 while searching for evidence of the Almas. They found footprints around their tents that had a stride of 4 feet, twice the average human stride. Their best print was 13.5 by 6.5 inches; the 1981 expedition found a four-toed print 19.5 inches long. There have also been sightings further north in Siberia; and reports have come from Karelia in north-west Russia. Professor Valentin Sapunov led expeditions in search of the Wildman there, and was shown rock carvings of giant feet. They are known as *Besov sled* (demon's footprints) and are said to symbolise the wildmen of the forests.[33]

The man-beasts seem able to survive successfully in places with extreme climates, judging by the quantity of footprints found in the snow. The best-known of the man-beasts – the Yeti or Abominable Snowman – inhabits the seemingly hostile environment of the Himalayan mountains of Nepal and Tibet, from where there are several reports of footprints found on the snowy slopes. Sceptics have argued that the seemingly man-like tracks are merely animal tracks made by bears or monkeys that have enlarged or merged through exposure to the sun. However, sometimes the footprints are accompanied by sightings of man-like creatures, such as that seen in 1970 by mountaineer Don Whillans when he was scaling Mount Annapurna. While searching for a campsite he heard a sound like bird cries, which a Sherpa said was a Yeti. Whillans said he briefly saw a black shape on a distant ridge. Next day there were human tracks impressed deep into the snow close to the camp, and the same evening he saw in the moonlight a black, ape-like shape pulling at tree branches. There may be more than one kind of Yeti, tall ones and small ones: certainly very little can be deduced from the ephemeral footprints in the snow.[34]

While it may appear feasible that man-beasts are alive and well in the remoter parts of the world, their presence in more densely populated areas like Europe seems most unlikely. However, reports of giant footprints do occasionally emerge from Europe, such as that in 1955 from France, when it was reported that Britain's Olympic skiers had found the tracks of an 'abominable snowman' while training high in the Alps near Val d'Isère. According to the team manager Peter Waddell, 'Each imprint was the size of a small dinner plate, with clearly distinguishable pads and claws. The imprints were in groups of three and all in a dead straight line... We followed the tracks till they disappeared down a virtual precipice where no human being would walk in his right senses.' The tracks 'very much resembled photographs I have seen of the footprints of the Himalayan yeti.'[35] A giant hairy creature was seen in Spain in 1968, in the Vilovi district near Barcelona, where witnesses surprised it drinking from a pond. It ran away, leaving manlike footprints 40 cm long.[36] Even Scotland has its legendary mountain giant: the so-called Big Grey Man of Ben MacDhui. Several apparently normal people have described their encounter with something frightening on the mountain, and have told how they heard footsteps crunching on the gravel path though nothing could be seen. The writer of one report even claimed that he did see something: a 10-foot tall figure which passed close by him seen through the

A frame from the cine film of Bigfoot taken by Roger Patterson in 1967 at Bluff Creek in northern California.

swirling snow and mist, and afterwards footprints were found, 14 inches long with a 4–5 foot stride.[37]

Common sense tells us that it is impossible for a 10-foot giant to be living on a Scottish mountaintop: the mountains are busy places these days, and anyway what would it find to eat? However, when it comes to the North American continent, we cannot be so certain about the non-existence of Bigfoot (aka Sasquatch). There are forests and mountains extending for hundreds of miles which are rarely penetrated by humans: America may have huge metropolises teeming with people, but it also has vast areas of country that are devoid of anyone. Then there are the sighting reports. I co-wrote a book in 1982 which listed 1,000 such reports covering the period 1818–1980. I only used reports where the witness actually saw a Bigfoot: there were so many other reports made by people who saw footprints but no Bigfoot, that it would have been impossible to include them all. It is probable that a certain proportion of the footprints are hoaxed, and that some are misidentifications, but is it safe to conclude that all the footprints fall into these two categories, and that all the witnesses who have claimed to see a Bigfoot are either liars or deluded? I cannot answer these questions – all I can do is offer a few descriptions of the footprints that have been seen.

'With a human footprint nineteen inches long, the big toe alone measuring five inches, it is left to the imagination to fill in the superstructure of this huge monster that has frightened the inhabitants of this smiling valley. Men, women and children have turned out to look with awe and wonder at the mysterious and enormous

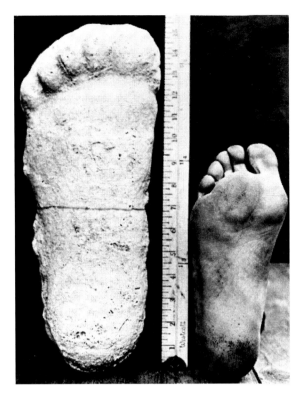

A man's foot compared with a cast of a footprint found at Bluff Creek after the Patterson sighting of a Bigfoot in 1967.

"hoof". It is a naked human foot in all the essentials, and its partner is on the other side of a six-foot creek, giving some idea of the prehistoric stride of the creature.' So begins a report from Vernon in British Columbia (Canada), dated 22 October 1907.[38] A steady stream of similar reports has continued throughout the 20th century, and still continues in the 21st. However, not all the tracks reveal 'a naked human foot in all the essentials', and some of them appear decidedly odd. The so-called Traverspine gorilla which plagued that small rural community near Goose Bay in Labrador in 1913 left footprints 'about 12 inches long, narrow at the heel and forking at the front into two broad, round-ended toes'. As I commented when reporting this event in *The Bigfoot Casebook*, 'Although a high proportion of apparent Bigfoot tracks are five-toed, with some four-toed found and a surprising number of three-toed, we do not have many other two-toed tracks on record.'

It was not until mid-century that tales of Bigfoot began to enter the national consciousness, and the major event that really brought the creature to public awareness was Roger Patterson's revelation that he had obtained 30 feet of 16mm colour footage of a female Bigfoot at Bluff Creek in northern California. On 20 October 1967, he and Bob Gimlin were in remote country 25 miles from the nearest proper road, riding around on horseback in search of Bigfoot. As they rounded a bend they saw one squatting beside the creek, and as it walked away, Patterson ran after it. He filmed as he ran, and got some reasonably clear shots. They also made casts of the footprints it had left, and these were found to measure 14.5 inches long by 5.5 inches wide. The Patterson footage has remained controversial, but no one has managed to prove conclusively that it was faked.

It is tempting to think that because a large number of footprints is found at a location, perhaps extending for a mile or more, they must be genuine, for who would bother to go to all the trouble of hoaxing *en masse* when just a few prints should do the trick. We must never forget the lesson of the giant penguin tracks, which prove that hoaxers can sometimes go to extreme lengths when they are determined enough. Was this what happened at Bossburg in Washington State in 1969? Over 1,000 footprints were found in the snow at the end of that year, and they were all made by the same creature because the footprints clearly showed it was crippled. Veteran Bigfoot researcher John Green was impressed by a report of footprints from several elk hunters on Coleman Ridge near Ellensburg, Washington State, in November 1970. They found a lot of footprints in the snow at their campsites: they were 17 inches long and 9 inches wide. They sank deep into the snow, which was hardpacked like ice where it had been trodden on. The men thought a hoax was unlikely: the stride was too long, the footprints too deep in the snow, and they could see snow kicked up by toe action and heel drag. They followed the tracks through the wood, and where the tracks crossed a log, the men, one of them over 6 feet tall, had to crawl over and the Bigfoot had clearly stepped over, showing his legs must be around 5 feet long. They followed the tracks for about half a mile and saw nothing to indicate a hoax. They felt that anyone wearing false feet the same size as the tracks would have been unable to impress them so deeply into the snow, as they would have been like snowshoes.[39]

The experiences of witnesses like the elk hunters suggest the presence of a real creature, albeit one that science does not recognise. But however amazing the footprints, and however reliable the witnesses, only a body which scientists can study will prove that giant man-beasts are alive and well and living in the American wilderness areas. Exactly the same sentiments apply to aliens: there have been literally thousands of reports of sightings of UFOs, and an awful lot of people claim to have seen their occupants, but without a body, the reports remain interesting but unproven. Reports that the American military *do* have bodies of aliens hidden away are, I should add, suspect on many counts. Physical evidence in support of alien landings is in short supply: they rarely seem to leave anything behind for analysis. This may in some cases be because both craft and aliens hover above the ground and don't actually touch it. However some clearly do touch down, since there are reports of footprints being found, and also other marks that may show where craft landing gear stood. The following chronological listing of relevant cases will prove intriguing but hardly conclusive.

At the end of the nineteenth century there was a spate of sightings of mystery airships, mostly in the United States: this was of course long before the flying saucer or UFO was thought of, and also before air travel of any kind became accepted. It is unclear whether the sightings were of early terrestrial flying machines, or extraterrestrial craft, or were part of a mass delusion. Some witnesses claimed to have seen people in the airships, and there was also the occasional landing report. One such occurred on 13 April 1897 at Lake Elmo, Minnesota, where two men saw a figure and then a strange 'wagon' which had rows of lights and rose quickly above the trees. In the mud they found '14 footprints… each two feet in length, six inches wide, arranged seven on each side, and in an oblong pattern.' It is not clear whether

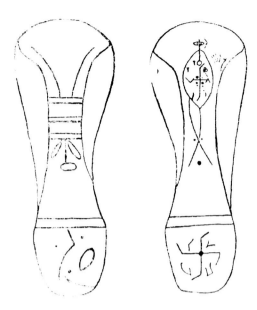

*The symbols seen in the
Venusian's footprint.*

these 'footprints' were made by the occupants of the airship or by the airship itself.[40] UFO reports of the kind we are familiar with today did not surface until after Kenneth Arnold's momentous experience in 1947: while flying a small plane through mountainous country in Washington State, he saw a formation of bright objects darting quickly in and out of the mountain peaks. When this sighting was publicised, it caught the public imagination and 'flying saucers' were born.

One of the many diverting offshoots was the category of witnesses who came to be known as contactees (because they had made contact with spacemen), the most famous of whom was George Adamski. One of his many extraordinary experiences took place on 20 November 1952, when in the desert between Desert Center, California, and Parker, Arizona, he encountered a landed spacecraft and a Venusian with long blond hair. After the craft had taken off, the Venusian's footprints were found in the sand, and one of Adamski's companions, George Hunt Williamson, described what they saw. 'I was the first one to arrive at the footprints after the contact had been made. I could see where the spaceman had deliberately scraped away the top soil in order to get down to a more moist sand that would take the impressions from carvings on the bottom of his shoes. I got down on the ground in order to get a close observation of the symbols. The carvings on the shoes must have been finely done for the impressions left in the sand were clear-cut, well-defined and evidently of a high order of workmanship. The footprint symbols tell why men from outer space have come to earth and what might happen if men on Earth refuse to live the Universal Laws of the Infinite Father.' This is followed by many more pages of interpretation: suffice to say that it is pure speculation.[41]

Most spacemen have not proved to be so friendly and forthcoming as the ones met by Adamski and other contactees. Nor are they usually so human-looking as

168

Adamski's Venusian. In a strange wave of sightings in France in 1954, the aliens that were seen were normally dwarfish. In one landing at Quaroble, a man was alerted by the barking of his dog and went outside, where he found an object on the railway tracks, and saw two beings in diving suits who were less than 3.5 feet tall. A light shone from the object and blinded the witness. After it had flown off, he was able to see that five imprints had been left, and investigators said it would have taken a weight of 30 tons to make them.[42] In the same year of 1954, hairy dwarves were also seen in South America on numerous occasions. A man out running at night in Venezuela came upon six hairy little men loading rocks into a hovering craft. They paralysed him with a violet light and after they had gone, strange footprints which could not be identified as either human or animal were found.[43]

The footprints found near Coldwater, Kansas, again in that busy year of 1954, must have been made by the alien rather than the craft, because it hovered and did not land, according to the 12-year-old boy who witnessed the events. He said that the alien visitor was the size of a 5-year-old child. However his footprints were not conventionally foot-shaped, being 'wedge-shaped' according to one report, or pear-shaped with narrow heels, according to another.[44] A man who saw a UFO land near Montville, Ohio, in November 1957 drove home to fetch another witness, but when they returned, it had gone. When the landing site was visited next day by officials, they found footprints that 'came from nowhere and went nowhere' with a heel print, then little holes in the ground 'like golf shoes would make' – but, he added, 'no one around there has golf shoes'. Two holes 3 feet deep were also found, 6 inches in diameter, and readings on a Geiger counter were high.[45] Only the day before this event, another soon-to-be contactee was experiencing something rather more extreme in the way of UFO contact, though there is nothing to suggest that the two events were linked. While driving near the Platte River in Nebraska, Reinhold O. Schmidt saw a landed UFO and was paralysed by a beam of light. Two men took him inside the craft where he met the crew: they were talking High German. After his release he contacted the sheriff and they went back to the landing site, finding three sets of footprints in the sand. Over the next few years Schmidt claimed ever more bizarre experiences, including journeys into space and under the ocean, but his UFO career ended when he was jailed for theft.[46]

One fact that is emerging from the reports so far is that no two are alike. Some are more bizarre than others, but no pattern is seen to be emerging. The next report could be interpreted as linking the Bigfoot and UFO phenomena, and it concerns a UFO sighting near Dorango, Colorado, on Christmas Eve of 1960. Wade Folsom saw a huge lit object that came down from the sky and disappeared among the trees on a nearby hill. Next day, a group of people went up the hill and found a place where tree limbs were broken. They also found a large number of footprints, human in shape, but some were 15 inches long and some were only 5 inches. They circled an abandoned mountain cabin and returned to the assumed landing site. Giants and dwarves together on the same craft, or Bigfoot meeting aliens? [47] Or perhaps the larger footprints were not left by Bigfoot, but by robots. A case from October 1963 in Argentina involved a truck driver who was driving early in the morning in heavy rain and found himself blinded by a bright light so that his truck went into a ditch. A huge metal object filled the road, and three huge robots were climbing out. He fired at

One of the depressions left by the spacecraft which landed at Socorro.
The stones were placed round it afterwards to protect it.

them and ran away. Next day investigators found some footprints 45–50 cm long by his truck, still there despite the heavy rain.[48]

Two 4-foot figures who said they were Martians visited the Newark Valley, New York, farm of Gary Wilcox in April 1964, arriving in an egg-shaped craft. They talked about manure and fertiliser, and after they had left, Wilcox found square depressions where they had been standing, 1–2 inches square and 1/16 inch deep. There was also a red jelly substance that he couldn't pick up.[49] On exactly the same day, 24 April 1964, a much-publicized sighting took place near Socorro, New Mexico, when police officer Lonnie Zamora saw a spacecraft that had landed in the desert, and beside it two figures. Later when the site was inspected, four depressions were found in the soft sand which were presumed to have been made by the craft, and four footprints made by small shoes, each with a crescent shape in the middle. Zamora sketched the imprints, and he also drew an insignia which he had seen on the craft. Zamora was a reliable witness, and no evidence of a hoax could be found, but a definitive solution to the mystery was not found either.[50]

At the other end of the reliability spectrum must be the Brooksville, Florida, landing of March 1965. John F. Reeves claimed that a UFO landed on his property, a 'robot' wearing a one-piece suit and glass helmet got out, flashed an object at him, dropped a piece of tissue paper with strange writing on it, and left numerous clear footprints in the sand while it was walking round. In the following years he claimed further encounters and footprints. As Jerome Clark commented: 'If any portion of Reeves's testimony is in any way authentic, we can only regret that he seems to have done

Some of the 'Martian' footprints
photographed by John Reeves.

everything in his power to hide that fact.'[51] No beings were seen during the strange events at Fort Beaufort in South Africa's Cape Province in June 1972, in fact the flying object would seem to have been too small to house any, for it was less than 2 metres long. First sighted by a labourer who had been sent to inspect the farm's water reservoir, the farm owner Bennie Smit then saw it, as did two policemen and more labourers. They also fired at it as it bobbed around in the trees and bushes. As they watched it kept on changing colour, and finally was lost to view in the thick undergrowth. In the area where it had been, nine imprints were found in damp clay soil, but no tracks were found leading to or from the clearing where the imprints were found. They were circular imprints 7 cm in diameter, in sets of three, and it was not clear whether they were made by a living creature.[52]

Also in South Africa, a UFO landed at Loxton on 31 July 1975 and was seen on his farm by Danie Van Graan early in the morning. It was like an oval caravan, and he could see people moving around inside. They were only about 1.5 metres tall and had long faces, pointed chins and slanting eyes. When he approached to within 5 metres of the craft, they suddenly noticed him and shone a beam of light at his eyes which made him feel ill, so he moved away. He could see that the craft was standing on legs, and when it had gone he found marks on the hard ground. There was 'a centre mark (consisting of three lines crossing one another to form a 6-point flattened star) and four marks on the outside perimeter, precisely the same distance from one another... Each of the four outside marks had the appearance of an arrow with all lines broken in the centre'. Danie also revealed that a couple of months after the

171

The mark left on the ground by a UFO at Loxton in 1975.

landing, he discovered footprints in the mud of an almost dry pool. He compared them with the feet of his labourers and found they were similar to 'a size 4 shoe but about twice as wide as a normal foot': his smallest labourer wore size 5 shoes. But it was not clear whether the footprints had any connection with the UFO landing. Investigator Cynthia Hind visited the site and found that 18 months after the landing, the soil at the landing site was hard and nothing would grow there.[53]

Scientific investigation has taken place in many of these and other UFO cases where physical traces have been found, but it is very rare for this research to produce any real answers. All that the mysterious imprints can tell us is: something strange happened here – possibly (hoaxing must always be borne in mind). None of the creatures or beings described in this chapter has actually been caught, and rarely have any of them been photographed: monsters and UFOs and aliens are as elusive today as they were 50 years ago. As we have seen, sometimes traces are left. But these enigmatic marks can no more prove that 'aliens were here' than a footprint in stone can prove that 'King Arthur was here'.

We have travelled a long way through this book, from footprints millions of years old, possibly telling of the earliest men on the earth, to recent footprints allegedly made by men from other worlds. All of them have been interpreted as proof of something extraordinary, be it the power of saints, the presence of giants, the existence of aliens, or whatever it is that the individual footprint symbolises for the witness. In this way the humble footprint provides a link to supernatural realms, and supplies a touch of magic and mystery to our mundane world.

Footprints to visit

I have here collected together some examples of footprints and other imprints which I believe it is still possible to see today, either from personal experience or using hopefully reliable information from other sources. I have given what I hope is sufficient information for the location to be found without too much difficulty. In some cases there will be a photograph either close to the entry, or in the chapter indicated, which will show you what you are looking for, since often the imprints are rather indefinite.

Argentina

Patagonia: Cueva de las Manos (Cave of the Hands): hand petroglyphs (The cave is a Unesco World Heritage Site, 40 miles from Perito Moreno: it is on private land, with access allowed by the owner). A massive quantity of hands (and also some feet) were stencilled on to the cave walls possibly 9,000 years ago: the effect is beautiful yet surreal. The meaning of the hand stencils is not known: 'There are many possible explanations: they could be signatures, property marks, memorials, love magic, a wish to leave a mark in some sacred place, a sign of caring about or being responsible for a site, a record of growth, or a personal marker – "I was here".[1] (See Chapter 2)

Australia

New South Wales: Ku-Ring-Gai Chase National Park: West Head rock engravings (North of Sydney: between West Head Walking Tracks nos. 12 and 13, on western side of West Head Road, signed by blue and white vertical boomerang signpost). One of many sites near Sydney with Aboriginal rock engravings, this site is easy of access and has many footprints (mundoes) – 75 altogether – along with several species of fish, shields and a spiny anteater. The feet may depict a path in a mythological event, or have been part of a ritual. (See Chapter 2)

Queensland: Carnarvon Gorge: hand petroglyphs (The Gorge is in Carnarvon National Park, 600 km west-north-west of Brisbane, and is 35km long). There is rock art, including hands stencilled on to white sandstone, to be seen in the rock shelters known as Art Gallery and Cathedral Cave. Walkways provide visitors with a good viewpoint while also keeping them away from the vulnerable rock art.[2] (See Chapter 2)

Austria

Saint Wolfgang: Church: St Wolfgang's foot, hand and body imprints (The village of Saint Wolfgang is on the shore of Saint Wolfgang lake between Salzburg and Bad

The impressions on the rock inside Saint Wolfgang church, Austria,
said to have been made by contact with the saint's body.
Photo: Andreas Trottmann.

Ischl; the church is above the 'Weisses Roessel Hotel'). The supposed body, hand and foot imprints of the saint are to be seen on a rock inside the church.[4]

Cambodia

Phnom Penh: The Silver Pagoda: Buddha's Footprint (In pagoda compound). The Silver Pagoda is floored with over 5,000 silver tiles and has a 90 kg solid gold Buddha. In the compound is Wat Phnom Mondap housing the Buddha's footprint.[5]

Canada

British Columbia: Prince Rupert: Metlakatla Man (On rock-face on south-west tip of Robertson Point west of Prince Rupert, near the Indian community of Metlakatla on the Tsimpsean 2 Reserve). The Tsimshian Indian tradition records that the human outline on the rock, with depressions marking the places where the head, arms, legs, feet and body would have been, marks the place where a chief fell back to earth after visiting the sky: he would have stayed up there longer, but there was nothing to eat.[6] (See Chapter 8)

174

The Devil's Stone showing his claw marks (Roskilde). Photo: Lars Thomas.

Denmark

Roskilde: The Devil's Stone (Located in a long flowerbed backed by a hedge, at the back of the square known as Staendertorvet, next to the cathedral). This large block of stone has deep striations which are said to have been made by the Devil's claws when he tried to hold on to the stone to stop himself being ejected from the town.[7] (See Chapter 7)

Egypt

Sakha : Jesus' Footprint (Sakha is in the present-day Governate of Kafr El-Sheikh). The Coptic name of the town is Pekha-Issous (or Lysous), meaning 'the foot of Jesus', named after an event during the visit of the Holy Family in their Flight into Egypt. They were thirsty, so Jesus placed his foot on a stone and a water source was discovered beneath it. The mark of Jesus' foot remained on the stone, which disappeared during the 13th century. In 1984, during digging by the main gate of the church, the lost rock was rediscovered, and the footprint is now to be seen in the Virgin Mary Church, where the rock is kept in a glass case.[8] (See Chapter 3)

The Giant's Footprint near Boscawen-un stone circle, Cornwall.
Photo: John L. Hall.

England

Bristol: Pool Farm cist cover (Now displayed in Bristol Museum: Bristol Museums and Art Gallery, Queen's Road, Bristol, BS8 1RL). This stone was the cover slab for a burial cist in the centre of an Early Bronze Age round barrow located at Pool Farm, West Harptree, in the Mendip Hills of Somerset. When first excavated in 1931 the cist was found to contain cremated human bone. The stone slab bears 10 carved cup-marks, and six human feet. They have splayed toes and are not placed in pairs, but scattered around the slab. They are not all the same size, and since the burnt bones found in the cist were of an adult and child, perhaps two of the feet represent those people, with the others also representing people buried in the barrow.[9] (See Chapter 2)

Cheshire: Jenkin Chapel: John Turner Memorial Stone (4 miles north-east of Macclesfield: half a mile north-east of Rainow on the A5002 Macclesfield–Whaley Bridge road, follow lane heading east to Saltersford/Jenkin Chapel, turning left at Blue Boar Farm. When the chapel is reached, the memorial is a short distance up Eurin Lane). The memorial commemorates John Turner, who died in a snowstorm around 1735. A single footprint, apparently made by a woman's shoe, was found in the snow beside the body, a mystery referred to on one side of the memorial stone.[10] (See Chapter 9)

Cornwall: Giant's Footprint (Near Boscawen-un stone circle, 3 miles south-west of Penzance). 'At the end of an old track leading from Boscawen-un Farm a stretch of open moorland rises up to a summit where, on the rocks of Creeg Tol, the farmer points out a large footprint, said to have been made by a giant who stepped there on

King Arthur's Footprint on the clifftop at Tintagel, Cornwall.
Photo: Paul Broadhurst.

his way up country from the Scilly Isles.' (John Michell in *The Old Stones of Land's End*)[11] (See Chapter 8)

Cornwall: Tintagel Castle: King Arthur's Footprint (13 miles north of Bodmin). Since, according to legend, King Arthur was born at Tintagel Castle, it is appropriate that his footprint can still be seen there. It is to be found on the highest point of the southern side of the island on which the ruins stand, facing Glebe Cliff and the parish church. It is a footprint-shaped hollow in the flat slate ridge. Also on the island can be found King Arthur's Seat, King Arthur's Cups and Saucers, and King Arthur's Bed, Elbow Chair or Hip Bath![12] (See Chapter 8)

Cumbria: Kirkby Lonsdale: The Devil's Bridge (10 miles south-east of Kendal). The famous old bridge, at least 700 years old, crosses the River Lune just east of the town. It was said to have been built by the Devil in one of his schemes to enslave more souls, but he was thwarted by an old woman. He left his claw marks on one of the coping stones, looking like parallel scratches.[13] (See Chapter 7)

Gloucestershire: Oddington: foot outlines in old church (Close to the Oxfordshire county boundary, just to the east of Stow-on-the-Wold). St Nicholas' church is along a track half a mile from the village and is well worth a visit even apart from the promise of feet inscribed in the porch. The church has an atmospheric interior, with a wonderful and huge Doom painting.[14]

Gloucestershire: The Tibblestone (At the Teddington Hands roundabout, junction of A453 and A438, 7 miles north of Cheltenham). This 4-foot stone was thrown by a giant who lived on Dixton Hill. His pastime was to throw rocks at ships sailing up the River Severn several miles away, but on this occasion he slipped and the stone fell short. It is said to bear the marks of his fingers. He also left a mark on the hillside where he fell.[15] (See Chaper 8)

Greater Manchester: Smithills Hall: George Marsh's footprint (Inside Smithills Hall, Smithills Dean Road, Bolton, BL1 7NP: Open all year – 1 April to 30 September open Tuesday–Sunday, 1 October to 31 March open Tuesday, Saturday and Sunday afternoons only; admission fee charged). The footprint on a stone slab inside the Hall was said to have been made by George Marsh after being interrogated at the Hall in 1555 about his adherence to the Protestant faith during the reign of a Catholic queen: he stamped his foot on the floor in testimony to his faith. The footprint sometimes appears bloodstained, according to some accounts.[16] (See Chapter 3 and Chapter 9)

Lancashire: Pendle Hill: The Devil's Footprints (Pendle Hill is 4 miles east of Clitheroe; the footprints are at OS map ref. SD 78523922. Best approached from the Nick o' Pendle, where the road from Sabden to Clitheroe crosses the ridge. From there follow the path towards the summit, but just after Apronful Hill – a tumulus also associated with the Devil – turn left and follow the footpath towards the edge of Deerstone Crag. Great care is necessary from here because a narrow path leads down the crag and threads its way through a tumble of loose rocks to where the footprints lie. As you approach, the increasing number of graffiti tells you that you are getting close). The Devil's Footprints are large foot-shaped depressions on a rock among the loose rocks of the Deerstones, made by the Devil when he jumped from Hameldon Hill across to Pendle. One observer noted that he appeared to have crossed his legs as he landed, since the left footprint is on the right side of the rock! One of the footprints is misshapen, said to be because the Devil has a club-foot.[17] (See Chapter 7)

Lincolnshire: Byard's Leap (Near Cranwell, 5 miles north-west of Sleaford). The marks of the hoof-prints of the horse known as Blind Bayard (pronounced Byard) are located on the car park of the Byard's Leap café and adjoining scrubland, near the junction of the A17 and B6403 roads. There is more than one version of the story explaining their presence, but they all involve a witch who terrorised the locality and had to be got rid of. During a knight's attempt to achieve this, she was on the horse's back and when her talons dug into his flesh he reared in agony and made 60-foot leaps, leaving the marks of his hooves on the ground. They are now marked by two sets of horseshoes fixed in the ground about 100m apart. The witch was killed, and buried under a large stone at the crossroads.[18] (See Chapter 6)

Merseyside: Liverpool: Calderstones foot outlines (Located in Harthill Greenhouses, Calderstones Park, Allerton – between Harthill Road, Calderstones Road, Menlove Avenue and Allerton Road). Six large stones from a Neolithic passage grave, which once stood at the mouth of the River Mersey, are decorated with carvings of spirals, cup and ring marks, lozenges – and footprints. Sadly some of the carvings are badly weathered and no longer clear. There are two foot-marks with toes on the front of Stone A, two foot-marks with toes and two partial feet on the front of Stone B (only

Some of the modern shoe outlines on the Calderstones. Photo: John Billingsley.

one foot-mark now visible), three or four foot-marks with toes, some no longer clear, on the rear of Stone E – and in addition on Stone D there are, on the rear face, 7 shoe outlines, probably dating from the 19th century. The recent ones may have been made by boys and men from nearby farms: an old man remembered working at Calderstones Farm as a boy when the stones lay on a roadside mound. He said it was customary for the men to lie in the sun on the stones after work; they would cut their names and initials on the stones as well as their boot outlines.[19] (See Chapter 2)

Norfolk: King's Lynn: Witch's Heart (Above the first-floor window of no.15 Tuesday Market Place). A lozenge-shape on the brick wall above the window contains a heart symbol. This is said to be the place where an alleged witch's heart struck the wall when she was hanged in the square below in 1616. The witch is said to have predicted that her heart would burst from her body at the time of her death, and fly to the window of the magistrate who convicted her.[20] (See Chapter 9)

Norfolk: Tilney All Saints: Giant's Finger-Marks (3 miles south-west of King's Lynn). In the churchyard opposite the church's south door stands Tom Hickathrift's Candlestick – in reality the shaft of an old cross. The five indentations on top are said to be the imprints of the giant Tom Hickathrift's finger and thumb. Inside the church is a stone said to be Tom's gravestone, but extensive building work at the time of my visit (2001) meant it was not possible to enter the church.[21] (See Chapter 8)

Northumberland: Birtley: Devil's Hoof-Prints (Birtley is a couple of miles north-east of Wark, and the location is a mile north of the village at NY 878793, where Holywell Burn crosses the lane: enter the field on your left (west) at that point and look for a rock pillar above the stream and waterfall). On the flat surface of the

The lozenge above the upper window contains the witch's heart. No. 15 Tuesday Market Place, King's Lynn.

Devil's Stone are some holes which are said to be the Devil's hoof-marks, made when he leapt to Lee Hall a couple of miles away across the North Tyne River. Unfortunately for him he did not make it, but fell into a deep section of the river, afterwards known as Leap Crag Pool, where he drowned (wishful thinking!).[22] (See Chapter 7)

Rutland: Barrowden church: foot outlines (The village is about 15 miles west of Peterborough, to the south of the A47). Several shoe outlines can be seen inscribed on the stone seats in the church porch.[23]

Suffolk: Blythburgh church: black dog's claw-marks (10 miles south-west of Lowestoft). On the same day, 4 August 1577, two Suffolk churches experienced a similar event, when a storm arose and a black dog appeared, which ran through the congregation, killing some of them as he did so. At Blythburgh, clear burn marks on the inside of the wooden door at the rear of the church were said to have been made by the black dog's claws as he quitted the church. The church is worth visiting for its own sake, being one of Suffolk's finest.[24] (See Chapter 6)

West Yorkshire: Cow and Calf Rocks, Rombalds Moor: Giant's Footprint (1 mile south-east of Ilkley town centre, close to minor road leading to Burley). An impression like a human footprint can be seen on the face of the Cow. The story is that it was made by Rombald, the giant who once frequented these moors: one day,

180

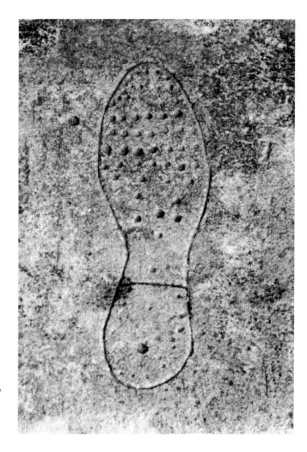

One of the shoe outlines to be seen in the porch of Barrowden church, Rutland.

while stepping from 'Almias Cliff' across the valley, his foot slipped, leaving his footprint. Or he was striding to Almescliffe Crag, and rock basins to be seen there are the footprints he made.[26] (See Chapter 8)

West Yorkshire: Great Rock (Devil's Rock), Stansfield: The Devil's Hoof-Print (2 miles west of Hebden Bridge, beside lane from Blackshaw Head to Cross Stone, Todmorden: OS ref. 960263). The Devil left his hoof-print on this rock when he stepped here from Stoodley Pike: his foot slipped and the rock cracked open.[27] (See Chapter 7)

France

Brittany

Finistère: Dirinon: St Non's Well (4 miles south-west of Landerneau: the well is by the side of a lane just to the south of the village of Dirinon). Close to the well is a stone marked with St Non's knee-prints, where she knelt to pray. A later version of the legend has her giving birth to St David here, and lying the new-born baby in a hollow above her knee-marks. St Non died at Dirinon and her tomb lies in a chapel beside the church.[28] (See Chapter 5)

Above:*The hill of Mont-Dol, where St Michael and Satan both left their marks.*
Opposite: *St Michael's footprint on Mont-Dol.*
Photos: Andreas Trottmann.

Ille-et-Vilaine: Mont-Dol: Site of struggle between St Michael and the Devil (Just to the north of Dol-de-Bretagne: summit of mound reached from Mont-Dol church along a steep road with a hairpin bend). During the epic struggle, St Michael threw Satan to the ground so hard that he made a depression in the rock and scratched it with his claw (sited to north of chapel Notre-Dame de l'Esperance). He made a hole in the hill with one blow of his sword and threw the Devil into it (Satan's hole to east of church). But he was not vanquished and reappeared again on Mont-St-Michel and mocked St Michael, so the saint leapt from Mont-Dol to Mont-St-Michel, leaving his footprint on a rock (to the south-east of the chapel)[29]. (See Chapters 4 and 7)

Morbihan: Carnac Museum. Here can be seen a cast of an elaborately carved stone from Petit-Mont passage-grave at Arzon (18 km south-west of Vannes), which once boasted some of the best prehistoric carvings in Brittany. Among meandering lines, cupmarks and other designs are two feet, side by side, with the toes at the top. Being located at a burial site, this carving may have had some connection with early beliefs about death.[30] (See Chapter 2)

Morbihan: Ile de Saint-Cado, Belz: St Cado's Slide (Roughly midway between Lorient and Auray). The *île* is a tiny islet linked to the mainland by a causeway, which was said to have been constructed by the Devil. He expected in payment the soul of the first person to cross, but St Cado sent over a cat instead. This annoyed the Devil, who seemed to be about to destroy the causeway, so St Cado rushed to stop him and slipped, leaving on a rock the mark of his foot, which became known as the *Glissade de St Cado* (St Cado's Slide). The mark can now be seen on a flat rock

Left: *St Cado's Slide, Ile de Saint-Cado,where the saint slipped and left the mark of his foot on the rock.*

Opposite *The statue of St Gildas near Saint-Gildas-de-Rhuys, below which are his well and his horse's hoof-print.*

outcrop by the calvary, which is located on the open area just before walking on to the causeway.[31] (See Chapter 4)

Morbihan: Noyal-Pontivy: Les Trois Fontaines (3 miles east of Pontivy; the wells are about a mile to the north of the small town of Noyal-Pontivy: follow the road to St Noyale but take a right turn (signed) before getting there). At the edge of the trees which are above the elaborate well structure at Les Trois Fontaines is St Noyale's prie-dieu or prayer stool, a stone with two hollows which were said to be the saint's knee-prints, where she would kneel to pray. Her bed, a larger flatter rock, is also close by.[32] (See Chapter 5)

Morbihan: Saint-Gildas-de-Rhuys: St Gildas' horse's hoof-print (17 miles south of Vannes). St Gildas spent some of his life here, and his tomb (now empty) is behind the high altar in the town church, where there are also reliquaries containing some of his bones. One of his legends tells how he had to fight a monstrous snake that was in fact Satan in one of his disguises. St Gildas vanquished him by hiding a needle in a ball of wool, the needle piercing the snake's throat when he tried to swallow the wool. At this point, Gildas mounted his horse and holding on to the wool he dragged the snake to Grand-Mont on the seashore. Here his horse made a mighty leap in the direction of the island of Houat, and as they sailed above the sea, St Gildas let go of the wool, so that the snake fell into the sea. His horse's hoof-print can still be seen

The Devil's Footprint in the Frauenkirche, Munich. Photo: Dr Elmar R. Gruber.

on the cliffs by walking along the clifftop in a westerly direction about half a mile to the Pointe du Grand-Mont. There are steps down the cliff to a statue of St Gildas, his well, and the hoof-print, which is a hollow in a rock at ground level in front of the well.[33] (See Chapter 6)

Normandy

Seine-Maritime: Fécamp: Trinity Church: Angel's Footprint (Between Le Havre and Dieppe). There are two important relics in the Church of the Trinity (*Eglise de la Trinité*): the blood of Jesus Christ, and the footprint of the angel who brought it there. The *Pas de l'Ange* can be seen inside the Chapelle de la Dormition. The angel left his footprint as a testimony, after having commanded the assembly of bishops to consecrate the church to the Trinity.[34]

Germany

Harz Mountains: Rosstrappe: Bodo's horse's hoof-print (The Rosstrappe is a granite rock that towers 1200 feet over the Bode valley near the town of Thale; there is a tourist footpath from Thale, the walk taking about an hour. Precise details obtainable from the Thale Tourist Information Office). On top of the rock is a so-called horse's hoof-print, made when the Princess Brunhilde's horse leapt across the gorge from the Hexentanzplatz to the Rosstrappe. She was being chased by the knight Bodo, who

The Hari ka Pairi ghat at Hardwar: The small temple on the left contains the stone with Vishnu's footprints.
Photo: Dr Elmar R. Gruber.

wanted to marry her and ignored her refusal. She landed safely on the other side, but when Bodo followed, he fell into the valley and turned into a black dog. He is still there, guarding the princess's crown which fell from her head during the jump.[35] Anyone visiting this location should be warned that the area is a witches' paradise: Hexentanzplatz means Witches' Dance Floor, and the site has been converted into a tourist attraction on the theme of witchcraft; also on the hill is the Walpurgishalle, a museum about witchcraft in the Harz Mountains.[36] (See Chapter 6)

Munich: Frauenkirche: Devil's Footprint (The Frauenkirche or Church of Our Lady is on Frauenplatz: the footprint is in the stone floor just inside the main entrance). The Devil is said to have come to see the building when it was completed, and he stood on that spot and stamped on the floor with delight when he couldn't see any windows, which he thought had been omitted in error. In fact the church does have windows, but none can be seen from that point. Another version of the legend says that there was a bet between the church architect and the Devil, the architect betting that he could build the church so that from one position no windows could be seen. He won his bet – and the Devil stamped his foot in rage at having lost.[37] (See Chapter 7)

India

Gaya: Vishnupada Temple: Vishnu's Footprints (Bihar, eastern India). An exposed rock inside the temple carved with Vishnu's footprints is set in a silver basin. It is the main object of worship within the temple, which may only be entered by Hindus.[38] (See Chapter 3)

Hardwar: Hari ka Pairi: Vishnu's Footprints (Uttar Pradesh, northern India). The Hari ka Pairi ghat, where most pilgrims come to bathe in the Ganges, is at the north end of town. A small temple stands over the stone which bears Vishnu's footprints, right by the waterside at the bottom of the steps: the temple bears the name 'Vishnu Feet'.[39] (See Chapter 3)

Kashmir: Srinagar: Jesus's Footprints ('The tomb of the prophet Yuz Asaf [Jesus] is in the middle of what is today Srinagar's old town, in Anzimar in the Khanjar quarter.

The footprints of Jesus at Srinagar: a plaster cast of the original prints found inside the shrine. Photo: Dr Elmar R. Gruber.

The building…is called "Rozabal"'). Jesus is said to have lived in India for many years: he did not die at the Crucifixion but went to live in the Near East and later in India, where he died an old man. In the building housing the grave of the prophet Yuz Asaf, who is believed to be the same as Jesus, his is the larger of two gravestones, and close by is a stone carved with the footprints of Jesus. These were discovered under layers of old wax from worshippers' candles. The scars of the crucifixion wounds had also been carved on the feet. Moslem, Hindu, Buddhist and Christian pilgrims visit the tomb in their thousands each year.[40] (See Chapter 3)

Iran

Mahmudabad: Shrine of Qadamgah (28 km from Nishapur). The shrine is 'on a small hill reached by a wide, shady turning on the left (north), in the middle of the village [Mahmudabad]' and 'contains what is believed by the faithful to be the footprints of the ninth century saint, Imam Reza.'[41] (See Chapter 3)

Ireland

Co. Antrim: Magheramully: St Patrick's Foot-Mark (At the site of the ruined Skerry church in Magheramully, which is 3 miles ENE of Broughshane: the church is said to be on the site of the home of Miliuc, to whom Patrick was sold as a slave). A hollow in a stone is identified as St Patrick's Foot-Mark, though confusingly it is also said to be the mark of the toe of the Angel Victor, made when he rose to Heaven after visiting Patrick.[42] (See Chapter 3)

Co. Cork: Coolineagh: St Ólann's Footprints (Coolineagh is 4.25 miles NW of Coachford: St Ólann's Stone is to be found 150 yards north of the ancient ruined church of Aghabulloge). The church was founded by St Ólann (Eólang), who was a teacher of St Finn Bárr of Cork. His stone is a boulder with the imprint of the saint's feet on it, and is one of three features to be seen here that are named for the saint. The others are St Ólann's Cap (a lump of quartzite on top of an ogham pillarstone, used to cure female complaints and headaches, and as a swearing stone) and St Ólann's Well. All three features are visited by pilgrims on the saint's day, 5 September.[43] (See Chapter 5)

Co. Derry: Derry: St Colum's Knee-Prints (In calvary outside Long Tower Church, south-west of Bishop's Gate). The knee-prints are two oval depressions or bullauns on St Colum's Stone, caused by St Columcille kneeling on it all the time. It was built into the calvary outside the church in 1898, and bears an inscription: 'This stone was removed from the street in 1897, near St Columba's Well [also known as The Three Holy Wells], where it had been for centuries. In 1898 it was solemnly enshrined on this Calvary to which our Holy Father, Leo XIII, has been pleased to attach many indulgences, both plenary and partial.'[44]

Co. Dublin: Skerries: St Patrick's Footprint (At the 'Springboards' swimming area, Red Island: on the north side of the concrete platform, an indentation in the rock is said to be the saint's footprint). When St Patrick was expelled from Wicklow he sailed north and landed on what became known as St Patrick's Island off Skerries. He had a goat which gave him milk, but when he was on the mainland making converts, people from Skerries stole his goat and ate it. Patrick was angry to discover what had happened. He stepped to the mainland in two strides, one to Colt Island, the second to Red Island. The people could only bleat when they tried to deny having killed the goat, but their normal voices returned once they told the truth. The people of Skerries were nicknamed Skerries Goat as a reminder of the event, and St Patrick's Footprint is permanently visible at Red Island. There is a also a bronze goat's head in St Patrick's Church, commissioned in 1989 to celebrate the 50th anniversary of the church, and to give St Patrick his goat back.[45] (See Chapter 5)

Co. Kildare: Colbinstown: Hound's paw-print (In the ancient cemetery of Killeen Cormac, in Colbinstown, 3.5 miles SW of Dunlavin (Co. Wicklow)). This was said to be the burial place of King Cormac of Munster. Because of a dispute about the site, the corpse was hitched up to a team of oxen and they were left to carry it unguided. When they reached Colbinstown, a hound leapt from a nearby hill to a stone in the cemetery, leaving its paw-print to mark the site of the king's grave. King Cormac's Grave comprises two pillarstones, one of which has two lines on it and the paw-print. There are also other ancient inscribed stones in the cemetery.[46] (See Chapter 6)

Co. Kilkenny: Kilcolumb: Cloch Cholaim (Colm's Stone) (6 miles NE of Waterford (Co. Waterford) are the remains of Kilcolumb church: the stone is 50 yards north of the church). The bullauns on this boulder were said to be the marks left by St Colm's head and knees, and people would visit the stone in search of a cure for a headache.[47] (See Chapter 4)

Co. Louth: Faughart: St Brigid's Shrine (3 miles north of Dundalk). The saint is believed to have looked after her father's animals here (he was a pagan chief) and when he wanted her to marry, she refused and took out one of her eyes. The story is recorded in three stones by the stream: one has her knee-prints where she knelt while praying for guidance; one has a recess where she placed her eye, and also bears her angry suitor's whip mark; and the third carries the impression of the suitor's horse's hoof-mark, made as he rode away.[48] (See Chapter 4)

Co. Roscommon: Oran: St Patrick's Well and knee-prints (About 7.5 miles north-west of Roscommon; on left before Oran graveyard and round tower). Pilgrims follow a course beginning at St Patrick's Bush where they pick up seven pebbles; they then walk seven times round the well, each time dropping a pebble by the bush. They end the sequence by kneeling on the stone with the knee prints.[49] (See Chapter 5)

Co. Sligo: Tobernalt Well: St Patrick's finger imprints (East of Sligo town by Lough Gill). Just below the well is a healing stone where people with back pain lie seeking a cure. Four indentations on top of the stone were said to be the marks of Patrick's fingers: it is believed that you can acquire power from the saint by placing your fingers in the marks.[50] (See Chapter 5)

Co. Tipperary: Ballyard: St Cominad's Bed (Ballyard is 3 miles NNW of Newport, and the saint's bed is at the ancient church of Kilcommenty). The 'bed' is actually a boulder marked with bullauns, and other impressions which have been interpreted as the marks of St Cominad's ribs and hands.[51]

Israel

Jerusalem: Mount of Olives: Christ's Footprint (in the Mosque of the Ascension). This site has been in Muslim possession since 1198. Marking the place where Jesus Christ ascended into Heaven, a right footprint, said to be his, can be seen inside the mosque, surrounded by a small rectangle. One guidebook comments that, over a period of time, 'the footprint has been so variously described that it must have been frequently renewed'.[52] However, this may be because pilgrims in the Byzantine period were allowed to take fragments away as souvenirs/relics. The left footprint was taken to the el-Aksa mosque in the Middle Ages.[53] (See Chapter 3)

Jerusalem: Convent of the Olive Tree: scourging stone (In the Armenian Quarter). The stone where Jesus was tied while being scourged is built into the north-east corner of the chapel of Deir el-Zeitouneh, and the shallow cavity is the mark of his elbow.[54] (See Chapter 3)

Italy

Genoa: Mandylion of Edessa (In the Church of St Bartolomeo degli Armeni, Piazza S. Bartolomeo degli Armeni, 2). This cloth bearing Christ's image was said to have been sent by him to King Abgar of Edessa after the king had invited him to visit Edessa. He had heard of Christ's reputation as a healer and hoped to be cured of his ailments. Christ washed and dried his face, leaving his image on the towel, which he sent to the king, who was cured and became a convert to Christianity.[55] (See Chapter 3)

Rome: Church of Domine Quo Vadis?: Christ's Footprints (Beyond the ancient walls, on the Appian Way). This church was built in the 9th century at the place where Peter had his vision of Christ. At the entrance is a copy of the stone with Christ's footprints, the original of which can be seen in the Basilica of San Sebastiano.[56] (See Chapter 3)

Rome: Church of Santa Francesca Romana: Knee-prints of St Peter and St Paul (Forum: near the Colosseum). When the magician Simon Magus was attempting to prove that his magic was stronger than that of St Peter, he jumped from a high tower and floated down, held by demonic power. St Peter and St Paul knelt together and prayed that the demons should release him, which indeed happened and he fell to his death. The paving stone with the marks made by their knees is kept in the Silices Apostolorum, in the wall of the transept, behind two small gates.[57] (See Chapter 5)

Rome: Basilica of Santa Sabina (Aventino): Devil's finger-marks. A stone with the Devil's finger-marks is still to be seen in this church. It is a black stone, on the left, seen when entering the church. The Devil threw it at St Dominic, angered by his devotion. It was blackened by contact with his burning hand, and three holes were made in it by the flames from his fingers. Some unknown force stopped it from touching St Dominic.[58] (See Chapter 7)

Rome: Basilica of San Sebastiano fuori le Mura: Christ's Footprints (Beyond the ancient walls, outside the Porta S. Sebastiano). In the Chapel of Relics can be seen the stone with the original footprints of Christ, which were made when he met Peter on the Appian Way.[59] (See Chapter 3)

Rome: Museum of the Souls of the Dead (Museo delle Anime dei Defunti): burned finger-marks (In Church of Santa Cuore in Suffragio, Lungotevere Prati 12). This is a small museum housing all kinds of articles that have burn marks on them supposedly made by souls in Purgatory: Bibles, hats, garments, a pillow, etc. This strange collection of scorched finger-marks has been collected from various locations in Europe.[60] (See Chapter 3)

Turin: Cathedral: The Shroud of Turin (In the Cathedral – Duomo San Giovanni – on Piazza San Giovanni, off Via XX Settembre). The shroud preserved in Turin is believed by many to have been Christ's shroud and to bear his miraculous image. Despite many tests, its antiquity has not been conclusively disproved. The actual

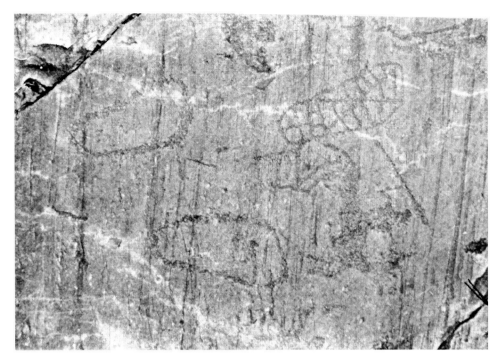

One of the rock faces carved with footprints at Naquane.
Photo: Andreas Trottmann.

shroud is rarely taken from its protective casket, but a replica is on display.[61] (See Chapter 3)

Val Camonica: Naquane: rock art (In the Lombard Alps north of Brescia). Val Camonica is an 80-km-long valley famed for its prehistoric rock art: it is a Unesco World Heritage Site. Naquane is the National Park of Engraved Rocks near Capo di Ponte (15 minutes away on foot) where there are 104 engraved rocks, with foot and hand engravings among the designs. (Closed on Mondays; access fee.) (See Chapter 2)

Lithuania

Sarnele: Devil's Footprint (Sarnele is a hamlet 8 km south-west of Seda, in north-west Lithuania). On the northern hillside of the Sacred Grove Hill in Mikytai Sacred Grove is a large boulder that has what is said to be the Devil's footprint upon it.[62]

Myanmar (Burma)

Yangon (Rangoon): Shwedagon Pagoda: Buddha's Footprint. This elaborate pagoda, a major pilgrimage site, houses some of the most important relics of the Buddha, such as hairs from his beard and a tooth. In a shrine to the Buddha a huge carved footprint is to be seen in front of the Buddha image.

*The Buddha footprint at the
Shwedagon pagoda.
Photo: Dr Elmar R. Gruber.*

Scotland

Aberdeenshire: Giant's Stone, Scurdargue (Near Rhynie, 30 miles NW of Aberdeen; exact location is at OS ref. no. NJ 482290, 2 miles NW of Rhynie, south side of Tap o' Noth, Scurdargue). There is the faint impression of a boot on the stone, said to be something to do with a fight between two giants.[63] (See Chapter 8)

Argyll and Bute: Dunadd: Inauguration stone (3 miles NW of Lochgilphead; Dunadd is signposted on the A816). This Dark Age fort is located on top of a rocky hill surrounded by flat marshland. On the north-west side of the hill can be found several intriguing rock carvings. There is a carved boar, an inscription in ogham, a hollow basin, and a footprint. The last two were probably used in ceremonies to inaugurate kings, of Dalriada and this is one of the few remaining inauguration footprints.[64] (See Chapter 2)

Argyll and Bute: Kilneuair church: Devil's hand-print (At the southern end of Loch Awe; the ruined church is just south of the B840). A tailor was being chased by the Devil, who left his hand-print behind: this is one of several places where the events have been located, but there is a mark in the church which purports to be the Devil's hand-print. Its precise location is 'on the inside face of the south wall on the left side of a former door.'[65] (See Chapter 7)

The footprint used for inauguration of kings of Dalriada at Dunadd fort.

Finlay Munro's footprints as they were in late 2000. Photo: Andreas Trottmann.

Argyll and Bute: St Columba's footprints (On the southern tip of Kintyre, 8 miles south of Campbeltown). St Columba is believed to have landed on the Scottish mainland at Keil Point, and there is a 13th-century ruined chapel dedicated to him about half a mile to the east. By the chapel is a small hillock, on top of which is a rock with two footprints said to be St Columba's. However one is at right-angles to the other, and both appear to be right feet! [66] (See Chapter 4)

Fife: St Andrews: Patrick Hamilton's face (On the tower of St Salvator's College, in North Street). A stone on the tower, about 24 courses up, has on it what looks like a face. This is said to be Patrick Hamilton, burned to death as a Protestant martyr in the early 16th century in front of the College in North Street. His face burned itself into the stone 'by the psychic power of his martyrdom'.[67] (See Chapter 9)

Highland: Glen Moriston: Finlay Munro's footprints (1 km SW of Dundreggan on A887: behind a prominent cairn opposite a layby before bend and bridge over River Moriston). The footprints were in soft ground, and were said to have been made by a travelling preacher called Finlay Munro early in the 19th century. The story was that he was preaching one day on the text of Amos 4:12 when some local boys (or some Catholics, depending on which source you read) disputed his words and called him a liar. He replied: 'As a proof that I am telling the truth, my footprints will forever bear witness on this very ground I stand on.' The cairn was built by visiting pilgrims who all added stones to it, and it was customary to stand in the prints: people reported that the hair on the back of your neck would stand up when you did so. Unfortunately the footprints were vandalised in the early 1990s – but the latest information I have is that they are returning, and so the location may still be worth

*The Ladykirk Stone bearing
St Magnus's footprints.
Photo: Jane and Ian Hemming.*

visiting. Apparently they have always returned following earlier destruction.[68] (See Chapter 3)

Orkney Islands: South Ronaldsay: Ladykirk Stone (St Magnus's Boat) (In the old St Mary's church at Burwick; key held by Mrs Nicolson at the Post Office about 3 miles away). The church is no longer used for services, and is described as 'sad' by my visiting friends, but in 2001 they were able to find the stone bearing St Magnus's footprints in the vestry 'surrounded by dusty old pews'. It is traditionally said to be the stone on which St Magnus sailed over the Pentland Firth when he couldn't find a more conventional boat.[69] (See Chapter 4)

Shetland Islands: Clickhimin: Inauguration stone (Less than a mile south-west of Lerwick on Mainland; signposted). This complex site on a promontory in the Loch of Clickhimin was occupied as a dwelling place in prehistoric times and later, and the surviving remains are of a broch and blockhouse. A stone with a pair of footprints is located at the threshold of the small outermost gateway at the end of the causeway, though this may not have been its original site. It was probably an inauguration stone.[70] (See Chapter 2)

Sri Lanka

Adam's Peak (Sri Pada): Buddha's Footprint (The conical mountain 7,360 feet high is in southern Sri Lanka, to the east of Colombo: the 'toilsome' climb to the top where the footprint is situated takes several hours). Buddha left his left footprint on Adam's Peak and strode in one step across to Thailand where he left his right footprint at Phra Sat. On top of the peak, broad steps lead to a walled enclosure containing the rock where Buddha's footprint is to be found: it is nearly 6 feet long because Buddha was 35 feet tall! To the Muslims it is Adam's footprint, to the Christians it is St Thomas's or Jesus's footprint, and to the Hindus it is Siva's footprint.[71] (See Chapter 3)

Footprints at Gladsax. Photo: Klaus Aarsleff.

Sweden

Gladsax: Bronze Age petroglyphs (2 miles west of Simrishamn in southern Sweden is the small town of Jarrestad. At the church, go north on the road towards the hamlet of Gladsax. About 1 mile north of Jarrestad the petroglyphs will be found on the lefthand side of the road (west): there is a sign at the roadside and the carvings are about 300 yards from the road. Petroglyphs are called *hallristningar* in Sweden). Scandinavia is rich in Bronze Age rock art, and one of the symbols often found is the human foot. Its meaning in this context is uncertain, but it may symbolise the journey to the next world, and hence act as a protection against the return of the dead. Gladsax is a good place to see petroglyphs of footprints, there being many at this site.[72] (See Chapter 2)

Switzerland [73]

Ardez: Hexenplatten (Witches' Stone) (Above the village of Ardez beside the old road to the village of Bos-cha, and easy to find: map ref. 810075/184300). The surface of the rock is covered with cup-marks, which folklore explains as the marks made by their broom handles as witches danced on the rock. There are also some possible footprints to be seen.

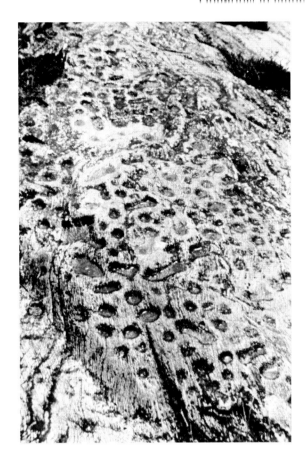

The Hexenplatten where the witches danced and left the marks of their broom handles. Photo: Andreas Trottmann.

Col du Pillon: Pierre-aux-fées (Fairies' Stone) footprints (On left of mountain pass road from alpine village of Les Diablerets to the Col du Pillon. The rock is in a field a little above the old footpath to the pass, on private property, and difficult to find. Enquire in one of the nearby mountain huts. The site is named on the map as 'Fenil Durand': map ref: 580535/133200). There are numerous small feet carved on the rock surface, and it may be that the discovery of naturally-formed 'feet' caused people to carve more. (See Chapter 9)

Garbela (Poschiavo): St Romerio's Footprint (After the Lago di Poschiavo, towards the town of Tirano, continue to the village of Piazzo and turn left on to mountain road to the hamlet of Garbela. Aim for the huge telecommunication mast, and park beside local grotto (restaurant). The prominent rock is easy to find, about 100 metres north of the mast: map ref. 806050/128000). There are cupmarks on the rock as well as the 26 cm long footprint said to be that of St Romerio.

Grimentz: Pirra Martera footprints (From the town of Fierre enter the Val d'Anniviers as far as Vissoie, then proceed to the charming car-free village of Grimentz. The stone is located, along with several cup-marked rocks, at a picnic site below a large parking area, and is easy to find: map ref. 610105/113240). The footprints, two side by side, are deep and easily identifiable.

Right: *St Romerio's Footprint.*

Below: *The Pirra Martera footprints.*

Photos: Andreas Trottmann.

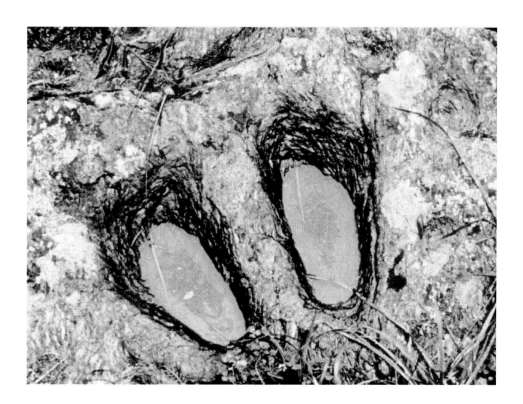

Stampa: Ciäsa Grande: Footprint stones (The village of Stampa is in the Bregaglia, a secluded valley between St Moritz and Chiavenna (Italy), and the stones are in the Ciäsa Grande museum). There are three stones with footprints to be seen here, one with fourteen footprints being the most impressive.

The Buddha footprint at Lamphun. Photo: Andreas Trottmann.

Thailand

Lamphun: Buddha's Footprint (670 km from Bangkok, 26 km from Chiang Mai – the Wat (monastery) is on a hilltop by Route 106 and is signposted). The main Wat houses a Buddha footprint.[74]

Samui: The Lord Buddha's Footprint (Samui is an island in the Gulf of Thailand south of Bangkok. Shrine not signposted: go up concrete slope on left, 2 km west of turn-off for Butterfly Garden on route 4170). The shrine containing the footprint is 150 steps up a steep hill. It actually consists of four footprints superimposed one on top of another.[75] (See Chapter 3)

Saraburi: Wat Phra Buddhabat: The Shrine of the Buddha's Footprint (140 km north of Bangkok: footprint is on a rocky outcrop about 25 km north of the town of Saraburi). There are several Buddha footprint temples in Thailand, but this is the most important. The footprint, which was discovered in the early 17th century, is covered by a pavilion called a *mondop*, with a canopy covered in gold and mirrors over the footprint itself. There are many other features of interest in the temple complex, including a cave with a seated Buddha, and assorted shrines: the temple and the footprint are popular with pilgrims.[76] (See Chapter 3)

Ukraine

Pochaev monastery: Our Lady's Footprint (the 'stopa') (Pochaev is a mountain-top monastery 20 km from Kremenetz in the southern Ukraine: the footprint is in a silver shrine in the largest of the monastery churches). A shepherd and two hermit-monks living in caves on the mountain saw a pillar of light and a vision of the Mother of God, some time in the 13th century. She left her right footprint on a rock, and afterwards a spring began to flow from it. Pilgrims came to visit it, and to use the water for healing purposes. Mary appeared again in 1675 when the monastery was besieged by the Turkish army. She appeared in answer to the monks' prayers, surrounded by angels with drawn swords, high above the church. The Turks shot at the angels, but they sent the arrows back, killing many of the soldiers and saving the monastery. An icon of The Mother of God Our Lady of Pochaev shows her footprint on the rock.[77] (See Chapter 5)

United States of America

California: Hollywood: stars' footprints (At Grauman's Chinese Theatre's Forecourt of Stars' Footprints, 6925 Hollywood Boulevard, Hollywood). All the major movie stars (for example Judy Garland, John Wayne, Frank Sinatra) have been immortalised in wet cement – usually their shoe-prints are present, but sometimes other trademarks have been imprinted, like Groucho Marx's cigar, Gene Autry's horse Champion's hoof-prints, Betty Grable's legs, R2D2's tread marks, Jimmy Durante's and Bob Hope's noses – but Marilyn Monroe's bottom and Jane Russell's top were not allowed.[78]

California: Willow Creek – China Flat Museum: Bigfoot footprints (Willow Creek is in north-west California, near the intersection of Route 299 and Route 96 in Humboldt County. The museum is open April – October, Friday – Sunday, and by appointment the rest of the year; admission free). In 1998 a new wing was built to house the collection of Bigfoot/Sasquatch research material (footprint casts, notes, photographs, etc) acquired during 40 years of research by the late Bob Titmus. Good examples of Bigfoot footprints (casts and photographs) can be seen in the museum.[79] (See Chapter 10)

Illinois: Shawnee National Forest: Gorham Bluff petroglyphs (in southern Illinois: 'Exit I-57 west on 13. Stay on 13 after it becomes 149. At Grimsby, turn south (left) on 3 to Gorham. Go west (right) on the first road past the bridge before the bluff ['an enormous, imposing bluff', standing alone on the horizon]. Turn left (south) at the first road west of the bluff. Stay on this unmarked road leading to the last house (white) before a large field, 500 feet past the house. Park the car and enter through the high weeds. Continue straight east, to the bluff. If you have not found the large movie screen-like setting for the petroglyphs, walk a few paces along the base of the bluff in either direction.') Here on the impressive Gorham Bluff are said to be the finest and oldest petroglyphs in the Midwest: along with hands are crosses within circles, and birds – child-sized palm-prints merge with birds in flight. A half-man

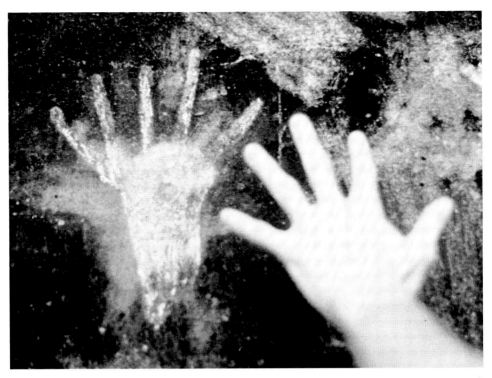

One of the hands to be seen at Gorham bluff. Photo: Frank Joseph

half-bird creature can be seen on the Rock of the Shaman: this is a powerful place with a 'lingering spiritual potency'.[80]

Massachusetts: Ipswich: Devil's Footprint (On Meetinghouse Green, in front of the First Church – which is the sixth on this site). The legend explaining the footprint on a rock in front of the church is that the evangelist George Whitfield confronted the Devil some time in the mid-17th century and they wrestled together, gradually moving upwards until they found themselves on the highest pinnacle. They each tried to push the other off, and the preacher won, throwing the Devil to the ground, whereupon he bounded away down the hill, leaving the mark of his cloven hoof on the rock.[81] (See Chapter 7)

New Mexico: Chaco Canyon National Historical Park: petroglyphs (The 35,000-acre park is south of Bloomfield: Route 57 crosses the park north–south). One of the many petroglyph sites is Atlatl Cave, which may have been occupied 4,000 years ago. Among the rock paintings in the cave are hand-prints: other symbols include spiral designs. One painting has a star and crescent with a hand-print over it, possibly depicting the sighting of the Crab Nebula supernova in AD 1054.[82]

North Carolina: Bath: The Devil's Hoof-Prints (From Greenville, 35 miles east on U.S. 264, 6 miles SE on S.R.92). The hoof-prints, 6 inches wide and 2 inches deep, are to be found 'on the old Cutlar farm' a mile west of Bath. Despite their designation

A section of Newspaper Rock, showing some of the hands and feet,
including a good example of one with six toes.

as the Devil's Hoof-Prints, according to the tale they were made by a horse ridden by
Jesse Elliot when he was racing the Devil and was thrown and killed. They carry an
aura of strangeness: it is said that nothing will grow in the depressions, and they have
remained unchanged since they were made in the early 19th century.[83] (See
Chapter 6)

Texas: Glen Rose: Creation Evidence Museum: anomalous footprints in rock (The
museum was established in 1984 'for the purpose of research, excavation, and
display of scientific evidence for creation'. It is currently housed in a temporary
facility while funds are raised to complete the permanent museum building). 86
human footprints have been excavated in Cretaceous limestone along the Paluxy
River, some in conjunction with dinosaur footprints, suggesting that humans lived
alongside dinosaurs. Among the artefacts housed at the museum are the Burdick
Track (a human footprint), the Meister Track (a fossil footprint found in Utah in
1968), and a handprint in stone.[84] (See Chapter 2)

Utah: Newspaper Rock State Park Monument: petroglyphs ('Take U.S. 91 out of
Moab, Utah, travelling 40 miles south, and take a right (or go west) on Route 211.
Drive 36 miles into the park.'). There are several hundred carvings on the cliff face
known as Newspaper Rock, some dating back 1500 years. Among them can be seen
hands and feet, some of the latter having six toes.[85]

Carreg Pumpsaint.

Wales

Carmarthenshire: Pumpsaint – Carreg Pumpsaint: The Stone of the Five Saints (6 miles outh-east of Lampeter; by the entrance to the Dolaucothi gold mines). Close to the car park for the mines, on a patch of mown grass beside a lane, stands a lone upright stone with large hollows around it. This stone illustrates a strange story of five Celtic saints who sheltered in one of the mine tunnels during a storm and slept with their heads on a stone pillow, thus forming the hollows.[56] (See Chapter 4)

Denbighshire: Corwen: Owain Glyndwr's Footprint (8 miles west of Llangollen). There are numerous links to the famous Welsh warrior in the Corwen area. The town of Corwen sits in the valley of the River Dee, immediately below the northern edge of the Berwyn Mountains. The footprint is to be found on a hill known as Pen-y-Pigyn that looks down on the church, so there is a climb involved to get to it. If you are standing in the main street (the A5 road) facing the entrance to the church, you will see the Post Office to your right. Walk towards it, and follow the lane that heads uphill immediately after the Post Office. When the lane ends follow the footpath into the woods: it gradually curves round to the left, climbing all the way. Follow the path and steps uphill until you reach the memorial and viewpoint, which is known as

The carving on Corwen church that has been interpreted as a mark left by Owain Glyndwr's dagger.

Glyndwr's Seat. The footprint is on a flat stone slab to your left, beside the path, just as you reach the memorial. Owain Glyndwr is said to have thrown his dagger at the church from his Seat, and the mark it made (actually a carved cross) can still be seen above the church's south door.[87] (See Chapter 8)

Denbighshire: Loggerheads: King Arthur's Horse's Hoof-Print (On the A494 Mold–Ruthin road, 3 miles south-west of Mold). On the north side of the road just before you reach the Country Park at Loggerheads is a structure marking the Denbighshire/Flintshire boundary and underneath it at ground level is a stone with a round hollow in it. This is Carreg Carn March Arthur (the stone of Arthur's horse's hoof) and the hollow is the hoof-mark made by King Arthur's horse when it leapt from Moel Fammau. The summit of this hill with its ruined tower can be seen as the highest point on the line of hills on the skyline.[88] (See Chapter 6)

Gwynedd: Aberdyfi: Carn March Arthur: Arthur's Horse's Hoof-Print (3 miles north-east of Aberdyfi: A circular walk of 2.5 miles begins at a car park in Happy Valley and passes through Tyddyn-y-Briddell Farm before heading up into the hills towards Llyn Barfog; the return route overlooking the Dovey/Dyfi estuary passes the hoof-print). King Arthur killed a monster that lived in the 'bearded' lake (Llyn Barfog); the rock with his horse's hoof-print is said to mark the place where his horse took off when it leapt across the wide estuary of the River Dovey/Dyfi while carrying King

In an alcove at the bottom of the county boundary marker at Loggerheads is a stone with a hollow said to be the imprint of King Arthur's horse's hoof.

Arthur to safety from his pursuing enemies. The hoof-print would be difficult to find without the aid of an upright stone bearing the words 'Carn March Arthur' (Arthur's horse's hoof) which has been erected right beside the flat rock which carries the hoof-print.[89] (See Chapter 6)

Gwynedd: Maentwrog church: St Twrog's Stone (Maentwrog village is 4 miles south-west of Blaenau Ffestiniog). The large stone, which gives its name to the village, stands to the left of the entrance to the church porch, and indentations on top were said to have been made by the saint's fingers when he threw it here from a nearby hill. Inside the church is a stained-glass window showing the saint standing with his hand on the stone.[90] (See Chapter 5)

Pembrokeshire: St Davids: The Devil's Footprints (Located in the cathedral grounds). The cathedral is sited in a hollow, and as you approach down the long flight of steps you will see that the path curves round to the left towards the entrance door to the cathedral. The footprints are carved on a gravestone which is lying flat on the ground, surrounded by closely mown grass, alongside the south wall of the cathedral, opposite the steps. They were said to have been made by the Devil when he was pushed off the cathedral roof by St David.[91] (See Chapter 7)

The Twrog Stone with indentations on top left by the saint's fingers.

Pembrokeshire: St Govan's Chapel: rib-marks (Among the cliffs at St Govan's Head a mile south of Bosherston, itself 5 miles south of Pembroke; there is ample parking on reaching the cliffs, but the road from Bosherston may be closed during army firing periods). The tiny medieval chapel and holy well (sadly now dry) are on the rocky shore, reached down a long flight of stone steps. Inside the chapel, beside the altar, is a narrow space barely large enough to squeeze into. It was believed to be a miraculous cell, 'that enables the largest person to turn round therein, and at the same time quite filled by the smallest'. If you look closely at the rock wall you can see striations, which were said to be the marks of Christ's ribs, made when he hid there from his enemies. The story is that he saw some men sowing barley in a nearby field and told them to fetch their reaping hooks. If anyone came looking for him, they were to say that they hadn't seen him since they were sowing the corn. When they returned with their hooks, the corn was ripe, and so when they answered the questions of Jesus' pursuers, they were truthfully able to say that they had not seen him since they sowed the field, and his enemies gave up the chase. In an alternative version, it was St Govan (or Gawain, one of King Arthur's knights) who hid in the cell.[92] (See Chapters 3 and 4)

The tiny chapel of St Govan in its rocky setting on the Pembrokeshire coast.

Powys: Llangynog church: foot and hand outlines (Llangynog is 10 miles south-east of Bala, and the church is in the centre of the village). The carvings are easy to find: walk up the steps into the churchyard and the flat table-top tomb on your right beside the path before you reach the church door has several shoe and hand outlines carved on top.[93]

The tombstone in Llangynog churchyard with carvings of shoes and hands on its flat top.

Notes and sources

Chapter 1 – The Meaning of Hands and Feet

E.A. Wallis Budge, *Amulets and Superstitions* (London: Oxford University Press, 1930; republished by Dover Publications, 1978), 467–71.

2 Edgar Thurston, *Omens and Superstitions of Southern India* (New York: McBride, Nast and Company, 1912), 119–20.

3 Bernard E. Jones, *Freemasons' Guide and Compendium* (London: George G. Harrap and Company, 1950), 547.

4 The quotation is from Gen. A. Hontum-Schindler of Teheran, in a letter dated 19 December 1888; quoted in Garrick Mallery, *Picture-Writing of the American Indians* (New York: Dover Publications, 1972), II, 714–15.

5 Many examples of hand and foot symbolism come from Gertrude Jobes, *Dictionary of Mythology, Folklore and Symbols* (New York, 1961), Vol.1, 592–3, 716–19.

6 Jones, *Freemasons' Guide and Compendium*, 547.

7 List taken from L.J.A. Loewenthal, 'The Palms of Jezebel', *Folklore*, vol.83 (1972), 31, where he also lists all his sources.

8 *Folklore of Blaenau Gwent* (Abertillery: Old Bakehouse Publications, 1995), 16.

9 Margaret Stutley, *Ancient Indian Magic and Folklore* (London: Routledge and Kegan Paul, 1980), 37.

10 E.S. Hartland, *The Legend of Perseus* (London, 1894–6), 1, 159.

11 W.G. Wood-Martin, *Traces of the Elder Faiths of Ireland* (London, 1902), II, 98.

12 Paul Sébillot, *Le Folk-Lore de France, I* (Paris, 1904), 406–9.

13 Herbert Kühn, *The Rock Pictures of Europe* (London: Sidgwick and Jackson, 1966), 176–7.

14 Maria Leach (ed.), *Funk and Wagnalls Standard Dictionary of Folklore, Mythology and Legend* (New York: Harper and Row, 1972), 410. The Maori lore is from Sir James George Frazer, *Aftermath* (A Supplement to *The Golden Bough*)(London: Macmillan, 1936), 50.

15 Ella Mary Leather, *The Folk-Lore of Herefordshire* (Hereford: Jakeman and Carver; London: Sidgwick and Jackson, 1912; Yorkshire: S.R. Publishers, 1970), 53.

16 Tony Wales, *Sussex Ghosts and Legends* (Newbury: Countryside Books, 1992), 66.

17 Colin Beavan, *Fingerprints: Murder and the Race to Uncover the Science of Identity* (London: Fourth Estate, 2002).

18 Otto Meinardus, 'A Typological Analysis of the Traditions Pertaining to Miraculous Icons', in *Wegzeichen: Festgabe zum 60. Geburtstag von Prof. Dr. H.M. Bidermann, O.S.A.* (Würzburg, 1971), 230.

19 More information on footprint magic, especially in Australia, the Solomon

Islands, New Guinea and parts of Africa, can be found in Frazer, *Aftermath*, 63–6.

20 A detailed study of the Graeco-Roman footprints is found in Katherine M.D. Dunbabin, 'Ipsa deae vestigia… Footprints divine and human on Graeco-Roman monuments', *Journal of Roman Archaeology*, 3 (1990), 85–109.

21 Laurette Séjourné, *Burning Water: Thought and Religion in Ancient Mexico* (London: Thames and Hudson, 1957; paperback edition 1978), 172–9.

22 Joseph Campbell, *The Hero With a Thousand Faces* (1949; London: Sphere Books, 1975), 193–4.

23 Brian Leigh Molyneaux, *The Sacred Earth* (London: Little, Brown, 1995), 72.

24 Jalmar and Ione Rudner, *The Hunter and His Art* (Cape Town: C. Struik, 1970), 8–9.

25 Thomas J. Larson, 'Spirits of the Kabiye', *Fate*, vol.50 no.8 (August 1997), 48–51.

26 Jobes, *Dictionary of Mythology, Folklore and Symbols*, 593.

27 Donald A. MacKenzie, *Crete and Pre-Hellenic* (1917; London: Senate, 1995), 35.

28 Peter Gelling and Hilda Ellis Davidson, *The Chariot of the Sun (and other Rites and Symbols of the Northern Bronze Age)* (London: J.M. Dent and Sons, 1969), 152–3.

29 Leach, *Funk and Wagnalls Standard Dictionary of Folklore, Mythology and Legend*, 410–11.

30 Sébillot, *Le Folk-Lore de France*, 410–11.

31 Molyneaux, *The Sacred Earth*, 70.

32 See Ian Wilson, *The Bleeding Mind* (London: Weidenfeld and Nicolson, 1988): the Appendix 'Stigmatic Biographies' gives a chronological list of the major ones from the 13th to the 20th centuries.

33 Joan Carroll Cruz, *Relics* (Huntington, IN: OSV, 1984), 230–1.

34 David Snellgrove, *Himalayan Pilgrimage: A Study of Tibetan Religion by a Traveller Through Western Nepal* (Oxford: Bruno Cassirer, 1961), 187.

35 Cecil F. Wright, 'Capel Ffynnon Fair: The Chapel of St Mary's Well, near Cefn, Denbighshire', *Transactions of the Ancient Monuments Society*, New Series, vol.15 (London, 1968), 60–1.

36 Richard Sheppard, 'Footwear outlines at Bolsover Castle', *Derbyshire Archaeological Journal,* 118 (1998), 142–6, noted in 'Abstracts', *3rd Stone*, 34 (April–June 1999), 45.

37 Hugh Montgomery-Massingberd, 'The Fight for Gulliver's House', *Telegraph Weekend Magazine*, 21 October 1989, 38–42.

38 John Billingsley, 'Looking for Clues', *Northern Earth*, 80 (Winter 1999–2000), 9, and 85 (Spring 2001), 21.

39 Stuart Boulter, 'Graffiti on the Tower Roof of St Michael, Cookley', *Church Archaeology*, vol.4 (2000), 55–7.

40 John Billingsley, 'Looking for Clues', *Northern Earth*, 90 (Summer 2002), 21–2.

41 S.W. Henley, 'Hidden History on the Roof', *Hidden History*, no.2/3, vol.2 (Nottingham: APRA Press, 1989), 10–12.

42 'Vindolanda', *Current Archaeology,* 178 (March 2002), 442–3.

43 *Antiquity* XXXVIII (1964), 150, 139.

44 I.J. Bromham, *Mysteries of Wales* (Swansea: Celtic Publications, 1979), 7–13.

45 Jim Thorpe web-site: www.visitjimthorpe.com

46 Alasdair Alpin MacGregor, *The Peat-Fire Flame* (Edinburgh and London: The Moray Press, 1937), 305–6.

47 *Folklore, Myths and Legends of Britain* (London: The Reader's Digest Association, 1973), 228.

48 Jennifer Westwood, *Albion: A Guide to Legendary Britain* (London: Granada Publishing, 1985), 126–8.

49 Mrs Gutch, *Examples of Printed Folklore Concerning the East Riding of Yorkshire* (London: Folk-Lore Society, 1912), 52, 208–9; John Nicholson, *Folk Lore of East Yorkshire* (London: 1890; Yorkshire: E.P. Publishing, 1973), 55.

50 Nicholson, *Folk Lore of East Yorkshire,* 55.

51 Giraldus Cambrensis, *Itinerarium Cambriæ* – translated by Sir Richard Colt Hoare as *The Itinerary through Wales and The Description of Wales* (London: J.M. Dent and Sons, 1908), 21–2.

52 David Hunt, 'Suicidal Architects', *FLS News,* 36 (Folklore Society, February 2002), 11.

53 J.R. Ackerley, *Hindoo Holiday: An Indian Journal* (1932; London, 1983), 262–3.

54 William Brockie, *Legends and Superstitions of the County of Durham* (1886; Yorkshire: E.P. Publishing, 1974), 137–8.

55 Alan Robson, *Grisly Trails and Ghostly Tales* (London: Virgin Books, 1992), 23.

56 Nicholson, *Folk Lore of East Yorkshire*, 62.

57 Tee Bee, vii, 281, noted in *Choice Notes from "Notes and Queries"* (London: Bell and Daldy, 1859), 215.

58 Benjamin Thorpe, *Northern Mythology*: *from Pagan Faith to Local Legends* (1851; Ware: Wordsworth Editions, 2001), 543.

Chapter 2 – Imprints from Prehistory

1 Brian Fagan, *New Treasures of the Past* (London: Quarto Publishing, 1987), 23–6; 'Steps to Preserve Oldest Footprints', *New Scientist* (14 January 1995).

2 Michael Baigent, *Ancient Tracks: Mysteries in Ancient and Early History* (London: Viking, 1998), 97–9; Michael A. Cremo and Richard L. Thompson, *Forbidden Archeology* (San Diego, CA: Bhaktivedanta Institute, 1993), 742–7.

3 Hazel Muir, 'Earliest Human Footprints Preserve Prehistoric Trek', *New Scientist* (15 March 2003), 15; David Derbyshire, 'Oldest Footprints Found on Volcano', *Daily Telegraph* (13 March 2003), 12.

4 Cremo and Thompson, *Forbidden Archeology*, 411–12.

5 Wendy Barnaby, 'Ancient Human Footprints', *Nature*, 254 (1975), 553, reprinted in William Corliss (compiler), *Ancient Man: A Handbook of Puzzling Artifacts* (Glen Arm, MD: The Sourcebook Project, 1978), 649–50.

6 'Forefathers' Footprints', *Fortean Times*, 104,17.

7 Spencer P.M. Harrington, 'Human Footprints at Chauvet Cave', *Archaeology*, 52: 5 (Sept/Oct. 1999); Nicholas Glass, 'The Oldest Art Gallery on Earth', *The Sunday Telegraph* (28 December 2003), 9.

8 Paul G. Bahn and Jean Vertut, *Images of the Ice Age* (London: Windward, 1988), 13–15; Martin Lockley and Christian Meyer, *Dinosaur Tracks and Other Fossil Footprints of Europe* (New York: Columbia University Press, 2000), 259–62.

9 Frances Lynch, Stephen Aldhouse-Green and Jeffrey L. Davies, *Prehistoric Wales* (Stroud: Sutton Publishing, 2000), 29 (photograph); Lockley and Meyer, *Dinosaur Tracks*, 262.

10 Gaynor Aaltonen, 'Sands of Time', *National Trust Magazine*, 91 (Autumn 2000), 36–9; Lockley and Meyer, *Dinosaur Tracks*, 262–4.

11 For more examples see William R. Corliss, *Archeological Anomalies: Small Artifacts* (Glen Arm: The Sourcebook Project, 2003), 65–87.

12 Earl Flint, 'Human Footprints in Nicaragua', *American Antiquarian*, 6 (1884), 112; Alan L. Bryan, 'New Light on Ancient Nicaraguan Footprints', *Archaeology*, 26 (1973), 146–7. Both reproduced in Corliss, *Ancient Man*, 640–3.

13 Gary S. Mangiacopra, Dr Dwight G. Smith and Dr David F. Avery, 'Homo Nevadensis of Carson City', *Fortean Studies 3* (London: John Brown Publishing, 1996), 211–22; Corliss, *Archeological Anomalies: Small Artifacts*, 77–8.

14 *Toronto News*, 1 August 1890.

15 Cremo and Thompson, *Forbidden Archeology*, 280–1.

16 Ulrich Magin, 'Footprints in Stone – Evidence for Initial Bipedalism?', *Bipedia*, 16 (France, March 1998), 14–15; Jerome Clark, *Unexplained!* (Farmington Hills, MI: Visible Ink Press, 2nd edn, 1999), 183–7; Corliss, *Archeological Anomalies: Small Artifacts*, 74–7.

17 Dr W.H. Ballou's report is quoted in Cremo and Thompson, *Forbidden Archeology*, 807–8.

18 U.S. Department of the Interior booklet, *The Story of the Great White Sands*, quoted in Brad Steiger, *Mysteries of Time and Space* (1974; London: Sphere Books, 1977), 31.

19 Burroughs' report and the subsequent discussion are covered in Cremo and Thompson, *Forbidden Archeology*, 454–8.

20 Reported in *Pursuit*, 3: 4 (October 1970), 78.

21 Wolfgang Haberland and Willi-Herbert Grebe, 'Prehistoric Footprints from El Salvador', *American Antiquity*, 22 (1957), 282–5, quoted in Corliss, *Ancient Man*, 643–4.

22 Magin, *Bipedia*, 16, 11–12.

23 *Seattle Post Intelligencer*, 15 April 1963; noted in *Pursuit*, 3: 4 (October 1970), 78.

24 Cremo and Thompson, *Forbidden Archeology*, 810–13. William J. Meister, Sr., 'Discovery of Trilobite Fossils in Shod Footprint of Human in "Trilobite Beds" – A Cambrian Formation, Antelope Springs, Utah', *Creation Research Society Quarterly* 5 (1968), 97. Magin, *Bipedia*, 16, 15; also Ulrich Magin, 'Footprints in Stone [Part II]', *Bipedia*, 17 (France, March 1999), 28–9. See also Corliss, *Archeological Anomalies: Small Artifacts*, 72–3.

25 Corliss, *Archeological Anomalies: Small Artifacts*, 73–4.

26 Cremo and Thompson, *Forbidden Archeology*, 458; Corliss, *Archeological Anomalies: Small Artifacts*, 82.

27 Magin, *Bipedia*, 16, 15–16.

28 Henry R. Schoolcraft, 'Remarks on the Prints of Human Feet, Observed in the Secondary Limestone of the Mississippi Valley', *American Journal of Science*, 1:5 (1822), 223–30, reprinted in Corliss, *Ancient Man*, 637–40.

29 Herbert P. Hubbell, 'Human Foot-Prints in the Stratified Rock', *Popular Science Monthly*, 22 (1882), 262, reprinted in Corliss, *Ancient Man*, 649.

30 *Toronto World*, 8 April 1890.

31 *The American Anthropologist*, IX (1896), 66, noted in *Pursuit* 3:4 (October 1970), 78.

32 'Footprints in the...', *Pursuit*, 4:3 (July 1971), 69.

33 Stan Morrison, 'Uncovering Prehistoric Anomalies in Oklahoma', *Alternate Perceptions*, 28 (Fall 1994), 4–7.

34 Steiger, *Mysteries of Time and Space*, 31–2.

35 Frank Joseph, 'Project Alta: Search and Discovery in the Bahamas', *Ancient American*, 3:23 (1998), 2–3.

36 Lockley and Meyer, *Dinosaur Tracks*, 267.

37 Bernadette Arnaud, 'Amputee Art', *Archaeology*, vol.56 no.6 (November/December 2003), 14.

38 Paul G. Bahn, *The Cambridge Illustrated History of Prehistoric Art* (Cambridge: Cambridge University Press, 1998), 112–15.

39 'Hiker finds rare Aboriginal cave art', *The Daily Telegraph*, 2 July 2003.

40 Roger Highfield, 'Research round-up: from supercomputers to cave art', *The Daily Telegraph* (8 October 2003), 16.

41 Bahn and Vertut, *Images of the Ice Age*, 135.

42 Philip Rawson (ed.), *Primitive Erotic Art* (London: Weidenfeld and Nicolson, 1973): Philip Rawson, 'Early History of Sexual Art', 9.

43 Jacqueline Simpson, 'Graffiti of Workmen', *FLS News*, 31 (June 2000), 9.

44 J.G. Frazer, *Spirits of the Corn and of the Wild* (London: Macmillan, 1912), II:338.

45 Johannes Maringer, *The Gods of Prehistoric Man* (London: Weidenfeld and Nicolson, 1960), 182, 184.

46 G.R. Levy, *The Gate of Horn* (London: Faber and Faber, 1948, 1963), 142–3. A precise description of Petit-Mont and its location can be found in Aubrey Burl, *Megalithic Brittany* (London: Thames and Hudson, 1985), 121–2.

47 O.G.S. Crawford, *The Eye Goddess* (London: Phoenix House, 1957), 103–4; *The Calderstones – A Prehistoric Tomb in Liverpool* (Liverpool: Merseyside Archaeological Society, no date): the carvings on all the stones are described and illustrated in this booklet.

48 'A Bronze Age Decorated Cist-Slab from Mendip': Bristol Museum Information Sheet. A drawing of the feet can be found in Stan Beckensall, *British Prehistoric Rock Art* (Stroud: Tempus Publishing, 1999), 70.

49 'A Bronze Age Decorated Cist-Slab from Mendip': Bristol Museum Information Sheet.

50 The origins of the story are complex. For some elucidation, see L.V. Grinsell, *Legendary History and Folklore of Stonehenge*, West Country Folklore no.9 (Guernsey: The Toucan Press, 1975), 14–15; Jerome F. Heavey, 'The Heele Stone', *Folklore*, 88 (1977), 238–9.

51 Bahn, *The Cambridge Illustrated History of Prehistoric Art*, 193.

52 Peter Gelling and Hilda Ellis Davidson, *The Chariot of the Sun* (London: J.M. Dent and Sons, 1969), 39–42, 152–3.

53 Richard Bradley, *An Archaeology of Natural Places* (London: Routledge, 2000), 140–6.

54 All aspects of sun-worship are covered in Miranda Green, *The Sun-Gods of Ancient Europe* (London: B.T. Batsford, 1991), with hands featuring especially on 50–2, 57, 74, 81.

55 *The Guardian*, 12 February 2000, noted in *Northern Earth* 82:34.

56 Bahn, *The Cambridge Illustrated History of Prehistoric Art*, 192–3.

57 Full details of Aborigine rock art which can be visited will be found in Peter Stanbury and John Clegg, *A Field Guide to Aboriginal Rock Engravings* (Sydney: Sydney University Press, 1990).

58 Full details of the carvings discovered along the Karakoram Highway by German-Pakistani expeditions between 1979 and 1984 can be found in *Between Gandhara and the Silk Roads* (Mainz am Rhein: Verlag Philipp von Zabern, 1987): the footprint and handprint are on plate 1.

59 Rudner, *The Hunter and His Art*, 185.

60 Rudner, *The Hunter and His Art*, 238.

61 Campbell Grant, *Rock Art of the American Indian* (New York: Promontory Press, 1967), 54–5. There are many sites to visit, and the best in the USA are listed briefly in the 'Stoneworks' section of Rosemary Ellen Guiley, *Atlas of the Mysterious in North America* (New York: Facts on File, 1995).

62 Paul Devereux, *Haunted Land* (London: Judy Piatkus (Publishers) Ltd, 2001), 7–17.

63 *Notes and Queries*, 3rd S. IX (13 January 1866), 39.

64 Dr O'Donovan quoted in R.R. Brash, 'On Ancient Stone Chairs and Stones of Inauguration', *The Gentleman's Magazine*, I (1885), 429–36, reprinted in George Laurence Gomme (ed.), *The Gentleman's Magazine Library: Archaeology: Part II* (London: Elliot Stock, 1886), 27–43.

65 Cary Meehan, *The Traveller's Guide to Sacred Ireland* (Glastonbury: Gothic Image Publications, 2002), 590.

66 Jennifer Westwood, *Albion: A Guide to Legendary Britain* (London: Granada Publishing, 1985), 419.

67 The full story of the Stone of Destiny can be found in Nick Aitchison, *Scotland's Stone of Destiny* (Stroud: Tempus Publishing, 2000).

68 Otta F. Swire, *The Inner Hebrides and Their Legends* (London and Glasgow: Collins, 1964), 92–3, 175–6.

69 Martin Coventry, *The Hebrides: A Guide to the Islands of Western Scotland* (Musselburgh: Goblinshead, 1999), 47.

70 Euan W. MacKie, *Scotland: An Archaeological Guide* (London: Faber and Faber, 1975), 280–1.

71 MacKie, *Scotland*, 147–8; Alan Lane, 'Citadel of the First Scots', *British Archaeology*, 62 (December 2001), 8–13.

72 Leslie V. Grinsell, *Folklore of Prehistoric Sites in Britain* (Newton Abbot: David and Charles, 1976), 186, 199.

Chapter 3 – Sacred Stones

1 John Wilkinson, *Jerusalem Pilgrims Before the Crusades* (Warminster: Aris and Phillips, 1977), 84.
2 I.G. Turbott, 'The Footprints of Tarawa', *Journal of the Polynesian Society*, 58 (New Zealand, December 1949), 4, noted in Erich von Däniken, *The Stones of Kiribati* (first published in Germany by Econ Verlag, 1981, as *Reise Nach Kiribati*; London: Souvenir Press, 1982), 62–6.
3 Brian Leigh Molyneaux, *The Sacred Earth* (London: Little Brown, 1995), 70.
4 Paul Sébillot, *Le Folk-Lore de France*, I (Paris, 1904), 363.
5 E.S. Hartland, *The Legend of Perseus* (London, 1894–6), 1: 130, 2:358, noted in Jeremy Harte, 'To Be a Joyful Mother of Children…', *Northern Earth*, 64: 8.
6 Advertisement for The Footprints Cross (available from Brooks and Bentley) printed in *The Telegraph Magazine*, 24 March 2001. There is also a Footprints Locket, with footprints across one face and words from the poem on the reverse. This was advertised by Brooks and Bentley in *The Telegraph Magazine*, 23 February 2002.
7 Maria Leach (ed.), *Funk and Wagnalls Standard Dictionary of Folklore, Mythology and Legend* (New York: Harper and Row, 1984), 9; Molyneaux, *The Sacred Earth*, 41; Clare Rettie, *Things Seen in Ceylon* (London, 1929), 94. The pilgrimage report was in *The Monthly Mirror*, xi 69 (January 1801). Information on the Buddha's footprint can be found in E.F.C. Ludowyk, *The Footprint of the Buddha* (London: George Allen and Unwin, 1958), 11–23.
8 *Notes and Queries*, 3rd S. VIII (25 November 1865), 434.
9 Richard Barber, *Pilgrimages* (Woodbridge: The Boydell Press, 1991), 32–3, 38–9.
10 E.A. Wallis Budge (ed., trans.), *The Book of Governors: The Historia Monastica of Thomas Bishop of Margâ A.D. 840* (London, 1893), 585 fn.1.
11 Sir Richard F. Burton, *Personal Narrative of a Pilgrimage to Al-Madinah and Mecca*, I (London, 1898), 203–4, 430.
12 Annemarie Schimmel, *Und Muhammad ist sein Prophet* (Düsseldorf: Diederichs, 1981), 36.
13 Norbert C. Brockman, *Encyclopedia of Sacred Places* (Oxford: Oxford University Press, 1997), 168–9.
14 Sylvia A. Matheson, *Persia: An Archaeological Guide* (London: Faber and Faber, 2nd rev. edn, 1976), 200.
15 Gregory of Tours, *The History of the Franks* (London: Penguin Books, 1974), 75–6.
16 E. Cobham Brewer, *A Dictionary of Miracles* (Philadelphia: J.B. Lippincott Company, no date; Detroit: Gale Research Company, 1966), 241; Wilfrid Bonser, 'The Cult of Relics in the Middle Ages', *Folklore*, 73 (winter 1962), 243.
17 Bede, 'De locis sanctis libellus', Ch.5, from *Works*, trans. Giles, 4 (1843), 417, quoted in Bonser, 241.
18 An anonymous pilgrim from Piacenza in Italy, c.570, translated in Wilkinson, *Jerusalem Pilgrims Before the Crusades*, 84.
19 Loretta Gerson, Silvia Mazzola, Venetia Morrison, *Rome: A Guide to the Eternal City* (London: Napoleoni and Wakefield, 1999), 22, 67; P. Charles Walker,

'"Domine, Quo Vadis?"', *The Catholic Fireside,* 12 July 1963, 22–3; Mary Sharp, *A Traveller's Guide to the Churches of Rome* (London: Hugh Evelyn, 1967), 81; P.J. Chandlery, *Pilgrim-Walks in Rome: A Guide to the Holy Places in the City and its Vicinity* (London: Manresa Press, 4ᵗʰ edn, 1924), 230, 241.

20 Sébillot, *Le Folk-Lore de France*: all three examples on 363.

21 Jean-Paul Clébert, *Guide de la Provence Mystérieuse* (Paris: Les Guides Noirs, Editions Tchou, 1998 (new edition)), 60–1.

22 Patrice Boussel, *Des Reliques et de Leur Bon Usage* (Paris: Balland, 1971), 135.

23 A.W. Smith, '"And Did Those Feet...?": The "Legend" of Christ's Visit to Britain', *Folklore*, 100:1 (1989), 73–4.

24 Francis Jones, *The Holy Wells of Wales* (Cardiff: University of Wales Press, 1954), 17.

25 Jonathan Caredig Davies, *Folk-Lore of West and Mid-Wales* (Aberystwyth: 1911; Llanerch Publishers, facsimile reprint, 1992), 319.

26 Otto F.A. Meinardus, *The Holy Family in Egypt* (Cairo: The American University in Cairo Press, 1986), 34, 47–8; Otto F.A. Meinardus, *Coptic Saints and Pilgrimages* (Cairo: The American University in Cairo Press, 2002), 89.

27 Herbert Kühn, *The Rock Pictures of Europe* (London: Sidgwick and Jackson, 1966), 176.

28 Information from website: www.bayanimagazine.com/bayani.arch61.html

29 Phyllis Benjamin, 'Is the Tomb of Jesus in Kashmir?', *INFO Journal*, 58 (December 1989), 22–4; Holger Kersten, *Jesus Lived in India* (Shaftesbury: Element Books, 1986), 208.

30 Paul Sieveking, 'Yard-long footprint in tree hailed as a "sign"', *Sunday Telegraph*, 28 January 2001.

31 Ross Kaniuk, 'Christ-Al Palace', *Daily Star*, 13 November 2000, 3.

32 Tristan Gray Hulse, *The Holy Shroud* (London: Weidenfeld and Nicolson, 1997).

33 Icons depicting the Mandylion are described and illustrated in Gabriele Finaldi, *The Image of Christ* (London: The National Gallery, 2000), 77, 98–101. The Veronica is to be found described and illustrated in several paintings in the same book, pp. 74–85. The most authoritative account of 'images-not-made-by-hands' can be found in Ernst von Dobschütz, *Christusbilder, Untersuchungen zur Christlichen Legende* (Leipzig: J.C. Hinrichs, 1899).

34 Peter Hough and Jenny Randles, *Mysteries of the Mersey Valley* (Wilmslow: Sigma Leisure, 1993), 147–8.

35 Raymond Crawfurd, *Plague and Pestilence in Literature and Art* (Oxford, 1918).

36 *Notes and Queries*, 3rd S, X (14 July 1866), 39.

37 Sydney Loch, *Athos: The Holy Mountain* (London, 1957), 126. See also Feodor S. Kovalchuk, *Wonder-Working Icons of the Theotokos* (Youngstown, Ohio, 1985), 43–5.

38 Paul G. Bahn, *The Cambridge Illustrated History of Prehistoric Art* (Cambridge: Cambridge University Press, 1998), 51; Marguerite Young, *Angel in the Forest* (New York: Charles Scribner's Sons, 1966), 11–17.

39 Brian de Breffney, *In the Steps of St Patrick* (London: Thames and Hudson, 1982), 33, 105; Lord Killanin and Michael V. Duignan, *The Shell Guide to Ireland* (London: Macmillan, rev. ed.1989), 83; Liam de Paor, *Saint Patrick's*

World: The Christian Culture of Ireland's Apostolic Age (Notre Dame and London: University of Notre Dame Press, 1993), 181.

40 Robert Hunt, *The Drolls, Traditions and Superstitions of Old Cornwall*, Second Series, no date (reissued by Llanerch Publishers, Lampeter), 272.

41 Robert Hertz, 'St Besse: A Study of an Alpine Cult', in Stephen Wilson (ed.), *Saints and Their Cults* (Cambridge: Cambridge University Press, 1983), 83.

42 Sébillot, *Le Folk-Lore de France*, 374.

43 *Notes and Queries*, 3rd S. X (18 October 1866), 299.

44 Katharine Briggs, *A Dictionary of Fairies* (London: Allen Lane, 1976), 108.

45 J.E. Hanauer, *The Holy Land – Myths and Legends* (London: Senate/Random House, 1996)(originally published as *Folklore of the Holy Land* (London: The Sheldon Press, 1907)), 46–7.

46 Peter Harbison, *Pilgrimage in Ireland* (London: Barrie and Jenkins, 1991), 127.

47 T.P. Ellis, *The Story of Two Parishes: Dolgelley and Llanelltyd* (Newtown, 1928), 55; W.J. Hemp and C.A. Ralegh Radford, 'The Llanelltyd Stone', *Archæologia Cambrensis*, CII, 2 (1953), 164–8.

48 Jeremy Bennett, 'Steps worn smooth by the passing feet of pilgrims', *Country Quest*, 15:12 (May 1975), 5–6.

49 *Notes and Queries*: 3rd S. IX (10 March 1866), 205; (17 March 1866), 227; X (8 September 1866), 189–90; 4th S. IX (15 June 1872), 494; (20 June 1872), 542.

50 John Nicholson, *Folk Lore of East Yorkshire* (London: 1890; Wakefield: EP Publishing, 1973), 55.

51 Jennifer Westwood, *Albion: A Guide to Legendary Britain* (London: Granada Publishing, 1985), 316–17; John Harland and T.T. Wilkinson, *Lancashire Folk-Lore* (Manchester and London: John Heywood, 1882; Wakefield: EP Publishing, 1973), 134–7.

52 Andreas Trottmann in *Athene* (autumn 1997), 8.

53 George Michell, *The Penguin Guide to the Monuments of India. Volume One – Buddhist, Jain, Hindu* (London: Penguin Books, 1990), 115, 236; *India's Sacred Shrines and Cities* (Madras: G.A. Natesan, no date), 332, 392, 395.

54 *Notes and Queries*, 3rd S. VIII (25 November 1865), 434.

55 Thor Heyerdahl, *The Maldive Mystery* (London: George Allen and Unwin, 1986; Unwin Paperbacks, 1988), 265.

56 Ludowyk, *The Footprint of the Buddha*, 11–23.

57 Heyerdahl, *The Maldive Mystery*, 265–7.

58 J.C. Cooper, *An Illustrated Encyclopaedia of Traditional Symbols* (London: Thames and Hudson, 1978), 71.

59 Two examples are illustrated in *Tantra*, introduction by Philip S. Rawson (Arts Council of Great Britain exhibition catalogue, 1971).

60 William Simpson, *The Buddhist Praying-Wheel* (London: Macmillan and Co., 1896), 42, where there is a drawing of the throne.

61 H.A. Giles (trans.), *The Travels of Fa-Hsien (399–414 A.D.), or Record of the Buddhistic Kingdoms* (Cambridge, 1923), 11, 18, 28, 48–9.

62 Karma Thinley Rinpoche, *The History of the Sixteen Karmapas of Tibet* (Boulder, Colorado, 1980), 92.

63 Tulka Thondup Rinpoche (ed. Harold Talbott), *Hidden Teachings of Tibet: An Explanation of the Terma Tradition of the Nyingma School of Buddhism* (London: Wisdom Publications, 1986), 121, 249.

64 Karma Thinley Rinpoche, *The History of the Sixteen Karmapas of Tibet*, 129–31.

65 Keith Dowman, *The Power-Places of Central Tibet: The Pilgrim's Guide* (London, 1988), 75, 192, and other examples are given in this book.

66 Andrea Loseries-Leick, 'On the Sacredness of Mount Kailasa in the Indian and Tibetan Sources', in Alex McKay (ed.), *Pilgrimage in Tibet* (Richmond: Curzon Press, 1998), Chapter 8.

67 William Edgar Geil, *The Sacred 5 of China* (London, 1926), 182.

68 Martin Palmer, *Travels Through Sacred China* (London: Thorsons, 1996), 20, 303.

69 Oliver Statler, *Japanese Pilgrimage* (London: Pan Books, 1984), 143–5, quoting from *The Confessions of Lady Nijo*.

70 J.G. Frazer, *Taboo and the Perils of the Soul* (London: Macmillan, 1911), 275.

71 *Ananova*, 16 September 2002; *Sunday Times*, 22 September 2002; noted in *Fortean Times* 166 (January 2003), 12.

72 Rev. Alban Butler (original compiler), edited by Herbert Thurston and Norah Leeson, *The Lives of the Saints* (London, 1931), 34.

73 Roger Peyrefitte (trans. Edward Hymans), *The Keys of St Peter* (London: Secker and Warburg, 1957; St Albans: Panther Books, 1972), 64.

74 Details of the Jasna Gora and Hackenberg burned hands come from Georg Siegmund, 'Mystery of the Burning Handprints', *Fate*, 34:6, issue 375 (June 1981), 42–51.

75 Ervin Bonkalo, Ph.D., 'The Fiery Hand', first published in *Fate* (June 1953), vol.6 no.6, and republished in vol.56 no.6 (June 2003); Dr Joe Nickell, *Looking for a Miracle* (Amherst: Prometheus, 1993), noted in Dr Karl P.N. Shuker, *Mysteries of Planet Earth* (London: Carlton Books, 1999), 124–5.

Chapter 4 – A Saintly Presence I

1 *India's Sacred Shrines and Cities* (Madras: G.A. Natesan and Co., no date), 223.

2 L'Abbé Guyard, *Life of St Antony of Padua*, noted in E. Cobham Brewer, *A Dictionary of Miracles* (Philadelphia: J.B. Lippincott Company, no date; Detroit: Gale Research Company, 1966), 241.

3 Paul Sébillot, *Le Folk-Lore de France*, Vol.I (Paris, 1904), 374.

4 Sydney Loch, *Athos: The Holy Mountain* (London: Lutterworth Press, 1957), 194–5.

5 Alan Smith, 'St Augustine of Canterbury in History and Tradition', *Folklore*, vol.89, I (1978), 23–8.

6 Elissa R. Henken, *Traditions of the Welsh Saints* (Woodbridge: D.S. Brewer, 1987), 256.

7 Robert Hertz, 'St Besse: A Study of An Alpine Cult', in Stephen Wilson (ed.), *Saints and Their Cults* (Cambridge: Cambridge University Press, 1983), 72–3.

8 John Ray, *Itineraries* (London, 1760), 228–30; Richard Fenton, *Tours in Wales* (1804–1813) (London: The Bedford Press, 1917), Extracts from Williams' MS (1814) in appendix III, 323.

9 Patrick Logan, *The Holy Wells of Ireland* (Gerrards Cross: Colin Smythe, 1980), 103–4; S. Baring-Gould and John Fisher, *The Lives of the British Saints*, vol.3 (London: The Honourable Society of Cymmrodorion, 1911), 7–8.

10 Sébillot, *Le Folk-Lore de France*, 377.

11 Sébillot, *Le Folk-Lore de France*, 373; S. Baring-Gould, *Brittany* (London: Methuen and Co., 1902; 4th ed. 1922), 104.

12 Cary Meehan, *The Traveller's Guide to Sacred Ireland* (Glastonbury: Gothic Image Publications, 2002), 292.

13 John Adair, *The Pilgrims' Way: Shrines and Saints in Britain and Ireland* (London: Thames and Hudson, 1978), 198; W.G. Wood-Martin, *Traces of the Elder Faiths of Ireland*, Vol.II (London, 1902), 97. St Brigid's imprints are listed in Patricia Jackson, 'The Holy Wells of Co. Kildare', *Journal of the Co. Kildare Archaeological Society*, vol.16 no.2 (1979–80), 139–40, 147, 158. 'Kilree' is from Lord Killanin and Michael V. Duignan, *The Shell Guide to Ireland* (London: The Ebury Press, 1962 edition) under Kells, Co. Kilkenny.

14 Otta F. Swire, *The Inner Hebrides and Their Legends* (London and Glasgow: Collins, 1964), 14.

15 Sébillot, *Le Folk-Lore de France*, 366, 376, 372.

16 Logan, *The Holy Wells of Ireland*, 79.

17 Logan, *The Holy Wells of Ireland*, 105.

18 Sébillot, *Le Folk-Lore de France*, 367–8; *Guide to Brittany* (London, no date), 163.

19 Sébillot, *Le Folk-Lore de France*, 367.

20 Clemens Jöckle, *Encyclopedia of Saints* (London: Parkgate Books, 1997), 108.

21 Sébillot, *Le Folk-Lore de France*, 365.

22 James M. Mackinlay, *Folklore of Scottish Lochs and Springs* (Glasgow: William Hodge and Co., 1893; Felinfach: Llanerch Publishers, 1993), 79; Killanin and Duignan, *The Shell Guide to Ireland* (London: 1962 edition) under 'Hollywood'.

23 'Irish Folk-Lore', *The Folk-Lore Journal*, vol. II part V (May 1884), 140–1, reprinted from William Shaw Mason, *A Statistical Account or Parochial Survey of Ireland*, drawn from the communications of the clergy (Dublin, London and Edinburgh, 1814–19), 3 vols.

24 Killanin and Duignan, *Shell Guide to Ireland* (1962 edn), 454.

25 Logan, *The Holy Wells of Ireland*, 40.

26 Thomas J. Westropp, *Folklore of Clare* (Ennis: Clasp Press, 2000), 68, 92.

27 Meehan, *Sacred Ireland*, 122.

28 Logan, *The Holy Wells of Ireland*, 63–4.

29 Meehan, *Sacred Ireland*, 623.

30 T.S. Muir, *Ecclesiological Notes*, quoted in Mackinlay, *Folklore of Scottish Lochs and Springs*, 80; Shirley Toulson, *Celtic Journeys* (London: Hutchinson and Co., 1985), 51.

31 Mackinlay, *Folklore of Scottish Lochs and Springs*, 76–7.

32 Sébillot, *Le Folk-Lore de France*, 368.

33 William Bottrell, *Traditions and Hearthside Stories of West Cornwall*, Second Series (published by the author, 1873; facsimile reprint by Llanerch Publishers, Felinfach, 1996), 277.

34 S. Baring-Gould and John Fisher, *The Lives of the British Saints*, vol.II (London, 1908), 211.

35 Baring-Gould and Fisher, *The Lives of the British Saints*, vol.II, 263.

36 Baring-Gould and Fisher, *The Lives of the British Saints*, vol.II, 276; Richard Fenton, *Tours in Wales*, 343.

37 Logan, *The Holy Wells of Ireland*, 42.

38 Richard Fenton, *Tours in Wales (1804–1813)* (London: The Bedford Press, 1917), 323.

39 Richard B. White, 'Excavations at Arfryn, Bodedern, long-cist cemeteries and the origins of Christianity in Britain', *Transactions of Anglesey Antiquarian Society* (1971–2), 30–1.

40 Anatole le Braz, *Les Saints Bretons en Cornouaille* (Paris: Calmann-Lévy, 1937), 64.

41 Sébillot, *Le Folk-Lore de France*, 373.

42 Sébillot, *Le Folk-Lore de France*, 373.

43 Sébillot, *Le Folk-Lore de France*, 377.

44 Logan, *The Holy Wells of Ireland*, 87.

45 Róisín ní Mheara, *In Search of Irish Saints* (Blackrock: Four Courts Press, 1994), 47; information on St Fiachra, 44–9.

46 Logan, *The Holy Wells of Ireland*, 104.

47 Agnes B.C. Dunbar, *A Dictionary of Saintly Women* (London: George Bell and Sons, 1904), vol.I, 321.

48 Dunbar, *A Dictionary of Saintly Women*, Vol.I, 345.

49 Henken, Traditions of the Welsh Saints, 258–9.

50 Fenton, *Tours in Wales*, 324.

51 Marie Trevelyan, *Folk-Lore and Folk-Stories of Wales* (London: Elliot Stock, 1909; Wakefield: EP Publishing, 1973), 134–5.

52 Baring-Gould and Fisher, *The Lives of the British Saints*, vol.III, 228.

53 Dunbar, *A Dictionary of Saintly Women*, Vol.I, 374.

54 Sébillot, *Le Folk-Lore de France*, 366.

55 Sébillot, *Le Folk-Lore de France*, 373.

56 Sébillot, *Le Folk-Lore de France*, 367.

57 Dunbar, *A Dictionary of Saintly Women*, I, 447.

58 Dunbar, *A Dictionary of Saintly Women*, I, 455.

59 Roger Peyrefitte (trans. Edward Hyams), *The Keys of St Peter* (London: Secker and Warburg, 1957; St Albans: Panther Books, 1972), 63.

60 Dunbar, *A Dictionary of Saintly Women*, I, 458.

61 Sébillot, *Le Folk-Lore de France*, 366.

62 Mackinlay, *Folklore of Scottish Lochs and Springs*, 73–4.

63 Westropp, *Folklore of Clare*, 95.

64 Sébillot, *Le Folk-Lore de France*, 404, 410, 374, 365, 368.

Chapter 5 – A Saintly Presence II

1 Ean Begg, *The Cult of the Black Virgin* (London: Arkana, Routledge and Kegan Paul, 1985), 189.

2 Paul Sébillot, *Le Folk-Lore de France* (Paris, 1904), 372.

3 Sébillot, *Le Folk-Lore de France*, 363.

4 Sébillot, *Le Folk-Lore de France*, 364.

5 Begg, *The Cult of the Black Virgin*, 166–7.

6 Sébillot, *Le Folk-Lore de France*, 372.

7 Sébillot, *Le Folk-Lore de France*, 364.

8 Full details of the footprint and its location are given in Marcel Baudouin, 'Le Pas de la Vierge et les Cupules du Rocher de la Fontaine Saint-Gré, … Avrill, (V.)', *Bulletin Société Préhistorique Française* (25 July 1912), 452–66.

9 Sébillot, *Le Folk-Lore de France*, 364.

10 Sébillot, *Le Folk-Lore de France*, 364, 404–5; for the present-day cultic recognition of the stone, Père A. Lecointre in letter to T.G. Hulse, December 1993.

11 Antoine Fave, 'A propos d'une pierre commémorative de la Peste d'Elliant', *Bulletin de la Societé archéologique du Finistère* (1893), 346–54; Fanch Postic, 'Le peste d'Elliant', in *Kerdévot: Livre d'or du cinquième centenaire 1489– 1989* (ed. Bernez Rouz) (Ergué-Gabéric: Association Kerdévot 89, 1989), 16– 27.

12 Herbert Kuhn, *The Rock Pictures of Europe* (London: Sidgwick and Jackson, 1966), 176.

13 Walter Starkie, *The Road to Santiago: Pilgrims of St James* (London, 1957), 14, 15.

14 William A. Christian Jr., *Apparitions in Late Medieval and Renaissance Spain* (Princeton, New Jersey: Princeton University Press, 1981, 1989), 70, 74, 75, 79, 80, 141.

15 Dom Bede Camm, *Pilgrim Paths in Latin Lands* (London, 1923), 88–90.

16 J.O.D., F.S.K., and D.F.A., 'Pochaev – Dormition Laura', *One Church* (U.S. Russian Orthodox journal, published in Youngstown, Ohio)(1956), 175–96.

17 Sonia Hillsdon, *Jersey: Witches, Ghosts and Traditions* (Norwich: Jarrold Colour Publications, 1987), 100.

18 Ruth and Frank Morris, *Scottish Healing Wells* (Sandy: The Alethea Press, 1982), 147.

19 James M. Mackinlay, *Folklore of Scottish Lochs and Springs* (Glasgow: William Hodge and Co., 1893; Wales: Llanerch Publishers, 1993), 79.

20 Oral accounts supplied by Llanfair farmer David J. Roberts to Tristan Gray Hulse in 1992, synthesising the accounts known to the informant via the older inhabitants of the community. Only fragments of this continuous narrative have been printed before: R. Richard and R.G. Lloyd, 'The Church of St Mary, Llanfair-Juxta-Harlech', *Archaeologia Cambrensis* (1930), 283–92 (291 – Our Lady's footprint); Frank Ward, *The Lakes of Wales* (London: Herbert Jenkins, 1931), 144 (Mary's footprints, and Hafod-y-Llyn).

21 Dafydd Guto, 'Cyfres Meini. Rhif 1: Llam Maria' – Llais Ardudwy 6 (Ionawr, 1987); *An Inventory of the Ancient Monuments in Wales and Monmouthshire. IV – County of Merioneth* (London: HMSO, 1921), 103.

22 Francis Jones, *The Holy Wells of Wales* (Cardiff: University of Wales Press, 1954), 47.

23 Alfred J. Butler, *The Ancient Coptic Churches of Egypt* vol.I (Oxford, 1884), 207.

24 Sébillot, *Le Folklore de France*, 367.

25 E. Cobham Brewer, *A Dictionary of Miracles* (Philadelphia: J.B. Lippincott Company, no date; Detroit: Gale Research Company, 1966), 241.

26 Gilbert H. Doble, *The Saints of Cornwall* (1970) Part Five, 52; Sébillot, *Le Folk-*

Lore de France, 366.

27 Christian, *Apparitions in Late Medieval and Renaissance Spain*, 101–2.

28 Sébillot, *Le Folk-Lore de France*, 366.

29 Christian, *Apparitions*, 100, 101, 102.

30 Chris Barber and John Godfrey Williams, *The Ancient Stones of Wales* (Abergavenny: Blorenge Books, 1989), no.99, p.118.

31 Agnes B.C. Dunbar, *A Dictionary of Saintly Women*, Vol.2, (London, 1905), 92–3.

32 J.W. James, *Rhigyfarch's Life of St David*: The Basic Mid Twelfth-Century Latin Text with Introduction, Critical Apparatus and Translation (Cardiff: University of Wales Press, 1967), 32.

33 Sébillot, *Le Folk-Lore de France*, 373, 405.

34 Tristan Gray Hulse, 'The Land of Holy Wells – 3: Santez Noaluen', *Source*, New Series No.3 (Spring 1995), 23–6; Michel Renouard, *A New Guide to Brittany* (Rennes: Ouest-France, 1982/1983), 210; Sébillot, *Le Folk-Lore de France*, 392–3.

35 Sébillot, *Le Folk-Lore de France*, 377.

36 Dunbar, *A Dictionary of Saintly Women*, II, 115–16.

37 Lord Killanin and Michael V. Duignan, *The Shell Guide to Ireland* (London: Macmillan, 1989), 113.

38 Rev. S. Baring-Gould, *The Lives of the Saints* (London: John Hodges, 1877), 161–3.

39 S. Baring-Gould and John Fisher, *The Lives of the British Saints*, vol.4 (London: Hon. Soc. Cymmrodorion, 1913), 52–3.

40 Shirley Toulson, *Celtic Journeys* (London: Hutchinson, 1985), 102–3.

41 W.G. Wood-Martin, *Traces of the Elder Faiths of Ireland* (London, 1902): vol.I, 163; vol.II, 97; Patricia Jackson, 'The Holy Wells of Co. Kildare', *Journal of the Co. Kildare Archaeological Society*, vol.16 no.2 (1979–80), 140, 152.

42 Brian de Breffny, *In the Steps of St Patrick* (London: Thames and Hudson, 1982), 86.

43 De Breffny, *In the Steps of St Patrick*: Ch.VII on St Patrick's Purgatory; footprint stone on p.127; Marion Dowd, 'Archaeology of the Subterranean World', *Archaeology Ireland*, vol.15 no.1, issue 55 (Spring 2001), 28–9.

44 John Hall, 'Haunted Roads on the Isle of Man: Part 4: Giants and Old Gods', *The Researcher*, vol.3 issue 1 (winter 2000), 34.

45 Mackinlay, *Folklore of Scottish Lochs and Springs*, 76; Morris, *Scottish Healing Wells*, 185.

46 Lady Wilde, *Ancient Legends, Mystic Charms, and Superstitions of Ireland* (London: Ward and Downey, 1888; Galway: O'Gorman Ltd, 1971), 216.

47 Philip Dixon Hardy, *The Holy Wells of Ireland* (Dublin, 1836), 30–2.

48 Patrick Logan, *The Holy Wells of Ireland* (Gerrards Cross: Colin Smythe, 1980), 88.

49 Anthony Weir, *Early Ireland: A Field Guide* (Belfast: Blackstaff Press, 1980), 151; Logan, *The Holy Wells of Ireland*, 79.

50 Logan, *The Holy Wells of Ireland*, 38.

51 See all these place-names in the 1962 edition of Killanin and Duignan, *The Shell Guide to Ireland.*

52 C.F. Tebbutt, 'St Patrick's Well, Oran, Eire', *Folklore*, 73 (spring 1962), 55–7.

53 Eily Kilgannon, *Folktales of the Yeats Country* (Cork and Dublin: The Mercier Press, 1989), 21.

54 Cary Meehan, *The Traveller's Guide to Sacred Ireland* (Glastonbury: Gothic Image Publications, 2002), 674.

55 Logan, *The Holy Wells of Ireland*, 38.

56 Information on the churches and prison is from Loretta Gerson, Silvia Mazzola, Venetia Morrison, *Rome: A Guide to the Eternal City* (London: Napoleoni and Wakefield, 1999), 21, 22, 89; see also Roger Peyrefitte (trans. Edward Hyams), *The Keys of St Peter* (London: Secker and Warburg, 1957; St Albans: Panther Books, 1972), 63; A.J.C. Hare, *Walks in Rome* (1909), 153; W. Bonser, 'Medical Folklore of Venice and Rome', *Folk-Lore*, vol.LXVII no.1 (March 1956), 14.

57 Gerson, Mazzola, Morrison, *Rome, A Guide to the Eternal City*, 107.

58 Sébillot, *Le Folk-Lore de France*, 377.

59 Sébillot, *Le Folk-Lore de France*, 374.

60 Sébillot, *Le Folk-Lore de France*, 394.

61 Sébillot, *Le Folk-Lore de France*, 373.

62 Sébillot, *Le Folk-Lore de France*, 366, 404.

63 Sébillot, *Le Folk-Lore de France*, 376–7.

64 Sébillot, *Le Folk-Lore de France*, 404; Renouard, *A New Guide to Brittany*, 172; Anatole Le Braz (trans. Frances M. Gostling), *The Land of Pardons* (London: Methuen, 1907), 235.

65 Le Braz, *The Land of Pardons*, 239, 246.

66 Bottrell, *Traditions and Hearthside Stories of West Cornwall*, 145–6.

67 Logan, *The Holy Wells of Ireland*, 101; Westropp, *Folklore of Clare*, 68, 90–1; Wood-Martin, *Traces of the Elder Faiths of Ireland*, II, 97; Lady Wilde, *Ancient Cures, Charms, and Usages of Ireland* (London, 1890), 70.

68 Sébillot, *Le Folk-Lore de France*, 406.

69 Anatole le Braz, *Les Saints Bretons en Cornouaille* (Paris: Calmann-Lévy, 1937), 111.

70 Paul G. Bahn, *The Cambridge Illustrated History of Prehistoric Art* (Cambridge: Cambridge University Press, 1998), 10, 11, 20.

71 S. Baring-Gould and John Fisher, *The Lives of the British Saints*, vol.4 (London: The Honourable Society of Cymmrodorion, 1913), 281; Edmund Pugh, *Cambria Depicta* (London, 1816), 170.

72 Baring-Gould and Fisher, *The Lives of the British Saints*, vol.4, 284; Jessica Lofthouse, *North Wales for the Countrygoer* (London: Robert Hale, 1970), 92.

73 Sébillot, *Le Folk-Lore de France*, 368.

74 Dunbar, *A Dictionary of Saintly Women*, 2, 208.

75 *Catholic Encyclopedia*, accessed via www.newadvent.org, and information from Andreas Trottmann.

Chapter 6 – The Hoof-Prints of Horses and Other Animals

1 D.R. Thomas, *A History of the Diocese of St Asaph* (London, 1874), 5; Sabine Baring-Gould and John Fisher, *The Lives of the British Saints* (London, 1907), vol.I, 183.
2 Edward Lhuyd, *Parochialia,* II:52, quoted in Elissa R. Henken, *Traditions of the Welsh Saints* (Woodbridge: Boydell and Brewer, 1987), 85.
3 Baring-Gould and Fisher, *Lives of the British Saints*, vol. I, 183; vol.II, 263.
4 Baring-Gould and Fisher, *Lives of the British Saints*, vol.II, 284.
5 Richard Fenton, *Tours in Wales (1804–1813)* (*Archaeologia Cambrensis,* Supplement 1917), 333.
6 Henken, *Traditions of the Welsh Saints*, 254–5; Baring-Gould and Fisher, *Lives of the British Saints,* vol.II, 423–4. The modern version is described in a letter from Megan Roberts dated 28 June 1990, and has not appeared in print before.
7 Browne Willis, *Diocese of St Asaph* (c.1720); D.R. Thomas, *A History of the Diocese of St Asaph* (London, 1874), 371.
8 Sabine Baring-Gould, *The Lives of the Saints* (London, 1898), vol.16, 314–16; Jennifer Westwood, *Albion: A Guide to Legendary Britain* (London: Granada Publishing, 1985), 262.
9 Paul Sébillot, *Le Folk-Lore de France*, vol.I (Paris, 1904), 381–2.
10 Sébillot, *Le Folk-Lore de France*, 385, 387.
11 Sébillot, *Le Folk-Lore de France*, 411, 406–8.
12 S. Baring-Gould, *Brittany* (London: Methuen and Co., 1902), 212–15.
13 Sébillot, *Le Folk-Lore de France*, 386.
14 Sébillot, *Le Folk-Lore de France*, 386.
15 Sébillot, *Le Folk-Lore de France*, 383–4, 388.
16 Sébillot, *Le Folk-Lore de France*, 387–8; Westwood, *Albion*, 182.
17 Westwood, *Albion*, 180–3; Ethel H. Rudkin, *Lincolnshire Folklore* (Gainsborough: Beltons, 1936; republished 1973 by EP Publishing), 77–9.
18 Charlotte Sophia Burne, *Shropshire Folk-Lore* (London: Trübner, 1883; republished by EP Publishing, 1973), Part I, 15–17.
19 Mary Corbett Harris, 'Legends and Folklore of Llanfachreth Parish', *Journal of the Merioneth Historical and Record Society*, vol.V (1965), no.I, 15–16.
20 Elissa R. Henken, *National Redeemer: Owain Glyndwr in Welsh Tradition* (Cardiff: University of Wales Press, 1996), 147–8.
21 Robert Hunt, *The Drolls, Traditions, and Superstitions of Old Cornwall*, First Series (3rd edition, 1881; facsimile reprint by Llanerch Publishers, 1993), 186.
22 Geoffrey Ashe, *The Traveller's Guide to Arthurian Britain* (formerly *A Guidebook to Arthurian Britain*) (first published 1980; retitled edition: Glastonbury: Gothic Image Publications, 1997), 91.
23 Richard Holland, *Supernatural Clwyd* (Llanrwst: Gwasg Carreg Gwalch, 1989), 14–16.
24 (no author), *Legends of the Black Forest* (Baden-Baden: C. Wild, no date), 100.
25 Sébillot, *Le Folk-Lore de France*, 388–9.
26 (no author), *India's Sacred Shrines and Cities* (Madras: G.A. Natesan and Co., no date), 406–7.

27 Leslie V. Grinsell, *Folklore of Prehistoric Sites in Britain* (Newton Abbot: David and Charles, 1976), 224.

28 (no author), *Folklore of Blaenau Gwent* (Abertillery: Old Bakehouse Publications, 1995), 12.

29 Sébillot, *Le Folk-Lore de France*, 383.

30 Sébillot, *Le Folk-Lore de France*, 384–5.

31 Information kindly supplied by Ulrich Magin, in a letter dated 31 January 2001.

32 Rosemary Ellen Guiley, *Atlas of the Mysterious in North America* (New York: Facts on File, 1995), 64.

33 Alan Roderick, *The Folklore of Gwent* (Cwmbran: Village Publishing, 1983), 74.

34 Rev. Elias Owen, *Welsh Folk-Lore* (Oswestry and Wrexham: Woodall, Minshall and Co., 1888, 1896; reprinted 1976 by EP Publishing), 162–4.

35 Edward Waring, *Ghosts and Legends of the Dorset Countryside* (Tisbury: The Compton Press, 1977), 39.

36 Janet and Colin Bord, *The Enchanted Land* (London: Thorsons, 1995), 111.

37 Cited in John Michell and Robert J.M. Rickard, *Phenomena: A Book of Wonders* (London: Thames and Hudson, 1977), 77.

38 Otta F. Swire, *The Highlands and Their Legends* (Edinburgh and London: Oliver and Boyd, 1963), 119.

39 Alasdair Alpin MacGregor, *The Peat-Fire Flame* (Edinburgh and London: The Moray Press, 1937), 174.

40 Charles Harry Whedbee, *Legends of the Outer Banks and Tar Heel Tidewater* (Winston-Salem: John F. Blair, 1966), 92–9; Jim Brandon, *Weird America: A Guide to Places of Mystery in the United States* (New York: E.P. Dutton, 1978), 168.

41 Sébillot, *Le Folk-Lore de France*, 383.

42 Sébillot, *Le Folk-Lore de France*, 381, 382.

43 Sébillot, *Le Folk-Lore de France*, 381, 385.

44 Sébillot, *Le Folk-Lore de France*, 382, 385.

45 Frances Parkinson Keyes, *The Land of Stones and Saints* (London: Peter Davies, 1958), 153.

46 Patrick Logan, *The Holy Wells of Ireland* (Gerrards Cross: Colin Smythe, 1980), 38.

47 Lord Killanin and Michael V. Duignan, *The Shell Guide to Ireland* (London: The Ebury Press,1962 edition), 267.

48 Martin Palmer, *Travels Through Sacred China* (London: Thorsons, 1996), 124–5, 235.

49 Noreen Cunningham and Pat McGinn, *The Gap of the North* (Dublin: The O'Brien Press, 2001), 65.

50 Thomas J. Westropp, *Folklore of Clare* (Ennis: Clasp Press, 2000), 58, 67–8.

51 Anthony Weir, *Early Ireland: A Field Guide* (Belfast: Blackstaff Press, 1980), 112.

52 Weir, *Early Ireland*, 202; Peter Harbison, *Pilgrimage in Ireland* (London: Barrie and Jenkins, 1991), 144, 145; Cary Meehan, *The Traveller's Guide to Sacred Ireland* (Glastonbury: Gothic Image Publications, 2002), 408.

53 Ronald Pepin and Hugh Feiss, OSB (trans.), *Two Mediæval Lives of Saint Winefride* (Toronto: Peregrina Publishing Co., 2000), 72.

54 *Vita Sancti Tathei*, in A.W. Wade-Evans, *Vitæ Sanctorum Britanniæ et Genealogiæ* (Cardiff: University of Wales Press, 1944).

55 MacGregor, *The Peat-Fire Flame*, 76.

56 Westwood, *Albion.* 158–9.

57 Henken, *Traditions of the Welsh Saints*, 242.

58 Owen, *Welsh Folk-Lore,* 132–3.

59 Sébillot, *Le Folk-Lore de France*, 390.

60 Ean Begg, *The Cult of the Black Virgin* (London: Arkana, 1985), 218.

61 *Folklore of Blaenau Gwent*, 12.

62 Sébillot, *Le Folk-Lore de France*, 372.

63 Westropp, *Folklore of Clare*, 69.

64 Sébillot, *Le Folk-Lore de France*, 390–1.

65 Lord Killanin and Michael V. Duignan, revised and updated by Peter Harbison, *The Shell Guide to Ireland* (London: Macmillan , 1989), 173.

66 Janet and Colin Bord, *Alien Animals* (London: Paul Elek/Granada Publishing, 1980), 88–90.

67 Westwood, *Albion*, 274–5.

68 MacGregor, *The Peat-Fire Flame*, 37–8, 39.

69 Otta F. Swire, *The Outer Hebrides and Their Legends* (Edinburgh and London: Oliver and Boyd, 1966), 74.

70 Otta F. Swire, *The Inner Hebrides and Their Legends* (London and Glasgow: Collins, 1964), 156.

Chapter 7 – The Devil Stamps His Foot (or Hoof, or Claw)

1 Paul Sébillot, *Le Folk-Lore de France*, Vol.I (Paris, 1904), 369.

2 See web-site of JaynesJersey: Legends and Folklore: www.jaynesjersey.com/legsnfolklr.htm

3 Joyce Miller, *Myth and Magic: Scotland's Ancient Beliefs and Sacred Places* (Musselburgh: Goblinshead, 2000), 174.

4 J.M. McPherson, *Primitive Beliefs in the North-East of Scotland* (London: Longmans, Green and Co., 1929), 143.

5 Leslie V. Grinsell, *Folklore of Prehistoric Sites in Britain* (Newton Abbot: David and Charles, 1976), 209.

6 Sébillot, *Le Folk-Lore de France*, 387.

7 Jacqueline Simpson, *The Folklore of Sussex* (London: B.T. Batsford Ltd, 1973), 20.

8 Personal communication from folklorist John Billingsley, 2001.

9 *Notes and Queries*, 3rd S. IX, 2 June 1866, 463.

10 Paul Bennett, *Circles, Standing Stones and Legendary Rocks of West Yorkshire* (Wymeswold: Heart of Albion Press, 1994), 24.

11 M.C. Balfour (ed. Northcote W. Thomas), *County Folk-Lore Vol.IV, Examples of Printed Folk-Lore Concerning Northumberland* (London: David Nutt, 1904, for The Folk-Lore Society; reprinted in facsimile by Llanerch Publishers, 1994), 148–9.

12 Ken Howarth, *Ghosts, Traditions and Legends of Old Lancashire* (Wilmslow: Sigma Leisure, 1993), 30; Jessica Lofthouse, *North-Country Folklore* (London: Robert Hale, 1976), 51.

13 *Cheshire Sheaf* (1906 volume), noted by Richard Holland in 'Is this where angels fear to tread?', *The Chronicle* (Chester), 18 September 1998, 6.

14 *Folklore, Myths and Legends of Britain* (London: The Reader's Digest Association, 1973), 205.

15 William Bottrell, *Traditions and Hearthside Stories of West Cornwall* (Penzance: published by the author, 1870; Felinfach: Llanerch Publishers, facsimile reprint, 1996), 171–2; Kelvin I. Jones, 'The Bucca', *The Cornish Antiquary*, no.1 (May 2000), 15–18.

16 Marie Trevelyan, *Folk-Lore and Folk-Stories of Wales* (London, 1909; reprinted by EP Publishing, 1973), 154.

17 Nona Rees, *St David of Dewisland* (Llandysul: Gomer Press, 1992), 30.

18 Jonathan Ceredig Davies, *Folk-Lore of West and Mid-Wales* (Aberystwyth, 1911; facsimile reprint by Llanerch Publishers, 1992), 324.

19 Rev. Elias Owen, *Welsh Folk-Lore* (Oswestry and Wrexham: Woodall, Minshall and Co., 1896; republished by EP Publishing, 1976), 190.

20 Charlotte Sophia Burne, *Shropshire Folk-Lore* (London: Trübner and Co., 1883; republished by EP Publishing, 1973), Part I, 19, fn.1.

21 Otta F. Swire, *The Highlands and Their Legends* (Edinburgh and London: Oliver and Boyd, 1963), 129.

22 Sébillot, *Le Folk-Lore de France*, 369.

23 Ulrich Magin, *Bipedia*, 16, 11.

24 Herbert Kühn, *The Rock Pictures of Europe* (London: Sidgwick and Jackson, 1966), 176.

25 Peter Kolosimo, *Unbekanntes Universum* (Berlin: Ullstein, 1991), 103–4.

26 Information from web-site: http://miskai.gamta.lt/parkai/a_34_3.htm .

27 Information supplied by Mark Edward through Doc Shiels.

28 Rosemary Ellen Guiley, *Atlas of the Mysterious in North America* (New York: Facts on File, 1995), 7.

29 Information from web-site: www.getnet.net/~dloucks/personal/neo/neo0816.htm

30 John Robert Colombo, *Mysteries of Ontario* (Toronto: Hounslow Press, 1999), 57.

31 Mike Dash, 'The Devil's Hoofmarks: Source Materials on the Great Devon Mystery of 1855', *Fortean Studies* (London: John Brown Publishing, 1994), vol.1, 71–150.

32 Numerous modern reports can be found in Dash, 'The Devil's Hoofmarks', 119–25.

33 James Alan Rennie, *Romantic Speyside*, quoted in Affleck Gray, *The Big Grey Man of Ben MacDhui* (Moffat: Lochar Publishing, 1989), 69.

34 Swire, *The Highlands and Their Legends*, 255–6.

35 *Michelin Brittany* (1983 edition), 83.

36 Sébillot, *Le Folk-Lore de France*, 379.

37 Sébillot, *Le Folk-Lore de France*, 378–9.

38 William Hone, *The Every-Day Book* (London: William Tegg, 1827), vol.II, 501 (entry for July 21).

39 Marcus X. Schmid, *Umbrien* (Erlangen: Michael Müller Verlag, 2000), 114.

40 Roger Peyrefitte (trans. Edward Hyams), *The Keys of St Peter* (London: Secker and Warburg, 1957; St Albans: Panther Books, 1972), 62.

41 Roy Palmer, *The Folklore of (Old) Monmouthshire* (Herefordshire: Logaston Press, 1998), 70.

42 Otta F. Swire, *The Inner Hebrides and Their Legends* (London: Collins, 1964), 56.

43 *Folklore, Myths and Legends of Britain*, 369.

44 *Folklore, Myths and Legends of Britain*, 328.

45 Burne, *Shropshire Folk-Lore*, Part II, 601.

46 *Folklore, Myths and Legends of Britain*, 247.

47 Jessie Payne, *A Ghost Hunter's Guide to Essex* (Romford: Ian Henry Publications, 1987), 2, 9.

48 Alan Smith, 'St Augustine of Canterbury in History and Tradition', *Folklore*, vol.89, I (1978), 25.

49 Raymond Lamont-Brown, *Scottish Folklore* (Edinburgh: Birlinn Ltd, 1996), 126.

50 Alasdair Alpin MacGregor, *The Peat-Fire Flame* (Edinburgh: The Moray Press, 1937), 185.

51 Terence Whitaker, *Scotland's Ghosts and Apparitions* (London: Robert Hale, 1991), 85–6; MacGregor, *The Peat-Fire Flame*, 184.

52 Davies, *Folk-Lore of West and Mid-Wales*, 325–6.

53 Roy Palmer, *The Folklore of Radnorshire* (Herefordshire: Logaston Press, 2001), 19; Jonathan Mullard, 'Beguildy Old Stone', *Earthlines/Northern Earth Mysteries* Joint Issue (nos. 5/31) Autumn 1986, 19–20.

54 Leslie V. Grinsell, *Folklore of Prehistoric Sites in Britain* (Newton Abbot: David and Charles, 1976), 98.

55 *Folklore, Myths and Legends of Britain*, 35.

56 Terence W. Whitaker, *Yorkshire's Ghosts and Legends* (London: Granada Publishing, 1983), 210.

57 Lofthouse, *North-Country Folklore*, 51.

58 Betty Puttick, *Ghosts of Bedfordshire* (Newbury: Countryside Books, 1996), 91–2.

59 Michel Renouard, *A New Guide to Brittany* (Rennes: Ouest-France, 1984), 37.

60 Sébillot, *Le Folk-Lore de France*, 378.

61 Information from Lars Thomas.

62 Loretta Gerson, Silvia Mazzola, Venetia Morrison, *Rome, A Guide to the Eternal City* (London: Napoleoni and Wakefield, 1999), 206–7.

63 Paul G. Bahn, *Prehistoric Art* (Cambridge: Cambridge University Press, 1998), 20.

64 Davies, *Folk-Lore of West and Mid-Wales*, 187–8.

65 Sébillot, *Le Folk-Lore de France*, 378, 375, 374, 375.

66 Doug Pickford, *Myths and Legends of East Cheshire and the Moorlands* (Wilmslow: Sigma Leisure, 1992), 10–11.

67 Sébillot, *Le Folk-Lore de France*, 395.

68 McPherson, *Primitive Beliefs in the North-East of Scotland*, 143.

69 Sébillot, *Le Folk-Lore de France*, 380.

70 Pickford, *Myths and Legends of East Cheshire and the Moorlands*, 11.

71 Marjorie Rowling, *The Folklore of the Lake District* (London: B.T. Batsford, 1976), 23.

72 Sébillot, *Le Folk-Lore de France*, 397, 399.

Chapter 8 – Giants, Villains and Heroes, Including King Arthur

1 T.C. Lethbridge, *Gogmagog: The Buried Gods* (London: Routledge and Kegan Paul, 1957), 17.

2 Charles Thomas, *English Heritage Book of Tintagel* (London: B.T. Batsford, 1993), 49–51, 96–8.

3 Chris Barber, *Mysterious Wales* (St Albans: Granada Publishing Ltd, 1983), 57.

4 This version was collected by the Rev. Francis Kilvert, and his diary entry is quoted in Jacqueline Simpson, *The Folklore of the Welsh Border* (London: B.T. Batsford, 1976), 22.

5 All the sources for these various versions are given in Leslie V. Grinsell, *Folklore of Prehistoric Sites in Britain* (Newton Abbot: David and Charles, 1976), 152. See also C.G. Portman, 'The Sacred Stones of Hay', *Mjollnir*, no.2 (winter 1979/80), 13.

6 Chris Barber, *More Mysterious Wales* (London: Paladin, 1987), 7.

7 The Rev. Ellis Davis, *Prehistoric and Roman Remains of Denbighshire* (Cardiff: William Lewis (Printers) Ltd, 1929), 312.

8 Geoffrey Ashe, *A Guidebook to Arthurian Britain* (London: Longman Group, 1980), 186.

9 Christina Hole, *Traditions and Customs of Cheshire* (London: Williams and Norgate, 1937; republished by S.R. Publishers 1970), 197.

10 Ella Mary Leather, *The Folk-Lore of Herefordshire* (Hereford: Jakeman and Carver, 1912; republished by S.R. Publishers 1970), 30.

11 B.C. Spooner, *John Tregagle: Alive or Dead* – West Country Folklore No.13 (St Peter Port, Guernsey: Toucan Press, 1979), 9.

12 John Hobson Matthews, 'Monmouthshire Folklore', *Folk-Lore*, vol.XV, no.3, (September 1904), 349; Roy Palmer, *The Folklore of (old) Monmouthshire* (Herefordshire: Logaston Press, 1998), 71–5.

13 Elissa R. Henken, *National Redeemer: Owain Glyndwr in Welsh Tradition* (Cardiff: University of Wales Press, 1996) is an impressive account: the knee-prints are mentioned on page 147 and the dagger on pages 152–5. A further account of the dagger is in Rev. Elias Owen, *Old Stone Crosses of the Vale of Clwyd* (London: Bernard Quaritch, 1886; republished for Clwyd County Council, 1995), 20–1.

14 Barber, *More Mysterious Wales,* 120; Wirt Sikes, *British Goblins* (London: Sampson Low, 1880; republished by E.P. Publishing 1973), 367.

15 Grinsell, *Folklore of Prehistoric Sites in Britain,* 196.

16 James MacKillop, *Dictionary of Celtic Mythology* (Oxford: Oxford University Press, 1998), 204–6.

17 Thomas J. Westropp, *Folklore of Clare* (Ennis: Clasp Press, 2000), 68–9.

18 W.G. Wood-Martin, *Traces of the Elder Faiths of Ireland* (London, 1902), vol.1, 163.

19 Noreen Cunningham and Pat McGinn, *The Gap of the North* (Dublin: The O'Brien Press, 2001), 124.

20 Cary Meehan, *The Traveller's Guide to Sacred Ireland* (Glastonbury: Gothic Image Publications, 2002), 681.

21 Paul Sébillot, *Le Folk-Lore de France,* Vol.I (Paris, 1904), 372, 369–70, 376, 370.

22 Sébillot, *Le Folk-Lore de France,* 370.

23 Alan Smith, 'Lucius of Britain: Alleged King and Church Founder', *Folklore,* vol.90 (1979), I, 29–36, with imprint on p.35.

24 William Henry Jones and Lewis L. Kropf, 'Magyar Folk-Lore and Some Parallels', *The Folk-Lore Journal,* Vol.I Part XI (November 1883), 362.

25 Paul G. Bahn, *The Cambridge Illustrated History of Prehistoric Art* (Cambridge: Cambridge University Press, 1998), 40; Jalmar and Ione Rudner, *The Hunter and His Art* (Cape Town: C. Struik, 1970), 4–5.

26 Information supplied by Dr Elmar R. Gruber.

27 Frank Joseph (ed.), *Sacred Sites of the West* (Surrey, BC, and Blaine, WA: Hancock House Publishers, 1997), 61–3; John Robert Colombo, *Mysterious Canada* (Toronto: Doubleday Canada, 1988), 364–5.

28 Robert Hunt, *The Drolls, Traditions, and Superstitions of Old Cornwall,* First Series (first published 1881; facsimile reprint by Llanerch Publishers, 1993), 73.

29 Tony Deane and Tony Shaw, *The Folklore of Cornwall* (London: B.T. Batsford, 1975), 141.

30 Craig Weatherhill and Paul Devereux, *Myths and Legends of Cornwall* (Wilmslow: Sigma Leisure, 1994), 14–15.

31 Wendy Boase, *The Folklore of Hampshire and the Isle of Wight* (London: B.T. Batsford, 1976), 100.

32 Roy Palmer, *The Folklore of Gloucestershire* (Tiverton: Westcountry Books, 1994), 38; Alfred Watkins, *The Old Straight Track* (London: Methuen and Co., 1925; reprinted by Garnstone Press, 1970), 31.

33 Phil Quinn, 'Land and Legend in Suburban Bristol', *3rd Stone* 24, (summer/autumn 1996), 11.

34 Enid Porter, *Cambridgeshire Customs and Folklore* (London: Routledge and Kegan Paul, 1969), 188–9.

35 Polly Howat, *Ghosts and Legends of Lincolnshire and the Fen Country* (Newbury: Countryside Books, 1992), 62.

36 'Local Curiosities' in *Lantern,* 17 (spring 1977), 9.

37 Charlotte Sophia Burne, *Shropshire Folk-Lore* (London: Trübner and Co., 1883; republished by EP Publishing, 1973), Part I, 2.

38 Jessica Lofthouse, *North-Country Folklore* (London: Robert Hale Ltd, 1976), 130–1.

39 Gutch, *County Folk-Lore, II, North Riding of Yorkshire,* 9, quoted in Katharine M. Briggs, *British Folk Tales and Legends: A Sampler* (London: Granada Publishing, 1977), 203.

40 A.W. Moore, *The Folk-Lore of the Isle of Man* (London: D. Nutt, 1891; republished by S.R. Publishers, 1971), 66.

41 Janet and Colin Bord, *Atlas of Magical Britain* (London: Sidgwick and Jackson, 1990), 139; John Rhys, *Celtic Folklore Welsh and Manx* (Oxford: Clarendon Press, 1901), 285–6.

42 Maxwell Fraser, *In Praise of Manxland* (London: Methuen and Co., 1948 – 2nd revised edition), 144.

43 T. Gwynn Jones, *Welsh Folklore and Folk-Custom* (first published 1930; reissued by D. S. Brewer, 1979), 80.

44 William Davies, *Casgliad o Len-Gwerin Meirion* (Blaenau Ffestiniog: Eisteddfod Transactions, 1898).

45 Myrddin Fardd, *Llen Gwerin Sir Gaernarfon* (Cwmni y Cyhoeddwyr Cymreig, 1909), 231.

46 D.E. Jenkins, *Bedd Gelert, Its Facts, Fairies, and Folk-Lore* (Portmadoc: Llewelyn Jenkins, 1899), 148–9, 217–18, 230.

47 Barber, *Mysterious Wales,* 4.

48 Rev. Ellis Davies, *The Prehistoric and Roman Remains of Denbighshire* (Cardiff: William Lewis, 1929), 294.

49 Joyce Miller, *Myth and Magic: Scotland's Ancient Beliefs and Sacred Places* (Musselburgh: Goblinshead, 2000), 186.

50 Otta F. Swire, *The Highlands and Their Legends* (Edinburgh and London: Oliver and Boyd, 1963), 135.

51 Grinsell, *Folklore of Prehistoric Sites in Britain,* 192.

52 Lethbridge, *Gogmagog,* 17.

53 G.F. Black, *County Folk-Lore Vol.III – Orkney and Shetland Islands* (London: David Nutt, 1903; facsimile reprint by Llanerch Publishers/Folklore Society, 1994), 260; Ernest W.Marwick, *The Folklore of Orkney and Shetland* (London: B.T. Batsford, 1975), 59; Burne, *Shropshire Folk-Lore,* 2.

54 James R. Nicolson, *Shetland Folklore* (London: Robert Hale, 1981), 90.

55 Marwick, *The Folklore of Orkney and Shetland,* 163.

56 W.G. Wood-Martin, *Traces of the Elder Faiths of Ireland* (London, 1902), Vol.I, 163.

57 Meehan, *Sacred Ireland,* 64.

58 Cunningham and McGinn, *The Gap of the North,* 130.

59 G.H. Kinahan, 'Connemara Folk-Lore', *The Folk-Lore Journal,* Vol.II Part IX (September 1884), 263–4.

60 Kinahan, 'Connemara Folk-Lore', 263–4.

61 Westropp, *Folklore of Clare,* 69, 85.

62 Sébillot, *Le Folk-Lore de France,* 376, 372, 362, 374.

63 Jones and Kropf, 'Magyar Folk-Lore', 361–2.

64 Letter from H.G. Pitout, with two photographs, in *Fate,* Vol.54, No.12, issue 621 (December 2001), 52.

65 I.G. Turbott, 'The Footprints of Tarawa', *Polynesian Society Journal* 58 (1949), 193.

Chapter 9 – Supernatural Beings

1 R. MacDonald Robertson, *Selected Highland Folk Tales* (Edinburgh and London: Oliver and Boyd, 1961), 40–3.

2 David Bell, *Derbyshire Ghosts and Legends* (Newbury: Countryside Books, 1993), 40–1.

3 Peter Underwood, *Ghosts of Cornwall* (Bodmin: Bossiney Books, 1983), 77.

4 Alasdair Alpin MacGregor, *Phantom Footsteps* (London: Robert Hale, 1959), 16.

5 Mark Turner, *Folklore and Mysteries in the Cotswolds* (London: Robert Hale, 1993), 15.

6 Angus Macnaghten, *Haunted Berkshire* (Newbury: Countryside Books, 1986), 45.

7 Tony Cornell, *Investigating the Paranormal* (New York: Helix Press, 2002), 178, 184–5.

8 Terence W. Whitaker, *Lancashire's Ghosts and Legends* (London: Robert Hale, 1980), 26–7.

9 John Girvan, *Ghosts of Devizes* (Devizes: Girvan Publications, 1995), 20.

10 Charles Fairclough, *Chester Ghosts and Poltergeists* (self-published, no publication details available), 51–2; Ken Webster, *The Vertical Plane* (London: Grafton Books, 1989), 14–15.

11 Norman Adams, *Haunted Scotland* (Edinburgh: Mainstream Publishing, 1998), 133.

12 Maria Leach (ed.), *Funk and Wagnalls Standard Dictionary of Folklore, Mythology and Legend* (New York: Harper and Row, 1984), 410–11.

13 Doug Pickford, *Myths and Legends of East Cheshire and the Moorlands* (Wilmslow: Sigma Leisure, 1992), 40–2.

14 Theo Brown, 'Fifty-Third Report on Folklore', *Report and Transactions of the Devonshire Association*, Vol. LXXXVIII, 251–2, quoted in Mike Dash (ed.), 'The Devil's Hoofmarks', *Fortean Studies* (London: John Brown Publishers, 1994), Vol.1, 122.

15 Jessica Lofthouse, *North-Country Folklore* (London: Robert Hale, 1976), 173–4.

16 Doug Pickford, *Staffordshire: Its Magic and Mystery* (Wilmslow: Sigma Leisure, 1994), 48.

17 Katy Jordan, *The Haunted Landscape* (Bradford on Avon: Ex Libris Press, 2000), 107.

18 Anne Bradford and Barrie Roberts, *Midland Ghosts and Hauntings* (Birmingham: Quercus, 1994), 96.

19 David Bell, *Ghosts and Legends of Staffordshire and the Black Country,* (Newbury: Countryside Books, 1994), 105.

20 Charles Walker, *The Atlas of Occult Britain* (London: Hamlyn, 1987), 145.

21 Mel Willin, 'Investigation of an Alleged Poltergeist Case', *The Paranormal Review*, issue 18 (April 2001), 3.

22 Adams, *Haunted Scotland*, 28.

23 Cornell, *Investigating the Paranormal*, 108, 109, 112, 117.

24 Richard Jones, *Haunted Britain and Ireland* (London: New Holland Publishers, 2001), 52–3.

25 John Girvan, *Ghosts of Devizes: Casebook II* (Devizes: Girvan Publications, 1997), 33.

26 'Mysterious Handprint Lasts Thirty Years', *Winnipeg Free Press* (Canada), 21 July 1928.

27 Terence W. Whitaker, *North Country Ghosts and Legends* (London: Grafton Books, 1988), 227.

28 *La Mano Morta, or Dead Hand*, a leaflet published by Ave Maria Publications, Co. Armagh.

29 Brackett K. Thorogood, *The Margery Mediumship: The 'Walter' Hands: A Study of Their Dermatoglyphics*, Proceedings of the American Society for Psychical Research, Vol. II (New York: ASPR, 1933).

30 Boczor Iosif, 'A Ghost With a Bad Conscience', *Fate* (May 2003), vol.56 no.5 (issue 637), 62–3.

31 Enid Porter, *The Folklore of East Anglia* (London: B.T. Batsford, 1974), 83–4.

32 Graham Dugdale, *Walks in Mysterious South Lakeland* (Wilmslow: Sigma Leisure, 1997), 150.

33 Sheila St. Clair, *Mysterious Ireland* (London: Robert Hale, 1994), 114.

34 Anne Bradford, *Haunted Worcestershire* (Redditch: Hunt End Books, 1996), 82–3.

35 Terence W. Whitaker, *Lancashire's Ghosts and Legends* (London: Robert Hale, 1980), 53.

36 Anne Bradford, *Unquiet Spirits of Worcestershire* (Redditch: Hunt End Books, 1999), 123.

37 Warren Brewer, 'Bloody Hand Print', *Fate* (June 2002), vol.55 no.5 (issue 626), 57.

38 Thomas J. Westropp, *Folklore of Clare* (Ennis: Clasp Press, 2000), 23.

39 Roy Palmer, *The Folklore of Warwickshire* (London: B.T. Batsford, 1976), 78.

40 *Folklore, Myths and Legends of Britain*, 105, 295.

41 David Bell, *Leicestershire Ghosts and Legends* (Newbury: Countryside Books, 1992), 64–5.

42 Peter Underwood, *A Gazetteer of Scottish and Irish Ghosts* (London: Souvenir Press, 1973), 103.

43 Antony D. Hippisley Coxe, *Haunted Britain* (London: Hutchinson, 1973; Pan Books, 1975), 187.

44 Charlotte Sophia Burne, *Shropshire Folk-Lore* (London: Trübner and Co., 1883; republished by EP Publishing, 1973), Part I, 114–16.

45 [author not named but known to be Rev. T. Brynmor Davies], *A Visitor's Impressions of Llansannan* (Abergele: J.H. Williams, no date), 13.

46 Bell, *Leicestershire Ghosts and Legends*, 42–3.

47 Ian R. Grant, *The Testimony of Blood* (London: Burns, Oates and Washbourne, 1929), 67–76.

48 William Worcestre, *Itineraries* (edited by John H. Harvey), (Oxford: Oxford University Press, 1969), 65.

49 J. Maxwell Wood, *Witchcraft and Superstitious Record in the South-Western District of Scotland* (Dumfries: J. Maxwell and Son, 1911; republished by EP Publishing 1975), 259–62.

50 William Brockie, *Legends and Superstitions of the County of Durham* (Sunderland, 1886; republished by EP Publishing 1974), 112, 65.

51 Alan Robson, *Grisly Trails and Ghostly Tales* (London: Virgin Books, 1992), 123–4.

52 *Folklore, Myths and Legends of Britain*, 266.

53 John Harland and T.T. Wilkinson, *Lancashire Folk-Lore* (Manchester and London: John Heywood, 1882; republished by EP Publishing 1973), 135–6; Fletcher Moss, *The Fourth Book of Pilgrimages to Old Homes* (Didsbury: the author, 1908), 19–26.

54 Polly Howat, *Tales of Old Norfolk* (Newbury: Countryside Books, 1991), 63–5.

55 Betty Puttick, *Ghosts of Bedfordshire* (Newbury: Countryside Books, 1996), 21.

56 Walker, *The Atlas of Occult Britain,* 182.

57 Maureen Waller, *1700: Scenes from London Life* (London: Hodder and Stoughton, 2000; Sceptre paperback, 2001), 291–2.

58 W.G. Wood-Martin, *Traces of the Elder Faiths of Ireland* (London, 1902), vol.II, 247.

59 Jim Brandon, *Weird America* (New York: E.P. Dutton, 1978), 98–9.

60 Fred H. Bost, 'A Few Small Steps on the Earth: A Tiny Leap for Mankind?', *Pursuit*, vol.10, no.2, 50–3.

61 Paul Sébillot, *Le Folk-Lore de France* (Paris, 1904), Vol.I, 361.

62 Aubrey Burl, *Megalithic Brittany* (London: Thames and Hudson, 1985), 54.

63 Sébillot, *Le Folk-Lore de France,* 361.

64 Sébillot, *Le Folk-Lore de France,* 361, 373–5, 396.

65 Alasdair Alpin MacGregor, *The Haunted Isle or, Life in the Hebrides* (London: Alexander Maclehose, 1933), 85–6.

66 F. Marian McNeill, *The Silver Bough: Vol. One, Scottish Folk-Lore and Folk-Belief* (Glasgow: William McLellan, 1957), 121.

67 Otta F. Swire, *The Inner Hebrides and Their Legends* (London and Glasgow: Collins, 1964), 197.

68 Alasdair Alpin MacGregor, *The Peat-Fire Flame*, (Edinburgh and London: The Moray Press, 1937), 308–9.

69 Walter Gill, *A Manx Scrapbook* (London: Arrowsmith, 1929), 347–9.

70 Otta F. Swire, *The Outer Hebrides and Their Legends* (Edinburgh and London: Oliver and Boyd, 1966), 228–9.

71 Khenpo Rinpoche Könchog Gyaltsen (trans.), *Prayer Flags: The Life and Spiritual Teachings of Jigten Sumgön* (New York: Snow Lion, 2nd ed. 1986), 38.

Chapter 10 – Footprint Evidence for Modern Mysteries

1 Information on all the discoveries can be found in Dr Karl Shuker, *The Lost Ark: New and Rediscovered Animals of the Twentieth Century* (London: HarperCollins, 1993) or the new updated version, *The New Zoo* (Thirsk: House of Stratus, 2002).

2 The text of the Russian hunter's account can be found in Bernard Heuvelmans, *On the Track of Unknown Animals* (London: Kegan Paul International, revised 3rd edition, 1995), 420–2; for more information on the living mammoth see Karl P.N. Shuker, *In Search of Prehistoric Survivors* (London: Blandford, 1995), 159–60.

3 Tony Healy and Paul Cropper, *Out of the Shadows: Mystery Animals of Australia* (Chippendale: Ironbark/Pan Macmillan Australia, 1994), 19. Chapters 1 and 2 are devoted to the Thylacine in Tasmania and on the Mainland. Malcolm Smith, *Bunyips and Bigfoots: In Search of Australia's Mystery Animals* (Alexandria, NSW: Millennium Books, 1996) also has a chapter on the thylacine on the Mainland.

4 Numerous ABC reports can be found in Smith, *Bunyips and Bigfoots*, from where the quoted case comes (p.135), and also in Healy and Cropper, *Out of the Shadows*.

5 Janet and Colin Bord, *Modern Mysteries of Britain* (London: Grafton Books, 1987), 96–8: the whole of Chapter 11 is devoted to alien big cats in Britain.

6 Karl P.N. Shuker, *Mystery Cats of the World* (London: Robert Hale, 1989), 167. As its title suggests, this book covers the whole range of mystery cats, including

plenty there is no room for here. In addition to the big cats of Australia, Great Britain and North America, briefly covered in this book, there are chapters on Continental Europe, Asia, Africa, Mexico and South America, all of which have their own mystery cats, all leaving plenty of footprints.

7 Some of Dr Shuker's books have already been cited: *The Lost Ark, The New Zoo, In Search of Prehistoric Survivors, Mystery Cats of the World.* Also worth obtaining are his *Extraordinary Animals Worldwide* (London: Robert Hale, 1991) and *From Flying Toads to Snakes with Wings* (St Paul, MN: Llewellyn Publications, 1997).

8 Nicholas Witchell, *The Loch Ness Story* (Lavenham: Terence Dalton, 1974), 60–3; Constance Whyte, *More Than a Legend: The Story of the Loch Ness Monster* (London: Hamish Hamilton, 1957), 103–6. Her so-called Mr Pilt is of course Mr Wetherall.

9 P.Y. Sébillot, *Folklore de France* (Paris, 1968), vol.2, cited in Michel Meurger and Claude Gagnon, *Lake Monster Traditions: A Cross-Cultural Analysis* (London: Fortean Tomes, 1988), 124.

10 *Medicine Hat News*, 21 July 1949; Ferenc Morton Szasz (ed.), *Great Mysteries of the West* (Golden, CO: Fulcrum Publishing, 1993), 35.

11 Meurger and Gagnon, *Lake Monster Traditions*, 229, 270–1.

12 '"Slimy Monster" is Only Large Alligator', *Calgary Herald*, 13 August 1953.

13 Jim Brandon, *Weird America* (New York: Dutton, 1978), 19.

14 Rosemary Ellen Guiley, *Atlas of the Mysterious in North America* (New York: Facts on File, 1995), 148.

15 Healy and Cropper, *Out of the Shadows*, 169.

16 Shuker, *In Search of Prehistoric Survivors*, 18–19.

17 Roy P. Mackal, *A Living Dinosaur? In Search of Mokele-Mbembe* (Leiden: E.J. Brill, 1987).

18 Bernard Heuvelmans, *In the Wake of the Sea-Serpents* (London: Rupert Hart-Davis, 1968), 391–2.

19 *Scottish Daily Mail*, 3 February 1962, quoted in Tim Dinsdale, *The Leviathans* (London: Routledge and Kegan Paul, 1966; Futura, 1976), 167.

20 Dr E.L. Dingwall, *Tomorrow* (1957), cited in John Michell and Robert J.M. Rickard, *Phenomena: A Book of Wonders* (London: Thames and Hudson, 1977), 76.

21 *The News* (now *Fortean Times*), no.10 (June 1975), 18–20; no.15 (April 1976), 12–13.

22 '"Abominable Seamen" in Atlantic?', *Ottawa Journal*, 11 September 1957.

23 Heuvelmans, *On the Track of Unknown Animals*: ch.17 is devoted to the Nandi bear. See also Shuker, *In Search of Prehistoric Survivors*, 153–8.

24 Shuker, *In Search of Prehistoric Survivors*, 142–5.

25 James F. McCloy and Ray Miller, Jr., *The Jersey Devil* (Wallingford, PA: The Middle Atlantic Press, 1976); James F. McCloy and Ray Miller, Jr., *Phantom of the Pines: More Tales of the Jersey Devil* (Moorestown, NJ: Middle Atlantic Press, 1998).

26 Ian Simmons, 'Strangeness at Skinwalker Ranch', *Fortean Times* no.169 (April 2003), 44–7.

27 The full story is given in Harry Price and R.S. Lambert, *The Haunting of*

Cashen's Gap (London: Methuen and Co., 1936).

28 Mike Dash, *Borderlands* (London: William Heinemann, 1997), 276–9.

29 Alasdair Alpin MacGregor, *The Peat-Fire Flame* (Edinburgh and London: The Moray Press, 1937), 82–3; Mike Dash, 'The Devil's Hoofmarks', *Fortean Studies*, vol.3 (London: John Brown Publishing, 1996), 329.

30 Mike Dash (ed.), 'The Devil's Hoofmarks', *Fortean Studies*, vol.1 (London: John Brown Publishing, 1994), 124.

31 James Alan Rennie, *Romantic Speyside* (or *Strathspey*) (1956), quoted in Affleck Gray, *The Big Grey Man of Ben MacDhui* (Moffat: Lochar Publishing, 1970, 1989), 70–1.

32 Healy and Cropper, *Out of the Shadows*, ch.5; Smith, *Bunyips and Bigfoots,* ch.6

33 *The Track Record*, no.43 (January 1995), 17.

34 Janet and Colin Bord, *The Evidence for Bigfoot and Other Man-Beasts* (Wellingborough: The Aquarian Press, 1984), chs 2 and 3.

35 *Regina Leader Post* (Canada), 14 December 1955.

36 Press report in *Arriba,* 27 February 1968, quoted in John Keel, *Strange Creatures from Time and Space* (Greenwich, Conn: Fawcett Publications, 1970), 125.

37 Gray, *The Big Grey Man of Ben MacDhui*, 69.

38 'An Immense Foot Print', *Calgary Herald*, 24 October 1907.

39 Janet and Colin Bord, *The Bigfoot Casebook* (London: Granada Publishing, 1982), 37, 80, and see the index references to 'footprints'. John Green, *Sasquatch: The Apes Among Us* (Seattle, WA: Hancock House Publishers; Saanichton, NC: Cheam Publishing, 1978), ch.19.

40 *St. Paul Pioneer Press*, 15 April 1897, cited on p.53 of 'Airship Sightings in the Nineteenth Century' in Jerome Clark, *The UFO Encyclopedia* (Detroit: Omnigraphics, 1998), 2nd ed., vol.1, 44–63.

41 Adamski described the events in Desmond Leslie and George Adamski, *Flying Saucers Have Landed* (London: T. Werner Laurie, 1953); Williamson's interpretation is in George Hunt Williamson, *Other Tongues – Other Flesh* (Amherst, WI: Amherst Press, 1953).

42 Aime Michel, *Flying Saucers and the Straight-Line Mystery* (New York: Criterion Books, 1958).

43 Coral and Jim Lorenzen, *Encounters with UFO Occupants* (New York: Berkley Medallion, 1976), 146.

44 Lorenzen, *Encounters with UFO Occupants*, 172; *Wichita Evening Eagle*, 8 September 1954, cited in Clark, *The UFO Encyclopedia*, vol.1, 218.

45 *Cleveland Plain Dealer*, 8 November 1957, cited in Clark, *The UFO Encyclopedia*, vol.2, 648.

46 Reinhold O. Schmidt, *Edge of Tomorrow: A True Account of Experiences with Visitors from Another Planet* (Hollywood: the author, 1963), cited in Clark, *The UFO Encyclopedia,* vol.2, 822–3.

47 Report in the Durango *Herald*, cited in Keel, *Strange Creatures from Time and Space*, 163.

48 Charles Bowen (ed.), *The Humanoids* (London: Neville Spearman, 1969), 106.

49 Clark, *The UFO Encyclopedia*, vol.2, 672.

50 Clark, *The UFO Encyclopedia*, vol.2, 856–67.

51 Clark, *The UFO Encyclopedia*, vol.1, 160–9.
52 Cynthia Hind, *UFOs – African Encounters* (Zimbabwe: Gemini, 1982), 44–51.
53 Hind, *UFOs – African Encounters*, 1–14.

Footprints to Visit

1 Paul G. Bahn, *The Cambridge Illustrated History of Prehistoric Art* (Cambridge: Cambridge University Press, 1998), 114–15, 149–51.
2 All information from Peter Stanbury and John Clegg, *A Field Guide to Aboriginal Rock Engravings* (Sydney: Sydney University Press, 1990), 68–9.
3 Bahn, *Prehistoric* Art, 115, 175, 269.
4 Information supplied by Andreas Trottmann in Switzerland.
5 See web-site: www.orientmagix.com/cambodia4.html
6 Information from John Robert Colombo, *Mysterious Canada* (Toronto: Doubleday Canada, 1988), 364–5; Frank Joseph (ed.), *Sacred Sites of the West* (Surrey, B.C. and Blaine, WA: Hancock House, 1997), 61–3.
7 Information from Lars Thomas in Denmark.
8 Otto F.A. Meinardus, *The Holy Family in Egypt* (Cairo: The American University in Cairo Press, 1986), 34; Otto F.A. Meinardus, *Coptic Saints and Pilgrimages* (Cairo: The American University in Cairo Press, 2002), 88–9 – there is also a photograph of the stone. See also web-site: www.sis.gov.eg/coptic/html/sakha.htm
9 Information on this slab was first published in *Proceedings of the Prehistoric Society*, vol.23 (1958), and summarised in Bristol Museum Information Sheet. Further information supplied by Gail Boyle at Bristol Museum in letter dated 6 March 2002.
10 Location information from Doug Pickford, *Myths and Legends of East Cheshire and the Moorlands* (Wilmslow: Sigma Leisure, 1992), 40–2.
11 John Michell, *The Old Stones of Land's End* (London: Garnstone Press, 1974), 16.
12 Location information from Charles Thomas, *English Heritage Book of Tintagel: Arthur and Archaeology* (London: B.T. Batsford, 1993), 49–51, 96–8.
13 Charles Walker, *Strange Britain* (London: Brian Trodd, 1989), 159.
14 Personal visit.
15 More details on the stone's history can be found in D.P. Sullivan, *Old Stones of Gloucestershire* (Cheltenham: Reardon and Son, 1991), 30–1.
16 Information on opening times supplied by Smithills Hall; story of footprint from Jennifer Westwood, *Albion: A Guide to Legendary Britain* (London: Granada Publishing, 1985), 316–17.
17 Ken Howarth, *Ghosts, Traditions and Legends of Old Lancashire* (Wilmslow: Sigma Leisure, 1993), 29–30. Location information supplied by Phil Reeder.
18 Location information, and one version of the story, from Polly Howat, *Ghosts and Legends of Lincolnshire and the Fen Country* (Newbury: Countryside Books, 1992), 20–1.
19 *The Calderstones – A Prehistoric Tomb in Liverpool* (Liverpool: Merseyside Archaeological Society, no date); Mike Royden's Local History Pages website gives a full illustrated history of the stones:

www.btinternet.com/~m.royden/mrlhp/local/calders/calders.htm

20 Information obtained from Polly Howat, *Tales of Old Norfolk* (Newbury: Countryside Books, 1991), 63–5, where the full story of the witch is given; and Charles Walker, *The Atlas of Occult Britain* (Twickenham: Hamlyn, 1987), 93.

21 Personal visit: details from Jennifer Westwood, *Gothick Norfolk* (Princes Risborough: Shire Publications, 1989), 39, and Enid Porter, *Cambridgeshire Customs and Folklore* (London: Routledge and Kegan Paul, 1969), 188–92, where the tales of Tom Hickathrift are told.

22 Personal visit. See also M.C. Balfour, *County Folk-Lore Vol.IV: Northumberland* (London: David Nutt, 1904; facsimile reprint by Llanerch Publishers, 1994), 148–9.

23 Personal visit; thanks to Bob Trubshaw for alerting me to this location by passing on information obtained by Sid Henley.

24 Personal visit. For more details of the events of 4 August 1577, see Janet and Colin Bord, *Alien Animals* (London: Paul Elek/Granada Publishing, 1980), 88–90.

25 *Yorkshire Notes and Queries* vol.2 p.311; Paul Bennett, *Circles, Standing Stones and Legendary Rocks of West Yorkshire* (Wymeswold: Heart of England Press, 1994), 25; Harry Speight, *Upper Wharfedale* (1900), 230.

26 Andy Roberts, *Ghosts and Legends of Yorkshire* (Norwich: Jarrold Publishing, 1992), 45.

27 Location information from John Billingsley, 2002.

28 Personal visit. See also Michel Renouard, *A New Guide to Brittany* (Rennes: Ouest-France, 1984), 89.

29 Michelin *Brittany Guide* (1983 edition), 83.

30 All details from Aubrey Burl, *Megalithic Brittany* (London: Thames and Hudson, 1985), 121–2.

31 Personal visit. See also Renouard, *A New Guide to Brittany*, 42.

32 Personal visit.

33 Personal visit. The legend is told in Renouard, *A New Guide to Brittany*, 325.

34 Information supplied by Andreas Trottmann.

35 See web-site: www.thale.de/english/frs.htm

36 Kristan Lawson and Anneli Rufus, *Weird Europe* (New York: St Martin's Press, 1999), 132–3.

37 Information from Dr Elmar R. Gruber in Munich.

38 George Michell, *The Penguin Guide to the Monuments of India. Volume One – Buddhist, Jain, Hindu* (London: Penguin Books, 1990), 236.

39 Visited in 2003 by Dr Elmar R. Gruber, who kindly supplied first-hand information and photographs. See also Michell, *Monuments of India*, 115.

40 Holger Kersten, *Jesus Lived in India* (Shaftesbury: Element Books, 1986), 206–9.

41 All information from Sylvia A. Matheson, *Persia: An Archaeological Guide* (London: Faber, 2nd rev. ed. 1976), 200.

42 Lord Killanin and Michael V. Duignan, *Shell Guide to Ireland* (London: The Ebury Press, 1962), 112; also in the same book revised and updated by Peter Harbison (London: Macmillan London, 1989), 83.

43 Killanin and Duignan, *Shell Guide to Ireland* (1962 edn), 166–7 (1989 edn), 113; Cary Meehan, *The Traveller's Guide to Sacred Ireland* (Glastonbury:

Gothic Image Publications, 2002), 544.

44 Tom Davies, *Stained Glass Hours: A Modern Pilgrimage* (Sevenoaks: New English Library, 1985), 73; Meehan, *Sacred Ireland*, 162–3.

45 See web-site: www.socc.ie/~skerries/springbrd.htm

46 Killanin and Duignan, *Shell Guide to Ireland* (1962 edn), 263–4 (1989 edn), 173.

47 Killanin and Duignan, *Shell Guide to Ireland* (1962 edn), 454 (1989 edn), 303.

48 Meehan, *Sacred Ireland*, 292–3.

49 Meehan, *Sacred Ireland*, 592–3.

50 Meehan, *Sacred Ireland*, 674.

51 Killanin and Duignan, *Shell Guide to Ireland* (1962 edn), 388 (1989 edn), 258.

52 S.M. Houghton, *Tourist in Israel* (London: The Banner of Truth Trust, 1968), 44.

53 Jerome Murphy-O'Connor, *The Holy Land* (Oxford: Oxford University Press, 1998 (Oxford Archaeological Guides), 125. See web-site: www.earlham.edu/~pss/jerusalem.htm

54 Murphy-O'Connor, *The Holy Land*, 67.

55 A general description of the Mandylion can be found in Gabriele Finaldi, *The Image of Christ* (London: National Gallery, 2000), 98–101. The church in Genoa has published a guidebook: P. Giuseppe M. Ciliberti, *Il Santo Sudario e la Chiesa di S. Bartolomeo degli Armeni* (1988).

56 Loretta Gerson, Silvia Mazzola, Venetia Morrison, *Rome: A Guide to the Eternal City* (London: Napoleoni and Wakefield, 1999), 21–2; P. Charles Walker, '"Domine, Quo Vadis?"', *The Catholic Fireside*, 12 July 1963, 22–3.

57 Gerson, Mazzola, Morrison, *Rome*, 20–1.

58 Gerson, Mazzola, Morrison, *Rome*, 206–7.

59 Gerson, Mazzola, Morrison, *Rome*, 67.

60 Lawson and Rufus, *Weird Europe*, 208.

61 Lawson and Rufus, *Weird Europe*, 229.

62 See website: miskai.gamta.lt/parkai/a_34_3.htm

63 Location information from Joyce Miller, *Myth and Magic: Scotland's Ancient Beliefs and Sacred Places* (Musselburgh: Goblinshead, 2000), 186.

64 Personal visit. More details of the layout and history of Dunadd fort can be found in any good guide to ancient Scotland, for example Euan W. MacKie, *Scotland: An Archaeological Guide* (London: Faber, 1975), 147–8.

65 Location information supplied by Andreas Trottmann.

66 Shirley Toulson, *Celtic Journeys* (London: Hutchinson, 1985), 51.

67 Charles Walker, *The Atlas of Occult Britain* (London: Hamlyn, 1987), 182.

68 Andreas Trottmann, 'Well of the Phantom Hand', *Athene*, 16 (autumn 1997), 8; more recent information, and local details, also supplied by Andreas Trottmann.

69 Visited in 2001 by Jane and Ian Hemming. See also Leslie V. Grinsell, *Folklore of Prehistoric Sites in Britain* (Newton Abbot: David and Charles, 1976), 186.

70 Full details of this site can be found in guide-books, such as MacKie, *Scotland: An Archaeological Guide*, 275–81.

71 Clare Rettie, *Things Seen in Ceylon* (London: Seeley, Service and Co., 1929), 94–8; see web-site: www.sripaga.org

72 Location information supplied by Klaus Aarsleff, Denmark.

73 All information kindly provided by Andreas Trottmann in Switzerland.

74 See web-site: www.inchiangmai.com

75 See web-site: http://samuiguide.com/islanddiscov-watstosee.html which also includes details of temples to visit on Samui.

76 See web-site: http://chiengfa.com/thailand/saraburi.html

77 J.O.D., F.S.K., and D.F.A., 'Pochaev-Dormition Laura', *One Church* (U.S. Russian Orthodox journal, published in Youngstown, Ohio)(1956), 175–96. The icon can be seen at the following web-site: http://puffin.creighton.edu/jesuit/andre/i_porchaev.html

78 See web-site: www.seeing-stars.com/Immortalized/ ChineseTheatreForecourt.shtml

79 See web-site: www.bfro.net/news/wcmuseum.htm

80 All information from Frank Joseph (ed.), *Sacred Sites: A Guidebook to Sacred Centers and Mysterious Places in the United States* (St. Paul: Llewellyn Publications, 1992), 151–6.

81 See website: www.getnet.net/~dloucks/personal/neo/neo0816.htm

82 Location information from Natasha Peterson, *Sacred Sites: A Traveler's Guide to North America's Most Powerful, Mystical Landmarks* (Chicago: Contemporary Books, 1988), 165–6.

83 The story is told in Charles Harry Whedbee, *Legends of the Outer Banks and Tar Heel Tidewater* (Winston-Salem: John F. Blair, 1966), Ch.10; more information and location details come from Jim Brandon, *Weird America: A Guide to Places of Mystery in the United States* (New York: E.P. Dutton, 1978), 168.

84 See website: www.creationevidence.org

85 Location information from Peterson, *Sacred* Sites, 127–8.

86 Personal visit. The full story is given in Marie Trevelyan, *Folk-Lore and Folk-Stories of Wales* (London, 1909; reprinted by EP Publishing, 1973), 134–5.

87 Personal visit.

88 Personal visit. The story of King Arthur in the Clwydian Hills is told in Richard Holland, *Supernatural Clwyd: The Folk Tales of North-East Wales* (Llanrwst: Gwasg Carreg Gwalch, 1989), 14–16.

89 Personal visit.

90 Personal visit.

91 Personal visit. See also Nona Rees, *St David of Dewisland* (Llandysul: Gomer Press, 1992), 30.

92 Personal visit. See also the description in Sian Rees, *A Guide to Ancient and Historic Wales: Dyfed* (London: HMSO, 1992), 201–2; Jonathan Ceredig Davies, *Folk-Lore of West and Mid-Wales* (first published Aberystwyth, 1911; facsimile reprint issued by Llanerch Publishers, 1992), 318–20.

93 Personal visit.

Index

Numbers in **bold** refer to illustrations.

Also from Heart of Albion Press

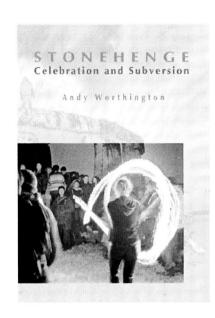

Stonehenge:
Celebration and Subversion

Andy Worthington

This innovative social history looks in detail at how the summer solstice celebrations at Stonehenge have brought together different aspects of British counter-culture to make the monument a 'living temple' and an icon of alternative Britain. The history of the celebrants and counter-cultural leaders is interwoven with the viewpoints of the land-owners, custodians and archaeologists who have generally attempted to impose order on the shifting patterns of these modern-day mythologies.

The story of the Stonehenge summer solstice celebrations begins with the Druid revival of the 18th century and the earliest public gatherings of the 19th and early 20th centuries. In the social upheavals of the 1960s and early 70s, these trailblazers were superseded by the Stonehenge Free Festival. This evolved from a small gathering to an anarchic free state the size of a small city, before its brutal suppression at the Battle of the Beanfield in 1985.

In the aftermath of the Beanfield, the author examines how the political and spiritual aspirations of the free festivals evolved into both the rave scene and the road protest movement, and how the prevailing trends in the counter-culture provided a fertile breeding ground for the development of new Druid groups, the growth of paganism in general, and the adoption of other sacred sites, in particular Stonehenge's gargantuan neighbour at Avebury.

The account is brought up to date with the reopening of Stonehenge on the summer solstice in 2000, the unprecedented crowds drawn by the new access arrangements, and the latest source of conflict, centred on a bitterly-contested road improvement scheme.

ISBN 1 872883 76 1

Perfect bound, 245 x 175 mm, 281 + xviii pages, 147 b&w photos, **£14.95**

Explore Shamanism

Alby Stone

Shamanism is a complex and confusing subject. There are many different ideas about what shamanism is, who is a shaman, and what a shaman does. *Explore Shamanism* provides a much-needed up-to-date guide to the study of shamanism.

Focusing mainly on the shamans of Siberia and Central Asia, *Explore Shamanism* includes a historical survey of academic approaches to shamanism, an overview of the various theories about shamanism, and a discussion of the origins of shamanism based on the latest ideas. There are also more detailed explorations of the initiation of shamans; the costumes, drums and other tools of the shaman's trade; journeys to the spirit world; and the place of trance, spirit possession and ecstasy in shamanic performance.

Explore Shamanism also surveys revived and reconstructed shamanisms in the world today.

Alby Stone has been studying and writing about shamanism for twenty years.

ISBN 1 872883 68 0.
Perfect bound, Demi 8vo (215 x 138 mm), 184 + x pages, 2 photographs; 17 line drawings, **£9.95**

Explore Green Men

Mercia MacDermott
with photographs by
Ruth Wylie

Explore Green Men is the first detailed study of the history of this motif for 25 years. Dr MacDermott's research follows the Green Man back from the previous earliest known examples into its hitherto unrecognised origins in India about 2,300 years ago.

The book starts by discussing the 'paganisation' of Green Men in recent decades, then follows backwards through the Victorian Gothic Revival, Baroque, Rococo and Italianate revivals, to their heyday in the Gothic and the supposed origins in the Romanesque. As part of this discussion there is background information on the cultural changes that affected how Green Men were regarded. The author also discusses the comparisons that have been made with Cernunnus, Robin Hood, Jack-in-the-Green, woodwoses, Baphomet, Al Khidr and Bulgarian *peperuda*. She also investigates which pagan god Green Men supposedly represent.

Explore Green Men is illustrated with 110 photographs and drawings, mostly of Green Men who have never before showed their faces in books.

This book will appeal to all with an interest in Green Men and to art historians looking for a reliable study of this fascinating decorative motif.

ISBN 1 872883 66 4

Perfect bound, demi 8vo (215 x 138 mm), 216 pages, 108 b&w photos, 2 line drawings **£9.95**

Explore Mythology

Bob Trubshaw

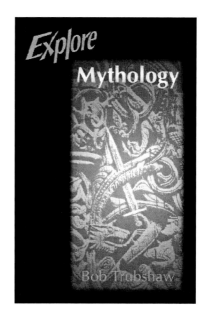

Myths are usually thought of as something to do with 'traditional cultures'. The study of such 'traditional' myths emphasises their importance in religion, national identity, hero-figures, understanding the origin of the universe, and predictions of an apocalyptic demise. The academic study of myths has done much to fit these ideas into the preconceived ideas of the relevant academics.

Only in recent years have such long-standing assumptions about myths begun to be questioned, opening up whole new ways of thinking about the way such myths define and structure how a society thinks about itself and the 'real world'.

These new approaches to the study of myth reveal that, to an astonishing extent, modern day thinking is every bit as 'mythological' as the world-views of, say, the Classical Greeks or obscure Polynesian tribes. Politics, religions, science, advertising and the mass media are all deeply implicated in the creation and use of myths.

Explore Mythology provides a lively introduction to the way myths have been studied, together with discussion of some of the most important 'mythic motifs' – such as heroes, national identity, and 'central places' – followed by a discussion of how these ideas permeate modern society. These sometimes contentious and profound ideas are presented in an easily readable style of writing.

ISBN 1 872883 62 1

Perfect bound. Demi 8vo (215 x 138 mm), 220 + xx pages, 17 line drawings. **£9.95**

Explore Folklore

Bob Trubshaw

'A howling success, which plugs a big and obvious gap'
Professor Ronald Hutton

There have been fascinating developments in the study of folklore in the last twenty-or-so years, but few books about British folklore and folk customs reflect these exciting new approaches. As a result there is a huge gap between scholarly approaches to folklore studies and 'popular beliefs' about the character and history of British folklore. *Explore Folklore* is the first book to bridge that gap, and to show how much 'folklore' there is in modern day Britain.

Explore Folklore shows there is much more to folklore than morris dancing and fifty-something folksingers! The rituals of 'what we do on our holidays', funerals, stag nights and 'lingerie parties' are all full of 'unselfconscious' folk customs. Indeed, folklore is something that is integral to all our lives – it is so intrinsic we do not think of it as being 'folklore'.

The implicit ideas underlying folk lore and customs are also explored.   There might appear to be little in common between people who touch wood for luck (a 'tradition' invented in the last 200 years) and legends about people who believe they have been abducted and subjected to intimate body examinations by aliens. Yet, in their varying ways, these and other 'folk beliefs' reflect the wide spectrum of belief and disbelief in what is easily dismissed as 'superstition'.

Explore Folklore provides a lively introduction to the study of most genres of British folklore, presenting the more contentious and profound ideas in a readily accessible manner.

ISBN 1 872883 60 5
Perfect bound, demi 8vo (215x138 mm), 200 pages, **£9.95**

Masterworks

Arts and Crafts of Traditional Building in Northern Europe

Nigel Pennick

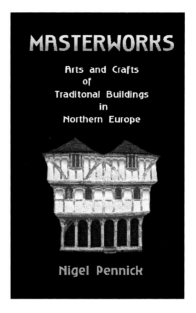

Masterworks is about the traditions of arts and crafts in northern Europe, taking as a starting point the use of timber in building. Timber frame buildings have been constructed over a long period of time over a large territory, mostly northern and north-west Europe. Various regional and local styles have come into being.

Timber buildings display a rich diversity of techniques, forms and patterns developed by generations of master craftsmen working with local materials under similar limitations. The 'arts and crafts' used in the construction of these buildings acknowledge and celebrate the knowledge, traditions, abilities and spiritual understanding of how to work effectively with natural materials. They are living traditions that remain relevant today.

Masterworks is a celebration of this arts and crafts ethos that is present in the traditional buildings of northern Europe.

> "*Masterworks* ... is written by a man who is not only in tune with his subject matter but is, in fact, a master wordsmith in his own right and deserves credit for this. I personally found this one of his most intriguing and important works to date and cannot recommend it too highly to the discerning reader."
>
> Ian Read *Runa*

ISBN 1 872883 63 X Perfect bound, Demi 8vo, 163 + viii pages, 23 b&w photos, 15 line drawings **£9.95**

Snake Fat and Knotted Threads

An introduction to traditional Finnish healing magic

K.M. Koppana

What did the Finnish cunning man carry in his magic pouch? How does one learn the language of the ravens? What is the Origin of the Cat? How do you attract a partner at Midsummer? These and much more are to be found in *Snake Fat and Knotted Threads*.

Snake Fat and Knotted Threads provides a unique resource about traditional Finnish healing magic and spells, folk customs and myths. All this detailed information is based on the author's research and practical experience.

K.M. Koppana has been interested in spells since she was small, being a keen reader of fairy stories. This interest has persisted and she still has an urge to pick up pebbles on walks. She is also a poet and used to edit small magazines, such as the long-gone *Starlight*, which was about the Finnish magical scene. In 2001 she moved from Helsinki to England, settling in the Midlands.

> *Snake Fat and Knotted Threads* '... is a study of the *tietaja* or cunning folk who used such items as human skulls, graveyard dirt and hangmen's nooses in their magical work. They invoked both the old Finnish gods and Christian deities. This is a highly recommended study of a bygone era of magical belief that in modern Finland has been sadly usurped by New Age therapists and neo-pagan Goddess worship.'
> Michael Howard *The Cauldron*

1st UK edition (originally published in Finland).
ISBN 1 872883 65 6 Perfect bound, demi 8vo, 112 pages, 14 b&w photos, 2 line drawings. **£7.95**

Further details of all Alternative ALbion and Heart of Albion titles online at **www.hoap.co.uk**

All titles available direct from Heart of Albion Press.
Please add 80p p&p (UK only; email
albion@indigogroup.co.uk for overseas postage).

To order books or request our current catalogue
please contact

Heart of Albion Press

2 Cross Hill Close, Wymeswold

Loughborough, LE12 6UJ

Phone: 01509 880725

Fax: 01509 881715

email: albion@indigogroup.co.uk

Web site: www.hoap.co.uk